W9-ADQ-729

Fawcett Crest Books
by Isaac Bashevis Singer:

THE FAMILY MOSKAT *(1950)*
24066-5 $2.95

SHORT FRIDAY *(1964)*
24068-1 $2.50

ENEMIES, A LOVE STORY *(1972)*
24065-7 $2.50

A CROWN OF FEATHERS *(1973)*
23465-7 $2.50

PASSIONS *(1975)*
24067-3 $2.50

The
FAMILY MOSKAT

Isaac Bashevis Singer

Translated from the Yiddish by A. H. Gross

FAWCETT CREST • NEW YORK

THE FAMILY MOSKAT

THIS BOOK CONTAINS THE COMPLETE TEXT OF
THE ORIGINAL HARDCOVER EDITION.

Published by Fawcett Crest Books, a unit of CBS Publications,
the Consumer Publishing Division of CBS Inc., by arrangement with Farrar, Straus & Giroux, Inc.

ISBN: 0-449-24066-5

Printed in the United States of America

First Fawcett Crest printing: March 1975

14   13   12   11   10   9   8   7   6   5   4

ACKNOWLEDGMENTS

I wish to express my gratitude to those who made possible the publication of this book.

To my sorrow A. H. Gross died before finishing his translation, and I wish to record the passing of a highly gifted and lovable man. The work was completed by his friends Maurice Samuel and Lyon Mearson, and by his daughter Nancy Gross. Mr. Samuel translated a number of chapters; Mr. Mearson corrected and edited most of the manuscript; Miss Gross did additional translation and editing. For their selfless efforts I thank them from the bottom of my heart.

I wish to thank the *Jewish Daily Forward,* in which this novel ran as a serial for two years, and Radio Station WEVD, over which a dramatization of this novel has been broadcast.

Finally, I wish to thank Mr. Alfred A. Knopf and his editors Mr. Herbert Weinstock and Mrs. Robert Shaplen for their advice, most helpful in bringing the book to its final state.

I dedicate these pages to the memory of my late brother I. J. Singer, author of THE BROTHERS ASHKENAZI. *To me he was not only the older brother, but a spiritual father and master as well. I looked up at him always as to a model of high morality and literary honesty. Although a modern man, he had all the great qualities of our pious ancestors.*

—ISAAC BASHEVIS SINGER

THE FAMILY OF

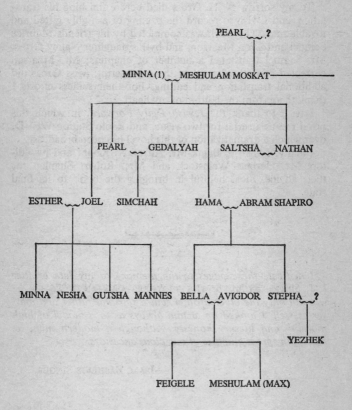

PEARL___?

MINNA (1)___MESHULAM MOSKAT_____

PEARL___GEDALYAH   SALTSHA___NATHAN

ESTHER___JOEL   SIMCHAH   HAMA___ABRAM SHAPIRO

MINNA   NESHA   GUTSHA   MANNES   BELLA AVIGDOR   STEPHA___?

YEZHEK

FEIGELE   MESHULAM (MAX)

MESHULAM MOSKAT

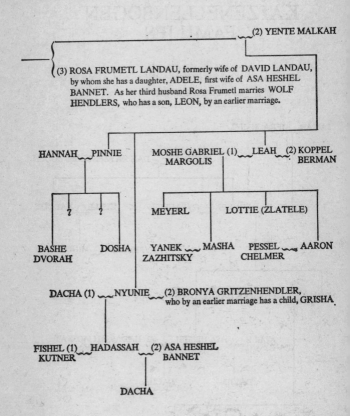

(2) YENTE MALKAH

(3) ROSA FRUMETL LANDAU, formerly wife of DAVID LANDAU, by whom she has a daughter, ADELE, first wife of ASA HESHEL BANNET. As her third husband Rosa Frumetl marries WOLF HENDLERS, who has a son, LEON, by an earlier marriage.

HANNAH __ PINNIE

MOSHE GABRIEL (1) __ LEAH __ (2) KOPPEL
MARGOLIS   BERMAN

?   ?

MEYERL   LOTTIE (ZLATELE)

BASHE   DOSHA
DVORAH

YANEK __ MASHA
ZAZHITSKY

PESSEL __ AARON
CHELMER

DACHA (1) __ NYUNIE __ (2) BRONYA GRITZENHENDLER, who by an earlier marriage has a child, GRISHA.

FISHEL (1) __ HADASSAH __ (2) ASA HESHEL
KUTNER   BANNET

DACHA

THE BANNET AND KATZENELLENBOGEN FAMILIES

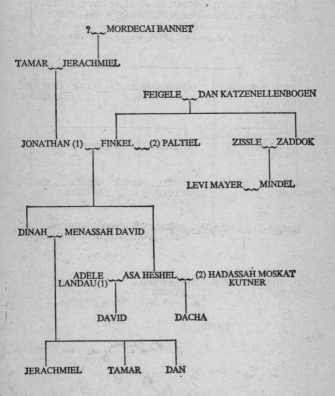

THE FAMILY
OF KOPPEL BERMAN

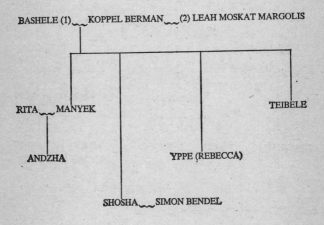

PART
ONE

CHAPTER ONE

1

Five years after the death of his second wife Reb Meshulam Moskat married for a third time. His new wife was a woman in her fifties, from Galicia, in eastern Austria, the widow of a wealthy brewer from Brody, a man of erudition. Some time before he died, the brewer had gone bankrupt, and all that was left to his widow was a bookcase full of learned tomes, a pearl necklace—which later turned out to be imitation—and a daughter named Adele; her name was properly Eidele, but Rosa Frumetl, her mother, called her Adele, after the modern fashion. Meshulam Moskat made the widow's acquaintance in Karlsbad, where he had gone to take the waters. There he had married her. No one in Warsaw knew anything about the marriage; Reb Meshulam wrote to none of his family from the watering-place, nor was it his habit to give anyone an account of his doings. It was not until the middle of September that a telegram to his housekeeper in Warsaw announced his return and gave orders that Leibel, the coachman, was to drive out to the Vienna Station to wait for his employer. The train arrived toward evening. Reb Meshulam descended from the first-class car, his wife and stepdaughter after him.

When Leibel came up to him Reb Meshulam said: "This is your new mistress," and lowered a ponderous eyelid.

All the luggage Reb Meshulam was carrying was a small, well-worn portfolio thickly plastered with colored customs labels. He had checked his large metal-strapped trunk through on the baggage car. But the ladies were weighted down with all sorts of valises, packages and bundles. There was hardly enough room in the carriage to stow the stuff away; it was necessary to pile most of it on the driver's box.

Leibel was far from being a timid man, but at the sight of the women he turned red and lost his tongue entirely. The new Madame Moskat was of medium height and thin. Her shoulders showed the beginnings of a stoop, her face was heavily wrinkled. Her nose was red with catarrh and her eyes were the sad, moist eyes of a woman of gentle birth and breeding. She wore the close-fitting wig of the pious Jewish

12

matron, covered with a soft black shawl. Long earrings hung, glittering, from her earlobes. She was dressed in a silk outer coat, in the style of a pelerine, over a cloth dress, and pointed-toed, French-style shoes. In one hand she carried an amber-handled umbrella; with the other she held fast to her daughter, a girl in her early twenties, tall and slender, with an irregularly shaped nose, prominent-boned features, a sharp chin, and thin lips. There were dark rings under the girl's eyes; she looked as though she had gone sleepless for nights. Her faded blond hair was combed tightly back into a Greek knot and was thickly peppered with hairpins. She was carrying a bunch of withered yellow flowers, a package tied with red ribbon, a large box, and a book, from the edges of which a little bundle of twigs protruded, reminding Leibel of the osier branches used in the ritual on the Feast of Tabernacles. The girl gave off a scent of chocolate, a faint flavor of caraway-seed perfume, and something arrogantly foreign. Leibel grimaced.

"A show-off!" he muttered to himself.

"Adele, my child, this is Warsaw," Rosa Frumetl said. "A big city, isn't it?"

"How do I know? I haven't seen it yet," the girl answered in a flat Galician accent.

As always when Reb Meshulam left on a trip or came back from one, a ring of curious onlookers gathered around him. Everyone in Warsaw knew him, Christians as well as Jews. The newspapers had published stories about him and his enterprises more than once; even his picture had been printed. In appearance he was different from the Warsaw Jews of the old school. He was tall and lean, with thin features, sunken cheeks, and a short white chin beard, each individual hair separated from the next. From below his bushy eyebrows peered a pair of greenish eyes, steely and piercing. His nose was hooked. On his upper lip there was a scant mustache like the whiskers of a sea lion. He was wearing a cloth cap with a high crown. His overcoat, with a gathered waist and split back, managed to look like an aristocratic caftan. From a distance he might have been taken for one of the Polish gentry or even for a Great Russian. But a closer view showed indications of the sidelocks of the pious Jew on his temples.

Reb Meshulam was in a hurry. Every once in a while he poked Leibel in the shoulder to drive faster But the loading of the luggage had taken a long time. Besides, the road from Vielka Street to the Gzhybov was blocked with fire engines and it was necessary to drive by way of the Marshalkovska and the Krulevska. The street lights were already lit, and around the spherical greenish-blue lamps flew swarms of flies, casting darting shadows onto the sidewalk. From time to time a red-painted tramcar rumbled by, the electric wires overhead giving off crackling blue sparks. Everything here was familiar to Reb Meshulam: the tall buildings with the wide gates, the stores with the brightly illuminated windows, the Russian policeman standing between the two rows of car tracks, the Saxon Gardens, with densely leaved branches extending over the high rails. In the midst of the thick foliage tiny lights flickered and died. From inside the park came a mild breeze that seemed to carry the secret whisperings of amorous couples. At the gates two gendarmes stood with swords to make sure that no long-caftaned Jews or their wives ventured into the park to breathe some of the fragrant air. Farther along the road was the Bourse, of which Reb Meshulam was one of the oldest members.

The carriage turned into Gzhybov Place, and abruptly everything changed. The sidewalks were crowded with gaberdined Jews wearing small cloth caps, and bewigged women with shawls over their heads. Even the smells were different now. There was a whiff of the market place in the air—spoiled fruits, lemons, and a mixture of something sweetish and tarry, which could not be given a name and which impinged on the senses only when one returned to the scene after a longish absence. The street was a bedlam of sound and activity. Street peddlers called out their wares in ear-piercing chants—potato cakes, hot chick peas, apples, pears, Hungarian plums, black and white grapes, watermelon whole and in sections. Although the evening was warm, the merchants wore outer coats, with large leather money pouches hanging from the belts. Women hucksters sat on boxes, benches, and doorsills. The stalls were lighted with lanterns, some with flickering candles stuck on the edges of wooden crates. Customers lifted and pinched the fruits or took little exploratory nibbles, smacking their lips to savor the taste. The stall-keepers weighed purchases on tin scales.

"Gold, gold, gold!" a beshawled woman shouted out from beside a crate of squashed oranges.

"Sugar-sweet, sugar-sweet!" sang out a plump girl guarding a basket of moldy plums.

"Wine, wine, wine!" shrieked a red-faced, red-headed peddler, displaying a basket of spoiled grapes. "Nab 'em, grab 'em! Nuzzle 'em, guzzle 'em! Try 'em, buy 'em!"

In the middle of the street, truckmen guided overloaded wagons. The heavy, low-slung horses stamped their iron-shod hoofs on the cobbles, sending out sparks. A porter wearing a hat with a brass badge carried an enormous basket of coal strapped to his shoulders with thick rope. A janitor in an oil-cloth cap and blue apron was sweeping a square of pavement with a long broom. Youngsters, their little lovelocks flapping under octagonal caps, were pouring out of the doors of the Hebrew schools, their patched pants peeping out from between the skirts of their long coats. A boy with a cap pulled low over his eyes was selling New Year calendars, shouting at the top of his voice. A ragged youth with a pair of frightened eyes and disheveled earlocks stood near a box of prayer shawls, phylacteries, prayerbooks, tin Channukah candlesticks, and amulets for pregnant women. A dwarf with an oversized head wandered about with a bundle of leather whips, fanning the straps back and forth, demonstrating how to whip stubborn children. On a stall lit by a carbide lamp lay piles of Yiddish newspapers, cheap novelettes, and books on palmistry and phrenology. Reb Meshulam glanced out of the window of the carriage and observed: "The Land of Israel, eh?"

"Why do they go around in such rags?" Adele asked, grimacing.

"That's the custom here," Reb Meshulam answered with a show of impatience. For a moment he played with the idea of telling the two women that he remembered when these tall buildings were put up; that he himself had had no small part in the street's development; that at night, years before, this very same neighborhood had been as black as Egypt, and that goats and hens had meandered in the street in the daytime. But in the first place there was no time for reminiscences—the carriage was almost at its destination—and in the second place Reb Meshulam was not the man to sing his own praises or dwell on the past. He knew that the women sitting beside him were not particularly taken with Warsaw, and for a moment he felt a pang of regret over his hasty marriage. It was all Koppel's fault, he thought to himself. That bailiff of his had him too much in his clutches.

The carriage came to a halt at the gate of Reb Meshulam's house. Leibel jumped down from the box to help his master

and the women. The group gathered about at once broke into
a torrent of remarks.

"Take a look!" one woman called out. "Strangers in town!"

"Who's the scarecrow?" shouted a boy in torn pantaloons,
with a paper cone on his head for a hat.

"As I live, the old goat's got himself married again," the
woman said, this time louder, to make sure the others would
hear. "May I drop dead!"

"Oi, Mamma, it's too much!" a fat girl howled; she
clutched a basket of fresh rolls against her chest.

"Hey, make room!" Leibel shouted at the top of his voice.
"What the devil are you standing around for? A convention of
idiots, may a plague take you all!"

He pushed a path through the throng and carried three valises to the steps leading to Reb Meshulam's flat. The janitor
and his wife came out to help. A barefoot boy in pants too big
for him darted in from the outskirts of the crowd and jerked a
handful of hair from the horse's tail. The horse started violently. The baker's girl shouted at him: "Hey, you bastard!
May your hands rot!"

"You too, you two-kopek whore," the boy yelled back at
her.

Rosa Frumetl hurried her daughter along after her to get
away from the vulgar talk. Soon the three of them—Reb Meshulam, his wife, and his stepdaughter—made their way
through the front entrance of the house and climbed the single flight of stairs to the Moskat apartment.

2

Naomi, the domestic, and Manya, her assistant, had been preparing for the master's arrival ever since Reb Meshulam's
wire had come. Now they were dressed in their finest. The
lamps in the salon, the library, the master's study, the dining-
room, and the bedrooms were alight—Reb Meshulam liked
everything to be bright against his homecomings. The place
was large, had twelve rooms; but half of them had been
closed up since the death of his second wife.

The news that he had married again and was bringing a
third wife and a stepdaughter back with him was passed on to
the servants by Leibel the coachman. He whispered the tidings
into Naomi's ear and she clutched at her enormous bosom

and let out a shriek. The janitor, entering with the luggage, confirmed the news, but there was no time to discuss it because Meshulam and the newcomers were on the way up. Naomi and Manya waited for them at the door, their white aprons spotless, like deferential servants in an aristocratic household. When Reb Meshulam opened the door and greeted them, they answered together: "Good evening, master, a blessed homecoming."

"I suppose you know already—they told you—this is your new mistress, and this is her daughter."

"Good luck! Good luck! May you have good fortune!"

Naomi threw a quick glance at the two women, and her sharp eyes almost popped out of her head. Her first impulse was to give Manya a pinch on her well-rounded rump, but the girl wasn't standing near enough.

The fat Naomi, in a blond matron's wig, her own hair artfully combed about its edges, was herself twice widowed. She was already in her late thirties, but looked younger. The neighborhood—half of Jewish Warsaw, in fact—knew of her shrewdness and the energy and dispatch with which she carried on the affairs of the Moskat household. "Naomi the Cossack," people called her. When she walked around the house, the floors trembled beneath her heavy tread. When she shouted at Manya, her powerful voice could be heard out in the courtyard. Her sarcastic remarks and devastating retorts were renowned all through the Gzhybov section. She was well paid, far above the usual scale for a domestic, and it was reputed that she had a respectable sum invested with Reb Meshulam at substantial interest.

"A cunning specimen," Leibel the coachman said about her. "A lawyer in a cook's apron!"

Manya was ten years younger than Naomi. In actuality she wasn't in Reb Meshulam's service, but in Naomi's. Reb Meshulam paid Naomi and she had hired the girl to carry the basket after her to market and to scrub the floors. Manya was dark, with a flat face, prominent jaw, wide nose, and slanting Kalmuk eyes. She wore her hair braided in rings at either side of her face. Below them large earrings dangled, bobbing up and down like springs. Around her throat she wore a circlet of silver coins. Naomi didn't need her so much to help in the running of the house—most of the work she liked to do herself—as to have someone around to talk to. When Reb Meshulam was away on a journey the two women ran the household as though it was their own. They drank mead, munched on chick peas, and played cards. Manya had a kind of gypsy luck, and Naomi kept on losing to her.

"She's always beating me," Naomi would complain. "The luck of a provincial idiot!"

Passing by the two servants as they stood bobbing and giggling, Meshulam led his wife and stepdaughter into the flat. In the dining-room stood an oversize table with extension wings at each end, and around it heavy oak chairs with high-railed back rests. A credenza covered one entire wall, the shelves loaded with wine beakers, spice- and herb-holders, samovars, all sorts of carafes, trays, and vases. Behind the glass panes were porcelain dishes and quantities of silver utensils, dented and worn from constant scouring and polishing. From the ceiling hung a heavy oil lamp that could be raised or lowered by means of bronze chains and a gourd filled with small shot to serve as a counterweight.

In Reb Meshulam's private study there were an iron safe and a closet full of old account books. The room smelled of dust, ink, and sealing wax. Book-lined shelves covered three walls of the library. On the floor in a corner lay an enormous volume bound in leather and stamped in gold: a Bible concordance that Reb Meshulam preferred to keep apart from the orthodox volumes. Rosa Frumetl went over to the shelves, lifted out a book, looked at the title page, and said to Reb Meshulam: "I wonder if you have my late husband's book here."

"What's that? How should I know? I don't know all of them."

"Written by my late husband, may he rest in peace. I still have a lot of his manuscripts."

"The things Jews write—there's no end to them!" Reb Meshulam commented with a shrug.

He showed them his bedroom with its twin oak beds, and the salon, a spacious room with four windows and a carved ceiling with traces of gold paint. Around the walls stood easy chairs upholstered in yellow satin, and sofas, taborets, and cabinets. On a piano covered with a linen throw stood a pair of gilt candlesticks. A candelabrum descended from the ceiling in a cluster of glass prisms. A large Channukah lamp hung on a wall. A seven-branched candlestick, a Menorah, stood on a mantel.

Rosa Frumetl breathed a gentle sigh. "May it witness no evil. A palace!"

"Ha! It cost a fortune," Reb Meshulam remarked, "and it isn't worth a pinch of snuff."

Abruptly he left mother and daughter alone in the room and went to his study to recite the evening prayers. Adele took off her coat, revealing a white blouse with pleated sleeves and a neck ribbon tied in a bow. She had narrow shoulders, thin arms, and a flat chest. In the light of the kerosene lamp her hair took on a coppery tinge. Rosa Frumetl sat down on a small divan and rested her pointed shoes on a footstool.

"Well, daughter darling," she said in a mournful tone, "what do you say? A paradise, eh?"

Adele threw her a cross glance. "It makes no difference to me, Mamma," she answered. "I'm not staying here. I'm going away."

Rosa Frumetl shuddered. "Woe is me! So soon! But I did it for you. So that you'd be able to stop wandering around."

"I don't like it. I don't like anything about it."

"What are you torturing me for? What is there not to like?"

"Everything. The old man, the house, the servants, the outlandish Jews here. The whole business!"

"What have you against him? With God's help you'll get married. He'll give you a dowry. We made an agreement."

"I'm not interested in any agreements and I'm not going to get married. This place is too Asiatic."

Rosa Frumetl took a batiste handkerchief from her bag and blew her nose. Her eyes reddened. "But where will you go?"

"I'll go back to Switzerland. I'll study again."

"Haven't you studied enough? Adele, Adele, what will become of you? An old maid—" Rosa Frumetl covered her face with her wrinkled hands and sat still. After a while she got up and went into the kitchen. Some preparations would have to be made—a bite of food, a place for her daughter to sleep. Careless servants, not to offer them so much as a glass of tea.

The kitchen was large, its main feature an enormous tiled oven. Copper pots and pans hung from hooks on the walls; kettles stood at either side of a wide fireplace. The room was redolent of freshly baked cakes and cinnamon. Manya, her shoulders wrapped in a red flower-embroidered shawl, sat at a table laying out a deck of cards. Naomi had taken off her apron and put on a coat preparatory to going out.

"Excuse me," Rosa Frumetl said timidly. "This place is so strange to us. Where will we find our rooms?"

"There are plenty of rooms here," Naomi answered in an irritated voice. "There's no lack of 'em."

"Please be good enough to show them to me?"

Naomi threw a doubtful glance in the direction of Manya. "The rooms used by the last mistress are closed," she said shortly.

"Then maybe you will be good enough to open them."

"They've been locked for years. Nothing's in order."

"Then it will be necessary to put them in order."

"It's too late now."

"At least come and light a lamp," Rosa Frumetl half pleaded, half ordered.

Naomi made a gesture to Manya, who grudgingly got up, took a ring of keys out of the table drawer, and started slowly out. Naomi snatched the keys from her hand and, walking ahead of her, opened the door to one of the bedrooms, a lighted lamp in her hand. The room was semicircular, the wallpaper shabby and beginning to peel. The windows were uncurtained, the torn blinds drawn down. Scattered about were rocking-chairs, footstools, empty flowerpots. There was a large clothes closet with a high cornice and with carved lion heads on its doors. A heavy coat of dust covered everything.

Rosa Frumetl at once began to cough. "How can anyone sleep in all this disorder?" she said plaintively.

"Nobody was expecting anybody to be here," Naomi answered, and put the lamp down on a writing-desk under a wall mirror.

Rosa Frumetl looked into the mirror and took a hasty step backwards. In the cracked, bluish-tinted glass her face had the appearance of being split in two. "Then where will my daughter sleep?" she said, not addressing the question directly to Naomi.

"There's another room with a bed in it—but it's more upset than here."

"And we didn't bring our own bedclothes."

"All the bedclothes that belonged to the last mistress—may she rest in peace—are packed away," Naomi said. Her voice called back an echo, as though some unseen presence were bearing witness to the truth of what she was saying.

She went out. Rosa Frumetl, left alone, crossed over to the commode and tried to open it, but it was locked. She tried a door communicating with another room, but that was locked too. The dried-out wood of the furniture creaked. Rosa Frumetl suddenly thought of how her first husband, Reb David Landau, had lain dead on the floor, his feet toward the door, a black pall covering him, and two wax candles burning at his head. Hardly three years since she had buried him and now she was the wife of another man. A shiver darted up her spine.

"It wasn't for me. It wasn't for me. It was for your daughter," she murmured, as though the dead man were in the room with her. "So that she might find a proper marriage...."

Unable any longer to contain her melancholy, she burst into tears. From the salon came the sound of rumbling bass notes on the piano, like distant thunder, as Adele ran her fingers over the keys. From elsewhere in the flat came the voice of Meshulam Moskat chanting in his study, his tones deep and resonant, for all his close to eighty years.

From outside came the clanging of heavy, sonorous bells, the bells of the Gzhybov church opposite the Moskat flat, the crosses on its two tall towers rearing up against a ruddy evening sky.

3

The word that Reb Meshulam Moskat had married for the third time flew speedily along the streets of Warsaw's Jewish quarter. His sons and daughters, of both his first and his second wives, were struck dumb. There was hardly anything that could not be expected of the old man, anything to spite them, but that he would marry again had occurred to no one.

"An old goat—plain and simple," was the general comment.

The news was debated over and over again and the conclusion everyone arrived at was the same: this was Koppel's work. Koppel, the bailiff and chief factotum, had married off his employer in order to cheat the Moskat children of their rightful due. In the Chassidic prayerhouses along the Gzhybov, Tvarda, and Gnoyna the story was known even before the evening prayers were over. There was such chattering that the reader was hardly able to finish the recitation of the service. He thumped on the stand for silence, but the congregation paid no heed. There were neither responses nor murmured "Amens" to the fervent Kaddish of the mourners. On their way home practically all the worshippers went by way of Reb Meshulam's house. They expected that the Moskat sons and daughters would be hurrying over in a fever of excitement and that the tumult would be heard clear out to the street. But not even a whisper came from the eight lighted windows.

In the almost fifty years since Meshulam's wealth had begun to accumulate, many unusual stories had been told about him. At times it seemed that everything he did had been carefully calculated in advance to confuse the Warsaw merchants and make fools of them. He undertook enterprises that everyone predicted were doomed to disaster; instead they turned out to be gold mines. He bought property on the deserted outskirts of the city, but in no time at all a building boom started and he sold the land for ten times its cost. He invested in stock of companies that were on the verge of bankruptcy, but somehow the stock shot up in value and paid handsome dividends. He was always doing what seemed strange. Most of the rich Warsaw Jewish merchants were followers of the Chassidic rabbi of Ger, whose repute was mighty among Polish Jewry; Reb Meshulam went on pilgrimages to the modest Chassidic court of Bialodrevna, whose rabbi had only a small following. The Warsaw Jewish community council had wanted to make him an elder, as was suitable for a man of his wealth, but he refused to take any part in civic affairs. When he did stick his nose into such matters, he managed to offend everyone, taunting the wealthy, the learned, and the rabbis, calling them peasants, simpletons, thick-skulled fools. He was one of the few Jewish businessmen who knew Russian and Polish, and it was rumored that he was in favor with the Russian Governor-General. For that reason attempts had been made several times to send him on missions of mediation and conciliation, but he had consistently refused, and had been roundly berated for his indifference. He followed his own way in everything. For breakfast, instead of having rolls and butter and coffee—mostly chicory —like other people, he would gnaw at some cold chicken and black bread. In the Moskat household the midday meal was taken, not at two o'clock, as was the custom in Warsaw, but at five. At first everyone had prophesied that he would come to a fall, as had happened to so many of those who had suddenly grown rich and arrogant. But the years went by and Meshulam did not slip. His wealth grew so great that something like terror began to seize hold of his enemies. Besides, he did not seem to be satisfied with one type of business, but branched out into all sorts of undertakings, so that no one could be sure exactly what it was that he was making his money at.

The things he occupied himself with! He bought lots and built houses; acquired ruins and put them in repair or pulled them down for junk. There would be reports that he had taken over a brick factory or that he had purchased a partnership in a glassworks or that he had bought a forest from some Polish landowner in Lithuania and was shipping lumber to England for railroad ties or that he had taken over the representation of a foreign tannery. For a while Warsaw seethed with the news that he had become a dealer in rags; he had opened a warehouse in Praga, on the other bank of the Vistula, and the ragpickers brought their pickings to him. He also bought bones; they were used to purify sugar. In recent years Meshulam had narrowed his interests; his wealth was so great that it increased on its own fat. He owned houses on the Tvarda, Panska, Shliska, Gzhybovska, Prosta, and Sienna; the buildings were old and half crumbling, but they were packed with tenants. It was rumored that he had a round million rubles in the St. Petersburg Imperial Bank. Whenever the subject was discussed someone would always say: "He doesn't know himself how much he has."

But so far as his children were concerned he had no luck at all. He had to support practically every one of them; he had made them administrators of his various properties and paid them the niggardly wage of twenty-five rubles a week. Of the two wives he had outlived, it was said that he had made their lives miserable. There were various opinions about his philanthropy; some said that he did not give a copper, others that he believed in secret charity. It almost seemed that whatever he did was with a view toward giving evil tongues something to wag about. When anyone ventured to tell him that all of Warsaw cursed him roundly, he would say: "The more curses the better."

He had an office in his home, but the administration of his affairs was carried on from Gzhybovska Street in a building surrounded by a large courtyard where Meshulam had warehouses and storerooms. The only tenants were his current or former employees. The courtyard was hidden from the street by a fence and flanked on three sides with old-fashioned buildings, low, with long wooden balconies and outside stairs. On the roofs swarms of pigeons perched. There was a stable where Meshulam kept his carriage horses. One of his Christian employees kept a cow in the yard. The unpaved ground was usually dotted with pools of water. A stranger entering through the gates might have the impression that he was in a small village, with cocks and hens cackling, and honking geese swimming around in the pools. In recent years Meshulam had employed only a few people. Most of the tenants worked elsewhere now, and paid no rent—as a matter of custom and because in any case there would have been no takers for the tumbledown flats. The only ones now employed by Reb Meshulam were Leibel the coachman; the janitor; a bookkeeper, Yechiel Stein, who had become half blind with age; and Shmuel, the carpenter, who was handy at all sorts of manual jobs. There were also a couple of aging gentiles who had once worked for Reb Meshulam and who received weekly pensions of a few rubles. Meshulam did not employ a cashier. He would take the money that had been collected, put it into his pocket, and then transfer it to his iron safe at home. When the safe was full he would take the notes and currency to the bank, accompanied by Koppel. Several times the accusation had been made that his books were not kept in order and he had been required by the tax offices to make an accounting, but the accusations had come to nothing. Those who had happened to see Yechiel Stein's books reported that his handwriting was like fly tracks and that he needed a magnifying glass to read what he himself had written. Every time Reb Meshulam walked in on the bookkeeper he would boom: "Scribble away, Reb Yechiel! You're a wizard of a penman."

The only one who knew about Meshulam's affairs was Koppel. He was known simply as "the bailiff." But he was more than that; he was the old man's adviser, confidant, and bodyguard. It was even whispered that Koppel, during his service with Reb Meshulam, had become rich on his own account and was now actually the old man's partner. Everything surrounding Koppel had a secretive quality. He had a wife and children, but none of the Moskat family had ever seen them. He lived in Praga, on the other side of the Vistula. He was fifty or thereabouts, but looked like a young man in his thirties, of middle height and lean, with a dark tanned face, curly hair, and wide-set flashing eyes. Summer and winter he wore a derby hat, pulled low over his forehead, and boots with high uppers. A pearl tie pin was stuck in his cravat. A cigarette always hung from the corner of his drooping mouth, and a pencil was stuck behind his left ear. He was clean-shaven. His features customarily wore a half-meek, half-contemptuous smile. Meshulam ordered him about like an errand boy. When the two walked together on the street, Koppel would linger a pace or two behind to avoid any implication that he considered himself the old man's equal. Whenever the two rode in Reb Meshulam's carriage, Koppel would sit with the coachman. If Meshulam addressed him in the presence of others, Koppel would incline his head deferentially. He would take his cigarette out of his mouth and keep his head lowered in a slight bow, the heels of his boots together, military syle. He had been a soldier in the Czar's army and it was rumored that during his service he had been a general's orderly.

4

But all this was for outside appearance. The truth was, as everyone knew, that Meshulam did not commit himself to any course of action without consulting his bailiff. The two would often have long talks. The administrators of the houses he owned—his sons included—had to make their accountings to Koppel. People who came for favors knew that in the last resort they would have to depend on Koppel. For years the Moskat sons and daughters had been carrying on a campaign against him, but it was Koppel who had won out. In his quiet way he put his nose into everything: matches for the grandchildren, dowries, philanthropies, communal affairs, even Chassidic disputes. On one occasion when Koppel was sick Reb Meshulam went about in a daze. He hardly heard what was said to him, scolded everyone, stamped his foot, and took refuge in a single answer to all questions: "My bailiff isn't here. Come tomorrow."

When Reb Meshulam made his yearly summer visit to the hot springs, Koppel went along with him, sharing his hotel quarters and taking the mineral waters that had been prescribed for the old man. It was even said that when the doctors had ordered mud baths for Reb Meshulam, Koppel had soaked in the ooze with his employer. In Karlsbad they strolled together up and down the promenade—here Koppel, instead of lagging behind, walked by Reb Meshulam's side—and talked about business affairs, about the wasters who lost all they had in Monte Carlo, and about the Galician rabbis who were visiting Karlsbad with their elegantly dressed daughters and daughters-in-law. Gossiping tongues said that

Reb Meshulam had signed over to Koppel a part of his fortune and had named him in his will as executor of the estate.
Koppel himself maintained an attitude of subservience toward
the younger Moskats. Whenever they came to ask his help in
some matter of preferment, he would put on a meek look and
say: "Who am I to decide?"

Koppel was with the old man at Karlsbad during the summer when he had met and married the Galician widow. Reb
Meshulam had met her at the springs while he was taking the
waters and had started a conversation with her, first in an attempt at an elegant Judæo-German, then in the familiar Yiddish. It pleased him to find that she had the habit of including
a few Hebrew words in her conversation; that she wore an orthodox matron's wig—although its elegance disturbed him a
little—that her dead husband, Reb David Landau, had been a
wealthy brewer in the city of Brody, and that her daughter,
Adele, had finished the preliminary college course in Lemberg
and had studied in Krakow, Vienna, and Switzerland. Rosa
Frumetl was suffering from some sort of liver ailment. She
was not staying at a hotel, but in a furnished room in the
poorer section of the city. She was frank to confess that she
had very little money. Nevertheless she conducted herself like
a woman of means. Each day she wore different attire. A
string of pearls hung about her throat, earrings dangled from
her earlobes, and a precious stone glistened from a ring on
her finger. She had invited Reb Meshulam to her lodgings and
had served him a glass of cherry brandy and some aniseed
cookies. There was a pleasant odor of lavender about her.
When Reb Meshulam raised his glass to wish her good health
she said: "Health and happiness to you, Reb Meshulam. May
your blessings increase."

"I've had enough blessings in my time," Reb Meshulam answered in his abrupt manner. "There's only one thing I can
look forward to now."

"May God forbid! What kind of talk is that?" Rosa Frumetl scolded him gently. "You'll live to be a hundred and
twenty—and maybe a span more!"

When the idea of marrying Rosa Frumetl and taking her
and her daughter back to Warsaw occurred to Reb Meshulam, he was afraid that Koppel would talk him out of it. But
the bailiff neither dissuaded nor encouraged him. Meshulam
asked him to find out what he could about the widow and he
brought back a detailed report. When, after a good deal of
hesitation, Reb Meshulam decided to go through with the af-

fair, Koppel attended to all the details. A thousand and one formalities had to be arranged so that Rosa Frumetl should be permitted to cross the Russian-Austrian border. A wedding ring had to be provided, as well as quarters for the married pair, and a rabbi to perform the ceremony. Koppel was as busy as though he were the groom's father. Rosa Frumetl wanted Reb Meshulam to settle some money on her and promise to provide a dowry for her daughter. Reb Meshulam agreed and even put it in writing. Adele went away for a week to Franzensbad, near by, and in her absence the marriage took place.

"The man's a lunatic," elderly gossips declared. "The old lecher."

Reb Meshulam had hoped for a quiet wedding, but it turned out to be a noisy affair. The hall was crowded with visiting rabbis, their wives, sons, daughters, and in-laws; Rosa Frumetl had been quick to make a host of acquaintances. Among the guests there was also a Galician *badchan,* a professional wedding jester, who had stumbled into the place and who at once began to improvise verses, bawdy and impudent, in a mixture of Yiddish, German, and Hebrew. There were all sorts of gifts, the kind that could be bought in the Karlsbad souvenir stores; fancy jewelry boxes, tablecloths, slippers with gilded heels, pens with magnifying glasses at the ends through which one might peer at a pretty colored view of the Alps. The large salon was full of sables, fur-lined silk coats, silk hats, and fashionable millinery. After the wedding ceremony there was a feast that lasted until late in the night, the women gossiping maliciously about the bride, who the day before had been practically a pauper.

"Who knows where good luck will strike next!" they said in their flat Galician dialect. "It took a miracle from heaven."

"She did a quick job on him!"

"And she plays the saint, too."

But directly after the wedding Reb Meshulam began to come to his senses. The masculine ripple that had awakened in him during his courtship soon flickered and died. In their bedchamber his bride revealed herself to be a broken shell. Under the wig of silken threads her hair was gray, cropped close like sheep's wool. Around her middle she wore a rupture belt. She lay in bed sighing and talking of her first husband, his learning, his devotion to his daughter, and his manuscripts, which she was so eager to have printed in Warsaw. She wagged on and on about the daughters of the rabbinical dignitaries who were becoming more wanton every day and who, here in Karlsbad, walked around openly with Austrian officers. She sneezed, blew her nose, took valerian drops for her heart. Reb Meshulam got up and climbed out of the bed.

"Enough babbling," he said in a loud voice. "Is there no end?"

For a moment it occurred to him that the best thing to do would be to get himself a divorce right here in Karlsbad, pay her off with a few thousand, and put an end to the comedy. But he was ashamed; he was afraid too that such a course might begin a long-drawn-out business of recriminations and lawsuits. He felt, too, a sort of blind resentment toward Koppel, although he knew in his heart that his bailiff was not to blame. For the more than sixty years that Reb Meshulam had been his own master he had never imagined himself capable of committing such a piece of foolishness. Had he not always carefully pondered his actions before he took a step? He had always arranged things so that it would be the other fellow and not himself who would be the fool. Let the hotheads do things in a hurry, flounder into impossible dilemmas, reduce themselves to poverty, sickness, disgrace, even death. But now he himself, Meshulam Moskat, had committed an outrageous blunder! What good could this marriage do him? His children would have something to laugh at. Besides, there were the financial commitments; he certainly couldn't break the promises he had made. No, he was not the man to break a promise; his bitterest enemies couldn't say that of him.

After a good deal of brooding he decided to follow the wisdom of the sages—the best thing to do is to do nothing. All right, what if there was a wife rattling around the house! So far as her dower rights were concerned, he would sign over to her one of his half-toppling houses; he would see to it that she didn't come in for any grand prize in the lottery. As for his new stepdaughter, there was something about her that set him on edge. She was educated, talked German, Polish, and French. But there was something too tense, too arrogant about her. She seemed to be staring past people, always thinking her own thoughts. No, she didn't fit in with his family, or with his business, for that matter. Besides, he was sure that she was secretly an unbeliever. He decided to arrange a match for her as soon as he got back to Warsaw and to give her a small dowry, not more than two thousand rubles.

"Just wait till she gets to Warsaw," Reb Meshulam said to himself. "Her nose'll come down."

With these thoughts weaving through his mind Reb Meshulam returned to Warsaw. He was not the one to moon over
past mistakes. He was the shrewd Meshulam Moskat, the victor in every encounter, not only against external enemies, but
over his own weaknesses as well.

CHAPTER TWO

1

A few weeks after Meshulam Moskat returned to Warsaw another traveler arrived at the station in the northern part of the
capital. He climbed down from a third-class car carrying an
oblong metal-bound basket locked with a double lock. He was
a young man, about nineteen. His name was Asa Heshel Bannet. On his mother's side he was the grandson of Reb Dan
Katzenellenbogen, the rabbi of Tereshpol Minor. He had with
him a letter of recommendation to the learned Dr. Shmaryahu
Jacobi, secretary of the Great Synagogue in Warsaw. In his
pocket rested a worn volume, the *Ethics* of Spinoza in a Hebrew translation.

The youth was tall and thin, with a long, pale face, a high,
prematurely creased forehead, keen blue eyes, thin lips, and a
sharp chin covered with a sprouting beard. His blond, almost
colorless earlocks were combed back from his ears. He was
wearing a gaberdine and a velvet cap. A scarf was wrapped
around his throat.

"Warsaw," he said aloud, his voice strange to himself,
"Warsaw at last."

People milled about the station. A porter in a red hat tried
to take the basket from him, but he refused to surrender it.
Though the year was well into October, the day was still
warm. Low clouds floated about in the sky, seeming to merge
with the puffs of steam from the locomotives. The sun hung in
the west, red and large. In the east the pale crescent of the
moon was visible.

The young man crossed to the other side of the railing that
separated the railroad station from the street. On the wide
thoroughfare, paved with rectangular cobblestones, carriages
bowled along, the horses seeming to charge straight at the
knots of pedestrians. Red-painted tramcars went clanging by.
There was a smell of coal, smoke, and earth in the moist air.

Birds flew about in the dim light, flapping their wings. In the
distance could be seen row upon row of buildings, their window panes reflecting the daylight with a silver and leaden
glow or glinting gold in the path of the setting sun. Bluish
plumes of smoke rose from chimneys. Something long forgotten yet familiar seemed to hover about the uneven roofs, the
pigeon cotes, the attic windows, the balconies, the telegraph
poles with their connecting wires. It was as if Asa Heshel had
seen all of this before in a dream, or maybe in a previous existence.

He took a few steps and then stood still, leaning against a
street lamp as though to protect himself against the hurrying
throngs. His limbs were cramped from the long hours of sitting. The ground seemed still to be shaking beneath him, the
doors and windows of the houses receding as though he were
still watching them from the speeding train. It had been long
since he had slept. His brain was only half awake.

"Is it here I will learn the divine truths?" he thought vaguely. "Among this multitude?"

Passers-by brushed past him, shoving the basket with their
feet. A coachman in a blue coat and oilcloth hat, whip in
hand, said something to him, but in the general tumult he
could not hear what the man asked him nor tell whether he
was speaking in Yiddish or Polish. A heavy-set man in a
ragged coat came to a stop near him, looked at him, and
asked: "A provincial, eh? Where do you want to go?"

"To Franciskaner Street. To a hotel."

"Over there."

A legless man rolled by on a small wooden platform. He
stretched out his hand toward Asa Heshel.

"Help a cripple," he whined in a singsong. "May the new
month bring you fortune."

Asa Heshel's pale face became bloodless. He took a copper
coin from his pocket. "And according to Spinoza I should feel
no pity for him," he thought. "What did he say about a lucky
month for me? Has another month rolled around?"

He suddenly remembered that he had neglected to pray
both this day and the day before. Nor had he put on his phylacteries.

"Has it gone as far as that with me?" he murmured.

He picked up the basket and started walking quickly. Another winter. So little time left.

The streets became even more crowded. The Nalevki was
lined with four- and five-story buildings with wide entrances,

plastered with signs in Russian, Polish, and Yiddish. A world of trade: shirts and canes, cotton and buttons, umbrellas and silk, chocolate and plush, hats and thread, jewelry and prayer shawls. Wooden platforms were piled high with wares. Draymen unloaded crates and yelled out in hoarse voices. Crowds went in and out of buildings. At the entrance to a store a revolving door spun around, swallowing up and disgorging people as though they were caught in some sort of mad dance.

The lodging-house where Asa Heshel hoped to find a room had three courtyards. It was almost like a town in itself. Peddlers called out their wares, artisans repaired broken chairs, sofas, and cots. Jews in faded coats and heavy boots fussed about their carts, which were hung with wooden buckets and lanterns. The meek-looking nags with their thin protruding ribs and long tails nuzzled at a mixture of oats and straw.

In the middle of the courtyard a group of jugglers was performing. A half-undressed man with long hair was lying on the ground, his naked back resting on a board studded with nails, while with the soles of his raised feet he juggled a barrel. A woman in red pantaloons, her head cropped close, padded back and forth on her hands, her feet waving in the air. A rag-picker, with a dirty white beard and a sack on his shoulder, came in from the street, raised his eyes to the upper stories, and cleared his throat.

"What'll you sell? What'll you sell?" he shouted in a rasping, hoarse voice. "I buy pots and pans, old shoes, old pants, old hats, rags, rags."

The ragpicker must have some deeper meaning, it seemed to Asa Heshel. What he really meant was: "Rags, that's all that's left of our striving."

"And Rabbi Hiyah taught: One man says, you owe me one hundred gulden, and the other answers, I owe you nothing." The words came in the traditional chant from a study house in a room off the courtyard. Through the dust-laden window pane Asa Heshel caught a glimpse of a dark face framed in disordered sidelocks. For a moment the singsong voice prevailed over the tumult in the court.

The steps up to the hotel were littered with mud and refuse. At the left, in a kitchen, a woman bent over a steaming washtub. At the right, in a room with four windows, and with moist, sweating walls, a group of men and women sat about a large table. A fair-haired man was gnawing at the leg of a chicken; an old Jew with a beard growing askew from his chin and a parchment-yellow forehead, furrowed with wrinkles, muttered over an open volume. A plump young man in a sweat-stained vest held a stick of sealing wax to a candle and dabbed the heated end on an envelope. The women sat somewhat removed from the men, the older of them with kerchiefs over their matron's wigs. A man in a quilted jacket, below which protruded the fringes of a ritual garment, was repairing a sack with a heavy needle and ropelike thread. A gas lamp snored and flickered. The hotelkeeper, a youngish man, came forward. He was wearing gold-rimmed glasses and under his collar a stringlike, typical Chassidic tie.

"A newcomer? What can I do for you?"

"Is it possible to get lodging here?"

"What else? First I have to see your papers. A pass or birth certificate."

"I have a pass."

"Good. A hundred per cent. What's the name?"

"Asa Heshel Bannet."

"Bannet. Any relation to Rabbi Mordecai Bannet?"

"Yes. A great-grandson."

"An aristocratic family, eh? And where are you from?"

"Tereshpol Minor."

"What brings you to Warsaw? To see a doctor, I suppose."

"No."

"What, then? To go into business?"

"No."

"Maybe to enter a yeshivah?"

"I don't know yet."

"Who else would know? How long do you want to stay? Overnight or longer?"

"In the meanwhile just overnight."

"You'll have to share a bed with someone else. It'll come out cheaper."

Asa Heshel made a wry mouth and started to say something, but he composed his lips and was silent.

"What's wrong with it? It isn't good enough for you? This is Warsaw. You have to take things the way you find them. This isn't the Hotel Bristol. The biggest merchants sleep two in a bed when the place is full."

"I thought I could get a room for myself."

"Not here."

A silence fell on the group at the table. The man who was repairing the sack lifted his needle high in the air and stared at Asa Heshel with perplexed eyes. A woman with a triangular face broke into a laugh, showing a mouthful of gold teeth.

"Look who wants to pick and choose!" she said in a sharp Lithuanian accent. "Count Pototski!"

The other women giggled. The glasses on the landlord's nose seemed to gleam with triumph.

"Where did you say you come from, your highness?" he asked, his mouth close to Asa Heshel's ear, as though the newcomer were deaf. "Show me your pass."

He looked long and carefully at the passbook with its black covers and wrinkled his forehead.

"Aha! From over there," he said. "From one of those one-horse villages."

He raised his voice. "All right, put down your basket. Warsaw'll put you in your place."

2

Asa Heshel came of distinguished stock on both sides of his family. His maternal grandfather, Reb Dan Katzenellenbogen, had a genealogical chart of his own, inscribed on parchment with gold ink in the form of a many-branched linden tree. The root was King David, and the branches bore the names of other illustrious forebears. Reb Dan himself had on his forehead a scar that, it was said, was the mark only of those descended from kingly stock and privileged to wear the crown when Messiah came.

Asa Heshel's grandmother on his father's side, Tamar, had worn a ritual fringed garment, like a man, and had made the New Year pilgrimages to the Chassidic court of the rabbi of Belz. His paternal grandfather, Tamar's husband, Reb Jerachmiel Bannet, was a man of fervent and inordinate piety, who never touched food before sunset, mortified his flesh with cold baths, and in the winter rolled his body in the snow. He paid no attention to household or business affairs, but day and night sat locked in his attic room, studying a volume of the Cabala. Sometimes he would disappear for days on end. It was said that on these journeys he would meet in some humble place the six-and-thirty hidden saints, by whose virtue and humility the entire earth is enabled to exist. Since Reb Jerachmiel refused to take part in any civic affairs, it was Tamar who participated in the community council's deliberations. She sat at the end of the table, alongside the propertied men of the town, her brass-rimmed spectacles perched on the end of her nose. She took snuff from a horn snuffbox, gnawed at sticks of licorice, and talked in determined accents. It was said that the rabbi of Belz himself stood up and put a chair in place for her when she came in.

She had brought eight children into the world, but only one of them had survived to adulthood. Some were stillborn, others had died in their cradles. She had not permitted the little bodies to be carried away until she had herself prepared them for burial. As a charm the last-born had been given five names, Alter, Chaim, Benzion, Kadish, and Jonathan, and to fool the Angel of Death they dressed the child in trousers of white linen and a white cap, like a shroud. Around his neck he wore a little bag containing an inscribed amulet and a wolf's tooth to ward off the evil eye. At twelve he was pledged to Finkel, the daughter of the rabbi of Tereshpol Minor. At fourteen he was married. Nine months after the wedding the young wife was delivered of a daughter, Dinah, and two years later of a son, who was named Asa Heshel, after one of his great-grandfathers. At the circumcision ceremony both grandmothers lifted the hems of their skirts and hopped and bobbed to each other as though they were at a wedding.

But there was little peace in the house of the young pair. Every couple of weeks Jonathan—they called him by the last of his five names—would climb into a coach and ride off to his mother in Yanov. Tamar stuffed him with pancakes, eggnogs, roast chicken, egg noodles, and preserves. In the spring she made him take a tonic against worms, as though he were still a schoolboy. The delicately reared Jonathan could not stand his father-in-law, who was always engaged in some dispute or other with half the town; or his mother-in-law, who kept the food pantry locked against her daughters-in-law; or his brothers-in-law, Zaddock and Levi, who, for all their learning and education, sat around playing chess or exchanging witticisms. When his father died—it happened in an almshouse during one of his trips away from home—Jonathan went to his mother and stayed there, dispatching a divorce to his wife by a messenger. Finkel was barely nineteen years old at the time.

Asa Heshel went through all the diseases of infancy; Gimpel, the Tereshpol Minor barber-surgeon, gave up all hope for him time and again. He had measles and whooping cough, diphtheria and diarrhea, scarlet fever and ear abscesses. He would weep all night long, get fits of coughing, and turn blue, as though he were dying. Finkel had to carry him around in her arms all night. Very early he began to suffer from fright;

anything might frighten him—the blowing of the ram's horn, a mirror, a chimney-sweep, a hen. He had dreams of gypsies stowing children in a sack and spiriting them away, of corpses that walked about the cemeteries, of ghosts that danced about behind the ritual bathhouse. He was always asking questions: How high is the sky? How deep is the earth? What's at the other side of the end of the world? Who made God? His grandmother would put her hands to her ears. "He drives me crazy," she wailed. "He's a dybbuk, not a child!"

He attended cheder for only half a day. He quickly got the reputation of a prodigy. At five he was studying Talmud, at six he began the Talmudic commentators, at eight the teacher had no more to give him. At the age of nine he delivered a discourse in the synagogue, and at twelve he was writing learned letters to rabbis in other towns. The rabbis would send him back long epistles, addressing him as "The Keen and Eagle-eyed" and "Uprooter of Mountains." Matchmakers flooded the family with matrimonial offers; the townsfolk predicted that he was sure, in God's good time, to inherit his grandfather's rabbinical chair, for what were his uncles Zaddok and Levi but empty heads and dawdlers. And then what does the promising youth do but abandon the roads of righteousness and join the ranks of the "moderns"? He would start endless disputes with the others in the study house and criticize the rabbis. He prayed without putting on the customary prayer sash, scribbled on the margins of the sacred books, made mock of the pious. Instead of studying the Commentaries he delved into Maimonides's *Guide for the Perplexed* and Jehuda Halevi's *Khuzari*. Somewhere he got hold of the writings of the heretic Salomon Maimon. He went about with his coat unbuttoned, his earlocks unkempt, his hat pushed to one side, his eyes looking into the distance beyond the rooftops. His Uncle Levi would chide him: "Don't think so much. The sky won't fall." The town agreed that it was Jekuthiel the watchmaker, follower of the heretic Jacob Reifman, who had brought the youth to grief. Jekuthiel Watchmaker had once studied under Reb Dan Katzenellenbogen, but later had gone in for worldly learning. He lived in a small house at the end of an alley, kept away from the religious folk, and fraternized mostly with the town musicians. He had a thin beard, a wide and lofty forehead, and big black eyes. All day he sat in his tiny workroom over his work bench, a jeweler's glass in his eye. In the evening he read, and sometimes to pass the time he played on the zither. His wife had died during an epidemic, and the children had been taken by her mother. Asa Heshel became a familiar at Jekuthiel's place. The watchmaker had in his library old copies of the modern Hebrew journal *Hameasef* and the Pentateuch in Moses Mendelssohn's German translation, besides a collection of the German poets, Klopstock, Goethe, Schiller, Heine, as well as some old textbooks of algebra, geometry, physics, and geography. There were also the works of Spinoza, Leibnitz, Kant, and Hegel. Jekuthiel gave Asa Heshel the key to his house and the youth spent entire days there, reading and studying. He only half understood the German. He struggled over the problems in mathematics and drew geometrical figures with a piece of chalk on a board. When his grandfather learned that the boy had thrown himself into the study of worldly books he disowned him. His mother's eyes were swollen with weeping. But Asa Heshel stuck to his new path. Often he would stay for the evening meal at Jekuthiel's. While the older man prepared the food, he discussed philosophy with Asa Heshel.

"All right, let's assume that the earth was torn away from the sun"—Jekuthiel spoke with the traditional prayerhouse chant—"Does that settle the matter? There still has to be a First Cause."

Asa Heshel swallowed all the books at a gulp. He managed to plow his way through the Russian and Polish with the help of a dictionary, the Latin from a Vulgate that Jekuthiel had borrowed from the priest. The "emancipated" Jews near by in Zamosc heard of him and began to send him books from their own library. Jekuthiel even wrote out for him a list of works that might help him go on to higher education without the help of a university. But years passed and little came of his undisciplined efforts. He began courses of study but never completed them. He was reading without system, browsing here and there. The eternal questions never gave him rest: Was there a God or was everything, the world and its works, mechanical and blind? Did man have responsibilities or was he accountable to no higher power? Was the soul immortal or would time bring everything to oblivion? In the long summer days he would take a crust of bread, a pencil, and paper and go off into the forest, or he would climb up to the attic of his grandfather's house, sit himself down on an upturned water barrel, and daydream. Each day he would make up his mind anew to leave the town, and each day he stayed. He had neither money for travel nor any idea how he might earn his keep out in the great world. Ever since he had departed from the accepted ways, his mother had begun to ail. She had taken off her matron's wig and went about with a shawl over her head, in the manner of a mourner. She lay in bed for days at a time, reading her prayerbook. His sister, Dinah, complained that because of him she could not find a husband. Reb Dan Katzenellenbogen's enemies began to discuss bringing a new rabbi to the town.

His grandmother Tamar was no longer alive. His father had disappeared. Some people said that he was somewhere in Galicia and had taken another wife; others said that he had died. Whenever Asa Heshel talked about going away, his mother would tremble and red spots would flare up on her cheeks.

"You, too, will leave me," she wept. "Dear Father in heaven."

During this time it happened that Reb Paltiel, one of the synagogue elders, lost his wife. After the prescribed thirty-day mourning period he sent a matchmaker to Finkel. Asa Heshel's grandmother seized on the idea and his uncles hastened to talk his mother into it. Reb Paltiel promised to sign over to Finkel a house he owned and put aside a dowry for Dinah. But he stipulated that Asa Heshel leave the town.

"He's too smart for me," Reb Paltiel declared. "I don't like his goings on."

These things Asa Heshel brought with him to Warsaw—his grandfather's maledictions and predictions that he would come to no good; his mother's prayer that Elijah the prophet, the friend of the friendless, would intercede to save him in his trials; a nickel-plated watch from Jekuthiel. Todros Lemel, head of the modern Jewish school in Zamosc, gave him a letter of recommendation to the learned Dr. Shmaryahu Jacobi, secretary of the Warsaw synagogue, written in Hebrew, in a flowery and ornate script.

The letter read:

To my illustrious teacher and guide, world-renowned sage in Law and Enlightenment, Reb Shmaryahu Jacobi, long may his light shine forth!

        Your worthiness has undoubtedly long forgotten my humble person. It was my elevated privilege to be your pupil at the seminary in the years between 1892 and 1896. I am now in the town of Zamosc, the director of the school, Torah and Learning, to teach the youth of Israel the doorway of modern knowledge. The youth who brings this letter to your distinguished self is, according to the unworthy opinion of your former pupil, one of those high and aspiring spirits which are so few in number. His grandfather, Reb Dan Katzenellenbogen, is a sage of great repute, and has been for fifty years the shepherd of his flock in Tereshpol Minor. Of this young man, Asa Heshel Bannet, it can be said that he is the true limb of his grandfather. Even in his tender youth he won renown. Learned men who heard him deliver a discourse spoke words of mouth-filling praise. Secretly, and away from the censorious eyes of the fanatics of the town, with the help of dictionaries he taught himself to read European languages. In the study of algebra he has traveled as far as logarithms. His soul also yearns toward philosophy. In his removed village there are all too few enlightened books, and through a traveler who visits us on the market days I have sent him books on history, natural science, psychology, and whatever else his heart has longed for. But it is difficult to satiate his spiritual hunger. I know that your honor has always striven to strengthen the hand of the youth who yearns to taste of the waters of wisdom, and I am prayerful that this neophyte will find favor in your eyes. It is his aspiration to complete high school as an extern and to enter a university, which is the Temple of Knowledge and also a threshold to an honorable livelihood. I add that many matches were bespoken for him with daughters of wealthy houses and he has turned away from them because of his thirst for enlightenment. He has also suffered many persecutions out of his search for truth. He is ready to eat bread and salt and to drink water by measure in order to reach the exalted goal of his heart. I could write many more words of praise for the youth Asa Heshel Bannet, and I could recount much of my town Zamosc and the struggles we must wage against the fanatics; the illumination that lights up all the corners of the Western lands has not yet penetrated into our towns, to our great shame be it said, and many still walk about in darkness at noon. But this paper is too small.

> *I remain bound to you, my teacher and guide, with stout ropes of love. I sign myself, your pupil Todros Lemel, founder and director of the school Torah and Learning for the young sons of Israel in the town of Zamosc.*

3

Dr. Shmaryahu Jacobi, secretary of the synagogue on Tlo-matska Street, had in recent years had little to do with the ac-count books of the temple; he was occupied with more learned matters. His wife had long been dead and his children had all married. He spent his days and half his nights writing a book on the history of calendars. In addition he was engaged in translating Milton's *Paradise Lost* into Hebrew. He was in his seventies, short, with rounded shoulders and a small head on which he wore a six-cornered skullcap. His sparse beard had passed through the stage of grayness and was now a faded yellow. A pair of blue-tinted spectacles was perched in front of his gray eyes. Now he was climbing a wall ladder to get a book from an upper shelf of the bookcase. He climbed slowly, one rung at a time, halting after each step. He put out his hand and took a volume from a lower shelf, peer-ing at its pages through a magnifying glass.

"Yes, yes, yes, babble, babble, idle talk . . ." he muttered to himself, giving the Yiddish an elegant German intonation.

The door opened and the chief sexton entered, a red-faced man with a wavy beard. He was dressed in an alpaca surtout, striped trousers, and a wide cap shaped like a casserole.

"Herr Professor," he said, "some young man has come with a letter."

"What? Who is he? What does he want? I have no time."

"I told him, but he has a letter, a document of some kind from a pupil of the professor's."

"What kind of pupil? I have no pupil!" The old man began to shake, the ladder shaking with him.

"Then I'll tell him to go."

"Wait. Send him in. Always they bother me."

The sexton left the room. The old man climbed down off the ladder and stood on his tottering legs, lifting the magnify-ing glass to his face as though ready to peer through it at the visitor. Asa Heshel opened the door and stood uncertainly on the threshold.

"Well, well, come in," the old man said in an impatient voice. "Where is the letter?"

He snatched the envelope that Asa Heshel held out to him, clawed at the leaf of paper with his thin fingers, and brought it up close to his tinted eyeglasses. For a long time he made no move. He might almost have fallen asleep on his feet. Suddenly he whipped the paper over to the other side. Asa Heshel took off his velvet cap. His flaxen-white earlocks were already half shorn away; only little tufts were visible behind his ears. After some hesitation he put his cap on again.

"*Nu, ja.* So, so," the old man said in a dry voice. "The old story. The son of a rabbi, a philosopher, an extern—always the same—just like fifty years ago."

He turned the letter over again, as though there were something else he might find between the lines, then suddenly dropped his elegant German enunciation and changed over to an unadorned Yiddish.

"Why didn't you learn a trade, instead of all this nonsense?"

"They didn't want me to."

"It's never too late."

"I would rather study."

"What do you mean, study? With these logarithms of yours you'll not impress anybody. How old are you?"

"Nineteen."

"It's too late to begin now. All the externs fail in the examinations. And if they do manage to pass they can't get into the university. They travel away to Switzerland and come back well-trained *schnorrers.*"

"I'll not be a *schnorrer.*"

"When you get hungry enough you'll be one. You're still young and inexperienced. All right, let's admit that we have heads on our shoulders, we Jews. But no one wants our brains. Read the ancient sages—the poor man's wisdom is despised!"

"I want to study for my own sake."

"*Quatsch!* Where there's no bread there's no learning. What about your health? Do you cough? Do you spit blood?"

"God forbid."

"Most of them get sick and then they have to be sent to a sanatorium. And some of them get so despondent that they get themselves converted."

"I won't convert."

"Yes, you all know everything in advance. But when your boots are torn and you have no roof over your head, you run to the missionaries fast enough."

"Maybe I can give some lessons," Asa Heshel ventured. He

wiped the perspiration from his face with a blue handkerchief.

"What are you talking about? You know little enough yourself. Forgive me for my frankness; I'm an old man, I will die soon, and so I speak the truth. You don't understand the way things are." His voice became milder and he took a step or two closer to Asa Heshel. "There's no shortage of education these days. Everybody studies. Here in the synagogue we have a janitor, and the janitor has a son, and the son knows logarithms, too. And maybe better than you do. He certainly knows Polish and Russian better, and he's younger than you are, besides. And in addition he's a Christian; all doors are open to him. How do you think you can compete with him?"

"I don't want to compete with anybody."

"Just the same, you have to. That's the way life is—constant competition. Our young men don't get a chance anywhere. Even in other countries. Why is it you're not married?"

Asa Heshel was silent.

"Why not? A young man must get married sooner or later. At least there's a wife and food and lodging in her parents' house. And as for tomorrow—let the Almighty worry about that. Here you can starve, for all anyone cares. I regret it, young man, but there's nothing I can do to help you. I am, as you see, half blind."

"I understand and I ask your pardon. Thank you and good day."

"Wait, don't go. Others make pests of themselves, and you want to run away. If you're proud, into the bargain, then you'll certainly go under."

"But you probably have no time."

"My time isn't worth a pinch of snuff. First I'll give you a note to Shatzkin, the manager of the free kitchen for intellectuals. You'll be able to get dinner there for nothing."

"I don't want any free dinners."

"My, my! Stubborn, too! It isn't free. Rich people pay for it. Rothschild won't get poor on account of you."

The old man waved Asa Heshel to a small leather sofa, while he sat down at the writing-desk and dipped a pen into a half-dry inkwell. He made a few scrawls, groaning as he wrote. He shook the pen, dropping a small blot on the paper. The door opened and the sexton came in again.

"Herr Professor, Abram is here."

"What Abram? Which Abram?"

"Abram Shapiro. Meshulam Moskat's son-in-law."

A mild smile showed on the old man's parchment-yellow face.

"Ah, that one. That cynic. Let him come in."

Even before the words were out of his mouth the door was flung open and a large man entered. He had a square, pitch-black beard and wore a flowing cloak and a broad-brimmed plush hat, with a silk knotted scarf around his neck in place of a cravat. On his velvet waistcoat a gold chain bobbed up and down. In his hand he carried a twisted walking-stick with a two-branched handle, like the horns of a stag, ornamented with silver and amber. He was so tall that he had to lower his head to get through the door. His broad shoulders brushed against the doorposts. His flushed face was a winy red. A big cigar was stuck between his lips. He brought with him the mingled odors of tobacco, scented soap, and something pleasant and cosmopolitan. Dr. Shmaryahu Jacobi came forward to greet him. The newcomer grabbed the old man's outstretched hand between his own hairy paws.

"Ah, professor!" he boomed in a thunderous voice. "Here I was, strolling around between Tlomatska and Bielanska, and suddenly it hit me—why shouldn't I go in and see how our dear Professor Jacobi is getting along? I had—if you'll permit me to say so—a rendezvous with a lady. But she let me stand and whistle. She was to meet me at the Hotel Krakow. Well, the devil take her. My God, professor, you're getting younger every day. As for me, I'm getting as old as Methuselah; I climb a single flight of stairs and my heart begins to pound like a thief's with the police after him. My, my, all the books! They write and expound, these wise men of yours, but when it comes to the real stuff, it's nothing but wind. Well, how are you, my dear professor? How does it go with your book on calendars? What's the latest news from the sky? After all, you're an astronomer. On the earth here it's nothing but one colossal mistake. Enough to drive you out of your mind. The day I've had today—may the anti-Semites have such a day! Fights with everybody! My wife, my father-in-law, the children! Even with the servant girl. I've covered every corner of Warsaw. I went to Dr. Mintz. 'Don't get yourself excited,' he says. 'Bad for your belly-button.' 'Aha,' I tell him, 'a fine trick if you can do it. Suppose you try, doctor,' I tell him. He imagines that all I have to do is stretch out on the sofa, close my peepers, and everything is settled. That's not my way, professor. I have to roar like a lion. Do you hear me, professor? If I wasn't ashamed I would let out such a roaring that Warsaw would collapse. Who is this young man? What's he sitting there for like a kitten?"

All the time Abram had been talking the old professor had stood smiling, showing his empty gums and shaking his head from side to side. He had apparently forgotten all about the youth from Tereshpol Minor. Now he turned around, looked at him, and rubbed his hand over his ivory forehead.

"This young man? Ah, yes. I must give him a note. To the free kitchen."

"No, thank you. I don't want it, I don't need it," Asa Heshel said timidly. "I have money."

Abram made an astonished gesture and clapped his hands.

"You hear that, professor? He has money," he said violently. "The first time in my life I hear anyone acknowledge that he has money. What are you so quiet about? For forty years I've been searching for a man like you, and here he sits like a nobody! Shame on you, professor. What does he need the free kitchen for!"

"He came to Warsaw to study—the grandson of a rabbi—a prodigy."

"Really? There are still specimens of that kind around? And I thought they'd gone for good, the whole species extinct, like the aurochs, if you'll forgive the comparison. Let me take a look at him. Tell me, professor, what sort of blessing does one recite over such a rarity? What does he want to study?"

"He has a letter, from Zamosc."

"Where is it? Let me see it."

Asa Heshel took from his pocket the creased sheet of writing-paper. Abram snatched it out of his hand and turned it from side to side. Then he began to read out loud the pompous, flowery Hebrew phrases, cantillating them in the synagogue style. His face shone, his beard quivered, his eyebrows lifted and fell, his cheeks puffed in and out. The words as he mouthed them with his Polish intonation had a bedraggled sound, with deep echoes and overtones. After every word in praise of Asa Heshel, Abram darted a glance at him from his large and blazing eyes. When he finished he gave the table a mighty pounding with his fist. The inkwell almost leaped off to the floor.

"Then there's something to go on living for!" he cried out.

"We still have Torah, Jews, sages, enlightenment! And I, idiot that I am, thought that we were through. Come here, young man. You'll not eat your meal at the free kitchen tonight!"

He grabbed Asa Heshel by the shoulders and pulled him to his feet.

"Tonight you'll eat at my house," he shouted. "I'm Abram Shapiro. Don't worry, it'll be kosher. Even if you want pork you'll get kosher food."

He started to laugh, a throaty gurgle that tore out of him in a mighty, almost unearthly echo. The tears poured from his eyes. His face took on an apoplectic hue. He snatched a silk handkerchief from his pocket and blew his nose, remembering that Dr. Mintz had warned him to stop going into a frenzy over every petty occurrence if he didn't want to get another heart attack.

4

The steps that led down from Shmaryahu Jacobi's office were broad and newly scoured. Below on the landing, cuspidors reposed at either side. Through the tall window a pale winter sun shone. The air was dry and frosty outside. In the synagogue courtyard, around a garden plot enclosed by iron railings, sparrows hopped about on their fragile legs and picked at seeds. From the rabbiner's window, hung with blue curtains, came the soft tinkling of a piano. Abram took a few long strides and pounded his cane into the asphalt. He stopped dead for a moment, clutching at his left side.

"Do you know anything about these things? Here I am walking slowly and my heart's galloping. Wait a few minutes. I'll take a rest."

"I have plenty of time."

"What's your name?"

"Asa Heshel Bannet."

"Yes, Asa Heshel. Well, look, the situation's this way. I would like to take you to my house, but I just had an argument with Hama, my wife. A shame! And I have two fine daughters. Too good for me. But don't worry. A quarrel can't last forever. In the meanwhile I've been invited for dinner to my brother-in-law's; Nyunie his name is. He's a brother of my wife, a dear fellow, a character. His wife, Dacha, is a pious woman, strictly orthodox, a rabbi's daughter. Maybe you've heard of my father-in-law, Meshulam Moskat."

"No."

"A Jew with a head on him, but no heart. A robber. Rich as Croesus. Well, we'll take a droshky and ride over to Nyunie's. You'll be welcome. Come to think of it, there's a sort of gathering there today, a few guests. My father-in-law—may the law catch up with him—took it into his head to get married again—some woman from Galicia. That makes her my stepmother-in-law. She's got a daughter, that makes her—let's see—my wife's stepsister. Yes, the whole thing's finished—wrapped up and knotted with a double knot. Wife number three—"

"Please forgive me," Asa Heshel ventured after a slight hesitation. "Maybe I'd better not go with you."

"What? Why not? Are you embarrassed, or ashamed? Listen to me, my boy, Warsaw isn't that one-horse village of yours—what do you call it, Tereshpol Junior? This is a place where you've got to show your face. And my brother-in-law is a simple man, and a bit of a scholar. And his daughter, Hadassah—she's a beauty. One look at her and you're finished. Believe me, if I wasn't her uncle, I'd go after her myself. Besides, maybe she'll be able to give you some tutoring. Just let me see how late it is. Exactly half past one. They eat dinner at two. They live on the Panska. A droshky'll take us there in no more than fifteen minutes. First I'll go into the restaurant over there and make a telephone call. I want to find out why that female kept me sweating. Come along and wait for me."

They crossed over to the other side of the street and through an all-glass door entered a large eating-place with red-painted walls and a profusion of mirrors. From the carved ceiling an elaborate crystal chandelier hung. Waiters with white napkins draped over their arms hurried back and forth. Their reflections repeated themselves on and on in the opposing mirrors. Someone was playing a pianoforte. There was the smell of brandy, beer, roast meats, and spices. A tall, heavy man, with a bald spot round as a plate and a smooth, red neck, was dipping his mustaches into a froth-topped mug. A little man with a serviette tucked in his collar bent over a plate of meat, making a clatter with his knife and fork. A girl with blond hair, in a white apron, her eyelids blued and her cheeks rouged, stood behind a buffet loaded with a variety of bottles, glasses, trays, and plates, pouring a greenish liquor from a carafe into a goblet. Abram went off somewhere. Asa Heshel felt his head spinning, as if the mere vapors were making him drunk. The room seemed to sway and his vision dimmed. Suddenly a figure materialized in front of him, horrifyingly familiar and at the same time puzzlingly strange. It was his own face, his own features he was seeing in a mirror near by.

"You!" he murmured to the reflection. "Beggar!"

The night before, he had shaved his face clean. But now a faint growth again covered his chin. The collar of his shirt was wrinkled. His Adam's apple moved about under the skin of his throat. He had bought an overcoat just before he left Tereshpol Minor, but in the brilliant light of the restaurant it seemed shoddy, too tight for him, with awkwardly fitting shoulders. The toes of his shoes curled upwards. Asa Heshel knew that it was only common sense to establish contact with the wealthy familes to whom this stranger wanted to take him. Timidity, according to Spinoza, was an emotion one must struggle to overcome. But the longer he remained in this ornate restaurant, the meaner he felt himself. It seemed to him that everyone was looking at him, winking and smiling contemptuously. A waiter brushed against him. The girl at the buffet grinned, showing a mouthful of brilliantly white teeth. A mad impulse swept over him to open the door and run away. At that moment he saw Abram walking rapidly toward him, his approach reflected in the mirrors.

"All right, let's go!" Abram said. "It's getting late."

He took Asa Heshel's arm and went out with him. A droshky drew up. Abram pushed Asa Heshel before him, climbed into the carriage, and dropped onto the seat, the springs groaning under his massive posterior.

"Is it far?" Asa Heshel asked.

"Don't worry. They won't eat you up. Don't be a greenhorn."

Abram pointed out the streets and houses as the carriage drove on. They passed a bank fronted with pillars; stores with show windows displaying gold coins and lottery tickets; a row of shops, in front of each of which were a sack of garlic, a case of lemons, and hanging strings of dried mushrooms. At Iron Gate Square there was a confusion of sights: a garden, an open space lined with benches, a wedding hall, a market place. Janitors swept together piles of refuse. A poultry dealer's apprentice, with bloodied sleeves, struggled with a flock of turkeys. They were trying to scatter, and another man blocked their flight by waving a stick. Through the bedlam a funeral procession wound its way. The horses pulling the hearse were draped in black; through the eyeholes the eyes peered, with their enormous pupils. Abram made a grimace.

"I don't mind anything in the world, brother," he remarked, "except to be a corpse. Anything but that."

He held a match to his cigar, but the wind puffed out the flame. He half stood up and struck another match; the droshky almost overturned with the shifting of his weight.

He blew a cloud of smoke and turned to Asa Heshel. "Tell me, young man," he said, "were you carrying on some sort of love affair in that town of yours?"

"Oh, no!"

"What's the idea of blushing? When I was your age I chased after every *shikse*."

As the droshky drove through the Gzhybov, Abram pointed out his father-in-law's house. A baker's girl standing in front of the gate with a basket of fresh loaves nodded her head at him; Abram good-naturedly waved his hand. On the Tvarda he nudged Asa Heshel and pointed with his finger.

"Over there used to be the Bialodrevner prayerhouse. That's where I go."

"Then you're a Chassid?"

"On the holidays I even wear the Chassid's fur hat."

A cold gust of wind blew into the carriage. Heavy clouds hid the sun. The sky turned a greenish blue. There was a tang of hail and snow in the air. Asa Heshel put up his coat collar. He had not yet got over the fatigue of the journey. There was a tight feeling in his nostrils, and his head ached. It seemed to him that he had been away from his home for years. "Where am I letting myself be dragged to?" he thought. He closed his eyes and held on to the iron side handle. In the darkness before his eyelids he saw the image of a phantom flower, dazzlingly sunlit, half opened and unsubstantial. It was an apparition that always came to him in moments of perplexity. He felt a longing to pray—but to whom should he pray? The divine laws would not be altered for his sake.

The droshky came to a halt. Asa Heshel opened his eyes. He climbed out of the carriage in front of a four-story building on a narrow, irregular street cobbled with round-surfaced stones. Abram took a silver coin out of a deep chamois purse. The horse turned his head with the queer appearance of curiosity with which animals sometimes seem to imitate human gestures. The two men entered Nyunie Moskat's house through a front door with frosted glass panels. They climbed a flight of marble steps, dust-covered and unswept. From a dentist's office on the second floor there was a strong smell of iodine and ether and in a spittoon on the landing there was a wad of bloodstained cotton. On a mahogany double door on the third floor was a brass plate with a name engraved on it in Polish and Yiddish—"Nahum Leib Moskat." Abram pressed the bell; there was a shrill ringing. Asa Heshel set his hat on straight and glanced back over his shoulder, as though he might make a dash for it at the last minute.

5

The door was opened by a stout servant girl with an enormous bosom and with a flowered scarf over her shoulders. Her bare feet were stuck into a pair of plush carpet slippers. There were dimples in her cheeks. Seeing Asa Heshel, she threw a questioning glance at Abram. He nodded his head.

"This young man is with me," he said. "You don't faint with ecstasy that I'm here, Shifra, my dear? After I went to the trouble of bringing you a present."

He took a little box out of his pocket and handed it to her. Shifra wiped her hand with her apron before taking it, so as not to soil the gaily colored cover.

"You never forget to bring something," she said. "And you shouldn't."

"Never mind that female babble. Tell me, is her ladyship from Galicia here already?"

"Yes, she's here."

"And that daughter of hers?"

"They're both in the salon."

"What are you cooking there? I can smell it all the way out here."

"Don't worry, it won't poison you."

Abram took off his cape. His white starched cuffs protruded from his sleeves; diamonds twinkled from his gold cufflinks. He took off his hat and stood before a wall mirror to comb his long hair carefully over his bald spot. Asa Heshel got out of his overcoat, too. He was wearing a gaberdine, and a thin string tie was knotted around his soft collar.

"Come along with me, young man," Abram said. "Nothing to be afraid of."

The salon they entered was large. It had three windows. Gold-framed portraits of bearded, skullcapped Jews and their bewigged and bonneted wives hung on the walls. Wide easy chairs with long golden fringes stood about. In a corner there was a wall clock, elaborately carved. Rosa Frumetl was seated on a sofa covered with brocade. In one hand she held a small glass of brandy and in the other a tiny cake. Near her was a low table with a telephone. Dacha, Nyunie's wife, an emaciated woman, dark as a crow, wearing a matron's wig, with a silk shawl over her shoulders, was talking into the mouthpiece.

"What? Talk louder!" she was saying, in a flat accent, drawing out the vowel sounds. "I don't hear a word. What?"

Adele sat at the piano at the other side of the room, wearing a pleated skirt and an embroidered white blouse with lace at the wrists, and a wide, old-fashioned starched collar. The sunlight shining through the curtains and hangings was reflected in her hair. Abram took Asa Heshel by the elbow as though to assure himself that the bashful youth would not flee.

"Good morning, good day!" he called out. "Where is Nyunie?"

Dacha, at the telephone, waved her hand. Adele put down the music score she had been leafing and stood up. Rosa Frumetl turned toward them.

"What's the good of standing on ceremony?" Abram addressed Rosa Frumetl and her daughter. "My name is Abram —Abram Shapiro, Reb Meshulam Moskat's son-in-law."

"I know, I know," Rosa Frumetl hastened to say, in her strong Galician accent. "He told me about you. This is my daughter, Adele."

"Very honored," the girl murmured, in Polish.

"This young man is someone I just met, Asa Heshel Bannet. A friend of the secretary of the synagogue on Tlomatska, a great Talmud scholar—very learned. Maybe you've heard of him. Dr. Shmaryahu Jacobi."

"I think I have."

A door opened and Nyunie came in. He was a small man, with a round belly and a huge head of hair on which a tiny skullcap was perched. The blond beard on his chin was carefully combed. He was wearing a wine-colored dressing-gown. Abram let go of Asa Heshel's elbow, leaped across the room to Nyunie, grabbed him by the waist, and lifted him up in the air, up and down, three times. Nyunie kicked back and forth, his small feet in well-polished slippers. Abram set him down on the floor, as though he were a dummy, and boomed out his thunderous laughter.

"Greetings, my friend, my brother-in-law!" he shouted. "Give me five!" He held out his hand.

"Lunatic! Madman!" Nyunie gasped. "Who is this young man?"

"What's going on here? What's everybody shouting for? Abram, stop carrying on!" Dacha had finished her telephone conversation and put down the instrument. "Who is this young man?" she continued, and held out her tapering fingers.

"It's a long story. Here, I'll begin it from the beginning. He's a prodigy, a genius, a mathematician, a sage, a jack-of-all-trades. He's one of those kind who are dumb as a fish today, but tomorrow they'll be standing in the University of Brussels, proclaiming that we Jews are a religion, not a nation, and that the *Ostjuden* stink up the atmosphere."

"The man's gone crazy. What are you getting the young man all confused for? Pay no attention to him; he's just baaing like a goat. Where are you from, young man?"

"Tereshpol Minor."

"Teresh—what?"

"Tereshpol Minor."

"Where on earth is that? What a queer name!"

"Near Zamosc."

"Dear God preserve us! So many strange towns! Is it true that you're a mathematician?"

"I studied a little."

"You're modest and he brags. Well, whatever it is, you stay here for dinner. Here, meet our guests. This is my father-in-law's wife, Rosa Frumetl, and this is her daughter—what's your name, my dear?—oh, yes, Adele."

"May I ask where you studied mathematics?" Adele asked in a precise and elegant tone.

Asa Heshel flushed. "I studied by myself," he stammered. "From books."

"Elementary mathematics—or higher mathematics?"

"I really don't know."

"Well, analytical geometry, for example, or differential calculus."

"Oh, no! I'm not as far advanced as that."

"Well, I went as far as that, but I don't count myself a mathematician."

"Oh, I don't make such claims."

"Adele, why do you cross-examine the man?" Rosa Frumetl broke in. "If they say he's a mathematician, then he's a mathematician."

"That's the style these days. Every yeshivah student is a Newton."

"It isn't the style—it's the truth," Abram boomed. "In our poor seminaries there are more geniuses than in all their universities put together."

"Oh, I've been to Switzerland and I've seen all these geniuses of yours. They lack elementary education."

"Adele, my darling, what are you saying? Everybody knows that the study of the Torah sharpens the mind," Rosa Frumetl interrupted; she seemed to be constantly on the watch, ready to curb her daughter's sharp tongue.

"That's a lot of nonsense! I studied the Torah myself—and when it comes to anything important I've got a head like a barrel," Nyunie remarked.

"You always had a head like a barrel," Dacha said.

"Quarreling already!" Abram shouted. "Whenever I have a squabble with my Hama it's a signal for the rest of the family to go at it. The young man's got terrific recommendations—he's a philosopher into the bargain. Show them the letter!"

"Please! I'm not a philosopher."

"The letter from Zamosc says you are."

"I'm only a student, I have some ideas."

"Ideas! The whole world's busy with ideas," Dacha put in with a sigh. "My Hadassah—every day she's writing down her ideas. In my time nobody bothered with ideas and we lived just the same."

"I'm getting hungry. Why are we waiting with dinner?" Nyunie asked impatiently. He had a reputation as the family glutton. Besides, he hadn't taken a fancy to this pretentious new stepmother whom Dacha had invited, or this newly acquired and irritating stepsister, or this green youth whom Abram had brought along. He was afraid that because of them he would not be able to stretch out on the sofa for a nap after his meal. His nerve-ridden wife, the typical daughter of a rabbinical house, who had to take pills to give her an appetite as well as to settle her stomach afterwards, darted an angry glance at him.

"Hadassah is not here yet."

"Where's she running around? We can eat without her."

"No, we'll wait," Dacha ruled. "When he reminds himself of food, your life's in danger!"

There was a ring of the outer doorbell. "It's Hadassah," Nyunie exclaimed, and started to run toward the door on his short legs. Dacha sat down on her cushioned chair, pulled out of her sleeve a monogrammed handkerchief, and held it up to her long nose.

"Abram," she said, "come here. Tell me where you found this young man."

"I found him and he's here; that's all there is to it. Don't be embarrassed, young man. Their Newtons don't scare us. Any one of our sages can tuck them under his belt. Just let us be a nation in our own land and we'll show what we can do. Ah, the geniuses'll tumble out of their mothers' bellies six at a time—like in Egypt. Our Jewish genius'll flood the world, damn their filthy belly-buttons—or my name isn't Abram Shapiro!"

"Woe is me, he's off again," Dacha moaned in a singsong. "Come here, young man; sit down, near me. My brother-in-law is a bit mixed up, but he's really all right. We all love him."

Asa Heshel sat down in the chair she indicated. Rosa Frumetl took a sip of her cherry brandy and a delicate bite from the almond cake she held. Adele started to say something, but at that moment the door opened and Nyunie came in with his daughter.

CHAPTER THREE

1

Nyunie, holding Hadassah by the arm, was a good head shorter than his daughter. Hadassah appeared to be about eighteen, tall and slender, with blond hair coiled in braids. Her face was pale, her nose slightly snub, the throat long, the forehead high and with a bluish tint at the temples. She wore a little velvet beret, schoolgirl style, a short jacket tied with ribbons; and although the day was not too cold, she had heavy socks over her stockings. She reminded Asa Heshel of the aristocratic young ladies in the romantic novels he had read. Her light-blue eyes had an embarrassed expression as though she were not in her own home but entering some strange house. Rosa Frumetl immediately began to shake her head from side to side, pursing her lips as though she were preparing to spit and ward off an evil eye. Adele eyed her from head to toe.

"This is Hadassah? May no evil befall her!" Rosa Frumetl murmured. "Beautiful!"

"Hadassah, this is your grandmother, your grandfather's wife. And this is her daughter, Adele."

Hadassah bent forward—something between a schoolgirl curtsy and an adult bow.

"Come here, you lovely child. Let me feast my eyes on you," Rosa Frumetl sang out. "Your grandfather never stops praising you. This is my daughter, Adele. You may talk Polish with her; she doesn't speak Russian—we're from Galicia."

"They told me about you," Hadassah said to Adele in Polish. "You're from Krakow, I think."

"I went to school there."

"Why don't you introduce her to the philosopher?" Abram bellowed. "Hadassah, my jewel, this young man is a Jewish Lomonosov."

Hadassah looked at Asa Heshel. Both of them blushed.

"Naprawde—is it true?" she asked; it was hard to say whether she was addressing her uncle or Asa Heshel.

"You're making fun of me," Asa Heshel stammered. He, too, might have been speaking to either of them.

"He's modest into the bargain," Abram continued in his booming voice. "He wants you to give him some tutoring. His tongue twists a bit on this pagan language—but he's got the head of an Aristotle. He studied algebra—in the attic."

"Really, in the attic?" Hadassah asked in bewilderment.

"Well, when it was raining—and there was no place—"

"It seems Mr. Shapiro likes to exaggerate," Adele put in, in her cold voice.

Nyunie broke in plaintively: "I'm dying of hunger. Why does it take so long?"

"Quiet, Nyunie, you won't starve," Dacha interrupted. "Hadassah, my pet, take off your coat. Where have you been?"

"We were walking—in the Saxon Gardens."

"Who's this 'we'?"

"You know, Mamma. Me and Klonya."

"Traveling around with a gentile girl! Ts, ts."

"At least it's better than going around with a gentile boy," Abram commented.

"Hold your tongue with those jokes of yours. Aren't there enough Jewish girls in Warsaw? This Klonya is from a common family. That father of hers—a foreman in a bakery. And the mother's so fat she can hardly get through the door."

"Well, what difference does that make? I like her."

"I'm surprised that your mother has that point of view," Adele remarked. "Back home in Austria, Jews and gentiles live together like one family."

"I don't know how it is in Galicia, but here they're a bunch of anti-Semites. Even now there's a boycott against us. Wherever you go you hear them grunting: 'Buy from your own kind.' They'd swallow the Jew alive if they could."

"Well, to tell the truth, when you take a look at all these Warsaw Jews, in their long gaberdines and skullcaps, it's as though you found yourself in China all of a sudden. One can see why the Poles don't want to stand for it."

"Adele, my precious! What are you saying?" Rosa Frumetl warned. "What kind of talk? Your father—may his virtue intercede for you—wore a long coat, and sidelocks, too."

"Please don't mention Papa. Papa was a European—a European in every respect."

"I see Miss Adele is in favor of assimilation," Abram commented in Polish.

"Not of assimilation—only of living together respectably and intelligently."

"And I suppose if we all put on Polish hats and twist our mustaches into points, then they'll love us," Abram rejoined, and twisted at his own mustache. "Let the young lady read the newspapers here. They squeal that the modern Jew is worse than the caftaned kind. Who do you think the Jew-haters are aiming for? The modern Jew, that's who."

"Oh, that can't be true."

"It is true, my dear young lady. You'll soon find out."

Shifra put her head into the room. "Dinner is ready," she announced.

Nyunie immediately started to move. The others went after him. In the dining-room the large table with its heavy carved legs was set with plates, knives, forks, and spoons, the silver scratched with age and use. At the door stood a table with a crock of water, a copper dipper, and a small tin basin. The men washed their hands first. Dacha produced a skullcap, which she placed on Abram's head. He leisurely dried his hands on a linen towel and loudly recited the prescribed blessing. Asa Heshel, in his nervousness, wet his sleeves. Rosa Frumetl carefully folded back the cuffs over her scrawny wrists and poured two dippers of water over her fingers. Adele looked at Hadassah as though to say: "Do we have to go through this?" Hadassah filled a dipper with water and held it out to Adele.

"Please, you first," she said.

"I'll wet the lace." She carefully bent back the embroidered cuffs of her sleeves and poured water over her fingers with their filed nails. Hadassah followed suit. Asa Heshel noticed that her fingers were ink-stained. Nyunie took his seat in a leather-covered chair at the head of the table and cut slices from a loaf of white bread. He murmured the blessing and handed the slices around. A currant loaf and small white rolls lay in a tray at the center of the table. Shifra brought in the appetizer—liver and tripe. Abram looked at Hadassah and lowered one eyelid. She got up, left the room, and returned with a carafe of brandy. Dacha scolded her.

"You're not doing him any favor," she said. "It'll only mean more visits to the doctor."

"Your health, Nyunie! You, young man! Your health, young ladies! May we drink at your weddings!"

"Health and peace, amen!" Rosa Frumetl murmured reverently.

The men had taken their seats first. At the right of the table sat Abram, Hadassah, and Dacha; at the left Asa Heshel, Rosa Frumetl, and Adele. There was a mist before Asa Heshel's eyes; everything seemed to be swaying—the glass-paned credenza and its porcelain dishes, the pictures on the wall, the faces of the others. He seemed to have lost his senses of hearing. The knife and fork trembled in his hand and tapped against the plate. He did not know whether to take a bite out of the slice of bread in front of him or break off a piece. With his fork he took up a piece of sour pickle from a plate, but it seemed to disappear—and fell out of his sleeve a moment later. When the servant placed a bowl of soup before him the rising steam completely obscured his vision.

"Hey, young man," he heard Abram's voice, "maybe you'd like a drink."

Asa Heshel wanted to say no, but his lips said yes. The women were busily talking to one another. A glass of some red-colored liquid appeared before him. He whispered: "Your health," and swallowed it at one gulp. Abram let out a howl of laughter. "That's the stuff, my boy," he shouted. "You'll be all right!"

"Take a bite of something," Dacha urged him. "Give him a cookie, somebody."

Hadassah left the table again and returned with some macaroons. In the meanwhile Asa Heshel had managed to swallow a piece of bread. Tears stood out in his eyes; he wiped them away with his fingers.

"You shouldn't have given it to him," Rosa Frumetl said accusingly. "He's delicate."

"Abram's ideas," Dacha grumbled.

"Tell me, young man," Nyunie broke in, "what do you have in mind to do in Warsaw?"

The question came unexpectedly, like all of Nyunie's remarks. The others were silent. Asa Heshel began to answer, first so softly that he could hardly be heard, and then in a stronger voice. He told them about Tereshpol Minor; about his grandfather, his mother and sister, his father, who had disappeared, and about Jekuthiel Watchmaker. His face was pale; only his ears were flushed. His eyes shifted about uncertainly, now at Dacha, now at Hadassah. His words came in bursts of disconnected phrases. Hadassah blushed. Dacha turned a bewildered gaze on him. Without knowing the reason, Rosa Frumetl felt the tears starting to her eyes.

"A fledgling—away from the nest," she murmured. "A-ah, the pain of a mother!" She lifted her batiste handkerchief and blew her nose. She was overcome by a strange feeling, as though the boy were somehow her own flesh and blood.

2

After dinner they all went into the salon. Abram lit a cigar; Nyunie began to fidget, peer around, and grumble to himself, like a rooster before settling on its perch. Just as desperately hungry as he had been before, so desperately drowsy was he now. He left the room and went to his small study, stretched out on a couch, and picked up a volume of Graetz's *History of the Jews,* which he was reading unbeknown to his wife; Dacha, in common with all the pious, thought it a heretical work. In less than five minutes he was snoring soundly. Nyunie was the administrator of two of his father's houses, although it was his assistant, the hunchbacked Moishele, who collected the rents. Moishele turned over the money and gave an accounting to Koppel and every Thursday brought to Dacha the family's weekly allowance. Nyunie paid no attention to the administration of the real estate or of his own household economy. The wedding settlement he had received from his father—five thousand rubles—still lay untouched in the bank, and in the years that had passed, a lot of interest had been added to it. Now he lay on the couch, limbs relaxed, his mouth half open, his head resting on a small cushion, which he had had since childhood and which he had never allowed himself to be parted from, either at home in Warsaw or when he was traveling.

For Dacha, too, the hour after the midday meal was always the most restful part of the day—especially when Abram was visiting. She would forget all her ills—the headaches, the rheumatic pains, the stabbing darts in her side, the tightness in her joints. Nyunie would be asleep in his study. Hadassah would have gone to her own room, the maid would be visiting a neighbor. Dacha would wrap her shoulders in her silk shawl, embroidered with two peacocks, sink into a deep chair, put her feet on a hassock, and half close her eyes. The stove with its gilded eaves spread its heat through the room. The sunlight shining in through the window curtains was reflected in the oven tiles with all the colors of the rainbow. The noise of the street was shut out by the double windows, the sills and sashes stuffed with cotton padding. Abram would sit near her, his lips puffing out rings of cigar smoke, his fingers playing with the gold chain that stretched across his vest. At such times Dacha would half doze, half listen to the gossip and intrigue about her father-in-law, brothers-in-law, their wives and children, and the rest of the kin—the dozen and one families to whose fortunes she was tied. Despite the fact that she was a pure-minded and chaste woman—the decorous daughter of a pious family—Abram recounted to her all his love affairs, transgressions, and carryings on. Dacha would shudder and put on an expression of disgust at his loose talk, drawing her silk shawl tighter about her shoulders. Occasionally she would open wide her half-closed mournful black eyes and stare at him.

"Feh, Abram, you're going too far! I won't listen to any more."

And when Abram would remain silent she would murmur: "Well, all right, go on and talk. I won't have to share the Gehenna that will be your portion."

But this day the chairs in the salon were drawn close so that they could all sit and talk together. The servant girl brought in tea, cakes, and preserves. Adele turned the pages of a gold-stamped album. Rosa Frumetl in a languishing voice told

Dacha about the brewery that her first husband, Reb David Landau, owned near Brody; of the eighty acres of ground planted with hops that were part of the business; of the peasants and servants they employed, and of the distinguished rabbis who came to visit them. Abram sat on the sofa next to Asa Heshel. He called Hadassah over to join them.

"Come here, my girl. Don't be bashful. I'm here to protect you."

Hadassah went over and sat at the end of the sofa. She glanced at Asa Heshel and then lowered her eyes.

"Maybe you'd like to give this young man some lessons. It'll be a good deed; you'll be earning a portion in paradise."

Hadassah looked questiongly at Asa Heshel. "I don't know if I know enough," she said shyly.

"For him it'll be plenty," Abram commented.

"Maybe my Adele can help," Rosa Frumetl interrupted. While she was talking to Dacha she had had an ear cocked to the conversation of the others.

"Mamma, you know I'm leaving Warsaw," Adele said hastily.

"You're not going so soon, my darling. A lot of water will flow under the bridge before."

"I'll be going sooner than you imagine."

"Too bad the dear young lady is leaving us," Abram remarked.

"What's too bad about it? Nobody will miss me."

"You can never tell. There's such a thing as love at first sight."

"Abram, you're starting your nonsense again!" Dacha scolded. "You seem to forget that you're getting to be an old graybeard. You've got marriageable daughters."

"Ah, my misfortunes! And suppose I am getting old; do you have to remind me of it? Besides, who said I meant myself? Maybe I meant this young man."

"Leave the young man alone."

Rosa Frumetl turned to Abram. "Maybe you can persuade her. Only here a little while and now she wants to go. And if you ask me why—"

"Probably someone she wants to see."

"Only the good Lord knows."

"Don't worry, my dear mother-in-law! If her destined mate is here in Warsaw, then she'll not go away. And if she does go away she'll come back," Abram said unctuously, not knowing himself where his tongue was leading him. "They all think I'm

a heretic, a runaround, a corkscrew, but destined mates—
that's something I believe in. Take me and my Hama. We fit
together like a square peg in a round hole. But when the angel
in charge of the business of seeing that children are conceived
shouted out: 'Daughter of Reb Meshulam, take Abram!'
nothing could help me."

"Abram, shame!" Dacha glared at him and gestured with
her hand to indicate that he should hold his tongue in the
presence of the girls. Abram struck his forehead with the
palm of his hand.

"Who changed the subject! We were talking about lessons.
Take him into your room, Hadassah, and listen to what he
knows. Young man, I forgot to ask you, where do you live?"

"Me? In a hotel on the Franciskaner."

"I know it. The Hotel de Bedbug. How much do you pay?"

"Fifteen kopeks a night."

"Listen to me, Dacha. I just got an idea. Maybe we ought
to fix him up at Gina's."

"What are you talking about?"

"She took a big apartment on the Shviento-Yerska and
rents rooms. It'll cost him ten rubles a month, but it'll be a
home."

"Abram! You ought to be ashamed of yourself!"

"What's there to be ashamed about? Back to her father, the
rabbi, she'll certainly not go. I hear that Akiba will be divorcing her any day now, and, God willing, she'll be married to
Hertz Yanovar according to the law of Moses and Ishmael—I
mean Israel."

"I don't know what'll happen later. All I know is that now
it's a scandal and disgrace. Why should you drag the young
man into a swamp like that?"

"Nonsense. It's a fine, lively place. All of Warsaw's Jewish
intelligentsia congregate there. It's a real salon. I'd hang
around there myself—if not for the bedbugs."

"Abram, I asked you not to talk that way," Dacha called
out angrily. The story about Gina, her husband, Akiba, and
Hertz Yanovar was not for the ears of the eighteen-year-old
Hadassah. Rosa Frumetl put down her teacup and raised her
eyes, full of curiosity. Adele leafed the album pages more vigorously.

When Hadassah and Asa Heshel had left the living-room
Adele got up from her chair and walked over to the window.
Twilight was coming on. The first snow of the winter was
falling, wet and soft, the snowflakes swirling in the wind,

melting away before they touched the ground. The smoke rising from the chimneys merged into the white mistiness. Birds, singly and in flocks, flew by. At the other side of the street stood a dray loaded with sacks and covered with a canvas. The two squat draft horses with their scarred hides were huddled together, their ears cocked. From time to time they turned their heads to each other as though whispering some equine secret. Adele stood at the window, her warm forehead pressing against the pane, and it suddenly came to her that her mother was right, there was no reason for her to go away —and there was no one to whom she would be going. She was tired of reading books, tired of thinking of her father, who had died too soon, of the Brody love affair that she had broken off out of pride, and of her entire uneventful life. She regretted now that she had been so sharp with the homeless youth from Tereshpol Minor and that she had needlessly irritated Abram and Dacha.

"I could have tutored him, too," she thought. "Anything rather than always be alone."

3

Hadassah's room was long and narrow. The window gave on the courtyard. The wallpaper was light-colored. Some landscapes and family photographs hung on the walls, among them one of Hadassah. At one side of the room stood a metal bed covered with an embroidered spread. A needlepoint cushion lay against the pillow. In a small rectangular aquarium bedded with moss, three tiny goldfish swam about. From the window the rays of the setting sun shone into the room, heightening the color of the gold-framed pictures, throwing patches of light on the wallpaper, the polished floor, and the gold-stamped bindings of the books on the bookshelves. On a round table stood a volume and a vase of faded blue flowers. Hadassah crossed the room quickly, took the book from the table, and put it into a dresser drawer.

"These are my books," she said, pointing to the shelves. "If you like you can look at them."

Asa Heshel looked them over. Most of them were school books—a grammar, a Russian history, a geography, a world history, a Latin dictionary. Przybyszewski's *The Outcry* leaned against a copy of Mickiewicz's *Pan Tadeusz.* Strindberg's *Confession of a Fool* reposed next to a thick

novel that bore the title *Pharoah*. Asa Heshel picked up some
of the books, glanced at the title pages, leafed them, and put
them back on the shelves. "The trouble is," he said, "I'd like
to read all of them."

"I'll be glad to lend them to you. Whichever you want."

"Thank you."

"Maybe you'd like to light a lamp—although I love this
half-light, between day and night."

"I like it too."

"Tell me what you'd like to study. I'm very weak in mathematics."

"Well, I want to take the university examinations—as an
extern."

"Then you'll need a tutor. I didn't get through them myself;
I became ill—before the examinations were given."

She sat down on the edge of the bed. In the setting sun's
rays her hair took on the color of molten gold. Her small face
lay in shadow. She looked toward the window, at a large ex-
panse of sky, a row of rooftops, and the tall chimney of a factory. Snowflakes pattered against the window pane. Asa Heshel sat on a chair near the bookshelves, his face half-turned
toward Hadassah. "If I had a room like this," he was thinking, "and if I could only stretch out on a bed like that . . ." He
took a book from the shelf, opened it, and put it on his lap.

"Why did you leave your home?" Hadassah asked.

"Just so. For no real reason. It was impossible for me to
stay."

"And your mother let you go?"

"Not at the beginning. But then later she could see for herself that—" his voice trailed off.

"Is it true that you're a philosopher?"

"Oh, no. I've read a few books, that's all. What I know
amounts to nothing."

"Do you believe in God?"

"Yes, but not in a God who demands prayer."

"Then what God do you believe in?"

"The whole universe is part of the Deity. We ourselves are
part of God."

"That means that if you have a toothache, it's God's tooth
that's aching."

"Well, I suppose it's something like that."

"I really don't know what to tutor you in," Hadassah said
after a slight pause. "Maybe Polish. I don't care for Russian."

"Polish will be all right."

"Do you understand the language?" She asked the question in Polish.

"Oh, yes, I understand it well enough."

The moment she went over to Polish the entire tone of the conversation seemed to change. Before that her voice had had a youthful, almost childish quality, the sentences sometimes drawn out, sometimes tumbling. Now the Polish accents came from her lips precisely and definitely, with the soft consonantal sounds carefully formed. Asa Heshel's Polish came slowly and stumblingly; he had to stop to think of the proper word forms and tense endings. Hadassah crossed her knees and listened carefully to him. He spoke with grammatical correctness, not substituting, as her father did, the dative for the accusative. It was his sentence structure that was unusual. In his mouth the language took on a languid sort of intimacy, as though the Polish had suddenly, by some sort of miracle, become the homey Yiddish.

"How do you plan to establish yourself in Warsaw?"

"I don't know yet."

"My Uncle Abram can be of great help to you. He knows everyone. He's a very interesting person."

"Oh, yes, I noticed that."

"He's a bit wild, but I love him. We all love him—Papa, Mamma, everyone. If a day passes without him coming here, we miss him. I call him 'the Flying Dutchman'; that's the name of an opera."

"Yes, I know."

"He has a daughter—my cousin, that is—her name is Stepha. She's the one who'd really be able to teach you. When she finished school she got a gold medal. She's just like her father—runs around, always jolly. We're altogether different."

"Forgive me, Miss Hadassah, but you talk so beautifully—like a poet." Asa Heshel's own words surprised him. They escaped his lips as though of their own volition. The unfamiliar and formal language and the dimness of the room seemed to have conspired to banish his timidity. Or maybe it was the glass of brandy he had had.

"A poet? You're making fun of me."

"Oh, no, I assure you."

"I don't write poetry—but I love to read it."

"I mean in your soul."

"Ah, now you're being just like Uncle Abram. He scatters compliments around on all sides."

"Oh, no, I'm in earnest."

"Well, anyway, it's agreed that I'll give you lessons in Polish. How many times a week?"

"Why, I leave that to you. Just as you like."

"Then let's say Sunday, Tuesday, and Thursday. Between four and five."

"I'm very thankful."

"And be sure to come on time."

"Oh, yes, on the dot."

"Now we'd better go back into the living-room or Uncle Abram will be making all sorts of remarks."

They went back through the corridor. It was dark. Asa Heshel took a step or two forward, then halted. The apparition of the fiery blossom that he had seen when he got into the droshky with Abram suddenly arose again before his vision, huge, sunlit, with a deep cup, surrounded with grays, purples, and blues, a whole spectrum of fantastic colors. Hadassah took his elbow and led him along, as though he were a blind man. He stumbled, almost overturning a wooden clothes rack. The lamps were on in the living-room. Adele was standing between the two windows. She was still holding the album. Asa Heshel could hear Dacha say to Abram: "A fine professor he must be! With neither Russian nor Polish."

"In Zurich all you need is German."

"The way I hear it, he doesn't know German either."

"What language did he lecture in, good Lord? Babylonian?"

"Whatever you say is all right with me. The whole thing's simply not true."

"Oh, Dacha, you're talking nonsense. I saw it myself, black on white, that Hertz Yanovar is going to lecture at the university. I don't remember the subject. The apperceptions of the conceptions or something or other."

"Well, so what? That doesn't make him a professor."

"What then? A wet-nurse?"

"If he were a professor in Switzerland he wouldn't be here in Warsaw thirteen months in the year."

"And I tell you, Dacha, that he can tuck all the professors in his vest pocket."

"Well, we'll see. I don't believe that Akiba will give her a divorce. It'll drag out till Messiah comes."

Dacha caught sight of her daughter and indicated to Abram to drop the subject. Rosa Frumetl nodded her head toward Asa Heshel and smiled broadly at him, showing a flash of her false teeth. She had an idea of something he might do for her

to earn a little money. Since she had come to Warsaw she had
called on several printers with the manuscript that her first
husband had left her. But the printers had not wanted to un-
dertake the job. They complained that the handwriting was illegible. Besides, pages seemed to be missing—or the numera-
tion was faulty. It would be necessary first for the manuscript
to be rewritten and corrected. While Asa Heshel had been out
of the room Rosa Frumetl had asked Abram's advice. He told
her that it would be impossible to find anyone better than the
young man from Tereshpol Minor, who, besides his rabbinical
studies, was expert in Hebrew and Hebrew grammar. Rosa
Frumetl had called Adele to another part of the room and
had discussed the matter with her.

"What do you think, my darling? The young man looks as
though he might be capable," she whispered. "Maybe it's just
the thing."

And Adele had said: "Very well, Mamma. Let him come to
talk it over."

4

When, later in the evening, Asa Heshel left the house with
Abram, he hardly recognized the outdoors. Panska Street was
magically changed. Pavement, gutters, balconies, and roofs—
everything was covered with snow. White bonnets sat on the
tops of the street lamps. Misty beacons streamed from the gas
flames, reminding Asa Heshel of comets' tails. The few pedestrians hurried along, their elongated shadows shifting after
them. At the end of the avenue a street peddler was putting
potatoes up to bake on the glowing coals of a small hand
wagon with a tin chimney. Porters, coils of rope around their
waists, warmed their hands at the fire. Abram took Asa Heshel by the arm.

"Guess where we're going now."

"To—what did you call her? Gina's?"

"Correct, brother! But remember, m—u—m—mum's the
word."

There was no droshky in sight and the two went over to the
end of the Tvarda. A snow-topped tramcar labored up the
winding street. The overhead wires were heavy and thick as
ropes. The plastered walls of the brick buildings shone like
polished glass. Scattered flakes of snow still fell from the red-
dish-hued sky, as though reflecting some distant conflagration.

"There's a droshky. Hey, you!"

Abram's shout echoed in the misty air, and the droshky pulled to a stop. They both climbed in.

The droshky rolled along through the same streets that had brought them to Nyunie's house. Against the green-blue light of the evening and under their blankets of snow the houses now seemed rich and luxurious, like palaces. The market stalls before Iron Gate Square were already cleared away. In the hall a wedding was going on. From the upper floor came the sound of music. Dancing shadows flitted past the window panes. On the street brightly lighted tramcars rumbled by, singly and in pairs, their headlights throwing a blinding glare on the polished steel rails. Clumps of snow hung from branches of trees, like white fruit. Abram puffed on his cigar.

"Well, they didn't eat you up over there after all."

"No."

"When are you having your first lesson?"

"The day after tomorrow."

"A fine girl! But not altogether healthy. She just got back from a few months at Otwotsk. That Adele is a dangerous one."

"What was the matter with her?"

"Who? Oh, Hadassah! Just before she was supposed to take her examinations for the university she got a fever of some kind. Her lungs aren't good. Now she's better—and already they're worrying about marrying her off. This Gina we're going to visit now is an interesting woman. Her father is the Bialodrevna rabbi. Her husband, Akiba, is a crazy man. They made her marry him against her will. His father is the Sentsimin rabbi, a madman himself. The court is conducted by the rabbi's mother, a woman in her eighties, a shrewd piece. This Akiba is a specimen you find only in our Polish towns. He goes to the *mikvah* for total immersion three times a day. When he prays he repeats every word ten times. How they could have saddled Gina with such a husband is a puzzle to everybody. She's been in love with Hertz Yanovar since her childhood. His father was the head of the yeshivah in Bialodrevna. Well, they married her off and the damage was done. She ran away. Meanwhile, Hertz Yanovar had gone to Switzerland and was studying. He amazed all the professors. He became an instructor even before he learned how to speak German. She raised hell to get a divorce, but years have passed and she's still bound to that idiot. He's madly in love with her, although he's as useful as a capon. The Sentsimin rabbi has a grudge against the Bialodrevna rabbi. It's an old quarrel. Where am I, ha? Yes. Suddenly Hertz Yanovar came over to Warsaw. He came just for a visit, to take Gina to Switzerland. Instead he established himself in an apartment on the Gnoyna and began to play around with all kinds of nonsense."

The droshky came to a stop. A wagon loaded with lumber had overturned and was blocking the road. All along Leshno Street a line of empty tramcars stretched; it was a long time before the way was clear. At last the droshky was able to move. It came to a stop on the Shviento-Yerska, opposite Krashinski Gardens, near a large house fronted by an enormous court. Gina lived in the second wing, and on the second floor. Climbing the stairs, Abram stopped several times to rest.

"You said, over there at the professor's, that you have money. How much have you?"

"Thirty-five rubles."

"You're richer than me. Anyway, first you'll pay a month's rent in advance. We'll worry about afterwards later."

"Why doesn't she want to get married?"

"Oh, you mean Hadassah. The man they picked out for her is a snotnose. It's all that grandfather of hers, Meshulam Moskat. He lets his bailiff talk him into anything." Abram lifted his stick and whacked the air with it, as though he were smiting someone unseen.

The steps that led up to Gina's apartment were lit by naked gas jets. From the near-by apartment came the whirring of a sewing-machine, from another the scratchy sounds of a phonograph. Some sort of celebration must have been going on in one of the flats; a number of well-dressed men and women were going up the stairs.

Abram pressed the button at Gina's door. After a little wait the door opened. In the doorway stood a woman in her thirties, tall and dark, with large black eyes, a curved nose, and a too large mouth. There was a little mole on her left cheek. A faint mustache dimmed her upper lip. Her black matron's wig—or was it her own hair, Asa Heshel wondered—was heavily braided, studded with combs, and covered with a tulle net. She wore a velvet dress and buckled shoes. Asa Heshel retreated a step or two. The woman brought her hands together in a gesture of surprise.

"See who's here! It's too bad we weren't talking about Messiah instead; he would surely have come."

"Gina, my love, I'm bringing this young man to you—a genius of geniuses."

"Forgive me, I didn't even see him; you're hiding him with your broad shoulders. Come in, please come in."

The two went into the entrance hall. This was a long corridor with a number of doors along it, all of them paned with frosted glass. The sound of voices came from beyond it. The air was heavy with the smell of cigarette smoke. The walls had been newly painted and there was a strong odor of oil and turpentine. On the freshly waxed floor sacking and newspapers were spread. The wooden coat hangers were laden with overcoats. Against the wall stood an assortment of galoshes and umbrellas. Gina helped Abram out of his cape and took Asa Heshel's coat.

"I could swear this young man is the son of a rabbinical house," Gina said.

"A miracle! The woman's a prophetess!" Abram exclaimed in exaggerated awe. "Deborah the prophetess!"

"You can see it in his face. Tell me, my dear child, what is your name?"

"Asa Heshel Bannet."

"And where are you from? One thing is sure, you're no Litvak."

"Are you mad!" yelled Abram. "Would I bring a Lithuanian into your house?"

"Don't shout. I have enough trouble with those lunatics in there."

"You mean Broide and Lapidus?"

"The whole bunch of them. Well, come inside."

"Just a minute, Gina. This young man needs a room."

"But, my dear Abram, all my rooms are rented. They're sleeping on the sofa, on the floor, on the mantelpiece. It's a poorhouse, not a lodging-house. If you'd brought him a couple of weeks ago it would have been different. But—wait a moment, I have an idea. There's a girl living here—studying to be a pharmacist—or a nurse—or God knows what. Anyway, last night she got a telegram—her mother died—so she packed up and went away. To Pintshev, I think."

"Well, then, that settles everything. Give him her room."

"And what'll happen if she comes back?"

Gina opened a door at the end of the corridor and led the two into a large crowded room. People lounged all over the place sitting on sofas, chairs, even on the windowsill and on a low chest of drawers. The walls were hung with oil paintings and drawings. The carpeted floor was strewn with cigarette mouthpieces. Clouds of tobacco smoke wove about under the ceiling. Everybody seemed to be talking at once, a jumble of Yiddish, Polish, and Russian. A small man, sunburned as a gypsy, in a torn blouse, with a jet-black beard and enormous flashing eyes, was expostulating in a hoarse voice with a peppery Litvak accent, gesticulating violently and flinging his head from side to side. His Adam's apple bobbed up and down; the hairs of his forelock stood upright, like wires. A girl with a mannish voice was shouting: "Clown! Idiot!"

"Don't mind him, Miss Lena," a younger man addressed her. He was wearing a pair of large, polished eyeglasses. He had a high forehead, an irregular, flat nose, and curly hair. Behind his twinkling glasses his eyes were smiling jovially. "He knows himself that he's just babbling. He's putting on a show."

"It's no show. The matter concerns our very life, our whole existence as a people!" the short man shouted. "We dance at everybody's wedding but our own. And they don't even thank us. All we'll get is a kick in the behind!"

"Feh! Gutter talk."

"It's the truth, the truth! You're all a bunch of traitors!"

"Ah, me! There's never an end to it!" Gina said with a sigh. "That Lapidus is like the ocean; he never rests a minute."

"The ocean spews out seashells—he spits out garbage," the younger man stated.

"Quiet, Broide! You're not so innocent yourself. Here, I want to acquaint you with this young man—from the provinces. Abram brought him. He's a genius, Abram says."

The argument broke off and the disputants stared at Asa Heshel. Lapidus was the first to break the silence.

5

"Where are you from?" Lapidus asked, putting out his hand. "I could swear you come from somewhere in the province of Lublin."

"Yes," Asa Heshel said. "From Tereshpol Minor."

"I thought so. There are still Jews in those towns. Real Jews, who aren't ashamed of the Jewish nose—and the Jewish Torah. Here, my friend, a new generation has arisen that has only one thing in mind—humanity! They weep bitter tears

over every Ivan, every Slav. There's only one nation they've
got no use for—their own flesh and blood!"

"Hey, Lapidus, back to your propaganda?" Broide exclaimed, in the vibrant voice of the trained orator. "That's really swinish!"

"What do you mean, swinish! I just want to let him know
what kind of a den he's fallen into. Look at them all"—he
turned to Asa Heshel. "A flock of humanitarians, all of them.
All they worry about is the social revolution and the Russian
peasants. There's not a single one of them that cares so much"
—Lapidus put his thumb to the tip of his little finger to illus-
trate how small was their regard—"about what happens to the
Jew!"

"As true as I live, Lapidus," Gina interrupted, "now you're
going too far! If you want to become a nationalist, or even to
go back to the prayerhouse of your young days, then for
God's sake do it! What's all the carrying-on for? A person
would think the place is a madhouse."

"It is! I was once in a village where they assemble them before sending them away to Siberia—what was the name?—
Alexandrovka—in a peasant's hut, and I saw a bunch of Jews,
with scrawny beards, black eyes—just like mine. At first I
thought it was a *minyan* for prayers. But when I heard them
babbling in Russian and spouting about the revolution—the
S.R.'s, the S.D.'s, Plekhanov, Bogdanov, bombs, assassina-
tions—I started to howl. I laughed until I became hysterical."

"You're not over it yet."

"I'm not nearly so hysterical as you are, Broide. You've not
gone through what I've gone through. While I was rotting in
prison, you played around with your father's servant girls."

"All right, so you've gone through a lot of experiences.
What good has it done you? All it's done is to make you a reactionary."

"And I tell you, Broide, you're more reactionary than I am.
It's people like you who'll ruin the world."

"Not the world, Lapidus. Only capitalism and chauvinism,
the things that people like you hold onto for dear life."

"I'm no chauvinist. I don't lust for anyone's territory. All I
want is a corner of the world for our own."

"That's fine. I'm glad you're not out to do some territory-
grabbing. But just wait. The appetite, they say, grows with
eating. Ha-ha-ha!"

"Ha-ha-ha!" Abram echoed him ironically. "It's a great
joke, Broide, isn't it? In what commandment is it written

down that we're supposed to spill our blood for every pig of a ruler while we stay homeless and in exile? Why should we do it? Because that's the way Karl Kautsky decided it's got to be?"

"It's got nothing to do with Kautsky, my dear Shapiro. If you can get a charter from the Turk it's all right with me. And if the Sultan decides not to give it to you, I won't rend my garments either, I assure you."

"But for a new Constitution you'd rend not only your garments but your own mother."

"The Constitution is something of world importance, and your charter is nothing but an idle fantasy for Zionist orators."

"It's starting all over again," Gina cried out. "They never get tired! Shouts and insults! Smoke and babble! Come, Abram; come—what's your name?—Asa Heshel! I'll show you the girl's room. The argument will stay fresh, don't worry."

She went out, Abram and Asa Heshel after her. In the corridor Gina stopped and turned to them.

"I really think, Abram, that this isn't the place for him. What do you think, young man?"

"I don't know, it's interesting."

"You hear what he says? Give him a few days and he'll be more European than the rest of them. If it wasn't so late I'd take him out to the Old Market and buy him a stylish suit and a modern hat," Abram said.

"Please, Abram, I beg of you! Before you start fixing other people's lives, think it over first."

"What's there to think over? He came here to study, not to chant psalms in a prayerhouse."

Gina opened a door and turned on a light. Asa Heshel saw a small room with a metal bed, covered with a dark spread. Near by was a table and on it a book, some vials, powder boxes, powder puffs, a glass with a toothbrush stuck in it, and a photograph of a young man with the face of a butcher and the epaulets of a student. A few dresses hung in a corner. The room was cool and quiet.

"This is it," Gina said. "How do you like it, young man?"

"Oh, very much."

"By the way, how are you feeling, Gina darling?" Abram asked suddenly. "You look wonderful. A princess!"

"It's only because I'm dressed up. Not because I've got anything to be particularly joyful about."

"What's the news from Akiba? What's he dragging the divorce out for?"

"God knows. It gets worse from day to day. When he's ready, his father decides to raise some objection; and when the rabbi finally agrees, that grandmother of his butts in. They're at him from all sides, and me they call the worst names you can think of. God knows, I must be made of iron to survive it. And *my* dear father has been kind enough to tell me that he's disowning me—that I'm no longer a daughter of his."

"A fat lot you should care."

"Yes, but it oppresses me, Abram. I knew beforehand it would be nothing but war. But it's all of them against poor me. Everybody throws mud at me. And on top of all that there's something else—but maybe I'd better not talk about it."

"What is it? What do you mean?"

"You'll only call me crazy."

"Come on, speak up! What do you mean?"

"I'm afraid that Hertz is getting tired of the whole business. He's a wonderful person, big-hearted, a scholar. But, between us, he's weak. All those experiments of his don't please me one bit. That woman—the medium—what's her name? Kalischer. She's nothing but an ordinary crook. She's got contact with spirits the way I'm Rasputin's mistress. All of Warsaw's laughing at him."

"Let them laugh. He's a great man."

"Just the same, I get more melancholy from day to day. I sit among those sardonic people in there and my head spins. I've got only one prayer to God—at least to spare me from going insane. . . . But what's the good of talking! Forgive me, young man." She turned to Asa Heshel. "Where is your hotel?"

"On the Franciskaner."

"If it's not comfortable for you over there, bring your things here. One way or another we'll manage."

"Are you staying on?" Asa Heshel asked Abram.

"No, I've still got to go to Praga tonight. But don't worry; I'll see you. I'll invite you to my house. You'd better hurry for your luggage."

Asa Heshel left. Outside the snow had begun to fall again, slowly and steadily, in big flakes. He put up his collar. The day seemed to him to have lasted an eternity. Words and phrases he had heard echoed and re-echoed in his ears. He hurried along the street, now and then breaking into a run. Something strange, secret, and Cabalistic seemed to pervade the atmosphere from the still red-tinted sky, from the snow-covered roofs, balconies, and doorsteps. The gas flames in the street lamps quivered and cast flickering lights. Shadows fled across the snow. Every once in a while the quiet was broken by a shout or an explosion, as though someone had shot a gun in the night. He suddenly remembered that this morning he had known not a single soul in Warsaw; now, only twelve hours later, he had a lodging, a tutor, the offer of a job to copy a manuscript, a promise to be invited to Abram's house. In the darkness before him he seemed to see Hadassah's features, alive and glowing, as in a dream.

When later he rang the bell and Gina opened the door, she looked at him and then at the dilapidated straw basket that constituted his luggage. She felt a pang in her breast. That was how—years ago—Hertz Yanovar looked when he left for Warsaw seeking an education. "He, too, will make someone unhappy," she thought. "Already—somewhere—the victim is being prepared for the sacrifice."

CHAPTER FOUR

1

Meshulam Moskat had long made it a practice to distribute the seasonal gifts to his family directly after the ritual of blessing the first Channukah candle. This year, as in previous years, sons and daughters, their wives and husbands and children, gathered at the old man's home for the holiday. Naomi and Manya put in long hours of preparation for the event.

Meshulam and the adult males of the family returned to the house after the evening services at the Bialodrevna prayer-house. The women and grandchildren were waiting for them.

In Meshulam's living-room there was an enormous Channukah lamp, elaborately etched. With his own hand he poured the olive oil especially imported from the Holy Land, recited the prescribed benediction, and applied a light to the wick. The flame spluttered and smoked; the large red "sexton" candle threw a wavering illumination on the tarnished silver. In honor of the day Meshulam had put on a flowered dressing-

robe and an ornate skullcap. To his sons he gave envelopes
containing banknotes; the women received coral necklaces
and bracelets, each appropriate to her age and prestige. To
the grandchildren he distributed tin tops and small coins. Neither the two servants nor Leibel the coachman were overlooked.

After the gifts were distributed, the servants brought in
large trays laden with *latkes,* pancakes made of grated potatoes, fried in oil and sprinkled with sugar and cinnamon.
After tea and perserves had been served, the family gathered
in groups to play games, as was the Channukah custom. Meshulam preferred to play with the children, making sure to
lose a few coppers to them. Only one of the old man's sons-in-
law had put in an appearance, Moshe Gabriel. Of the other
two, Pearl's husband had died in the past year, and as for
Abram Shapiro, Meshulam had little use for him. Moshe Gabriel was a learned man, the son of a rabbi, and one of the
honored few who sat at the rabbi's table at the Bialodrevna
Chassidic court. As soon as the Channukah lamp had been
lighted, he had returned to the prayerhouse; his visits to his
worldly father-in-law were for him occasions to be suffered
and endured.

The living-room was full of noise and excitement. Joel, Meshulam's oldest son, a man in his late fifties, unusually tall,
with a big belly and a mottled red neck, had the reputation of
being a gambler. Everything about Joel was enormous: the
bulging blue eyes, the fleshy, pitted nose, the large ears with
the thick lobes. Carefully, and with ponderous movements, he
shuffled the cards and kept his eyes open to see that everything proceeded according to the rules. Good cards or bad, he
kept throwing coins into the plate at the center of the table.

"A gulden!" he said in his deep bass voice.

"Aha, Joel! Who're you trying to frighten? You've probably
got nothing," remarked his brother Nathan.

"Then put your money in," Joel retorted. "Let's see how
clever you are!"

Nathan was shorter than Joel, but stouter, with the high
round belly of a pregnant woman, a short fleshy neck, and a
double chin. Only a few sparse hairs sprouted on his face; the
family had always felt that he was a bit lacking in masculini-
ty. He had no children. He was troubled with diabetes, and
his wife, Saltsha, small and round as a barrel, would remind
him promptly every hour to take his pills. He looked at his

cards, tugged at the few hairs in his beard, smiled craftily, and said to his brother: "You don't frighten me with your gulden; here's another one on top of that."

Pinnie, Meshulam's son by his second wife, was short and thin, with a withered, jaundiced face framed in a yellowish-green beard. He was almost dwarfed by the massive bulk of Joel and Nathan. It was his custom to call attention to himself by throwing out witty remarks and sage Talmudic quotations; but no one paid any heed to him. He was an atrocious card-player; and it was partly as a result of this that his wife, Hannah, limited him to a half-ruble spending money.

"I'm done for," he kept on saying, throwing his cards aside. "With cards like these a man can go bankrupt."

Nyunie, the younger of Meshulam's sons by his second wife, was in a constant lather of quivering, perspiring, flushing—and making one mistake after another. He stood somewhat in awe of his older brothers, Joel and Nathan, and as a result constantly picked on Pinnie.

The women's table was a buzz of talk, most of the conversation monopolized by Joel's wife, Esther—Queen Esther, as the family called her—an Amazonian woman with a triple chin and a vast bosom. She was drawing little tablets from a canvas bag and calling out the numbers written on them. The others busily searched for the number on squares of the cardboard that lay before them on the table. Although she had just consumed a quantity of the holiday pancakes, she had beside her a variety of delicacies—a sectioned orange, some cookies and caramels, halvah, anything to satisfy the tapeworm that yawned voraciously inside her, so the doctors had told her. Saltsha, Nathan's wife, was apparently in luck. Hardly had the game started when she yelled out in triumph and showed her chart, with a horizontal line of figures completely filled out. Although they were playing for tiny stakes—groszy—the noise at the women's table was deafening. They talked, laughed, and interrupted one another, making a clatter with their glasses of tea and teaspoons. Esther and Saltsha, the two senior daughters-in-law, kept up a continuous flow of gossip, mostly at the expense of Dacha, who had come without her daughter, Hadassah. Pearl, Meshulam's oldest daughter—a widow, and a hardheaded businesswoman, the true daughter of her father—sat apart with her daughters and daughters-in-law. They were sufficient unto themselves, living in the northern quarter of Warsaw, in a part of the city the others referred to as "that section." They visited Meshulam's house no more than twice a year. Hannah kept only half an eye on the game. Most of the time she watched Pinnie, always afraid that he would commit some outrageous blunder. At the end of the table sat Hama, Abram's wife. She was short, ailing, and always in a state of melancholy, with nose red and eyes dim from weeping. She looked like a nondescript pauper who by some miracle had found herself the daughter of a wealthy house. Her clothes were worn and her matron's wig was the worse for wear. She made little futile gestures with the chips she held in her hand, unable to find the numbers on her chart. Every other minute her eyes turned toward her two daughters, Bella and Stepha, and a sigh escaped her lips. She bitterly resented the few gorszy she and her daughters were losing to those gluttonous sisters-in-law of hers, Esther and Saltsha.

"What number did you call?" she said. "Seventy-three? Ninety-eight? I can't hear a word."

Leah, Meshulam's youngest daughter—she was Moshe Gabriel's wife—sat with the unmarried girls. For all that they called her Aunt, she thought of herself as belonging to their generation. She was stout, with large breasts and full cheeks, well-padded hips, and fleshy legs. Her big blue eyes had a sharp and calculating look about them. In her youth something had happened to her that the family considered a disgrace—she had fallen in love with Koppel, the bailiff. When Meshulam had found out about it he had given Koppel a sound drubbing and had at once married off his daughter to Moshe Gabriel Margolis, a childless widower. There were squabbles and arguments between husband and wife year after year; there was always talk of divorce. Now Leah was whispering to the daughters of her brothers and sisters and pinching and poking them. The girls were almost expiring with laughter.

"Aunt Leah! Please stop! Oh, you'll be the death of me!" they kept on shrieking. They shook with laughter, fell into one another's arms, and made such a hubbub that Meshulam banged his fist on the table; he did not like female giggling and chattering.

Rosa Frumetl was not playing with the others. She swore that she neither knew the game nor had the head to learn it. She made a show of ordering the servants about in the kitchen, serving the older guests tea and anise cakes and the younger ones little paper cones of candy, raisins, almonds, figs, dates, carob beans. If one of the children coughed she at once showed the deepest concern; the child should be given rock candy or an eggnog. Whenever Meshulam scolded one of the boys at the game table or called him names, she immediately rushed to the victim's defense.

"The poor darling! What language to use to such a little treasure!"

"All right, all right!" Meshulam grumbled. "What difference does it make to you! I know all about it."

Adele had not wanted to come out of her room at all. But when Rosa Frumetl put her handkerchief to her eyes and pleaded with her not to shame her, she consented to put in an appearance while the blessing was being recited over the Channukah light. Then she retired to her room with her head at an elegant angle. Queen Esther poked Saltsha in the ribs.

"Playing the proud lady, that skinny hen," she said behind her hand, and then whispered something salty into the other's ear. Whatever it was, the younger girls were not permitted to hear it, but they laughed and blushed just the same.

2

After Meshulam had managed to lose a dozen or so five-kopek pieces to the children, he got up from his chair and threw a meaningful glance toward Pinnie. Pinnie was considered the family chess-player; the old man played only rarely, but everyone knew that he liked the game. Pinnie dropped his cards and set up the chessboard. Father and son took their places opposite each other, ready for a lengthy struggle. Nyunie had to go home—Dacha was complaining of a headache—so Joel and Nathan sat around to watch the contest.

As was his custom, Meshulam plunged directly into an offensive. He moved his bishop out and then his queen, in the mating position. Pinnie blocked him by bringing out a knight and later maneuvered a simultaneous attack on queen and rook. This was a surprise to the old man. He clutched his thin beard. He had not expected such a development.

"If you'd like, Papa, you can take the move back."

"A mistake is a mistake," the old man answered sharply. "A move is a move."

"But you just happened to overlook—"

"When you overlook something, you've got to take the consequences," the old man declared with finality.

"I warned you to move the pawn," Joel remarked.

"If people listened to everything you say—" Meshulam dismissed him. He stroked his beard, contemplating the board and humming a synagogue melody. Nathan hummed along and Pinnie joined in. After much deliberation Meshulam gave check with his knight. True, the piece would be captured, but at least it would serve to postpone disaster for a while. He thumped the knight down and said: "Check!" then resumed the melody.

As he did so, the shrill ring of the outer doorbell echoed in the room. Everyone turned toward the corridor, expecting Naomi or Manya to answer. But both of them must have been occupied elsewhere, for after a pause the bell rang again. Rosa Frumetl had gone to Adele's room. Saltsha went to the door and after a while came back.

"A stranger," she said to Meshulam, "some young man is here to see you."

"A young man? What sort of young man?" Meshulam asked angrily. "Let him go back where he came from."

"He says he was asked to come here to look over a manuscript."

"Who knows anything about manuscripts? Tell him not to annoy me."

"Maybe it's something important, Papa," Pinnie said. He would have been glad to see the game broken up to avoid his father's bad temper over his defeat.

"If it's anything important let him come to see me at my office," Meshulam growled. He could see that the game was hopeless.

"It's a pity. Somehow he makes you feel sorry for him," Saltsha said. "What shall I tell him?"

"You know what, Papa? Let him come in. You've lost the game anyway," Nathan advised.

"Yes, you're right, it's lost."

Saltsha did not wait to hear anything else. She went out into the corridor and in a moment returned with Asa Heshel. Everyone in the room looked curiously at him; a stranger had never found his way into the Moskat household on the first night of Channukah.

Asa Heshel hesitated for a few moments at the threshold. He had completely forgotten that this was a holiday night; the roomful of people embarrassed him.

"Well, don't stand at the door. Come in," Meshulam called out in his deep voice. "We don't eat people alive here."

Asa Heshel threw one last fearful look over his shoulder, as though preparing for his escape, and came forward. He stopped a few steps from the chess table and said: "You're Reb Meshulam Moskat?"

"Who else did you expect? Who are you?"

"Your lady—that is, your wife—told me to come here."

"Aha! So that's it! You came to see my wife." Meshulam allowed one eyelid to drop ponderously down and cover his eye. Everybody burst into laughter.

"I met her at your son's house."

"My wife! At my son's!" There was another outburst of hilarity. They all knew that the old man was given to heavy humor once in a while, and no kind of flattery pleased him as much as laughter at his jokes. Besides, this was a good opportunity for him to take away the sting of defeat. Asa Heshel looked around in confusion.

"It's about a manuscript," he said haltingly.

"What kind of manuscript? Speak up, young man. Make yourself clear!"

"It's a commentary—written by her first husband—on Ecclesiastes."

"Aha, I see. Where is she? Call her in!" Meshulam ordered.

Stepha, Abram's daughter, went out of the room to get Rosa Frumetl, who came in quickly, blushing, as though she, too, were embarrassed by the sudden intrusion.

"An unexpected visitor!" she exclaimed. "I was sure you wouldn't come at all. Why did you wait so long?"

"I was busy. I didn't have time."

"Do you hear that? I want to give him a chance to earn something—and he has no time! You must have found a fortune all of a sudden. Even my daughter was wondering why we didn't see you."

"I didn't have time. I couldn't help it," Asa Heshel repeated.

"But you had time for your lessons—or so I hear," Rosa Frumetl said.

Asa Heshel moved his lips, but no sound escaped. Rosa Frumetl shook her shoulders mournfully back and forth. "And your sidelocks—you've cut them off," she said. "Well, I suppose I'm not the Lord's watchman, to keep an eye out for orthodox ways. Come into the library with me; I'll show you the manuscript. I was already thinking of finding someone else."

She went out of the room and Asa Heshel followed her. Immediately the women began to whisper and giggle. Meshulam scowled. "Who is this young man?" he asked. "What kind of lessons is she talking about?"

"Hadassah is tutoring him," Stepha informed him. "My papa told me about him. He could have been a rabbi—and he studied mathematics in the attic."

"So now she's become a teacher," Meshulam said angrily. "Well, I'll see to it that the marriage contract is fixed right away. Right after the Sabbath."

He scattered the chess pieces and stood up. Dacha, that daughter-in-law of his, was taking things into her own hands too much. More than nine months ago he had given orders that the preliminary arrangements be drawn up for Hadassah's marriage to Fishel, Reb Simon Kutner's grandson. Zeinvele Srotsker, the *shadchan,* had even been given a fifty-ruble advance for his services. The dowry was ready and waiting. But Dacha was always managing to postpone things, pleading that the girl was sick, or giving some other excuse. Meshulam knew what the truth was: Dacha was opposed to the match, Hadassah was too much interested in this modern nonsense, and Abram, that charlatan, that no-good, was egging everybody on to pay no attention to Meshulam Moskat's wishes. He, Meshulam Moskat, would settle things once for all—and now! He would show all of them who was the boss—he, Reb Meshulam, who provided for all these hangers-on and gluttons, and married off their children, or Abram, that goat in heat, that woman-chaser, who was good for nothing except spending money and neglecting his family.

He began to pace back and forth, his shoes squeaking. He felt a tingling in his fingertips and a surge of strength, as always before he embarked on some enterprise. There was a glint in his pale eyes. He rubbed his forehead with the palm of his hand and began to map out a plan for crushing the stubbornness of this arrogant daughter-in-law and of that "delicate" and "precious" granddaughter.

"*Schlemiels,* parasites, time-wasters!" he rumbled. "Who asks for their advice!"

For the hundredth time he made up his mind to cut Abram out of his will entirely. He wouldn't leave him a copper, even if his own daughter and her children should—God forbid!— have to eat the bread of charity.

3

In the library Rosa Frumetl took a manuscript down from a shelf. It was held together by boards and tied with green ribbon. She placed it carefully on the table.

"Here it is," she said. "Take off your overcoat and make yourself comfortable."

Asa Heshel took off his coat and Rosa Frumetl carried it out into the corridor. He sat down on a leather chair and began to leaf the pages. The manuscript was yellowish and faded, the pages of varying sizes, most of them unnumbered. The handwriting was small and angular, with many erasures and emendations in the margins and between the wavering lines. He glanced at the introduction. The author had undertaken the writing of the work, it said, not with the hope of seeing it in print, but for himself and the issue of his loins. The introduction went on to say that if the grandsons or great-grandsons of the writer should consider the work worthy of publication they were first to get the consent of three rabbis, whose task it would be to judge whether the author had not unintentionally erred and interpreted the Biblical text falsely. The work itself was a mixture of research, speculation, and hairsplitting. There was a complete lack of punctuation. The style was awkward, full of high-flown and artificial phraseology.

"Well, what do you think? Will you be able to manage it?" Asa Heshel heard Rosa Frumetl ask him.

He looked up. She had brought him a glass of tea and a little tray of cakes. Adele had come into the library with her mother. She was dressed in the same pleated skirt and embroidered blouse he had seen her in at their first meeting. In the reddish glow of the lamp her face seemed thinner, and her forehead, with her hair combed back, loftier. She had the yellowish appearance of someone just up from a sickbed.

"Good evening," she said. "I'd made up my mind that you didn't want to see us any more."

"Oh, no," Asa Heshel stammered. "I had no time. Each day I wanted to come but—"

"What do you think?" Rosa Frumetl interrupted. "Can you read it?"

"I'm afraid it'll all have to be written over."

"Too bad!"

"And in some places additions will have to be made—in brackets. It's too concise; there'll have to be some explanations."

"Well, go ahead with it." Rosa Frumetl sighed heavily. "No hurry. Come here every day, whenever you have time, and work on it. Make yourself at home. And about money—I'll talk to my husband."

"Please don't bother about that."

"No, I'll talk to him now. Have your tea. I'll be back in a minute."

Rosa Frumetl gathered the folds of her skirt and went out, the door hinges creaking after her. Adele came closer.

"I thought we'd offended you or something," she said.

"Oh, no!"

"I have the same temperament as my father. I speak frankly—and I make enemies. I'm afraid that I'll come to a bad end."

She sat down on the step of a ladder that leaned against the bookshelves. Her pleated skirt spread before her like an open fan.

"Tell me, what's the manuscript like? I tried so many times to look into it, but I didn't understand a word."

"Oh, it wouldn't be of interest to a girl."

"Tell me something about it. I'm not so ignorant."

"Well, I really don't know where to begin. It's what they call scholasticism."

Asa Heshel began to finger the pages, Adele looking curiously at him. He read a few passages to himself, his lips moving silently while he gave a negative shake of his head; then a few minutes later he clutched at his chin and read intently. His brow creased into deep wrinkles. The expression on his face kept changing rapidly—from the rapt attention of a youth to the thoughtfulness of a mature man. An unexpected idea struck Adele—this was the way her father must have looked when he was young.

"Well," she said, "I'm listening."

"You see, there's a certain passage in Ecclesiastes—'The wind goeth toward the south, and turneth about unto the north; it whirleth about continually, and the wind returneth again according to his circuits.' Now, you see, the wind is interpreted to mean the soul. When a man sins, his soul, after he dies, might be transmigrated into all sorts of things—a dog, a cat, a worm—even into the whirling wings of a windmill. But at the end the soul returns to its beginnings."

While Asa Heshel was talking, Adele kept her wide-eyed gaze fixed on him. There was something of awe and astonishment in her look. The tiny blue veins in her temples throbbed.

"I hope I made it clear," Asa Heshel said after a while.

"Oh, yes."

"And what do you think?"

"If only these things could be written in a European tongue!"

Asa Heshel was about to answer, but at that moment the door opened and Meshulam came in, followed by Rosa Frumetl.

"So we've got a scholar here, eh?" the old man said. "Tell me, young man, do you think you can fix the book up?"

"I think so."

"Myself, I don't hold with this writing business. Everybody in the world thinks he's a writer. But I promised her to have it printed, so—How much do you expect for your trouble?"

"Whatever you like. That isn't the principal thing."

"What do you mean? You don't expect to do it as a favor?"

"Yes; that is—no."

"Tell me about yourself. What are you—one of these 'modern' Jews?"

"Not exactly."

"If a young man like you runs away from home—from his parents—he's certainly no saint of a Jew."

"I don't aspire to be a saint."

"What then? A sinner?"

"All I want to do is to study."

"Study what? How to answer ritual questions? When some frightened woman gets worried because a pig's shadow passed over her milk bucket—"

"No. That I know already."

"I hear that my granddaughter's giving you lessons—what's her name?—Hadassah."

Asa Heshel flushed. "Yes," he answered, stammering. "She's giving me Polish lessons."

"What good'll Polish do you? In the first place Russia's the ruler here. And in the second place Hadassah will be betrothed this Saturday night. It won't do for a bride to be giving lessons to anyone."

Asa Heshel wanted to say something, but he had lost his voice. He felt a dryness in his throat. His face turned white, and the tea glass he held in his hand trembled.

"Do you really mean it?" Rosa Frumetl brought her hands together. *"Mazeltov!"*

"She'll marry Fishel Kutner. His grandfather, Simon Kutner, has a business in oil on the Gnoyna. Not much learning, but an honest man, a follower of my rabbi—the Bialodrevner. The groom studies in the prayerhouse, and in the afternoons he keeps the books in his grandfather's store."

"What wonderful news!" Rosa Frumetl exclaimed. "Dacha didn't say a word about it."

On the old man's face a sly smile showed. "Next Saturday night," he said. "You'll be invited. You'll eat honey cakes." He peered at Asa Heshel from beneath his heavy eyebrows and made a motion with his mouth as though he were swallowing his own mustache.

4

For a while there was silence in the room. Asa Heshel picked up a cake from the tray and then put it back again. Rosa Frumetl played with the string of pearls she was wearing around her throat. Meshulam sat down, picked up a page of the manuscript, and held it close to his eyes. He turned to Rosa Frumetl.

"Where's my magnifying glass?"

"I haven't any idea."

"Is there anything you do know? What kind of thing is this?" he asked Asa Heshel.

"Biblical commentary."

"Ha! Everybody brings me new books—rabbis, peddlers—but I've no time to waste. The office is full of books."

"Why don't they bring them here?" Rosa Frumetl inquired.

"And who's going to take care of them? Koppel's an ignoramus. Bundles of letters, from rabbis, teachers, God knows who else. And no one to answer them."

"Ts, ts, ts! Rabbis write to you and they get no answer."

Meshulam gave his wife a wry look. "What's to stop you from answering them? You're supposed to be an educated woman. Besides, my eyesight's not so good."

"Suppose you ask this young man. He's a learned youth."

"What? That's an idea. Come to see me in my office, on the Gzhybovska. My bailiff has a shrewd head, but in such matters he's a peasant."

"When shall I come?"

"Any time, any time. And you can tell me what they're all writing about. In two words."

Meshulam went out. Rosa Frumetl turned to cast a triumphant glance at Asa Heshel. Instead she met her daughter's gaze and left without another word. Silence fell again. From a corner came a faint squeaking, as though a mouse were scurrying along back of the woodwork. Adele shifted on the ladder. Asa Heshel wanted to raise his eyes, but his eyelids hung heavy. He had a queer feeling that the chair he sat on was keeling over.

"Why are you so disturbed?" Adele asked. Her eyes were fixed on him, measuring him deliberately.

"I'm not disturbed."

"You're in love with her. What else can it be?"

"In love? I don't know what you mean."

"She's superficial. Everything's on the surface. She knows practically nothing. She never passed her examinations."

"She became sick."

"All bad students somehow manage to get sick before the examinations."

"She had to go to a sanatorium for her health—for almost a year."

"Yes, I've heard about those cases before. They've a way of fooling themselves and others."

From the living-room came a muffled ringing. Nine o'clock.

"It was my first impression that you were a serious person," Adele said.

"What have I done?"

"When a man starts to study—at your age—you have to apply yourself day and night, not run around after girls."

"But I run after nobody."

"And you certainly don't go to live in a house like that."

"Who told you about it? There's nothing wrong with the house."

"Oh, I know. That Gina is just a wanton woman. And Abram Shapiro is a fraud. Fine company for a student."

Asa Heshel made an involuntary movement. The manuscript fell from his hands and spilled onto the floor. He bent down to pick the pages up, but could not grasp them. The helplessness that had suddenly overwhelmed him had something of a dreamlike quality.

"I don't want to hurt you," the girl continued. "It's only

that you've got something in you; otherwise I'm sure I
wouldn't bother to speak to you about it at all."

Asa Heshel murmured a faint "Thank you."

"Don't bother to thank me—and look straight at me.
You're not such a pious Chassid that you have to be afraid to
look at a girl. And don't hunch down with your shoulders
bent that way. You're not eighty years old."

Asa Heshel straightened up and turned his eyes toward her.
Their eyes met. A quick smile passed over her sharp features.

"You're a queer combination," she said. "The small-town
yeshivah student and the cosmopolitan."

"You're making fun of me."

"No, I'm not. The ones I met in Switzerland are the dark
and curly-headed kind. Beggars, every one of them. What you
need is someone to be a real friend to you—and you need a
lot of discipline."

"Yes, I think that's true."

"If you're really serious about studying, I can help you. I
can be more help to you than Hadassah."

"I thought you said you were going away."

"I am. But not immediately."

She got up from the ladder and bent down to help gather
the scattered manuscript. Her fingers touched his. He felt the
sharp stab of her filed fingernails. As he straightened out the
manuscript on the desk, she leaned over his shoulder; the feminine odor of her body and the perfume she used filled his nostrils.

She walked away from the table. "Well, I'm going now,"
she said. "Good night."

"Good night," he answered.

"If you want, I can give you your first lesson tomorrow."

"Well—yes—thank you."

"And please don't be so bashful all the time. It isn't becoming. Certainly not for a cosmopolitan."

CHAPTER FIVE

1

To the court of the Bialodrevna rabbi on this Channukah
more than a hundred of the faithful came to make the pilgrimage. The rabbi did not have more than two thousand fol-

lowers, and these were scattered all over Poland. Even on
Rosh Hashona, the New Year holiday, not more than two or
three hundred of the devout had forgathered. Since the rabbi's
daughter, Gina Genendel, had left Akiba, her husband, the
son of the Sentsimin rabbi, and was carrying on with that
heretic Hertz Yanovar, some of the rabbi's followers had fall-
en away. The resident students and permanent attendants at
the rabbi's court had hardly reckoned on a Channukah attendance of more than a score.

The train, which made a stop at the station five versts from
Bialodrevna, brought Chassidim who had not shown their
faces at the court for several years. They came from as far as
Radom and Lublin. The drivers waiting at the station with
their sleighs could not pile all the visitors in; the overflow had
to wait for the return trip. A few set off on foot, in the manner of the old days. They took swallows of brandy from
flasks, sang Chassidic chants, and cut a few Chassidic capers.
On these lonely roads a peasant was seldom seen. The fields
on both sides of the road, sown with winter wheat, stretched
to the distant horizons, like a frozen sea. A solitary crow flew
low over the vastness, emitting its lonesome caw.

With the news that a crowd of the faithful was approaching, the town-dwellers broke out into a rash of excitement.
Inn and lodging-house keepers made haste to prepare more
beds; storekeepers got ready for a rush of trade. The butchers
had the ritual slaughterer slit the throat of a cow they had
been fattening in its stall for the following Sabbath week. The
fishermen went out to the lake on the near-by estates of
Count Dombrowski and bargained with his manager for a
catch of fish. What impressed the townsfolk most was the
news that Reb Meshulam Moskat had arrived from Warsaw.
It was his custom to come only for the Rosh Hashona holiday; if he was coming on Channukah it meant that at last
Bialodrevna would be lifted up from its low estate.

By Thursday afternoon the prayerhouse had an entirely altered appearance. Young boys who had been brought along
by their fathers were busy studying or playing at holiday
games. The older men peered into volumes of commentaries
or strolled about, chatting. The pale light of the winter sun
shone through the tall windows, touching the tops of the long
tables, reflecting back from the pillars that set off the reader's
platform. Newcomers were constantly arriving, and there was
a continual exchange of greetings. Aizha, the old sexton, who
had served the original Bialodrevna rabbi, the grandfather of

the present incumbent, was the first to greet each newcomer.
"Welcome and peace to you, Reb Berish Izhbitzer!" his
hoarse voice could be heard through the length and breadth
of the prayerhouse. "An honored guest!" *"Sholem aleichem,*
Reb Motel Vlotzlavker!"

Although it was nearing time for the late afternoon services, several of the Chassidim were still putting on phylacteries for the morning prayer. The Bialodrevna rabbi was
known for being unconventionally late in the synagogue routine. Some of the worshippers were standing for the recitation
of the Eighteen Benedictions, others were sipping brandy and
nibbling at honey cakes. One old man had brought with him a
large teapot of boiling water and was brewing tea. A lanky
youth had stretched himself out on a bench near the stove and
was dozing. It was all right for those stultified Jews, opponents of the Chassidim, to study the Law in luxury, and sleep
on feather beds; a true Chassid could make do with any hard-
ship so long as he was near his rabbi.

The moment they arrived, the faithful wanted to catch a
sight of their blessed rabbi and receive his greetings, but Israel
Eli, the beadle, passed the word along that the rabbi was receiving no one.

Ever since the trouble with his daughter the rabbi had practically secluded himself, spending his time in his own
chamber. His room was a sort of combination library and
chapel. Shelves of volumes stretched along the yellow-papered
walls. There was an Ark of the Law, a reading-stand, and a
table. The window, hung with white draperies, looked out
over a garden, now snow-covered. Through the panes could
be seen terraced fields, stretching into the distance, toward the
west. The rabbi liked to stand and look for hours at the rang-
ing landscape.

"Ah, sweet Father in heaven," he would sigh, "what will
the end of it be! Woe and woe and woe!"

The rabbi's tall figure was bent. The skirts of his green silk
sleeping-robe with the yellow girdle reached to his heels.
Through the front opening of the robe could be seen his knee-
length breeches, the wide four-cornered ritual fringed garment, white hose, and low shoes. The rabbi was in his late fifties, but his thin beard was still black; only here and there a
few white hairs gleamed. He took a sudden step forward and
just as suddenly stopped. He stretched out his hand, as though
about to take a book from the shelves, and then let it drop to
his side. He glanced at the square-faced clock on the wall,

with its long spring-weights and the Hebrew characters on the dial, the wooden framework carved with clusters of pomegranates and grapes. It was a quarter past four; soon the early winter darkness would descend.

The stove was burning, but a chill ran along his spine. Every time he remembered that his daughter, his Gina Genendel, had departed from the paths of virtue, had left her husband and was roaming about somewhere in Warsaw among heretics and mockers, he felt a bitterness in his mouth. It was his fault. His. Whose else could it be?

Tired from pacing up and down, he seated himself in his leather-upholstered chair. His eyes closed and he half dozed, half brooded. The paradise of the world to come was not to be his portion. Where was it written that Yechiel Menachem, the son of Jekatriel David of Bialodrevna, must eat of Leviathan in the dining-halls of heaven? There were hot coals, too, that had been decreed as the sinner's portion. But what of Israel, what of the people Israel! Heresy was growing day by day. In America—so he had heard it said—Jews violated the Sabbath. In Russia, in England, in France, Jewish children were growing up in ignorance of Holy Writ. And here in Poland, Satan roamed openly through the streets. Youths were running away from the study houses, shaving off their beards, eating the unclean food of the gentile. Jewish daughters went about with their naked arms showing, flocked to the theaters, carried on love affairs. Worldly books were poisoning the minds of the young. Never had it been as bad as this, even in the times of Sabbathai Zvi and Jacob Frank, may the names of the false messiahs be blotted out for eternity. Unless the cursed plague were halted, not a remnant would be left of Israel. What was He waiting for, the almighty God? Did He want to bring the Redeemer to a generation steeped in sin?

Israel Eli opened the door slowly and put in his head. He was a plump man, with red cheeks, deep-set eyes, and a round beard. His velvet hat was perched square on top of his head.

"Rabbi, Reb Meshulam Moskat has come," he announced triumphantly. "His youngest son, Nyunie, is with him."

"So."

"Also Reb Simon Kutner, with his grandson, Fishel."

"*Nu!*"

"It's said that there'll be a match between Fishel and Nyunie's daughter, Hadassah."

"*Nu*, a good match."

"Reb Zeinvele Srotsker is here, too."

"Aha! The *shadchan*."

"And I hear that the girl doesn't want the match."

"Why not? Fishel is a decent youth."

"She went to those modern schools of theirs—she's probably looking for a modern husband."

The rabbi shuddered.

"Yes! First they poison them with heresy—and afterwards it's too late. They lead their own children to the slaughterhouse."

"They probably want you, rabbi, to intervene in the match."

"How can I help them when I am helpless myself? My own daughter a wanton—"

"God forbid, rabbi! What are you saying! Maybe she's one of their 'enlightened' ones—but a pure Jewish daughter."

"If a married woman runs away with a man she's a wanton!"

"But—may even the suspicion of the words be forgiven me —they don't live together."

"What difference does that make? If they've lost all faith, then what else matters?"

Israel Eli hesitated a moment, then said: "Rabbi, they're waiting for you."

"There's no hurry. I'll come down later."

The beadle went out. The rabbi got up and went over to the reading-stand. He enjoyed looking at the complicated, symbolic tablet that hung on the eastern wall. Although it had been painted almost a century before, the colors were still bright. Above were the names of the seven stars. In the corners were the figures of a lion, a stag, a leopard, and an eagle. Around the edges ran the symbols of the twelve signs of the zodiac—the Ram, the Bull, the Twins, the Crab, the Lion, the Virgin, the Balance, the Scorpion, the Archer, the Goat, the Water-bearer, the Fishes. Over the side was inscribed a verse:

Why do you weep for your gold that is gone,
But not for your days that depart one by one!
Your gold goes not with you beyond the bourne,
And the days that depart will never return.

When the rabbi stood like this at the stand, the Ark of the Law, with its scrolls on one side, the bookshelves on the other, and in front of him the Unutterable Name of God, he felt safe from all storms and tempests, from all the temptations and lusts of the flesh. He put his lips to the fringes of the curtain that hung before the Ark and kissed them. With his fingernail he scratched off the wax drippings that had gathered on the Menorah stand. He closed his eyes and with both hands clutched the stand, as though it were the horns of the altar, which give the sinner sanctuary from the judgment of death. His body shook to and fro. His lips moved in prayer—for himself, for his daughter in the outer darkness of the world, for the faithful who had journeyed to his court, and for all of Israel scattered among the nations, among the uncircumcised and the unbelievers, the prey of plunderers and assassins. He raised his clenched fists and cried out: "Dear Father! Dear God! Is the cup not yet full?"

He remembered a wry remark of his father: "Cancel out, dear Father in heaven, the capital You've invested in Your people Israel. For surely it is plain, almighty God, that it will return You no profit."

2

The night had fallen and the stars were high when the rabbi repaired to the prayerhouse. To maintain the pretense that it was still twilight and thus not too late for the afternoon services, the naphtha lamps had not been lighted. Only the stump of a memorial candle flickered in one of the uprights of a Menorah stand. As the rabbi came in, the faithful crowded around him, each of them eager to be the first to extend greetings. In the gloom the rabbi could see Moshe Gabriel Margolis, Meshulam Moskat's son-in-law. The rabbi took the other's soft hand in his own and held it for a few moments. Moshe Gabriel, a smallish, neat man, in a glossy alpaca coat and a silk peaked hat, was silent. His face was pale; his tobacco-colored beard, in the glimmer of the single candle, took on an amber glow. His gold-rimmed spectacles were circles of light.

"Peace to you, Reb Moshe Gabriel; how are you, Reb Moshe Gabriel?" the rabbi said. He repeated the name twice, a mark of affection.

"God be praised."

"You came with your father-in-law?"

"No. I came alone."

"Come to me after the lighting of the Channukah candles."

"Yes, rabbi."

The rabbi exchanged greetings with Meshulam, Nyunie, Simon Kutner, and Fishel, Simon Kutner's grandson, but he spent no time conversing with them; it was not his habit to show favor to the wealthy among his followers. Immediately after the combined afternoon and evening services the rabbi officiated at the lighting of the candles. When his wife was alive and Gina was still a child, they had come to witness the ceremony; but it was years now that the rabbi had been alone. The ritual was performed quietly and somberly. Aizha poured the oil into the copper container and trimmed the wicks. The rabbi changed the prescribed blessing and applied the flame. An aroma of hot oil and scorched canvas filled the air. The rabbi began to cantillate the phrases of the Channukah song. It was not a tune he sang, but a murmuring, a mixture of sighs and fragments of melody. The worshippers chanted along with him. When the ritual was over, the youngsters hurried to the long tables to play their games. Some of the Chassidim permitted themselves to join in. This was no sacrilege; benches and tables are not holy in themselves; the important thing is the feeling in a man's heart. For the man of piety is not the whole world a house of prayer?

Later the rabbi left for his own quarters, while most of the faithful returned to their lodgings, where the evening meal was waiting for them—soup, meat, bread, and cracklings—and where they could begin their meal with a swallow of brandy and a bite of egg cake. The wealthier Chassidim paid for those who could not afford so lavish a repast. For all that there was no moon in the sky, the night was bright in the light of the stars and the brilliance of the snow. Columns of smoke rose from chimneys. A sudden frost had descended, but there were plenty of logs for the stoves and a goose or two stored away in every pantry.

Meshulam, Nyunie, Zeinvele Srotsker, Simon Kutner, and his grandson, Fishel, were staying at the same inn. A common reason had brought them together to Bialodrevna. Dacha, Hadassah's mother, was squarely opposed to the match between her daughter and Fishel. Hadassah herself had flatly refused to marry him. Zeinvele Srotsker was known for being able to talk to young people in their own language. For all his staunch Chassidic piety he was a daily reader of the *Warsaw Courier*, a Polish paper, and knew all about the affairs of the Polish gentry. He had even arranged a match between two gentile households. He had argued with Hadassah until his throat was dry, but had accomplished nothing. All the girl would do was flush and murmur some half-intelligible arguments. She was more of a *shikse* than any of the gentile girls he had ever had anything to do with, Zeinvele complained. He would go away from her exhausted and bathed in perspiration.

"Stubborn as a goat," he announced, and he informed Meshulam that he refused to humiliate himself any further.

It looked very much as though Meshulam would not be able to make good his intention of settling the match by the Sabbath eve. But he refused to admit defeat. In his long career he had overcome more formidable opponents than Dacha and Hadassah. Besides, he had convinced himself that his long life was the result of all the victories he had won in the countless struggles in which he had engaged. If he were to lose a single one, it would be the signal for his death. The stubbornness of his daughter-in-law and granddaughter threw a sort of terror into him.

After a good deal of thought Meshulam found the way out. He would go to the Bialodrevna rabbi with Nyunie, Simon Kutner, and the prospective groom and there draw up the preliminary engagement contract. The bride's signature was necessary for the final contract, but the preliminaries could be arranged without her. Later he would find some way to deal with these stiffnecked females.

Both Meshulam and Simon Kutner were sure that if the rabbi were a witness to the preliminary arrangements and approved them, Dacha would certainly give in. Her own father, the Krostinin rabbi, had been a staunch follower of the Bialodrevner. Surely she would not dare to put herself in opposition to the wishes of personages like these.

The four now sat at the table eating the evening meal. Simon Kutner, broad-shouldered and with a fan-shaped white beard and a ruddy face, was dipping pieces of bread in the gravy of the roast, heaping horseradish on them with the point of his knife, and exchanging comments with Meshulam. Fishel, with red cheeks and black eyes that darted constantly from side to side, was wearing a slit coat, a small hat, and well-polished boots. He threw in a remark now and then. The talk had to do with some Talmudic observations concerning an accidentally extinguished Channukah candle. Fishel had some knowledge of the point in question. His grandfather skillfully managed the conversation so that whenever the talk roamed, Fishel was able to interject an appropriate remark.

Meshulam knew the trick, but he also knew that all prospective bridegrooms went in for the same mild deceit. Not all bridegrooms were geniuses. What pleased Meshulam about the youth was his calmness and poise, his shrewd business head. He could feel confident that Fishel was the kind who would add to his worldly goods after his marriage and would remain a loyal Chassid at the same time. He turned to Fishel and remarked: "Well, what are you waiting for? Let's have your interpretation"—and he poked Zeinvele in the ribs as a sign that he, Meshulam, was not the man to be taken in by a hoax.

While this was going on, Aizha informed Moshe Gabriel, who was waiting in the prayerhouse, that the rabbi was ready to receive him. Moshe Gabriel patted his curled sidelocks, tugged at the sash he wore around his waist, and followed the beadle. The way led through a small courtyard. In the rabbi's room a lamp and a candle were burning. The rabbi was smoking a long, curved pipe. He waved Moshe Gabriel to a chair.

"Tell me, Reb Moshe Gabriel, what is this business with Nyunie's daughter? I am told that she refuses Fishel."

"What is there to be surprised at? Her mother sent her to these modern schools; the books they read are full of adulteries and abominations. And now she's not content with a Chassidic youth. Like the rest of them she's taken the bit between her teeth."

"Maybe she's fallen in love—God forbid."

"I don't know. Some young man came to Warsaw, a youth from Tereshpol Minor—a prodigy they say, but already spoiled, the grandson of the rabbi of Tereshpol Minor."

"That would be Rabbi Dan Katzenellenbogen."

"Yes."

"A great man."

"What good does it do? This young man goes around with my brother-in-law, Abram Shapiro. Hadassah is giving him lessons of some kind. Abram and my father-in-law are at daggers' points. Nyunie's wife, again, does nothing without him. He's using them to prick the blister."

"What has he against his father-in-law?"

"It's an old quarrel."

"*Nu.* . . . But it is wrong to compel a child. Gina Genendel was opposed to Akiba, too. But her mother, may she find peaceful repose, forced her."

"It's bad one way and it's no good the other."

"Man has free will. Without free will what is the difference between the throne of glory and the depths of the nether world?"

The rabbi put the stem of his pipe between his lips and began to puff. He made up his mind to warn Meshulam that if the girl proved firm in her refusal she should not be compelled to go through with the match. Better that she remain single for a few years more than that she depart from the path of righteousness after the wedding.

PART
TWO

CHAPTER ONE

1

In the middle of the night Rosa Frumetl heard her husband groan. She asked him what troubled him, but Meshulam grumbled impatiently and said: "Go to sleep. Don't bother me."

"Maybe you'd like some tea," she persisted.

"I don't want any tea."

"Then what is it you want?"

Meshulam thought for a moment. "What I want is to be thirty years younger."

Rosa Frumetl sighed tenderly. "A silly idea! There's nothing wrong with you, thank God. Like other men of fifty—may no evil eye."

"Pah, you're babbling nonsense," Meshulam growled. "Anyway, leave me alone. What bothers me is none of your business."

"I honestly don't understand you," Rosa Frumetl said mournfully.

"I don't understand myself," Meshulam said in the darkness, half to himself, half to his wife. "I spin and I spin and nothing comes out of it. I've had two wives, seven children, given out dowries, supported sons-in-law. It's cost me millions! And what have I got out of it? A bunch of enemies, gluttons, parasites. A fine generation I've spawned."

"Meshulam, it's a sin to talk that way."

"Let it be a sin. As long as I've got a tongue I'll speak, and if God wants to lash me for it, it'll be my behind that gets the whip, not yours."

"Feh! Meshulam!"

"Feh as much as you please! You've got one child, I've got seven—and in every one of them there's a worm gnawing—" He broke off, as though undecided whether to voice his complaints to this woman who was so unexpectedly his wife, whether it was below his dignity. "That my children are worthless," he resumed, "is nobody's fault. I myself am a hard man, stubborn, spiteful, something of a villain. I don't deny it. And the apple, they say, doesn't fall far from the tree. And my wives weren't any bargains either. The first one—may her

96

spirit not hold it against me—was a common woman. The second one was plain unlucky. But at least I could expect to have decent sons-in-law. Those, at least, you can buy for cash as you buy cattle in the market."

"Meshulam, what kind of talk is this?" Rosa Frumetl broke in.

"Quiet, woman! I'm not talking to you. I'm talking to the wall," Meshulam rumbled. "What are you shivering about? I'll roast in hell, not you!"

"Matches are made in heaven," Rosa Frumetl protested weakly.

"Sure, it looks that way, doesn't it! That Abram—an idolator and a heretic, a lecher, a breaker-up of homes. He's slandered me and robbed me. Now he's breaking his neck to spoil *her* life—what's her name?—Nyunie's daughter—Hadassah. Or take Moshe Gabriel, Leah's husband—a beggar. And my daughters-in-law—useless, worthless except maybe Pinnie's wife."

Rosa Frumetl made an effort to comfort him. "At least," she said, "you'll rejoice in your grandchildren."

"Good-for-nothings! The same as their parents!" Meshulam shouted. "Those fancy schools have turned my granddaughters into *shikses,* every one of them. And the boys—pumpkin-heads! Give 'em Channukah money—that's all they're interested in! Bribe them with presents! The moment they leave the cheder they're through with learning."

"You can change it, Meshulam," Rosa Frumetl said. "You've got the power. You can dictate to them."

"You talk like a fool! What sort of power have I got? I'm nothing but an old man, an old Jew of eighty. Soon it'll be time for me to die and leave them to haggle over everything I've got. They can hardly wait for it. They'll swarm around like locusts and devour whatever they find."

"You ought to make provision, Meshulam," Rosa Frumetl sighed softly.

"When there's six feet of earth over you, you can't make provision. But while I'm alive I'm the master, do you hear?" He raised his voice to a roar. "I'm alive and I'm the boss!"

"That's what I've been telling you, Meshulam."

"Hadassah will marry before the winter's over. That's final. Nothing they can do will stop it." He lowered his voice to a growl. "And what about that daughter of yours? What's she sitting around for? How old is she already? Thirty?"

"What are you saying, Meshulam! She's not even twenty-four yet—I can show you the birth certificate! May He whose name I'm not worthy to mention only send the right man."

"God isn't a *shadchan*. Zeinvele Srotsker has been to see her time and again, and she refuses to talk to him. Another aristocrat! Nose in the air!"

"Excuse me, Meshulam, my Adele comes from a finer family than—you'll pardon me—Hadassah."

"That'll look good on a gravestone. I'll give her a dowry, only for God's sake let there be an end to it! I don't want any old maids moping around the house."

Meshulam suddenly knew that there would be no sleep for him. He wanted to get up and go into the library; there was a sofa there where he would manage to get through the night somehow. But his legs felt heavy, his head ached, and there was a bitter taste in his mouth. Disconnected thoughts chased each other through his mind. He wanted to sneeze and at the same time to yawn. His nightcap had fallen from his head. He swung his legs off the bed and got his feet into his slippers.

"Where are you going?" Rosa Frumetl asked.

"Don't worry. I'm not running away. Stay where you are and go to sleep."

He poured a few drops of water over his fingers from the pitcher that stood beside the bed—the orthodox ritual on rising—put on his robe, and with unsteady steps went out of the bedroom. In the darkness of the corridor he could not see the library door. He put out his hand, clutched a doorknob, and pushed against it. It was Adele's room. She was sitting at the edge of the bed in a blue house robe and plush slippers reading a book. Meshulam took a step backwards.

"Oh, it's you! A mistake! Excuse me."

"Is anything wrong?"

"Nothing. Don't be afraid. I wanted to go into the library. Why aren't you asleep? What is it you're reading so late?"

"A book."

"What kind of book? Maybe you've got a match. I want to put the light on in the library."

"One minute." Adele, holding on to the book, lifted the lamp and preceded the old man out of the room. For a moment the shadow of the old man's head hung motionless on the wall, with a long nose and pointed beard, like a wedge. The two went into the library and Adele lit the lamp.

"Maybe you'd like me to make you some tea," she said.

"No, no. Tell me, what is the book you're reading?"

"It's just a book—by a man called Swedenborg."

"Who is he? I never heard the name."

"A Swedish mystic. He describes Paradise and Gehenna."

"Idiocy! You can find it in our own books. Isn't there enough time in the day for you to read?" he asked, and looked at her curiously from under his shaggy eyebrows.

"I couldn't sleep."

"Why not? What makes you so restless?"

"I don't know."

"Listen to me. It's true you're a smart girl, an educated girl. But you're not practical. From all these books you'll get nothing. All they'll do is drive you into a melancholy. A girl like you should be a bride—get married."

"It doesn't depend on me."

"Who, then? Zeinvele Srotsker has suggested a couple of good matches."

"I'm sorry. But that way of getting married is not for me."

"Why not?"

"I can't go in for an arranged match."

"That means, I suppose, you want to fall in love."

"If I happen to meet someone and I like him—"

"Nonsense! You're liable to wait around till your hair's gray and never find anyone. Or maybe you've taken a fancy to that greenhorn that's fixing up your father's manuscript."

"He's from a fine rabbinical family—and he's cultured and intelligent. If he fell into the right hands he could become a—"

"A what? A starving Hebrew teacher somewhere! A beggar in rags! From what I hear, he's a heretic, a *goy*. They say he's turning Hadassah's head around."

"It isn't his fault. She's got some sort of notion in her mind. He's not for her and she's not for him."

"Good! Exactly what I think. Come here, sit down—here on the sofa. Don't be embarrassed on my account—I'm an old man—"

"Thank you."

"Hadassah's going to marry Fishel. Nyunie has already agreed and Dacha will give in. I'll see to it that the wedding takes place before Passover. So far as you're concerned, do what you think is best. I'll put aside two thousand rubles for you, and I won't forget you in my will either. But take my advice; marry a businessman. All these budding geniuses go around with the toes sticking out of their shoes."

"I'll see. I have to feel that a man is sympathetic to me. Otherwise—"

"All right, all right. And don't read in the middle of the night. Something new in the world—young girls, and they have to know about everything. What'll you do when you're old? Ah, the world's turned upside down."

"Life's not easy if you don't have some understanding about things."

"And do you think knowing is going to make it easier? And in the next world it won't help either. A human being's got to give an accounting. Well, go ahead. And tell that young genius to come to my office. I want to talk to him."

"But, please, don't scold him. He's proud."

"Don't be scared about him. I'll not eat him up. Still water, I tell you, but he runs deep."

"Good night."

"Good night. A simple life, I tell you, that's the best. No questions, no philosophy, no racking your brains. In Germany there was a philosopher, and he philosophized so long that he began to eat grass."

The old man took a book down from the shelves and tried to read, but the letters seemed to change color—first green, then gold. The lines bobbed up and down and in the center of his vision there was a yawning emptiness on the page, as though the type had suddenly flown away. For a moment he closed his eyes. The book he was holding was a commentary on the laws relating to death and mourning. He picked up the spectacles lying on the table, settled them on his nose, and read:

Know that before he expires the Angel of Death comes to the man in the agony of dying, a thousand eyes blazing on his fearful image, the unsheathed sword in his hand. And he tempts the moribund to blaspheme God and worship idols. And because the man is frail, and the fear of death is upon him, he may stumble and lose his world in a single hour. Therefore it is that in the olden times, when he fell upon his bed in his final anguish, he called in ten witnesses and made void and annulled the words he would utter before the parting of the soul and the wicked thoughts that come from the Evil One. And it is a fitting custom, meet for the God-fearing man.

Meshulam closed the book. That he had chanced to pick this volume out of all the books on the shelf was a bad sign. Yes, his time had run out. But he was not ready. He had not yet made his repentance, had not distributed his money to

charity, had not properly executed his testament. Somewhere
in his iron safe there were a few sheets of paper with some directions written on them, but they had not been signed by witnesses or sealed with sealing wax. He tried to recall what he
had written, but he could not remember. He lay down on the
sofa and rested his head on the raised end. A single snore
escaped his lips and he fell into a deep sleep. When he awoke,
the bright light of early morning was shining through the
misted window panes.

2

On that same night Hadassah, too, was sleepless. The wind,
blowing against the window, had awakened her, and from
that moment she had not been able to close an eye. She sat up
in bed, switched on the electric lamp, and looked about the
room. The goldfish in the aquarium were motionless, resting
quietly along the bottom of the bowl, among the colored
stones and tufts of moss. On a chair lay her dress, her petticoat, and her jacket. Her shoes stood on top of the table—
although she did not remember having put them there. Her
stockings lay on the floor. She put both hands up to her head.
Had it really happened? Could it be that she had fallen in
love? And with this provincial youth in his Chassidic gaberdine? What if her father knew? And her mother—and Uncle
Abram? And Klonya! But what would happen now? Her
grandfather had already made preliminary arrangements with
Fishel. She was as good as betrothed.

Beyond this Hadassah's thoughts could not go. She got out
of bed, stepped into her slippers, and went over to the table.
From the drawer she took out her diary and began to turn the
pages. The brown covers of the book were gold-stamped, the
edges were stained yellow. Between the pages a few flowers
were pressed, and leaves whose green had faded, leaving only
the brittle veined skeletons. The margins of the pages were
thick with scrawls of roses, clusters of grapes, adders, tiny,
fanciful figures, hairy and horned, with fishes' fins and
webbed feet. There was a bewildering variety of designs—circles, dots, oblongs, keys—whose secret meaning only Hadassah knew. She had started the diary when she was no more
than a child, in the third class at school, in her child's handwriting, and with a child's grammatical errors. Now she was
grown. The years had gone by like a dream.

She turned the pages and read, skipping from page to page. Some of the entries seemed to her strangely mature, beyond her age when she had written them, others naïve and silly. But every page told of suffering and yearning. What sorrows she had known! How many affronts she had suffered—from her teachers, her classmates, her cousins! Only her mother and her Uncle Abram were mentioned with affection. On one page there was the entry: "What is the purpose of my life? I am always lonely and no one understands me. If I don't overcome my empty pride I may just as well die. Dear God, teach me humility."

On another page, under the words of a song that Klonya had written down for her, there was: "Will he come one day, my destined one? What will he look like? I do not know him and he does not know me; I do not exist for him. But fate will bring him to my door. Or maybe he was never born. Maybe it is my fate to be alone until the end." Below the entry she had drawn three tiny fishes. What they were supposed to mean she had now forgotten.

She pulled a chair up to the table, sat down, dipped a pen in the inkwell, and put the diary in front of her. Suddenly she heard footsteps outside the door. Quickly she swung herself onto the bed and pulled the cover over her. The door opened and her mother came in, wearing a red kimono. There was a yellow scarf around her head; her graying hair showed around the edges.

"Hadassah, are you asleep? Why is the light on?"

The girl opened her eyes. "I couldn't sleep. I was trying to read a book."

"I couldn't sleep either. The noise of the wind—and my worries. And your father has a new accomplishment; he snores."

"Papa always snored."

"Not like this. He must have polyps."

"Mamma, come into bed with me."

"What for? It's too small. Anyway, you kick, like a pony."

"I won't kick."

"No, I'd better sit down. My bones ache from lying. Listen, Hadassah, I have to have a serious talk with you. You know, my child, how I love you. There's nothing in the world I have besides you. Your father—may no ill befall him—is a selfish man."

"Please stop saying things about Papa."

"I have nothing against him. He is what he is. He lives for

himself, like an animal. I'm used to it. But you, I want to see
you happy. I want to see you have the happiness that I didn't
have."

"Mamma, what is it all about?"

"I was never one to believe in forcing a girl into marriage.
I've seen enough of what comes of such things. But just the
same you're taking the wrong road, my child. In the first
place, Fishel is a decent youth—sensible, a good businessman.
You don't find men like him every day. And in the second
place, his grandfather is stuffed up to here with money, and
one day—though I wish him long life, dear Lord—it'll all go
to Fishel."

"Mamma, you may as well forget it. I won't marry him."

"At least let me finish what I've got to say. I suppose you
have the idea that you're the child of a rich home. Unfortunately, you're mistaken. Your father has a few rubles—just
enough for a rainy day, if one should come. He wouldn't
touch that money for any other purpose. You're a girl without
a dowry, and a sick girl, too. That's the way it is. That's the
whole truth."

"I don't understand what you want of me, Mamma."

"Your grandfather's decided to be as stubborn as a mule.
He's already given Koppel orders to stop paying our weekly
allowance. He swears he won't leave us a grosz in his will.
And you can believe him. We'll all be left helpless. Your
father—I don't have to tell you—is useless when it comes to
making a living. All he can do is eat and sleep. And I'm a sick
woman—sicker than you imagine. God knows how long I can
keep on driving myself."

"Mamma!"

"Don't interrupt me. I don't want to say anything about
your Uncle Abram. So far as I'm concerned he's all right, and
I'm devoted to him. But he's nobody to be depended on. He's
made his own wife miserable and he's been no blessing to that
other one—what's her name?—Ida Prager. His daughters are
penniless. And now he's attached himself to us. He wants to
use us to spite your grandfather."

"I won't let you say anything about him. I love him."

"I feel for him too. But what good does it do? The man's a
key that's turned the wrong way, a busybody mixing into
other people's business. And that new one—whatever-you-
call-him—Asa Heshel—doesn't make such a hit with me. I
won't have him in this house, do you hear? I'll throw him
out."

"He doesn't come here any more."

"You're a poor girl. Don't forget it. It's true you're not so ugly—may no evil befall you. But a person's not always young and not always beautiful. Fishel will be grabbed up before you can turn around, and what'll you be left with?"

"Let them grab him. Today for all I care."

"And where'll you be? Especially without a dowry. Your grandfather won't give you a copper."

"I don't need his money."

"You'll change your mind, my child. There've been plenty of others like you. When you were in the sanatorium—God grant you health from now on—it cost hundreds and hundreds of rubles. God knows I don't want to frighten you, but when it's a question of weak lungs a person can never be sure."

"Then I'll die!"

"Ah, Hadassah, you're sticking a knife into my heart! Don't think I haven't thought things over. Night after night I lie awake thinking. What closer friend have you than me! You're in danger, I'm telling you. Great danger."

"Oh, Mamma, stop wailing over me. I'm not dead yet. I'm telling you finally, once and for all, I'll not marry Fishel."

"And that's your last word?"

"Yes."

"Well, may God stretch out his arms of mercy to you! Yes, what they say is right—a child is an enemy. Your father wasn't to my taste either, when I was young. But when my mother—God rest her soul—wept and pleaded, I said: 'So be it; lead me to the canopy.' No, the children of today have no hearts, only stones. Well, let it be. I'll be quiet. But your father won't. We'll be without a piece of bread."

"I'll work."

"Sure, my fine lady'll go to work! Simpleton, you can't lift a finger! It's a miracle you're alive. If I didn't wait on you hand and foot you couldn't stand on your own legs. You need comforts. You need money. If I die your father'll bring home a stepmother for you before I'm cold in my grave."

"Let me alone!" Hadassah covered her face with her hands.

"All right. I'm going. Some day you'll remember my words. But then it'll be too late."

She went out and closed the door behind her. The moment she was gone, Hadassah flung herself out of bed. She went to the table, picked up the diary, thought for a moment, and then put it away in the drawer. She turned out the light and stood quietly in the darkness. Through the window she could see a heavy snow falling, the wind driving the flakes against the window pane.

CHAPTER TWO

1

For some time Asa Heshel had given up his triweekly visits to Hadassah. Meshulam Moskat's announcement that the girl was to be betrothed and that tutoring was unbecoming to her frightened him off. Several times he had thought of telephoning her, but the complexities of the instrument, so new to him, were too much for him. He lay in bed in his room at Gina's until late in the afternoon. Every night the flat was crowded with lodgers and visitors. He could hear doors opening and closing, long conversations on the telephone, Broide and Lapidus at their eternal arguments, girls singing Russian songs, applause. Gina had asked him several times to join them in the living-room, but he always managed to make some excuse. What sort of appearance would he make among these sophisticated people in his Chassidic clothing? He had bought a soft collar and a black silk tie, but they seemed only to add to his provincial look. The noisy phonograph music that came from the living-room, the shouting and laughter, the silhouettes passing back and forth on the other side of the glass-paned door of his room, embarrassed him, making him think that all of them knew he was waiting only for Hadassah. That's what they must be giggling about.

He started up in bed. What was happening to him? Why was he wasting his time in idle fantasies? He had come to Warsaw to study, not to moon about love. Ah, how he envied those ancient philosophers, the Stoics, whose determination no amount of suffering could disturb; or the Epicureans, who, even when their house was in flames, ate their bread and drank their wine! But he would never be able to achieve such heights. His emotions were constantly returning to plague him. All he could do was think about Hadassah, her room, her books, her father and mother, even about Shifra, the maid. If only he knew whether she ever thought about him! Or had she forgotten him altogether? He would make an attempt to telephone her—or maybe he would write her a letter.

He got off the bed, turned on the lamp, and sat down to write to Hadassah. After the first few lines he dropped the pen. What was the sense of it? He would plead with no one; he would sooner die. When he fell asleep, the gray dawn already showed through the window. He got up late, his head aching. He dressed and went out to the food store to buy a couple of rolls and some cheese and then went back to his room. He leafed through a geography, a Russian grammar, a world history. His eye caught a sentence about Charlemagne, founder of the Holy Roman Empire. The author described Charlemagne as a great man, defender of the Church, a reformer. Asa Heshel shook his head.

"The crueler the tyrant, the greater the world's praise," he said to himself. "Mankind loves the murderer."

He tried to clear his mind and go on with his reading. But his thoughts would not be dismissed. What sort of world was this, where the order of things was continual murdering, looting, and persecution and where at the same time the air was filled with phrases about justice, freedom, love? And what was he doing? Poring over children's primers, hoping that some day, maybe in ten years, he would manage to earn a diploma. Is this what had become of his youthful dreams? What was he but an inconsequential nobody, with inconsequential and futile notions?

He got up and walked over to the window. He took the nickel-covered watch from his vest pocket; it was half past three, but the winter dusk was already beginning to fall. There was a deep quiet in the courtyard that the window overlooked. A thin snow fell from the rectangle of sky he could see above the surrounding roofs. A crow had perched atop a weathervane on the opposite rooftop; against the pale white sky it took on a bluish color. It seemed to be peering into the vast distances of another world. At the roof's edge, along its gutter, a cat carefully paced. Down below in the courtyard a beggar woman bent over a box, a sack on her shoulders, poking with a hook among the refuse. She pulled out a couple of rags and stuffed them into the sack. She lifted a shrunken, worn face toward the upper windows and sang out in a thin voice: "I buy bones, I buy rags. Bones, bones."

Asa Heshel leaned his forehead against the pane. Once, he thought, she too was young, and the ox whose bones she now sought to buy was a calf leaping about the meadows. Time makes refuse of all things. No philosophy could alter that.

He stretched himself out on the bed and closed his eyes.
Hadassah would grow old, too. She would die and they would
carry her corpse in the funeral procession along the Gensha to
the cemetery. And if time did not exist, then she was a corpse
already. Then what was the sense of love? Why should he
yearn for her? Why should it grieve him that she was to be
the bride of Fishel? He must acquire the indifference of the
Hindu yogis. Enter Nirvana while he was yet alive.

He fell into a half doze. The sharp ringing of the outside
doorbell woke him. It stopped and then after a moment began
anew. Again there was silence, then he heard a knocking at
his own door. He got off the bed. He must have fallen into a
heavy sleep. His limbs were numb. The ceiling seemed to rise
up and the walls recede. He could see two silhouettes against
the glass door pane. He knew that there was something he
should say, but he could not think of the words. Finally he
called out: "I'm here."

The door opened and Gina put her head in. "A young
lady's asking for you," she said. "Can she come in?"

She stepped back and Hadassah entered. She was wearing a
jacket fastened with loops, a velvet beret, and woolen socks
over her stockings. Her cheeks were flushed from the cold.
Scattered flakes of snow clung to her shoulders. She was carrying a black handbag and a thin book with red covers. She
waited at the threshold until Gina closed the door.

In Polish she said: "You stare at me as though you don't
recognize me."

"Of course, Hadassah."

"You were sleeping—I waked you."

"No, no—it's only that I didn't expect—"

"Why haven't you come to see me? I thought you were
sick."

"No, I wasn't sick. Please sit down."

"I expected you for your lessons, but you disappeared. My
Uncle Abram gave me your address."

They were both silent. He knew that Hadassah's visit was
something out of the ordinary, but he could not yet grasp its
meaning.

"I thought maybe I'd offended you or something," he heard
her say.

"Oh, no, how could you offend me?"

"Because you didn't even telephone."

"I was forbidden to visit you," Asa Heshel said.

"Who forbade you?"

"Your grandfather. Not really forbade, but he said you were going to be betrothed."

"Oh, it's not true!" She sat down on the edge of a chair, pulled off one of her gloves, and put it on again. "Maybe you're busy now," she said after a silence. "I'd better go."

"Please stay."

"I thought that apart from the lessons I could consider you a friend. Every day I asked Shifra if you'd telephoned. My Uncle Abram asked for you too."

"What is that book?" Asa Heshel asked, as though deliberately changing the subject.

"Knut Hamsun's *Victoria.*"

"A novel?"

"Yes."

Again there was silence. Then Hadassah said: "You're studying alone, I see."

"What else can I do? But I'm afraid I won't be able to manage it—the examinations, the textbooks. I'm too old."

"But you can't give up."

"Why not? What's the use of it all? There's such a thing as being resigned."

"You're too pessimistic. I know, because I'm very melancholy too. Everyone is against me—my grandfather, Papa, even Mamma."

"What do they want of you?"

"You know. But I can't."

She started to say something else, but suddenly stopped. She walked to the window. Asa Heshel went after her and stood beside her. There was a twilight blueness outside. The snow fell slowly, broodingly. Lights gleamed from the opposite windows. There was a faint rumble of noise, which sounded at one moment like the sighing of the wind and again like the rustling of the forest. Asa Heshel held his breath and let his eyelids close. If only the sun were to stand still in the skies, as it had stood still for Joshua, and the twilight last forever, and the two of them, he and Hadassah, to stand there at the window, close to each other, for eternity!

He glanced toward her and met her own eyes turned toward him. Her features were hidden in the dimness. Her eyes, deep in pools of shadow, were opened wide. It seemed to Asa Heshel that he had experienced all this before. He heard himself say: "I longed for you very much."

The girl quivered. There was a movement in her throat, as though she were swallowing something.

"I too," she answered. "From the beginning."

2

Hadassah had left. It was dark, but Asa Heshel had not turned on the light. He was lying fully dressed on the bed, his eyes staring straight in front of him into the darkness, broken from time to time by passing reflections of light moving over the ceiling and losing themselves in the corners of the room. Could what had happened be true? Was it real or was it a dream? What difference did that make? Was not all of reality, according to Berkeley, a perception of the divine mind? Ah, what nonsense! They were two people, a man and a woman, and they were in love with each other. She would marry him, and they would kiss and embrace and have children. No, the whole thing was madness. Her grandfather would never permit it. Maybe she regretted already what had happened? But the words she had said could never be taken back. They were already a part of the history of the cosmos.

There was a knock at the door, then another. Gina looked in. By the light in the corridor he could see her hairdress, the braids wound like a coronet and studded with combs. Her long earrings sparkled and glittered.

"Asa Heshel, are you asleep?"

"No."

"What's the matter? Why didn't you answer when I knocked? Why are you lying here in the dark? Just because a young lady calls on you do you have to get so confused? Although, to tell the truth, I don't blame you. She's beautiful. May I put on the light?"

"Yes, please."

Gina pressed the electric-light switch, and Asa Heshel sat up on the bed. For a moment the brightness blinded him and he rubbed his hand over his eyes. Gina remained standing, leaning against the doorpost.

"Tell me, my dear boy, are you planning to eat or is this one of your fast days?"

"Of course I'll eat. What made you think—"

"Where do you plan to eat? I want you to have your meals here. Maybe you'd like something now. Some fresh bread and butter, and cheese, or eggs."

"Thank you. I'm not hungry."

"How can you not be hungry? You've been in your room for hours and hours. Forgive me for mixing into your private affairs, but I'm old enough to be your mother."

"I'm really not hungry."

"Then please get up and come into the other room with me. You've not even seen my dining-room yet. My lodgers are all away, and there'll be nobody to disturb you. As you see, I'm not a young girl any more, so you have nothing to be afraid of."

He got off the bed, straightened his collar, and followed her through the long corridor into the dining-room. He sat down. Gina went out and in a few moments returned with a tray of cakes and a flask of brandy. "Have some brandy and cake before you wash your hands for eating," she said. "And if you prefer to eat without washing your hands, that's all right, too. And you needn't be afraid of the brandy. It's sweet, not strong—woman's brandy."

Asa Heshel murmured his thanks. Gina poured some of the liquor into a glass and he took a piece of the cake. He moved his lips and whispered something—whether the ritual blessing or the courteous "your health" Gina could not tell. Gina went out again and returned with a dish of butter, some cheese, and a little basket of seed rolls.

An old-fashioned clock that hung on the wall, with a long pendulum and gilded weights, began a hoarse creaking and then rang out nine. Gina looked at the dial.

"Only nine o'clock," she remarked. "I thought it was much later. Ah me, I sit here all alone and the hours fly by. By the way, who was the young lady who called on you? I could have sworn it was Nyunie Moskat's daughter."

"Yes, it was."

"I've heard a lot about her, but I've never met her. Just imagine, Abram, her own uncle, is in love with her. But really in love."

Asa Heshel convulsively swallowed a mouthful of food.

"Her Uncle Abram! That's impossible!"

"When you live as long as I have you'll know that anything is possible. It's supposed to be a secret, but everybody knows it. Just imagine. An old goat like that."

"But he has a wife."

"A wife makes no difference to Abram. He's not just a man —he's a volcano! Naturally he can't marry her—even if he got a divorce, they'd never allow it. But if he can't, no one

can. I hear they're proposing all sorts of matches for her, but
he won't allow any of them."

"But why?"

"He's jealous, green-eyed. Why he permits her to be friendly with you I can't understand. How did she find out your address?"

"Abram gave it to her."

"You see! Abram's at the bottom of everything. He has his
own way of doing things. He bosses the entire household—
Nyunie, Dacha, Hadassah. They don't make a move without
him. He's got them practically hypnotized."

Asa Heshel opened his mouth to say something, but the
words seemed to have flown away. Suddenly he saw everything double—Gina, the lamp, the tiled stove with the gilded
cornices, the wall clock. He tried to reach for a piece of roll,
but his hand found only empty space.

"I believe she was giving you some tutoring," Gina said.

"Yes."

"If it's not comfortable for you to go to her house for lessons, maybe she can come here. But don't fall in love with
her. In the first place she has weak lungs—she had to spend
months in a sanatorium. And in the second place Abram will
tear you apart. Although, on the other hand, maybe that's
what he wants. He has his own crazy ways of figuring things
out. Please believe me, I'm telling you all this without any ul-
terior motives. What difference does it make to me? I'm just
talking along because I'm lonely. I'm sad, so sad that I'm
ready to die."

"Oh, no! You're still a young woman."

"Not so young and not so smart. I don't know what people
say about me—certainly nothing good—but I assure you I'm
the exact opposite of Abram. He can fall in love with anyone,
so long as she wears skirts. But I can only love one person. If
I'd fallen into decent hands I'd have been a faithful wife. But
my mother—God rest her soul—wanted to see me settled.
You've probably heard—I'm the daughter of the Bialodrevna
rabbi."

"Yes, I know."

"It's a long story. If I wanted to tell you the thousandth
part of it I'd have to sit with you seven days and seven nights.
But why should I burden you with my tragedy? You're still a
youth. I suffered with my husband, Akiba, eleven long years. I
never loved him—may God not punish me for saying it. I
hated him from the beginning. And I've known Hertz Yano-

var ever since I was a child. His father was the head of the yeshivah in my town. Why am I telling you all this? I don't know—my mind's just wandering. Oh, yes, I want you to meet him. Have you anything to do tonight?"

"No, nothing."

"Maybe you'd like to come with me to visit him. I told him about you and he's eager to meet you. If you like we can both ride over there in a sleigh. Don't refuse; it'll be a pleasant ride and it'll cheer me up. You'll probably laugh at me, but I'd like to have your opinion of him. I'm so confused myself that I don't understand anything any more. Don't hurry. Finish your food. The evening's just beginning over there. He's one of those late birds."

Gina laughed, her eyes filling with tears. She got up from her chair and went out. Asa Heshel could hear her in the adjoining room sobbing and blowing her nose.

3

Hertz Yanovar lived in a flat on the Gnoyna in a large block of houses with enclosed courts. It was dark on the stairs and Gina kept striking matches to light the way. The apartment was on the second floor. Without ringing or knocking she pushed the door open and the two went in. The corridor was dim, illumined only by the pale glow of a naphtha lamp that burned in the kitchen. A small, thickset servant girl with red, peasant cheeks and heavy bare legs was washing dishes. When she saw Gina she came to the doorway and put her finger to her lips.

"Hilda is here?" Gina asked, with a grimace of distaste.

"Sh-sh-sh. Mr. Yanovar told me to let no one in."

"What is he afraid of? The spirits won't run away," Gina said angrily. She took off her coat and hat.

"I hope you're not easily frightened." Gina turned to Asa Heshel. "My professor plays around with spiritualism. You know what that is?"

"Yes. I've read about it. Calling up the spirits of the dead."

"It's all a lot of foolishness, but what can I do? Every genius has a touch of the lunatic. Tell me, Dobbie"—she turned to the girl—"who's here?"

"Finlender, Dembitzer, Messinger, and that one—Hilda. Oh, yes, Mr. Shapiro is here too."

"Abram! Just imagine."

Asa Heshel started. "I think I'd better go. Good night." He glanced toward his overcoat and hat, which he had hung on the rack.

"What's the matter with you? What are you running away for? A fine cavalier!" Gina exclaimed. "I'm ashamed of you."

"I'll only be in the way—I'd better go home."

"Maybe the gentleman's afraid of the dead ones," the servant suggested.

"No, not of the dead ones," Asa Heshel answered.

"Then don't make a fool of yourself," Gina said impatiently. She took him by the arm and drew him toward a door with frosted panes. She opened it and the two entered a large room with peeling wallpaper and a faded ceiling. The lighted floor lamp was covered with a red kerchief; a reddish, shadowy glow flowed from it, like a sickroom light. In the middle, at a small square table, five men and a woman sat. All had the palms of their hands resting on the table edge. They were silent. The first one to look up at the newcomers was Abram, who sat facing the door. His beard was disheveled, his face cinder-red in the glow of the lamp. He nodded at the newcomers half-mockingly and put his fingers to his lips. At his right sat a smallish man, with a tapering chin and a wide, creased forehead. He had the guilty expression of a youngster caught misbehaving. His hair, which began to sprout somewhere halfway back on his skull, was uncut and bunched at the back of his neck. A loose black silk cravat was tied about his throat. Asa Heshel had seen his photograph at Gina's. It was Hertz Yanovar.

At Abram's left sat a woman with flowing black hair, an oval forehead, and a triangular face, which ended in an elongated chin. She wore a silk shawl around her shoulders. A high collar enclosed her throat. She was staring straight ahead of her with stern eyes, obviously angry at the interruption. Her look reminded Asa Heshel of the female Nihilists whose pictures he had once seen. One of the other men was tall and thin, with ash-gray hair combed low around his head and with flabby bags under his eyes. The others had their backs toward the door; Asa Heshel could see that one of them was hunchbacked.

"H'mm, h'mm . . ." Hertz Yanovar began to murmur, like a pious Jew interrupted at his devotions. "H'mm, h'mm. . . ." He gave a mild shake of his head in Gina's direction.

"Back to the table again, I see," Gina said in a loud voice, as though deliberately provoking them. "I thought you were raising up the dead."

Hertz Yanovar shook his head more violently and made some unintelligible sounds.

"Put an end to the comedy," Gina said. "I didn't come here to play at witchcraft."

The medium cast a furious glance at Gina and took her hands off the table. She pushed her chair back and stood up. She was wearing a long dress and low-heeled shoes. "It's no use," she called out. "Let it be enough!"

The rest let their hands drop from the table and began to look about, talk, adjust their collars, like students when the teacher ends his lecture. Abram got up, clapped his hands, and rushed toward Asa Heshel and Gina in the manner of one who had long been anticipating their arrival and could hardly wait to greet them. He threw his arms about Gina and pressed her cheek to his, then grasped Asa Heshel by the shoulders.

"It's telepathy," he shouted, "or else the prophet Elijah guided you here! I've been looking for you for days!"

"Gina, you've spoiled everything," Hertz Yanovar said petulantly. He looked at the medium supplicatingly, as though apologizing, and then came forward to Gina. Asa Heshel noticed that he was wearing velvet trousers, and slippers ornamented with pompons. "I really mean it, Gina darling," he continued, half tenderly, half remonstratingly. "You said you weren't coming."

"So now I'm not supposed to come any more," Gina exclaimed. "Don't be afraid, the spirits won't run away. And if a certain spirit's insulted and decides to stay away for good, it won't bother me at all!" And she darted a contemptuous glance toward the medium.

"I'm going, professor," the medium said shortly. "Good night."

"Gina! Hilda, don't go, I beg you," Yanovar pleaded, turning first to one and then to the other. Hilda was angrily gathering her loose hair up on her head and stabbing hairpins into it. "Why all the argument? This is a serious matter! We are searching for new truths—and you—ai, ai! A calamity! We are sitting here barely fifty minutes. Another ten minutes and the table would have responded. You could at least have waited."

"Wait? For what? Why? Every time I come here you're either carrying on with your nonsense about ghosts or you're raising the table! I'll take that cursed table and break it to pieces, and be done with it once and for all!"

"A tiger! Not a woman, a tiger!" Abram remarked judicially.

"Good night, professor." The medium held out her long fingers with well-manicured nails.

"Good night, good night—please don't go," Yanovar said frantically. "Tell me, Gina," he continued, "who is this young man?"

"I told you about him. Asa Heshel Bannet. He's my new lodger."

"Greetings. A pleasure to meet you. This is Hilda Kalischer. This is Dr. Messinger"—he indicated the tall man with the round-cut hair and the bags under his eyes—"this is Finlender, and this is Dembitzer. I've heard of you. Your grandfather, if I'm not mistaken, is the Tereshpol Minor rabbi. A sage. This business with the table is not foolishness, I assure you. Some of our greatest scientists believe in it. Lombroso, for instance, the idol of all the materialists—"

"Professor, I must go now," the medium said with finality.

"What can I do? If you must go, then you must. But please, I beg of you, telephone me. And please don't take offense. Gina means no harm. It's only that she's nervous."

"You don't need to apologize for me," Gina interrupted. "And leave my nerves alone. If Miss Kalischer is such a loss to you, you can go along with her."

"Hey, Gina, now you're starting to quarrel in earnest!" Abram remarked, waving a warning finger.

"Everything I do is in earnest. I'm not an actress like some people. At least not such a bad actress."

Hilda Kalischer flashed out of the room, overturning a chair and letting out a muffled shriek. Hertz Yanovar wrung his hands and ran after her on his short legs. The glass-paned door banged shut. From the corridor came the sounds of sobbing. The hunchback drew a comb from his breast pocket and began to comb his hair, at the same time looking at Gina wryly. He was the one who had been introduced to Asa Heshel as Finlender. Dembitzer, a broad-built, clumsy-looking man, with a huge, fleshy face full of moles, took from his pocket a packet of cigarette papers and a bag of tobacco and expertly rolled a cigarette.

"Women, eh?" he said good-naturedly, winking at Abram. "What a race of people!" He bent down and picked up the chair that Hilda had overturned in her flight.

The only one who remained sitting at the table as though nothing untoward was happening was Dr. Messinger. His tall, lean figure seemed to have frozen into a fixed position. His long arms hung down. His small eyes, half-hidden behind folds of flesh, looked toward the window, past the curtains. He seemed to be gazing beyond the room, totally unaware of what was happening inside it.

"Messinger, are you asleep?" Abram shouted at him.

And Messinger answered, in a Germanized Yiddish: *"Ja! Nein! Um Gotteswillen,* be good enough to leave me alone!"

4

"Madness! Lunacy!" Abram remarked to himself and the room at large. "What difference does it make to you, Gina, if the children amused themselves?"

"It makes a lot of difference. Intelligent people should devote themselves to something sensible, not playing around with fortune-telling like a bunch of old midwives. It's a shame and a disgrace. And I don't want that woman around here! I'll tell Hertz straight out. It's either her or me. I'm not going to have any brazen females hanging around."

The door opened and Hertz Yanovar came back. His small face was bloodless. The perspiration stood out in beads on his high forehead. He looked at Gina with his sad eyes and his lips turned down, as though he were on the point of tears. "A shame, Gina," he said. "To drive her out! A shame!"

"I warned you that this is what it would come to. It's all your fault. First it was hypnotism, and then automatic writing, and now it's pulling ghosts out of your sleeves. Listen to me, Hertz. I've suffered plenty on your account, but there's a limit to everything. I'm the one that's being put to shame. I'm the one they talk about as though I were a slut. I won't have it, you hear! That woman makes my flesh crawl. Either go off with your fine medium and spend your time with black magic or sit down and attend to your work. I can't stand it any more."

She bent her head, covered her face with her hands, and started to cry. Abram took his silk handkerchief out of his pocket and held it out to her. Messinger got up from his chair and drew himself up to his full height.

"Good night, professor," he said. *"Adieu."*

"Please don't go," Hertz begged. "These things happen. I thought you'd demonstrate for us."

"Not tonight. I'm not in the mood. *Au revoir.*" He went out with long strides.

"I think I'd better go, too," Dembitzer remarked.

"Why are you all running away?" Gina asked. She took Abram's handkerchief and blew her nose. "None of you is to blame. It's all my fault. I'm to blame—for everything."

She ran out of the room, letting the door bang after her.

"I really don't know," Yanovar sighed. "It's nothing but nerves—no more than that. It's true that she gets it from all sides. Nothing but trouble—" He went out after Gina.

"It's nothing but hysteria," Finlender remarked.

"It's not hysteria," Dembitzer said, rolling a cigarette. "Oh no. She's jealous—and not without reason."

"You hear that, Asa Heshel?" Abram remarked. "Trouble and trouble, wherever you go. Come here, I want to talk to you. I think you and I had better leave. The two of them'll make up without us."

"Very well. I'm ready."

They went out into the corridor. Abram put on his long sable-collared coat and tall fur hat. He hooked his umbrella over his arm and lit a cigar. Asa Heshel put his coat on, and they both went out into the street. Abram sniffed the air. "A bit frosty," he said. "Everyone makes a fool of himself in his own way," he continued after they had walked along a few yards. "One chases money, another chases women, and a third makes faces at ghosts. Well, the devil with 'em. Let's change the subject. Tell me, did Hadassah come to visit you?"

"Yes."

"When?"

"Today."

"What did she say? What did you talk about?"

"She's going to keep on giving me lessons. At my place."

"She looks bad, eh?"

"A little pale."

"I tell you that girl's life is a tragedy. The family's running wild. Trying to talk her into a match—with a snotnose, a worm. All he's thinking of is the dowry, nothing else. He's as worthy of being Hadassah's husband as I am of being chief rabbi. The girl can't stand the sight of him. But her grandfather's bailiff—a bootlicker, a fawner, a hypocrite, the dirtiest dog in Warsaw—he's become the judge and jury for the fami-

ly. And they get that other one to help them—Zeinvele
Srotsker—that specimen, with his rupture dragging on the
ground. And all of them—every one of them—against one
weak child. I'm so furious about it, I tell you, I have to hold
myself back from running to that old bastard and breaking his
bones."

Abram lifted his umbrella and began to wave it furiously in
the air.

"But I don't understand," Asa Heshel said. "They can't
drag her to the canopy."

"What? That bunch can do anything. Hadassah was practically born in my hands. I love her as though she were my own
child. That father of hers, that Nyunie, is a yellow-livered
coward, a pinhead, an idiot. He trembles at the thought of his
father. The old man is constantly threatening to disinherit
him. He's been scaring the whole family that way for the last
thirty years. The damn fools have talked themselves into
thinking that he'll leave millions to 'em. I know what he'll
leave them—he'll leave 'em his fingers to his nose. He'd rather
throw his money into the Vistula. So to hell with him. But
what's the good of talking? He's gone to the rabbi, the Bialodrevner! And they've made the preliminary arrangements.
Didn't Hadassah tell you about it?"

"Yes, she told me something."

"I must tell you that you've made a great impression on
her. Something unusual. I really don't understand it myself.
Piff-paff! That you're intelligent and accomplished—that I can
see for myself. But I suppose girls see other things in a young
man. I'll speak frankly—and I want you to answer me truthfully. What do you think about her? Do you like her or
not?"

"I—I like her very much." It was all Asa Heshel could do
to keep his teeth from chattering.

"Come on, don't be ashamed. And don't tremble! Or go
ahead and tremble if you like. It was my opinion, I must tell
you, that they shouldn't be discussing matches now at all.
She's a delicate girl—a hothouse flower. One touch from a
coarse hand and she'll perish. And rather than have her fall
into the clutches of that pipsqueak, Fishel, and that grandfather of his, the usurer, I'd rather see her dead! You'll think
I'm crazy, but I tell you I'd sooner follow her coffin to the
cemetery than dance at that kind of a wedding."

Abram came to a halt and clutched his left side. His big

eyes became soft and tear-rimmed. Asa Heshel felt a moistness in his own eyes.

"And what is there to do?" Abram said reflectively, as though talking to himself.

"Oh, I would do anything—anything. Even if I knew that my whole life—"

"Yes, brother. I know—I know. I see how it is. Well, good night to you. We'll be talking to each other." Abram raised his umbrella and waved toward a passing sleigh. He held out his hand and pressed Asa Heshel's fingers. The sleigh moved off swiftly, its bells jingling. Asa Heshel walked along with a strange lightness, as though he were suddenly buoyant. His elongated shadow ran on before him. The icy wind blew against him, billowing out the skirts of his coat. He had the feeling that he was not walking, but flying with the unimaginable speed of one who was being borne along to meet his destiny.

CHAPTER THREE

1

When Abram climbed into the sleigh after leaving Asa Heshel, he ordered the driver to take him to his apartment on the Zlota. Halfway there he poked the driver between the shoulders with his umbrella and commanded him to turn around and go to the Stalova in Praga, on the other side of the Vistula. The driver halted his horse and scratched his head under the peak of his cap. He did not feel up to making so long a trip on a cold night. But when he turned around and took another look at his passenger, elegant in his fur coat and fur hat, he wheeled the sleigh around, flourished his whip, and shouted: "Vyeh, little one, giddap!"

The horse galloped forward, clumps of snow flying from beneath its hoofs. The sleigh slid along, bounced and careened, its bells jingling. Abram leaned his shoulders against the back of the seat. He knew that Hama would shout to the high heavens when he got home. She had warned him that if he stayed away from the house all night once more, she would take the two girls with her and go to her father's. But Abram could not resist the temptation of going to his one love, his true love, Ida, who had divorced the rich Leon Prager on his account, and had taken a flat in a mean section of the city to be near him, Abram. Over the telephone he had given her all sorts of excuses for his long absence, and only the day before he had sent her a bouquet of flowers and a box of bonbons by messenger. But Ida was not the kind who could be fobbed off with presents.

The sleigh turned in on the Senatorska. The clock in the tower of the city hall showed five minutes before midnight. Soon the sleigh emerged on Platz Zamkovy. On the left stood the palace, where in the old days Poland's kings had lived and where the Russian Governor-General now had his residence. At the gate greatcoated sentinels stood on guard, bayonets fixed to the barrels of their rifles. A single window on an upper floor was brightly illuminated. At the right, down the slope, stretched streets dimly lighted with gas lamps, the midnight sky stabbed here and there by factory chimneys.

The bridge, which by day was thick with tramcars, wagons, trucks, and automobiles, was now half empty. The Vistula lay frozen, the snow that covered it obliterating its banks. In the blue mistiness the landscape took on the appearance of a painted canvas. It was difficult for Abram to believe that only a few months before he had cavorted around the men's bathing pavilion, showing off, doing tricks. In Praga there was a suburban tang in the air. He smelled the smoke of the locomotives that whistled and puffed their way from the two railroad stations to the distant Russian provinces.

It was close to one o'clock when the sleigh pulled up at a four-storied house on a small street. Abram handed the driver a silver ruble and waved the change away. He pulled the doorbell. The janitor appeared, opened the gate with an enormous key, and bowed low over the twenty-kopek piece that Abram put into his hand. He passed by two enclosed courts and entered the last of the buildings near a stable from which came the whinnying of horses. It was on the fourth floor of the building that Ida had her flat and studio.

Abram climbed the stairs, halting at every landing to rest. He could hear cats mewing and there was the acrid odor of lard and carbonic acid. His legs felt heavy and his pulse was pounding. The dinner he had eaten earlier at a restaurant—brandy, fish, and roast goose—lay heavy on his stomach. "Ai, ai, I'm killing myself," he muttered. "If Dr. Mintz could see me now."

He found the doorbell in the darkness. He heard its strident ring. He thought he would have to wait for a long time before Zosia, the servant, opened the door, but he heard her footsteps the moment he rang. When she saw Abram she squealed.

"Pan Abram! As I love my grandmother, it's Pan Abram!"

"Is your mistress sleeping?"

"Not yet. Come in. What a welcome visitor!"

Zosia was in her thirties, but she looked younger. She was the widow of a sergeant who had died ten years before in Siberia. She was more than a servant to Ida Prager; she was her friend and confidante. Whenever Abram brought a gift to Ida he was sure to bring something to Zosia too. She was plump, with a large bosom, a wide face, and a snub nose. Her blond hair was combed back on each side of her head and coiled over her ears. She did the cooking, washed the clothes, scrubbed the floors, sewed, darned, and always seemed to have plenty of time on her hands. In her leisure she devoured crime stories issued in serial pamphlets and pored over a thick book that gave interpretations of dreams, keeping it under her pillow at night. Now she helped Abram off with his coat, took his fur hat, and put away his umbrella. Abram was breathing heavily, but he was not so far gone as to forget to give her a playful poke in her plump side.

"Where's your mistress?" he inquired.

"She's in the studio."

Abram pushed open the studio door. On the walls hung an array of Ida's canvases, among them a portrait of Abram. Tropical plants stood in tubs near the windows. Carved figures and figurines stood on tables and small taborets. Magazines and books were scattered on the bookshelves. Red candles were stuck in an ornamental glass stand. Abram knew that this bohemian disarray was all carefully planned to the minutest detail. Ida was sitting on a low easy chair. She was wearing a black silk house dress, a wide embroidered sash around her waist, and red sandals on her feet. She was puffing at a cigarette with a long mouthpiece. In the old days she had been renowned as a beauty and had won prizes at balls. Now she was close to forty. Her black hair, bobbed short, was beginning to show traces of gray. There were dark rings under her eyes. When she saw Abram she raised the corners of her mouth in a vexed smile.

"So, he's here at last! My great hero!" she said in Polish. "God's miracle!"

"Good evening, Ida darling. How beautiful you look! How lucky that I find you still awake!"

"I've been to bed and I got up again. What kind of cigar is that you're smoking? It stinks!"

"Are you crazy? It's a pure Havana! Half a ruble each!"

"Throw it away. What evil spirit brought you here?"

"Are you beginning to quarrel? You know very well what brings me here."

"You could have telephoned. After all, I'm not your wife."

The door opened and Zosia appeared. She had put on a fresh blouse and around her waist she wore a tulle apron with lace edges. A comb was stuck in her hair. She smiled at Ida and asked: "Shall I make something to eat?"

"I couldn't swallow a mouthful if you killed me," Abram said.

"A glass of tea, maybe?"

"Tea is something else."

"Get him some food," Ida ordered. "Otherwise he'll howl with hunger in the middle of the night."

"No, please—" Abram growled. "The doctor gave me strict orders not to take a single bite after ten o'clock."

"You do a lot of things you're not supposed to."

Zosia shook her head doubtfully and went out. Abram got up from his chair and then sat down again.

"What are you doing these days? How are you feeling?" he asked. "What are you so sarcastic about?"

"What am I doing? I'm going crazy. The studio's freezing, the stove smokes, the canvases get covered with soot—it's too much for me."

"Is Pepi sleeping?"

"She's with her father."

"I don't understand."

"He came to Warsaw. He has two rooms at the Bristol. He insisted that I send the child over to him."

"And she was willing to go?"

"Why not? Tomorrow he's taking her to the circus."

"Well, tell me, did you get the flowers and the candy?"

"Yes. Thanks. I've told you a thousand times not to send me those bonbons. We stuff ourselves so much with sweets that we're ready to burst. What are you so disheveled for? Have you been in a fight or something?"

"A fight? God forbid. Though as a matter of fact there is someone I ought to smash over the skull. Just imagine. Hertz Yanovar invited me to a seance—that Kalischer woman was calling the spirits. All of a sudden Gina comes storming in and practically chases her out. Hertz and I have big plans. We're preparing to issue a journal."

"What kind of journal? Some more madness?"

"A journal for self-education. Here in Poland and in Russia there are thousands—hundreds of thousands—of your Jewish boys who are dying to get some education. We'll teach them trades, too. Watchmaking, electricity, mechanics, God knows what else. All by mail. A tremendous idea. I'll be the director."

"I thought that Hertz was going to Switzerland."

"How can he go? Akiba refuses to divorce her. The old man's trying again to force Hadassah into a marriage."

"What difference does it make to me? I'm going to Paris. This spring. Pepi will stay with her father. Everything's decided."

"Did you see him?" Abram asked suspiciously.

"Yes, I met him and talked the thing over. He'll send me a hundred rubles a month. Pepi'll be sent to a private school."

She took a deep pull on her cigarette and puffed a cloud of smoke into Abram's face. Abram sat still. He took out his handkerchief and wiped his bald spot. As always when he was upset, one side of his forehead flushed an angry red. He plucked at his beard, threw away his cigar, and stared at Ida with his big moist eyes. He was getting too old for all these arguments. No matter how he tried to smooth things over, she kept on nagging. He started to say something, but Zosia entered with the tea things. To banish his melancholy Abram started to tell a joke to Zosia, but for the first time the spirit was lacking.

2

Ida's bedroom held a wide bed and a couch. There were Japanese silk paintings and landscapes on the walls. The lamp, shaped like a Chinese lantern, threw a subdued glow. There was a rag carpet on the floor. Although Ida confined her painting to the studio, the bedroom had a strong odor of turpentine and oils. Abram undressed and lay down on the couch. Following a new hygienic fad, the small pillow was stuffed with some kind of straw instead of feathers. He pulled a plaid blanket over him. Ida was in the kitchen, and Zosia was in the studio, shuffling about on her low-heeled shoes, humming a tune as she cleaned the dishes. Abram lay on the unyielding couch, the hard pillow against his shoulders, gloomy thoughts crowding in his mind. What if Hama made good her threat and went off to her father? Koppel would take the administration of the building away from him and he would be left without a copper. And Ida? She was already as good as lost. And his own daughters? The older one, Bella, was her mother all over again. Not a single *shadchan* came calling on her. They avoided her like a plague. The younger one, Stepha, was a good-looking enough girl—but no luck. Twice she had been on the brink of a match, but they had both vanished into thin air. What for example, does a girl like that think when her father stays away from home all night? Once he had found her reading Artzybashev's *Sanine*. Who could know?—maybe some of those students, those cadets, had already managed to talk things into her. After all, what difference was there between Stepha and some of the girls he had himself managed to persuade?

He rubbed his hand against the back of his head. What was the use of torturing himself with thoughts like these? His heart was thudding, and there was a sour taste deep in his throat. Every sin has its own punishment, he thought.

Ida came in, bringing with her the scent of salves and perfumes. He could tell from the heightened gleam in her eyes that she had taken a glass of something; lately she had adopted the habit of coming to him half-intoxicated. She banged the door shut and called out in a high-pitched and unnatural voice: "Are you sitting up or are you asleep, my pasha?"

"Listen, Ida, if you want, we can finish it now. This minute."

"What's bothering you? Has the grand vizier been insulted?"

"I've never forced myself on anybody and I'm not going to start now."

"What are you talking about? Who's saying anything about forcing?"

"I don't like these tricks—these carryings-on. I'm going."

He heaved himself up. The couch creaked under him.

"Are you out of your mind? Where are you running? Zosia'll think we've gone mad."

"Let her think what she likes. Everything's got to have an end."

"Abram, what's the matter with you? Is it because I'm going to Paris? But I'm not going yet. You know it's bad for me here. I daub and daub and I don't know where in the

world I am. What's the point of going on painting? Who
needs it? Who cares about it? I was never so lonesome in my
life as in this cursed Praga."

"I didn't exile you here. This isn't Siberia, and I'm not the
Czar."

"You are! Here I sit and wait for you every night and you
wander around the devil knows where. You promised me
you'd divorce Hama and we'd get married. On account of
you I left a rich husband."

"That story's got a beard on it by this time."

"What'll happen to me? I'm getting old and sick. I'm so
upset I have to drink to quiet my nerves."

"That's all you need. To be a drunkard."

"Don't shout. She can hear every word. I can't paint; that's
the God's truth. I've got no talent; I can't draw. Today I got
back all the pictures I sent to the gallery. Zosia brought them
back. All they do is laugh at me."

"If they laugh here what'll they do in Paris?"

"Let them laugh. You're the one who started to raise all the
fuss about my being a genius. It was only your way of getting
me away from my husband."

"Shut up!"

"Go on, beat me! What have I got to live for?"

She burst into tears and threw herself on the bed. In the
other room Zosia took a single step and then remained stock-
still. Abram hesitated for a moment, then turned out the light.
Another victory. How many of them in the thirty-five years
since he'd been playing around with women? He knew in advance what would happen. They would make up in the darkness. They would kiss and caress and murmur to each other,
make adventurous plans, and indulge in all sorts of abandoned love-making. However tired and ill he might be,
Abram was still a mighty lover.

He opened his eyes and glanced at the clock. He had
barely two minutes. He got off the bed and put your overcoat
went to look for his things. She was gone. There was a telephone
little tree. But she all took her away, she would be

3

At noon the next day Abram took the tramcar home. It was
cold and cloudy, presaging a storm. The sun, which from time
to time peered out of a break in the overhang, was small and
had an icy whiteness. The snow had drifted into frozen heaps.
Icicles hung from roofs and balconies. Pedestrians slid along
the sidewalks. Horses slipped and stumbled. Abram took a
small mirror from his breast pocket and looked at his reflec-

tion. His face was yellow, his beard uncombed. There were bluish discolorations under his eyes. "I'm getting to look like an old tramp," he thought. He would have liked to go to his barber on the Zlota to get a haircut and massage and have his beard trimmed; but he owed the man three rubles and change. He would have to cover some notes today, meet payments on loans, and find endorsers for new loans he must take. He had let Zosia talk him into having an enormous breakfast—hot rolls, fried sausage, an omelet, and black coffee. Now he had heartburn. He wanted to get home as quickly as possible, go to bed, and sleep off his debauch. But he was aware that there would first have to be angry words with Hama. He knew by heart the complaints that would come rolling off her tongue, the names she would call him, the threats and dire predictions she would make. All he prayed for was that the girls would not be at home. He went up the stairs slowly and rang the bell. Hama stood before him in a black, shabby dress, her face jaundiced, three hairs descending from the mole on her chin. She looked at him with more scorn than anger.

"God help me," she said. "What you look like! Something the cat dragged in."

"Let me pass."

"Who's stopping you! Go in. It makes no difference to me. I've moved out of here already. I only came back to get some things."

Abram passed the living-room and went into his bedroom. The girls were not home. There was silence and disorder in the house, as in the summer months when the family had left for the country. He eased himself out of his coat and tossed his hat onto a chair. He threw himself down heavily on the bed. He closed his eyes. "Whatever happens," he thought, "the devil with it! Let everything go to the dogs!" He dozed off.

He opened his eyes and glanced at the clock. He had slept barely ten minutes. He got off the bed and with unsteady steps went to look for Hama. She had gone. There was a telephone on the desk in the small room that served as a writing-room. He called Nyunie's house. Shifra, the servant, answered and inquired who was calling.

"It's me, Abram Shapiro," he answered. "How are you, my dove? Is Hadassah at home?"

"Oh, Mr. Abram! Yes. I'll call her."

He waited several moments. Through the receiver he could hear a confusion of voices. Then he heard a cough and Dacha's voice asking: "Who is this?"

"Dacha, it's me! Abram!"

"Yes, Abram."

"What's the news? How are you? I wanted to talk to Hadassah."

"Forgive me, Abram, but you've got nothing to say to her. Leave the child alone."

"Are you out of your mind?"

"You've caused enough trouble. I'll not let you ruin my household."

"What the devil is the matter?"

"Good-by!"

The receiver slammed in his ear.

Abram got up from the chair and shook his head in bewilderment. The line in his forehead deepened. His shoulders were bowed. "So that's the way matters stand," he said aloud. "All of them at once." He grabbed the telephone book and slammed it down on the floor. He strode over to the wall mirror and lifted a hairy fist. "Keep your pants on!" he yelled to his reflection. "Idiots! Savages!"

And in the mirror the image with the ragged beard and the uncombed hair waved its own fist and shouted back at him: "Idiots! Savages!"

4

When Hama left home with Bella, she had little hope that her father would receive her with any friendliness. For years Reb Meshulam had been grumbling that she ought to leave her husband, the worthless runaround, and come with her daughters to his house. Nevertheless Hama knew that the moment she took his advice he would begin to nag at her, scold her for not having listened to him earlier, and treat her like a stepchild. So humble did she feel that she did not take a droshky. She had filled one valise with clothing, Bella another, and they had gone on foot like people burned out of house and home. Neighbors looked out of their windows, dolefully shaking their heads. The janitor's wife came out from her cubicle, wringing her red hands, wiping away her tears with the corner of her apron. A one-eyed mongrel ran after them. Hama had re-hearsed beforehand what she would say: "Father, give me only a crust of bread—but don't make me go back."

But things did not turn out the way she had expected. When Naomi went into Meshulam's study with the news that Hama had run away from her husband together with her older daughter, the old man's eyes filled with tears. With un-steady steps he went out to the kitchen, where Hama was waiting with her luggage. He put his arms around her and kissed her, the first time he had done so since her wedding. He kissed Bella, too, and said: "Why do you have to wait in the kitchen? My home is your home."

He spoke in a loud voice, so that everyone in the house should hear him. Manya, who had been sitting at the kitchen table drinking coffee, indifferently watching what was go-ing on, got up and picked up the valises. Naomi went to pre-pare a room for the new arrivals. Rosa Frumetl, who had been standing at the window in the living-room murmuring the morning prayers, read on to the end of a verse, closed the book, kissed it, and went out to the kitchen. Her eyes were soft and mournful. She kissed Hama on both cheeks, nodded her head to Bella, and said: "Welcome, welcome. Since it had to be this way, may it be in a happy hour."

Meshulam had already had his breakfast of black bread and cold chicken and was ready to go to his office. But in honor of his daughter's arrival he stayed home for a while. He sat with the women—Adele had joined them—in the dining-room, sipped a glass of black coffee, and talked away with more warmth than was his custom. He recalled now how Hama had been born on the Sabbath before the Passover; he had been eating a warmed-over meal when the midwife had come to tell him that his wife had given birth to a girl. The in-fant was so weak that they had been afraid she would not live and that her death would darken the joyous Passover holiday. "But thank God," Meshulam concluded, "the child lived."

Rosa Frumetl laughed and blew her nose in her batiste handkerchief. Hama listened to her father and tears fell from her eyes. She was unaccustomed to hearing her name men-tioned in her father's house. Ever since his quarrel with Abram the old man had got into the habit of venting his anger on her. When Bella and Adele left the table, Hama began to recount all of Abram's goings-on; his staying out all night, his running around with servant girls and *shikses,* his taking things from the house and pawning them, his collecting rents from the tenants months in advance and using up the money. He had even borrowed a few rubles from the janitor; the man had come to her to get them back. Rosa Frumetl wrung her fingers and sighed.

The old man's sparse mustache seemed to stand erect. When Hama was through he shouted: "Why did you have to keep quiet about it? I'll tear the dog limb from limb!"

"Father, if you only knew!" Hama broke into loud sobbing.

Meshulam got up and began to pace angrily back and forth in the confined space near his chair. "All right, enough crying," he growled. "The blister's pricked. You'll never have to look at his face again. Quiet, quiet. Give her a drink of water," he said to Rosa Frumetl. "Where's the other one— what's her name?"

"Stepha is home," Hama replied, her voice choked with sobs. "She—she had some things to—to attend to."

"What is there to attend to? Anyway, the first thing is to get the older one married. She's a good girl, a fine girl. She'll have a three-thousand-ruble dowry. You'll stay here—till you get a divorce."

With the word "divorce" a shudder ran over Hama's body. "What's the good of a divorce?" she moaned. "I'm finished. I live only for the children."

"You're not old yet. When you've had a chance to rest up a bit and get some decent clothes you'll be a new woman. I'll give you fifty rubles now; go and get yourself some new dresses."

He went out and came back with two twenty-five-ruble notes. After some hesitation he added another ten-ruble note to them from his purse. "For pocket money," he said.

Hama took the money and wept afresh. This unexpected kindness made her misfortune seem all the greater. Naomi came and led her to the room that had been prepared for her. An extra bed had been moved in for Bella. The linen smelled of starch, bluing, and lavender. Naomi, Manya, and Bella fussed about. Adele opened the door, stood at the doorsill, and gave advice, half in Yiddish and half in Polish. Rosa Frumetl came in to inquire what Hama would like for dinner— beef, or fowl, or a roast, or a stew with a savory gravy. To Hama it seemed for a moment that she was a girl again and that her mother was still alive. She had not slept a wink the previous night. Now she tied a damp towel around her forehead and lay on the bed, occasionally sighing or groaning. Bella went with Naomi to the market. She was used to handling household affairs. At home she was servant, cook, and laundress. Naomi realized that she would be able to make use of her. Manya, a little afraid that she would be superfluous now, grabbed a cloth and began to dust the furniture.

When, after all the talk and fuss, Meshulam put on his coat and overshoes to leave for the office, his limbs felt astonishingly light. He even found himself humming an old tune that he had long forgotten. It was as though his daughter's homecoming had made him younger, reminding him of the time when the house was full of children. Besides, her return represented for him a victory over Abram. Just let him divorce her, and then everything would be all right. True enough, she was no beauty, but when she got hold of herself and he, Meshulam, put up a decent dowry, Zeinvele Srotsker would manage to dig up a husband for her—a widower or a divorced man. No, he was not through yet; with God's help he would live to have something to rejoice over.

It was windy in the street. There was a hint of hail and snow in the air. The hawkers near the gates were shouting out their wares. Sleighs jingled past. Drivers yelled at their horses and snapped their whips. Gzhybovska Street smelled of horse-droppings and cart grease. Passers-by, some of whom Meshulam either did not know or did not recognize, bowed greetings to him. A gentile took off his hat deferentially. "No," he thought, "the world's not upside down yet." A dog ran out of a courtyard, barking at the old man's heels; Meshulam waved it away with his umbrella. The janitor opened the courtyard gate. The unpaved walk was covered with snow; in spite of that, someone had released flocks of fowl from their cages. Pigeons were picking at kernels of oats, tiny sparrows hopped about. Koppel was already waiting in the office, which was on the first floor. He was pacing back and forth in his polished boots, glancing at his watch, puffing at a cigarette, and taking an occasional look at the newspaper on the desk. When Meshulam told him that Hama had left Abram, he made no comment. Meshulam threw him a wondering look. He had expected Koppel to be overjoyed at the news. For the thousandth time he realized that Koppel's ways were unpredictable. Reb Meshulam sat down in the leather-covered chair at the desk, piled high with papers. Koppel went into the adjoining room and in a little while returned with a glass of tea for his employer.

5

Most of that day Abram spent in bed. The clock rang the
hours and half hours. From the courtyard came the cries of
peddlers. A beggar sang a doleful song about the sinking of
the *Titanic*. A parrot screeched. Abram only half heard the
sounds. The gold chain that stretched over his belly heaved
with his breathing. He snored, groaned, and murmured, from
time to time opening his eyes and looking about him with a
sad, wide-awake look, as though he had only been going
through the motions of sleeping. When he finally got off the
bed it was dark. He held his breath and listened intently. Why
was it so quiet? "Hama is gone," he said half aloud. "Bella,
too. And where is Stepha? I'm all alone, alone with the four
walls."

He was hungry, but he did not have enough money to go to
a restaurant. His limbs heavy, he dragged himself into the
study. He did not turn on the lamp. Through the curtains
came a pale shaft of light, throwing a shadowy pattern that
lingered on the wall opposite the window.

He sat down at the writing-desk and automatically lifted
the receiver of the telephone. When he heard the operator's
voice he gave Ida Prager's number. Zosia answered the telephone.

"Zosia, my love, this is me—Abram," he said into the
mouthpiece. "Is your mistress home?"

"No."

"Where is she?"

"I don't know."

"What are you doing there all alone?"

"What should I be doing? I'm lonely—ready to die."

"Why so melancholy all of a sudden?"

"Last night I dreamed of three crows. Two of them picked
out my eyes and the other one kept on cawing: 'Zosia, dead
Zosia, dead, dead'—"

"Nonsense. You're a healthy, bouncing wench. You'll live
to be ninety."

"No, Pan Abram, my dead husband is calling me. I
dreamed about you too."

"Me? What about me?"

"You want to know, eh? Well, I'm not a gypsy fortune-
teller, but something not so good has happened to you."

"Correct."

"You see. I know everything. My mistress went to the circus with Pepi and the child's father. But don't get jealous."

"Who cares? If she leaves me, I'll take you."

"Me? You're making fun of me. And me an orphan."

"I'm not joking, Zosia."

"What could I do for you? Be your servant?"

"You're a woman, not a servant."

"You shouldn't talk like that. Never, never would I betray my mistress. She's like a sister."

"Well, so what? Sometimes one sister fools another."

"Oh, no, Pan Abram. Not my mistress. You ought to come here more often. When you come around it's like a holiday."

"Zosia, I'm hungry as a wolf."

"Then come around. I'll satisfy the wolf."

"I'll come, Zosia, maybe tonight. Look, Zosia, maybe you can lend me a few rubles."

"How much do you want?"

"Ten rubles."

"Even fifty if you want it."

"That's more than I'd lend to myself. But it's good to hear you offer it. Don't tell your mistress."

"Don't worry. You can be sure I know how to keep my tongue between my teeth."

Abram put down the telephone and breathed a sigh of relief. So that was the way things stood. She was with her husband. He was losing everything and everybody.

He went back to the bedroom, put on a fresh shirt, his fur coat, and his Russian fur hat. He did not bother to turn on the light; he could see in the dark, like an animal. He left the house, locking the door behind him. "Ah, Abram," he murmured to himself, "you're as good as six feet under."

When he got down to the courtyard he saw Koppel standing near the street lamp in his short overcoat with the velvet collar, his derby hat pushed to the back of his head, a cane hanging on his arm. He was engaged in conversation with the janitor. Abram froze in fright. When Koppel saw him he made a movement as though to leave. The janitor lifted his hand to his hat.

"What does he want, Jan?" Abram asked in a stifled voice.

The janitor turned to Koppel. "Here's Pan Shapiro now," he said.

"What do you want with the janitor?" Abram said to Koppel, half shouting. In Polish he said to the janitor: "You can go."

The man hesitated, then went back to his cubicle.

After a short silence Koppel said quietly: "I've come on your father-in-law's orders."

"It's always someone else's orders. What do you want?"

"Your houses are being taken over."

"Who's to take them over? You?"

"You're through as manager. You'll turn the books over to me."

"And if I refuse, what'll you do? Throw salt on my tail?"

"I won't do anything."

"Then go to hell."

"Whatever you say. It's not my affair. I only want to remind you that the notes are with us."

"What notes? What are you babbling about?"

"You know what notes. We paid them, but we didn't tear them up."

"You're talking Turkish! Get out before I take this stick and break your skull."

"You'll not be breaking any skulls. The endorsements are forged."

"Get out," Abram shouted in a voice that was hardly his own. "On your way." He raised his stick threateningly. Koppel walked off.

Abram remained motionless where he stood. His heart was beating fast and seemed to be fluttering about in his chest, as though it were suspended by some fragile thread. He left the courtyard and began to pace along the Zlota toward the Marshalkovska. He took deep breaths of the frost night air and exhaled with hoarse sighs. Suddenly he heard a familiar voice. He turned and saw his daughter Stepha on the opposite side of the street. She was not alone; a young student was with her. She had apparently not seen her father. She was wearing a green, caracul-bordered jacket with a broad-brimmed hat. A fur piece hung from her shoulders. Her hands were tucked into a muff. Calf-high Russian boots enclosed her legs. Her round face was flushed. The student was no taller than she. In the dim light Abram could see a thin mustache sprouting on his upper lip. Was it possible that she was taking him to the apartment? Who could he be? This was something new.

He wanted to call out to her, but somehow he was dumb. He turned to follow them. Stepha was talking in a loud voice. He could hear her saying: "Silly! Insane!"

The student remained at the gate while Stepha went up alone. Abram stood in the shadow of a balcony to watch. The youth began to stroll back and forth, his hands clasped behind him, with the measured walk of a man patiently waiting for a woman who he is determined will not escape him. Abram could see him clearly. Small features, a thin nose, a long chin. A sly fox, Abram reflected. When a scoundrel like that gets after a girl, he gets what he's after. With quick decision Abram crossed the street, went into the house, and climbed the stairs. "What am I doing this for?" he thought. "I must be out of my mind."

He took the door key from his trousers pocket and tried to insert it in the lock, but at that precise moment the door opened and Stepha stepped out. She bumped full into him. Her hatpin stabbed his ear. He could smell pomade and narcissus perfume.

"Papa, it's you!" she exclaimed in surprise.

"Yes, it's me. Where are you running to? I haven't seen you for about a year."

"Oh, Papa, I'm in a hurry. I'm going to the theater."

"Who's taking you?"

"What's the difference? A gentleman."

"When will you get home?"

"About twelve—or one—I'm not sure."

"Wait a minute. I've got to tell you something. Your mother's left me and gone to your grandfather's."

"I know. Oh, Papa, you're such a scoundrel. I've just got to kiss you." She threw her arms around him and kissed him on the cheek and on the nose.

"What theater are you going to?"

"To the Letni Theater. What are you so curious for? Don't worry, I won't get myself seduced."

"I'm not so sure."

"Don't start preaching morals to me, Papa. It doesn't become you."

"Have you got any money with you? I'm down to my last grosz."

"All I have is twenty kopeks." She went down the stairs quickly and energetically. Abram scratched the back of his neck, undecided whether to go into the house or return to the street. "So that's the way it is. Koppel has the notes. And I, idiot that I am, thought I was fooling them. They can throw me in jail—even tonight."

He lit a cigar, then peered by the match flame at the brass plate on the door with his name engraved on it: "Abram Shapiro." He reflected a moment and then snapped his fingers. "I'll go in and take a drink. I'm done for anyway." He went inside. In a glass-paned cupboard there were a bottle of brandy and some vishniak. In the darkness he went into the kitchen and took from the cupboard some bread, a piece of cheese, and the remains of a herring. "To hell with Mintz and all doctors," he thought. "Damn them with their lousy diets and prescriptions. To hell with all of them—bailiffs, wives, daughters—whores, all of them."

He looked toward the window. He could see the full moon high through the upper pane. At the top of his voice he shouted: "To hell with you! Let the pious hypocrites recite the blessing over the new moon. Not me! I'm through! They can all politely crawl on their hands and knees and stick their noses here." And he pointed violently with his index finger toward his rump.

6

Half an hour later Abram was down in the street again. This time he directed his steps to Gnoyna Street, toward Hertz Yanovar's place. He passed by the Vielka and the Bagno and came out on the Gzhybov. On the Bagno some of the secondhand stores were still open—dealers in old furniture, valises, whips. Draymen were loading furniture from platforms onto their trucks. The draft horses were nuzzling into the feed bags, scattering oat kernels on the snow. On the Gzhybov Abram went past Meshulam Moskat's house. He threw a single glance at the brilliantly lighted windows on the upper floor and walked quickly by. Strange to think that Hama, the mother of his children, was now up there, and that he could no longer even approach her. He shrugged his shoulders. Ah, the miserable creature. To rebel all of a sudden in her old age.

At Hertz Yanovar's he ran into the familiar group: Hilda Kalischer, Dembitzer, and Finlender. Dr. Messinger had been there, but had gone. Apparently there had been no seance; the table was standing against the wall with Dembitzer's overcoat draped on it. Yanovar, in dressing-gown and slippers, ran forward both hands outstretched.

"Welcome, Abram! It's good you came. I was going to call you."

"Why didn't you? I tell you, brother, I'm in trouble."

"What's happened?"

"What hasn't happened? The whole world's come crashing down on me. My wife, my father-in-law, Koppel, Dacha. They're out to tear me apart. But a fig for the lot of 'em. I spit on 'em. What are you sitting around for like drenched chickens? How are the ghosts?"

"Please, Abram, no sarcasm."

"Believe me, no sarcasm, not today. I've got a question I'd like to ask the table myself—what's going to be the end of me?"

"Come around tomorrow and we'll ask it," Hilda Kalischer put in. She was seated on a sofa, a silk shawl over her shoulders. She looked cross. A thin cigarette dangled from the corner of her lips.

"Your affairs are your affairs. What'll happen about the journal?" Dembitzer asked. "A thing like that can't be dragged out. It's got to be one way or the other."

"I'll talk with the printer today. The important question is the board of editors."

"We have to start small," Yanovar said. "Let's get out a sample issue of thirty-two pages. Then we can see how the provinces will respond. What do you think, Finlender?"

The hunchbacked Finlender had been standing at the bookcase, fingering a volume. Now he turned around.

"You know my opinion," he said sharply, emphasizing each word. "We have to approach the undertaking systematically. You've got to have a definite program. And first of all, you'll have to have a capital of at least thirty thousand rubles."

"That's a lot of money," Abram said, and winked toward Dembitzer. Finlender, a bachelor, bookkeeper in a tea firm and compiler of a dictionary, had a reputation for making unreal and impossible plans. Everyone laughed at the contrast between his fabulous projects and his pedantic manner of speech.

"I wouldn't begin the project with a ruble less," Finlender continued.

"Nonsense! Who needs thirty thousand! Three hundred rubles will do," Hertz Yanovar interrupted. "We'll get credit. I know someone who'll provide the paper."

"The question is where do we get the three hundred."

"Three hundred rubles I can put up myself, for all I'm a pauper," Abram remarked.

"In that case there's nothing to prevent us from going ahead," Yanovar said.

"And what'll there be for me to do on the project?" Hilda Kalischer inquired. It was evident that all the talk about the journal bored her. Impatiently she poked at a loosened hairpin in the Greek knot at her nape.

"You'll be the treasurer, Hilda. With your intuition you'll know whom to trust and whom not to."

"Joke as much as you please, but I don't think anything of the whole plan. Professor Yanovar shouldn't give up his time to such trifles. Especially since he expects to go abroad."

"Seriously, Hilda," Hertz said, "I don't understand why you're opposed to it. An ignorant and coarsened generation is growing up. This is an opportunity to educate them. That young man who lives at Gina's, for instance. He's got to make a start when others of his age are finishing."

"Golden words! Words of wisdom!" Abram interjected. "He's got more in his little finger than all the university students have in their heads put together. And he's got to grabble around in textbooks for children! And before you know it the damn conscription'll come around and he'll either have to run away or put on a uniform for the Czar. They're all disappearing—all our Jewish youth."

Dobbie, the servant, came to the door. "The food's on the table," she announced.

They all went into the dining-room.

On the table, which was covered with a stained tablecloth, stood bowls of borsch flanked by tin soup-spoons. Instead of chairs there were benches. Abram poured some brandy into a glass from a flask on the sideboard, his large, hairy hands trembling. Dembitzer dipped a small roll into a glass of wine.

"Here's good fortune to the new journal!" he said.

"Good fortune without end. May this be the beginning of a Jewish university—just to spite Hilda."

"For all I care—I'm leaving the country anyway."

Hertz Yanovar had taken a mouthful of bread and sardines; the food stuck in his throat. "What? When? What are you saying?"

"I've had a proposal to go to London. They guarantee all expenses. I didn't want to tell you, but as long as you're all going to become printers or editors or whatever it is, there'll be nothing for me anyway."

"I don't understand a word of what you're saying. Who's doing the guaranteeing? What'll you do in London?"

"I'll show you the letter. Let's not talk about it any more." Hilda nervously spooned up some borsch from her plate and let it drip back.

"I have an idea," Abram exclaimed. He pounded his fist on the table. "I'll go abroad too. I can see everything clearly now. Finlender, you're right. We've got to start big. Thirty thousand's not enough. I'll raise fifty thousand or my name isn't Abram Shapiro. Maybe a hundred thousand!"

"What's happened to you all of a sudden?"

"Thank God, I've never begged for a grosz in my life. But I'm sure—I'm convinced—that I could raise money abroad. I'll go to Germany, to France, Switzerland, England. Let the fancy Jews there be assimilationists, anti-Semites, whatever there is in the book, but education is something they have regard for. Jacob Schiff alone could hand over fifty thousand rubles."

"Jacob Schiff is in America."

"America doesn't scare me either. We'll put out a big magazine. We'll engage the best pedagogues. We'll send out instructors to teach crafts. We'll create a fund to send promising youths to study in universities in other countries."

"You know, maybe it's not so fantastic," Hertz Yanovar said musingly.

"It's all clear. Clear as day. I'll leave right away. The thing can't be postponed for a single minute," Abram thundered. "The moment she mentioned London it was like a flash of lightning. I'll tell you a secret. My wife has left me. She's left everything and gone to her father. I'm a grass-widower. Thank God, my daughers are grown up. One way or another the old man will see that they're disposed of. I want to do something big, something important—not for me, for the people. As true as I'm talking to you, I was thinking about going to Palestine and starting a colony—Nachlat Abram, that would be the name. But the climate's bad for me. At least, not now. My heart—it's overstrained. All right—if I can't do something in the Jewish homeland, then let me at least do something in the Exile. We have thousands, tens of thousands, of prodigies in our Polish Jewish villages. Thousands of Mendelssohns, Bergsons, Ashkenazis are lost in our provinces, I tell you. There's nothing the anti-Semites are afraid of so much as of our education. That's why they keep us out of their universities."

"As I live, the man's eloquent," Dembitzer said with a laugh.

"He'll raise money, too," Finlender commented. "If only he doesn't cool off just as quick."

CHAPTER FOUR

1

At about ten o'clock at night there was a sharp ring at Gina's door. Gina left the group in the living-room and went to answer it. On the dim outside landing, a few steps away from the threshold, she saw a slight, round-shouldered man in a long gaberdine and a wide-brimmed low hat. A mendicant, Gina thought. She started to take a coin from her purse. Suddenly she trembled and stifled a shriek. It was Akiba, her husband. "He's dead," flashed across her mind; "he died and he's come to strangle me." She stepped out into the hallway and closed the door behind her. She clasped her hands.

"Akiba—it's you!"

"Yes."

"What are you doing here? When did you come? What is it you want?"

"I'm ready to agree to the divorce."

"Now? In the middle of the night? Are you out of your mind?"

"Then it can wait till tomorrow."

"Where are you lodging? Why didn't you write to me?"

Akiba made no answer. Gina opened the door a trifle. She peered into the inside hall to make sure no one was there, and said: "Well, come in."

Akiba followed her with shuffling steps. He seemed to bring with him the odor of ritual baths, prayerhouse candles, sweat, and mold, the provincial aroma that Gina had long forgotten. She opened the door to Asa Heshel's room and they both went in. She turned on the light and saw him clearly. He seemed to have shrunk. His beard was uncared for, wisps of lint and dust clinging to sparse hairs. His sidelocks were lank and bedraggled. His coat was split at the seams, the padding showing. A scarf was tied around his throat. His arms hung limply down, like those of a straw man. His eyes shifted from side to side under the thick brows. Gina shuddered.

"What's been happening to you? Have you been sick or something?"

"I want to bring the thing to an end," Akiba muttered. "It's got to be finished. One way or another."

"The rabbi—your father—does he know?"

"My grandmother is the one who objects. I don't care. I'm not taking the sin on my shoulders."

"Well, anyway, sit down. I'll bring you a glass of tea."

"No. Never mind."

"What are you afraid of? That the tea won't be kosher? At least you could have written me a card—you could have let me know. You'll excuse me, but you still act like a fool."

She went out and closed the door. There was a flush on her cheeks, and tears stood in her eyes. She thought of calling Hertz Yanovar on the telephone, but she was afraid someone might come out of the living-room and overhear her. She went into the kitchen and came out with a pitcher of water, a basin, and a towel. Akiba had taken off his hat and was wearing a crumpled skullcap. Below his open gaberdine she could see the ritual garment with the knotted fringes.

"You can wash," she said. "Maybe you'd like me to bring you something to eat. Downstairs there's a wurst store, certified kosher."

Akiba waved the suggestion away.

"At least you can have some bread, and maybe an apple."

"I'm not hungry. Sit down. I want to ask you something."

"What?"

"I want the truth. Have you been living in sin with him?"

Gina felt a wave of heat engulf her. She went toward the door and then turned to face him. "You're starting again," she said. "Excuse me, Akiba, but you make yourself ridiculous."

"According to the Talmud, a woman who commits adultery is unclean to her husband as well as to her seducer."

"Don't quote the Talmud to me. If you want to get a divorce, then get it, but spare me your accusations."

"It isn't a question of accusation. What good would a divorce do if the abominations go on? The Talmud compares it to a man performing his ablutions while he holds on to the carcass of a reptile."

"You won't have to serve my term in Gehenna. And even if I'm doomed to be pricked with daggers, I've had plenty of experience in suffering. I don't have to tell you the things I've gone through. Our marriage was no marriage from the beginning. Let it be over and done with."

Akiba was silent for a while. Then he said: "It looks as though you're doing well for yourself here in Warsaw."

"May my enemies do no better! It's a miracle I manage to keep alive. And I have trouble with gallstones. When I get an attack I could tear at the walls with my fingernails. I should go for a cure to the warm baths, but I haven't a grosz. God knows how long I can carry on."

"If you hadn't decided to ruin your life you'd have everything—comfort in this world and paradise in the next."

"Well, what's the use? Everything is destined beforehand. You can stay here tonight. There's someone living in this room—a young man from the provinces—but I'll get him a bed somewhere else. I have to go; I have guests."

"I didn't notice a mezuzah on the door."

"There's one on the outside door."

"There should be one on every door. I'll find a place to sleep somewhere else."

"Where will you find one at this time of night?"

"On the Franciskaner."

"Do what I say and stay here. If you want, I'll nail a mezuzah on the doorpost. As long as you're here already, you may as well stay, and tomorrow, if we live, we'll settle things once and for all. Who knows, maybe they'll begin to talk it into you again and the whole thing'll have to start over."

"A mezuzah's got to be examined before it's put up."

"All right, then you'll examine it."

"It takes a qualified scribe. Sometimes there may be an imperfection, a letter missing."

"You'll drive me crazy. Dear God! I'm not accustomed to this fanaticism any more. You wait here. The sin'll be on my shoulders."

She went into the hall. There was the sound of a key being turned in the outside door. Asa Heshel entered. Gina threw a frightened glance at him and blocked his path.

"Please excuse me," she said. "Someone's in your room."

"Did she come back?" Asa Heshel exclaimed.

"Who? Oh, you mean the pharmacy student. No. It's this way. You'll have to sleep somewhere else tonight. I'll tell you what—take the tramcar over to Hertz Yanovar's. I'll telephone him. Something's happened here, something unexpected. My husband arrived. As you know, I've been waiting for a divorce, and now, all of a sudden—he must have gone out of his head. There was no place to put him. One moment—"

She went quickly to the telephone, hastily banged the hook up and down, then gave the number. "Hertz? I'm glad I got you. When I tell you what happened you'll faint. Imagine, Akiba's here! He agrees to a divorce. Tomorrow . . . What? . . . Of course; unexpected. Charged in, like a bull in a china shop. I thought I'd die. . . . What ? . . . In Asa Heshel's room. I was afraid to let him out of my sight. Today he got the idea and tomorrow he might— . . . What? . . . I don't suppose he's got a grosz. We'll have to pay the rabbi and the scribe and the lot of 'em. . . . What? Then you'll have to go and borrow some. . . . What? No, I can't borrow from anybody. The pawnbroker doesn't open until late in the day and I've got nothing left to take there anyway. How much? I don't know; at least twenty-five . . . What do you say? . . . Hertz, I'm pleading with you, don't make things worse. You've got to get it. Maybe Abram—Oh God, if only I'd never been born!"

She flung the receiver down, leaving it dangling on the cord; then she reached for it and hung it on the hook. She turned and went back to Asa Heshel. "Tell me, I beg of you," she half sobbed. "Why should unfortunates like me have to drag out a tortured existence?"

"I can lend you twenty-five rubles," Asa Heshel said. He put his hand in his pocket and took out the banknote that Rosa Frumetl had given him some days before.

"Dear God. Where did you get such a fortune? An angel must have sent you." She blew her nose violently. "You're a noble youth. You'll get the money back soon, before the week's over. Ride over to Hertz's. Dobbie'll prepare a bed for you. What is it I wanted to tell you? Yes. Someone called you twice. Hadassah, I think."

"What did she say?" Asa Heshel's face flushed a deep red.

"She did say something, but I don't remember exactly. That you should call her, or go over to see her, or—forgive me; I can't seem to think. But don't worry; she'll call again, I'm sure. And thank you, and God bless you."

2

On the Gnoyna, not far from the house where Hertz Yanovar lived, Asa Heshel caught sight of Abram. He was standing in his fur coat and tall fur hat and was poking with the point of his umbrella into the trodden snow on the sidewalk. When he saw Asa Heshel he threw him a relieved glance and shouted: "At last you're here. I've been waiting for you."

"For me?"

"I know about everything—about Akiba and the twenty-five rubles. Gina told me everything; I called her on the telephone. She said you were coming to Hertz's for the night. So that's what you are. A philanthropist. Don't go up there. The place is a madhouse. That Hilda Kalischer's just started to carry on. Plates are flying through the air like birds. It's a great life, I tell you."

"I don't understand," Asa Heshel said in bewilderment.

"It's easy enough. She's jealous. Like two cats tied up in a sack, that's the way it is. That I got out of there without a cracked skull is God's miracle. I tell you she's got her claws into him, that Kalischer woman. Either she's in love with him or she needs a professor for that black magic. Who knows? It's probably a mixture of both. You should hear the things she said. And that pinhead—weeping like a beaver. It was something, I tell you. You'll stay at my place tonight. You can sleep in my wife's bed. Don't get excited. She's left me. She's a virgin again and I'm a bachelor. I'm going abroad to raise money for a journal we're starting. I think I told you about it. It's a grandiose project. For youths like you—so that they won't have to rattle around without hope in the big cities. We'll prepare them for the universities. The brainy ones we'll arrange to send abroad. It's even likely that I'll be able to do something for you. And very quickly, too. And now tell me how you're getting along. Have you seen Hadassah? They've given me orders to keep away from there; not even to telephone."

"Me too."

"Who? When did it happen?"

"I telephoned her, and her mother told me not to dare call up again."

"So you see, we're both in the same boat. Look, it's late. I've had a few drinks, my tongue is loose—so I'll spill it out straight. The way it looks to me, you're in love with each other."

Asa Heshel was silent.

"Silence is confession. I'm an old-time woman-chaser myself. All this stuff is an open book to me. I can spot it before the victims themselves know what's happening. But what's the good of it if they're going to tie her to that snotnose?"

"She telephoned tonight. Twice. I wasn't in the house."

"She did? You see, I know what I'm talking about. She doesn't want him, that Fishel, with the whole business of the *mikvah*, and wearing a matron's wig, and his grandfather, and his lousy oil business, and the whole stinking mess. The damn fools. First they send their daughters to decent, modern schools and then they expect them to forget everything they've learned and suddenly become old-fashioned, orthodox, meek Jewish housewives. From the twentieth century straight back to the Middle Ages. Tell me about yourself. Is your health all right?"

"I don't know. Sometimes I think I'm not so well."

"What bothers you?"

"My head hurts. And my heart. I seem to be always tired."

"At your age you don't have to worry about your heart. You're such an unbeliever that you don't even believe in your own energy. I don't have to flatter you, but I'm telling you that there's no reason you can't get to be a doctor, a professor, a philosopher, anything you want. You look like one of these rabbi-worshippers from the provinces, but just the same there's something about you that makes a hit with a woman. I tell you that if I were in your shoes I'd turn the world upside down."

"I'm grateful for your encouragement. If I hadn't run into you here, I'd be finished."

"You're talking things into yourself. Your destiny wouldn't change. I believe in destiny. What does Hadassah see in you? It's an astonishing combination."

"I don't think anything'll ever come of it."

"Why not? Throw away the gaberdine and you'll be a regular European. Hadassah has an intuition. Don't worry. You'll be falling into each other's arms and you'll be tearing each other apart. But that's the way love is. If I were in your place I'd be running off with her—anywhere."

By this time they had reached Abram's house. The janitor opened the courtyard gate. There was a strong smell of liquor about him. Abram inquired if Stepha had come home, but the janitor could not remember whether or not he had let her in. The stairways were dark. Abram struck a match. He opened the door and let Asa Heshel enter ahead of him. There was a shrill ringing; it was the telephone in the study. Abram hurried through the dark corridor. By the time he picked up the receiver his head was spinning and he felt on the verge of a faint. He could hardly catch his breath.

"Hello, hello. Who is it?" he panted into the mouthpiece. "This is Abram Shapiro."

But there was nothing but silence at the other end of the wire. Whoever had been calling had apparently hung up.

3

While Abram Shapiro was fixing the beds, Asa Heshel went into the study. Near the writing table stood a glassed-in bookcase. In the lower section was a set of volumes of the Talmud bound in leather, the backbone stamped in gold—a wedding gift from Meshulam Moskat. The upper shelves were filled with works of commentaries, a Pentateuch, volumes of Maimonides, a Code of the Law, a Zohar, and collections of sermons. To Asa Heshel it seemed like years since he had held one of these volumes in his hand.

He took down a copy of the First Tractate of the Talmud, put it on the table, and opened it. The opening initial was lavishly bordered, decorated with scrolls and fancy designs. He began to chant the words to himself.

"Look at that," Abram's voice interrupted. "Reading the Talmud! The forest calls to the bear."

"It's so long since I've looked into a Jewish book."

"As true as I'm standing here, I was once a student myself. When I was married to Hama I remember I recited a whole section by heart. The old man beamed all over."

"Then he's learned in these matters too?"

"He knows—but not too much. He's half Chassid, half anti-Chassid. The scholar in the family is Moshe Gabriel, my brother-in-law, Leah's husband. And Leah, I must tell you, makes his life a torture. If he happens to come home late from the prayerhouse, she won't let him through the door. And the oldest daughter, Masha, is her mother all over again."

"It's a large family?"

"An army. All kinds, like in Noah's ark. But what's the good of numbers. We Jews, I'm telling you, are building on sand. We live in the air. They don't give us a chance."

"Do you really believe in Palestine?"

"Why? Don't you believe in it?"

"What'll we do if the Turks refuse to hand it over? You can't force them."

"They'll have to turn it over. There's such a thing as the

logic of history. Let's go to bed. It's half past one already. I can't imagine who telephoned so late."

In the bedroom Abram began to take his things off. Asa Heshel stooped for a long time over his shoelaces, ashamed to undress in front of the older man. It was only when Abram had left the room for a few minutes that he found the courage to undress hastily and climb into Hama's bed. The beds stood at right angles to each other, in the old-fashioned manner. Abram sighed and tossed around so that the bedsprings groaned.

"A mad idea of that Akiba's—to fall in at Gina's practically in the middle of the night," he said. "Did you see him, the dolt?"

"No."

"I know him from back in Bialodrevna, when he was living with his father-in-law, the rabbi. Everything we Jews do we do lopsided. We match a flea with an elephant. And what comes out are cripples, *schlemiels*, lunatics. Ah, the Exile, the Exile! It's demoralized us."

In less than five minutes Abram was snoring. Asa Heshel squirmed in bed, pushed away the pillows, pulled them back again, covered and uncovered himself with the blanket and was unable to fall asleep. It seemed to him that the clock in the other room ticked away at a furious pace. Abram was right. The only thing to do was to leave Poland, to go abroad. She too would have to leave—if she wanted to avoid clipping her head, putting on the matron's wig, immersing herself in the ritual bath.

He turned to the wall and dozed off. Suddenly he started up. He heard a key turning in the lock of the outside door. "It's Abram's daughter," he thought; he had heard Abram asking the janitor about her when they came in. He listened, all his senses alert. He could hear her firm steps advancing along the corridor. She yawned and then murmured something to herself in Polish. Through the partly opened door he could see a light go on in another room, then go out again. The door of the bedroom opened wide and he saw her image in the doorway. She had taken off her dress and was standing in a bodice and petticoat. She called: "Papa, are you asleep?"

Abram stirred. "What? Who is it?"

"Papa, I waked you. I'm sorry."

"What do you want? What time is it?"

"It's not so late. Papa, what'll I do? I have no money."

"Do you have to bother me now? Can't you wait till morning?"

"I have to leave early."

"What for? I haven't a grosz."

"I owe the dressmaker. My shoes are torn."

"Quiet! I'm not alone. There's a young man sleeping in the other bed. What's his name—the one who lives at Gina's."

"So what? I have to have ten rubles."

"I haven't got ten kopeks."

"Unless you want me to go to grandfather's."

"Nothing makes any difference to me any more. I'm leaving the country. I'm bankrupt in more ways than one."

"Papa, you're drunk."

"Who's that student you're dragging around with?"

"How do you know he's a student?"

"I saw him."

"You manage to see everything. Well, he's a wonderful fellow. He's finishing medicine. A very interesting talker."

"They all talk fine, but when it comes to the real thing, they run like hares."

As Stepha started to answer, the telephone rang. Abram heaved himself out of bed and ran barefooted to the other room, brushing past Stepha. Asa Heshel could hear him shouting into the mouthpiece, but could not make out what he was saying. In about fifteen minutes Abram returned.

He went over to Asa Heshel's bed. "Young man, are you asleep?" he asked.

"No."

"Hadassah didn't come home tonight. Nyunie, the idiot, slapped her. The damn fool."

4

When Asa Heshel opened his eyes the sun was shining in through the window curtains. Abram was up, wearing a colored robe, half open and revealing a hairy chest.

"Get up, brother," he shouted. "It's the day of judgment. The fish in the water tremble."

"How late is it?"

"What difference? Dacha telephoned again; Hadassah has

disappeared. She's probably spent the night with her friend, Klonya—she lives in Praga. They have no telephone there. What a girl!"

Asa Heshel knew that he should get up, but having neither slippers nor robe, he was ashamed to go into the kitchen. He wondered whether Stepha was still in the house, but he was too embarrassed to ask. When Abram left the room, he dressed and looked at himself in the mirror on the commode. A stubble of beard had sprouted. In spite of all his troubles he seemed to have put on some weight since his arrival in Warsaw. There was a glint in his blond hair. He raised his arms, flexed them, and smiled. He had developed muscles. The night's sleep, broken though it was, had refreshed him.

"Well, what are you gaping at? Go into the kitchen and wash up," came Abram's voice at the door. He went into the kitchen. Stepha was there, in a petticoat and a short-sleeved white blouse, her bare feet stuck into bedroom slippers. She was washing some stockings in a pan, rubbing so energetically that bubbles arose. She looked curiously at Asa Heshel, measured him from top to toe, and said: "So it's you."

"A thousand pardons."

"Go ahead and wash. I won't look. My name is Stepha. I saw you at my grandfather's, but you looked different. Here's the soap."

"Thank you very much."

"My father's been talking about you day and night. Don't let him lead you around by the nose. Whatever he tells you, you do the opposite."

Asa Heshel washed hurriedly and went out of the kitchen. In the hallway Abram stopped him. "We'll have a quick bite," he said, "and then we'll go to look for Hadassah. We'll ride out to Klonya's. Though Dacha'll get there before us, I suppose."

He led Asa Heshel into the dining-room. On the table there was half a loaf of bread, some cheese, some herring. They ate quickly, Abram chewing fast with his strong and powerful teeth. Stepha kept coming in and going out. She looked at Asa Heshel curiously, as though she would have said something to him if her father had not been there. Then she disappeared into the kitchen, where they could hear her singing a Polish song in a high, strong voice. When the meal was finished, Abram went into his study to telephone. He called Ida, Dacha, a lawyer he knew, Hertz Yanovar, and Gina. Akiba had had a bad attack during the night and they had had to call a doctor. They were not sure yet whether it was acute indigestion or a fit of some kind. The divorce had had to be put off. Hertz Yanovar told Abram that Hilda Kalischer had left Warsaw early in the morning to go to visit her mother in Otwotsk. "I just don't know what to do," he said into the telephone. "There's such excitement that I can't think." Dacha was not in the house. Shifra, the maid, had answered the phone. She told him that Dacha had already left for Praga; the telephone had rung earlier, but when Shifra had picked up the receiver, whoever it was at the other end had hung up; it must have been Hadassah. "Such nonsense," Shifra complained. "She'll catch her death of cold and get inflammation of the lungs." Ida had gone down to do some marketing. Zosia told him that her mistress had come home early the previous evening, about ten o'clock, and she had been very nervous. She already knew that Hama had left Abram and was waiting impatiently for him to telephone her or come over to see her.

Abram came out of his study bouncing with energy. "Things are going on," he murmured. He loved nothing so much as excitement, days and nights full of motion. He even enjoyed the knowledge that he did not have a grosz in his pocket and that the law might be at his very heels. The lawyer he had called had told him that the penalty for forging a note might be as much as three years. No matter, he thought, the old man wouldn't go so far as to let him go to prison. "It wasn't from a stranger I took anything—from my own children's grandfather." Any decent man of his age would have died long ago and given his heirs a chance to have a little pleasure out of his money. "Come on, youngster, let's go," he said to Asa Heshel. "First I'll have to borrow fifty rubles somewhere. Someone promised me a loan yesterday. Then I want to take you to get a decent suit on credit. We'll get you a new hat too. Then we'll go on the search for the lost princess. I have a plan, wait till you see. I'll cook up such a stew that all Warsaw will be laughing in their sleeves."

The two went into the street. The day was mild and sunny. Housewives were shaking out pillows in red ticking at the windows opening on the courtyard. Servants were splashing water against window panes. There was an aroma of milk and fresh-baked bread in the air. Abram asked Asa Heshel if he had any money.

"Three rubles."

"Hand 'em over."

Abram summoned a droshky and the two climbed in. They got off at the Elektralna, where an old friend of Abram's had a ready-made clothing store. The road was crowded with automobiles, droshkies, and bicycles. A funeral procession made its way along. At its head marched a stout priest in a lace-trimmed surplice, murmuring from an open prayerbook. After him came four men in silver-edged coats, wearing triangular hats, and with lanterns in their hands. A bell rang; passers-by took off their hats and crossed themselves. A flock of pigeons flew over the procession, swooping down to pick at the horse-droppings.

Abram's clothing-store friend was a short, stout man, with a high round belly. He embraced Abram and kissed him on both cheeks. Abram whispered something in his ear. Asa Heshel left the store in a brand-new suit. The store-owner wrapped the old clothing in a bundle and put it behind the counter. Abram borrowed a couple of rubles from his friend and bargained for a hat for Asa Heshel at a store a few doors away.

Then the two went to a barber's where Asa Heshel was shaved, given a haircut, and even doused with cologne, while the master barber himself trimmed Abram's beard. Asa Heshel looked at his reflection in the long mirror. He hardly recognized himself.

"Count Pototski, or my name isn't Abram! You look like a *goy*," Abram boomed.

He was right. With the doffing of his Chassidic garments Asa Heshel had also doffed his Jewish appearance.

5

It was close to noon when the droshky came to a stop at the house in Praga where Klonya lived. Abram sent Asa Heshel up to call the girl, while he remained in the carriage. Klonya's family lived on the second floor. Asa Heshel climbed the well-scrubbed, sand-covered steps. He knocked at the door. It was opened by a stout girl whose flaxen hair was plaited into two large braids. She was wearing an alpaca smock. There was a thimble on her finger and she was holding a needle and thread.

"Does Miss Klonya live here?" Asa Heshel asked.

"I'm Klonya."

"Hadassah's uncle is waiting downstairs in a droshky. He would like you to come down for a minute."

"Which uncle? Abram?"

"Yes."

"Hadassah spent the night here, but she's gone now. Are you—"

"I'm the one she was tutoring."

The girl's eyes smiled. "I recognized you right away. She described you to the life. Too bad you didn't come an hour earlier. Her mother was here. It isn't the first time that she's spent the night with us. Come inside for a while."

"I'm sorry. Mr. Shapiro is in a hurry."

"It'll only take a minute. I'll just introduce you to my mother." She took his arm and drew him inside, along a small corridor and into a large room. In the middle of the room was a table with chairs around it. On one of the walls hung a deer's head with twisted horns, an ancient double-barreled hunting rifle, and gilt-framed portraits of a young man with wide mustaches and a high-bosomed woman with her hair up in a coil. Against the window hung a canary cage and below it stood a sewing-machine. Over a dresser hung a picture of Jesus, the beard curled and a crown of thorns on the head. Below it a small red lamp was burning. On a sofa, from whose broken sides tufts of horsehair protruded, lay a big sheep dog, his paws extended. When Asa Heshel entered, the animal began to growl, but a smallish woman, fat and round, with a generous double chin, called out: "Quiet! Lie down!"

"Mamusha, this is the young gentleman who's taking lessons from Hadassah. Hadassah's Uncle Abram is downstairs in a droshky."

"Why doesn't he come up? This is a respectable house. Very honored to meet you. Hadassah is like my own child. She's not a girl; she's a flower. Clever and beautiful like the sun in the sky. Lucky man who gets an angel like that. And you, young man? They tell me you came to Warsaw to study."

"Yes. I just started."

"There's nothing better than an education. Whatever you are, Jews or Christians, as long as you've got some learning in your head, everybody'll lift his hat to you. Hadassah isn't for one of those gaberdines, one of those Chassids. She's too delicate. That specimen from the Gnoyna, in the oil business, with the sidelocks, isn't the man for her."

"Oh, Mamma, you talk too much."

"I'm the kind of woman who tells the truth. Straight out. She told me everything, although she's got a discreet nature. I told her plain, parents have to be obeyed, but first of all comes your own heart."

While her mother talked, Klonya fixed her hair, put on a coat, and picked up a shiny pocketbook with a brass handle. Asa Heshel said good-by to the older woman. She held out a fat hand, scarred from housework, and asked him to come again. The dog jumped down from the sofa, sniffed at Asa Heshel's ankles, and wagged his tail. On the stairway Klonya said: "Hadassah will be here again at one o'clock."

"Where did she go?"

"To apply for a job. It was advertised in the papers."

He stood at the yard gate while Klonya talked to Abram. Abram was gesturing with his hands, tugging at his beard, striking his forehead. He called Asa Heshel over.

"She'll be back at one o'clock. It's now twenty past twelve. You wait for her. Don't let her get away. I'll be back in about an hour."

Abram spoke in Polish so that Klonya should understand, in a voice so vehement that passers-by paused to stare. It was decided that Asa Heshel would wait in the restaurant on the opposite side of the street; Klonya would send Hadassah over to him the moment she came, then both would wait there for Abram. The droshky-driver began to show signs of impatience, snapping his whip and cursing at the horse. Soon the carriage rolled away with Abram inside. Klonya said something to Asa Heshel, but although he understood each word separately, he did not seem to be able to fit them together. The stone floor of the restaurant was sprinkled with sawdust. A sharp odor of beer and frying food assailed his nostrils. The place was empty, the tables were covered with soiled cloths. Asa Heshel sat down. A short, squat man came over to him. His shirt sleeves were rolled up above the elbows.

"What would you like?"

Asa Heshel wanted to say "A glass of beer," but instead he said: "Some tea."

"This isn't a tea house."

"Then a glass of brandy." His own words surprised him.

"Something to eat with it?"

"Yes."

"Some sausage?"

"That will be all right."

He immediately regretted it. Of course the sausage wouldn't be kosher, but now it was too late. The man came back with a glass and two thick sausages on a plate. He looked at Asa Heshel with his keen gray eyes.

"Where are you from?" he asked.

"I'm staying in Warsaw."

"What street?"

"Shviento-Yerska."

"What do you do for a living?"

"I'm a student."

"Where? In a school?"

"No. Private."

"With a rabbi?"

"With a teacher."

"Why don't you go back to Palestine?"

The saloonkeeper apparently was ready to carry on his cross-examination, but a barefooted young girl, her face thickly freckled, called him from the other room. Asa Heshel took a sip of the raw liquor. It burned his throat and brought tears to his eyes. He picked up the sausage and bit off a piece. "I'm lost anyway," he thought. "Yes, Abram is right. I've got to get out of Poland. If not to Palestine, then to some other country where there's no law against Jews going to college. If only Hadassah would come with me. I've got to think it all out."

He drained the glass of brandy, feeling a simultaneous wave of warmth and dizziness sweep over him. He did not hear the door open or see Hadassah come in. She stood at the open door in a long, fur-collared winter coat, a black velvet beret on her head. She was holding a newspaper under her arm. Her face, in the few days since he had seen her, had become even paler, as though she had just got up from a sickbed. She nodded and smiled shyly, her gaze fixed on him. The new clothes had changed him beyond recognition. Only the black string tie under his collar reminded her of the green youth of a few days before.

6

When Asa Heshel told Hadassah of his decision to go to Switzerland, her eyes moistened.

"Take me with you. I can't stand it here any more." There was a rush of blood to her cheeks. Her small hands, in the black gloves, played nervously with the tin ashtray on the table. She kept glancing at him and then turning her eyes away. It seemed to Asa Heshel that in the last couple of days she had become maturer. She talked on, telling how her father had gone into an uncontrollable rage, how her mother was siding with her grandfather, and how everyone in the family had now taken a hand in the affair—uncles, aunts, cousins, her stepgrandmother—even Koppel. Nothing was right. Even the job she had applied for had turned out to be no good. The woman had expected her to wash clothes, besides taking care of the child.

There was a long pause. Then she said: "Are you really going? Or is it just something you're thinking about?"

"If you would come with me I'd go today."

"You've just put on city clothes and already you're talking like a man of the world."

"I mean it with all my heart."

"But you need a pass or something to cross the borders."

"There are ways of going without it."

"I just don't know. Everyone in the house is furious at me. Even Shifra. They don't let me alone for a minute. Not even to read a book. But I don't care. They can't force him on me. I'd rather die. I've even thought of putting an end to it."

"Hadassah, don't say such things!"

"You said yourself that suicide was the greatest affirmation of man's freedom."

"But I didn't mean in a case like this."

"I'm not afraid. When I was in the sanatorium I made my peace with death."

The saloonkeeper came in. Seeing a girl at the table, he twirled one end of his mustache and said: "What will you have?"

"I—I don't know," Hadassah said nervously. "It's so cold in here."

"I suggest the young lady have some soup. It's just ready—tomato and rice."

"All right."

"For you too?" Asa Heshel shook his head, and the man went out.

"Everything seems so topsy-turvy," Hadassah continued. "I look at you, but I hardly recognize you."

"I hardly recognize myself."

"You made such a good impression on Klonya and her mother. I got there just a little while after you left. I didn't sleep all night, or the night before, either. I telephoned you twice, but you weren't home."

"Gina's husband came home; I spent the night at Abram's."

"Everything's so complicated. My Aunt Hama's gone to Grandfather's. Did you meet Stepha?"

"Yes."

"What did you think of her?"

"She's like her father."

"Yes, you're right. They told me you telephoned and Mamma told you not to call any more. I was so upset I cried. Shifra told me."

"It wasn't your fault."

The saloonkeeper came in and put a bowl of soup in front of Hadassah. She picked up the spoon.

"What will you study in Switzerland?"

"Mathematics is what I like best."

"I thought you were going in for philosophy."

"The philosophers know nothing. Everything has to be started over from the beginning."

"What I'm interested in is biology. I love to work with a microscope. I'm sure Papa would change his mind after a while and send me some money."

"I'm sure of it."

"How much does the trip cost?"

"Less than fifty rubles. I have twenty-five already. I loaned it to someone, but they'll pay it back."

"Who? Never mind—it isn't important. I have two diamond rings and a gold watch. They're worth a few hundred rubles."

"Then you're really in earnest! But they'd never let you go."

"What's the alternative? To stay here and get married." She spooned up some soup, raised it to her lips, and then put it untasted back in the plate.

"Don't you like the soup?"

"Yes. I always knew that a day would come when I'd have to leave everything behind me. I walk around the house as though it were a deserted ship. A few days ago I dreamt that you went away on a train, a long train with the windows covered with curtains. I ran after it—but it was too late."

"I dreamed about you, too," he said, his face flushing. "We were together, all alone, on an island, near a brook; we were lying on the grass, and you were reading to me."

"I always dreamed of islands, even when I was a little girl."

She was suddenly silent. She caught her lower lip between her teeth and smiled, a far-away smile. Then her face took on an expression of deep seriousness. Something he had thought before returned to Asa Heshel. "How can I aspire to her? She's all belief, I'm all doubt. I'll only do her harm." He started to say something, but the door opened and Abram came in, stamping his feet. His fur hat was aslant on his head. The familiar cigar was stuck between his teeth. For a moment he stood in the doorway and looked at the pair. Then he shouted:

"My God, the world's turned upside down and they sit there like a couple of doves! Look at them! Romeo and Juliet or my name isn't Abram!"

"Uncle!" Hadassah got up from her chair and rushed over to him, almost overturning the bowl of soup.

He caught her in his arms and kissed her. Then he held her away from him and growled: "Let me take a look at her, the lost heiress, the enchanted princess. Your mother's running around like someone insane. She's convinced you're somewhere at the bottom of the Vistula. You telephone her right away! You hear? This minute."

"There's no telephone here."

"All right, I'll call her myself. There's a telephone not far away. And suppose your father did slap you around a bit. Does a girl run away from home? My father almost killed me. And he was right."

"Mamma was already over at Klonya's. She knows I slept there."

"That's no excuse. Ah me, ah me! A new generation! And I thought that I was full of adventure."

While Abram was talking, Asa Heshel managed to empty the sausages off the plate and drop them to the floor so that Abram should not see what he had been eating. A cat, which had been waiting watchfully on the other side of the room, sprang down from the chair and padded over. The saloonkeeper, hearing Abram's voice, came in from the other room.

"Nothing to worry about," Abram shouted at him. "These are my children. Give me the bill. I'll pay."

He took a silver ruble out of his purse and threw it onto the table. The saloonkeeper rubbed his forehead. That's the way it always was. Let one Jew into the place and they'd draw a thousand others, like flies, and the place gets to be a madhouse. The plate of soup was standing untouched. The cat was gnawing at the sausages. A pack of devils, these Jews, with their stylish clothes. The newspapers were right; that gang would eat up Poland like a flock of locusts, worse than the Muscovites and the Swabians. He felt like making some insulting remark, but decided to say nothing. That big man with the blazing eyes, the fur hat on his head, and the black beard looked like someone who wouldn't stand for anyone spitting in his porridge.

He gave Abram his change—eighty kopeks. Abram picked out a ten-kopek piece and flung it on the table. "Buy yourself a drink," he boomed. "Good luck!"

7

When Abram heard that Asa Heshel was going to go to Switzerland and that Hadassah wanted to go too, he stared at her in wonder. "That was my plan for them," he thought in surprise. "How did they know it? I don't remember mentioning it to either of them. It must be telepathy," he decided. Aloud he said: "That's not so simple."

"Asa Heshel says that it will cost only fifty rubles and that you don't need a pass."

"And what'll you do there? Even in Switzerland you've got to eat."

"I'll earn something. And Papa'll send me money."

"And suppose he doesn't, what'll you do? Call him a bad boy?"

"He'll send it."

"Well, do what you like. You're not a school child. At your age my mother had three children."

He walked with Hadassah back and forth on the sidewalk near the restaurant. Asa Heshel had gone to buy a tie; Abram had insisted that the Chassidic string tie was ridiculous now that he was wearing city clothes. He puffed furiously at his cigar.

"So that's the way it is," he growled. "Without my advice. I'm telling you, look before you leap. Don't do things in a rush. He has nothing to lose. But you! Suppose you get sick, God forbid. You'll be all alone. Although, come to think of it, the air in Switzerland is supposed to be good for people with weak lungs. They go there from everywhere."

"You see, Uncle."

"But just the same, think it over. A girl of your age, a respectable girl, from a decent family, to pick up and go off like that! Your grandfather'll tear the roof down. Your mother will go out of her mind. The whole neighborhood will buzz. I'll just ask you one favor; don't tell me anything about it. I haven't heard a word, and I want to know nothing. If you'll excuse me, I'm deaf in my left ear. Besides, I'm leaving the country myself. If we happen to run into each other, then we can celebrate."

Hadassah's face lighted up. "When are you going? Where?" she exclaimed. "You're only joking."

"What's so wonderful about it? Even a horse can go abroad. I told you about the new journal, didn't I? Hertz Yanovar is the editor; I'm the manager. We have to raise fifty thousand rubles. I'm going all over. To Switzerland, too."

"Is it really true?" Hadassah jumped for joy. "It would be wonderful! You could live with me."

"Thank you very much. I'm already provided with lodgings. Look at her; carrying on a love affair and springing around like a calf! What do you think Switzerland is? Sky, earth, and water, like everywhere else."

"I just can't stand it here any more. It's disgusting. Day and night, Fishel, Fishel. It sticks in my throat. Besides, I want to study. A girl has a chance to become a doctor there."

"And what do you think you'll do if you get to be a doctor? Give an enema to some old Jew? Marvelous. But anyway, what's it got to do with me? If you want to go, go. And what about Asa Heshel? What'll you do with each other there? Get married?"

"Why do we have to do anything? We'll both study. What'll happen later—well, we'll see."

"What d'you mean, later? It takes seven years to become a doctor."

"What about it? We're not so old."

"Idiots! May I drop dead if I understand you. Either you're a drooling baby or I'm a doddering ancient. My God, what a generation! I don't know any more where in the world I am."

"Uncle darling, I love you! If I miss anyone at all, it'll be you and Mamma."

"You'll miss us all right. I miss you already. The whole thing's too much for me. To pick up and go all of a sudden! To leave Warsaw! It doesn't make sense to me. I can understand going to the warm baths for a couple of months, or God knows where else. But to leave your home, your family, everything—"

"I tell you I can't stand it here any more."

"All right, then go. *Bon voyage,* drop me a postcard once in a while. Still waters, that Asa Heshel. I tell you I'm sorry I ever started with him."

"You're the one that praised him so much."

"Come to think of it, your grandfather's had it coming to him. Don't let him have the illusion that he and that Koppel of his can play God almighty. In principle you're absolutely right. You don't drag decent girls to the canopy. Just the same, I can't see how you can be so light-hearted about it. Even a bird returns to its nest."

"I'll come back—when I've finished studying."

"Go and wait seven years! Ah, youth, youth! You'll singe your wings. You'll both get scorched. But it's your affair. Just don't ask me for any advice, and don't tell me anything. They'll blame me anyway."

He took a last puff of his cigar, threw it in the gutter, and started to walk off. Near by, a blind man was playing an accordion. Abram took a coin out of his pocket and threw it into the beggar's hat as he passed. Then he turned around, his overcoat unbuttoned, his hat askew, and strode back.

"Well, if you're going, go!" he shouted back at Hadassah. "Say good-by to me and on your way!"

"My God, I'm not going today. What are you so sarcastic about?"

"Where's Asa Heshel? Does it take a year to buy a tie? A fine business I started. I clothe him, I dress him, and he runs away with my niece. Like a play by Shakespeare. I'll tell you the truth, I wouldn't trust my Stepha to him."

"You're so inconsistent."

"He's an adventurer. I don't wish him any harm, but that's the way it is. Yesterday he runs away from his own town, today he runs away from Warsaw. Tomorrow he'll run away from you. I'll admit I'm no angel myself, but just the same, I don't want to see my own flesh and blood suffer."

"He won't need to run away from me. I'm independent."

"I've seem them proud like you before. But when there's a little brat kicking around inside, they don't feel so high and mighty."

"Don't worry about me. I'll never get married, anyway."

"What then? Free love?"

"Marriage is a mockery. The whole thing is false."

"What's the matter all of a sudden? Been reading Artzybashev? Some of Asa Heshel's ideas?"

"What difference does it make?"

"Ah me, a couple of lousy books and the things they've done! I'll tell you the truth; it looks to me as though you don't begin to grasp how serious the whole thing is."

"That's not so."

"What are you, anyway? One of these socialists, nihilists?"

"I know; you think I'm still a child. But I have my own thoughts."

"What are they, good God? Tell them to me. Let me know them."

"You know very well. You're just being a hypocrite."

"What's that? Well, all right, I admit it. I'm afraid that I'm plain jealous."

"Oh, Uncle, stop talking like that. I'll always love you."

"Call me crazy, but, believe me, all my life I've yearned for real love. Your Aunt Hama isn't much of an Amanda. I've had plenty of affairs, all sorts, but here—here"—Abram thumped himself violently on the chest—"I'm an idealist. And suddenly a God-knows-what comes crawling out of some hole, and he gets the real thing. Well, I can't wait for him any more. I've got a thousand things to do. Here's the key to my apartment. Tell your hero that as long as Akiba's at Gina's he can stay at my place. I'm sorry I got excited. I suppose it's because of my bad heart."

"You ought to go to the doctor. You shouldn't run around so much."

"What's the good? I've been running around like this for the last thirty years: I can't stop in the middle. An express train. Call me tonight or early tomorrow morning."

"Yes, Uncle. I love you, you know that, but if I stay here I'll have to marry Fishel."

"You're right. Come here and let me kiss you. If your grandfather at least had the decency to close his eyes at last—"

"Oh, shame on you." Hadassah reached her arms up to him and kissed him on both cheeks. Tears came to his eyes. He had a strange feeling that the whole course of events was his own doing, although, God knew, his mixing into other people's business brought him nothing but trouble. "There must really be a devil in me," he thought. A droshky wheeled up. Abram tore himself away from Hadassah and climbed in. He waved his hand and gave Ida's address to the driver. "What's come over me today?" he wondered. "I hope I don't get an attack." From his breast pocket he took out a small box of pills and swallowed two of them. He told the driver to stop at a florist's, went inside, and bought a bouquet of roses for Ida and a bunch of yellow blossoms for Zosia—after all, she had just loaned him fifty rubles. Ida hadn't been home when he was there earlier. Now he decided to spend the rest of the day there. "Whatever happens will happen," he thought. "A man can't die twice."

At Ida's house the janitor looked at him curiously as he went through the gate carrying both bunches of flowers. A be-shawled gentile woman, a steaming tin of food in one hand, shook her head somberly. She, a decent Christian soul, had to plod on foot all the way to the factory to take her husband his lunch, while these Masons and Christ-killers rode around in droshkies and lugged flowers to their whores.

He climbed the stairs and rang the doorbell. Zosia opened the door. Abram handed both bunches of flowers to her.

"Is your mistress home?"

"Not yet."

He put his arms about her and embraced her ardently, bending his head down and pressing his mouth to hers.

"God save me, you're a piece all right," he mumbled in Yiddish. "Your lips taste like paradise."

"What are you saying? What are you doing to me?"

"Shut up, you unbeliever! You forbidden morsel! God damn the whole tribe of Esau!" And he began to kiss her on the mouth again, fervently and desperately.

8

Asa Heshel and Hadassah walked back from Praga. As they crossed the bridge, they could see the Vistula still and frozen, its surface covered with snow. Off in the distance a small fig-ure was plodding across the ice; it was difficult to make out whether it was a grown-up or a child. To their right, across another bridge, a locomotive pulled a train of red freight cars. Birds circled above them. There was a smell of smoke and a touch of the coming spring in the air. The ancient buildings on the Warsaw side of the bridge peered at them with their ir-regular rooftops, turrets, balconies, and thickly set rows of windows. It seemed to Hadassah that she was seeing these sights for the first time, as though it was she who was the pro-vincial, and Asa Heshel was showing her the glories of the great city.

They wandered through Old City, into alleyways Hadassah

had never seen before, the sidewalks so narrow that it was difficult for the two to walk side by side. Householders drew water from old-fashioned outdoor pumps. The shop fronts were covered with iron bars. Some of the buildings had bricked-in windows. Streetwalkers sauntered near the unlit street lamps.

Near the Freta, Asa Heshel suggested that they go into a coffee house. They were the only ones in the place. The window was made up of varicolored panes of glass. Hadassah began to talk about her cousin Masha, the daughter of her Aunt Leah, who in spite of the objections of her father, Moshe Gabriel, had taken courses at the university. "She hasn't spoken to him for years," Hadassah said. "Anyway, he's practically a stranger in the household. Peculiar, isn't it? No one in the family is really happy." She took a sip of coffee, looked at Asa Heshel, and raised the cup to her lips again. "Why can't I tell him all I am thinking?" she wondered. "What is it that stops me?" Asa Heshel sat silent, his head bent, his face pale. "I've got to get over it," he was thinking. "I've got to get rid of this cursed timidity."

For all their new-found freedom, the two still talked in broken phrases, their eyes averted. What, after all, had really been decided? All their talk about Switzerland—was it more than idle conversation? The whole idea was too simple to have any real substance. Could they seal their destiny as easily as this, in a half-empty coffee house on the Freta, in a wintry twilight? When Asa Heshel looked at Hadassah, it seemed to him that she was entirely too fragile ever to be his wife and that he was too uncouth ever to please her. Back of it all there must be a trick somewhere, an error that at the last moment would arise to negate everything. Through his mind fled a patchwork of strange thoughts, vague and childish. He did not know why, but ever since his adolescence he had been haunted with the obsession that he would never be able to bring himself to any intimacy with a woman and that his wedding night would be a humiliation. Hadassah stole glances at him. She had not slept all night, the sofa at Klonya's house had been so bumpy. She had got up when it was still dark, and the demarcation between the events of the now and yesterday was misty. She was still amazed at the change his new clothes made in Asa Heshel's appearance. She kept thinking about her Uncle Abram's mystifying remarks. She felt certain now that the love she had so long awaited had at last arrived. But it had come in a welter of complications she had thought existed only in books. Why on earth should she run away? Her mother would die of grief. "I must have lost all feeling of responsibility," she thought. Aloud she said: "But, God in heaven, we know each other so little!"

"We must have known each other before, in another incarnation," Asa Heshel answered.

"Do you really believe that?"

"The soul is eternal."

Through the varicolored pane the setting sun cast a red glow on Asa Heshel's face. There he sat, opposite her, proud, yet somehow humble, full of secrets she could not know, and ready—so it seemed to her—to disappear out of her life as suddenly as he had entered into it.

The evening was coming on when they left the coffee house. They passed the prison at the corner of Nalevki and Dluga and went along Rymarska Street and the Platz Bankovy. On the Iron Gate Square the street lamps were already burning. A cold wind came from the direction of the Saxon Gardens. Tramcars rolled along. Crowds of people thronged the market stalls. Hadassah held Asa Heshel's arm tightly as though afraid she might lose him. Farther along, at the bazaars, stall-keepers presided over mounds of butter, huge Swiss cheeses, bundles of mushrooms, troughs of oysters and fish. The torchlights were already ablaze. They passed a slaughterhouse. Floodlights blazed in the building. Porters with hoses were swishing water on the stone floor. Slaughterers stood near blood-filled granite vats, slitting the necks of ducks, geese, and hens. Fowl cackled deafeningly. The wings of a rooster, its throat just slit, fluttered violently. Hadassah pulled at Asa Heshel's sleeve, her face deathly white. A little farther on, in the fish market, stood tubs, barrels, and troughs. In the stale-smelling water, carp, pike, and tench swam about. Beggars sang in quavering voices, cripples stretched out stumps of arms. Away from the glare of the lights inside, the darkness of the court was intensified. Asa Heshel and Hadassah walked a little way along Krochmalna Street and emerged on the Gnoyna. A cold wind swept along the street. Hadassah began to cough.

"I'd better go home now," she said. "I suppose I'll have to face them. When shall I see you again?"

"Whenever you say."

"I'll telephone you at Abram's tomorrow, early, about ten o'clock. The day seems to have gone by so quickly."

"Since I met you time has become even more illusory."

A droshky stopped near them. Hadassah climbed in. She nodded her head toward Asa Heshel and touched her fingers to her lips. He returned the gesture awkwardly and then hurried away.

At Abram's house he climbed the steps to the apartment and opened the door with the key Hadassah had given him. It was dark and cold inside. He turned on the electric light and went into the study. He lay down on the sofa and closed his eyes. How rich the day had been! He had thrown off his provincial garments; he had been with Hadassah. His life was beginning. The only problem was—where was there room for love in a world built on hatred and destruction? Until that question was answered, life had no meaning. He had started to doze off when the telephone rang. Should he answer it? Maybe it was for him. No that was impossible. Yet somehow the feeling persisted that the call was for him. He lifted the receiver. It was Hadassah, to tell him that she was thinking of him and that she would call him in the morning. She spoke in a hurried voice. She started to say something else, but then he heard the click of the receiver; her mother must have come in.

Asa Heshel went over to the window. There had been an intensity in her voice that shook him. He knew now that the decision was made. There would be no retreat.

CHAPTER FIVE

FROM HADASSAH'S DIARY

February 3.—It is now midnight. Papa's sleeping. Mamma has just gone to bed. Only I cannot close my eyes. Everything around me is beginning to seem so strange. I never dreamed that the day would come when I would long for the Panska, our courtyard with its refuse boxes, our old-fashioned apartment, and my own room, where I have so often been sad and lonely. Yet I have started to long for them even before I leave them. The last few nights I have been dreaming that I am already in Switzerland. How foolish one's dreams can be! I imagined that the peaks of the mountains were made of gold. Eagles flew back and forth in the air, huge as human beings. My dreams are so strange. I seem to be talking all night long with someone. Sometimes I imagine that Asa Heshel and my Uncle Abram are one and the same person.

February 4.—He seems so pale. He says he isn't afraid and that he is ready for anything, because anyway everything has been predestined. He is really a fatalist, like Pechorin. But I can tell he *is* afraid. It is too bad that he is so young. I always wanted my "knight on a white horse" to be at least ten years older than I.

For myself I have no fear at all, though sometimes I'm sure that I am making a mistake and that everything will end in disaster. Something inside me—a spirit or another self—wants to lead me to perdition. I remember that other self from my childhood.

February 5.—Yesterday I spent several hours with him. We walked in the Saxon Gardens. We stood by the pond where swans paddle in the summertime. Now it is ice-covered. Boys and girls were skating, gliding and cutting all sorts of fancy figures. We went into the Alley of Roses. He wrote my name on the snow. Sometimes he is gay and carefree. But then he gets morose. He looks so well in his new clothes. We talked about Weininger's *Sex and Character;* he agrees with Weininger that woman has no soul.

How foolish it all is!

We took the tramcar to the Zlota. He wanted me to go up to Abram's apartment with him, but I told him that a respectable girl doesn't go into an apartment alone with a man. He was very resentful. Actually I was afraid we might run into Stepha. And the janitor knows me, too. But later I did go up with him; we decided that if Stepha came in I would hurry out through the rear door. It was all so embarrassing.

He didn't put on the light. We sat for a long time on the sofa in Uncle's study and talked. He is so full of contradictions. And he's so pessimistic. He says that the world is a jungle and that morally man is lower than the beasts. He talks with so much conviction that I feel like crying. I *have* to believe in Man, and in an almighty God, and in love, and in the soul. If I didn't I simply would not be able to go on living.

While he was sitting so close to me in the darkness, I had the feeling that he was much older—thirty or forty years old.

Let him destroy all my illusions, I don't care! It is so good to hear his voice. I am sure that his faith in mankind will be restored. In Switzerland we'll recover our ideals together. We are young, we love to read and discuss things. What else matters? When I think that I might have given him up for Fishel, my flesh crawls.

We kissed for a long time. He said I was the most beautiful girl in the whole world. Was he sincere? Sometimes he is so naïve, like a child of seven. Enough for now. I am very happy.

The middle of the night.—What will happen if our secret is discovered? What if I get sick? How tragic to build one's happiness on chance. Before I went to sleep I read Tolstoy's *My Confession.* He says that man must develop within himself a love for all mankind. Then I would have to love everybody—Shifra, Koppel, my stepgrandmother, Adele, my former mathematics teacher, Miechislav Knopek, and Zeinvele, the *shadchan,* too. Can a human being really attain such a love?

My dreams give me no rest. The moment I close my eyes I see fantastic visions, flowers of all colors—I hear bells ringing. Sometimes I imagine that the whole world's on fire. What is it that's going through this poor brain of mine?

I'm sitting on the edge of my bed, and everything inside me is in a tumult.

February 8.—I had to promise Mamma and Papa that I would consent to be engaged to Fishel in two weeks. Of course, I deceived them, poor souls. My Uncle Abram is playing a strange role—he is talking me out of my "adventure"— but at the same time he is helping us. He is trying to get a subsidy for Asa Heshel; there is a sort of fund in the Jewish community here for poor students. It looks to me like plain begging. Uncle is getting ready to travel abroad. How wonderful it would be if the three of us could be together in the Alps. Mamma is very weak; her face looks yellow. She looks at me as though she knew instinctively that I was preparing to leave.

Gina has got a divorce from that fanatical husband of hers. I suppose she will get married to Hertz Yanovar very soon. They'll probably go to Switzerland, too. There'll be a whole group of us there.

February 11.—Klonya and I and Asa Heshel went together to the moving pictures on Iron Street. He simply couldn't understand what he was seeing. We had to explain everything to him.

I have the feeling that everything that is happening is also a sort of cinematographic play. Nothing seems real, neither life nor death. I wonder what he is thinking of at this moment.

Sometimes it seems to me that he isn't one person, he is several persons in one.

February 12.—I have an idea that Mamma knows everything. But she doesn't say a word.

At night.—I went to a jeweler's on the Chlodno and asked how much he would give me for my rings. When I was standing at the counter and he was examining the rings through his magnifying glass I suddenly realized that I was preparing to do something that would affect my entire life.

Why has Papa become so strange to me? He has begun to smoke cigars and he spends his time solving chess problems from the newspaper. They're starting to get the house ready for the engagement ceremony. The rabbi from Bialodrevna, Gina's father, is going to be there. They all take it so seriously while I, the heroine of the story, am getting ready to run away. It's like a comedy at the Letni Theater.

February 14.—My throat hurts me. I coughed all night. I'm afraid I have some fever. I'm to meet him today, but who knows whether they'll let me go out of the house. It's snowing. There's a droshky at the gate. The janitor is sweeping the entrance with a long broom. The weathercock on the roof of the building opposite is turning back and forth. I'm reading Zeromski's novel *The Labors of Sisyphus.* I went into the kitchen and watched Shifra draining and salting the meat on the salting board. It is Thursday today—the day when the mendicants go from door to door. I gave an old man ten groszy and he wished me health. He said it twice and thumped with his staff on the floor. I know it is all so simple and ordinary, but to me it was unusual.

Warsaw, dear city of mine, how sad I am! Already, before I have left you, I long for you. I look at your crooked roofs, your factory chimneys, your thickly clouded skies, and I realize how deeply rooted you are in my heart. I know it will be good to live in a strange country, but when my time comes to die I want to lie in the cemetery on the Gensha, near my beloved grandmother.

PART THREE

CHAPTER ONE

1

The Gzhybov section had plenty to talk about: Reb Meshulam Moskat had suddenly been taken ill, and his granddaughter Hadassah had run away from home with some raw youth from the provinces. Warsaw's Jews put two and two together: the girl's flight was responsible for the old man's illness. In the Chassidic prayer and study houses confusion piled on confusion. Tongues buzzed everywhere—in the food stores, the market stalls, at tailors' tables and cobblers' benches, in the furniture shops on the Bagno, even as far away as the Nalevki. In the homes of Meshulam's sons and daughters the telephones started ringing early in the morning. In front of the old man's house Dr. Mintz's carriage waited, and there was a constant stream of droshkies. Meshulam's oldest son, Joel, and his wife, Queen Esther, both of them heavyweights, puffed up the steps that led to the Moskat flat. Nathan, the younger son, had been ordered to keep to his bed; in addition to his diabetes he had a bad heart. But he persuaded Saltsha to go with him to his father's house. She carried with her a bagful of medicines and pills. Pearl, Meshulam's oldest daughter, the widow, was out of the city; she had gone to Lodz on business, and the others sent her a telegram to return. Pinnie came dashing on foot. At the door he ran into his sister, Leah. The crowd gathered on the sidewalk made way for them. They heard Pinnie ask: "What happened? What happened?" and saw Leah wring her hands as she answered: "What's the difference what happened? What he needs now is God's mercy."

A crowd of the curious gathered around Dr. Mintz's carriage, peering through the shiny windows at the cushioned seats and back rests. They gawked at the gentile coachman in his high silk hat and silver-buttoned uniform, and at the horses with bobbed tails, shiny pelts, and heads held high. Another coach wheeled up, the carriage of Dr. Frankl, and immediately there was a murmur that the situation was critical and that a consultation was being held. Naomi appeared in the doorway, red and excited, shouting at the top of her lungs:

"What the black year goes on here! It's impossible for people to get in the door!"

"How's the boss?"

"Go on, go home! We'll send a messenger to give you a report. Standing around like dummies." She made a threatening gesture.

"She's stolen plenty from them, the old witch," the baker's girl said. "A fire in her guts."

"What's happened to Koppel, the bailiff?" one woman asked. She was holding a basket of groceries against her pregnant belly.

"Here he comes now."

Koppel was getting out of a droshky. He tossed a few coins to the driver, and before anyone had a chance to say a word to him he was up the steps and the door had closed behind him. Porters, draymen, laborers, and idlers stood around on the opposite sidewalk, rolling cigarettes, looking curiously toward the windows of the Moskat apartment, and talking in loud voices.

"Just let him close his eyes for good and the scramble'll start for fair."

"I should have the money this business is going to cost."

"There'll be plenty left."

"And he had to find himself a third wife, the old goat."

"Don't worry your head about it. She'll have a good juicy bone to gnaw at."

"They say that Nyunie's daughter ran off with someone," a man remarked.

"What! Mamma darling! I'll die!" the baker's girl hugged herself in an ecstasy of excitement.

"Which one? What's her name?"

"Hadassah."

"God's curse! Punishment from heaven! The Almighty takes His time, but He hands it out, it's a double portion!" the pregnant woman said piously. "They stuff themselves and cram it into their bellies, and the poor people—they throw 'em out with their lousy few sticks of furniture—may their bones be thrown about in Gehenna."

"Hey, loose-mouth! Reb Meshulam never threw anybody out into the street."

Old Jews, idlers who knew everybody's business and followed everybody's funeral, declared that it was Abram Shapiro, the heretic and loose liver, who was responsible for

Nyunie's daughter's fall from grace. Though all of them acted
as though they were privy to everything that went on in Warsaw's wealthy Jewish households, the truth was that none of
them knew anything at all about the troubles that had struck
the Moskat family. It was only toward the evening, when
Zeinvele Strotsker, the *shadchan*, arrived at the Bialodrevna
prayerhouse, that some details were forthcoming. Hadassah
had a friend, a gentile girl; early on Monday morning she had
told her mother that she was going with this friend to a party
in Praga and would remain at her house overnight. It wasn't
the first time Hadassah had spent the night with the *shikse*,
and Dacha had raised no objection. As it turned out, instead
of going to Praga the girl had gone to the railroad station,
where this man was waiting for her—some student from
Tereshpol Minor, the grandson of a rabbi, but an apostate.
Everything was so carefully planned that Hadassah's mother
and father discovered their misfortune only the next day.
When the news reached Meshulam, the old man had fainted.
His power of speech was gone and his face was contorted.
The girl's mother was sick, too; they were putting ice packs to
her head. The police had been informed, but the pair had dis-
appeared into thin air.

Zeinvele's listeners heard and were silent in amazement.
True, the Bialodrevna faithful were used to sensations. Had
not their own rabbi's daughter departed from the paths of
righteousness? What things had not happened in Warsaw
since the Revolution of 1905! Chassidic youth had cast off
their gaberdines, shaved their faces, become strikers, Zionists.
Daughters of respectable homes had fallen in love with university students and had run off with them to New York,
Buenos Aires, or Palestine. Mothers of children had discarded
their matron's wigs and let the wide world see their naked
hair. It was these worldly books, printed in Yiddish so that
anyone could understand, that had poisoned decent people's
minds. And these "reformed" schools, where parents were
sending their daughters lately, were nothing but nests of paganism and wantonness. Nevertheless, who could have expected that a thing like this would happen to Nyunie's daughter,
Meshulam Moskat's own grandchild! It was a sign that no one
could be sure of his own children any more. And the way Meshulam had reacted only went to prove that with all his faults
he still remained a Jew of the old school, a Chassid.

"A-ah, world's end," they sighed.

Almost every one of the worshippers had a son or daughter

at home who was falling victim to the new ways. They brought home novels from the libraries. They went to all sorts of meetings. Speakers were thundering that Jews should not wait for Messiah to come, but build the Jewish homeland with their own hands. Boys and girls met in secret cellars and attics and conspired against the Czar. The truth was that the Jews were being persecuted more and more. Day by day it became harder to earn a living. What would be the end of it all? There was only one hope left—for Messiah to come, to come quickly while there were still a few pious Jews left.

Zeinvele Srotsker sat on a bench, his hands on his knees, his head bowed down. Hadassah's flight meant a serious loss to him. He was to have received five hundred rubles as his fee. The Passover season was approaching—and he had a daughter of his own to marry off.

2

In the sickroom where Meshulam lay, the lamp was turned low. Beside the bed sat a nurse from the Jewish hospital. The patient was propped up against two pillows. His eyes were closed. His sunken face was like parchment. From time to time his thin beard and mustaches quivered. Once in a while a flush appeared on the pads of his cheeks.

Rosa Frumetl opened the door and looked in. In a whisper she asked the nurse whether the sick man had awakened. The nurse shook her head, and Rosa Frumetl closed the door again.

The other rooms were crowded with the Moskat sons, daughters, in-laws, and grandchildren. There were, besides, a handful of people whom nobody seemed to know, who had managed to make their way into the flat. Joel and Nathan, the old man's sons by his first wife, were sitting in armchairs in the living-room. Joel was combing his amber-colored Franz-Josef-style beard with his fingers. Every once in a while he took a large gold watch out of his vest pocket, carefully released the three spring-covers, and looked at the dial. There was nothing he could do here; he had his own affairs to attend to. He kept on suggesting to Queen Esther that maybe they ought to go. But each time she whispered back that it would be unfitting to leave. She murmured something about the will, but he could not for the life of him figure out what difference their staying would make so far as the inheritance was concerned. He smoked one cigar after another. He calculated idly that if he were to live to be as old as his father was now, he would have to last another twenty years, whereas if he were to die in his seventies, he would have to wander about in the land of the living for a matter of only ten years or so more. What then, he reflected philosophically, was all this mad chase after money? Unless it were for the children—and who could say that they wouldn't wait around his deathbed the same way he and the others were now waiting around their father's? He coughed out a cloud of smoke and said to his brother Nathan: "It's all vanity. Vanity of vanities."

"A pinch of snuff," Nathan answered, and swallowed one of his pills.

Nathan followed his routine as though he were in his own home. Saltsha had taken off his shoes, put a pair of slippers on his feet, and then propped them on a hassock. She kept on bringing him things—tea with saccharine—he couldn't take sugar because of his diabetes—a slice of orange, a chicken liver, a small glass of brandy. Instead of letting his thoughts dwell on unpleasant matters he looked through an almanac that contained a perpetual Jewish calendar and gave dates for the market fairs held in Russian towns. It had descriptions, too, of China, Siam, India, and other far-away countries, and accounts of the intense cold in the regions near the North Pole, where night and day were six months long. How did the Jews up there manage to observe the Sabbath, Nathan wondered—"unless they go by the clock" he decided. He had an impulse to tell Saltsha about it, but he was ashamed to say anything in front of Joel. A complicated world, he thought. To be able to figure out such a thing!

Pinnie wandered aimlessly from room to room, his hat on the side of his head and his coat unbuttoned. He had had nothing to eat since early morning. Hannah had telephoned him twice to come home to dinner, but he stayed on. He talked to everyone—the relatives, his brothers, the servants, and even the strangers. "I should be doing something," he said to himself. "The place can't be left upside down." But he couldn't think of anything he ought to do. Finally he wandered into his father's study and looked through the papers in a drawer of the writing-table—torn notes, letters from rabbis, merchants, kinsfolk; long-expired contracts, stamped receipts from yeshivahs and Talmud torahs; columns of figures whose purpose was unclear. How could Papa keep all this in his mind, Pinnie wondered. Koppel must have fleeced him from head to foot. Pinnie tried to open the iron safe that stood against a wall, but it was locked.

Leah, Meshulam's youngest daughter, was sitting in the kitchen talking with Naomi about Hadassah. Naomi was saying that the young man Rosa Frumetl had engaged to revise the manuscript had made a bad impression on her from the beginning. She never trusted these provincials; they wormed their way in everywhere and then walked off with anything they could pick up. Every once in a while Koppel came into the kitchen, to light a cigarette from the glowing coals in the stove and to exchange a few words with Leah. Naomi knew that Koppel was still in love with Leah. Whenever he came in she left the two to themselves, going over to join Manya, who was at her eternal occupation of laying out a deck of cards. Manya still could not be sure whether her destined lover would be light or dark.

It was Hama who was most upset by Meshulam's illness. Nothing was going right for her. First she had left Abram, now her father was deathly sick. Her brothers and sisters would get their hands on everything and there would not be a copper left for her. She was afraid that the old man had written not only Abram out of his will but her and her daughters as well. Most of all, in the last few days she had begun to feel the old love for her father. Now she sat in a room with Rosa Frumetl, feeling that her new stepmother was in somewhat the same position as herself, uncertain whether Meshulam had made some provision for her. Both women wept, blew their noses, and urged each other to eat something.

Adele had locked herself in her room. Her stepfather was a man well along in years, and it was only to be expected that some day the end would come. But that that provincial Asa Heshel should pick himself up and run off with Hadassah— that was something she could not accept. She wasn't jealous, no; she wished them both luck. But just the same—what was the good of denying it?—it was like a slap in the face. She regretted bitterly that she had agreed to have him work on her father's commentary. She was ashamed that she had spoken to him the way she had, and had volunteered to tutor him. She had degraded herself, and all he had done was jeer at her. That's the way it had always been with her—in Brody, in Vienna, and now here in Warsaw. When it came to men she was simply an unfortunate. Was she really so ugly, or did she have faults she was not aware of?

She lay down on the bed. Let it be so; she would make peace with her destiny. She would reconcile herself to never having a husband, children, a home of her own. She would live alone. She suddenly thought of her father, whose body was turning to dust in the Brody cemetery.

"Papa, *you* loved me," she murmured aloud. "You were the only one."

3

All the time Meshulam Moskat lay on his sickbed, Rosa Frumetl, Leah, Naomi, and Koppel prowled and sniffed about the house, each suspecting the other of having the keys to the iron safe in the study. Where, each of them wondered, had the old man hidden the jewels and ornaments that had belonged to his first two wives, as well as the diamonds and precious stones they knew he had hoarded in recent years? Once, while the others were out, Naomi tried to force the door of the safe with a poker, but it refused to budge. True enough, in all the confusion it would have been easy to grab some of the silver cups and beakers, the candlesticks and trays, but Naomi had not sunk quite so low as that. Then there were the trunks full of muffs, fur coats, dresses of silk, satin, and velvet, packed away in camphor. But one would have to be insane to go to the trouble of taking any of these ancient fineries.

Anyway, Naomi had managed to accumulate a small fortune—more than seven thousand rubles—and at the end she decided to remain honest. She and Manya kept a sharp eye on everyone. Leah made no secret of her searchings. She peered into trunks, emptied wardrobes, went through piles of papers, shook out every article of apparel that belonged to the old man. The key was not to be found.

In the meanwhile the Moskat sons and sons-in-law, who were administrators of individual buildings, stopped turning the rents over to Koppel. It was a long-established custom for them to make an appearance at the old man's office on the Friday after the eighth of each month and turn in an accounting. At such times the writing-desk would be piled high with paper money, heaps of silver and coppers. Each of the administrators would present a list of those who were late in paying. Meshulam had never been known to evict any delinquent tenant, yet there was constant talk of evictions and legal action. Joel always had news of some bargain in real estate that could be got for next to nothing, and Meshulam would tell Koppel to make a note of the address and take a look at the property after the Sabbath.

Koppel went to the office every day. He sat at the desk, smoked cigarettes, read the newspapers, and yawned. The old retainers who collected a pension would come in, hat in hand, to ask respectfully how the boss was getting along. Koppel told them that things were no better. Yechiel Stein, the bookkeeper, had also taken to his bed; his daughter came around to complain that for two weeks now there hadn't been a grosz of wages and that there wasn't a copper for food for the sick man. To which Koppel answered: "If it were up to me you could have it," and let her know that he himself had not collected his salary either.

He got up from the chair, planted himself at the window, and looked down into the courtyard. Everything was falling apart with neglect. The stairways that led up to the upper floors were half-rotten. Panes were missing in windows, the holes covered with cardboard or stuffed with rags. The impoverished tenants, with no money for coal, burned up the lumber that belonged to Reb Meshulam. Koppel had said hundreds of times that the parasites ought to be thrown out, the building demolished, and a decent court of houses put up. But of late it had been impossible to persuade the old man to make any changes.

Yes, everything was different. When Koppel had become bailiff, Meshulam had carried on vast enterprises. The money poured in from all sides. Meshulam was constantly building, speculating on the Bourse, acquiring partnerships, and making investments. In those days Koppel was always on the move. He had traveled second-class, had stopped overnight at hotels, taken drinks with merchants—wealthy ones—and Polish gentry. Meshulam's sons had trembled before him; his daughters and daughters-in-law had flattered him. Traders and commission men had tried to win his favor with gifts. As a matter of fact it was from the money he had made in those days that Koppel had managed to acquire the two-story house in Praga where he now lived and to accumulate the thousands of rubles he had in the bank. In the old days he had hoped that he would be Meshulam's son-in-law one day. He had not given up hope even when Leah had been married off to the widower, that prayerhouse bench-warmer Moshe Gabriel.

Then, when he had turned seventy, Meshulam had pulled in his horns. He had liquidated most of his holdings and had held on only to the tenements. He had put his cash into the Imperial Bank in St. Petersburg, which paid a low rate of interest, and purchased stocks and bonds, which had never fluctuated over the years and which paid conservative dividends. According to Koppel's figuring, the old man should have been worth a round million, apart from what he had in his safe and the other treasures he had hidden away.

Koppel thought more than once that the common-sense thing would be to spit at the whole mess and go his own way. He could start some real-estate brokerage, or even live comfortably on what he had. His wife, Basha, was no spendthrift; out of the fifteen rubles a week he gave her for household expenses, she always had something left over. His children, Manyek, Shosha, Yppe, and Teibele, were growing up nicely and giving him no trouble. Manyek was studying at a commercial school. Shosha was a real beauty. Yppe, unfortunately, limped a bit; she had to wear a brace on her left leg, but a dowry was ready for her. Teibele was still a child. Yes, Koppel could afford to tell all the Moskats to go to the devil. Just the same, there were a lot of accounts he had to settle with them.

His feeling for Leah had not diminished over the years; instead, it had grown stronger. Leah already had a grown daughter. If Masha should get married, Leah might find herself a grandmother within the year. But in Koppel's eyes she was still a young girl. Whenever he saw her, with her high bosom and her rounded hips, the lace hem of her petticoat showing, desire for her would overwhelm him. She lived a life of perfect respectability, but Koppel knew well that she was straining at the leash. Moshe Gabriel was not the husband for her; only a few days before, she had said to Koppel: "I'll bring the thing to an end. It's only that I don't want to upset my father."

But to divorce his own wife and marry Leah, Koppel would need a lot of money. And to that end he would have to stay around the family. He had worked carefully for years to reach the point where the old man would name him executor in his will. He often imagined himself married to Leah and head of the family enterprises. He would ride in a carriage with rubber wheels; he would become an elder of the community council, go to the Sabbath services in the Great Synagogue. He would arrange matches for the Moskat grandchildren which would unite the big Polish Jewish fortunes. He would open his own bank, "The Bank of Moskat and Ber-

man." He would have a seat on the Bourse, be held in esteem
by the Governor-General, go about in a tall silk hat. He
would journey with Leah to take the waters at the fashionable
spas.

But nothing had gone the way Koppel had hoped. Meshulam's sudden illness was the finishing touch. It was clear that
the old man had not made out a will. Koppel would not get a
copper. Besides, Leah had begun to suspect that he wasn't so
powerful after all. She had said something to him about the
key to the safe and had hinted about being ready to make
some sort of arrangement with him. But Koppel had acted as
though he didn't understand her. "And I was under the impression that there was nothing you didn't know," Leah had
said. "I thought that Koppel Berman wasn't one of your ordinary people."

And Koppel had flushed and answered: "What did you expect me to be? A magician?"

4

Late one afternoon, as Koppel sat in the office smoking one
cigarette after another, the toe of his boot dislodged a lower
drawer of the desk. He opened it. Inside were some seals, a
bottle of India ink, a few tablets of sealing wax, gummed
paper, a hodge-podge of articles. At the back of the drawer
was a small jar. Koppel took the cover off. Inside was the key
to Meshulam's safe; Koppel recognized it by the deeply in-
dented notches and the wide shank. The shock was so great
that he even forgot to be surprised. It was a duplicate key, he
could tell; it had never been used. Koppel hefted it on the
palm of his hand. "They've probably cleaned the safe out by
now," he thought, "but I might as well take a look just the
same."

He put on his coat and derby, picked up his briefcase, and
went out. On the steps he lit a fresh cigarette. "The first thing
is to be calm," he reflected. "Otherwise it won't do." In the
courtyard the janitor's wife greeted him and said something
about the goose he had asked her to fatten up for him for the
Passover. Koppel told her the Passover was still a long way
off. "There's plenty of time," he said. "The bird can keep on
gorging."

He turned his steps toward the Gzhybov. The sun was setting. There was an early tang of spring in the air. At the end

of the square a horse had fallen and broken its leg, and a crowd had gathered around. In front of Meshulam's house the baker's girl was quarreling with a customer who insisted on pinching every roll before making her choice. The inner stairway was dark, the lamp still unlit. Koppel rang the bell and Manya answered, in her hand the inevitable deck of cards. She looked at him with her short-sighted slanting eyes.

"Oh, it's you. Koppel."

"Yes. What's the news around here? How's the old man?"

"May his enemies have it no better."

"Where's Naomi?"

"Went out."

That was good. Naomi had kept her eye on him during the last few days as though he were a thief. In order to fend off any possible suspicion of his intentions, Koppel began to banter Manya.

"So you're still laying out those cards?" he asked jocularly.

"What else is there to do?"

"They say if you're unlucky at cards you're lucky at love."

"I'm unlucky at both."

Koppel looked at her appraisingly. Manya wrapped her shawl tighter about her; she didn't fancy having anything to do with a married man.

"I'll put on the light," she remarked.

"Don't bother." He struck a match and lit a fresh cigarette. Manya went back to the kitchen. Koppel coughed softly. Apparently there was no one in the house except the sick man and the nurse. No lights showed from any of the rooms. He pushed open the door of the study. The window shades were half-drawn and the faint glow of the gas lamps shone in from the street. Bars of light raced across the ceiling and lost themselves in the room's dark corners. The door of the safe shone dully, like a black mirror. Koppel listened intently, holding his breath. He took the key out of his pocket. It was now or never. He tried to fit the key in the lock, but it wouldn't go in; it slipped aside and scraped loudly against the steel door. He wanted to strike a match, but he did not dare. All of his senses were wary. He felt around the keyhole with the tips of his fingers; it was stuffed up—with wax or putty. He took a penknife from his pocket and picked the keyhole clean. Then he inserted the key carefully. This time the key fitted. He turned it toward the right. The lock gave with a creaking sound, but the door still remained tight. He tugged hard and the door yielded. The safe must have been packed full, for even in the darkness he could see bundles of papers tumbling down, one after another, helter-skelter, like something in a dream. They were unmistakably banknotes. He could tell by the even size and the wrinkled edges.

From then everything went quickly. Koppel got down on his knees, unloosed the straps of his briefcase, spread it wide, and began to stuff the bundles of money inside. It was hardly a moment before the capacious case was full; he had to struggle to close it again. He stuffed banknotes into his breast pockets, his side pockets, and his trouser pockets. He picked up the briefcase, amazed at its weight; he had not thought that paper could be so heavy. While he was buckling the strap the steel tongue pricked his finger, deep under the fingernail. "I'll get myself a case of blood-poisoning," he thought. He put his finger in his mouth and began to suck it. "I mustn't leave a trace of blood." He felt like a murderer removing clues.

For a while he stood still, thinking he heard footsteps. With trembling hands he closed the door of the safe and locked it. He went out into the hallway. In the dimness he thought he saw the pale outline of a face.

"Manya," he called.

There was no answer. The shape melted away as though his voice had exorcized it. His words sounded hollow in his own ears. On the floor he saw a banknote. Could he have dropped it? He bent to pick it up, but it was only a faint patch of light reflected on the floor. "I'm getting nervous," he thought. He felt his temples throbbing and the sweat pouring out under his collar. He began to shuffle about noisily. He opened the door to Meshulam's room. A dim lamp glowed. The enormous shadow of a head wavered back and forth on the ceiling. The nurse in her white cap turned toward him and put a warning finger to her lips.

On the outside stairway the lights had not yet been turned on. He saw no one as he went out. "What's happened to them all," he wondered, "to leave the old man alone?" Disconnected phrases, long-forgotten Hebrew words, went through his mind. For a while he stood in indecision about which direction to turn, whether toward the Tvarda or the Gnoyna. He started to walk toward the Tvarda. He slipped and almost fell. A group of worshippers were coming out of a prayerhouse. A peddler was hawking Purim noise-makers. Was it already so close to the holiday, Koppel wondered. A droshky drove by and Koppel signaled it. Climbing in, he barked his knee on the step. He sat down and put the briefcase alongside him.

"Where to?" the driver asked, and Koppel, astonished, realized that he could not remember his own address.

"Over the Praga bridge," he said.

The driver scratched the back of his neck, snapped his whip, and wheeled the carriage around, the swiftness of the maneuver almost sending Koppel to the floor. Suddenly he remembered the putty that had been stuffed into the keyhole of the safe. Whose work was that? Naomi's! That's what would give him away. "I'm done for. I'm finished. There'll be an investigation and everything'll be discovered. Maybe I'd better jump out and run away. No, hold on to yourself. Don't lose your head."

In a lightning burst of comprehension it was clear to him that he had blundered. If he had at least had the sense to gather up the bits of putty and cram them back into the lock! Now it was too late. Naomi must have already come home and telephoned for the police. They'd be waiting for him at his house. They'd put him in chains. They'd take everything away from him. All of Warsaw would sneer at his fall. He'd rot away in prison. He felt a cold sweat all over him. Good-by to Koppel Berman, Meshulam Moskat's right hand, respectable Warsaw householder, the father of decent children. He was Koppel Berman the thief, fleeing in a droshky with the loot he had stolen. Even the driver knew it! What else could be the meaning of that queer way he was bending his shoulders and inclining his head? Somewhere in the distance he heard a policeman's whistle, long and quavering. They were after him already.

He closed his eyes and waited. This was the end, he thought. What would Leah say?

He felt a sharp pain in the finger he had pricked. The vein in it was pulsing. He opened his eyes and saw by the light of a street lamp a black spot on the fingernail. A flake of rust must have lodged there.

The droshky came to a sharp halt. A tramcar was rolling by. They were somewhere on Senatorska Street. A cold gust of wind was blowing from the Vistula. He had the feeling that he had suddenly been awakened from a heavy sleep.

5

As the droshky approached the Praga bridge Koppel's nerves quieted down. There was no one after him. Naomi had probably not yet returned to the flat, and nobody had noticed the crumbled bits of putty. It must have been the old man himself who had stuffed up the keyhole long before he took to his bed. And even if somebody did get suspicious, it would certainly be a long time before the police were called in. Koppel wiped the sweat from his forehead. He took a pack of cigarettes from his pocket and expertly lighted a match in the face of the wind that was blowing from across the Vistula. He leaned against the upholstered back rest of the carriage, stretched out his legs, placed the heavy briefcase on his lap, and closed his eyes.

There was a bedlam of noise on the bridge. Tramcars rumbled on, clanging their bells. Automobiles rolled along; heavily loaded trucks lumbered by. Draymen yelled and snapped their whips. The driver turned toward Koppel. "Where are we going to, boss?"

Koppel gave him the name of a street a block beyond his own house. The driver flicked his whip over the horse's flanks. Huge clouds, dark and red-tinted, moved swiftly across the sky, now and then revealing a sliver of moon. The droshky went past Koppel's house. Koppel glanced at the entrance; nobody was lurking there. He turned up his coat collar and pushed his hat down on his head so as not to be recognized by any neighbor who might be about. He noticed that in his own apartment only one curtained window was lighted; Bashele was still as sparing of fuel as she had been in the first years of their marriage, when he had earned ten rubles a week.

"Here we are, boss—whoa!" the driver said. Koppel climbed out, gave the man a half-ruble, and watched while the carriage drove off. Then he slowly walked home.

At the door of his own flat Koppel stood still for a moment, listening. He could hear Bashele moving about in the kitchen and humming to herself. Everything was all right. He went inside. The kitchen was warm. A fragrant odor arose from the steaming pots on the stove. Bashele was bent over the oven. Her figure still had something slim and girlish about it. She had a wide face, watery eyes, and a slight snub nose. She had been a servant when Koppel had married her, the daughter of a peddler. She knew nothing about Koppel's affairs. She was continually busy with cooking, baking, and hunting for bargains. Her only amusement was to gaze at the troupes of jugglers in the courtyard or to listen to the street singers. On Sabbath afternoons she went regularly to visit her sister in Old City. The neighborhood knew Bashele as a faithful wife and a devoted mother. When Koppel chose not to spend the night at home, he would tell her that he had to take a trip for his employer, and Bashele never asked for details. She did not even know that the house they lived in belonged to her husband; Koppel had told her that Meshulam had simply registered it in his name.

"It's a legal business," he had said to her. "Don't go talking about it." And she never breathed a word.

"My Koppel knows how to handle himself," she would say to the neighbors, "believe me."

When he came into the kitchen she was at the stove, her back to the door, but she knew it was he. She knew his step; she had recognized it as he climbed the stairs and she was aware that he had lingered a bit before he opened the door.

"Is it you, Koppel?" she said.

She turned toward him, and the pan she held in her hands almost fell to the floor.

"Dear Father in heaven, you're pale as wax. Worse than a corpse!"

"Who's pale? What are you babbling about?"

"Pale as chalk! Are you sick? Does something hurt you?"

"Nothing hurts me."

"What are you carrying in the briefcase? It's almost breaking at the seams."

Koppel started. "Has anyone been here?" he asked.

"Nobody. Who should come?"

"Where are the children?"

"Who knows? Running around somewhere, wearing out their shoes."

Koppel went into the dark living-room, the "large room" as the family called it. Without putting on a light he felt his way to his own room. It was here that he sat on the Sabbath to work on his accounts and brood about Leah. He lit a cigarette and then set fire to a taper to light the naphtha lamp. No matter how much Bashele tidied it, the room was always crowded. There was a pair of yellow riding boots that he had never worn; a fishing rod; a saddle; a collection of canes of all styles; three antique wall clocks, which, no matter how carefully they were regulated, never kept the same time. On a table lay a mandolin. On the walls hung a calendar and pictures of emperors, hunters, generals, and opera singers. The air smelled of tobacco and leather. Koppel closed and bolted the door. He opened the briefcase and looked at the banknotes with which it was stuffed. With shaking fingers he took the bundles of money out of his pockets. A single glance was enough to tell him that he had taken much more than he had thought. Most of the banknotes were tied with string or held by rubber bands. One such package was made up of hundred-ruble notes; there must have been close to five thousand rubles in that one alone.

"A treasure!" he murmured to himself.

His voice sounded strange in his own ears. He felt as though some presence were with him and watching him. The flame in the lamp flickered as though a gust of wind had disturbed it. The panes in the windows rattled. Koppel started to count the money, but he kept on losing count. He wanted to moisten his fingertips so that the banknotes would not rustle as he handled them, but his mouth was dry. He stood in the middle of the room and looked around. He ought to hide the money—quickly, as soon as possible. But where could he put it so that it wouldn't be found by anyone who might come searching for it? A trunk wouldn't do, nor the cornice of the stove. Not even the attic, where the Passover dishes and utensils were stored. Maybe he might be able to lift a plank from the floor and conceal it there. But that would be an old trick to the police.

He walked over to the mirror and studied his reflection. "Ah, you devil," he said to his image. "You thief." Bashele was right; he was pale as chalk. The hair on his head was wet with perspiration. I'll get sick yet, he thought. I'll ruin everything and everybody. Suddenly he heard the noisy banging of the outside door and the sound of quick steps. "They're coming after me! The police!" He rushed to the pile of money and stretched his arms out over it as though to protect it. Again he felt a burning pain in his finger. There was a loud knock at the door. "Who's there?" he shouted in Polish, but it was Bashele, come to tell him that his meal was ready.

"Why do you lock yourself in?" she asked through the door. "The noodles are getting cold."

CHAPTER TWO

1

Hadassah's disappearance set off an unceasing squabble between her father and mother. Nyunie gave up sleeping in the bedroom; the girl made a bed for him on the couch in the study. He would stay up late, reading a book that described how the earth had been torn away from the sun and cooled off; how the first living things had grown out of the slime and had gone through their generations, microbe fish, and ape, until man had been fashioned. In comparison with the thousands of millions of years since the solar system had shaped itself out of the cosmic fog, the years in which he, Nyunie Moskat, had been crawling over the face of the earth were no more than a droplet in an ocean of eternity. Where Warsaw was now, there might have been—who knew?—a sea. And in what were today deep abysses, some day great cities might arise. Even the stars and planets could not last forever; they flared up and then they died. The caldron of nature was eternally bubbling and eternally bringing forth new worlds, new species, new ways.

When Nyunie read these words he forgot for a while that he had a sick and disagreeable wife; that his only child had run off; that he had not heard from her for more than a fortnight; that his father was on his deathbed, and that he, Nyunie, had made nothing of his life. For years he had tried to tear himself away from Warsaw and the family and travel, see the world, learn something. But he had remained buried here in Panska Street. One day was like another; he got up, observed the morning ritual, ate breakfast, exchanged a few words with Moishele, his assistant administrator, about the rent collections—and before he knew it, it was night again and time to go to the Bialodrevna prayerhouse for the evening services. During the day, after his midday meal, he would sleep soundly, but at night he would toss and turn on his pillow, a welter of thoughts passing through his mind. Since Hadassah had gone, Dacha had adopted the habit of speaking in the wailing half-chant of an ancient crone. Every word she said to him was like a pointed barb. Nyunie saw more clearly than ever

186

that his father, together with the *shadchans,* had finished him off for good.

Not a wife—a plague, he thought. A cursed mistake.

In the study Nyunie at least did not have to look at Dacha's soured face and listen to her eternal complaints. He had stopped worrying about Hadassah. "She's smarter than I was," he decided. "If only I'd had her courage!" He made up his mind that as soon as he heard from her he would send her thirty rubles a month until she had finished her studies at the university. Who knew? Maybe he'd be able to manage a visit to Switzerland himself. What would be so wrong about putting on some of those Western clothes and going in for a little education? Didn't he, too, feel the pull of the wide, free world outside of Poland?

Dacha was not sleeping. She was sitting up in bed, her back against three feather pillows. She had more things to worry about than that idiot Nyunie, spending the night on the couch in his study. Nevertheless she felt affronted. He was not a man, he was a pig, she thought. "His wife gets sick and he runs away. All he's interested in is stuffing his belly." Maybe he was having something to do with women outside. Who could know? With a man—any man—there was no telling.

It was almost dawn when she dozed off. She awoke at about ten o'clock, more exhausted than when she had fallen asleep. The postman had brought nothing. The girl had disappeared like a stone thrown into a pond. What was the verse in Job? "Naked came I out of my mother's womb, and naked shall I return thither." Shifra brought in some tea with milk and a roll and butter, but Dacha only drank the warm beverage. She had no appetite. Nyunie had already left the house. Where the empty-headed fool wandered about during the day she had absolutely no idea. He had probably made up with that other fine specimen, that brother-in-law of his, Abram. At noon Dacha was supposed to be at Dr. Mintz's office. He was giving her some sort of electrical treatment and injections of strychnine. He had told her that if she did not watch out for herself she was likely to be in great danger.

"It's not the daughter that bothers me," Dr. Mintz had said. "It's the mother I'm worried about."

Shifra stayed home alone. She put the afternoon meal on the stove—a piece of beef for herself, a quarter of a fowl for her mistress—and went into the living-room. She sat down, wrapped herself in her shawl, and warmed herself in the rays of the winter sun that shone in through the windows. She pulled her skirts high above her knees to get the warmth of the sun on her thighs, and opened the neck of her blouse, as she had seen the daughters of wealthy families do at their country places. Hadassah's flight had communicated something of a dissolute feeling to Shifra. If girls like that could ape the manners of the gentiles, then why could not she, for all that she was no more than a servant? The telephone rang and she got up to answer it. The call was for her, from someone she had recently met, Itchele, a drayman. He wanted to take her to the theater on Saturday night. Shifra smiled coyly into the mirror on the wall near the telephone.

"Why do you want to take me?" she asked flirtatiously. "Is it because I'm so good-looking?"

"You know why."

"Go on! You're not interested in me," Shifra insisted, feeling she was carrying on a spicy adventure. "It's that girl in Praga you're interested in."

"I forgot her long ago."

Shifra had her doubts whether it paid to have anything to do with this latest conquest of hers. It wasn't that he didn't earn a living, but people talked about him. It was said that a girl he was supposed to marry had broken off the engagement and that he hung around with the loafers on the Krochmalna. She had no faith in these smooth-tongued fellows with their polished boots and roving eyes. It mightn't do any harm to go to the pictures with birds of this kind, or to accept a treat at one of the delicatessens. But when it came to marriage, a girl had to keep her eyes open for someone settled.

Itchele wanted to keep on talking, but Shifra heard a ring at the outside door. She hung up the receiver and went to answer.

"Who's there?" she called.

"The police," came the answer.

Shifra's limbs shook. Maybe Itchele had done something. She opened the door a crack and saw a short, stout officer in a silver-gray uniform, wearing a peaked hat and with epaulets on his shoulders. She opened the door all the way and then shrieked. Hadassah was there. The girl was haggard-looking. Her coat was torn, she was wearing no hat, and her hair was disheveled. She was carrying a clumsy paper-wrapped package under her arm. She looked timid and afraid, like a provincial servant girl. Shifra's hands shot up to her livid cheeks.

"Is this where Nahum Leib Moskat lives?" the officer asked, reading the name from a slip of paper.

"Yes—here."

"Where is he?"

"He's not home now."

"His wife?"

"She's out"

"Do you know this girl?" The officer indicated Hadassah, almost poking her breast with his gloved hand.

"My God, it's my young mistress!" Shifra exclaimed.

"What's her name?"

"Hadassah."

"Ga-da-sa," the officer repeated, giving the name a Russian pronunciation. "When's your boss coming home?"

"I don't know. Sometime tonight."

"Who are you?"

"The maid."

"*Da.* I'll be back tomorrow at nine. And you—" he turned to Hadassah—"you don't leave this house, do you hear? *Do svedania.*"

The officer smartly brought his hand to the hilt of his sword, then raised two fingers halfway to the peak of his hat, and went down the stairs. Shifra started to wring her hands and move her lips, but it was a few moments before anything coherent came from her.

"Dear Father in heaven," she finally burst out, "what do my eyes see? What are you standing there like that for?"

Hadassah looked hesitantly after the retreating officer and then went into the entry hall. There was something frozen and stiff in her gait. She went into her room, Shifra following her. She stood motionless near the door, still clutching the bundle. Her eyes, which seemed to have shrunk in their sockets, were fixed straight ahead.

"Dear God, what happened?" Shifra moaned. Hadassah made no answer. "Maybe you'd like to wash." Hadassah looked at her strangely.

"No. Not now," she answered.

A chill flowed along Shifra's bones. She went into the living-room and pressed close to the tiled stove. "*Oi, gevald,*" she kept murmuring. "Wait till they come home—it'll be worse than Yom Kippur."

When she went back to Hadassah's room the girl was stretched out on the bed, her coat still on. Her head was turned to the wall. She made no sound; Shifra could not tell whether she was awake or asleep. The soles of her shoes were torn, her stockings ripped. The bundle, now open, was on the table. Shifra could see what it contained: a single garter, a broken comb, and a lump of black bread. Shifra stared at the objects. That kind of bread she had not seen in these parts, not even in the fare the soldiers ate. It looked heavy, half raw, doughy, full of bran. A lump rose in her throat. That was the kind of loaf they gave to inmates of jails.

2

It was about four o'clock when Dacha got back home. She rang the bell and waited for a long time before she heard Shifra's voice.

"Who is it?"

"Me."

The girl opened the door slowly.

"Mistress, there's a letter from Hadassah," she said after some hesitation.

"A letter! When did it come? Give it to me!"

"It's in Hadassah's room."

Dacha walked through the hallway and opened the door. Hadassah had started up and was sitting huddled over on the edge of the bed, her head bent down. There was a flush on that side of her face which had been resting on the pillow. When Dacha came in she made a move as though to get off the bed, but fell back. Dacha's face flamed red, as though in anger.

"So," she said at last. "You're alive."

Hadassah made no answer.

"Well, if you're here, you're here," Dacha continued in a harsh voice, surprised at what she herself was saying. She glanced back over her shoulder and saw Shifra standing at the open door. She closed the door with a bang. She had a desire to throw her arms around the girl and at the same time to seize her by the hair.

"When did you come?" she demanded.

Again Hadassah was silent.

"Have you gone dumb—or what?"

"I came today—before—"

"God help you, the way you look! That I should have lived to see this day," Dacha said in a half-chant. It was as though her dead mother, the pious wife of the Krostinin rabbi, was speaking through her lips.

For a long time she stared at her daughter. Hadassah's coat

was filthy. Two buttons had been torn away; some of the cloth
with them. The upper part of her dress was ripped. Her hair
was matted. Dacha's gaze fell on the bundle.

"What kind of bread is that?" she asked.

"Bread." Hadassah only repeated the word.

"All right. I can see that."

Dacha went out, slamming the door behind her. Shifra was
still outside.

"When did she come? How did she get here?"

"A police officer brought her."

"Police officer? That means she's been in prison."

"That's how it looks."

"What did he say?"

"He's coming back tomorrow morning, at nine o'clock."

"Who else was here?"

"The janitor was on the steps, with his wife."

"And all the neighbors ran to get a look."

"I suppose so."

"There's nothing to hide any more. Let the whole world
know my shame." There was a glare in Dacha's eyes. "She's
not long for this world, anyway."

"Please, mistress, don't say it."

"Quiet! Get a bath ready. She's filthy. Don't let anybody
in."

"The telephone's ringing."

"Don't answer it."

Shifra went into the bathroom to heat the water. Dacha
went into the living-room. She began to pace swiftly back and
forth, her hands folded over her breasts. Her fatigue had vanished; suddenly she felt strong. She stumbled against a low
stool and sent it out of the way with a kick of her foot. Unexpected broken words came to her lips: "Funeral . . . hospital
. . . pregnant . . . bastard. . . ." Louder she said: "And that
idiot, away all day, God knows where." She had an urge to
shout at the top of her voice, to pour out floods of curses. The
telephone rang again. She went over and answered it.

"Who is it?"

"Dacha darling, it's me, Abram."

"What do you want?"

"Dacha, please, listen to me. It's about Hadassah. It's important."

"Nothing's important any more. You've killed her. You can
forget she was ever alive."

"Listen to me, I tell you. I've received a postcard—"

"What kind of postcard! You murderer, you thief, you outlaw!"

"Excuse me, Dacha, but you talk like a market woman."

"May you be cursed the way you've brought curses on us! May your daughters come to the same end as my daughter! You Satan, you murderer!" She threw the receiver down; the instrument clattered to the floor.

Shifra came in. "Mistress," she said, "I've got the stove burning."

"Let everything burn! Fill the tub with water. Have you got some green soap?"

"Yes, mistress."

"Get an empty sack. Put all her clothes in it. Throw them into the garbage."

Dacha went back to Hadassah's room. The girl had taken off her coat, revealing the soiled dress she was wearing underneath. Her throat was thin and gaunt, flecked with brown and blue marks. She was standing by the dresser; when her mother came in she took a startled step backwards. Dacha snatched up the lump of bread from the table and weighed it in the palm of her hand.

"Heavy as stone."

Hadassah did not move.

"What are you standing there like a dummy for? What are you staring for? Where were you? Tell me. What miserable holes have you been in? Who ripped your dress?"

"Nobody."

"Where is he? Where has he gone? What's he done to you? I'll shout it from the rooftops."

"Mamma!"

"I'm not your mother! I blot you out, do you hear? What's he done to you? Tell me the truth!"

"Mamma!"

"We'll have to know what to tell the doctor. Maybe it won't be too late. Ah, dear God."

"I don't need a doctor."

"What do you need, then? A midwife?"

Shifra came to the door. "Mistress," she said, "the water's ready."

"Come on! At least we can get the lice off you."

"I can do it myself."

"Ashamed, are you? Creatures like you haven't got anything left to be ashamed for."

Dacha's face turned a greenish hue. Her eyes flamed, her

lips quivered. Her curved nose looked menacing. She grabbed Hadassah's shoulders with both hands and pushed her along.

"Come on, I'm telling you!" she shrieked. "Come on, you shameless animal!"

Hadassah let herself be pushed along. "I'm not living. I'm dead," she thought. "They're going to wash the corpse." She let her mother pull her clothes off her, the dress, the petticoat, the shirt and drawers and stockings. Shifra stuffed them into the sack and turned on the water taps. While the tub was filling, Hadassah stood motionless on the stone floor, her teeth chattering. She bent her head and closed her eyes. Over and over she kept telling herself that she was dead, nothing could harm her any more; she need no longer feel any shame.

3

Dr. Mintz, who had come in answer to Dacha's telephone call, looked at Hadassah for a long time. He listened to her heart and lungs, and held her wrist with his stubby fingers, gazing at his watch. After much hemming and hawing he announced that Hadassah would have to go back to the sanatorium. But she was not to be moved for another week or two. In the meanwhile no visitors were to be permitted; she was to have complete rest.

The short, big-boned doctor, with his enormous head and thick mustaches, snatched up his bag, put on his overcoat with the heavy fur collar and lapels and his plush hat with the professorial broad brim.

"The principal thing," he said, "is to ask no questions and make no accusations."

"Doctor, promise me that she'll be all right."

"I'm not God almighty and I'm not one of your miracle rabbis. We'll do what we can."

He went down a half flight of steps and stopped to rest. He had a bad heart himself.

Near his carriage stood a group of women with shawls over their heads. They clustered around him, complaining about their aches and pains and their various female ills. Dr. Mintz waved his umbrella at them.

"Leave me alone! Idiots! I'm sicker than you are," he shouted, stamping his foot. "You're not dying yet, none of you!"

He heaved himself into the carriage, sat down, leaned

against the back rest, and took a pencil and a small notebook out of his pocket. He made a note in the queer handwriting that only he himself could decipher, a reminder to speak to someone in the government about Asa Heshel, who must be rotting away in some stinking jail. He had been a poor devil of a Chassidic student himself once, and he had also had a love affair with the daughter of a wealthy house. Who would ever have dreamed in those days that she would grow up to be the shrew she was now! Hadassah wouldn't last long. Too bad.

Hadassah was left alone in her room. How strange, yet how familiar, this warmth and comfort, this lean body, this white silk nightgown she was wearing; the spotless bed sheets, the glowing stove warming the room; the landscapes and portraits looking down at her from the walls! On the small night-table were slices of orange, a bowl of cereal, a cup of cocoa. There were no bedbugs here; there were no prison matrons to paw her. Could it be true? Yes, she could die peacefully at last in her own bed.

She closed her eyes and then opened them again. How many days had gone by since she had returned home? She slept whole days through, but she was still tired. The time seemed to rush by so quickly. It was day and night and then day again. She heard the clock strike three and then, a moment after, it seemed, she heard it ring nine. Her dreams had a nightmarish quality. She imagined herself flying like a bat, and then falling precipitately through space like a stone. Shadowy forms whispered to her, speaking in a coarse mixture of Russian, Polish, and Yiddish. Abram and Asa Heshel seemed to be merged into a single dual-faced image. Her father and Dr. Mintz fused and separated. She seemed to be traveling abroad, but the borders kept receding ever farther away, then coming closer and changing form, appearing first like a mountain, then like a river. Her mother opened the door, looked in, and said:

"Cover yourself, my child. You'll catch cold."

"When is Purim?"

"What a question! God willing, next week."

"How is my Uncle Abram?"

"The devil knows and the devil cares!"

"How is Grandfather?"

"May his enemies have it no better."

Hadassah wanted to ask if anything had been heard of Asa Heshel, but she refrained. She turned to the wall and dozed

off. She had a queer feeling that her head was growing enormous, inflated with air, like a balloon, and that her fingers
were growing huge and thick. She started up. It must have
been dark outside, for the lamps were lit. Her mother, her
shoulders bowed, and in a long black dress, was holding a
thermometer.

"Just the same; no change," she said, as though to herself.

"Mamma, what time is it?"

"It's ten o'clock."

"Is it still today?"

"What, did you think it was yesterday? Here, take your medicine."

"She's awake?" She heard her father's voice and saw him
come into the room. It seemed to Hadassah that he had got
smaller. He looked at her and smiled. "A fine criminal" she
heard him say.

She must have fallen asleep again, because when she was
next aware of her surroundings the room was in total blackness. She could not remember where she was. She sat up in
bed, putting both her hands to her forehead. "Yes, I'm in prison. Everything is lost!" She held her breath and listened intently. Where had all the other women gone? She could not
hear a single sound. Had they died or had they all been set
free? She put her hand out. Her fingers touched a glass. She
lifted it and brought it to her lips. It was tea, cold and sweet-
ened, with some lemon in it. She drank down the cool
smoothness of the liquid, her dry palate sucking in the taste of
the lemon. All at once every detail of what had happened
came flooding back to her: how she had met Asa Heshel at
the Muranover railroad station; the trip in the third-class car
to Reivitz; the night in the cold station among the Ukrainian
peasants; the ride in a cart to Krasnostav; the inn crowded
with coachmen, commissionairies, Chassidim; the long journey to Kreshev and the wait at the water-mill for the gentile,
the dark one, who was to take them across the border to Austria. The name of the village was Boyari, she remembered.
Asa Heshel had not shaved. He had climbed to the hayloft
and read. A peasant had brought the news that the guard had
been changed at the border and it would be necessary to bribe
the new one all over again. Then the long walk in the dead of
night to the frozen river San. The man who led them told
them it was only half a mile, but the journey had taken weary
hours of plodding. They had crawled through frozen fields,
forests, marshes. It had rained and she had become soaked

The wind had blown Asa Heshel's hat away. She had lost one of her galoshes. Dogs barked. Someone had flashed a lantern and then it had become pitch dark again. Then suddenly they had heard shouts and shots. They had thrown themselves down on the ground. Asa Heshel had called her name. A soldier had grabbed her and hauled her off to a sentry booth, where another soldier was waiting with a bayonet. She had wept and pleaded with them to let her go, but they had stared stonily at her and said: "The law is the law."

She had been taken under guard to Yanov, then to Zamosc, Izbitsa, Lublin, Piask, Pulavy, Ivangorod, Zhelabov, and Garvolin. In Yanov she had shared a cell with a murderess. The woman told her that she had cut her mother-in-law's head off with a sickle. In other towns she had been thrown into cells with thieves and prostitutes. She had made the acquaintance of a political prisoner, a girl from Zamosc. In Warsaw she had been kept for a night in the Seventh Commissariat. The next morning they had brought her to the Fourth Commissariat, and from there the police officer had brought her home.

Now, in the darkness, she remembered everything. Their plan to flee to Switzerland had failed. Asa Heshel was lost somewhere. She was dangerously sick, she was disgraced. No, there was no point in staying alive. She had only one prayer to God: to take her quickly, now. She relaxed her limbs and tried to imagine her life slipping away from her. In her mind she said good-by to her mother, her father, Abram, and Asa Heshel. Was he alive or dead? She did not know.

CHAPTER THREE

1

It was the Moskat family custom to celebrate the Purim festival at Meshulam's home, where sons, daughters, in-laws, and grandchildren would gather for the feast. This year, although the old man lay ill, the custom was not broken. Naomi and Manya busied themselves baking cookies, tarts, and strudel, as well as preparing the traditional holiday chick peas and flat cakes. Nathan read the Book of Esther out loud. For the feast, which came in the late afternoon, Rosa Frumetl lit two stubby candles. Manya lowered the large chandelier from the ceiling and put a flame to the wick. It was at first expected that Meshulam would keep to his bed throughout the celebration, but the old man let it be known by unmistakable gestures that he intended to preside at the family feast. He was dressed and brought into the dining-room in a wheelchair. In the candlelight his face was as yellow as the saffron sprinkled on the pleated Purim loaf. The sick man was wearing an embroidered silk sleeping-robe. There was a velvet skullcap on his head. A shawl covered his lap to protect him from a chill. He rested his slippered feet on a small hassock. Nathan brought over a basin of water and a copper dipper; Joel poured the water over his father's hands and dried them with a towel. Naomi and Manya served carp in sweet-and-sour sauce, soup, meatballs with a raisin sauce, and a compote of apricots. There were *hamantashn*, the triangular, poppy-seed-filled pastries, almonds, walnuts, and preserves. There were wine, vishniak, and mead. Starting at noon, messengers began to come, bearing Purim gifts from relatives, kinsfolk, and friends. Rosa Frumetl and Naomi watched to see that each received a suitable reward and that appropriate gifts were returned to each sender. Meshulam sat at the head of the table, staring before him. He heard and understood everything, but his tongue seemed to be stuck to the roof of his mouth, and he felt a reluctance to emit unintelligible sounds or make motions with his head. He could see that Pinnie had his sleeve in the fish gravy, and that Joel's grandson, a boy of four, was stuffing himself with fruit and candy. He would overeat and spoil his little stomach, the old man thought. He would have liked to be able to say: "Hey, you, you rogue, enough!"

There was a constant procession of beggars, poor folk, and youngsters in holiday masks. Rosa Frumetl had provided twenty-five rubles in small coins. She had stacked the piles of change on a plate in front of her. She doled the money out to the young boys from the near-by yeshivah, the emissaries from the charitable organizations, soup kitchens, and orphanages, and the mendicants "in business for themselves." These came in arrogantly, ready to argue vehemently if the gift was below their expectations. They would throw Meshulam a contemptuous glance, which seemed to say he was meeting the just end of those who denied the humble their due. The Purim players came in singing. They wore cotton beards and tall paper hats with Stars of David pasted on them. Their excited eyes gleamed behind the slits of their masks. Some were girded with swords and daggers of cardboard. They sang, shuffled about in awkward dance steps, and made thrusts at each other with their sabers. One group of youngsters enacted a play about King Ahasuerus and Queen Esther. When Meshulam had been well, he had paid the players their fee and chased them out; he had had no patience with these carryings-on. Besides there were petty thieves among these Purim invaders. But now there was no one to protest. Ahasuerus stood with his long black beard, a paper crown on his head. He waved his golden scepter toward Queen Esther. Two executioners went through the motions of beheading Queen Vashti, who wore horns and from beneath whose dress a pair of boy's boots stuck out. Haman, with enormous black mustaches and a triangular hat, paid homage to Mordecai, while Zeresh, his wife, emptied a chamberpot over his head. Meshulam could hear the voices of the players, but could not make any sense out of their babblings. The others were laughing, giggling, and clapping their hands. Nathan was howling in glee, his belly heaving up and down, coughing and spluttering in ecstasy. Saltsha ran over to shake him and thump his back. Meshulam's eyes looked at them all contemptuously.

"A pack of fools! Idiots!" he thought.

He regretted everything now: that he had twice married daughters of undistinguished families and spawned children of no accomplishments; that he had not been more discriminating in the choice of sons-in-law; that he had made such a fool of himself as to marry for a third time; and especially that he had not made out a detailed will, with an executor and a seal, leaving a substantial part of his wealth to charity. Now it was too late. They would dissipate his fortune, every grosz of it. They would quarrel and tear at one another. Koppel would steal all he could. Abram would swindle the lot of them. Hama would be left penniless. They had told him that Hadassah had come back, but he didn't understand the whole thing clearly. Where had she come back from? What had happened to the one she had gone away with? How would they be able to marry her off, now that she had disgraced herself? He remembered a passage from Ecclesiastes: "All is vanity and vexation of spirit." He raised his eyes and looked toward the window. The sun had gone down, but the sky was still bright with sun-drenched clouds. They looked like fiery sailing ships, flaming brooms, purple windows, strange creatures. A wide patch of luminescence seethed and bubbled in the center, yellow and green, like boiling sulphur, reminding him of the fiery river in which his own soul would have to be cleansed. A hand made out of light, mist, and space was weaving and darting, making intricate patterns, writing some secret message. But what it all meant no ordinary son of man could hope to understand. Would he, Meshulam Moskat, at least find the truth of things at the other side?

"Your health, Father! May it soon be restored to you!" It was Joel speaking, raising a glass of wine to his lips.

Meshulam made no movement. What was he sopping it up for, the glutton? Wasn't his belly big enough?

Meshulam grimaced and made motions with his head, Naomi and Pinnie wheeled him back into the bedroom. They lifted him onto the bed and pulled the blanket over him. He lay awake for a long time, watching the twilight deepening. The clouds had scattered; only small puffs remained in the sky. Stars began to appear. From behind the spires of the church on the other side of the street, which still reflected the glow of the setting sun, a yellow moon swam into the heavens. Meshulam, as when he was a boy, still saw in the moon's pale face the features of Joshua. What did the affairs of the world mean to him now? He had only one desire, to see the splendors of the higher worlds that, iridescent with secret illumination, hovered over the roofs of the Gzhybov.

2

In the earlier years Abram had been in the habit of celebrating the Purim evening at Meshulam's house. Since his quarrel with his father-in-law Abram had held the holiday observance in his own home. Hama and Bella would bake honey cake and *hamantashn*. His in-laws would come late in the evening after the celebration at the old man's house, half-drunk and singing, and would stay until late in the night. The women and girls danced with one another. The men drank beer. Abram would put on an old dress of Hama's, a discarded matron's wig, and a blouse stuffed with a pillow, and would make believe he was a wife who had come to the rabbi to settle a dispute with her husband. He would squeak in a high falsetto voice that Nyunie, the husband, the good-for-nothing, did not make a living and spent all his time in the Chassidic prayerhouse. Besides he was always sticking his fingers into the pots on the stove. Abram would pull up his sleeves.

"Rabbi! I'm the mother of eight children! Just look at the way he's pinched me black and blue!"

"Feh! Shame on you. Cover your arms! Wanton!" Pinnie, in the role of the rabbi, would shout.

"Rabbi, my crown! Go on, take a look, it won't harm you. You're too old anyway."

They would go through the same masquerade every Purim, year after year, but it never failed to send the women into peals of laughter. They would fall into one another's arms, shrieking with delight. And the next month the tenant on the floor below would refuse to pay rent on the grounds that all the jumping about had broken the plaster on the ceiling.

Or there would be another performance. Abram would be possessed of a dybbuk and would be brought to Pinnie, the rabbi, to be exorcized. Pinnie would ask him what sins he had committed in his lifetime. And Abram would answer mournfully:

"Ai, rabbi, what sins have I not committed?"

"Did you eat forbidden meat?" Pinnie would ask sternly.

"Only when it was tasty."

"Did you carry on with women?"

"What else? With men?"

"Did you fast on Yom Kippur?"

"All I had was some pork between meals."

"And after that?"

"I took a ride over to the rabbi's married daughter's."

"What did you do there?"

"The rabbi was in *shul,* so I blew out the candles and we recited the Psalms."

"In the dark?"

"I knew them by heart."

The women would blush and giggle. Joel's face would become as red as a beet. He would emit one loud "Ha!" and the cigar would fall from his open mouth.

Year in, year out, Pinnie preached the same mock sermon. He demonstrated that the Biblical Mordecai was in reality a Warsaw Chassid. Haman was really Rasputin. Vashti was the Czarina, Esther was an opera singer and Abram's protégé. With nimble casuistry he so twisted the Biblical passages as to prove that Mordecai must have been a herring dealer. The women howled at Pinnie's gesticulations and his thin piping voice. Late at night they would sit down to another feast of chick peas, mead, cold meats, and horseradish. Then they would go home, laughing and talking noisily, knocking at the doors of neighboring apartments and waking up children. In the courtyard Nathan would sing a Purim song, and dance with the janitor. It had once happened that Nyunie had gone out on the balcony and emptied a jug of beer. A passing policeman had got his hat drenched. He had come upstairs ready to arrest the lot of them. They had had to slip something into his palm to quiet him.

But this year, with Hama gone, Abram's flat was deserted. Late in the afternoon he went down, bought a bottle of wine and a bouquet of flowers, and then took a droshky to Ida's. The daughter of a pious and well-to-do family, Ida had been used to joyous Purim celebrations. But now she, too, was alone. Zosia had gone to visit a friend. Ida sat reading a book. When Abram came in she did not raise her head.

"A good Purim to you," Abram said. "Why are you so gloomy? It's a holiday."

"A fat lot the holiday means to us," Ida answered.

During the years since Ida had left her husband she and Abram had separated more than once. Her friends had warned her that the man was a fraud. Leon Prager, her husband, had never given up hope that Abram would disappear from the picture and that Ida would come back to him. The child, Pepi, who had been three years old when her parents separated, had no real place to call home. Sometimes she was with her mother in Warsaw, sometimes with her father in Lodz, or with her grandmother, or in a boarding-school. There had been times when Ida had left Warsaw, sending Abram long letters of farewell and pleading with him to leave her alone. But he always managed to get her back. Abram would dispatch letters and telegrams or follow her to the resorts where she had fled for refuge. Ida swore that Abram had cast a spell over her. There was no peace for them either together or apart.

Meshulam compared the two to a dog and a bitch stuck together.

3

It was close to noon the next day when Abram left Ida. He decided to take a tramcar instead of a droshky; he had only three rubles in his purse, and he did not know where he might be able to borrow any more. But the moment he emerged from the courtyard a droshky rolled up. He got in and told the driver to take him to the Zlota. He lit a cigar. A spring sun was shining; rivulets of water ran along the gutters. A mild breeze blew from the Praga woods. When the droshky crossed the bridge, Abram could see that the ice on the Vistula was breaking up. As Abram looked at the icy flocks it seemed to him that the bridge was speeding along. The Warsaw side had even more of a springtime look about it. King Zygismund stood on his tall pedestal waving his bronze sword. The sculptured mermaids drank thirstily from their empty goblets. Columns of soldiers stood in formation in front of the castle. A military band was blaring. Officers called out commands in piercing voices. A Catholic funeral wound its way through the crowd that had gathered to watch the drill, the coffin covered with wreaths.

"A fine time to die," Abram reflected. "When everything is coming back to new life."

The droshky stopped near his apartment. Abram got out and went upstairs. He went into his bedroom, lay down on the bed, and dozed off. Through his heavy sleep he heard the outside door open. He struggled to his feet. Hama came in. He stared at her. Her face was a greenish hue, deep bags stood out under her eyes. There was an angry red blotch on one cheek, as though she had been slapped. She started to say something, but no sound issued from her lips. Then she began to sob: "He's dead! Father's dead!"

Abram's jaw fell. "Where? When?"

She swayed as though she were about to fall. Abram rushed over and held her.

"All right, enough crying," he muttered. "He was an old man."

"He was my father." Hama broke out into a fresh flood of wailing. "Dear God, what will become of me now! I'm alone in the world! Like a stone."

"Hama, quiet yourself. Here, sit down."

"What good will anything do me? Dear God, if only I were lying there with him!"

Abram got her into a chair. He paced back and forth across the room. "Yes," he said. "That's the way it is. Everything has an end."

Hama blew her nose. "And you—you quarreled with him," she wept. "And now he's there, stretched out with his feet toward the door."

"May God punish me if I was ever his enemy."

"Dear Lord, what'll I do now? I'm alone!"

"Foolish woman! You'll be rich! What nonsense are you

talking? You'll have houses and a couple of hundred thousand in cash besides."

"I don't want it! I don't want anything! If I were only lying there beside him!"

"What are you talking about? You've got daughters to marry off."

"What's my life? Nothing! Worse than a dog's." Suddenly she tore from the chair. "Abram! You've shamed me enough!" she howled. "Enough of it! It's got to come to an end!"

She made a motion as though to throw herself at him. Abram took a step backwards.

"I don't know what you want," he muttered, half afraid.

"Abram! I can't go on this way! Kill me, beat me, tear pieces of flesh off me, but don't leave me alone!" She stretched out her hands to him. "For God's sake, have pity on me!"

Now she was sobbing with convulsive spasms. Then, unexpectedly, she cast herself down on the floor and threw her arms around his legs, almost throwing him off his feet.

"Hama, for God's sake, what are you doing!"

"Abram, please, I beg, I plead! Let's start again—I can't stand it."

"Get up!"

"Let it be a decent home again. Let the children know what it is to have a father."

Abram felt a wave of heat rise to his face. Tears began to pour from his eyes.

"All right, all right."

"And you'll come to the funeral?"

"Yes. Get up from the floor."

"Oh, Abram, I love you, you know it. I love you."

He bent down and helped her up. She held on to him. He felt her tears moisten his face. There was a strange warmth exuding from her. Abram suddenly felt a long-forgotten desire toward this broken woman, the mother of his children. He bent his head and kissed her brow, her cheeks, her chin. It was suddenly lightning-clear to him that there could be no talk of divorcing her, whatever might be the consequences. They would have to finish what was left of their life together, especially now that the old man was dead and that a royal inheritance would be her portion.

4

The funeral of Meshulam Moskat was not held until two days after he had passed away, although it was the Jewish custom to perform the final rites on the day of death. The reason for the delay was that the officers of the Jewish community insisted on canceling the purchase through which, by virtue of payment of two thousand rubles, Reb Meshulam had acquired possession of a double burial plot in the Gensha cemetery. The officials of the burial association complained that Meshulam had tricked them out of the plot for a trifle and, according to the Talmud, a mistake annuls an agreement. They demanded now that the heirs pay an additional ten thousand rubles.

Joel flew into such a rage that he made wild threats: he would sue them, he would have them arrested; but the officials laughed at him.

"Let him go ahead," they said. "If that's what he wants, it's all right with us."

After much wrangling a compromise was reached; the family agreed to pay an additional three thousand rubles. The quarreling and negotiating lasted for more than a day; all of Warsaw's Chassidic circles discussed the affair. A large crowd stood in front of the community building. Every once in a while a droshky would drive up and an elder or some other important official would descend. The people in the crowd would shrug their shoulders.

"No, it doesn't pay to be a millionaire!"

"The way I look at it, when something's sold it's sold."

"A decent man doesn't try to find a bargain at the kehillah."

When the affair with the kehillah was settled, a dispatch came from Bialodrevna that the rabbi was at once boarding a train and that the funeral should be held up until his arrival. In all the excitement the family had forgotten to inform him of Meshulam's death. This meant another delay.

During the time the body lay at the Moskat apartment, the house was a bedlam. Naomi and Manya did what they could to keep out strangers, but the curious almost tore the doors down from their hinges. The corpse lay on the floor of the living-room, in a black shroud, and resting on scattered straw, two candles in silver candleholders burning at its head. The mirror was covered and the windows half-opened. Vigil-keepers from the organization, "Watchers of the Dead," sat on low stools chanting the Psalms. Those who had ever had a difference with him came to ask the dead man's pardon. Against the black shroud Meshulam's head seemed small, almost like a child's. Rosa Frumetl went about weeping and sniffling. She had taken off her matron's wig and wore a shawl over her close-cropped head. Adele stayed in her room. The old man's sons, daughters, in-laws, and grandchildren kept wandering in and out of the flat. The safe in the study had been sealed. The family kept a wary eye open to see that nothing was stolen by the hordes of visitors.

"Look at the mob," Naomi complained. "A person would imagine someone sent for them."

"It'll be impossible to clean up after that bunch," Manya commented. "A gang of nobodies!"

When word got about that the Bialodrevna rabbi was on his way to the funeral, the Gzhybov became black with people, surging back and forth like a sea. The tramcars could not force their way through the Gzhybov and detoured along the Mirovska off in the direction of the Jewish hospital. A disgruntled passenger shrugged his shoulders. "What is this? Palestine?"

In addition to the Bialodrevna rabbi, other Chassidic rabbis came to the funeral—the Novominsker, the Amshinover, the Kozhenitzer. Akiba, who had only shortly before divorced Gina, was in a carriage with his father, the Sentsimin rabbi. He was sitting on a cushion he had brought along with him, to make sure that his person would have no contact with the linsey-woolsey material of the upholstery, a cloth mixture forbidden by the Mosaic law. Policemen were on hand to keep the crowds in order. They shouted at the tops of their voices and laid about them with the sheaths of their swords. Some of the Talmud Torahs to which the dead man had made contributions sent their pupils to march at the head of the procession. Women wept as though the dead man had been a close relative. Most of the storekeepers on the Gzhybov had closed their shops. Because a funeral of this size would demand a lot of droshkies, coachmen from all parts of Warsaw descended on the neighborhood. A couple of doddering ancients complained to each other that the dead man had not deserved these honors.

At around two o'clock the hearse began to move. The horses, draped in black cloth, with holes cut out for the eyes, paced slowly. The carriages stretched along the whole length of the Gzhybov, the Tvarda, the Krochmalna, and the Gnoyna. The horses reared and neighed. Young boys tried to catch a ride on the sides of the coaches, but were treated to a lash of the whip. There was no event the Jews of Warsaw enjoyed so much as a grand funeral. Long before the hearse reached the cemetery a mob was waiting. Youngsters were perched on tombstones to get a better view. Every balcony along the Gensha was packed. Cemetery attendants in caps with shiny peaks and coats with polished metal buttons were carrying planks of wood and shovels. Beggars and cripples besieged the gates and the path to the burial plot. The spectators from the balconies and windows were afraid that the crowd pressing forward in the cemetery would overturn the hearse, or that some of the rabble would be pushed into the open grave. But Warsaw's Jews were used to handling themselves in mobs like this. For all the confusion, everything went along according to law and custom. The corpse was prepared for the interment, arrayed in its shrouds, and wrapped in a prayer shawl. Shards were placed on the eyes. A twig was thrust between the fingers, so that the dead man, when Messiah came, would be able to burrow his way to the Holy Land. The onlookers heaved a sigh. The women broke into noisy lamentations. The gravedigger recited the passages tradition required:

"He is the Rock, His work is perfect; for all His ways are judgment: a God of truth and without iniquity, just and right is He."

After the earth was thrown back into the grave, the Moskat sons recited the Kaddish. Those gathered around the grave tore up clumps of the withered grass from the ground and tossed them over their shoulders. Abram was standing near Hama and their two daughters. While the body was being lowered into the grave, tears fell from his eyes. Hama sobbed convulsively all through the ritual.

Moshe Gabriel was standing silent and a little away from the others. His gaze was fixed toward the cloudless sky. "He is up there already," he was thinking. "He's rid of the burden of the flesh. He'll go through the ordeal of purification, alas, but he'll find paradise. Already his eyes can see what no one of us can see." Stepha, Masha, and the other "modern" Moskat granddaughters all wore black dresses, hats draped with black crepe, and veils, in the modish manner. They looked fresh and charming in spite of the somber attire, and the younger men around threw glances at them. Leah dropped her hand-

kerchief; Koppel picked it up. Some of the crowd left the
cemetery to go to the prayerhouses. Others went into restaurants or delicatessen stores. When the crowd thinned out, those
who remained had a chance to gape at the visiting rabbis;
some black-bearded, others red-bearded; in sable hats and
fur-lined silk coats. Their dangling sidelocks fluttered in the
wind. Their throats were wrapped in woolen scarves. Each of
them was surrounded by a protective circle of beadles and retainers. They sighed, took pinches of snuff from enormous
snuffboxes, extended courtly greetings to one another, but
spoke little. There were long-standing differences between the
various Chassidic courts. When the Bialodrevna rabbi saw the
Sentsimin rabbi, he turned his face away; now that Akiba and
Gina were divorced, the relationship they had shared by virtue of the marriage of their children had vanished. Nevertheless Akiba, naïve fool that he was, went over to the Bialodrevna rabbi and said: "Peace to you, father-in-law."

And the other shrugged his shoulders impatiently and muttered: "Peace to you."

5

The Moskat sons sat out the *shiva,* the prescribed week of
mourning, at the flat where the dead man had lived. The four
of them, Joel, Pinnie, Nathan, and Nyunie, sat in their stockinged feet on low benches. The mirrors on the walls were still
covered, on the windowsill stood a small basin of water with a
linen rag soaking in it, so that the soul of the dead man would
be able to perform its ritual ablutions. A memorial wick
burned in a glass holder. Early in the mornings and late in the
afternoons a quorum of men gathered to hold prayer services.

For the Sabbath the Moskat sons went to their own homes,
and on Saturday evening, with the appearance of the first
three stars, they came back to finish the mourning period. But
after the interruption it was not quite the same. Joel and
Nathan began to discuss practical matters: the property their
father had owned, his will, his bank deposits, the contents of
the safe. Koppel came over from Praga, and all were busy
making computations on sheets of paper. Pearl, Leah, and the
in-laws, Esther and Saltsha, went into another room to talk in
private. The jewelry that had belonged to Meshulam's first
two wives had disappeared; they suspected Rosa Frumetl of
having taken it.

"It's her work. No doubt about it. She's got the eyes of a thief," Leah remarked.

"Where could she have hidden it?" Saltsha asked.

"There are those who would help her."

In a day or two the real quarreling and wrangling began. The whispered suspicions turned to open accusations. The women demanded that Rosa Frumetl take an oath that she did not have the jewelry. Rosa Frumetl immediately burst into a flood of tears protesting her innocence, reciting her distinguished lineage, and lifting her hands to call God to witness that the accusations were false and the accusers evil. But the more she wept, the more convinced were the others that she was guilty. Koppel called her into the library and locked the door.

"Wives have the right to take whatever they want," he said craftily, "and the daughters have the right to complain." He suggested that he was ready to give her a promise in writing, on behalf of the daughters, that as soon as the jewelry was recovered she would get her full share of it. But Rosa Frumetl pursed her lips contemptuously and said: "I don't need any of your promises. You're no better than the best of them."

The unsigned will that had been found in the old man's desk disinherited Hama and provided that her portion was to be divided between Stepha and Bella three years after their marriage. Meshulam had also made bequests to charities. After a good deal of discussion the family agreed to disregard the will, on the ground that in recent years the old man had had too many things on his mind. But before that decision was reached, Abram and Nathan almost came to blows. Then Joel insisted that he, as the oldest, was entitled by Mosaic law to a double share. Pinnie put in a demand for his uncollected dowry of three thousand rubles, together with the accumulated interest. The others asked if he had any kind of note or document, and Pinnie shouted: "I had it, but I lost it somewhere."

"In that case you're a jackass," Joel observed.

"And if I'm a jackass you're a thief," Pinnie answered.

Many years before, Meshulam had registered a building in the name of his first wife. Pearl, the widowed oldest daughter, maintained that this house should go to her, Joel, and Nathan, since this was an inheritance from their mother. Rosa Frumetl offered a document, black on white, to the effect that Meshulam had agreed in Karlsbad, before they were married, to leave her a house and to provide a dowry for her daughter. She banged her fist on the table and declared that she would summon them all to a rabbinical court. Joel bit his cigar in anger.

"You'll not scare us with any rabbis," he declared.

"Is there no fear in your heart for God?" was her answer.

It looked as though the division of the estate would be a long-drawn-out affair. There were scores of documents to be prepared, deeds and certificates to be copied, appraisals of buildings and lots to be made, and searching around in archives. Every one in the family knew that Naomi had placed a substantial sum of money in Meshulam's hands, but, with all her reputation for shrewdness, she had not had the foresight to get a receipt for it. The others had now to take her word for the details of the investment. Meanwhile, by common agreement, Koppel carried on the family business affairs. On the Friday following the eighth of every month the Moskat sons and sons-in-law turned over the rents to him. They soon found that Koppel was just as necessary to them as he had been to their father. Joel and Nathan came to the office every forenoon, and Koppel brought them glasses of tea and gave them an accounting of the way things were going.

Abram bellowed that Koppel would steal everything in sight. He called his brothers-in-law asses. But nobody paid any attention to him. Instead they tried to talk him into making up with the bailiff, but Abram sneered.

"Not while I'm alive!" he shouted.

In the changed situation Abram had some money again. True, he no longer collected rents; Hama and Bella took care of that. But every Friday he received forty rubles for the family expenses. He bought some presents for Ida and began to think seriously of making preparations for his travel abroad. Two or three evenings a week he was at Hertz Yanovar's place. Adele was preparing to leave Poland, too. Now that her stepfather was dead, she had only one wish—to get out of Poland as soon as possible and resume her studies—although she had no clear idea of what or why she should study. After a family council the Moskat sons agreed to allow her a weekly stipend of ten rubles and to put aside a dowry of two thousand rubles to be given her if she should marry within the next eighteen months.

On a rainy May afternoon, when Adele was returning home from the municipal library, she found a letter waiting for her, postmarked Switzerland. She tore open the envelope. It was from Asa Heshel, written in Polish, in an uneven hand, on a page torn from a notebook.

Highly esteemed Miss Adele (the letter began):

I cannot hope that you still remember me. I am the young man who worked on your late honored father's manuscript and who, unfortunately, fled, like a thief, before the task was completed. Yes, I am still alive. I can well imagine what you, your mother, and the rest think of what I have done. I hope that at least I will be able to return the money that was paid to me for the work.

I would not venture to annoy you except that I am in a difficult and awkward situation. When I was fleeing across the border, everything I had was lost, including my notebook. The only addresses I remember are your own and Madame Gina's, in whose flat I had my lodgings. I wrote to the last-named person, but the letter was returned to me; unfortunately, I did not know her family name.

I would venture to ask a most important favor. Could you inform me of the address of Abram Shapiro? This information is of the utmost importance to me. And I will never forget your kindness.

I do not expect, of course, that you can have any interest in my personal circumstances. I would only say that I am living here in Berne, in the home of a man who comes from Galicia, but who formerly resided in Antwerp. I am teaching his children Hebrew and other Jewish subjects. I am also permitted to attend lectures at the university as a free listener and I am preparing to take my entrance examinations. I have long since abandoned all ambition and am resigned to my lot; only the eagerness to acquire knowledge is left to me. Switzerland is beautiful, but I can unfortunately take no joy in nature. I am always alone, as though I were living on the moon.

I extend a thousand thanks in advance for your kindness, and I sign myself with deep respect,

Asa Heshel Bannet

Adele locked the door of her room and at once sat down to answer the letter. She covered eight pages in her ornamental handwriting, full of question marks and exclamation points. Her tone shifted from the light to the earnest. She enclosed a lilac blossom and her photograph, on the reverse side of which she wrote: "A memento to a provincial Don Quixote from an unsuccessful Dulcinea." She forgot completely to enclose Abram's address.

PART
FOUR

CHAPTER ONE

1

Letter from Adele to Her Mother

Dearest Mother:

It is almost two weeks since I sent you the telegram about my marriage. In that time I have received a telegram and two letters from you. I have been meaning every day to write, but I have been so occupied that I have literally not had a moment to myself. But now I will tell you everything.

When I left Vienna I went to Switzerland. My object, as you know, was to enter the university again. I knew that Asa Heshel was in Berne, but that wasn't really on my mind. I never dreamed that things would turn out the way they have with us. After all, we knew each other so little, and we are such different types. When I saw him for the first time at Nyunie Moskat's house, he didn't make any particular impression on me. Just the same, I thought it was the right thing when I got to Switzerland to go to see him and tell him about the people he knew in Warsaw. I thought, too, that I might be able to be of some help to him. It turns out that he has been in love with me all the time. When he saw me he practically threw himself at me. It was quite plain that Hadassah has completely gone out of his mind. The whole thing was never anything more than an adventure for him; he hasn't even bothered to write to her. Without intending to, I let it slip that she was engaged to be married, and then it was very evident to him that she was really only a fickle person.

You will hardly believe it, Mother, but the very first evening we were together he told me he loved me and asked me to marry him. I was really surprised by his words, and I told him that an important thing like marriage wasn't decided on the spur of the moment. But all he would talk about was getting married. He said that he had been thinking about me all the time, and so on, and so on. I could tell that he was being sincere; you know, Mother, that I'm not fooled by empty compliments. He is a very strange young man, so

212

full of feeling and so inhibited. All the time he was talking to
me I felt such sympathy for him. I really can't describe to you
the condition I found him in. He didn't have a grosz to his
name. I am sure he must have been going hungry, although
he's too proud to admit it. I had to persuade him to let me
lend him a few francs—I was careful to call it a loan. It
would take too long to write you in detail how we finally decided to get married. He practically forced me into it, although I wanted to wait awhile. I have really never before
met such an impulsive nature. I must say that here in Switzerland I saw him in an entirely different light. He is so romantic, and so deeply in love. Sometimes he talks such playful
nonsense, yet he mixes it up with so much philosophy and so
many Talmudic quotations that you really never know exactly
where you are. It appears that the Talmudists were great ad-
mirers of our gentle sex. All I keep thinking is—if only Papa
were alive to see me married. Papa always said that he wanted
a youth of learning as a son-in-law, even if he were one of the
"emancipated" kind. And he has so much of Papa in him!
Sometimes, when he begins to talk, I really have the illusion
that it is Papa speaking. Just like two drops of water. It's really impossible to make you understand what I mean in a letter.

　　　　He wanted to go to the rabbi here in Berne the
very next morning, but I absolutely refused to be hurried that
way. And he almost went wild with impatience. Then I
thought, well, the whole thing must be destined to happen this
way. Once, Mamma, you said something to me that I've always remembered: "Marriage and death are things that can't
be avoided." When you come to think of it, how strange it is
that the young man who came to us to edit Papa's manuscript
took Papa's place, in a manner of speaking! Now I really
know that I love him, and he is very close and dear to me.
I've fallen in love with him after the wedding—just as it was
with you and Papa.

　　　　Naturally, the wedding was quiet. Asa Heshel
had managed to become acquainted with a few young men
from Russia. He met them in the restaurant they all took their
meals in, and they all came to the ceremony. We bought a
ring, some honey cake, and wine, and that was all. The sexton
wrote our names and filled out a certificate. It's very comical
to mention, but I noticed that the Jewish law says that if, God
forbid, we should ever be divorced, he would have to pay me
two hundred gulden separation money. Two candles were
lighted in the rabbi's study and they put a white robe on Asa

Heshel. I was really so moved I wanted to cry. I was wearing my black silk dress and the hat I bought before I left Warsaw. The rabbi's wife escorted me to the canopy. I don't need to tell you, dearest Mamma, that never had I imagined that you wouldn't be with me when I got married. I was thinking about you and Papa. I remember I used to laugh whenever I saw a bride weeping beneath her veil, but I must confess that this time I cried myself. I had to cover my eyes with my handkerchief. The rabbi said the words of the ceremony and held a glass of wine for us to sip from. And then Asa Heshel put the ring on my finger. Four men held up the wedding canopy. And that was all. Then we all went to my hotel and we ordered a fine dinner, with wine. One of the guests bought a bottle of champagne.

We spent the night at my hotel and we were so happy, I really can't tell you. In the morning we started on our trip. First we went to Lausanne. The train travels along between the ranges of mountains and you just can't imagine the beauty of the mountains in the early summer. It seemed to me that all nature was rejoicing because of our happiness. Later the train runs along Lake Geneva. We stayed two days in Lausanne, at a Jewish pension, and we made the acquaintance of some very interesting people. It was strictly kosher. Everyone there seemed to know that we were just married, and there were all sorts of jokes at our expense. Asa Heshel almost got into a fight with one of the men, who was quite a fool. He is as bashful as a child and wants to conceal everything from other people. And at the same time he says things that are simply unbelievable. I have to watch him all the time, to make sure that people don't get the wrong impression. I must tell you that in these last two months he had done very little studying. He has to take a qualifying examination here, but instead of preparing for it he wasted his time with a whole mass of useless books. He has absolutely no sense of discipline, but you may be sure that I'll be watching out for him from now on. He is really very capable, and I'm sure that he'll go far. He doesn't realize how lucky he is that he has me as his wife. Without me he would literally have died here.

From Lausanne we went to Montreux. The town is below, and up above rise terraces of vineyards and sheep pastures. You really expect that at any moment everything will come tumbling down. There was some sort of celebration going on while we were there. The boys and girls were dressed in their national costumes. The Swiss are as carefree as children. We foreigners really don't exist for them. We spent a night in Montreux, and from there we went to a village called Visp, where there's a little train that goes to Zermatt. From this village you can see the Matterhorn clearly, with its peak covered with snow as though it were the middle of the winter. Asa Heshel was so enthusiastic about it all. We spent two nights there and we were almost out of our minds with delight. I really can't communicate to you even the thousandth part of the things we experienced. From there we were supposed to go to Italy, which is very near, but Asa Heshel wasn't willing to let me spend so much money. When I think back, I really must admit that he's very comical in some respects. He writes down in a little book every penny we spend. He puts it down under the word "Debts" and he watches over every centime. Oh yes, he has some sort of teaching job that pays him a few francs.

Mamma dearest, now we're back in Berne. We're still living in a hotel, but we're looking for a regular place. I am sending you in this letter a note from the rabbi, certifying our marriage, so that the Moskats will be able to send me the two thousand rubles that were promised to me. I really could have kept on postponing the wedding and kept on collecting the ten rubles a week for months; you will remember that according to the agreement I had eighteen months to get married in. But I didn't want to take advantage of that. I'm sure that if they have any pride they won't want to see me the loser financially, and will make it up to me in the way of a gift. If your late husband were alive he would certainly have been lavish with his gifts. You must remember that we're both students and we have no chance to earn any money. I kiss you many times and offer a sincere *Mazeltov* for you as well as for us, because I know that this is as much your joy as it is ours. Asa Heshel sent a telegram to his mother, but he hasn't received an answer yet. From what he tells me about his family it's quite clear that they're a bunch of religious primitives. Their way of life is just as though they were still in the Middle Ages. Even Asa Heshel himself is a mixture of backwardness and modernity. That's why it's often so hard to understand him.

Please write me how everything is with you, and whether they've already made over to you the house that my late stepfather left to you. I am very eager to hear about every detail. Has Hadassah been married already? Did you go to the wedding? What does the family say about my marriage?

Please write me everything. Asa Heshel promises to write you a separate letter. In the meanwhile he sends his heartfelt regards. I kiss you many times. From me, your daughter who hopes to see you soon in peace and in joy—

Adele Bannet

2

FROM HADASSAH'S DIARY

July 3.—He has married Adele. In Switzerland.

July 4.—A sleepless night. An awful suspicion kept on torturing me: he must have written to me, and Mamma concealed his letters. I lay awake until daylight burning with anger. I kept on seeing pictures of myself fighting with Mamma and tearing the letters out of her hands.

In the evening.—Why don't we have the kind of religion where a Jewish girl can go into a synagogue and kneel in prayer before God? I've been reading the Psalms, translated into Polish. Once I remember seeing my grandmother weeping over her prayerbook, and I laughed at her. God forgive me. Now I myself stain the pages with my tears. Please, Father in heaven, give me back my faith. I want to die—but not before Mamma. I am afraid to imagine her walking after the corpse of her only daughter. I have caused her so much suffering already.

The middle of the night.—God created everything, the heavens and the earth and the stars. And all according to His will. What a great comfort this is. If God wants us to suffer, then we must suffer with thankfulness. (I must never forget this!!!)

July 5.—A wedding announcement has come, printed in Hebrew and German. Shifra brought it in to me. I suppose Adele had it printed especially to send here to Warsaw. So that she could gloat over all of us. It's so childish and so disgusting. They are in Berne. I'm sure that he's unhappy, but not like I am.

July 6.—There must be some sort of devils racing around in my brain. I fight with all my strength not to hate poor Mamma. I love her, but somehow I can't abide her presence. Please, God, do not take away from me the last object of my love. My Uncle Abram doesn't want to have anything more to do with me. It seems to me that everybody rejoices over my misfortune. But that can't be true. They are making so many dresses and clothes for me that it's really terrible. They've engaged seamstresses, and they are in the living-room sewing all sorts of shirts and underwear, all trimmed with lace. It's so old-fashioned and unpleasant, just as though we're all stuck somewhere in the Middle Ages. They're making me a fur coat. I'm so happy that Klonya is in Miedzeshin. I'm more ashamed to face her than anyone else. They've taken my measurements for a matron's wig. I tried it on and in the mirror I hardly recognized myself. With all of the tragedy, I really wanted to burst out laughing. Well, I'll wear it, just as though it were my cross.

Dawn.—I slept for six solid hours. I dreamed that I was at the cemetery on the Gensha. There was a slanting plank of wood there, and dead children were sliding down it. One little girl had a ribbon in her blond hair and a scar on her forehead. I can see her now. If everything comes from God, what is the sense of dreams like this? The wedding is to take place at grandfather's old flat, not at a hall. They're already printing the invitations. It's my own fault. I've willingly bent my shoulders to receive the yoke. And I know there is more suffering waiting for me.

I received a letter from my bridegroom. He has such a round handwriting, and there's a little curlicue at the end of each word. The letter was in a mixture of three languages, Yiddish, Polish, and Russian. It's quite evident he copied it out of one of those books that print sample letters of all kinds·

July 8.—I was sitting on one of the benches in the Saxon Gardens, and a wild thought came to me—to write a letter to *him*. I know his address in Switzerland. I knew that I wouldn't really dare to send it, but just the same I went into a shop and bought a sheet of paper and an envelope. I wrote the word *"Mazeltov"* in Yiddish, and then I tore the sheet into pieces and threw them away. It's all so foolish. And all the time I cried so much that people stared at me.

July 9.—Yesterday I met my Uncle Abram in the street. When he saw me he made a movement as though to turn away, but instead he took off his hat, bowed, and hurried on. I never believed that my Uncle Abram would ever lift his hat to me and then go on his way, like a stranger. Apart from the fact that he doesn't like my husband-to-be, my marriage is a personal calamity to him. What it means is that Koppel has won out over him. How strange it is that in our family everything is complicated by strife and personal ambition. Papa is in Otwotsk; he doesn't even write to me. After Grandfather died I could have had my way in everything; that is the truth. I could even have got Papa to agree to my going away to Switzerland. But I was too broken. I am plunging into the abyss of my own free will. I really don't understand it. It's as though I were committing suicide.

In the evening.—It's so difficult for me to imagine him with Adele. It's simple enough, but my mind can't grasp it. I know for sure that he's thinking of me day and night. It can't be otherwise. Our beings have a sort of electrical affinity for each other. Thank God I don't feel any hatred toward Adele. (This very second I *did* feel a twinge of hatred; she has such a hypocritical nature. Dear God, protect me!) The only thing I'm afraid of is that I might go out of my mind. There's a sort of childish terror that seems to hold me enchained. I can't describe it. For some reason I've developed a frantic fear of dirt of any kind; I'm always washing myself. And every few minutes I imagine that I have to go to the bathroom. It's all so unpleasant. Stepha brought me a volume of Forel to read. I read it once before, but this time it all seemed so loathsome. Why is everything in the world profaned?

Later.—There's something I must do and I don't know what it is. I'm envious of the nuns that I see walking on the street; they all seem so at peace. If not for my mother, I would become one of them. I have a strange premonition that my marriage to Fishel will not take place. Something will happen. Either I'll die, or I'll run away at the last moment. My mother gave me half of her jewels. It suddenly occurs to me that I could sell them all and run off to America. People have done things like that before. But what's the sense of such thoughts? All hope has gone forever.

Morning.—I've completely forgotten the date. All I know is that in about two weeks I'll have to stand under the wedding canopy. They've just brought the wedding dress. I tried it on, and when I looked in the mirror I saw to my astonishment that I'm still good-looking. The dressmakers kept on exclaiming how beautifully the dress fits. It has a lot of folds and a long train. For a moment I felt better, and I thought to myself that things weren't so terrible after all. I am young, and good-looking, and I'm not poor. I could see how the others envied me, and that made me more cheerful for a while.

Monday.—This Saturday my bridegroom will be "called up" for a reading at the prayerhouse. Mamma called Papa on the telephone at Otwotsk. He promised he would come back right away. The wedding will be on Friday, and on Saturday night there'll be a reception. Mamma is doing all the work. Day and night she's busy cooking and baking. She worries about everything, and that aggravates her gall-bladder condition. How can I help her, when I just can't stand being near her? And while I am suffering so much, *he* is somewhere in a pension in the Alps with Adele. Shifra brings me all the news. All the things I didn't even dare to hope for myself. I am sure that she doesn't even love him. How she must rejoice over my misfortune!

The middle of the night.—How easy it would be to put an end to everything. I found a piece of cord and made a noose in it. There's a hook on the wall, and I have a stool. Everything that is needed to be rid of all my troubles. But something holds me back. I suppose it's sympathy for Mamma. I know, too, that God doesn't want us to run away from His punishment. And deep inside me there's still a hope that everything is not yet lost.

Tuesday.—Dear diary, dear friend, it's almost three weeks since I've written in your pages. She who writes now is not the Hadassah you knew before. I am sitting at a writing-desk, a matron's wig on my head, and my own face is as strange to me as my soul. I have gone through all of it: the ritual bath, the wedding ceremony, and all the rest. I will confide no more of my secrets to you, my diary. You are pure; I am unclean. You are honorable; I am false. I hardly have the courage to turn your pages. I will hide you away, together with a few other mementos that are precious to me. Even my name is changed now. Now I am Hadassah Kutner. And that name is just as meaningless as everything else that's happened to me. Adieu, my diary. Forgive me.

3

Letter from Rosa Frumetl to Adele

To my precious and devoted daughter Adele Bannet:

        I open this letter by informing you that my health, thank God, is good; and may God grant that I may hear the same from you always and forever, amen. Second, I again wish you a heartfelt *Mazeltov*, and many joys and long years of satisfaction and all good things; may your marriage be an omen of peace and prosperity and may the years cover you with health and honor. For who else is left to me in all the world save you, my daughter? True, it would have been well if I might have had the merit of leading my only child to the canopy, but probably in God's eyes I am not worthy of so great a blessing. When your telegram came to me I shed tears of gratitude and rejoicing. If only your sainted father could have lived to see this day. May he be an intermediary and a pleader for mercy before the divine throne for you and your husband and for all of us, amen. I am sure that his spirit hovered over your wedding canopy and that he prayed to God that you may have blessings and benedictions and know no more of sadness, and that your husband may treasure you with honor. For it is true that he has acquired a rare jewel, such as one might search for all over the world, intelligent and beautiful and—may no evil befall you!—with all virtues. And I pray to God that you may be an exemplary wife; undoubtedly it is so decreed by Heaven, for everything is determined in heaven even before we are born. And I must tell you further that when I saw Asa Heshel for the first time at Nyunie's house, I felt a strange pang in my heart, which seemed to be telling me that he was the one who was to be your destined husband. And now it is as though he were my own child. I cannot tell you of my eagerness to meet his mother and his grandmother, and his grandfather, the rabbi of Tereshpol Minor. May God be thanked, my daughter, for you have acquired a husband of noble birth, as is fitting for your own distinguished lineage, and you may hold your head high. The foolishness of his youth is long forgotten, and if the end is good, then all is good.

I must write you further that your good news has rejoiced everyone and that everyone has come forward to wish you everything that is best, even Dacha, though—the truth must be said—she did so not with an open heart. The two thousand rubles have already been placed in your name in the bank. About the ten rubles' weekly allowance there have been many words. The matter would have been well arranged except that that scoundrel Koppel interfered, and Leah, too, let herself be heard. You are aware, my daughter, of all the gossip that has been whispered concerning these two —and now I can see that they were true words. One hand washes the other. I gave them warning that if no fair settlement were arrived at I would summon them to an arbitration. Nor is the matter of the building left to me by your late stepfather yet settled. It would seem that they are anxious to drag the affair out until I weary of it. But I may tell you, my daughter, that this I will not permit. The truth is that they are overflowing with riches; they do not know themselves the limits of their wealth. Many people are saying that that abandoned villain Koppel has looted the family from head to toe. In spite of that he has become the real head of the family affairs and he is the one who holds the reins; especially since the others are, unfortunately, thick-skulled. How often did I warn your stepfather! But now it is all too late. In the meanwhile I was required to move from the large apartment and was given a flat of two rooms on the Tvarda. Joel moved into the large flat. I could, of course, have made difficulties, but I did not want to enter into any quarrels with them, for they are, may I be forgiven the words, a coarse lot.

      My dearest daughter, as I sit now and write to you, it seems to me that you are sitting next to me, and that we are talking face to face. There has been a big and noisy wedding here. Hadassah was married to Fishel on Friday, and on the evening following the Sabbath there was a reception. I did not have the desire to go, as you can understand, but it was not befitting that I should refuse and give rise to who knows what gossip. It was necessary, too, that I give her a wedding gift—a jewelry box that I had lying around for many years, from the Brody days. The wedding was noisy and vulgar, probably to drown out the truth that the bride had brought scandal on the family. I can imagine how the bile rose in her when she heard the news of your marriage. All Warsaw was talking about it. Fishel comes from a family of wealth, but he is a fool. It is easy to see that after Asa Heshel he can find no favor in her eyes. People say that the bride kept up a constant wailing, and that she had to be watched to see that she did not run away; and that the marriage came off only because of Koppel—so that he might have another fortune to control. No one dares to say a word against him, except Abram Shapiro. Abram didn't attend the wedding; you can imagine what a turmoil that created. Not long ago he saw me on the street, and he turned his face away. The whole world's his enemy, the way he runs around with his women.

      The wedding took place in your late stepfather's flat. The bride had fasted all day, and believe me she looked like a corpse. She wouldn't be so bad-looking, but she was as white as chalk. The women who led her to the canopy practically had to drag her. And the girls who were there wept bitterly. The whole thing was more like a funeral. The wed-

ding march they played was different from the kind we used
to have in Brody; all the customs here in Poland are different.
For instance, they don't have the dance where the old women
hop up and down in front of the bride with a loaf of bread.
They didn't serve cake and brandy, because it was getting so
close to the Sabbath and the women had to go home to light
the candles. Even so, it lasted so long that it turned out to be
almost a desecration of the Sabbath. The rabbi was one of
those government rabbis, in a high silk hat. The Bialodrevna
rabbi was supposed to come to officiate, but he didn't. It was a
real slap in the face for them.

For the Friday evening only the family stayed.
I went home, because to me the Sabbath is the Sabbath. But
on Saturday night I had to go. The place was so crowded it
was impossible to move, and the heat was so great that the
perspiration was dripping off everyone. The people who were
doing the serving pushed their way through as though they
were frantic. Some of the guests got double portions and others got nothing. The food wasn't the best 'either. The fish
wasn't fresh and the soup was watery. If you could have seen
what went on! There were a lot of wedding presents, but all
cheap stuff. You should have seen "Queen Esther" and Saltsha. They were behung with so many pieces of finery that
they were almost hidden.

Joel and Nathan danced a *kozak,* both of them
with their enormous bellies, like a couple of elephants. The
Chassidim started to yell out against the men and women
dancing together, but nobody paid any attention to them.
Koppel came to the wedding without his wife, and I heard
that he danced a waltz with Leah; but I didn't see it. Moshe
Gabriel, a saintly man, left the place early; he couldn't abide
the goings-on. And the bridegroom's grandfather protested
too. Never in my life have I seen such a madhouse. It was
more like a wedding at some peasant's. The musicians were
playing military marches. Hannah, Pinnie's wife, lost a
brooch in all the excitement—or someone stole it—and she
fainted. I tell you with all my heart, my dear daughter, that
before having any part of a wedding like that a quiet wedding
like yours is a thousand times better. And I understand it cost
a fortune.

And now, my dearest daughter, I want to re-
mind you that you are the pure daughter of a distinguished
Jewish house. In worldly matters I cannot counsel you; but I
pray that you do not forget that a Jewish daughter must give

constant heed to the ablutions that are required of her. It is written that it is because of three sins that a woman dies in childbirth—may God forbid—and one is when she doesn't heed the ritual laws of purification. The children of such a union are likened to those illegitimately born. Do not be angry if I remind you of these things; it is only because the world of today takes them too lightly. I am sending you a copy of *The Pure Well*, where you will be able to find all the laws of ablution, and I pray that you heed them. I know that it will not be easy in a strange country like Switzerland, but if a person really wants it, then she can manage to find a ritual bath, and a rabbi of whom to ask questions, because there are pious Jews everywhere.

Write to me and tell me when and how much money to send you. Believe me, my dear daughter, when I realize that with God's blessings you are at last a wife, it is as though new health were poured into my body. I only hope that your dear husband will understand and appreciate the treasure that has come into his keeping, and that he will be good to you as is your desert. Write to me at once, and a long letter, because now that you are away, there is nothing left for me but your letters. This from me, your mother, who yearns to hear nothing but good news from you—

Rosa Frumetl Moskat

CHAPTER TWO

1

This year, two years after Hadassah's marriage, the Moskat clan, as in all the previous summers, left Warsaw for the cool countryside. Joel, Nathan, and Pinnie took up their quarters in their father's villa in Otwotsk. Hama, with her older daughter, Bella, moved in with them. Pearl, Meshulam's oldest daughter, the widow, had a house of her own in Falenitz. Nyunie and Leah shared a villa in common in Shvider. Before his marriage to Hadassah, Fishel had acquired a house with thirty acres of ground near Usefov. The year before, Rosa Frumetl had spent the summer in Meshulam's villa. At that time her stepdaughters Queen Esther and Saltsha had done everything they could to spite her, making fun of the way she chanted out of her prayerbook, the way she poked her bony

fingers into the flesh of a chicken, the way she put on her matron's wig, the way she washed her hands and made the appropriate benediction after leaving the bathroom. Rosa Frumetl had so much anguish that instead of gaining weight that
summer, she lost five pounds. This year, however, Rosa Frumetl did not have to depend on the Moskats. Now she had a
new husband, Wolf Hendlers, a man of means, and learned
besides. He had a cottage of his own in Shvider. Now in the
letters she wrote to her daughter in Switzerland Rosa Frumetl
could sign herself "Rosa Frumetl Hendlers," and she made a
proud flourish at the end of her new name.

The first one to leave Warsaw for the summer was Queen
Esther. Directly after the Passover holidays she began to complain that her tapeworm was drawing the life out of her. The
Warsaw air was too thick—you could cut it with a knife. The
clothes she had had made for herself during the winter were
already miles too big, she had lost so much weight. Her
daughters, too—Minna, Nesha, and Gutsha—had become
nothing but skin and bone; her son Mannes as well. Joel made
a face. He could not bear staying in Warsaw all alone, and at
the same time he could not abide this business of fresh air,
and trees and fields—and a flock of babbling women all
around him. Joel used to say that going off to the country for
the summer was a lot of nonsense. When it's hot, you sweat
no matter where you are, he said, and the cold night winds
only give you catarrh. But Queen Esther generally had her
own way. Early in the summer two wagons rolled up in front
of Joel's house; there was a bustle of loading huge quantities
of bedclothing, apparel, pots and pans, dishes, stocks of foods.
The draymen pleaded that the load be lightened, because the
horses were scrawny old nags. Besides there was always the
danger that everything would tumble off along the roads. But
Queen Esther kept on adding to the load—a bowl, a clothes-
press, or a sack of old potatoes that had already begun to
sprout. It always turned out that the samovar was the last
thing to be piled on the heap, tied on with a rope so that it
would not fall off. The janitor's one-eyed dog barked. Children pulled hairs out of the tails of the horses. Less prosper-
ous housewives looked out of their windows, their bewigged
heads bobbing, murder in their envious looks.

"Out to the green pastures already! They go crazy with too
much prosperity."

Nathan had to leave Warsaw early because of his diabetes,
Saltsha insisted. It was a warm day when they left, but Saltsha

made him put on a heavy vest and saw to it that his overcoat was buttoned tight. Queen Esther accused Saltsha of going for her own pleasure more than for Nathan's, for the sharp country air only stimulated his appetite and there was hardly anything he was allowed to eat.

Pinnie's chief reason for going was that not one of his four daughters was yet bespoken. Everyone knew that it was easier for a girl to catch a man "along the line" than in Warsaw, where the girls stayed at home most of the time and a prospective husband never got a real chance to have a look at them. It was the same reason that prompted Hama to hurry off, too. Bella was getting along in years. Stepha was going around with some student, but it didn't look to Hama as though he was much of a bargain. Besides, what was the point of sweating in Warsaw? It was little enough they saw of Abram. Day and night he was with that woman of his, Ida Prager, although Hama had heard rumors that he was getting tired of his old flame and was looking for a new conquest. Anyway, in the summer he would come out to the country for the weekend, like most Warsaw householders, and sometimes even bring a gift with him.

Dacha went because Dr. Mintz told her to, and because Nyunie, fool that he was, made her life miserable at home. There was nothing better for Dacha's ailments than to settle back in a hammock, a pillow under her head, a pair of glasses on her nose, and read the Yiddish newspaper. She read everything: the news items, the feature articles, the serial stories. There was so much a person could find out: what the officials in Petersburg were saying; what manner of life the Rothschilds lived in London, Paris, and Vienna; who had died lately in Warsaw and who had got married or become engaged; how Jews lived in far-away places like Yemen, Ethiopia, and India, and what was the favorite food of the Czar's uncle, Nikolai Nikolaievich.

Rebecca, her maid ever since Shifra had gone to work for Hadassah, would bring out a cup of cocoa, some cookies, and a dish of preserved fruit. Dacha would wash her hands from a jug of water that she always had by her, recite the appropriate blessing, and refresh her spirits with the food. Then she would set the tray down and stretch out comfortably. Dacha's back and limbs did not ache so much here in the country. Her gall bladder bothered her less. The only thing she did not like about the place was that she had to put up with Leah as her neighbor. This summer Leah's husband, Moshe Gabriel, was staying with his son, Aaron, in Bialodrevna. It was an open secret that matters were rapidly approaching a divorce between husband and wife, and evil tongues wagged rumors that the moment the divorce took place Koppel would leave his wife and he and Leah would marry. A shudder shook Dacha's spine whenever she heard these reports. That was all she needed—to have Koppel for a brother-in-law! Even after all these years Dacha had never been able to accustom herself to Leah's strident voice, which carried all the way over from her cottage; to the phonograph that Leah had brought up from Warsaw, which she kept going day and night, grinding out theater music and cantorial arias; to Leah's short-sleeved blouses and the short dresses she wore, with her bare legs showing beneath them, like an unbeliever. That sort of thing might be all right for a young girl; a person could understand that. But what madness did Leah have in her mind? Did she think she was much younger than Dacha?

Dacha would close her eyes and fall into a doze. All through the years she had had complaints against her father-in-law, considered him arrogant and callous. Now that he was dead she could understand the troubles he had had. The estate had not yet been divided. Koppel the bailiff still held all of them in the palm of his hand. Leah was behaving scandalously. Queen Esther and Saltsha were acting the great ladies. Abram had lost every bit of decency. Even her own husband, Nyunie, had not shown so much ill will toward her as long as the old man had been alive. And what of her child, her Hadassah? Dacha preferred not even to think about that. She was a sick woman. Every day she lived was a gift from heaven. What was the sense of eating herself up alive? That was all Nyunie was waiting for, for her to close her eyes for good.

2

A Letter from Hadassah to Asa Heshel

Dear Asa Heshel:

I came across your address today quite by accident. You probably know all about us. I really don't know why I'm writing this letter. It's silly and I frankly don't expect an answer. You have a wife and I a husband. I've learned that you have settled down, and it makes me happy to think that at least one of us has reached his goal. I'm certain that you have not completely put me out of your mind. You are a philosopher and you are aware of the fact that the past cannot be eradicated. I picture to myself your astonishment at learning that I was going to be married This must have proved to you once again that women are indeed frivolous creatures. I was always aware of your feeling of contempt and it was this that pained me most. I was sick for weeks. I looked forward to death, to an end to all this pain. But you remained silent and it was your silence that drove me to despair. I admit that my parents are not responsible for what happened. It is all my fault. When I saw the road to happiness would forever be closed to me, I chose the opposite. Even as a child I knew that at the crucial moment I would fail.

How are you? How are you getting along? Are you studying at the university? Did you meet any interesting people? Is Switzerland really so beautiful as you imagined it? When I recall our trip it becomes almost dreamlike. I had the opportunity to observe great human suffering on my way back. I never foresaw during my strolls on the Pavia and Dluga that one day I too would be behind bars. It gives me satisfaction that I know how it feels.

Everything here is as it always was. Mother is ill most of the time and ill-tempered. Father spends a good deal of time with Uncle Abram. They were not on speaking terms, but they are friends again. I live on the Gnoyna (Garbage Street). And how well this name describes my position! In the summer I go to the country near Otwotsk. Here I can at least be alone with my thoughts.

You can address a letter to me at Usefov should you decide to answer. I hope that you are happy with your wife and I send my regards to her.

Hadassah

PS. Klonya got married.

A Letter from Asa Heshel to Hadassah

Dear Hadassah:

You will never know the joy your letter gave me. I read and reread it countless times. I awoke in the middle of the night, pulled the letter from under my pillow and read it by the light of the moon. I still cannot believe it. But the handwriting is yours. I want you to know that although we both made a stupid decision, my love for you has not altered for a minute. My thoughts are always of you. How many times I decided to put all thoughts of you out of my mind! I told myself that it was hopeless. But I could not. Somehow I knew that you had not forgotten me and that sometime I would hear from you. When I read your letter I said to myself—now I am prepared to die. I want you to know that I wrote to you, not one letter but many. When Adele came to Berne, she told me that you were engaged. She didn't mention your having been ill or having been imprisoned. How horrible! I have often felt that the higher powers are warring with me. Since my childhood things have never worked out. With you I suffered the hardest blow. If I had known that there was even a slight chance, I would have come back. During the first few weeks my senses were dulled by the catastrophe that had befallen me in this strange land. I could not enjoy the mountains and the beauty that surrounded me. I cannot describe my utter loneliness! I was sure that you hated me and did not want to answer. When I heard the news that you were going to be married I was certain that my fears were correct. I too wanted to destroy all hopes. Your letter revived these hopes in one moment. From now on I have a single goal: once again to be near you. I will not rest until it is so. I have never loved anyone except you. That is the truth. I pray God that you will answer soon. I understand all the obstacles that stand between us, both physical and moral, but it cannot be otherwise. Write me everything, everything! I am attending courses in the philosophy faculty, but as a nonmatriculated student. One has to pass an examination here too. The material studied here is so negligible compared to the ideas that keep running through one's head! My personal life is senseless from beginning to end. I blame no one. The thought that you have a husband is strange to me, but it nevertheless is a fact. Switzerland is beautiful, but everything is so strange: the people, the scenery, the customs. I am sometimes even a stranger to myself. If I were here with you, everything could be different. Warsaw seems so distant, like a bewitched city.

Asa Heshel

PS. I am giving you another address. You understand the reason.

3

Letter from Adele to Her Mother

Darling Mother:

         I don't know exactly why I'm writing this letter. Maybe it's because my heart is full of pain and I can no longer contain it. You've often asked me in your letters how things are going with me, whether my husband is approaching any real goal, and how he is treating me. Before, when I wrote to you, I tried to smooth things over and to paint them brighter than they are. I didn't want to cause you any suffering. But now I really can't keep things locked up inside me any more. My darling Mother, you may as well know that your daughter has fallen into a living grave. In the two years that I've been married I can honestly say that I haven't had one happy month. The first few days I was really happy. I thought that at last I could see the end to all my years of loneliness. But soon it was plain that my miserable fortune was still following me. I am my father's daughter. I was born to suffer, and I'll probably die before my time, too.

         Now I will write you everything, without concealing a single thing. Asa Heshel has his good sides; he can make himself agreeable to strangers who never did anything for him and to whom he owes nothing. In his own way he's an idealist. Day and night he's dreaming of ways to cure the world and day and night he carries around some book on philosophy. But this doesn't stop him from being cold-hearted and cruel, and on top of that really a crazy person. If I should sit down to write you all his madnesses it would fill an entire book. To tell it to you briefly, it is like this: I was ready and willing to do everything possible so that he could complete the university course and really make something of himself. I was ready to spend on him all the money I had. All I wanted was for him to study honestly and to behave like a normal human being. But the whole two years have been nothing but bitter disappointment for me. I wanted to rent a house and furnish it, so that it could be a real home, but he absolutely refused, and after all this time we still live in lodgings. I thought that as time passed he would want to have a child, like all normal people, but he warned me that if I became pregnant he would run away and I would never hear from him again. And I could believe it, too, because he's got absolutely no sense of responsibility. It happened that twice I got caught—it was his fault both times—and he made me get rid of it and put my whole life in danger. The second time I had a hemorrhage and a very high fever. It's impossible to get a doctor here to do it, and I had to go to an old gentile woman, a midwife. Thank God that at least I wasn't fated to die.

Darling Mother, I know I shouldn't write you such things. I know what suffering it will cause you, but to whom else can I pour out my heart? Right after the wedding he began to be ashamed of me, as though I were a leper. He forbade me to come into the restaurant where he meets his Russian friends, a bunch of ne'er-do-wells who belong in a zoo or some such place. Can you imagine, I'm not good-looking enough or educated enough to show myself before these creatures! He's even denied that he's married, and has really caused me terrible embarrassment. And he's never invited anyone to come to visit us. Instead of studying he wastes half the day tutoring children. He simply allows himself to become a measly Hebrew teacher or an assistant tutor—so long as he doesn't have to take a copper from me. He tells me quite frankly that he's carrying on this way because he wants to separate from me and he doesn't want to be under any obligations. When he gets angry he shouts and says things that you'd expect from an escaped lunatic. He's filled himself up with ideas from a book by some philosopher who hates women, some crazy man—a Jew who got converted and committed suicide at the age of twenty-three. And he says—Asa Heshel, I mean—that he doesn't want to have a child out of fear that it might not be a boy. That's just one example of his madness. It's the custom here for everyone to go to bed early; by nine o'clock the whole town is asleep. But he lies awake until three in the morning reading or writing all sorts of useless stuff which he throws away later. In the morning he stays in bed until noon like a dead man. On account of the way he carries on we already have been asked to move a few times from our lodgings, because in this part of Europe people are civilized and they don't understand these wild Russian goings-on. So far as cooking and eating at regular times is concerned, that's absolutely out of the question. All day he practically fasts, and in the middle of the night he suddenly gets hungry. God knows I would have picked up and left him long ago, but when it serves his purpose he turns so delicate and attentive,

and says things that are like a warm poultice to an aching
cheek, and insists that he loves me.

Darling Mother, you are certainly wondering
how your daughter is able to stand all this shame and disgrace. I have stayed with him only because I didn't want to
break up our life and because I know my own nature. I'm not
one of those women who love one man today and another tomorrow. I'm like those insects that can love only once. I
didn't want to come back to you after three months, a complete failure. So I just gritted my teeth and I stood it. I always
kept on hoping that things would get better. I felt that as he
got older he would see where his best interests were. Some
time ago he began to talk about wanting to go back to Warsaw. I always suspected that he had never forgotten that Hadassah, although he assured me with the most sacred oaths
that he had put her out of his mind. But he's told me so many
lies. Now I know definitely that they're carrying on a corre-
spondence. He gets letters from her addressed to a different
place. Now he says he's going to Warsaw whether I go with
him or not. He's not much over twenty, and I know that
they'll conscript him, because there's nothing the matter with
him physically. But he doesn't pay any attention to the danger
of such a thing happening. That Hadassah creature is simply
false to her husband. I have absolutely no illusions about that.
He's going to her, that's the whole truth of it. In the last couple of weeks he seems to be out of his mind entirely, and
wanders around as though he's on some strange planet. He's
ready to put everything in jeopardy—himself, me and other
people. Now I've discovered that his father died of melancholy in some dreary village in Galicia. There must be a streak of
quiet insanity in him, too.

Darling Mother, forgive me for not writing to
you to wish you *Mazeltov* on your marriage. I appreciate
your position and God knows I've got no resentment against
what you decided to do. Those Moskats are just a bunch of
ruffians. What else was there for you? I hope that at last you
will find real peace and contentment.

I haven't decided yet what I'm going to do. He
wants us to travel together, and he still promises all sorts of a
wonderful future. He wants to make a stop in Tereshpol
Minor and have me meet his mother and sister and his grandfather, the rabbi. The truth is he is really still a child and he
has a child's thoughts and ideas. I was thinking his mother
might have some influence on him. She wrote me some very

warm and heartfelt letters. But I know at the same time that Hadassah is waiting for him to come back to Poland and that sooner or later matters between us will come to a divorce. I am so confused that I'm sure that this letter will just be a jumble of nonsense to you. But honestly it's a real reflection of what's going on in my mind. Please pray to God for me, darling Mother, because He's the only one who can help me. Your unfortunate daughter,

Adele Bannet

CHAPTER THREE

1

In Tereshpol Minor the puddles and floods of melting ice began to dry up in the strong sunshine of the days after Passover. The trees and bushes that ringed the village put out little green apples and pears, gooseberries, cherries, and raspberries. Wheat, as in every year before harvest time, went up in price a few groszy the bushel. At the same time fowl and eggs were plentiful. The peasants prophesied an abundant year, because the days were getting warmer and there was plenty of rain; nevertheless, during the month of May they repaired to the roadside shrines to offer special prayers for the crops, the men dressed in linen cloaks and old-style four-cornered hats hung with tassels, the women in flowered dresses, and with wooden hoops under their headgear, the girls in gay frocks and wearing strings of colored beads. They marched piously along, carrying crucifixes, holy pictures, and wax candles, and chanting as though they were following a coffin.

Among the Jews in the town, life flowed along its accustomed ways. The tradesmen in the market place carried on with their affairs. In the bystreets and alleys artisans worked at their benches. In the houses in the poorer streets men and women busied themselves making the horsehair sieves that were sold throughout the province. The street leading to the bridge was full of these sievemakers. Girls combed out bundles of horsehair, all the while singing doleful songs of unhappy orphans and kidnapped brides. Men wove the hair on wooden looms, singing snatches of synagogue melodies.

In the summer months there was little business in the market place, and it was mostly the womenfolk who sat in the shops, so that their husbands could take time to devote themselves to Jewishness. From the study houses could be heard voices lifted in Talmud chants. In the cheders the teachers struggled with the children from early morning until evening. The Evil One was busy, too. Jekuthiel the watchmaker had brought a collection of "forbidden" modern books from Zamosc and had started a library. A few of the younger men had even become Zionists. It was rumored that some of the sieve-makers and the tannery workers were getting together to plan a strike, just as in 1905. Others had gone off to America.

There was a report in the Lublin newspaper that in Sarajevo a Serbian student had shot the Austrian Crown Prince and his wife, and that the Austrian Emperor, Franz Josef, had sent a note to the Serbs. The doctor, the pharmacist, and the surgeon-barber of Tereshpol Minor discussed the matter in the evenings, while their wives poured tea from the samovar and played cards. But the ordinary Jews of the town paid no attention to the news. The things that went on in the big world outside!

Reb Dan Katzenellenbogen, the rabbi, no longer had the power he had wielded of old. First of all, he was close to eighty now. Second, was not his own grandson a deserter from Israel? Third, there was little comfort he could take in his two sons, Zaddok and Levi, or in his daughter, Finkel. Zaddok was to have been his father's successor; he already held the post of government rabbi. But he did not conduct himself as a man in his position should. The prominent householders in the village were already saying that when the rabbi should leave them—might it not happen for a hundred years! —they would have to bring in someone from outside. Levi had begun to look for a rabbinical post directly after his marriage, but nothing had come of it; and now for more than twenty years he had been idling away his time at his father's home, and at his father's expense. Finkel's husband, Jonathan, had divorced her a couple of years after the two were married and had left her with two children, Asa Heshel and Dinah. For almost nineteen years she had been alone, and then she had married a town elder, Reb Paltiel, who had died a few months later. Reb Dan was convinced that for some reason Heaven was persecuting him. The Chassidim said that too much poring over the philosophy of Maimonides had driven the rabbi into a melancholy.

The rabbi carried on his daily life as he had done in the old days. He lay down in bed directly after the evening prayers, in his white trousers and stockings, and with the ritual fringed garment still on him, and got up again at midnight to wail over the destruction of the Temple. He wrote with a pen made of a goose quill. He ate only once a day, some bread, beet soup, and a dry piece of beef. The house in which he lived—it was the rabbinical residence, maintained by the community—was old and decrepit. The community elders wanted to put everything in order, but the rabbi refused to allow it.

It might have seemed as though Reb Dan was hiding away from the world behind the yellow window hangings that separated his study from the Shulgass. All matters of arbitration or ritual decision he left to his sons; the only community problems to which he would give any consideration were those of great complexity and importance. Rabbis from other communities wrote epistles to him, but he never answered. He was invited to grace weddings and circumcisions with his presence, but he rarely accepted any of these honors. All his life he had hoped that in his old age all worldly temptations would depart from him so that he might be able to serve the Eternal in full faith. But even now, at the very threshold of the grave, he still found himself carrying on interminable wrangles with Satan, confusing his mind with alien thoughts, troubling himself with questions into which a man of piety should not inquire. The old riddle remained: the pure in heart suffered and the wicked flourished; the people chosen of God were still ground into the dust; Israel's people, instead of living a life of penance, were turning to heresy. What would the end be? What had Reb Dan accomplished during his span on earth? What meritorious deeds would he be able to offer on the scales of judgment in the world to come?

He would get up from his chair and go out to the study house, his wide skullcap pushed aslant on his forehead, his velvet coat wrinkled and unbuttoned. His beard, which had been white for years, was again taking on a parchment-yellow tinge. His heavy eyebrows almost hid his eyes. Sometimes he felt an urgent need to speak with someone, not simply idle conversation, but words of substance. But there was rarely anyone in the study house to whom he might talk. He would go over to a youngster who sat hunched over an open volume and pinch him on the cheek.

"You're studying, my son? You want to be a God-fearing Jew?"

"Of course, rabbi."

"And you have faith in the almighty God?"

"What else, rabbi?"

"It is good, my son. The righteous shall live by his faith."

2

The wagon that was bringing Asa Heshel and Adele from the
railroad station to Tereshpol Minor followed the main road-
way at first and then turned onto the so-called Polish road.
The fields stretched out on both sides. The wheat was already
high. Along the furrows peasants were bent over, pulling out
the clumps of weeds. Scarecrows held out their wooden arms,
their ragged sleeves flapping. Birds wheeled and circled overhead, chattering and cawing. As the wagon went by, the peasants lifted their straw hats in greeting to the passengers, the
girls turning their covered heads and smiling. Fresh as he was
from the scenery in Switzerland, southern Germany, and Austria, nevertheless Asa Heshel found something in the Polish
landscape that none of these other countries possessed. It
seemed to him that the difference lay in the strange silence
over everything. The sky hung low over the earth, descending
to form a circular horizon. The small silver clouds that floated above appeared to have a peculiarly Polish shape. All the
sounds merged into a single stilled murmuring: the chirping
of field insects, the humming of bees, the croaking of frogs in
the marshes. The sun seemed to be standing slightly askew in
the sky, glowing with a strange ruddiness, as though it had
lost its way in the low-hanging spaces. From a distance the
farms with their straw-covered cottages appeared like the rel-
ics of ancient settlements. Shepherds had built a fire on pasture land. The smoke ascended in a straight column, as though
from some pagan altar. An open roadside shrine revealed a
figure of Mary holding the Christ child. The sculptor who had
carved the statue had given the figure of the mother a big
round belly, like a pregnant woman. In front of the shrine a
candle burned. The air was filled with the sharp odor of cow-
droppings, upturned roots, and a faint pre-harvest tang. A
timeless tranquillity seemed to exude from the white birches,
which gazed far off into space, and the silver-gray willows,
bent like old men, with long, dangling beards. Asa Heshel was
reminded of the Emperor Casimir and of the Jews who had
come to Poland a thousand years before, asking to be permit-

ted to trade, to build their temples, and to acquire ground to bury their dead.

Adele had not been able to sleep the previous night. Now she reclined on the piled straw in the bed of the wagon, dozing. The driver, a small, broad-shouldered man wearing a sheepskin hat, sat motionless, the reins dangling limply in his hands. It was difficult to tell whether he had fallen asleep or whether he was just lost in thought. The horse crept along slowly, its head lowered. At the edge of a forest Asa Heshel noticed a gypsy camp. A short man with a wide coal-black beard fussed over a copper pan. A swarm of children, mother-naked, ran around in the sun. Women in gaily colored calico dresses were cooking pots of food over fires burning in shallow trenches. Asa Heshel had never come across any gypsies outside of Poland; they were a sign that he was home again.

The wagon entered the forest, and at once it got darker. The fir trees lining both sides of the path stood motionless, trancelike in their dense greenness. There were the shrill whistle of a bird and the call of a cuckoo. The horse cocked its ears and came to a dead stop, as though a disaster that only a beast could sense lay ahead. The driver started up.

"Hey, on with you!"

Asa Heshel sat on a sack of straw and gazed about him. He was back in the familiar region of his youth; each moment was bringing him nearer to Tereshpol Minor. He had gone through a lot in the less than three years since he had left, a green youth, for Warsaw. He had fallen in love with one woman and had married another; he had stolen across borders; he had studied in a university. Jekuthiel the watchmaker had written him that all the youths of the town envied him his great good fortune. But now he felt low in spirits. His suit was wrinkled from the long journey, covered with wisps of straw and hay. In order to save his mother and grandfather the shock of seeing his clean-shaven face, he had refrained from shaving for several days, and now his cheeks and chin were covered with a thick stubble. His eyes were bloodshot from nights of insufficient sleep. What had all his adventures amounted to? He had married a woman he didn't love. He had broken off his studies before they were ended. He would soon have to report to the military. How many times had he sworn to hold fast to the Ten Commandments, the foundation stone of any ethical system! Instead he was carrying on a love affair with a married woman. Well, and what of his dreams of revaluating all values, of discovering Truth, of bringing salvation to the world? His marriage to Adele had trapped him in every way.

As though she had sensed the thoughts that were going through his mind, Adele awoke and sat up. She was wearing a white blouse and a skirt with black and white checks. Red welts covered her cheeks from the hard wagon bed. Her hair had come undone. She adjusted the loose tresses, sticking hairpins in place. She looked at Asa Heshel with her pale, wide-open eyes.

"Where are we?"

"We're getting close to Tereshpol Minor."

"Where's my bag? Where's my comb? What's happened to the valises?"

She broke into a flood of complaints. What did he mean by dragging her around this way? What did she care about Tereshpol Minor? Their whole life together was a mistake. What had he against her? Why had he decided to ruin her young life? She knew very well why he was coming back to Poland. She was mad, out of her mind, to have come along with him. She should have gone directly to Warsaw and let him go wherever he wanted by himself. Dear God in heaven! The best thing for her would be to swallow a vial of iodine and put a finish to the whole degrading business. All of these complaints came flooding from her lips in German, so that the driver should not understand. As she talked every one of her features quivered—her throat, her chin, her temples. Every once in a while her upper lip would draw back convulsively, revealing a row of small teeth, sharp and widely spaced.

Asa Heshel looked at her, but he did not answer. What was the use of all this babbling? They had an agreement, hadn't they? Before they left for Poland he had promised to introduce her to his family and to spend at least a few days with her at her mother's. That promise he was going to keep. All her talk about her love for him and his treachery was hopeless repetition. She had known, the very day she dragged him to the canopy, that he loved Hadassah, not her. She herself had called their marriage an experiment—two people living together without love. He could show her these words in her own handwriting.

The wagon reached the approaches of the town, near the Christian section. The white-painted houses stood a little distance apart from each other, with small garden patches between them. Here and there a potato field stretched between two cottages. The windows were hung with curtains, and the sills were covered with flowerpots. A cat sunned itself behind one of the panes. A barefoot girl drew up a bucket of water from a well. As she bent over, the embroidered edge of her petticoat showed beneath her dress. At the end of the street stood a Catholic church with its two spires. The Orthodox Russian church was behind a row of chestnut trees, its walls covered with figures of bearded apostles.

Soon the wagon rumbled into the market place. Here the houses were taller, dilapidated-looking, and huddled closer together. The shops displayed a motley of goods—textiles and iron pots, kerosene and writing-stands, leather and brooms. On the tower of the town hall the hands of the clock pointed to twelve, as they had for nobody knew how many years. Asa Heshel ordered the driver to stop in front of Jekuthiel the watchmaker's shop. Jekuthiel came out, a small man, with crooked shoulders, almost hunchbacked, in an alpaca coat, striped trousers, and a silk skullcap perched on top of his head. There was a jeweler's eyepiece in his left eye. He stared at the conveyance, saying nothing. Asa Heshel climbed down.

"You don't recognize me?"

"Asa Heshel!"

The two threw their arms about each other.

"Welcome! Welcome! You didn't let me know. This is probably your wife."

"Adele, this is Jekuthiel. I've told you about him."

"I knew your husband before you did," Jekuthiel said, smiling.

They talked for a while, then Asa Heshel climbed back into the wagon and directed the driver toward the Shulgass. The village now revealed itself to Asa Heshel in all its familiarity. The house in which his grandfather lived seemed to have shrunk through the years. The windows hung awry in their frames. A white plume of smoke rose from the chimney. Someone had apparently rushed to carry the news of Asa Heshel's arrival, for as the wagon approached, three women appeared at the door, Asa Heshel's mother, his grandmother, and his sister Dinah. His grandmother's shoulders were bowed with age, her face dried up like a fig. There were yellowish pouches beneath her eyes. Sparse white hairs descended from her chin. She peered over her eyeglasses and shook her head.

"It's you, my child. God knows I wouldn't recognize you. A real foreigner!"

His mother was wearing a loose house robe, with slippers on her white-stockinged feet and a scarf wound tightly over her close-cropped head. Since Asa Heshel had seen her, her chin seemed to have become smaller and her nose sharper. A fine network of wrinkles stood at the corners of her eyes. When she saw him she held her arms wide. An embarrassed flush flamed over her pale cheeks.

"My son, my son! That I have lived to see this day!"

Asa Heshel kissed her. She seemed light and thin in his embrace. His nostrils breathed in her familiar odor. His lips were wet and salty with her tears. Dinah had married the year before; her husband, Menassah David, was away from the village just now. She had changed beyond all recognition. She was wearing a loose dress and a wide matron's wig. She had become stouter. A queer alarm peered out of her eyes.

"Mamma, Mamma, just look at him!"

"This is Adele, my wife." Asa Heshel addressed the remark to all of them.

Finkel fluttered slightly, not knowing what to do. After a momentary hesitation Adele came forward and kissed her.

"My mother-in-law is the image of her son," she said. "Just like two drops of water."

"You're Asa Heshel's wife—now you're my daughter."

"Asa Heshel wrote to all of us," Dinah broke in timidly. "He told us all about you. It seems so strange. As though it were only yesterday when we were children playing together." She put her hand up to the braided matron's wig. The gesture made her seem again a young maiden.

It did not take long for the entire family to gather. There was Uncle Zaddok, his wife Zissle, Uncle Levi and his wife Mindel, and Asa Heshel's cousins as well. The neighbors began to pour in, and soon the kitchen was full of noise and hearty talk. In the meanwhile the wagon-driver unloaded Adele's large trunk and the four valises, pasted over with customs labels. The house was soon filled with the fragrant odor of cakes, milk, and freshly brewed coffee seething in a pot on a tripod over the fireplace. The flames rose from the burning pine branches and cones which the girls of the family gathered in the forest.

3

As evening approached, the bell rang in the church tower, calling the pious Christians to Mass. From the gentile neighborhoods the women began to stream toward the church, in their long black dresses, old-fashioned shoes with pointed toes and low heels, with rosaries and crucifixes dangling from their throats, and with their heads wrapped in black shawls. In their hands they carried gold-stamped prayerbooks. The Jewish townsfolk walked slowly to the prayerhouses and study houses.

Asa Heshel's aunts and uncles and cousins had already gone home, and the neighbors had departed. His mother had a headache and had gone to lie down on her bed. Dinah was preparing the evening meal. Asa Heshel's grandmother was standing at the east wall reading the evening prayer. Adele had gone to the rear room that the couple were occupying. Asa Heshel went out into the yard at the back of the house, separated from the synagogue yard by a fence. The ground was covered with wild growths and vegetation. There was an apple tree that yielded its fruit late in the summer; now its leaves shone like little spears of flame. The weeds grew tall, almost to the height of a man. Among the grasses were clusters of buttercups, puff blossoms, and other blooms whose names Asa Heshel did not know. The air was full of the rustlings and chirpings of field mice, moles, and crickets. Asa Heshel looked about him. In the few hours he had been back with his family he had already listened to all sorts of strange stories. His Uncle Zaddock had hinted that his own brother, Levi, was digging the supports from beneath him and seeking to take away from him his government rabbinical post. His Aunt Mindel accused his Aunt Zissle of having cast an evil spell on her; from what Asa Heshel could make out, Zissle had put into Mindel's trunk an elflock and some reeds of a broom. The girls, his cousins, were carrying on all sorts of feuds; the boys made derogatory remarks about each other. The family, small as it was, was compact with hatred, intrigue, and jealousy. His mother had whispered to him that her two sisters-in-law were her blood enemies.

"They eat me up when they look at me," she told him. "May the evil things they wish me fall and be consumed in a wilderness."

Asa Heshel glanced back at the window of the room that had been given to him and Adele. There was a light inside. He could see Adele bending over and emptying the trunk, as though she were planning on a lengthy stay. In the glow of the lamp her face looked intent. There were dark rings under her eyes. She lifted up some white garment, looked at it, hesitated, and then put it back. How queer it was to think that of all women this was his wife, who had joined her fate with his!

As he stood in the courtyard he saw his grandfather. The old man appeared suddenly and without warning, like some other-world apparition. His long velvet coat flared wide. The fringes of the ritual garment fluttered against his white breeches. His beard hung awry from his chin, as though it were being blown by a gust of wind. He took a step to the left, then back to the right, coming to a halt a little distance from Asa Heshel. Ada Heshel made an involuntary movement backwards.

"So it's you, Asa Heshel."

"Yes, Grandfather."

"I see, I see. You've grown. I think you've grown."

"It may be, Grandfather."

"I know all about everything. You're married. A letter came. Well, *mazeltov*. I didn't send you a wedding gift."

"It doesn't matter, Grandfather."

"Did you at least marry her according to the laws of Moses and Israel?"

"Yes, Grandfather. She comes from a pious household."

"And you count that as a virtue?"

"Of course, Grandfather."

"How is that possible? Apparently the last spark of faith hasn't been extinguished."

"I do not deny the existence of God."

"Then what is it you deny?"

"The pretensions of man."

"You mean the Torah of Moses?"

Asa Heshel was silent.

"I know, I know. All the arguments of the heretics: there is a Creator, but He has revealed Himself to no one; Moses lied. And others maintain that Nature is God. I know, I know. The sum and substance of it all is that any sin is permitted. That's the root of the matter."

"No, Grandfather."

"I'm going to the evening prayers. If you want, come with me. What is there that you can lose?"

"Yes, Grandfather. Of course."

"At least let them see that you have a little Jew left in you."

The old man put his hand on Asa Heshel's elbow, and the two walked slowly along. They came to the antechamber, stopping to wash their hands at the copper urn, and went into the prayerhouse. A candle flickered in the Menorah. The pillars that enclosed the reader's stand threw elongated shadows. The shelves around the walls were packed with books. Some of the students were still bent over the tables, reading in the dim light. Worshippers paced back and forth, softly chanting. A youth swayed fervently in a corner. Near the Ark was a framed inscription in red: "God is always before me." On the cornice of the Ark two carved gilded lions held up the Tablets of the Law. There was a heavy odor that seemed to Asa Heshel to be compounded of candle wax, dust, fast days, and eternity. He stood silent. Here in the dimness everything he had experienced in alien places seemed to be without meaning. Time had flown like an illusion. This was his true home, this was where he belonged. Here was where he would come for refuge when everything else failed.

4

After the evening prayers Asa Heshel returned home with his grandfather and sat with him for a long time in his study. The rabbi asked him many questions about the world outside of Tereshpol Minor. What was it like, this Switzerland? What sort of people lived there? Were there Jews there, and if there were, did they have synagogues, and study houses, and ritual baths, and rabbis? Asa Heshel told him that he himself had attended synagogue services in Lausanne on the holiday of the Rejoicing of the Law; the elder, who called up members of the congregation to the reader's stand to read from the scroll, had spoken French. In Berne and in Zurich, on the other hand, the synagogue officials and the congregation spoke German. The rabbis in Switzerland wrote books on worldly philosophy; their wives did not wear the matron's wig of the pious east European Jewess. Reb Dan listened and puffed at his pipe. He passed his hand over his forehead and pulled down his eyebrows. Yes, it was not a new story to him that the Jews in the Western countries were aping the Christians. In their temples organs played, just as—it was a desecration to mention them in the same breath!—in the churches of the gentile. Nor were there partitions that sectioned off the women from the men in the synagogues; what then was there to keep unclean thoughts and desires from the worshippers? And he had heard, too, that many of the Jews in those Western countries went to the synagogue only on the high holy days, the Days of Awe, Rosh Hashona and Yom Kippur. Why, he had often wondered, did Jews like that remain Jews at all? And what, the rabbi wanted to know, were the thoughts of those Jews who had become complete heretics? If God had lost all meaning for them, and the world was without design, how could they justify calling themselves Jews? Asa Heshel made an answer to the effect that Jews were a people like every other people, and that they were demanding that the nations of the world return the Holy Land to them. But the rabbi was far from satisfied. If, he insisted, they had no further belief in the Bible, then why should they have any longing for the Biblical land of the Jews? Why not some other country? Any country? And besides all that, who could be foolish enough to think that Turkey would give Palestine up to them? The rewards of this world were for the strong, not the weak.

The rabbi passed on to questions concerning Asa Heshel's personal affairs. What had he learned there in the universities of the gentiles? And would what he had learned at least enable him to earn a livelihood? What would he do if he were called to serve in the army? Did he want to put on the Czar's uniform? It struck Asa Heshel that even for simple questions like these he could not find answers that would really satisfy the old man. He had not finished his studies, he told him; nor would the study of philosophy be much of a help when it came to making a living. As for serving the Czar, of course he was not eager to become a recruit, but he did not intend to inflict some sort of physical disability on himself. The old man wanted to say to him: "Then why did you come back to Poland? What have you accomplished with your frenzied chase after the fleshpots of the world?" But he decided to refrain. Had he not discovered time after time that people of this sort remained stubborn to the end? The rabbi got up from his chair.

"*Nu*," he said, "go and have something to eat. There'll be plenty of time to talk."

He paced back and forth. He furrowed his brow, plucked

at his beard, and sighed. Asa Heshel sat where he was for a while, but his grandfather paid no further attention to him. He got up and left the study.

In the kitchen the evening meal was already waiting for him. His grandmother had prepared some soup with kasha, some beef and peas, and plum stew for dessert. They all fussed about him, his mother, his sister Dinah, and a servant girl whom he had not noticed earlier. He was barely through eating when the relatives and neighbors began streaming into the kitchen again. Asa Heshel saw grown women in matron's wigs with whom he remembered playing children's games when they were all young together. They stole curious glances at him, smiled and nodded their heads. Adele had already established a comfortable intimacy with everybody. She had wrapped a scarf tightly over her hair, and somehow the provincial touch gave her face a more familiar appearance. She showed Asa Heshel's cousins an apron that she had embroidered herself and a silk underbodice that she had bought in Vienna. She took out of her purse the foreign coins she had with her, and the others gaped at them in wonder. His mother drew Asa Heshel into a corner and whispered to him that the daughter-in-law he had brought to her was a treasure, intelligent and good. She wanted him to promise her that he would honor Adele loyally and guard her against all harm. His sister Dinah winked knowingly at him, a clear sign that her sister-in-law was to her liking. His aunts and cousins hung on her every word and gazed at her with adoration.

His grandmother brought him a small skullcap to wear instead of the modern hat he had kept on his head. They all sighed when he put it on. Adele brought him a hand mirror so that he might look at himself: he hardly recognized his own face; the sprouting beard on his chin and cheeks and the traditional skullcap on his head had taken away the last bit of his resemblance to the Westerner.

All during the meal Adele kept throwing triumphant glances toward him, as though she were saying: "Your family, and they're all on my side! To them *I'm* your wife, not Hadassah." She seized every opportunity to address Finkel as "mother-in-law" and went into a long account of the distinguished family she came from, reciting the names of famous rabbis. Asa Heshel's grandmother was hard of hearing, and from time to time Adele would have to repeat what she had said, putting her lips close to the old lady's ear. The aging woman shook her head solemnly; they had been afraid, here in Tereshpol Minor, that Asa Heshel would marry someone of a common family; thank God, he had taken a woman befitting his station.

After the meal Adele went with the other women to sit on the benches outside. Asa Heshel walked off alone through the village. For a while he stopped at the study house. Near the door, at a long bare table, a few old men bent over open volumes dimly illuminated with flickering candles. From the Shulgass Asa Heshel turned into the Lublin Road. He halted for a moment at a water pump with a broken handle. There was a legend current in Tereshpol Minor that although the well underneath had long since dried up, once during a fire water had begun to pour from the spout, and the synagogue and the houses around it had been saved from destruction.

He turned to the road that led to the woods. It was lined with great trees, chestnut and oak. Some of them had huge gashes torn in their sides by bolts of lightning. The holes looked dark and mysterious, like the caves of robbers. Some of the older trees inclined their tops down toward the ground, as though they were ready to tumble over, tearing up with them the tangled thickness of their centuries-old roots.

5

Near the woods, not far from where the barracks had once stood, Asa Heshel came upon a small, one-story building, its front window brightly lighted. He went closer. Through the glass he could see a room lined with bookshelves to the ceiling. A kerosene lamp hung from a chain. What, he wondered, was a study house doing here, so far away from the Shulgass? Then he noticed on the far wall a portrait of Theodor Herzl. So this was the library they had told him about. He climbed the three steps to the door, knocked, and, getting no answer, pushed against the knob and went in. The group of men and women in the room turned toward him. Jekuthiel the watchmaker came hurrying up on his short legs. The others crowded forward. Asa Heshel recognized most of them, but he had forgotten their names. The majority of the men were in the familiar caftans; other wore Westernized clothing, with stiff collars and ties. The girls were wearing calico dresses or skirts and colored blouses, and shoes with high uppers. On one of the walls of the room, he noticed, there was a blackboard, and on it a carefully written sentence in Hebrew: "The inkwell is on the table"; the translation in Yiddish was written below.

"It's you at last," Jekuthiel said to him with satisfaction. "We were this moment talking about getting you to visit us."

"I'm David Katz." A short, youthful man came up to Asa Heshel and held out his hand. "You must meet our comrades here." He turned to the others. "This is Asa Heshel Bannet, who has just come back from Switzerland."

They pressed forward to introduce themselves, the men first, filing past and extending moist palms, at the same time calling out their last names: Rosenzweig, Meisner, Beckerman, Silbermintz, Cohen, Frampolsky, Rappaport. It was puzzling to Asa Heshel to realize that these were the playmates of his childhood; Meisner was Chaim, the youngest child of the owner of the junk yard; Frampolsky was the son of Leibush the coachman; and Rappaport was the one they had called "Scabbyhead"—they had gone to cheder together. Their faces were a puzzling medley of the intimate and the strange. There was something bewildering in these brows, eyes, noses, mouths, these shapes hidden somewhere in Asa Heshel's memory, hovering on the brink of being blasted from all recollection. The girls were huddled in a separate cluster. They smiled and giggled, trying to push each other forward, their cheeks flushed. In their expressions there was an embarrassment as well as a warmth he had seldom noticed in the outside world.

"Don't let me interfere with what you were doing," he said. "I just happened to drop in."

"Oh, it doesn't matter at all."

"Has the library been here long?"

"Tell him, Jekuthiel," David Katz said.

"Why me? You're the director."

"You know the troubles we've had better than I do."

"What's the difference? It's a bit of a library, that's all. Your grandfather thunders to the heavens, but, to tell the truth, no one pays any attention to him any more. The Chassidim have lodged complaints against us with the authorities three times, but so far we've been able to manage."

"Tell him about the time they broke in and burned all our books."

"It's true. The fanatics broke in through the windows. Now we have heavy shutters. But if it isn't one trouble it's another. Just now it's factions: Hebrew versus Yiddish, Zionism versus

Socialism, God knows what else. Making fools of themselves
—just as in the big cities."

Asa Heshel looked over the shelves of books. Most of the
volumes were well worn and thumbed, the stamping on the
covers faded. He opened a book or two at random; there were
sentences underlined and copious marginal notes. Some of the
names of the authors he was not familiar with; apparently a
few new writers had emerged since he had been away from
Poland. On a table lay magazines and a literary anthology in
paper covers, its pages stapled together. He leafed through it,
and saw poems with lines consisting of only a couple of words
and many dots—a sort of European quality penetrating the
Yiddish characters. In an article under the title "Jews with a
Mission" one author had written:

*We Jews are tired of all these metaphysical missions which
the German rabbiners and the other Jewish leaders have saddled on our weak shoulders. We reject the argument that we
must turn back the clock of history and return to Palestine.
The Jewish masses love their homes. They want to live in
brotherhood with their neighbors and to fight shoulder to
shoulder with them for a better world, where there will be
neither nations, classes, nor religions, but only one united, advancing humanity.*

It was nearly midnight when the library closed. Asa Heshel,
Jekuthiel, and David Katz walked on ahead, the others trail-
ing behind them, the men and women arm in arm. There were
loud conversations and laughter. One of the girls began to
sing a song; the men joined in. Their footsteps echoed sharp
and clear on the cobbled road. Shadows moved on ahead of
them, the shapes converging, mingling, and separating as in
the rounds of a dance. Jekuthiel smoked a cigarette and
smiled.

"If your grandfather could see this!" he said.

"There are worse sins than this committed in Tereshpol
Minor," someone commented.

The others left Asa Heshel at the entrance to the Shulgass.
He shook hands with each one of them; a girl in spectacles
pressed his hand with special fervor, her glasses blinking in
the moonlight. Soon they were gone and Asa Heshel was left
alone. He took a deep breath and listened intently. Somewhere an owl hooted, a mournful wail as though over some
unbearable sorrow. Asa Heshel knew that Adele would be

lying awake waiting for him, ready to welcome him with accusations, complaints, and nagging. He already knew by heart
what she would say and what he would answer. Then there
would come the making up, the caresses in the dark, and the
lies.

CHAPTER FOUR

1

One evening, when Hadassah was home alone and sat reading
a book on the porch of the summer cottage in Usefov, she
heard someone cough. She looked up. Rosa Frumetl was
standing on the lawn below, her hand resting against the trunk
of a pine. She was wearing a flowered dress and white shoes.
Her wrinkled face was burned from the sun, her nose was red,
and her lips were pressed tightly together. She stared at Hadassah with the determined look of one who has come bent
on some mischief. Hadassah let the book fall from her hands.

"I'm not the guest you expected, eh?" Rosa Frumetl said in
a harsh voice. "I've come to tell you that we know all your
carryings-on. The truth comes out like oil on the top of
water."

"What is it you want?" Hadassah stammered.

"You know all right. You're not the saint you make yourself out to be. Don't think that the world's gone crazy altogether. There's still a God in heaven who sees everything and
hears everything. The Almighty takes His time, but He pun-
ishes with a heavy hand."

"You'll pardon me—"

"I didn't come to pay you a neighborly visit. I'll talk plain
words. You're false to your husband. And you're stealing
someone else's husband. I just want to warn you that you're
playing with fire. Whatever you do with yourself is your affair. If you choose to run around with your naked hair showing, like any slut, well, I'm not God's Cossack. In God's good
time you'll get His punishment. But I'll not allow you to break
up my daughter's life. I tell you I'll raise such an alarm that
people'll come running from all over the neighborhood."

Hadassah felt the blood leave her face. "I don't know what
you mean."

"You write him love letters. You make a mock of everything decent in a Jewish woman. You're getting ready to run away with him and be his mistress. Do you think that people's eyes are blind? In the first place it'll only take a few weeks before he gets sick and tired of you. And in the second place—do you hear me?—I'll not let it get as far as that. I'll let your husband know and I'll let your mother know. God help us, she's a sick woman, and what you're doing'll send her to her grave. And besides, it's against the law. In Poland whores must carry a yellow pass."

"You'll be good enough to go."

"I'll go when I'm good and ready. You keep on acting like a wanton and I'll pull the hair out of your head! Don't forget, you're no stranger to the inside of a prison."

Hadassah tore herself up from her chair and started to run into the house. Rosa Frumetl ran after her, taking short, mincing steps, and shouting out: "Wanton! Prostitute! Help!"

Hadassah closed the glass-paned door. Rosa Frumetl started to bang with her fist against the framework. The caretaker's dog awoke and ran toward her, barking. There was a stick leaning on the rail of the veranda. Rosa Frumetl picked it up and waved it at the dog.

"Away! Away! So you turn your dogs on me. There is still a world to come, dear Father in heaven! May the plagues of Egypt afflict you! May the epilepsy toss you as high as the roof!"

The caretaker's wife came out of her cottage and quieted the dog. Rosa Frumetl said something to her in Polish. Hadassah went to the closet, snatched an overcoat, hat, and bag, rushed through the kitchen door, and ran to the gate that opened on the meadow. She hurried to the Usefov station. Every once in a while she stopped to look back, as though afraid that Rosa Frumetl was behind her. There was a train waiting at the platform. She climbed in without buying a ticket. It was only when the train started that she found it was bound for Otwotsk. Near Shvider some men and women were bathing in the river. The sun had gone down, and purple shadows lay on the smooth surface of the water. A big bird flew low. Phonographs could be heard grinding out music in the cottages near the tracks. Couples strolled along the wooded paths. A venerable-looking Jew stood near a tree, piously shaking his body back and forth, reciting the evening prayers. At the Otwotsk station Hadassah got out and bought a ticket to Warsaw. There was a train already in, but it wasn't due to leave for another twenty minutes. She climbed into the dark coach and sat down. She was the only one there. She closed her eyes. Ahead of her the locomotive emitted a muffled puffing and snorting. The smoke from its stacks came in through the window. A deep calm seemed to have fallen on Hadassah's spirit. The blow she had suffered was so cataclysmic that it was as though she were left without the possibility of pain. But at the same time she was aware that the real anguish would come later. She felt cold and put up her coat collar. If he had been there to hear all that! the thought flashed through her mind. If only he knew how much she was paying.

In the last letter she had written to him she had given him detailed instructions for finding her. He was to come to meet her at the cottage; Fishel was never there during the week, and she had so arranged matters that there would be none of the usual visitors around. And now all the plans were shattered, and she didn't know what to do next. Maybe she should go to Klonya's. But how would he know that she was there? No, she would have to go home to the apartment on Gnoyna Street. But what sort of excuse would she be able to give to Fishel for coming back to Warsaw in the oppressive summer heat? And what would Shifra say when she returned to the cottage and found her gone? What would the caretaker think? Rosa Frumetl must have told her everything, and now the busy tongues would spread the news throughout the region. Besides, how could she be sure that Rosa Frumetl wouldn't tell Fishel? She might even call him on the telephone from the country. No question but that she had gone straight to Hadassah's mother, and then Mamma'd get another attack.

The common-sense thing would be to go back to Usefov at once. What was the use of running away? The secret was no secret any longer. But how was it possible for her to go back? Rosa Frumetl's insults, her banging on the door, her calls for help, had thrown Hadassah into a panic. The whole thing had the aspect of one of those childish nightmares which came back every time something frightened her, the same gnawing in her stomach, the chill at her ribs, the tingling at the roots of her hair.

The train started. The conductor came in and lit the lamp. He took Hadassah's ticket and punched two holes in it. Hadassah looked out of the window. The Shvider River lay still in the night. The woods around were bathed in darkness. At Falenitz, Hadassah caught a glimpse of the inside of an inn, with porters and draymen playing dominoes. At Miedzeshin, where Klonya lived, Hadassah got to her feet, as though to get off, but she sat down again. After the train passed Vaver, factory buildings could be seen near the tracks. Smoke rose from chimneys. Workers moved about behind barred window panes. Soon the train passed the Praga cemetery. A strange envy gripped Hadassah. What was it like under those mounds of earth? A lighted tramcar rumbled past the cemetery railings. A raised signal light changed color, from red to green. In a few moments the train reached the bridge. The Vistula flowed clear and limpid between its banks. A divine peace lay upon the waters, like the silence before Creation.

The train came to a stop. Hadassah got out. Where was her valise? Yes, she remembered, she hadn't taken one with her. How oppressive it was here in the city! The heat beat up in waves from the concrete platform. Hadassah walked past the locomotive, huge and black, emitting a foul stench of coal fumes. Oil dripped from the massive wheels and axles. The chimney still coughed hoarsely. Through the window could be seen a half-naked man in front of the open furnace. His face was covered with soot. His eyes reflected the flames of the fire, like a devil in Gehenna. Outside the station, droshkies darted along. Newsboys were calling out extras; Hadassah caught a phrase, something about a note that Austria had sent to Serbia. So apparently all the talk about war had not been idle. And it was at such a time that Asa Heshel was coming! Because of her he would fall right into the maw of disaster!

She stopped at a store on the Muranov and telephoned Abram's house. There was no answer. He was apparently out of the city with Ida or maybe hanging around somewhere with the actress of whom Hadassah had heard talk. Then she telephoned her Aunt Leah. She wanted to talk to Masha, but Masha wasn't at home; she must be with that painter, that gentile boy of hers. Dear God in heaven, was there no one she could talk to? She picked up the telephone again and called her father. There was no answer there either. She went out of the store and hailed a droshky. She climbed in and told the driver to take her to her flat on Gnoyna Street.

2

It was Wednesday evening of the next week. The telephone in the corridor rang. Hadassah got up to answer it. She picked up the receiver, her fingers trembling. *"Proshen,"* she said in Polish, "Please." There was no answer; all she could hear through the receiver was a hoarse scratching and whistling. Then suddenly a low voice came through clearly.

It was he. Hadassah tried to speak, but there was a tightness in her throat. It was as though the power of speech had left her. Her teeth chattered. "It's me, Hadassah."

There was silence for a few moments, then she said: "Where are you?"

"In a druggist's, on the Krochmalna."

"When did you come? Dear God in heaven."

She heard him murmur something, but she did not make out what he was saying.

"Speak louder."

He again said something, but although she heard every word separately, she could not grasp the meaning. She could hear him saying: "Last night—I mean the night before—from Shvider." What was he doing in Shvider, she wondered.

Aloud she said: "Wait for me. At the corner of Krochmalna and Gnoyna. Do you know where I mean?"

"Yes."

"I'll be there soon. I'm leaving now."

She tried to hang up the receiver, but her fingers were powerless to release it; it was a second or two before she could put it on its hook. Thank God Fishel wasn't at home! She went into her room and opened a closet. Dear God, the day had come at last! She looked over the row of clothes. They were all winter things; her summer dresses were in Usefov. She opened a cupboard and took out a black belt. She put on a broad-rimmed straw hat. Where was her key? And her bag? She wanted to turn off the gaslight, but she couldn't reach it. Well, never mind, let it burn. She went out and let the door close on the snap lock. She began to hurry down the dark staircase, but slowed her pace. She had better be careful; she might fall. She felt a pain in her left breast. "If only I don't die before I get to Krochmalna Street!" She passed Fishel's store. The glass-paned doors were already locked, but a gaslight burned inside. A dim glow fell on the greasy walls, the stone floor, the casks and vats, the tin containers. Fishel was not to be seen. He was probably somewhere in the back. Gnoyna Street was crowded. Faces flashed by, half-hidden in the shadows. Newsboys were hawking another extra; Hadassah could see the enormous scareheads on the page, but she couldn't make out what the words were. How the people were snatching the papers! How adroitly the newsboy was making change! A coin fell on the sidewalk; she could hear the sharp ring. A porter passed her, an enormous load strapped to his shoulders. A baker's boy, in a patched shirt and long drawers, balanced a tray on his head, with fresh-baked cakes on it. Who had scattered these apples on the sidewalk? It was a policeman. He was poking with the point of his boot into a basket, and the peddler woman was weeping. Children were scrambling for the apples. Hadassah hurried on to the end of Krochmalna Street. Asa Heshel was not there. Had she imagined the whole thing? Suddenly she caught sight of him. The way she remembered him, yet somehow changed. He had grown taller, and somewhat fuller. He had a foreign look about him.

"Hadassah!"

"Asa Heshel!"

They were both silent.

For a moment she hesitated, then she embraced him. Her face became hot and moist. She kissed his cheek and he kissed her on the brow. She felt the salt taste on her lips. People stopped to stare. They were not far from Fishel's store, but that did not occur to her now. She grasped both his hands.

"Come."

"Where?"

"Come with me."

"You mean to Usefov?"

Hadassah was not aware of what she was saying or of what he was asking her.

A droshky passed by. She waved and the driver brought it to a stop. She climbed in, banging her knee against the step. Asa Heshel hesitated for a moment, then got in after her. The driver turned around.

"Where do you want to go?"

"Just drive ahead," Hadassah said. "Anywhere."

"To Lazhenki Park?"

"Yes."

The driver wheeled the droshky about. Hadassah lost her balance and swayed. She clutched Asa Heshel's sleeve. Everything seemed to be turning around—the sky, the rows of buildings, the street lamps.

"When did you come?"

"Monday. Today."

"Today's Wednesday."

"I was in Shvider. At her mother's. I mean at her stepfather's."

Hadassah was silent; it was as though she were pondering

some hidden meaning in what he had just said. For the moment she had forgotten that he had come back to Poland with Adele, and that Rosa Frumetl lived in Shvider with her new husband.

"Now we'll be together. For always."

"Yes. For always."

"No one will separate us."

"No one."

The droshky swayed, as if it were going downhill. They were driving past the Saxon Gardens. Sparks of light glowed and died among the thickness of the tree branches and foliage. There was a crescent moon in the sky; a star shone brightly. Only a few hours before, Hadassah had been here; now they were different streets, different lamps, different trees. The droshky rolled on. The moon raced ahead. The hindquarters of the horse rose and fell. Two girls carried huge bunches of flowers. Dear God, how many moths there were flying about those lampposts! And what shadows they threw! And the perfume of the acacias. "This is the happiest moment of my life," Hadassah thought. She suddenly remembered that he was to have met her in Usefov.

"Were you in Usefov?"

"Twice. The woman told me you'd left."

"I'd been waiting for you."

"I couldn't understand. Why didn't you stay there?"

"Because—never mind. We're together now. Until death."

"If they don't take me into the army."

"Please God, no. Take off your hat. I want to see you."

She pulled off his hat. It tumbled down and she bent to get it. Asa Heshel bent down too. The droshky swerved to the side. For a moment the two seemed to be suspended in midair. The momentum almost flung them to the floor. They held on to each other. The driver pulled on the reins and brought the droshky to a halt. He turned and pulled his cap to the side of his head, looking at them with the good-natured patience of one who is used to the foolishness of enamored couples, especially in the summer evenings.

"Careful," he said. "You'll tumble out."

Hadassah looked at him with a radiant expression on her face.

"Forgive us," she said. "We're just so happy."

3

The droshky turned into Marshalkovska Street and went past the Vienna Station. The clock in the station tower showed fifteen minutes to eleven, but the square was as crowded as though the evening were still young. The tramcars were packed. Droshkies rolled along in all directions. The sidewalks were jammed. Men in light-colored suits and straw hats, swinging canes jauntily, sauntered along with girls in flowered dresses, white gloves, and hats bedecked with blossoms and cherries. In the light of the electric lamps the bare arms and throats of the women seemed extraordinarily livid. Beneath wide hat brims and behind veils their eyes glowed with a midsummer amorousness. Asa Heshel had never seen Warsaw in the summer. The city seemed to him vaster, richer, and more elegant. Hardly two weeks had gone by since he had left Switzerland, but he felt that he had been traveling for months. Ever since his visit to Tereshpol Minor he had not had a decent night's sleep. First there had been the endless rides in trains and wagons. Then there had been the night he spent with Adele at a hotel on Nalevki Street. She had quarreled with him until dawn. He had let her talk him into going with her to Shvider, to the house where her mother was staying with her new husband, Wolf Hendlers. When he had got there, Rosa Frumetl immediately started to upbraid him. Adele had gone off into hysterics. Wolf Hendlers, too, had chided him for his behavior.

Twice he had gone to Usefov to find Hadassah. The first time he had been unable to locate the cottage. The second time the caretaker had told him that Hadassah had left. When he returned to Shvider he saw Adele getting off the same train. She had apparently trailed him. She had grabbed him by the arm on the platform and had screamed at him: "Now I know everything. You dog!" She had yelled and sobbed. He had taken to his heels and had not stopped running until he reached Falenitz. There he had caught a train to Warsaw. He had at once telephoned to Hadassah's house but had got no answer. He had gone to Gina's. She welcomed him warmly, but was unable to provide him with a room. She had taken him to a flat where two girls, seamstresses, lived, and they consented to rent him a dark room.

All this he blurted out to Hadassah in broken phrases.

"What kind of seamstress?" she asked. "I don't understand the whole thing."

"Gina didn't have any place for me. All of her rooms were taken."

"Why did you stop off at your grandfather's? I thought that you had already begun to regret the whole thing."

"No, Hadassah. I love you. I love you more than anything else in the world."

At Jerusalem Alley the droshky came to a halt. Laborers were digging up the street, repairing the sewers. Electric flares were burning in the trenches. A spotlight threw a stark yellow glare. There was a smell of asphalt, gas, and mold. Down below they could see mud-covered pipes and half-naked men. It was some time before the droshky could continue on its way.

Hadassah said something, but because of the noise Asa Heshel could not hear what it was. On Uyazdover Alley the benches were crowded with people. Asa Heshel looked at Hadassah.

"Where are we going?"

"I told him to drive to Lazhenki Park."

"Is it open?"

"I don't know."

"What will we do if it's closed?"

She looked at him and didn't answer. The droshky came to a halt.

"Here you are."

Asa Heshel put his hand in his pocket and drew forth a silver coin. The driver looked at it and tried to bend it.

"This is foreign money, panie."

"Oh, I made a mistake." Asa Heshel reached again in his pocket and brought out a half-ruble. He handed it to the driver and motioned him to keep the change.

The driver raised his whip. "Thank you, sir." The two got out and the droshky wheeled off.

The park gate was still open, but a watchman was standing near it to prevent newcomers from entering. Asa Heshel and Hadassah walked along the street. After they had taken a few steps Hadassah stopped abruptly.

"My God," she said, "I didn't even ask you if you were hungry. How did you happen to be on the Krochmalna?"

"Because it was near your house."

"I was getting ready to leave. If you had called five minutes later you'd have found me gone. The moment the bell rang I knew it was you."

"All day you weren't at home. I must have telephoned twenty times."

"How can that be possible? Oh, yes, I went to Stepha's, Abram's daughter. Her sister, Bella, got married. Oh, if I had known that you were in Warsaw! I was talking about you to Stepha. She knows all about us. Masha, too."

"What about him?" Asa Heshel asked after some hesitation.

Hadassah turned pale. "I wrote you everything. It was an act of despair. Now it's over. I wanted to punish myself. You'll never understand."

"Yes, I do understand. We were both desperate. Why didn't you stay in Usefov?"

"Didn't I tell you? Her mother came and made a scene. It was terrible."

"We'll have to go away somewhere."

"Yes. We must go away. But where? I'd have to pack a few things. But now it would be impossible. He's home."

"I see."

"Everything is against us, but they won't separate us. There's something I want to tell you. Papa's in Warsaw. There's trouble between him and Mamma. Sometimes he goes out to see Abram. They had a quarrel, but they made up. Papa's just practically in love with him. He imitates whatever he does. It's all so crazy. If Papa's not home I'll be able to get the key from the janitor."

"Maybe it would be best to telephone."

"There's no place to phone from here. Let's sit for a while on that bench."

They sat down, looking at a villa that stood opposite, nestling among a group of acacias. The tall windows were lighted behind the brocaded hangings. From time to time a silhouetted figure fluttered by. Above the windows was a carved balcony, supported by three sculptured figures of Hercules. A cool wind was blowing. Asa Heshel glanced at his wrist watch. It had stopped at five minutes to eleven. It must be a good deal later than that now. Most of the benches were empty.The tramcars arriving from the heart of the city were rolling up empty, swaying drunkenly on the tracks. Shadows passed over Hadassah's face. Asa Heshel's love for her, quiet beneath his travel fatigue, suddenly flared up. "Dear God, I'm actually sitting beside her," he thought. "I'm holding her hand in mine. It isn't a dream." He bent toward her, but at the moment someone sat down at the other end of the bench.

"Hadassah," Asa Heshel murmured, "is it really you?"

"Yes, it's me." The foliage of a tree threw a network of shadow over her features. She bent her head. "Maybe we can go to your place," she said.

"We would have to go through their room."

"Who? Oh, the seamstresses." She lapsed into silence, mystified by all these intricate complications that were closing in around her.

4

When the two again climbed into a droshky it was late, long past midnight. Hadassah told the driver to take them to Panska Street. The driver was apparently drunk; in the middle of the ride, near Jerusalem Alley, the carriage came to a stop. The horse raised his hoofs and brought them down heavily on the cobblestones. The driver's head dropped to his chest, and at once his heavy snoring could be heard. Asa Heshel leaned forward and tapped him on the shoulder. He awoke with a start and picked up his whip. Before starting he turned around and asked again for the address. Hadassah told him to stop at the end of Vielka Street. They got off, and Asa Heshel paid the man a half-ruble. Hadassah murmured something about his spending too much, and Asa Heshel made some answer. Both of them were so tired that they had little idea of what they were saying.

There was no sign of life on Panska Street. The street lamps, standing widely separated, threw a yellow glow on the pavement. The stores were locked and shuttered. Hadassah had to ring the bell for a long time before the janitor at her father's house came to open the gate. Hadassah asked him if her father was home, but the janitor did not know. She wanted him to open the door—all this while Asa Heshel was standing a little distance off—but he swore that he did not have the key. She joined Asa Heshel, took his arm, and the two walked along Tvarda Street to the Gzhybov. Hadassah pointed out Meshulam Moskat's house. The windows were dark, except for a red lamp glowing behind one of the panes.

"My grandfather's house. My Uncle Joel lives there now."

"Gina told me he's sick."

"Yes. Very sick."

From the Gzhybov they turned onto Gnoyna Street. Hadassah, it seemed, was turning her footsteps toward home. At a courtyard entrance she came to a halt. At the right Asa Heshel could see a sign with an inscription on it: "Fishel Kutner." She pulled the bell. Asa Heshel stared at her. Was this her way of saying goodby to him? She took him by the arm and smiled. Her face was unusually pale. Golden points of light shone in her eyeballs. They heard steps.

"You follow me," Hadassah whispered in his ear.

He wanted to ask what she meant, but now there was no more time. A heavy key turned in the lock, and the door opened. Asa Heshel saw the long, red face of the janitor, one-eyed, and with a black patch instead of a nose. He put his hand in his pocket, took out a silver coin, and thrust it into the other's calloused paw, their fingers fumbling against each other's.

"Where's the gentleman going?"

"It's all right, Jan. He's our guest," Hadassah answered and pulled at Asa Heshel's sleeve. She hurried through the gate, Asa Heshel following her uncertainly. For a moment he could see nothing, as though he had been swallowed up in darkness. Apparently the walls enclosing the court were blank. A small rectangle of sky reared high up over his head, studded with stars. It was as though he were at the bottom of a pit. For a moment he was alone, then Hadassah materialized near him. They put their arms around each other. Her hat fell to the ground.

"Come with me," she whispered. Her lips touched the lobe of his ear.

She took his wrist. He followed blindly. "Whatever happens will happen," he thought. He was full of fear and recklessness. "She's taking me to her husband. I don't care. I'll tell him openly that she belongs to me." The yard was a long one. He stumbled against a cart, barrels, and boxes. There was a smell of oil and brine. Hadassah drew him after her into a doorway. He followed her to the stairs. They went silently, walking on tiptoe. Hadassah halted on the third floor. She tried to open a door, but it was locked.

"One second."

She disappeared somewhere and he was alone, with the feeling of a small boy who has been left to wait for his guardian to return. He put his hand on the door, felt the wood, the knob, the keyhole. He pushed the door open. How was that possible? Only a moment before it had been locked. He wanted to call Hadassah, but he didn't dare to make a sound. Inside it was pitch black. His nostrils sniffed the dust of a long-uninhabited apartment. Where had she gone? Maybe to get a key. Yes, she had brought him to an empty flat in the house belonging to her husband. Everything was explained now. Where was she? She might stumble and fall. Was he happy now? Yes, this was happiness. Now he would be ready to die.

He heard footsteps.

"Hadassah, where are you?"

"I am here."

"The door is open."

"Did you force it?"

"No. It opened."

"But how? Never mind."

He opened the door wide and went in, Hadassah after him. He reached out to take her hand, but his fingers met something warm and wooly. She was carrying a shawl, or a blanket. They entered a narrow corridor. Then they were in a large room, crowded with furniture. Asa Heshel brushed against a rocking-chair; it began to sway back and forth. He bumped his head against the edge of a tiled stove. Hadassah took his hand and led him after her. She pushed open a door with the toe of her shoe and they passed into a smaller room. Now his eyes were getting accustomed to the darkness. He could make out wallpaper, a metal bed, a dresser, a looking-glass. A ray of light flashed across the mirror. A torn curtain hung over the window. Hadassah put the blanket down on the mattress.

"What room is this?"

"Our room."

They embraced and stood close to each other in silence. He could hear the beating of her heart. She took his wrist in her hand and pressed it tight.

She let go of him and spread the blanket on the mattress. They lay down. A patch of sky showed through the torn curtain at the window. A strange and secret, never before experienced warmth enclosed Asa Heshel. He passed his hands over Hadassah's body, like a blind man, touching her eyes, her forehead, her nose and cheeks, her throat and breasts. They gazed at each other, the pupils of their eyes enormous and filled with the mystery of night.

PART
FIVE

CHAPTER ONE

1

A few days after the war broke out, the Tereshpol Minor town crier read aloud in the market square an order that all Jews were to leave the town within twenty-four hours. Immediately pandemonium set in. To the elders of the Jewish community the magistrate announced that the orders had come from Zamosc. Two of the town's prominent Jewish householders immediately took a coach into Zamosc, but the *nachalnik* would not even receive them. The order, he sent out word, had come from the Czar's uncle, Nikolai Nikolaievich, commander-in-chief of the Russian armies.

Those who had horses and wagons immediately began to pack their belongings together. The others tried to hire or buy any sort of conveyance from the neighborhood peasants. The Poles who lived in the town acted as though what was going on was none of their affair. They went unconcernedly about their daily chores. Markevich, the slaughterer, slit the throat of a pig; Dobush, the butcher, went on with his cornthreshing and apple-gathering. Anek Liss, the bootmaker, left his bench to stroll over to the shop of Mottel, the leather dealer, and propose that the stock of leather be sold to him for a third of its value.

"They'll take it away from you anyway," he announced. "And there are rumors that they're going to kill all the Jews." He drew his finger suggestively across his gullet. "K-k-k-k!"

The Jewish housewives ran to their gentile neighbors to wail and sob, but the gentiles were too busy to listen to them. They were occupied with sifting flour, putting up preserves, churning butter, making cheese. The older women sat spinning flax, while the children played with dogs and cats or dug in the ground for worms. They could get along very well without the Jews.

Some of the Jewish housewives tried to store furniture with their neighbors for safe keeping, but the latter complained that their houses were already too crowded. Just the same, they were ready to take bundles of clothing, linen, silverware, and jewelry.

It was on a Monday morning that the town crier read out

the proclamation. By noon on Tuesday three quarters of the Jews had left. The Lublin road was jammed with wagons, carts, and pedestrians. The Jewish butchers drove their live-stock ahead of them. The poor folk had packed their few pos-sessions in bundles and were carrying them on their backs. The scrolls of the law from the synagogue had been carefully placed on beds of straw in a wagon, the holy objects covered with prayer shawls and Ark curtains. A group of men and women walked alongside to guard them. The peasants and their wives came to the doors of their cottages. Some brought out pannikins of water to the fleeing Jews; others laughed and jeered.

"Oi, oi! Sheenies! Pappele, Mammele!"

Rabbi Dan and his family left the village with the last group to go. The old man had given orders that the books in his study be hidden in the garret. He was carrying with him his prayer-shawl bag and a couple of cherished volumes. He crammed his manuscripts into the mouth of the stove and then watched them burn.

"The world will survive without them," he remarked.

The rabbi leaned against the doorpost as the papers burned. Three sackfuls of manuscripts and letters had accumulated in the more than forty years that he had occupied the rabbinical chair. How, he wondered, could he have written so much? There had been a time when he had entertained the idea of publishing some of his commentaries. Now that was all in the past. The flames were in no hurry. Gusts of down-drafts blew some of the pages out of the fire, and the rabbi had to pick them up and throw them back. The thick bundles of manu-scripts were too slow to catch on; it was necessary first to tear the pages apart. In the heart of the flames a yellowed sheaf of paper lay for a long time uncharred as though by a miracle. When at last it did burn, the pages kept their shape for a while, the glowing lines of writing standing out in fiery char-acters.

When the sacks were emptied the rabbi went out of the house to the waiting wagon. He kissed the mezuzah on the lin-tel of the door and took a last glance backward over the yard, thickly overgrown with wild grasses and weeds. He looked at the apple tree, the shingled roofs, the chimney, the windows, the outdoor booth built for the Feast of Tabernacles. Over the roof of the prayerhouse a stork hovered. The panes of the study-house windows threw back the golden rays of the sun. A column of smoke rose from the chimney of the communal

bathhouse; the village Christians were going to use it now that
the Jews were being driven out. The hearse still stood at the
door of the poorhouse. The rabbi's wife, his daughter, Finkel,
and her daughter, Dinah, were already seated in the wagon
among pillows, packages, and bundles of bedclothes. The old
woman was weeping. Dinah's head was bandaged with a
towel. Her husband, Menassah David, was lost somewhere in
Galicia. Reb Dan took his seat in the wagon and looked up at
the sky.

"Well, it's time to go," he said.

The wagon went by the *shulgass* and the market place. A
crowd of people stood near the church; there was a funeral
going on, or a wedding. The gilded crucifixes shone in the
sun. From the dim interior came the sound of the organ and
the chanting of the choir. A little farther on, on the left, was
the Jewish cemetery. Among the gravestones, beneath the
white beeches, stood the tomb of the great rabbi Menachem
David, who here, in Tereshpol Minor, had written fifty-two
books of Talmudic commentary: on top of the tomb a crow
perched, gazing off into the distance. At the far side of the
turnpike the wagon came to a halt near an inn. The owner
was a Jewish widow. Since this was in a different administra-
tive district it was probable that the expulsion order did not
apply, and the innkeeper had stayed on. In one of the back
rooms some of the sick from the poorhouse lay on straw pal-
lets. Reb Dan's wagon drew up alongside the cart on which
Jekuthiel the watchmaker sat, the tools of his trade piled
around him. He looked at the rabbi and smiled sadly.

"*Nu*, rabbi?" he said.

It was clear that what he meant was: Where is your Lord
of the Universe now? Where are His miracles? Where is your
faith in Torah and prayer?

"*Nu*, Jekuthiel," the rabbi answered. What he was saying
was: Where are your worldly remedies? Where is your trust
in the gentiles? What have you accomplished by aping Esau?

The innkeeper came out and invited Reb Dan and his family into the house, where a separate room had been prepared
for him. There would be a wait while the horses were watered
and plans were made for the next stage of the journey. The
rabbi took his prayer-shawl bag, got down from the wagon,
and went to the room that had been prepared for him. For a
long time he paced back and forth. A Channukah lamp hung
on a wall; a few books stood in a small bookcase. There were
two high, canopied beds. In the courtyard near the window a

goat stood. The animal shook its white whiskers, raised its head to scratch its back with its horns, and pawed with its hoof. The rabbi looked at the goat, and the goat stared back at him. He suddenly felt a rush of affection for the creature, the "valiant among the grass-eaters," which the Talmud compared to Israel, the "valiant among the nations." He felt like caressing the poor beast or giving it some tasty tidbit. After a while he took a copy of the Talmud from his bag and began to read. Not in a long time had the rabbi found so much sweetness in poring over the ancient texts.

His wife came in to tell him that they were ready to continue the journey. She looked at him as he sat, a transported expression on his face. She started to say something, but could not because of the lump in her throat. In these strange surroundings her husband seemed to her like one of the venerable ancients, a *tanna*. She felt a wave of ecstasy mixed with sadness at the thought of the goodly portion that was hers in having lived for nearly sixty years with this saint.

2

It was about two o'clock when the wagon started off again. The rabbi's sons, Zaddok and Levi, with their wives and children, had gone on ahead. It was expected that the ride to Zamosc would take no more than four hours, but the procession of vehicles stood motionless more than it moved. The road was crowded with soldiers, mounted cannon, and military wagons, moving toward the river San, where the Austrians were launching an attack.

There was a bewildering variety of uniforms to be seen: Cossacks with long spears and round hats, earrings in the lobes of their ears; Circassians in fur caps and ankle-length coats, with an array of daggers thrust into the front of their uniforms; Kalmuks small as pigmies, with slanting eyes. Teams of eight or ten horses pulled the heavy cannon along, the powerful wheels crushing the stones on the road. The yawning mouths of the cannon were hung with branches and festooned with flowers. In the middle of the fields at either side of the road army cooks at field kitchens were preparing huge vats of food. Mounted soldiers dashed back and forth shouting and cracking the air with their whips. The horses neighed and reared up on their hind legs, foam spattering from their mouths. Flocks of birds flew noisily overhead.

Clouds of dust glowed in the sun above the columns of bayonets. The few vehicles carrying the fleeing Jews aroused the scorn of the soldiers.

"The Christ-killers are on the march already," they grumbled. "Like rats from a sinking ship."

Some of the fugitives tried to explain that it was not of their own choice that they were leaving their villages, but the officers ordered them to turn back, lashing at them with their crops. The women began to sob and the children to wail. The gentile peasants who were driving the wagons complained that they did not intend to drive around forever with this Jewish junk; they wanted to get rid of the whole pack of them and get back to their farms. The one the soldiers gaped at most was Rabbi Dan. His white beard, his velvet hat, his silk caftan, all of these seemed strange to them. Where the devil were they dragging themselves to, these cursed Antichrists? What side were they on in the war? What did they want? Why didn't the dogs adopt the true Orthodox faith? They felt like seizing these unbelievers by the beards or by those damned sidelocks of theirs, or sticking a bayonet into them. Their hands itched to tear the wigs off their women, to find out what was under the dresses of the younger ones. Why wait until they could confront the Austrian enemy at the other side of the San?— the Jewish enemy was right here, stumbling around under the wheels of their military carts.

"Sons of dogs! Unbelievers! Spies! German swine!"

Some of the soldiers spat into the faces of the Jews; others smashed their fists into the pleading mouths or aimed kicks with their heavy boots. Most just stared passively at these long-coated, disheveled, frightened people. At every roadside shrine the drivers crossed themselves and murmured prayers to Mary and Jesus that they be permitted to return home safely with their horses and carts.

The sun was beginning to set, but no village was yet in sight. The soldiers sang savage-sounding songs in their untamed voices. The cavalry shouted and cursed, waving their unsheathed swords. Horses stumbled and fell. Already some of the wounded were being brought back from the battlefront. They lay on the bare ground, their yellow faces agonized, with bloodstained bandages wrapped around them. The air stank with the smell of sweat, urine, and cart grease. Rabbi Dan sat huddled on the straw packing of the wagon. He had never doubted that Israel was a lamb among the wolves, surrounded by idolaters, murderers, lechers, and drunkards. This

was the lower world, where Evil reigned. Where else would
Satan build his fortress? Where else would the hosts of darkness lie in wait? But he comforted himself with the knowledge
that everything came from God. Even the Devil had his roots
in the divine creation. The important thing was that man had
free will. Every blemish would find its purification. Uncleanliness was in reality an illusion.

Here, stumbling along the wanderer's path, the rabbi met
the powers of evil face to face. It was as though the noise and
the stench of corruption and death had extinguished in him
the spark of godliness. He had lost the pillar he leaned against
for support. He wanted to pray, but his lips were powerless to
form the words. He closed his eyes. He felt that he was falling
into an abyss. He gripped the sides of the wagon and began to
recite the afternoon prayer, but in his confusion he forgot
how the words went. Over and over he found himself repeat-
ing the same phrase: "Happy are they that dwell in Thy
house."

In the evening the procession reached the village of Modly-
Bozhytz. Here there was no sign at all of war. The market
place was still and empty. Oil lamps glowed through the windows. In the study house boys and older men sat at the tables
studying. The local rabbi and some of the elders came out to
greet Reb Dan and his sons, and escorted them into the synagogue, while the women went into the rabbi's house. Reb Dan
stood against the eastern wall to murmur the evening prayers.
It was good to stand again near an Ark of the Law. From the
tables came the low voices of the devout, reading the Talmud.
Reb Dan breathed deep the familiar prayerhouse fragrance.
Outside there were foulness and uncleanliness; here there was
the odor of holiness and piety. "Forgive us, O our Father, for
we have sinned; pardon us, O our King, for we have trans-
gressed." He murmured the words and pounded his fist
against his chest in repentance for the doubts that had assailed
him.

A youngster with long sidelocks and big dark eyes came up
to the rabbi and asked for an interpretation of a difficult passage in the Commentaries. There seemed to be a contradiction in an analysis of the renowned Rabbi Tam. Reb Dan
took the candle from the boy's hand and peered at the open
volume with its yellowed pages, dotted with melted wax.
"There is no contradiction," he said. "The Rabbi Tam is correct," and he explained to the youth the complications of the
passage.

It had been Reb Dan's intention to establish the family in Lublin until things became more settled. But Levi, who fancied himself an expert in political matters, declared that the battle would soon be shifting in that direction. It would be better, he argued, to go on to Warsaw. After some discussion Reb Dan dispatched two letters, one to his grandson, Asa Heshel, and the other to a former disciple of his, Godel Tsinamon, who had become wealthy in the capital city. The letters requested that lodgings be arranged for him and the family. The others added postscripts to the letter to Asa Heshel—his grandmother, mother, sister, uncles and aunts, and cousins as well, greeting his wife, Adele, with warmth and affection, and, even though she was not known to them, they sent their respectful wishes to his mother-in-law, Rosa Frumetl, and to his stepfather-in-law, Reb Wolf Hendlers.

CHAPTER TWO

1

Most of the well-to-do Warsaw Jews who maintained cottages along the Otwotsk line usually stayed on in their summer places until the Rosh Hashona holidays began. Others remained until the New Year period was over. But this year all of them returned to Warsaw early. This was wartime. There was a dearth of food, and the scarcity grew from hour to hour. The German armies were winning victory after victory; the Russians were steadily retreating; the fighting was coming closer. In times like these who had the peace of mind to loll about in the country?

As in the years past, the Moskat women had put on some weight and the men were tanned by the sun. They came back to find their apartments in need of painting and overhauling, but all such activities were postponed. The women immediately went to the market places to stock up with food, but it was hard to find any substantial supply. The stores were for the most part shuttered, the storekeepers standing outside the doors in their long coats. They held whispered conversations with steady customers and let them in through rear doors. Some of the storekeepers refused to accept paper money and insisted on being paid with silver or gold coin. The tenants of the Moskat houses, as though they had conspired together, stopped paying rent. The Moskat family found itself without any income.

Nathan, Pinnie, and Nyunie went to call on Koppel at the office, but Koppel could not be of any help. It was impossible to attach furniture or start eviction proceedings. The young men were being mobilized. Meshulam's estate had not yet been divided among the heirs. Nathan, who was inclined to be most optimistic when things looked blackest, insisted that the war could not last long.

"They'll beat each other black and blue, the stubborn fools," he said, "and then they'll have to come to an understanding."

But Pinnie, who read all the newspapers and fancied himself shrewd in political affairs, maintained that the war could well last a year, or even two.

"They're not short of soldiers," he declared. "The rulers have plenty of time."

"So what is there to do?" Nathan asked.

"Pull in your belt and wait for it to be over. It won't harm you if you lose a few pounds."

While the others talked, Koppel paced back and forth. The war wasn't doing him any good, either. He owned two houses himself, one in Praga and one in Warsaw proper. He bit his lip and blew out thin puffs of cigarette smoke. The old man had been right, he reflected. Most people were thieves, frauds, and scoundrels, a curse on their corrupt souls!

Koppel had reached the goal to which he had long aspired. He was to all intents and purposes the trustee and guardian of the Moskat wealth. Queen Esther, Joel's wife, complained that she was left without a copper; Joel was sick and there was not enough money in the house for a sack of flour or a bag of potatoes. Hannah, Pinnie's wife, demanded that a family meeting be called and the estate be divided up without delay; she was ready, as a matter of fact, to sell her share. Nyunie talked in a way that told no one where he really stood. The fact was that he had ten thousand rubles in cash put safely away, and besides, his son-in-law, Fishel, was a wealthy man.

Reb Meshulam's oldest daughter, Pearl, the widow, did not come to call on Koppel. She had her own properties and business interests. Besides, she was a sick woman and the doctors had warned her to avoid any excitement. Leah did not put in an appearance, either; Koppel would not let her go under. What was it they said?—"Old love doesn't get rusty."

Hama wanted to rush to Koppel and plead for help, but

Abram warned her sternly that if she dared to humble herself before his blood enemy he would never again set foot in the house.

"I'll not ask that bootlicker for any favors," Abram yelled. "Not as long as I live!" He pounded his fists on the table until the lamp shook.

"But, Abram," Hama complained, and blew her nose, red with catarrh, "it's getting worse and worse. We'll be left without a piece of bread."

"Then we'll eat cake."

He went out banging the door behind him. He could not understand her panic. Suppose she went hungry for a while? Anyway she ate less than a bird, and Stepha was hardly ever home, always hanging around with that student of hers. With Bella it was different; she was nursing a child; she needed milk for her breasts. Ah, what a grandchild that was!

For all that he did not fancy being classified as a grandfather, Abram simply could not help adoring the infant, the very image of himself—two drops of water. The only thing that annoyed him was that the family insisted that the child be called Meshulam, after his great-grandfather. What a name for a helpless baby! When it came to children, the women were the ones who managed everything. After all, they had to carry them and bear them and rear them. A man could get to be a parent without any bellyaches.

In the street Abram lit a cigar and started to walk slowly toward Marshalkovska Street. He reminded himself that he still had not seen Asa Heshel. The outbreak of the war, the hurried journey home from the country, the mobilization, the scurrying around for food, the trouble with Koppel, had driven thoughts of anything else out of his mind. Besides, Bella had had a difficult childbirth. For three days she had been in labor. Hama had run to pray at the graves of her parents. The grandmother on the father's side had run to the synagogue. The doctors had talked of taking the child with instruments. At such a time how could he, Abram, have had in his mind the affairs of Hadassah and Asa Heshel? But now that Bella and the child, thank God, were all right, he could take an interest in things again. The world had to go on, even if the war was between Gog and Magog. He went into a druggist's and telephoned to Gina.

"Gina, darling, it's me, Abram."

"What? You're still talking to common people?" Gina exclaimed scornfully. "I thought you were too high and mighty

for that. After all, a grandfather! It's no small thing. Well,
anyway, congratulations and good luck. How's the child?"

"Ah, what a boy! Never anyone like him since they started
to spawn 'em. A voice like a lion. He takes one look at me
with those eyes and I'm done for. I don't envy the girls who'll
fall into his hands."

"Shame on you. An infant, a dove, and you're talking about
such things already. You must be crazy."

"You're crazy yourself. Just wait fifteen or sixteen years
and you'll see what this nursling can do. Tell me, Gina, I hear
that Asa Heshel is back in Warsaw."

"My God, Abram, have you just thought of it? What an
egotist you are! The young man's been searching all over for
you. He's called a thousand times, but go and look for the
wind in the fields."

"Where is he?"

"You ask me that? And you were at one time his patron!
Anyway, he came running in on me—that was before the war
broke out—pale as chalk, as though he were being led to the
gallows. I tell you, he was terror-stricken. 'What's the matter?'
I asked him, and, to make a long story short, he had quarreled with his wife and run away from her."

"Where is he? What's he doing? Where's he living? Has he
seen Hadassah?"

"How do I know? I haven't been spying on him. He lives
here, in this building. All of my rooms were taken and I got
him a place at those seamstresses', the socialists. He has a hole
of a room, but it's better than wallowing around in the gutter."

"What? That's fine. Fine. Has he got a telephone?"

"Are you out of your mind? How would paupers like that
get a telephone?"

"Listen to me, Gina. Don't think for a minute that I forgot
about the young man. Abram Shapiro doesn't forget his
friends. I've been thinking about him day and night. But when
a man's got a daughter in labor and she's shrieking to the
rooftops, it's a different thing. This business of having a baby
is no joke. And I've been thinking of you, too, Ginusha. Tell
me, how are you?"

"Me? The world's forgotten me."

"Fool. There's only one Gina in the world. All I have to do
is think of you and I feel warm all over."

"Never mind the flattery."

"Well, all right. Anyway, I'm coming to see you soon."

The tramcars had stopped on Marshalkovska Street. Columns of soldiers marched by toward Mokotov. Troops of cavalry rode by. Fully equipped infantry companies plodded along shouting out some piece of doggerel about a girl who went gathering mushrooms. Horses went by, drawing cannon after them. Machine guns stood on wagons, covered with waterproofing. A military band trumpeted away. Yes, this was war. Abram followed the tramping soldiers. His feet, of their own volition, began to march in time to the music. "What sort of business is this?" Abram thought. "Men are marching off to be killed, and they serenade them to their death. Ah, dear Lord, what a mess You've made of things! A fine world You've managed to turn out. I'd give anything to know what You're thinking of up there on Your throne of glory in the seventh heaven. Do You know, I wonder, that there's a man called Abram Shapiro here on the earth? Ah, Father in heaven, You've got the heart of a bandit."

Near Iron Gate Square Abram climbed into a droshky and told the driver to take him to Shviento-Yerska Street. He could hardly wait now until the carriage reached Gina's address; he had an urgent need to speak to her and find out all about Asa Heshel. "How could I have waited so long?" he wondered. "He must surely think that I don't want to have anything to do with him any more. The cursed war—it's responsible for everything."

"Hey, driver, faster. I'll give you a good drink."

He felt ashamed at his own words. When the war had started, the government-controlled liquor stores had been given orders to pour their stocks into the gutters. Old Nicholas had probably become afraid that a drunken population might get a notion to topple him off his throne, together with that Czarina of his, and Rasputin, too.

2

The droshky came to a halt. Abram paid the driver and went into the building in which Gina had her flat. For a while he stood at the gate looking out toward the Krashinski Gardens. Whether it was only a trick of his imagination or it was really happening, Abram seemed to hear in the distance the blowing of a shofar, the traditional ram's horn, going through all the customary staccatos and glissandi. "The Day of Atonement is getting close," Abram thought gloomily. "The fish in the water

tremble. The day of judgment approaches. And what will the
end of everything be? What judgment will be inscribed for me
for the things I've done this year? My God, the way I've been
behaving, who would know that I'm a Jew?"

A ragged beggar came up to him, hand outstretched.
Abram handed him a silver forty-kopek piece. The beggar
stammered: "I have no change." "It's all for you," Abram
told him, and listened while the beggar fervently wished him a
blessed new year and the merit of always having something to
spare for the poor.

He went inside the gate, the tears starting to his eyes. At the
entrance door he hesitated. It had been his intention to call on
Gina, but now he decided to visit the flat of the seamstresses
first. Maybe Asa Heshel would be there.

He called to a little girl playing in the courtyard.

"Where's the apartment where the dressmakers live? Franya, one of them's called."

"You mean the dark one? The pretty one?"

"Yes."

"And the other is lame?"

"Yes."

"In the last house over there. On the third floor."

"Tell me, little girl. Would you like to have a ten-groszy
piece?"

"I don't know."

"Here's ten groszy to buy caramels."

"My mamma told me I mustn't take anything from strangers."

"I won't tell anybody. It'll be a secret between us."

He pushed a coin into the child's hand. She looked at him
in bewilderment and said: "Thank you."

"God bless you, my child," Abram answered.

He watched as the girl hurried away, noticing her pitifully
thin legs and the ribbon bound in her little pigtails. He put a
match to his cigar. "Ah, how easy it is to do good! Dear God,
why do I do nothing? I've given myself over altogether to material things. I've completely forgotten that a man has a soul.
Dear Father in heaven, forgive me."

Struggling up the three flights of stairs was difficult. He had
to stop frequently to rest and catch his breath. The stairs were
covered with dust and refuse. On one of the landings a girl sat
grating horseradish. From the doors of the flats came the
smell of fried foods, beet soup, and groats. Apparently some
artisans lived in the flats; Abram could hear the sound of

hammering and sawing, and the whir of a machine. On the third floor, not knowing which door led into the seamstresses' flat, he listened for the sound of a sewing-machine. His nostrils caught a whiff of the charcoal used for heating the pressing iron and of burnt wool. It must be there, through that door.

He knocked, opened the door, and entered a large room. Yes, this was it. Not only were the two girls, Franya and Lila, there, but a third woman, occupied in trying on a dress. She was wearing only bloomers; the corset around her enormous hips reminded him of a suit of armor. When Abram entered, she squealed and ran behind the screen. Franya went out. Lila stopped the machine and looked at him questioningly.

"Excuse me," Abram said. "I knocked but no one answered."

"What can I do for you?"

"I'm looking for a young man who lives here. Asa Heshel."

"Over there, on the left."

Abram went toward the indicated door. Behind him he could hear the whispering of the women. "I charged in like a bull in a china shop," he thought with chagrin. He put out his hand to knock at the latch, but his touch thrust it open. He gaped at what he saw. Asa Heshel and Hadassah were seated on the bed, Asa Heshel in his shirt sleeves. Hadassah had taken off her hat, and her hair was drawn back in a Greek knot. She was wearing a white blouse and a striped skirt. A gas lamp was burning. Asa Heshel started up from the bed, almost overturning the small table near by. Hadassah started up too.

Abram began to shout—his custom whenever he found himself in an embarrassing position. "So you don't recognize me, eh? So you've got too high and mighty to recognize me!"

"Uncle!"

"Who else? I'm at least thankful you know me."

He closed the door behind him, seized Asa Heshel by the shoulders, and kissed him fervently on both cheeks. Then he pushed him away and grabbed hold of Hadassah.

"Yes, me! Your Uncle Abram!" He kissed her on the lips. Hadassah held him tightly and pressed kisses on his cheeks and beard.

"Well, all right, enough! First you forget that I'm alive and then you make a fuss over me!"

His cigar had fallen to the floor. His stick stood upright, leaning against him. It clattered and slid to the floor.

"Well, all right," Abram growled. "Don't be afraid. Call me anything you want—murderer, swindler, rascal. But even a villain wouldn't harm his own flesh and blood."

"I've looked all over for you," Asa Heshel said.

"None of that or I'll let you have this stick over your head! When you came back, the first thing you should have done was to call on me. My God, here I am thinking and talking about him day and night—and here he is, in Warsaw all the time, hiding away God knows where, like a mouse in a hole. I was so furious that if I'd run into you I'd have torn you apart. But now I've calmed down. The devil with you. If you don't give a damn for me, then I return the compliment. That's the first thing. And so far as you're concerned"—he turned to Hadassah—"I've got a different kind of reckoning to make with you. If you weren't a female, one of the weaker sex, look-at-me-but-don't-dare-touch-me, I'd let you have it so hard you'd have to go crawling around to collect your teeth."

"If that's the way you feel, then go ahead."

"Mind your business. I'll do as I like. Consider yourself whatever you like—a beauty, a *grande dame,* a pish-pash—to me you're nothing but a child, a baby in diapers."

"Uncle, they can hear every word in the other room."

"Let them hear. I'm telling the God's truth. What's the idea of spending your time in this stinking hole? My God, the world's bright and sunny outside, and here the two of you sit in the darkness! Let's get out! Come with me! Let's carry on and paint Warsaw red! We'll yowl and shout till the houses fall in like the walls of Jericho!"

"Oh, Uncle, if you only knew—" Hadassah stopped short.

"What is there to know? I don't know a thing. I'm an idiot. Look at him! Look how he's grown, that bargain of yours! A regular *boulevardier,* a European dandy! My God, how the years fly by! Come here, closer to me. I must kiss both of you!"

Abram grabbed both of them and began to shake them back and forth. The table fell to the floor. The door opened timidly and Franya looked in, smiling.

"What's going on here? A pogrom?"

"So you know me, eh? I thought you didn't recognize me when I came in."

"It's easy to remember you, Mr. Abram."

"If I knew he was living here with you I'd have been here day and night."

"Please excuse him," Hadassah said. "My uncle has no control over his feelings. I'll put everything right."

"Oh, don't bother about that at all," Franya replied. "There's a woman asking for you," she continued, addressing Asa Heshel.

"For me?"

"I took her into the kitchen. You can go out to see her there."

Franya went out, closing the door behind her. Asa Heshel flushed a painful red. Abram shook his head meaningfully. Hadassah sat down on the edge of the bed and got up again.

"Who is it?" Abram asked. "My God, do all the women chase you?"

"I don't know. Nobody's visited me here. I can't understand." Maybe it was Adele, or her mother! How had they found out where he was?

"Well, go and see who it is. We'll wait here."

Abram walked over to the window and stared out at the blind wall opposite. Hadassah picked up the overturned chair and table. Asa Heshel put on his coat and straightened his tie.

"The whole thing doesn't make sense," he murmured.

He went out. Hadassah picked up a book and sat down, turning the pages with trembling fingers. The gas lamp flickered. Abram kept staring out of the window, looking up to the rectangle of sky visible between the rooftops. That Asa Heshel and Hadassah would be meeting each other Abram knew. But that she would come to him in this dark hole in a house where they were known, that was more than he could have imagined. If Dacha heard about it! he thought. It would finish her off!

He shook his head. All of a sudden he felt a strong distaste for this new generation. He remembered that his own daughter Stepha had been dragging around with that student of hers for the last four years and nothing seemed to come of it. It occurred to him again that Yom Kippur was not far off, that he had a bad heart, and that the time when he would have to make his final reckoning was drawing closer and closer.

3

It was his mother whom Asa Heshel found waiting for him in the other room. She was wearing a long wide-sleeved coat, and her matron's wig was covered with a net scarf. In one hand she was carrying a satchel and in the other a cloth-wrapped bundle. Asa Heshel was so astonished that it was several moments before he could find his voice.

"Mamma!"

"My child!"

She embraced him, still holding on to the bundles.

"When did you come? How did you get here?"

"I came on the train. Your grandfather wrote you a letter. Why didn't you answer? I thought—God knows what."

"I couldn't find any lodgings."

"Is that a reason not to answer? My God, to survive what I've gone through I must be made of iron. Where are you living? Where's your wife? Who's that girl that opened the door?"

Asa Heshel felt his mouth go dry. "I don't live here. I just have a room here," he managed to say.

"What do you need a room for?" His mother looked at him, her gray eyes wide open. Her beaked nose was pale; her chin sharp.

"I'm studying here. Wait a second."

He left his mother and went back to his own room.

"It's my mother. My mother is here," he announced in a forlorn voice.

Abram and Hadassah were seated on the edge of the bed; they had apparently been talking about him.

"Your mother?" Hadassah repeated.

"Yes."

"Well, an exciting day," Abram remarked, and struck his hands together. "Where did she come from? Did you expect her? Where are you going to talk to her? You can't bring her in here."

"I'll go down with her somewhere. The whole thing's so unexpected."

"All right, all right, brother. Just don't lose your head. Your mother's more important than anything else. I'll tell you what: tonight I'll be at Hertz Yanovar's. Come over there if you can. You too, Hadassah."

Hadassah did not answer. She got up and put on her hat. Her face was pale, and her expression as she looked at Asa Heshel was a mixture of doubt and fear.

"I should like to meet her," she ventured after some hesitation.

"When? Now?"

"No. Maybe not."

"It's all so mixed up. I can't understand it. My grandfather wrote to me. I was supposed to find lodgings for them. And now, all of a sudden—"

"Is the family coming here?" Abram asked.

"They've been driven out."

"A fine complication!" Abram said. "Ah, brother, now you're in trouble. Where are you going to take her? You go down first, and we'll wait here for a while."

"I'm sorry. I really don't know how to—"

"Don't worry about it. A mother's a mother."

"Good-by, then. I don't know how to thank you for coming."

"All right, all right, brother. You better hurry along."

"Good-by, Hadassah. I'll telephone you. I really—" He went out. In the few minutes he had become bathed in perspiration. His mother was waiting for him, standing up and facing the door.

"Mother, let's go downstairs," Asa Heshel said to her.

"Where'll we go? I'm dead tired. I've been walking around all day. The streets are so long. Where is Adele?"

"Give me the package. We'll take a droshky."

"Where to? Well, all right."

He took the bundle from her and they went out.

"What kind of a place is this?" his mother inquired. "So many steps. Enough to give you heart failure."

"This is Warsaw. The buildings are tall."

"Walk slower."

Asa Heshel took his mother's arm. She was walking unsteadily and holding on to the banister carefully as she went down.

"I'll take you to get something to eat. There's a kosher restaurant near here."

"How do you know it's kosher? How can you be sure?"

"The owner's a pious Jew."

"What do you know about him?"

"He's got a beard and sidelocks."

"That's no guarantee."

"He's got a rabbinical license."

"Today's rabbis! They give out certificates to anyone that asks."

"What do you expect to do? Fast?"

"Don't worry. I'll not starve. I've got some cookies in the bundle. Tell me, is it always so crowded and noisy here, or is it on account of the war?"

"It's always this way."

"I walked the whole way, and the din was enough to make you deaf. It's impossible to get across the streets. Some strange woman helped me. How can people live in a Gehenna like this? The moment I stepped off the train I got a head-ache."

"You get used to it."

"Your grandfather wants to come here. Godel Tsinamon— maybe you've heard of him, an old disciple of your grandfa-ther's—found a flat for us. He promises we'll be all right. The minute we wrote to him he answered. And a stranger."

"I don't know what to say, Mamma."

"Not to write a line! And at a time like this. The things I've gone through. As though I haven't suffered enough in my life. I haven't closed an eye for God knows how long. All sorts of bitter thoughts—I don't even want to mention them. You can imagine how things were if they let me travel here by myself. The train was full of soldiers. Tell me the truth, what's going on between you and your wife? I'm suspicious about the whole thing."

"We've separated."

His mother's cheeks showed red flecks.

"So soon! A fine thing! The joy I have out of my life."

"We couldn't get along with each other."

"Do you think that explains anything? What's the matter with her? What have you got against her? My life! First Din-ah's husband gets lost somewhere in Austria and now you run away from your wife. What's the use of being born?"

"Mamma, I'll tell you everything."

"What's there to tell? Where are you taking me? My bones ache all over."

"I'll get a room for you in a hotel."

"I don't need your hotels. Where is she, your wife?"

"What's the difference? You don't want to see her."

"Why not? She's my daughter-in-law."

"There'd be no sense to it."

"What do you think you're going to do? Hide her?"

"I can't go to where she is."

"Then I'll go myself. I suppose it's my fate to be shamed and degraded. Give me her address."

"She lives on Sienna Street. Number eighty-three."

"Where is that? How will I find it? God help me, I'm all alone."

Asa Heshel tried to persuade her again to go into a restaurant, but she refused. He reconciled himself at last to taking her to Wolf Hendler's house, but there was no droshky in sight. His mother looked about her, shaking her head in bewilderment.

"What's this garden right here in the middle of the streets?"

"Krashinski Gardens. A park."

"My, the heat. Let me take another look at you. You don't look so good. What do you eat? Who takes care of you? Your wife is a decent, intelligent woman. And an orphan. You've caused her enough anguish. She tried to hide it, but I could tell. Your father's son, God help me!"

"Mamma!"

"How much can a human being stand? Ever since I've been old enough to face anything it's been nothing but misfortune. I've got no more strength left. I come to visit my own son; like a fool I expect to have a little joy in my life, and what do I find? She's a decent Jewish girl, a girl of a fine family. May God forgive you for what you're doing."

Asa Heshel started to answer, but just then he saw Abram and Hadassah on the other side of the street. He was holding on to her arm, and her head was lowered. Abram raised his cane and waved it. Asa Heshel noticed for the first time that he seemed to be aging; his shoulders were bent and his beard was graying. He felt a sudden surge of love for Abram, for Hadassah, for his mother. The tears rose to his eyes. He saw Abram talking earnestly to Hadassah. He must be warning her not to throw her life away, he thought. Ah, God, what a dilemma to be in! He watched them. They seemed so near and yet so distant, like close kin to whom one bids good-by before one sets out on a long journey. He turned toward his mother and kissed her cheek.

"Don't worry, Mamma," he murmured. "Everything will turn out all right."

"When? In the next world, maybe."

Asa Heshel sat with his mother in the droshky he had hailed to take them to the Hendlers' flat. With one hand she held on firmly to the side bar, and with the other to Asa Heshel's elbow. For years and years she had been accustomed to apologizing for him to his grandfather, his grandmother, his uncles and aunts. She had forgiven him all his irregularities. She had deprived herself of necessities to send money to him in Switzerland. Now he was dragging her over the streets of a big city, telling her stories that made no sense, bringing her nothing but shame and aggravation. But how could she find her way alone? What would she do if she found Adele's door closed to her? In big cities anything was possible.

The droshky came to a halt. Asa Heshel paid the driver and led his mother into a doorway. In front there was a panel of nameplates and bells. He pressed a button and waited until he heard the answering buzz. Then he kissed his mother, saw her in through the door, and hurried away.

He wanted to go along Tvarda Street, but instead he found himself walking on Iron Street. He passed by Panska, Prosta, Lutska and Gzhybovska and emerged on Chlodno Street. Near the church he stopped. How could he be sure, it occurred to him, that Adele was at home? Maybe the servant had not let her in. Maybe she was standing at the door this very moment, not knowing what to do next. "Dear God in heaven, what has become of me? I'm sinking deeper and deeper." The thought suddenly flashed through his mind that there was a profound connection between the fourth and the seventh commandments. He resumed his aimless walking. He kept his eyes open for a delicatessen store where there might be a telephone he could use. On Solna Street he went into a store, but the telephone was in use. The proprietress, a woman in a white apron, wearing a wig piled high with braids, was holding a long conversation with someone. She was laughing, showing a mouthful of gold teeth, apparently talking to a man about some business matter, but at the same time making frequent references to her husband. Every once in a while he heard her say: "And what about my husband? Do you think he'll keep quiet?"

Asa Heshel wanted to stalk out of the store, but all at once the woman ended her conversation with a request that the other send her ten pounds of liver and five pounds of turkey. The moment Asa Heshel picked up the phone, the operator asked him for the number. He gave it to her and waited. Who would answer the phone? The servant? Wolf Hendlers? Rosa Frumetl? Adele? He heard Adele's voice.

"Who is calling?"

"It's me. Asa Heshel."

There was silence at the other end. Then she said: "I'm listening."

"My mother came to Warsaw. She insisted I take her to your house."

"She's here."

"I suppose you understand that—"

"The least you could do is have enough decency not to carry on this comedy in front of your mother," she said in Polish. "Maybe it makes no difference to you, but the servant thought she was a beggar. She wanted to give her a coin."

Asa Heshel felt a pang of pain.

"I couldn't—that is, I didn't have the time. I was ashamed."

"You needn't be ashamed of your mother. She is an honorable person and intelligent, too. My mother liked her at once. So did my stepfather."

"You don't understand. I didn't say I was ashamed of my mother. I was ashamed because of the situation."

"You ought at least to have the courage to face things. Please don't imagine for a minute that I want to get you to come back. When you ran away from Shvider you showed the things you're capable of. You can imagine what my mother and stepfather thought. I tried to look for you, but you hid somewhere like a thief. And without a clean shirt to your back. But anyway, nothing surprises me now. If a son can abandon a woman like your mother, then—How are you getting along? I hope you're happy with her."

"What are you talking about? She's married. She's with her husband."

"You mean she's disgracing her husband. Your mother's going to stay here with us. If you've got an ounce of honor in you, you'll come to see her."

"How can I?"

"There's nothing complicated about it. You can't go on hiding. People have to face each other, even to get a divorce."

"When shall I come?"

"Now if you want. My stepfather is going out soon. The others will be taking a nap. We'll be able to discuss things privately."

"I'll be there in an hour."

"I'll be waiting. Good-by."

Asa Heshel had shaved earlier, but he went into a barber shop and had his hair cut and his face shaved again. Then he stopped at a restaurant and had some food. He boarded a tramcar and rode to Sienna Street, instead of walking the short distance. He would get there cool, clean, and composed-looking. He would tell them all the naked truth. He climbed the stairs to the flat slowly. The moment he pressed the bell, the door opened and Adele stood facing him. She was wearing a blue skirt and a white blouse. At her throat was the medallion that his mother had given her in Tereshpol Minor. He saw the flash of the gold wedding ring on her finger. She seemed to him somewhat stouter. The scent of caraway-seed perfume pricked at his nostrils. She said: "Come in," and held the door wide open.

She led Asa Heshel into her own room, which had once been the study of her stepfather's son, a surgeon. She indicated a chair, and Asa Heshel sat down. She herself sank down on the couch, tucking her feet under her. She looked at him with a curious glance.

"Well, my fine hero, how are things with you?"

"Where is my mother?" he asked.

"She's asleep."

She wanted the whole truth from him with no concealment, she said. He admitted everything. He had been with Hadassah, at her father's apartment, at Klonya's in Miedzeshin, in an unoccupied flat in Fishel's house. She demanded all the details, her pale eyes never abandoning their faint smile. How could she feel any anger at this awkward youth, with his Chassidic gestures—this strange mixture of embarrassment and shameless confession? She could see now that he would never change. That quick brain, behind that high forehead, would find a justification for any transgression.

"At least you have the decency to tell me the truth," she said at last.

She got up and went out, returning presently with a tray of tea and cakes.

"I don't want anything," Asa Heshel said.

"What are you afraid of? I won't poison you."

He drank some tea while she watched him. His thin lips sipped the liquid, like a child. A cake fell from his hand. He bent down to pick it up, but instead let it lie. She could see the blue veins in his temples pulsing and his face twitching. "The poor fool," Adele thought. "I'll not divorce him. Why make her respectable? Let her stay the whore." She got off the couch and said: "What's the use of concealing things. You're going to be a father."

The tea glass shook in Asa Heshel's hand.

"Are you serious?"

"It's the truth."

"I don't understand."

"I'm in the fourth month."

He involuntarily dropped his eyes and looked at her stomach.

"What's the matter? You're pale as a ghost. I'll be the one to bear the child, not you."

In the corridor outside the door there was the sound of footsteps. Both mothers had awakened from their naps.

CHAPTER THREE

It was Fishel's custom to go back to his store after the evening services at the prayerhouse. On this evening, however, he had decided to go directly home. Under wartime conditions there was little to do at the store anyway. Oil, soap, and fats were getting scarcer by the day, and Fishel was not eager to sell what he had. At the prayerhouse the youths who would soon have to present themselves to the military for recruitment huddled together and talked in low tones of doctors who might be bribed, of a barber-surgeon who was adept in piercing eardrums, bringing on a rupture, pulling out a mouthful of teeth, or stiffening finger joints. They told one another about some official who was willing to supply forged birth certificates and identification papers. Most of them were already doing what they could on their own: eating herring, drinking brine and vinegar, and smoking countless cigarettes, all reputed to result in losing weight. When Fishel joined the group they stopped their talk, not because they were afraid of him—he certainly wasn't an informer—but because, just the same, he wasn't one of their own. Fishel had a blue ticket of rejection from the army, a handsome wife, a store, a house of his own in the country, a gold watch, a rich father-in-law. How could a man like that know what went on in the heart of someone who couldn't buy his way out of the Czar's uniform?

Fishel left the prayerhouse and turned homeward. He walked along slowly. What would Hadassah be doing now, he wondered. Still running around? "Her mother is sick, and her father wastes his time with that fool Abram. He'll probably marry again the moment his wife dies. Who knows, he might still father half a dozen children." Fishel knit his brow. That's the way it always is, he reflected. All these inheritances fritter

away to nothing. With God's help, he'd manage to hold on to
what he had. Who was it had told him that that student had
come back from Switzerland? Was it possible that she was
meeting him somewhere? No, she was not a loose woman.
And she certainly was not a liar. She had told him the whole
truth about everything right after they were married.

He climbed the stairs to his flat and knocked at the door.
Hadassah came to open it. He murmured: "Good evening" as
he went in.

"Oh, it's you."

The telephone, which hung on the corridor wall, began to
ring. Hadassah hurried to pick up the receiver.

"Yes, it's me. What's that? Please talk a little clearer. What?
My Uncle Abram? We just walked around for a while and
then had lunch together. Where did you go? Oh, yes, I understand. I guessed it. The tickets? Please wait at Nyetsala Street
near the Saxon Gardens, at quarter past eight." She hung up
the instrument.

"Who was it?" Fishel asked.

"A girl friend of mine. Someone I went to school with."

"What does she want?"

"Nothing. Just to talk."

"You said something about tickets."

"Tickets? Oh, yes, we're going to the theater."

"Again?"

"Why not? What else have I to do?"

"Lately you've got the habit of running around. It's lunch
with Abram in the afternoon and theater in the evening. Our
sages call such women gadabouts. According to the Talmud,
they can be divorced without a settlement."

"Then divorce me."

"I'm just joking. The weather's getting colder. It's best for
you to stay home. You might catch cold."

"Then I'll die."

"That's childish. You've got plenty to live for. We'll be
rich. Oil is worth its weight in gold these days."

"I suppose that should make me happy."

"Why not? Money is an important thing. When will supper
be ready? I'm hungry."

Hadassah went into the kitchen. Some pots stood steaming
over the small flames on the stove. Shifra was away; her
sweetheart had been taken into the army, and she spent her
time running around to the other servant girls in the neighborhood to see if the letters they received contained any news of

him. And now she had left the kitchen alone and the food had burned. Hadassah poured a cup of water into one of the pots. There was a cloud of steam and noise of seething. No matter how diligently Hadassah followed the instructions in the cook book, she could somehow never manage to learn. She stood at the stove, the cup in her hand, and thought of Asa Heshel's mother's unexpected arrival. Now he'd gone over to Adele's, and his mother would patch things up and make peace between them. Shifra charged into the room.

"Mistress, I have news from my Itchele!"

Hadassah started.

"Where is he?"

"In a town by the name of Zhichlin."

"So you see. You worried for nothing."

Shifra rolled up her sleeves, put on an apron, and busied herself over the pots. Hadassah went to the other room. Fishel was walking back and forth, his hands clasped behind him, murmuring something to himself. The lenses of his glasses glowed in the reflection of the gas lamp.

"You're really going out after supper?"

"Yes. Why?"

"Take my advice, don't go out."

"Why not? She's one of my closest friends."

"Listen to me, Hadassah. The holy days are coming soon, the Days of Awe. A person doesn't live forever."

"I don't know what you mean."

"You understand me. I'm warning you. You're traveling a dangerous path."

Hadassah went out, banging the door so that the glass panes shook. Fishel went over to the bookcase. He knew what he was talking about; he had heard clearly enough a man's voice at the other end of the phone. She was running off to meet him at the Saxon Gardens. Maybe they were kissing. Maybe she was carrying on a love affair. Maybe—God forgive him for the thought—maybe she had sinned with him.

Fishel felt his heart contract in his chest. "Dear God in heaven, what can be done now? How can I save her? Help me, dear Father." He fumbled among the books in the bookcase, his hands trembling. He opened a volume of the Code of Law and read over the regulation, which he already knew by heart: a woman who commits adultery is unclean to her husband as well as to the seducer. He put the book back and took out a volume of Psalms. He felt the need to pray, to pour out his heart to God, to confess his own sins, to plead that his beloved wife, Hadassah, the daughter of Dacha, be saved from evil. He sat down on a chair and shook back and forth, his eyes closed, his lips murmuring the verse: "Blessed is the man who walketh not in the counsel of the ungodly, nor standeth in the way of sinners, nor sitteth in the seat of the scornful."

Tears welled up in his eyes. His glasses misted, and he took them off to wipe them. His hunger had gone. There were spots on the yellowed pages of the book, like tearstains and fragments of candle wax. A funeral melancholy descended on him. This was his grandfather's book of Psalms. It was from this volume that the old man had chanted when his only son, Ben Zion, Fishel's father, had lain mortally ill at the hospital. Fishel felt a sudden urge to rend his garments like a mourner, to take off his shoes and sit on the bare floor. His grandfather was gone; his father was dead, too, and as for his mother— she was somewhere in Great Poland with another husband. There was no one left to him, no kith or kin, no child of his loins. Ever since he had married and his wealth had begun to increase, even the Chassidim in the prayerhouse had become his enemies, begrudging his good fortune. And now this final blow. What was the use of his life altogether? What was the good of all his prosperity? He began again to murmur the Psalm: "Lord; how are they increased that trouble me! Many are they that rise up against me. Many there be which say of my soul, There is no help for him in God. Selah."

CHAPTER FOUR

A few days before Yom Kippur, Reb Dan Katzenellenbogen reached Warsaw with his family. An apartment was waiting for him on the Franciskaner—three rooms and kitchen. Godel Tsinamon, his old pupil, had made the arrangements. As a poverty-stricken youth he had studied under the rabbi of Tereshpol Minor; he had eaten his Sabbath meals at the rabbi's house. Now that he had become a rich man, he paid his debt to his old benefactor. He put down several months' rent in advance and saw to it that the flat was furnished with beds, tables, chairs, and the necessary housekeeping equipment. For the middle room he had brought in an Ark of the Law and shelves for books. He waited for the rabbi at the railroad station. With him was Finkel, the rabbi's daughter, and her son,

Asa Heshel. Godel was a red-faced man, with a white forked beard. He wore a pair of gold-rimmed glasses on his coat. The rabbi hardly recognized him.

"Is it you, Godel?" he said. "An aristocrat!"

The rabbi's family made a substantial group: both his sons, Zaddok and Levi, his daughters-in-law, Zissle and Mindel, and a throng of grandchildren.

The women immediately began to prepare for the holy day. The rabbi made a minute inspection of the mezuzahs on the door lintels, and issued orders to the household not to buy any meats until he had first assured himself that the slaughtering had been done with strict ritual observance; he even forbade them to buy milk until he could be sure that all of the requirements had been observed in the milking.

Mindel complained tearfully. "What shall the children eat in the meanwhile?" she wept. "Coals?"

The rabbi wandered about the flat confused. It was on the second floor, with windows facing on the courtyard and the street. The rattling of the tramcars and wagons and the shouts of the stall-keepers came in from the outside. Street musicians were blaring away. Children were howling at the tops of their voices. The rabbi now comprehended the full significance of the Talmudic phrase: "In big cities life is difficult."

It was hard to become accustomed to Warsaw. There was a prayerhouse opening on the courtyard, but the ritual bath was on the other side of the street, and crossing over was an adventure that was attended with danger to life and limb. In the kitchen the cooking had to be done over a gas flame, and who could know whether the gas was manufactured under orthodox supervision? Water came from a tap, but who could know through what uncleanliness the pipes stretched their length?

Nevertheless, in spite of all difficulties, the preparations for Yom Kippur were completed.

The day before the holy day Rabbi Dan went to the prayerhouse for morning prayers, and after the prayer drank a glass of wine and nibbled at some cake with the other worshippers. At home his wife had prepared a breakfast of some carp, dumplings, and a stew of carrots. In the afternoon, the rabbi put on his silk gaberdine, his white rabbinical robe, his prayer shawl with the gold-embroidered edge. His wife put on her best dress and wore a pearl-embroidered shawl over her head. His daughter and daughters-in-law, too, were dressed in their holiday clothes. After the rabbi had pronounced the blessings, he went off to attend the *Kol Nidre*. The courtyard was noisy.

Women whose husbands had been taken off into the army wailed and wept. Bewigged and beshawled matrons, carrying gold-stamped prayerbooks under their arms, exchanged fervent wishes for the new year. It was still early, but the lights already blazed inside the prayerhouse. The floor was strewn with hay and sawdust. The sexton showed the rabbi to a seat near the east wall.

He did not approve of the style of the services here. They were different, not so strict as those he was accustomed to in Tereshpol Minor. There was less weeping, less groaning. Near the door a group of young men talked to each other while the reader read. In Tereshpol Minor the rabbi would have banged his fist on the pulpit and ordered silence. He wrapped his prayer shawl over his head and leaned against the wall. For the Eighteen Benedictions he remained standing for a long time. Reb Dan did not usually weep when he prayed, but when he recalled that on this holy evening Jewish soldiers were wandering about, God knows where, eating unclean food, suffering God knows what tortures, the tears came to his eyes. At the confessional prayer he enunciated each phrase distinctly and beat his chest with fervor.

The worshippers began to go home, but Reb Dan and a few other old men stayed on to spend the night in the prayerhouse. The rabbi pored over an ancient volume through the long night, brooding over Israel's old glory.

The priest kept watch at three places in the temple: at the Chamber of Abtinas, at the Chamber of Flame, and at the Chamber of the Hearth. . . .

This was the singing which the Levites used to sing in the Temple. On the first day they sang: "The earth is the Lord's and all that therein is." On the second day they sang: "Great is the Lord and highly to be praised." On the third day they sang: "God stands in the congregation of God." On the Sabbath Day they sang a Psalm, a song for the time that is to come, for the day that shall be all Sabbath and rest in the life everlasting.

But the iniquities of our fathers have caused the desolation of the Temple, and our sins have prolonged our captivity. We have no burnt offering, nor the trespass offering, nor staves of the Ark, nor Holy of Holies. . . .

The candles flickered and spluttered. An old man with a parchment-yellow face and a bushy white beard stretched out on a bench and dozed heavily. The star-faded sky and a three-quarter moon looked in through the windows. As he sat here in his prayer shawl and white robe Reb Dan could forget that he had been driven out of Tereshpol Minor. He was in a sanctuary, among his own people and among the familiar volumes of sacred law. No, he was not alone. There was still a God in heaven, angels, seraphim, a throne of grace. All that he needed was to stretch out his hand and he would touch one of the holy volumes whose words were the voice of the living God, the letters with which God had created the world. A sudden wave of pity swept over him for the unbelievers who wandered about in outer darkness, shooting and killing one another, looting, stealing, raping. What were they seeking? What would be the outcome of their endless wars? How long would they go on sinking into the morass of iniquity? He recalled the words of the prayer:

"And therefore inspire, O Lord our God, all Thy work with Thy name, and extend Thy dread over all Thou hast created, that all Thy work may reverence Thee, so that they may all unitedly perform Thy will with an upright heart, and be convinced like us, O Lord our Lord, that dominion appertaineth unto Thee, that strength is in Thy hand, might in Thy right hand, and that Thy name is tremendous over all Thou hast created."

Reb Dan leaned his forehead against his closed fist and fell into a doze. When the sun's rays came through the window he woke up. He poured water over the tips of his fingers at the bucket. Purple shadows wove in the corners of the prayer-house, as at sunset. The candle stubs had grown small, the flames flickering and pale. Outside there could be heard the crowing of a cock. Reb Dan had not noticed how far the morning was advancing, or that the worshippers were gathering for the day's devotions. Zaddok, his older son, came up to him.

"How are you, Father?" he asked. "Here. Take a pinch of snuff."

Reb Dan regarded him with a bewildered gaze. "See how old he has grown," he thought. "A gray beard. In his sixties." He took a pinch of snuff.

"Thanks." And suddenly he shouted angrily: "Enough! It is time! High time for the Messiah!"

CHAPTER FIVE

The opinion of the Moskat family was that it was Leah's own fault that Masha had wandered off to the paths of unrighteousness. The girl was twenty-five years old now, but she had been associating with older men ever since she was in the fourth class. Queen Esther and Saltsha, her sisters-in-law, had warned Leah countless times that a girl as pretty as Masha should not be left to her own devices. But somehow or other Leah had no power at all over her daughter. Everything Masha did was strange to Leah. Leah was fat and big-boned; the girl was lean and slender. Leah had an enormous appetite; Masha pecked at her food like a bird. Leah had been a poor student at school; Masha had graduated with a gold-medal award. Leah talked loudly, with violent gesticulations and abandoned laughter; Masha was reserved and delicate. On the coldest winter days the girl insisted on wearing a light coat; it was a wonder to everyone that she did not catch her death of cold. In the summer, when the family went out of town, Masha remained alone in the hot city. Just like her father, she was full of hidden ways. She would leave the house in the morning, no one knowing whither she was bound. She would come home late at night, when the rest of the family was sound asleep. She had made many acquaintances, visited wealthy homes, gone to balls and parties—but of all this Leah would find out only later, or from other people. For some time Masha had gone around with a student, Edek by name, the son of a wealthy family in Vlotzlavek, but Leah had never seen him. Then the girl had given him up and Leah had never known why the two had separated. Whenever the mother ventured to talk things over with Masha, the girl would smile and say:

"Don't worry, Mamma. Everything will be all right."

The range of Masha's talents left her mother in awe. Almost by herself she learned French, how to play the piano, dancing, drawing, painting, and how to make a sort of rag marionette for which rich ladies paid as much as twenty-five rubles. She designed her own hats, she had her clothes made by Polish seamstresses in the gentile section of Warsaw. She spoke the Polish of the aristocracy. Once Abram had encountered her riding horseback in Lazhenki Park, and when he asked her where she learned to ride, she had answered: "Oh, there's nothing difficult about it."

Leah, who was noisy and vituperative toward everybody, treated Masha with reserve. When the maid cleaned Masha's room Leah watched carefully to see that she disturbed nothing belonging to the girl. Masha kept an aquarium with goldfish, and Leah always made sure that the water was changed regularly. Whenever the subject came up, Leah said: "I'm not her mother, I'm her servant."

For months there had been whisperings in the family that Masha was going around with a gentile, but Leah could not figure out how to approach the subject. When at last she plucked up enough courage to ask Masha if the rumor was true, Masha answered in Polish: "I'm of age and I'm able to take full responsibility for my own actions."

Whenever Masha went over to Polish, Leah felt lost entirely. She went out of her daughter's room. She wanted to let the door bang behind her, but instead she closed it silently. Later, when she went to Koppel's office, she poured out the whole story to him.

"What do you think of such behavior?" she complained. "She'll heap shame and disgrace on me."

Koppel was silent for a while. Then he said:

"If you yell at her she'll move out of the house altogether."

Leah knew Koppel was telling the truth. Masha had hinted more than once that she did not like living on Tshepla Street. It was too far from the tramcar, and too near the Krochmalna. Leah realized that as usual Koppel was not talking idly, that he was weighing and measuring every word.

He sat opposite her at the writing-table that had been Reb Meshulam's. An account book and an abacus lay on it. He talked, puffed at his cigarette, and went over the account books at the same time. He looked straight at Leah and spoke bluntly:

"Divorce that rag of a husband of yours and put an end to the whole thing," he said. "We're not getting any younger."

"It's easy to say. My God, you can imagine the howls that would go up."

"They'll stop some time. They can't howl forever."

Koppel went into the adjoining room and returned with a glass of tea for Leah. She liked her tea sweet, and although sugar had become scarce because of the war, Koppel dropped three lumps into the brew. He always had some cheese cake and buns in the cabinet.

Leah stirred the tea for a long time. "What can I do? Squeeze a divorce out of him?"

"Get rid of him."

"And then what?"

"You know."

"And what about your wife? What'll she do, go begging?"

"She'll be taken care of."

"But—but haven't you got any fear of God in your heart?"

"I'll get over that."

Koppel turned pale as he said this, but he managed a smile. Leah looked at him doubtfully. She had never been able to make up her mind whether she loved or hated him. When Koppel's eyes bored into her breasts she felt a warm flush and at the same time an unpleasant sensation. She had a desire to spit in his face. True, Koppel vowed his love for her, but he had an eye for other women. Who knew what kind of life he led, what haunts he frequented? Whenever he pressed her to live with him without waiting for the divorce, to go off to a hotel with him, or to ride out to some village, a revulsion came over her and she would say: "No, Koppel. I haven't sunk to that level yet."

In the twenty-eight years of their acquaintance she had never really been able to tell exactly where she stood in relation to him. When she had been a girl he had kissed her and sent fervent letters to her. But after her marriage he seemed to have forgotten all about her. For years she had been kept sufficiently occupied bearing children and attending to her domestic duties. Two of the children she had borne were dead. Later Koppel had begun to pester her again, but quarrels and differences had always broken out between them. He had never succeeded in getting more than a kiss from her, but he had never conceded defeat. The moment the two found themselves alone, he would recite his love for her. He was not one of those men who come to your house, drink ten glasses of tea, and find themselves tongue-tied. On the contrary, his tongue was sharp and loose. He had all sorts of nicknames for Moshe Gabriel. He bragged about his power over women. Without any sense of shame he told her how worldly men dealt with easy females. When he left, Leah always felt ill at ease. And since Reb Meshulam's death Koppel had become even more presumptuous. When the war broke out and the tenants stopped paying rent, Leah was entirely in his hands. Whenever she came to him for money, he would say: "What is there in it for me?"

Koppel had a clear plan. He would divorce Bashele and give her a settlement of five thousand rubles. Leah would divorce that oaf her husband, and the two of them would get married. The hell with the rest of them. He wasn't their slave any more; he was the boss, in charge of the estate. He was a man of substance himself, the owner of a couple of houses. He had a good amount of cash; how much he would reveal after the wedding. True, he was in his early fifties, but he was in possession of his full powers. If she didn't delay the affair too long, they might even have children. He would buy a villa in Druskenik; he'd take a trip abroad with her—the war wouldn't last forever. They'd go to Monte Carlo, to the Riviera, to Switzerland, Paris, Berlin, everywhere. His properties and hers together would bring in six hundred rubles a week. For a song he'd buy Nathan's, Pinnie's, and Hama's interest in the estate, and he'd be one of the biggest operators in Warsaw, a second Meshulam Moskat.

"Listen to what I'm telling you, Leah," he urged her. "You and I together can overturn the world."

Koppel was right. Moshe Gabriel was no husband for her. It was an ordeal from beginning to end. But, just the same, how could she pick up, in the middle of everything and at her time of life, and marry Koppel? What would Abram say? Pinnie? Saltsha? Esther? What would the younger ones say—her own children and her nieces and nephews? My God, all Warsaw would laugh behind her back. They'd sneer at her and curse her and wish her a million plagues. And then how could she go cold-bloodedly about the business of breaking up Basha's home? True, the other was a cow, but after all she was the mother of his children. Surely there was a God in heaven who wouldn't overlook these goings on.

"Well, what do you say?" Koppel insisted. "Let's have it."

"It's easy enough to talk."

"The whole thing can be finished like that."

"And what about all your women? There must be a dozen of them."

"If I can have you, then the hell with all the rest of them."

"I'm not so sure."

Leah took the few banknotes Koppel handed her and went home. Out in the street Koppel's words kept ringing in her brain. "He's right," she thought. "I'm getting older. Before you know it, nobody'll want to even look at me. Moshe Gabriel is my misfortune. It's his fault that Masha wants to leave the house. What else should the girl do, with such a *schlemiel* for a father?"

She took a mirror out of her bag and looked at herself. Yes, her cheeks were still youthful, her throat was smooth. But the years would fly by and the blood would cool. She was a stubborn idiot. She would not permit her life to be ruined by that unworldly lump.

Koppel's words had fired her blood, like liquor. Her heels tapped briskly along the sidewalk. She took a deep breath.

"I'll put an end to it," she said aloud, "this very week."

CHAPTER SIX

Pan Zazhitsky told his son Yanek that he would never consent to the youth's marriage to Masha even if the girl was willing to become converted. There was no mistaking Pan Zazhitsky's ultimatum: the day after the wedding he would summon a notary and transfer all his possessions to his daughter Paula. Besides, the family home would be barred to the boy. The old man had a habit of accompanying his talk with constant doodling on a sheet of paper. He was seated at his writing-desk wearing an old-fashioned morning robe, his bare feet stuck into a pair of slippers with pompons. His few remaining gray hairs were uncombed over the bald patch on his head. Beneath his sharp eyes, under the thick brows, flabby pouches were visible. His nose was red and fleshy. His sparse mustache quivered with the restless movement of his lips. As he spoke, an asthmatic cough seized him.

"My son, you'll have to make your choice," he announced. "It's either your family or this Jewess. That's my last word."

"But why, Father? If she's willing to convert, then she'll be one of us."

"I don't want to have anything to do with her. I hate their guts. If you can't find a Christian girl that's to your liking in all of Poland, then—then—"

Pan Zazhitzky could not finish the sentence for a fit of coughing.

His small hands were knobbed and blue-veined. The

Adam's apple bobbed up and down in his scrawny neck. While he gasped for breath he picked up a book and opened it. It was a history of Freemasonry, written by some priests.

"What in the devil do they want, these Jews?" he said, half to himself and half to the boy. "For two thousand years everything Christian was unclean for them. If one of us so much as looked at a bottle of wine it became taboo. And now all at once they want to become our brothers."

"Father, that's got nothing to do with Masha."

"They're all the same. From the Jewish Freemasons in France to the scabby brats that play around in the filth in our Polish villages. They've ruined Poland. It's on account of them that I've got this asthma."

"It was Rybarsky who ruined us, not the Jews."

"Quiet, you traitor! I've sacrificed my whole life for you, and you run around with these fakers and their daughters. You paint naked whores. And now you want to bring that filth into your own house."

"Father, watch out for your words."

"What'll you do? Beat me? I'm an old, broken man. But at least I'll die with the pride that I've been a loyal son of Poland, not a Jew-lover. It is they who have set the Germans to destroy our Polish people."

Pani Zazhitzky, the old man's wife, came into the room. "What's happening now? Here, father, drink a glass of milk. What are you upsetting him for, Yanek?"

"I'm doing nothing. He just loves to talk and—"

"Well, you better be quiet, my son. All night he coughs. Can't close an eye. And now you upset him. What a son!"

Pani Eliza Zazhitzky was small and slender, with the typical dark eyes of a Jewess—the reason, probably that she always wore a heavy crucifix on a string of rosary beads. Her graying hair was gathered back in a Grecian knot. A bunch of keys hung from her waist. She was fifteen years younger than her husband, but her forehead was deeply creased. Ever since they had left their estate in Lublin province and settled in Warsaw she had been ailing. She was in constant terror of thieves, arsonists, big-city servants who poisoned their employers and stole the family jewels. Each day she carefully read every line in the *Warsaw Courier*, including the advertisements. She also borrowed the anti-Semitic "Two Groszy" from the janitor. She put a glass of milk before her husband. "Here, drink, father. It will soothe you."

"Ach, I can't stand all these drinks."

"It's good for your cough. Ah, dear Lord, milk gets dearer by the day. And they say there'll soon be no tea, either."

"Soon there'll be nothing left," Pan Zazhitzky interrupted. "Nobody pays rent any more. People have become robbers and thieves I tell you. The Jewish speculators are hoarding all the food, the food that our hard-working peasants produce with the sweat of their brows."

"Yes, yes, it's true. I've been through the Jewish streets and I saw for myself. The Jews stand in front of their stores with their yellow beards and they don't let in a customer. They've got cellars full of flour and sugar and potatoes. Just ask one of them for a pound of flour and he says 'Nothing, nothing.'"

"And your son wants to marry one of them."

"Then let him, papusha. We'll soon be dying anyway. He'll live to regret that he's brought shame on a good Polish name."

Yanek got up and went out. In the corridor he saw his sister, Paula, combing her hair at the mirror. The girl was twenty-one, five years younger than he. She was blonde, with blue eyes and dimpled cheeks. She had finished her schooling two years before and was now keeping company with a wealthy boy, a student at the Polytechnic. Yanek had the tall frame of his father and the dark eyes of his mother, the latter queerly inappropriate to the snubbed Slavic nose. His chestnut-colored hair was thin and set far up on his high forehead. At the academy where he studied painting, his fellow students were in the habit of teasing him by calling him Jew.

"What are you getting all fixed up for? Meeting Bolek?"

"Oh, it's you. Popping up, like a ghost. I thought you'd moved out already."

"Soon."

"Isn't it cold in that pigsty of yours?"

"You'll please be good enough not to call my studio a pigsty."

"My, how sensitive you've got! I saw a notice of the new exhibition in the *Courier*. Your name wasn't even mentioned."

"They'll be mentioning me yet."

"I notice they didn't forget the Jew painters."

"So what?"

"How laconic you've become! What sort of quarrel are you carrying on with Papa? One can hear your yelling all over the house."

"I beg your pardon if we woke you up."

"You'll kill them with your nonsense."

"Shut up."

"And if I don't? You Jewish onion!"

There was a time when Yanek would have slapped the girl's face for such impertinence; but now Paula was too grown-up to be treated so summarily, and besides, Yanek was too much estranged from the household even to carry on a family feud.

Yanek went out of the house. In the courtyard he noticed a Succoth booth, which every year had been the cause of much grumbling among the Christian residents of the building. The two Jewish families in the house erected the booth each holiday season, but each time Yanek's father had the janitor take it down. This year, however, aware that Pan Zazhitzky never left his apartment, they had taken advantage of the situation and had put up the symbolic booth. Yanek gazed curiously at the strange construction. He felt a desire to go inside and see what the thing looked like, but he was afraid that he might be taken for a scoffer. How interesting it would be, he thought, to do a canvas of a group of Jews at their feasting and singing in the holiday booth, the whole scene lit by candles, the women bringing trays of holiday food to their men.

Pan Zazhitzky's house was on Hozha Street. Yanek's studio was on Holy Cross Street. He shared it with three colleagues, all of them Jews. Strange, how his destiny had thrown him close to Jews from his very youth! In his high school there had been a single Jewish student, and the two had been close friends. Then when he went to law school, he was drawn to his Jewish fellow students. Later, when he changed over to the art academy, the few Jewish artists there had brought him into their circle. The Christian students had actually doubted that he was a Catholic, the son of a Polish nobleman. More than once they had said to him: "Hey, you Jew, why don't you go back to Palestine!"

There were times when Yanek hated his dark Jewish eyes, his chestnut hair, and the Jewish mob he so much resembled. He would draw caricatures of Jews, quarrel with his colleagues, act like an anti-Semite. He planned to go and settle in Italy, where the Christians were dark and where no one would throw it up to him that he had a Jewish face. In Poland it was impossible to keep away from the Jews. His father babbled about them day and night. The priest at the church assailed them in his sermons. His mother complained about them. The Warsaw streets were full of them. Whenever Yanek walked along, some Jewish man or woman would stop him and ask him a question in Yiddish. Day after day he was compelled to make the same embarrassed explanation: "I'm sorry. I'm not Jewish."

Not only did he look like a Jew, he knew, but he had all the qualities the others attributed to the Jews. He shunned fighting, could not stand liquor, suffered from bashfulness and shrinking. At school he read serious books, avoided athletic sports, visited museums and art shows. In those days he had painted fantastic canvases, strange beasts and foliage. He had studied law to please his father, but from the very beginning he had known he would never enter the legal profession. At art school he was in constant trouble with his professors, who had called him decadent, nihilist, Jew. At twenty-one he had presented himself for military service, but he had been rejected; his heart was bad. When he was driven to visit a brothel, destiny seemed to push him into the arms of a Jewish prostitute. Ever since he had read Kraushar's history of the Frankists, he suspected that he himself was descended from these converted Jews. His grandmother had once told him that his great-grandfather had been a Wolowski, a name that had been adopted by the sons of Elisha Shur.

Numerous times Yanek had decided to avoid all Jews, to forget all about them, but fate balked him. He fell in love with Masha the first time he saw her. His sculptor friend Yasha Mlotek was doing a bust of her, and the moment Yanek turned his eyes on her he had known she was the one he had always dreamed of. It took only a few words of conversation to put him at ease with her. The portrait he painted of her was the best thing he had ever done. Everyone admitted that. They had carried on their love affair in the alcove where stood the oven with the twisted chimney pipes, a stack of unfinished canvases, dust-laden frames, and an ancient sofa, its springs broken and the horsehair stuffing bulging out. In the large studio Mlotek would be singing Jewish melodies, full of sighings and wailings. Chaim Zeidenman, a Lithuanian, a former yeshivah student, would be boiling potatoes in their skins and eating them with herring. Felix Rubinlicht would be sprawled out on a couch reading magazines. There was no drinking in the studio, and no quarreling. There was something soulful, something words could not describe, that enveloped all that these Jewish artists did—their work, their talk about art, even their witticisms and shady jokes. The girls who came to the studio also had a queer mixture of freedom and religiosity. Masha had told him about her grandfather, the patriarch Meshulam Moskat, about her father, her uncles, and the Bialodrevna rabbi. She walked with him along the streets and pointed to the houses where they all lived—Nathan, Nyunie, Abram. Whenever he reminded her that they could expect nothing but trouble, he being gentile and she Jewish, she would wave away all fears with a gesture of her hands.

"It's simple," she would say. "Either I'll become a Christian or you a Jew."

Yes, some mysterious power was pushing him toward Jews. His children would be the grandchildren of Moshe Gabriel and Leah, of the blood of Meshulam Moskat. He seemed to be driven to take his walks in the Jewish streets and byways, where before his eyes there swam a strange sea of forms, characters, unusual scenes. Here in this section someone or other was always carrying on a heated debate about religion. Talmudists with long sidelocks spent the nights studying Holy Writ. Chassidim hotly discussed their rabbis and their gifts of driving out dybbuks. Their Zaddiks wandered off into the forests to commune in loneliness with God. Holy men with white beards spent their lives poring over the mysteries of the Cabala. Fantastic youths left their families and went off to Palestine to toil over the draining and restoration of swamp land and sandy wastes, abandoned for centuries. Young girls labored in attic rooms preparing bombs to hurl at Czarist officials. At their weddings these folk wept as though at a funeral. Their books read from right to left. Their section of Warsaw was like a bit of Bagdad transplanted into the Western World. Yanek never tired of hearing about this people who had lived for eight hundred years on Polish soil and had never acquired the Polish tongue. Where did they come from? Were they descendants of the ancient Hebrews? Were they, perhaps, the grandsons of the Khazars? What idea held them together? Where did they get those coal-black or fiery-red beards, those wild eyes, the pale aristocratic faces? Why did the peoples hate them with such a bitter hatred? Why were they chased out of land after land? What was the urgent drive that sent them to England, to America, Argentina, South Africa, Siberia, Australia? Why was it precisely this people who had given the world Moses, David, the prophets, Jesus, the apostles, Spinoza, Karl Marx? Yanek had an urge to paint these people, to learn their tongue, to know their secrets, to become part of them. For models he hired their poverty-stricken girls, porters, peddlers. The artists who shared his studio would shrug their shoulders and begin to talk Yiddish to him.

"You've gone crazy," Mlotek insisted. "Your Jews look like Turks."

"You don't know what you're after," Felix Rubinlicht declared. "A real *Goyisher kop.*"

CHAPTER SEVEN

During the intermediate days of the Feast of Tabernacles, Koppel, as usual, arrived at the office at eleven o'clock in the morning. There was not much to do. The tenants were not paying their rents, but there was some income from shops, bakeries, small factories, the scattered interests that were part of the Moskat fortunes. The few hundred rubles a month that did come in Koppel was careful to divide among the Moskat heirs according to their needs. The largest sum went to Joel, who was desperately ill. The smallest amount went to Abram. And when Koppel had finished with the family's affairs, he turned to the computing of his own business, shifting the beads on the abacus, letting clouds of smoke drift from his nostrils, and humming a current popular song:

> *It is a secret thing,*
> *This song I have to sing. . . .*

As Koppel sat at the desk which had once belonged to Meshulam Moskat, brooding about notes, interest, mortgages, and valuta, he heard firm footsteps on the stairs outside. He looked around. The door opened and Leah came in. It was raining outside and she carried an umbrella with a silver handle. She wore a caracul coat and a feathered hat. It had been long since Koppel had seen her so festively dressed. He rose from his chair.

Leah smiled. "Good morning, Koppel," she announced. "Why do you get up? I'm not a rabbi. I'm not even a rabbi's wife."

"To me you're more important than a thousand rabbis, or their wives either."

Leah suddenly became serious. "I want you to listen to what I've got to say, Koppel," she said almost angrily. "Are you still of the same opinion? I mean about me."

"About you? You know how I feel."

"And you still have some love for me?"

"I don't have to tell you."

"Then in that case I want you to know I've come to make a final decision."

Koppel turned pale. "That's good news," he said in a stifled voice, the cigarette dangling from his lip.

He quickly recovered his poise, went around the desk to help her off with her coat. Nor did he forget to take her wet umbrella and stand it in a corner. Leah was wearing a close-fitting black satin dress (Koppel had once remarked that the dress always excited him), which emphasized her rounded hips and high bosom. When she peeled off her gloves, Koppel noticed that she wasn't wearing her wedding ring.

"Everything goes your way, Koppel," she observed. "You're a lucky man. Why don't you ask me to sit down?"

"Please, Leah. You're the boss here."

"Really? Some boss! Listen, Koppel, we're no longer children."

"No."

"And before we do anything foolish we've got to think things out carefully. Last night I couldn't sleep a wink. Just look at my eyes. I thought the whole thing through. There's nothing I've got to lose. Once and for all I've got to get rid of my foolish pride. But if you have any regrets, Koppel, then I'll not hold it against you. It's not so easy to break up a home."

"I regret nothing. This is the happiest day of my life."

"Then why are you so pale? You look like Yom Kippur before sunset."

"I'm all right."

"Just before Rosh Hashona," Leah continued after a pause, "he went to Bialodrevna and took Aaron with him. He's there yet. The simpleton imagines that I'll play the part of a deserted wife and spend my time mourning for him. Well, he's mistaken. I'm going to go to Bialodrevna and demand a divorce. Twenty-five years of it is enough."

"I knew all the time that you'd come to your senses."

"How could you know? As long as my father was alive, I was willing to stand for anything. I didn't want to ruin his declining years. I suffered and I kept quiet. I used to lie awake, wetting the pillow with my tears, while Moshe Gabriel spent his time at Chassidic parties. He was more at home in Bialodrevna than in his own house. And all the responsibilities were mine—the household, providing enough money to get along, everything. The only thing he ever did was to nag me because I saw to it that the children didn't grow up to be useless fools like him. Now I've had enough. For the rest of my years I want to live like a human being, not like an animal."

"A hundred per cent right."

Koppel shook his head decidedly and drew on the cigarette between his lips, but it had long since burned out. He began to search about for a match, feeling in his pockets, rummaging on the desk and in the drawers. The abacus fell to the floor, its wooden disks turning with a humming sound before coming to rest.

"What are you searching for?" Leah exclaimed.

"Nothing. Some matches. Here they are."

"Don't be so confused. For twenty-eight years you've been telling me about your great love. Just the other day you made a whole speech. But if you've changed your mind, we'll still be friends. A thing like this has got to be gone into with one's whole heart or not at all."

"But, Leah, I don't know why you're talking this way."

"I don't know either. What I want is a clear answer."

"I'm ready to go through with it. You'll only have to give me a couple of days."

"You can even have a couple of weeks. The hurry isn't as great as that. There's only one thing I want. Try not to hurt your wife. She's got to have enough to get along on—for herself and the children, too."

"She'll never lack anything."

"How do you know she'll accept a divorce?"

"I don't claim to predict anything."

"I see. So what it amounts to is that all these years you've been just talking."

"No, Leah, that isn't true."

"You don't seem very enthusiastic. I suppose that twenty years ago I was younger and prettier."

"To me you're always beautiful."

"This isn't the time for compliments. You needn't think, Koppel, that it's easy for me to take a step like this. I've been up all night, tossing around like a snake. I'm not one of your young women any more. I'll soon be forty-four. People say I'm a smart one, but there's a bit of the fool in the smartest person. Everybody thinks of you as a swindler and a thief, ready to take away any trick in the deck; but I've trusted you. What are you getting so pale for? I'm not trying to insult you."

"Who thinks I'm a thief?"

"What's the difference? I don't think it."

"I *am* a thief."

Leah's breast ached with a sudden pang. "Who is it you've stolen from?"

"Your own father."

"Are you joking?"

"If everyone says it, I suppose it must be so."

"Koppel, don't be like that. You know how people talk. They'll say anything and they gossip about everyone. It went around that Masha was really your daughter."

"I wish she were."

"Tell me the truth, Koppel. What's bothering you? If you don't want to break up your home, then let's not start anything. So far the whole thing's a secret."

"It won't be a secret for long."

"What do you mean?"

"We'll get married in the Vienna Hall."

"Are you out of your mind? Divorced people marry quietly. What bothers you? Is it that you're sorry for Bashele?"

"I'm sorry for her, but that won't stop me."

"Maybe you're in love with someone else. You have a dozen women."

"Not even a half dozen."

"I think I'm beginning to understand you, Koppel. You always used to tell me that you had women, but that you didn't take them seriously. Just playing around. But, according to my standards, when a man goes around with a woman for a long time, she's no plaything. I don't know your affairs and I don't want to know them. Forgive me, such things revolt me. But if you're really in love with one of those females, then please, I beg of you, don't make a fool of me. After all, I'm still a daughter of Meshulam Moskat."

"I'm not in love with anybody and I'm not afraid of anybody."

"Who said anything about being afraid?"

"Didn't you?"

"Are you afraid she'll throw some vitriol at you?"

"What 'she' are you chattering about?"

"Just listen to me, Koppel. I can see that you're keeping something from me. I can't drag the truth from you, and I don't care to try. Forget about the whole thing. Pretend I haven't said a word. I'll divorce him anyhow, but that has nothing to do with you."

"So now you're changing your mind."

"Have it that way if you prefer it."

"Don't run away. You know I've loved you from the very first. Ever since I came to work for your father. Everything I've done has been for you. Every night I had dreams that a day like this would come, a day that would—I don't know how to express what I mean. I used to have dreams that I was calling the boss 'father-in-law.' "

Leah's eyes filled with tears. She took a handkerchief from her bag and blew her nose. "Then why do you torture me?"

"In your eyes I'll always be a servant."

"Don't talk like that. You're just trying to hurt me."

"Didn't you just call me a thief?"

"I called you? Would I marry a thief?"

"And if I did steal, that was for you, too."

The telephone rang. Koppel picked up the receiver and then put it down again. He took out his watch, glanced at it, then put it back in his vest pocket. He looked at Leah, half confused, half eager. He bit his lips, and the color in his cheeks faded, then flushed red again. An urge seized him to confess everything. He knew that he was doing something that he would later regret, but he was powerless to control his tongue. "Leah, there's something I've got to tell you."

"Go ahead."

"Leah, I've got more than sixty thousand rubles, cash, at my house."

Leah raised her eyebrows. "Well, what about it? I'm glad for your sake."

"It's your father's money."

Leah shrugged her shoulders. "Why do you tell me now? To ease your soul?"

"I can't stay here in Warsaw. I'll never be able to find any peace."

"What will you do?"

"I'll go to America."

It was like a stab in Leah's entrails. "Alone?"

"With you."

"How? There's a war going on."

"We can go through Siberia. What do you say?"

"What can I say? All I know is that I'm up to my neck in filth."

Leah could no longer control herself. She tried to swallow the lump in her throat and broke into sobs. Koppel went over to the window and closed it, though it had been open only a crack. Then he began to pace back and forth. Suddenly he felt an astonishing sense of lightness. A faint smile showed at the corners of his mouth. He had a distinct feeling that a load had fallen from him; it had oppressed him, somewhere on the left side of his chest. He went over to Leah, fell to his knees, and put his head in her lap. Something youthful and long forgotten welled up in him. Leah put her hand on his head, caressing his hair with the tips of her fingers. He did not know himself whether he was weeping or laughing. With both her hands she raised his face to hers. Her cheeks were wet. But her eyes smiled. "Koppel, what will we do in America?" she murmured.

And Koppel answered: "We'll begin a new life."

CHAPTER EIGHT

1

Already the reverberations of the cannon fire on the battlefront were causing Warsaw windows to tremble. The German line was advancing against a Russian counterattack. Regiments of soldiers were steadily marching through the Warsaw streets—Cossacks, Kirghiz, Bashkirs, Caucasians, Kalmuks. The hospitals of the city were full of the wounded. City officials had hurried to move their families out of town somewhere to the rear. There was talk to the effect that the Governor-General was preparing to leave and that the bridges across the Vistula were being mined. There were rumors that the retreating Russian armies would put Warsaw to the torch. Nevertheless, the Feast of the Rejoicing of the Law was celebrated as always. The official liquor shops were closed, but the celebrants managed to get enough of the spirits from unlicensed distillers. There was no lack of either wine or beer. In the Bialodrevna prayerhouse the faithful began their drinking on the eighth day of the Feast of Tabernacles. Early in the morning of the Feast of Rejoicing of the Law the Chassidim were already drunk.

It was stiflingly hot in the prayerhouse. The children carried paper pennants, and apples stuck at the end of sticks, candles spluttering in the apples. Women and girls crowded forward to kiss the silk covering of the Torah scrolls. Young men and boys engaged in every kind of mischievous play. They stealthily poured water into the pockets of the unsuspecting worshippers; they knotted the fringes of the men's ritual shawls; they hid prayerbooks and skullcaps. The reader intoned the additional service, but none of the congregation made the proper responses. Nathan Moskat was chosen as warden. He complained that he was a sick man and had no energy to devote to community affairs. Besides, his brother Joel was deathly ill. But the Chassidim refused to listen to his excuses, and when the formality of his election was completed, the younger men seized the new warden, stretched him out full length on a table, and pommeled him in good humor. Nathan groaned and protested, while the young men chanted:

> *"One and one,*
> *One and two,*
> *One and three. . . ."*

After Nathan's bottom had been well pounded, they let him go, and he rose good-naturedly and invited the celebrants to his house for a drink in honor of the day. Saltsha had known in advance that Nathan was to be elected warden and had made proper preparations: wine, vishniak, mead, tarts, flat cakes, and nuts. An enormous pot of cabbage mixed with raisins and saffron steamed in the kitchen. Two geese were roasting in the oven. The fragrant odors permeated the entire apartment. Abram brought with him a magnum of wine that he had been hoarding since before the war. He took off his coat and shoes and danced on top of Nathan's oaken table, singing a Bialodrevna ditty:

> *"Abraham rejoiced in the rejoicing of the Law,*
> *Isaac rejoiced in the rejoicing of the Law,*
> *Jacob rejoiced in the rejoicing of the Law,*
> *Moses rejoiced in the rejoicing of the Law,*
> *Aaron rejoiced in the rejoicing of the Law,*
> *David rejoiced in the rejoicing of the Law."*

Saltsha begged Abram to stop his nonsense, but Abram paid no attention to her. She warned the Chassidim that the floors had been highly waxed and that they might slip. They paid no heed to her. The ecstatic celebrants joined hands, forming a circle, and sang quavering Bialodrevna songs, stamping on the floor with their heavy boots. The boys thrust their way into the middle of the circle, hopping along with the oldsters. Housewives and girls from the neighboring flats came in to watch the merriment, clapping their hands and doubling over with peals of laughter. When Saltsha brought in one of the roast geese, the Chassidim fell on it, tearing pieces of the steaming fowl with their bare hands. In less than a moment nothing was left but a pile of bones. Pinnie, hoarse with shouting and singing, clutched Saltsha and tried to kiss her. Nathan laughed so uproariously that his belly shook.

"So Pinnie," he squeaked, "must I say to you what the King said to Haman: 'Will you force the Queen before me in the house?' "

"At the Rejoicing of the Law every Jew's a king," Pinnie answered firmly.

Saltsha ran away, but Pinnie lumbered after her. The women in the kitchen began to scurry around, squealing. Abram chased after Pinnie, grabbed him by the collar, and shouted: "Idiot! Woman-chaser!"

"Oh, mamma!" one of the women cried. "It's too much. I can't laugh any more."

"We know you, Abram," Pinnie squeaked in a comic falsetto, "you old chicken-thief!"

"Good people, hold me! I'll fall! I'll die with laughter!" howled an old woman with an enormous Greek knot at the nape of her neck.

"Oh, my sides! My sides!"

Abram lifted Pinnie up bodily and carried him out of the kitchen. Pinnie shrieked, kicking his feet like a school child being carried out for a whipping.

From Nathan's house the celebrants went in a body over to Pinnie's. His wife, Hannah, and his four daughters had expected the invasion and had been busy all day preparing for it. Hannah, known for her stinginess, had been careful to remove all the valuables and breakables from the living-room which the Chassidim might damage in their carryings on. She had prepared a mess of strudel and cherry punch. The Chassidim searched in vain for toothsome morsels in closets and chests, but all the hiding-places were locked tight. They quickly ate the strudel, drank the punch, danced a few of their dances, sang a few of their songs, and marched off to

Abram's. There, too, the visitation was not unexpected.
Hama and her married daughter, Bella, had cooked a savory
cabbage mixture and roasted a goose. There were honey
cakes, meat patties, cherry brandy. Even before the holiday
Abram had warned Hama not to shame him with her parsi-
moniousness. She was wearing a holiday dress with all her
jewelry. The earrings, the brooch, the golden chain, the rings,
looked out of place against Hama's uncouth form. Bella had
put on the clothes that had been part of her wedding outfit.
Avigdor, her husband, was present at the celebration, too. He
had been a widower with a drygoods store on Mirovska
Street. He was a fervent Chassid, a man of learning, with a
pale face and a pair of eyeglasses with enormous thick lenses.
Abram had wanted his son-in-law to join the Bialodrevna
prayerhouse, but Avigdor was a loyal Sochatshov Chassid.
Now, when Abram spotted him, he shouted: "A good holiday
to you, my fine ornament! Are you drunk or sober?"

"I'm never drunk."

"Then in that case the hell with you."

Hama ran up warningly. "Abram, watch your tongue. Is
that a way to talk to your daughter's husband?"

"A man's got to drink!" Abram shouted. "If not, he'll never
be able to spawn a kid."

"Shame on you, Abram! You're bringing disgrace to the
house."

Hama's nose immediately reddened and tears came to her
eyes. Apparently Abram was already drunk. Bella ran up to
him and tried to whisper something in his ear, but Abram
caught her and started to kiss her. "Ah, my daughter, your father is just no good."

"Drunk as Lot," Hama sighed.

"Lot took special care of his daughters," Abram boomed.

"Feh, Abram!" Pinnie warned him. "Nice talk for a grandfather!"

"Yes, Pinnie, you're right!" Abram mumbled. He grabbed
Pinnie's beard and began pulling him along like a goat. The
others began to laugh and squeal with delight.

Stepha came in from one of the other rooms. She was tall,
almost as tall as Abram. She had on a red dress and black lac-
quered sash. She was twenty-seven years old, but she looked
older, in her thirties. She had a large bust and large hips. Her
dark face was rich in charm. But something of fatigue was in
her look. The medical student with whom she had been going
about for the past four years had not completed his course.

Neither was he willing to marry. It was whispered in the family that Stepha had already found herself pregnant and that she had had an abortion.

When the Chassidim caught sight of Stepha, they began to smile shamefacedly and retreat shyly. The older men clutched their beards and whispered to each other.

"A good holiday to you, Sheba," Abram said. "For all good Jews today's a great holiday."

"A good holiday to you too," Stepha answered.

"Well, go and bring in the refreshments. You're a Jewish daughter, after all."

"I'm not denying it."

Stepha turned back and went to the room she had come from. She wasn't pleased that her father had called her by her Hebrew name, Sheba, nor did she like it when he carried on like those other orthodox Jews. What tricks was he up to now, the hypocrite? "He's a thousand times worse than I am," she thought. "It's his fault that I am as I am, without either God or husband."

In the living-room the celebration went on, the singing and the shuffling of feet. Abram climbed on a table, holding high the *babkes* that Hama brought in. He doled them out, as Israel Eli, the beadle, was wont to do in Bialodrevna, at the same time shouting:

> *"Rich and poor, young and old,*
> *See my* babke *and behold.*
> *Like a bee without a sting*
> *Is a* babke *without a drink. . . ."*

Hama tried to hide away some of the brandy and whisky for her own household use, but Abram managed to get his hands on all of it. He kept on pouring glass after glass for the celebrants. He sent some of the youngsters out to rouse up the owners of the closed shops, and they came back laden with apples, pears, grapes, watermelons, and walnuts. From the wine cellars in one shop they brought up a basket of dry wine, the bottles dusty and cobwebbed. Somewhere they had managed to get a small barrel of beer and a spigot. Abram knocked out the bung; the foam poured out over the vat. The singing and the dancing grew in ardor. More Chassidim arrived. Whenever the excitement started to flag, Abram was at hand to whip it up. "Livelier, brothers! No sleeping! Rejoice in the Torah!"

"Your health! Your health, brothers! Next year in Jerusalem!"

Hama stood in the doorway with several of the neighbor women. She alternately laughed and wept, blowing her nose and wiping her wet eyes. "If he could only be like this all through the year!" she thought. "What do they know of what I endure?" Abram brought her a glass of beer. "Drink, Hama! Your health!"

"But Abram, you know it isn't good for me."

"Drink! The devil isn't ready to take you yet!" And he planted a kiss on her cheek.

Hama flushed with joy and embarrassment. The women giggled. She managed to gulp down some of the beer. The first swallow seemed to spread a glow all over her. Mordecai, last year's warden, grabbed Zeinvele Srotsker's elbow. "A madman—but one of our own. A Chassid to his bones!"

2

This year Fishel did not take part in any of the family celebrations of the holiday. Directly after the services he left the prayerhouse. In the intermission he had taken a drink, as is the custom on the Day of Rejoicing, and now he felt dizzy. In previous years he had joined with the rest, dancing and drinking with his fellows, leading them along to his own house. Hadassah and Shifra had set out refreshments and wine. His father-in-law, his mother-in-law, and the whole family had joined them. Old and young had envied him his good fortune. But now he was going home alone. He hurried furtively along the streets. The door was not locked. He pushed it open and went inside. Neither Hadassah nor the servant was there. He took off his glasses and wiped them with a corner of his scarf. Things had come to a pretty pass when they went out and left the doors open. It was getting late. He was hungry. After some hesitation he went into the kitchen, took some white bread, fish, and a leg of the roasted goose in the oven. He was faint with hunger, but the moment he took a mouthful of food his appetite seemed to disappear. He tried to chant a ritual song as he ate, but it came out a mournful wail. A wanton —that's what she had become. A loose woman. In the ancient days they would have let her drink the bitter water. If she had been defiled, her belly would swell and her thigh would rot.

Feh, what thoughts were these! "I'm not her enemy. There's a dear God in heaven. He sees the truth."

Fishel heard the outside door open. Hadassah? he wondered. Or maybe Shifra? He raised his eyes and saw a strange woman. She had a shawl over her shoulders. Did he know her? There was something vaguely familiar about her.

"The lady isn't home?"

"What is it you want?"

"I work over at your father-in-law's, Nyunie Moskat's—"

"Oh, yes. What is it? What have you come for?"

"My mistress wants you both to come over, right away."

"What's the matter? My wife isn't in the house."

"My mistress says to come right over. She's very sick."

"What happened?"

"I don't know. Suddenly she felt very sick. She's a little better now, but—"

"All right. I'll come right away."

He put on his things and went out with the girl, locking the door behind him and putting the key under the mat outside. The two walked in silence along the street. "A ruined holiday," Fishel thought. "But what is there to do?" He felt a sense of satisfaction that he had been called, that he had not become entirely estranged from the family. In the differences between him and Hadassah, Dacha sided with him. He hurried along after the girl. Strange and unexpected thoughts kept crowding his brain. How would it be, he thought, if he divorced Hadassah and married this servant? She was probably an orphan. She would be loyal. And what if, instead, he just asked her to sin with him? He felt ashamed at his own thoughts and tried to drive them away; they persisted. And no wonder, he thought. Hadassah had not been to the *mikvah* for purification in months. After all, a man was made of flesh and blood.

He hurried after the girl, who was walking rapidly ahead of him. "Better to walk behind a lion than behind a woman. . . ." He suddenly remembered the Talmudic injunction. They reached the house and went upstairs. The girl opened the door and let him in. The moment he stepped inside he knew that his mother-in-law was very ill. The odor of medicines and the sickroom came pungently to his nostrils. He went into the living-room. His father-in-law stood in the middle of the room. He was smoking a cigarette and staring into space.

"Go inside. She wants to see you. But don't talk too much."

"What happened?"

"It looks very bad."

The sickroom opened directly off the living-room. One of the two beds was made up; in the other Dacha lay. Her face was pale and jaundiced. Fishel hardly recognized her.

"Come here. Don't be afraid." Dacha's voice was surprisingly loud and healthy. "Sit down near me. I suddenly felt very bad. A heart attack or something. They had to send for Dr. Mintz."

"What did he say?"

"I don't know. All I know is it's not good. Where's Hadassah?"

"She happened not to be in the house."

"Where is she?"

"Visiting a neighbor, or somewhere."

"Is the door closed?"

"Yes."

"Please lock it with the key."

Fishel did as she asked.

"Now come here. I want you to promise something. I want you to say Kaddish for me."

"But—but—you'll soon be well. You'll be all right."

"If it pleases God. Come closer. It's true you're a Chassid, but a sick woman's not a woman any more. I know everything. Hadassah's traveling a false road. Oh, God, that I should have lived to see it!"

"Please—don't excite yourself about it."

Tears began to fall from Dacha's big black eyes.

"It's all his fault. He's dragged me to my grave and he's ruined his daughter. I forgive him. But whether God will forgive him, only He knows."

"Please, Mother-in-law, it's a holiday. With God's help, you'll be all right."

"Whatever happens between you and Hadassah, promise me you'll say Kaddish after me when I'm gone. I'll see that you get my share of the properties. I'll make the papers out tomorrow."

"Please. I don't want them."

"I sacrificed my life for her. Day and night I thought only about her welfare. And this is how she pays me back. I'll not find any rest in the grave."

"She's young. She doesn't know what she's doing."

Dacha began to sob convulsively. Fishel felt a lump gather in his throat, and his eyes filled with tears. He started to say something, but he heard hurried steps in the other room, a knock at the door, and Hadassah's voice: "Mamma, Mamma, let me in."

"Let her in," Dacha said.

Fishel went to the door, but his fingers trembled so that it took a few moments before he managed to turn the key. The door pushed open and Hadassah almost stumbled over him as she burst in. She glared at him angrily. Fishel thought he had never seen so much hate in her eyes as now. He stepped aside and Hadassah went over to the bedside.

"Mamusha—"

Dacha opened one eye. "What do you want?" she said. "I'm still alive."

"Mamusha! What's the matter with you?"

"Nothing. A little pain in the heart, that's all. It'll pass."

Hadassah turned to Fishel. "Go into the other room," she said. "Leave us alone."

"Let him stay here. I sent for him," Dacha interrupted.

Dacha closed her eyes again. For a few moments there was silence. It was difficult to tell whether she was sleeping or thinking. Faint tremors passed over her forehead. Her lips were queerly curled in a smile. Hadassah bent over the bed. She lifted a bottle of medicine from the table at the bedside and sniffed it. "If this were only poison," she thought. "I can't stand it any more. It's all my fault." Dacha opened her eyes, as though she divined what her daughter was thinking. She spoke.

"Come here. Give me your hand."

Hadassah put her hand in her mother's bony fingers. Dacha wanted to get the girl to give her solemn oath that she would give up Asa Heshel. Instead she was silent. "She'll not keep her promise anyway," Dacha thought. "I'll only be making her add to her sins." She dozed off. The bed seemed to be flying off with her into space. "Is this death?" she wondered. "Is this what people are so much afraid of? No, it can't be as simple as this."

CHAPTER NINE

1

The family kept nagging at Asa Heshel: if he did not want to be conscripted and sent to the front he would have to make himself defective in some way. Asa Heshel's mother had already taken to reading the Psalms, bedewing every page of the Psalter with her tears. His Uncle Zaddok thought that the easiest way out would be for Asa Heshel to have all his teeth extracted. Uncle Levi advised him to have an eardrum punctured; Dinah, his sister, was of the opinion that if Asa Heshel starved himself he would be underweight and would be released. Every day Adele came to her mother-in-law on Franciskaner Street, complaining and lamenting. Her mother and her stepfather, Reb Wolf Hendlers, talked openly about a divorce. Adele kept on saying that if Asa Heshel would give up that vile woman, she, in turn, would give him enough money to buy himself out of the service. But Asa Heshel would neither make a cripple of himself nor remain with his wife. The fear of military service that had come over him during the first few days disappeared. The more Adele's pregnancy advanced, the stronger was his desire to run away. He could foresee the whole frantic mess: the confinement, the midwife, the hospital, the doctors. He had to find protection in the army, like a murderer in a city of refuge.

Asa Heshel's days were a confusion of festival and impending disaster. His grandfather had stopped talking to him. He passed the holidays with the seamstresses. For the New Year, Fishel went to Bialodrevna, to be with his rabbi. Her mother wanted Hadassah to attend synagogue with her on Panska Street, but Hadassah had bought a ticket for another synagogue on Granitchna Street. Immediately after the blowing of the shofar she left. Asa Heshel had got his overcoat, his suits, and his laundry back from Adele. He met Hadassah at the Saxon Gardens. They got into a droshky and Asa Heshel told the driver to pull down the top. They had found a little cafe on a side street not far from Lazhenki Park. There they drank coffee, ate cakes, chatted. Shifra had prepared a festive meal, but Hadassah had telephoned her to eat alone and gave her permission to stay overnight in Praga with her relatives.

Returning to the city, they took separate paths. They met at the gate of Hadassah's home on Gnoyna Street. Hadassah led Asa Heshel upstairs, then left him to go to the festival dinner at her mother's. Asa Heshel sat in the darkness and waited for her. The telephone rang, but he did not answer. He went to the window and looked out at the starry sky. He was filled with despair and hope. He was not going to the front yet. And even if he was killed, that might not mean the end. Was it possible that the whole cosmos was dead, and that life and consciousness were contained only in the cells of protoplasm? He began to walk back and forth. His eyes became accustomed to the darkness. How dramatic life was! She had a husband, he had a wife. She had gone to her father and mother to eat the holiday bread and honey. He was waiting for her body. Well, and what about the fetus in Adele's womb? That was going through its preordained process. The centrosomes were dividing, the chromosomes were winding up; every turn and fold carried the inheritance of countless generations.

During the Ten Penitential Days, Hadassah and Asa Heshel met daily. Hadassah came to the seamstresses'. Asa Heshel came to Hadassah's house. Shifra knew all their secrets. Fishel was busy all day long with his transactions. Even if he had turned up suddenly at the house, Asa Heshel could have left by a back door. The blinds of the bedroom were pulled down all day long. Hadassah had lost her sense of shame. She had learned to undress without hesitation. Her body was girlishly slender; her nipples were of a fiery-red color. She had strange desires. She would pretend that Asa Heshel was her lord and she his slave. He had bought her in the slave market and she had fallen at his feet. She was forever asking him about Adele. Why did he not love her? Why had he married her? What did she, Hadassah, have that Adele had not? Sometimes she talked about Fishel: how he had shivered during their wedding night, how he had come to her and gone away, had said magic formulas, and had wept.

For the *Kol Nidre* prayer Asa Heshel went to the same synagogue as Hadassah. She took her place upstairs, in the women's section; he stood downstairs. Every now and again he would raise his eyes to the grating round the women's balcony. The candlelight fused with the electric lights. The cantor intoned the traditional roulades and appoggiaturas. The sighing of the worshippers broke in on his artful singing. Old frequenters of the synagogue, in white ceremonial robes, with prayer shawls on their shoulders and gold-embroidered hats on their heads, alternately prayed and wept. From the women's section came a continuous wailing. The war had torn husbands from their wives, children from their mothers. At the door of the synagogue there was a throng of homeless men who had been expelled from the towns near the battlefront by Grand Duke Nicholas. These Jews prayed after their own fashion, in loud voices, with extravagant gesticulations. Asa Heshel stood speechless. He had gone to his mother's before nightfall in order to take his last meal before the fast. His grandfather had left for the Chassidic chapel. A big candle had been stuck in a pot of sand. His mother had already put on the gold-shimmering dress she had made for her wedding, the silk shawl, the satin headcover. She had run up to him, embraced him, and cried: "God guard and protect you from the hands of gentiles."

And she had been seized by spasms. Dinah had poured a couple of drops of valerian on a piece of sugar and had given it to her mother, to bring her to.

After prayers Asa Heshel and Hadassah met outside the synagogue. They went into the Saxon Gardens and sat down on a bench. A three-quarter moon hung over the fleecy clouds. Leaves pattered down between the branches. Their shadows were etched with queer sharpness on the ground. Asa Heshel and Hadassah sat in silence. They rose and went to Gnoyna Street. Shifra was not at home. Hadassah locked and bolted the door. She had committed the greatest crime. She was ready for her punishment.

Having profaned the holiest day she yielded to all his impulses. She gave herself to him on the chair, on the carpet, on Fishel's bed. Asa Heshel dozed off and awoke, frightened by a dream, blazing with passion. Hadassah sighed in her sleep. Asa Heshel got up from the bed and stood at the window. Yes, this was he, Asa Heshel. His father, half insane, had died somewhere in a filthy little hamlet in Galicia. Generations of rabbis, saints, rabbinical wives, had purified themselves in order that he might be born. And here he was spending the night of Yom Kippur with another man's wife! And he would probably finish up somewhere in a trench, with a bullet in his heart. He was not sad; he was only filled with wonder. Was this God's plan? Was it possible that he was a part of God, body of His body, thought of His thought? What would happen if he were to open the window and fling himself out? What would happen then to his love, his fear, his bewilderment? No, there was always time to die. He shivered, and turned to Hadassah's bed.

2

On the day of the Rejoicing of the Law Asa Heshel was to meet Hadassah before the Bank Square, near the pillars. But a half hour passed and Hadassah did not appear. Asa Heshel telephoned Fishel's home; there was no answer. He waited an

hour and ten minutes. Hadassah did not show up. The seamstresses had gone away that day. They would not be coming
home before two or three in the morning. He had his opportunity to spend the last day of the festival with Hadassah. But
now everything was spoiled. Asa Heshel returned alone. He
went into the dark room, lit the gas lamp, and sat down. He
pulled a valise out from under the bed. Among a pile of
shirts, socks, and handkerchiefs lay a manuscript handwritten
in German. The title was "The Laboratory of Happiness."
Asa Heshel took out the sheets of paper and began to leaf
through them. Most of the chapters were unfinished. On a
scrap of paper was written a group of theses: (1) time as an
attribute of God; (2) the Godhead as the sum total of all possible combinations; (3) the truth of falsehood; (4) causality
and play; (5) paganism and pleasure: (6) transmigration of
the soul in the light of Spinozaism. Underneath was a note:
"If I don't make an end of X, I might as well die!"

While he sat thus, fingering the manuscript, the doorbell
rang. He ran to answer it. It must be Hadassah! The corridor
was dark. He opened the door and was aware of the scent of
caraway perfume. He recognized Adele's figure. "Adele!"

"Yes, it's I. What kind of pigsty is this?"

"How did you come here?" he asked, and at once regretted
the question.

Adele caught at his words. "I hope you're not going to
throw me out."

"God forbid. Come in."

He led her into his room. In the lamplight her face was yellow and splotchy. She was wearing some kind of old-fashioned
hat like an inverted flowerpot. She sat down at once on the
chair.

"So this is where you live! A palace! Aren't you eating, or
what?"

"I'm eating."

"Mother has a saying for that: 'The way a corpse eats is the
way he looks.' "

Asa Heshel was silent.

"I suppose you're surprised by my visit. I had to speak with
you. You see my condition."

"I am going into the army. You know that."

"Yes, I know that. If a man wants to commit suicide there's
no way of stopping him. I want to speak openly with you."

"Well, speak."

"If you go way, I'm left absolutely at sea. You know the Jewish law better than I do."

"Do you want a divorce?"

"I don't know any more what I want. You've finished my life for me. Even if I go on living."

"It's too late for that kind of talk."

"It isn't too late at all. You're not seventy years old yet. What are you doing with your life? You're killing your mother—all for the sake of that idiot."

"Better tell me plainly what you want."

"What's the hurry? Are you expecting her?"

"Perhaps I am."

"Let her come. I'll spit in her face. Meanwhile I'm your wife and she's a whore. I'm your wife and you're my husband. I'm carrying your child under my heart."

"Adele, what's the use of all this talk? We have to make an end to this business. It's your fault if you're—"

He broke off.

"We don't have to do anything. If I want to, I'll drag you along for the rest of my life. Marriage isn't a plaything to me. I'll make it miserable for both of you."

"You speak like your mother."

"I'm speaking the truth. It's this woman who brought you all this misery. It's because of her that we came back to Poland on the eve of the war. You'd have been studying, you'd have accomplished something. What's going to become of you now? Whatever happens, you're going to lose your best years. Don't think she'll wait for you. You'll rot in the trenches and she won't give a damn. Just try coming back to her without a leg!"

"Tell me simply what you want."

"You don't deserve it, but I want to help you. And I won't fool you about it; I hope to get something out of it, too. You mustn't throw yourself into this insane war. We can save you. My stepfather, Mother. We've been able to get our money out of the bank. There's even a way of returning to Switzerland. You've only got to do one thing: put an end to this madness."

"Adele, I love her."

"Is that your last word?"

"It's the truth."

"You've talked yourself into it. You aren't capable of any kind of love."

Adele sat awhile with bowed head. Her lips were twisted. Her nose had become long and pointed. There was something mannish and rationalistic about her forehead, her lifted eyebrows. Asa Heshel had a strange feeling; it was as though, behind the feminine façade, the spirit of her father, the scholar, had broken through. Strange, but while she was near him he felt no repulsion. No, he did not hate her. What he was afraid of was the burden of becoming a provider; the shame of being a married man, surrounded by relatives, while he had achieved nothing. It occurred to him that could he live with her in secrecy as he lived with Hadassah, he would not have minded having both of them. He would have liked to explain it to Adele, but he knew beforehand that she would not grasp it. It was not even clear to him.

Adele rose suddenly. "What kind of room is this? Where does this window lead?"

She stood at the window facing the blind wall. From this point one could see the neighboring courtyard and the straw on the roofs of several festival booths. She leaned out so far that Asa Heshel became frightened.

"Adele, be careful!"

She drew her head in, straightened up, and turned toward him.

"It's you who are committing suicide, not I."

"Yes, that's true."

"Poor fellow!"

She looked at him and smiled. He was still attached to her! He did not want her to fall out. Who knew? Perhaps he already had a feeling for the creature she was carrying in her. It was his child. Adele suddenly realized that she would not listen either to her stepfather or to her mother. She would not divorce him. Never! Legally he would forever remain her husband, she his wife.

"Come here," she said. "You may still give me a kiss."

And then she did something utterly unexpected. She stretched out her hand and extinguished the lamp. She remained standing, frightened by her own foolishness.

CHAPTER TEN

1

After Leah left Koppel's office on that intermediate day of the Feast of Tabernacles, Koppel paced back and forth. His kid boots squeaked. His cigarette had gone out, although it still dangled from his lower lip. He went into the rear room, where there was a small gas heater and a pot of tea brewing. There was a mirror on the wall above the table. Koppel stared at his own reflection. "So the well-born wench hasn't managed to get out of my clutches," Koppel thought. "Ah, if the old man knew about it, he'd turn over in his grave." He grinned at his own reflection. "You're a smart bastard, Koppel."

He went back into the larger room, opened a window, and peered out into the courtyard. A small gentile girl sat on a pile of broken stones. A barefooted woman was emptying a slop pail. Koppel started to scrawl idly with the tip of his fingernail on the mist of the window pane. What would happen to the houses Reb Meshulam had left if he and Leah were to run off to America? Everything would fall to dust.

He put on his overcoat and went out into the street. There was a time when it had seemed to Koppel that if Leah would as much as kiss him he would go out of his mind with ecstasy. But that was the trouble with the desirable things of life; they had the quality of coming too late. It was easy enough to say: "Divorce Bashele! Go off to America!" But how could a man do a thing like that? She was a loyal wife, the mother of his children. If he should announce to her that he was going to divorce her she would take it as a joke. And what would people say generally? The whole town would be in an uproar.

He had never put in an appearance in his own house as early as he did this day. He felt a longing to be at his own home, in his own room. There, on the old sofa, stretched out, he was accustomed to think out his plans. He signaled a droshky, climbed in, and leaned his head against the back of the seat. He stretched out his legs and closed his eyes. He could tell what neighborhood he was passing through by the sounds and the smells. Along Zhabia Street the odor of faded leaves told him he was passing the Saxon Gardens. On Senator Street a tinge of the odors of the Vistula and the Praga forests was already in the air. Even the echoes of the cannon firing in the distance could not deaden the familiar sounds. Newsboys were calling extras: the Russian troops were holding off the German offensive. Koppel opened his eyes, called to a newsboy, and threw him a one-kopek piece. He looked at the paper as the droshky rolled along.

"The bear isn't finished yet," he murmured to himself.

At the bridge the droshky came to a stop. A train of ambu-

lance wagons, something like omnibuses, was entering the
bridge. Through the windows could be seen soldiers with bandaged heads and limbs. Nurses bent over the wounded men.
In one of the ambulances lay a figure completely swathed in
surgical dressings. Only the tip of the nose was visible. A couple of white-coated attendants were busying themselves with
some sort of apparatus and rubber tubing. A pang of anguish
shot through the pit of Koppel's stomach.

"Ai, mother," he murmured.

At home he found only Shosha, his oldest daughter, a girl
of sixteen; she was eleven months younger than Manyek. She
was taller than her father, but her face was childish. Two long
blond braids plaited with ribbons descended to her waist. She
was far from being a good student at school; she was attending the fourth class for the second year. Before Koppel could
say a word she threw her arms around him and leaned her
breast against his. "Tatush!"

Koppel managed to release himself. "Where is your mother?" he asked.

"She went to the grocer's."

"Where are Yppe and Teibele?"

"Teibele's sleeping. Yppe's at the carpenter's."

"Well, what's the news at school?"

Shosha's eyes brightened. "Oh, Tatush, what excitement we
had! Our history teacher fell down. And did we howl! I've
still got a pain from laughing." And the girl broke out in a
childish giggle that showed her mouthful of uneven teeth.

Koppel shrugged his shoulders. "What's there to laugh
about if somebody stumbles?" he asked. "That's a thing that
can happen to anybody."

"Oh, but Tatush! It was so funny. She took a flop right
down between the benches. I must kiss you!"

The girl clutched him again and showered a flood of kisses
all over his face. Koppel barely managed to release himself.
Just like her mother, he thought. Foolish and good-hearted. It
had occurred to Koppel more than once that if a calf like this
should happen to fall in love with some boy, before you knew
it she'd come home with a lump behind her apron.

He went into his own room, chained the door, and
stretched out on the sofa. The longer he smoked and pondered, the more astonished he was at himself. What sort of
mad idea was that? To break up a household and run off to
America? Who'd be around to keep an eye on Shosha? Who'd
be there to see to it that Yppe found a decent husband? Espe-

cially since the poor girl limped. And what would happen to
Teibele and Manyek? It wasn't as though Leah were a young
girl. She was forty-four, and maybe older. If she loved him, as
she said she did, then why shouldn't she be content to be his
mistress right here in Warsaw?

When Koppel remembered that he had told Leah about the
way he had looted her father's safe, he felt a sour bile rising
to his mouth. "I must have been crazy," he thought. "I've
stuck a knife into my own guts."

He turned to the wall and dozed off. His wife woke him at
about seven, when supper was already on the table. Koppel
got up and wearily dragged himself into the dining-room. Everything seemed strange to him, the glazed lamp that hung
from the ceiling, the set table, the children around it. Yppe
and Shosha were talking animatedly to each other, breaking
out into noisy giggling. Manyek sat quietly in his short school
jacket with the gold buttons. His close-cropped head threw a
gigantic shadow on the wall.

Bashele fussed about her husband, offering him more of the
meat, some sour pickles, some sauerkraut. "Koppel, you sit
here as though you were a stranger. Have you got a headache
or something?"

"What? I'm all right."

"It isn't like you to fall asleep in the daytime."

Koppel turned to Manyek. "What's the news at your
school?" he asked.

Before the boy could answer, Shosha burst out giggling.
"You should have seen the way our teacher took a flop!"

A man who has a cow for a wife has calves for children,
Koppel thought. He had no appetite left for the food. The
moment the meal was over he put on his coat and went to the
door.

"Koppel, don't come home late," Bashele called after him,
although he was not in the habit of turning in much before
two in the morning.

The stairways were dark. He turned left up the street. On
Mala Street, not far from St. Petersburg Station, lived the Oxenburg family, whom Koppel frequently visited. On the floor
above, in the same house, lived Mrs. Goldsober, the young
widow of an old carpet merchant. Koppel and his intimates
would gather at the Oxenburgs' a few times during the week.
The Oxenburgs had a large five-room flat. Rents were cheap
in the Praga section. The only drawback was that the whistling of the locomotives could be heard all through the night.

But the Oxenburgs were so used to the noise that in the summer months, when they went away to the country, they could not sleep.

"The silence rings in your ears," Isador Oxenburg would complain.

At one time Isador Oxenburg had owned a few restaurants, in Praga and Warsaw proper. Oxenburg's tripe was famous. But since his health had gone he had occupied himself renting out cooking utensils and dishes for weddings. His wife, Reitze, acted as agent for domestics. They had a son of whom it was reported that he was a fence, a receiver of stolen goods. But the parents had a good deal of joy from their daughters, Zilka and Regina. Zilka's husband, an employee in a piece-goods firm on Gensha Street, earned thirty rubles a week. Regina was engaged. Mrs. Oxenburg must have been a beauty in her youth, but now she was so fat that she had difficulty getting through a doorway. She weighed over three hundred pounds. Nevertheless she ran the household affairs, fussing about with the servant girl and quarreling with her husband. Oxenburg, tall and thin, with a scrawny, veined neck and a beer-colored mustache, carefully waxed and pointed in the Polish manner, was a drinker, spending more time on a sofa than on his feet. He was given to playing solitaire. Whenever he had an argument with his wife he would thump his fist against his chest and shout at the top of his voice: "Do you know who you're talking to? Isador Oxenburg! You've sucked me dry, like a leech! Look at what you've done to me!"

And he would point to his sunken cheeks, which had a sickly blue tinge, as though the flesh had been plucked clean.

2

Isador Oxenburg and Koppel both belonged to the Anshe Zedek Society. Koppel was practically a member of the family at the Oxenburgs'; he even had a key to the house. In the hallway he took off his overcoat and hat and hung them on a wall hook. Then he combed his hair with a pocket comb. When he entered the living-room he found the whole circle: David Krupnick, Leon the Peddler, and Motie the Red were playing cards with Mrs. Goldsober. Itchele Peltsevizner was playing dominoes with Zilka. They were all so absorbed that they hardly noticed Koppel's entrance. As he came in he heard Mrs. Goldsober say: "I'll drop out with my kings."

"I'll keep you company," remarked David Krupnick; he was a furniture dealer, reputedly wealthy. A widower, he was partial to Mrs. Goldsober.

"Pass."

"I bet six groszy."

"Raise you ten."

Mrs. Goldsober was sitting at the head of the table, wrapped in a knitted shawl. Her chestnut hair, which had reddish streaks, was combed back from her forehead. An ornamental comb was stuck on top of her coiffure. She had a round forehead, a small nose, and a girlish chin. Her upper lip pouted faintly and showed a mouthful of small white teeth. Her eyebrows were plucked. She had once been a victim of asthma, and ever since she had been in the habit of smoking a particular kind of long thin cigarette that was supposed to clear the bronchial tubes. Now she exhaled small clouds of smoke through her nostrils.

"Well, men," she said, "what have you got?"

"I have nothing but a headache," sighed Motie the Red, a small figure of a man with a pockmarked face and reddish, close-cropped hair.

"Three queens," declared David Krupnick, putting down his hand.

"All right, take it," answered Leon the Peddler, pushing the saucer full of money toward him. "The luck of a thief!"

Mrs. Goldsober turned and saw Koppel. She looked at him with a curious and half-roguish glance. "Why so late?" she asked. "I was beginning to think we'd have to do without you tonight."

Koppel raised his eyebrows. "I suppose you couldn't manage without me?"

"Of course not. Don't you know I'm longing for you all the time?"

"Do you hear what's going on?" Motie the Red shouted, banging his fist on the table. "She's longing for him."

"Oh, it's an old love. Been going on for years," Leon the Peddler remarked.

"Is that the way it is? And here I thought all the time she was in love with me." David Krupnick picked up the deck and began to shuffle the cards.

"You're too lucky at cards," said Mrs. Goldsober.

"What's that piece of goods want of me?" Koppel thought. "She's probably quarreled with Krupnick, or maybe she just wants to be cute." He walked out of the room and in the manner of one perfectly at home, went into the dining-room. He wanted to have a chat with Mrs. Oxenburg, but she was not there. At the head of the table, in an upholstered chair, sat her husband. He was laying out the cards in a game of solitaire. A flask of brandy stood near by. When Koppel walked in, Oxenburg quickly clutched the bottle, as though to hide it, but when he saw who his visitor was he withdrew his hand.

"Good evening, Isador."

The other's thin, bluish lips smiled crookedly. "Aren't you playing tonight?"

"What's the good of it? A lot of damn nonsense."

Oxenburg shook his head dolefully. "Ah," he said, "you call that card-playing? Nowadays they play marbles."

"My feeling exactly."

Oxenburg put his hand on the oilcloth-covered table. "What's new in the society? Are you still the first warden?"

"Not even the second."

"Are you on the board?"

"I haven't even that honor."

"What happened? Did they kick you out?"

"Nobody could kick me out."

"A tough guy, eh? You young men are fortunate. You don't take anything seriously. Things were different in my day. The society was then on Stalova Street. It was in the by-laws that we bring food to the Jewish hospital on Chista Avenue. There weren't any trolley cars in those days, only a horse-drawn bus, but we weren't supposed to ride on the Sabbath. We used to pack a basket with white bread, onions with fat, tripe, liver; and we went on foot. It was some walk! The Poles at the bridge used to throw rocks at us. If we caught one of the bastards, we'd beat hell out of him.

"On Krochmalna Street there was a gang that used to block our way. The first time they tore us to pieces. Our food spilled all over the street. They broke Yossel Batz's rib. I myself got a bump on the forehead. That evening we had a meeting. 'Listen to me,' I said. 'Are we going to be afraid of a few ruffians?' 'But what can we do?' our boys said. 'We're not supposed to use sticks on the Sabbath.' Our rabbi was from Lithuania. His name was Reb Feifke, and he said: 'If there's danger, you can.' 'Well,' I said, 'if this holy man says so, he knows what he's talking about.' He studied from a volume as big as a table.

"The next Saturday the women walked behind with the food, and we went ahead of them, in small groups. Near Yan-

ash's Court we heard a whistle. I was in front with four other
men. Suddenly the bastards were around us. Their leader was
Iche the Blind, a real fighter. The women peddlers had to pay
him protection money. 'Well,' Iche says, 'Krochmalna is my
precinct.' 'What do you want?' I says. 'We're not here for
pleasure, it's for sick people.' 'We don't need your Praga charity,' he says. 'Get out or I'll break your neck.' And he gave me
a punch on the chest. I saw there was no way out, so I lifted
up my stick and he got it right on the chin. He was so surprised that he stood there with his eyes popping out. 'Well,
babies,' I says, 'lend me a hand.' The fight began. Our boys
gave them what was coming to them. The news spread that
Iche the Blind was being slaughtered. There were shoemakers
on the Krochmalna who also paid Iche protection money so
he wouldn't annoy their women. When they heard that we
were giving it to the gang, they, too, came out. There was one
cop, but he beat it. To make a long story short, we kicked the
guts out of them. From that time on, everyone in Warsaw
knew that Isador Oxenburg don't take it lying down." Oxenburg wiped the perspiration from his forehead. "Maybe
you'd like a drink?"

"No."

"What's the news with the Moskats? How do you stand
over there?"

"What's on my mind is trying to get out of the country and
go to America," Koppel answered, hardly understanding why
he confided in this drunkard.

Oxenburg's face dropped and he chewed convulsively, as
though he were trying to swallow the ends of his mustache.
"What for? You're joking."

"I'm serious."

"What's the matter? Is Warsaw too small for you? What'll
you do in America? You've got to slave hard for a living
there."

"Where's your wife?" Koppel inquired.

"Who knows? I tell you, brother, here in Warsaw you're a
lord. In America you'll press pants."

Koppel made no answer. He got up and went out of the
room. He stood hesitating in the corridor, undecided whether
to go inside and join the others or to get out altogether. The
drunkard was right, he thought; what would he do in America? He imagined how it would be there, living in a tall building with Leah. Trains would speed by above the roofs; cars
thunder by under the ground, crowded with people who all

talked English. He'd be wandering about, all alone in a strange world, no children, no friends, no women. Leah would grow old and bad-tempered. Bashele would weep for him for a while and then she would marry that coal dealer on the other side of the street. He'd be sleeping in Koppel's bed, and Bashele would be waking him in the morning, telling him: "Chaim Leib, my sweet, the coffee's getting cold."

"Ah, a plague on all the women," Koppel thought. "Double-crossers and whores, all of them."

He suddenly felt mean and helpless, as he used to feel when he was a green, frightened orphan from the provinces, earning a bare two rubles a week. He had been so lonesome in those days that he would go to the prayerhouse early on Saturday and stay there till the Sabbath was over. Later his luck had changed. He had become a member of the congregation, he had got to know Meshulam Moskat, he had married a decent poor girl, had fathered a few nice children, had accumulated some money. What did he have to kick about? Why break up two homes? Where was it written that he had to be Meshulam Moskat's son-in-law?

As he stood with his brooding thoughts in the corridor, the living-room door opened and Mrs. Goldsober came out, her face flushed and smiling. Beneath her shawl he could see a lace-embroidered blouse. From under her pleated skirt the hem of her petticoat protruded. She gazed at him with some surprise. "Look at him. Standing there like a whipped school-boy."

"You're going home already? So early?"

"Where did you get that idea? I left my asthma cigarettes at home."

For a moment they were both silent. Mrs. Goldsober made a jerky motion with her head. "I'll tell you what," she said at last. "Keep me company up the stairs."

"Why not?"

They climbed the stairs, Mrs. Goldsober leaning against his shoulder. At her landing she opened the door with a key.

"Come in," she said. "Maybe you have a match."

Inside it was dark, the air heavy with the smell of floor wax. One was conscious of the orderliness of a home where a woman lived alone. Suddenly the widow threw her arms around Koppel's neck and kissed him full on the lips. She smelled of smoke and chocolate. Points of light swam before Koppel's eyes.

"So that's the way it is?" he murmured.

"Yes, that's the way," she answered.

Again she began to kiss him, with the abandon of a woman who had thrown off the last vestige of shame. "What the devil is going on?" Koppel thought. "This is too good. Something is bound to happen."

3

Mrs. Goldsober tore herself out of Koppel's arms.

"I've got to go down," she said. "God knows what Krupnick will imagine."

"What are you afraid of Krupnick for?"

"I don't want to give him any reason for talk. I'll tell you what. Come up later. Around eleven o'clock. I just want to show myself there once again."

Koppel thought for a moment. "I'm not hanging around the Oxenburgs' all evening. I'll come back later."

"Where are you going, Koppel? You're a strange one; always full of secrets. I'll tell you what, Koppel. You go down first. If we go in together it'll start them talking right away."

Koppel went downstairs. In the corridor of the Oxenburg flat he stopped to smooth his hair at a wall mirror. Then he went into the living-room. The card game had ended. David Krupnick was talking to Leon the Peddler, who dealt in antiques and jewelry. Zilka, the Oxenburgs' married daughter, had gone out of the room and the men were left with their stag talk.

"It's a lot of nonsense," Leon the Peddler was saying. "Every woman has her price." He clutched Krupnick's lapel, as though he were going to confide some secret to him. "Take my case. Here I am, not young and not handsome. I walk about—may it happen to none of you—with ulcers in my stomach. An operation is what I need. Last week, Wednesday I think it was, I get a telephone call to come up to some gentile house on Rose Alley. They were marrying off a daughter and they wanted some jewelry. I took a couple of samples from Yekel Dreiman and went over there in a droshky. I climbed up the marble steps and rang the bell. A woman opened the door. I took a look at the girl and I tell you I had to rub my eyes to make sure I wasn't seeing things. Tall, blonde, and with a smile enough to give you the shivers. 'Excuse me,' I say, 'are you the bride-to-be?' And she laughs and tells me she's the girl's mother. I tell you, I thought I'd faint. 'Well,' I say, 'I can imagine how the daughter looks if the mother's such a beauty.' She laughs again and tells me that her daughter is out getting fitted at the dressmaker's and that she'll be home soon. And there she was, at home all alone. I forgot all about business. I take out my merchandise. She looks at the stuff, puts it on, and sighs. 'What are you sighing for?' I ask her; 'I'll certainly not overcharge you.' Well, one word leads to another and she tells me her whole history. Her husband had squandered everything. The man her daughter was marrying was a Count. They'd have to do things in proper style, and there wasn't the wherewithal. So I let go with a little joke and say: 'Well, I'm not rich, I'm only the middleman in this transaction. But for my money you're worth the finest diamond pin money can buy.' I was scared she'd have my head and throw me down the steps. Instead she opens up those enormous eyes of hers—I tell you my limbs began to quiver—and she says: 'For my children I'm ready for any sacrifice.' If I didn't get a stroke on the spot, then I've got the strength of a lion."

Motie the Red slapped his hand on the table. "Well," he said, "did you get what you wanted?"

"And if I did, you don't think I'd tell you."

Koppel folded his hands behind him. "Go on with your inventions. We're listening."

"Where've you been?" asked Itchele Peltsevisner. "Chasing after Mrs. Goldsober?"

"I don't chase after anyone."

"Sit down and take a hand."

"I've got to go." Koppel went out into the corridor and put on his hat and coat. He went out into the street and turned toward the bridge. He was used to having good luck with women, but Leah's coming to him at the office and Mrs. Goldsober's sudden yielding surprised him for all that. He stood at a street lamp and lighted a cigarette. "I've got everything," he thought, "money, women, property. What else do I need? What's the sense of moving away from where I am?"

At the junction of Mala, Stalova, and Mlinarska Streets he stepped into a restaurant and, after some hesitation, telephoned Leah.

"Leah, it's me."

"Koppel!" Leah cried. "Here I've been sitting and thinking about you all day. The whole thing seems like a dream to me."

"Can I see you?"

"Where are you? Come over here. No one's in the house but the children."

Koppel got into the number-five streetcar. Leah lived on Tshepla Street. He climbed out of the car after it had passed the City Market. He still had a short distance to go by foot. He passed the barracks and a military bakery. Farther on was the gendarmerie. Lights flickered in the dark courtyard. An armed guard stood in a sentry box. In the quiet of the night the sounds of the cannon fire on the battlefront came clearer. A thin rain began to fall. Everything was hanging by a thread, Koppel thought. He suddenly recalled what, as a child, he had heard said in school: that the earth was supported by Leviathan, the monster creature of the seas, and if Leviathan were to take its tail out of its mouth, the whole world would collapse. On the stairway in Leah's house he took out a handkerchief and wiped his face. He rang the bell and heard Leah's footsteps. He opened his eyes wide; never before had he seen her so elaborately dressed. There was a silk scarf over her hair. She wore an embroidered satin lounging-robe and slippers with pompons. A diamond ring glittered on her finger. She took his arm and drew him into Moshe Gabriel's room. It was the first time Koppel had been there. He saw bookcases, a reading-stand with a volume of the Talmud on it. Had it not been for the couch, Koppel could have imagined he had stumbled into a Chassidic study house. A mood of embarrassment swept over him. "She looks like a rabbi's wife," he thought. He sat down with some hesitation. It seemed to him now as though he had not seen Leah for a long time.

"Would you like a glass of vishniak?"

She went out and came back with a tray on which were a flask of brandy, two glasses, and some honey cake. Her hands were unsteady; the tray trembled as she walked. "Help yourself, Koppel." Leah put the tray down. "Why are you so pale? Has something happened?"

"No, Leah. Nothing's happened," he answered. "It's only that I love you."

"Go on. Drink. I've been thinking everything over. Ah, Koppel, I'm afraid. What'll happen to the children? Zlatele and Meyerl still need a mother. How can I leave such swallows alone—perhaps I should take them with me."

"It's not impossible."

"But how? In the midst of all this shooting? Koppel, I—I just don't know what to say. Here, come closer to me, you're not a Chassid."

He moved closer to her and took her hand.

"Tell me," he asked, "do you regret what's happened?"

"Regret? No, Koppel. What is there to regret? What I've got here is no life. And the children are all on my side—except Aaron, of course. Only the other day Meyerl said to me: 'Mamusha, you're always alone.' Masha, too, knows my troubles, but she never says a word. Zlatele is soft as silk. She plays the baby, but she's got mature understanding. Tell me what to do, Koppel. What did you call me for? Were you longing for me?"

"Yes, Leah."

"I wanted us to be alone. That's why I brought you in here. Wait a minute. I'll get some tea."

She got up. As she did so, her knee brushed against his, and the fold of her robe parted. Koppel saw the smooth length of her leg. He got up and went over to the reading-stand. He opened the volume. On the page lay a fringe from a prayer shawl and a reddish hair. Probably from Moshe Gabriel's beard. A humbleness overtook Koppel. A rabbi—and she was his wife, he thought. She is Meshulam Moskat's daughter—and I am Koppel the overseer.

When the door opened again and Leah came in with a tray of tea things, cakes, and lemon, Koppel experienced an anguished desire to fall at her feet and kiss the hem of her robe, the way he'd seen the characters do at the Polish theaters. He went toward her and put his arm around her waist. The tray in Leah's hand shook.

"Koppel, what's the matter? You'll be scalded."

"Leah, you've got to belong to me," Koppel quavered. "I love you. I've loved you ever since that day you came into the office and your father called you *shikse*."

She put the tray down. Koppel put his arms around her and kissed her. Leah's full lips pressed ardently against his own. Her face was suffused with a girlish flush and her eyes seemed to grow wider and more intensely blue. Koppel glanced toward the sofa, but Leah broke away from his embrace.

"No, Koppel. God willing, we'll be married. There'll be enough time for that."

When Koppel left, the rain had stopped, but the sidewalks were still wet and glassy. The street lights were wreathed in mist. Koppel looked at his watch. It was a quarter to eleven. "The devil with the Goldsober woman," he thought. "All I need is to get mixed up with that creature." But he had no desire to go home. He was too much aroused. Yet something was missing. "What," he wondered, "am I hesitating about? Bashele won't be the only woman in the world who's been divorced. She'll be all right. I'll see that she doesn't want for anything. About God I'm certainly not going to worry. Who says there's a God, anyway? Squeeze a man's throat, and he's through."

Suddenly Koppel knew what it was he wanted. He had to confide in someone about the events of the day, to find an ear to listen to him. Not the way that damn fool Leon the Peddler babbled on about his conquests, but in his own way, with some understanding pal over a glass of beer. There was a time when he had had friends. David Krupnick had been a bosom pal. And in those days a man could exchange some intimate talk with Isador Oxenburg, with Motie the Red, or with some of Meshulam Moskat's people. But the years had changed everything. Krupnick was now his enemy, for all that his enmity was concealed. Motie the Red had a wife who led him by the nose, and he was no longer interested in bachelors' gossip. Isador Oxenburg had become a drunkard. Koppel stood still for a moment and listened to the distant rumble of artillery. No, the old days would never come back. Right before his eyes a whole generation had passed.

He took the streetcar back to Praga and alighted on Mlinarska Street. He had decided not to walk past Mala Street, but to go directly home. The street, however, seemed to draw him. It was too early to go to sleep. The gate to the courtyard of the Oxenburgs' house was already closed, but the janitor opened it at once. Koppel was a generous tipper. Koppel looked up and saw a light in Mrs. Goldsober's flat. He ascended the stairs and tapped lightly on the door.

"Who is it?" came a whispered voice.

"Me."

The door opened. Mrs. Goldsober was in a pink robe and red slippers. Her hair hung loose behind her. She had powdered and made up her face carefully. Koppel smelled the soft odor of carnation perfume. She took him by both hands and drew him inside. She giggled softly. "What a man!"

PART
SIX

CHAPTER ONE

1

At exactly eleven o'clock at night the train wheels began to move. Dinah, Asa Heshel's sister, ran along the platform, waving her hand. Half of her face was lighted in the glow of the moving cars, the other half was in shadow. Adele stood where she was, waving her handkerchief. Rosa Frumetl and Asa Heshel's mother were a few paces behind her. The train rolled along the dimly lit platform. The sky was tinted with a red and violet glow. The clouds hung low. Only when the train had crossed the bridge did Asa Heshel turn his gaze away from the window. A single candle glowed in the dim interior. The car was crowded with soldiers and civilians, men and women. The few Jews sat close together. All the seats were occupied. Asa Heshel put his valise down and sat on it. The floor was filthy, strewn with sawdust. The car stank of cheap tobacco. A cold wind from the open fields blew in.

Some of the passengers had already composed themselves for sleep. Others talked and smoked. The conductor came through, calling for tickets. He lowered his lamp, paned in red and white, and peered below the benches to make sure that no one was hiding under them. A gendarme came in, demanding identification papers. He stared for a long time at Asa Heshel's birth certificate. When the train stopped in Otwotsk one of the passengers brought in a kettle of tea. Asa Heshel unwrapped the package Hadassah had given him. There were cakes, chocolates, and preserves. A wave of love for Hadassah swept over him. He had been with her the previous night, but now that seemed long ago. No day before had ever been so crowded for him: their wanderings through the streets; the hotel; their leave-taking before the dawn; and then being at his mother's house, with Dinah, his grandfather, his grandmother, his uncles and aunts, his cousins. Dinah was now in the last month of her pregnancy. Some news had come from her husband, Menassah David; he was again on the Russian side of the border.

Now every minute, every second, was taking him farther away from all of them. The train rushed along. The night flew past the windows. Houses rose up and sank back. Trees

336

danced by. The searchlight of the locomotive lit up a scarecrow. Against the gray sky the tattered figure with its straw
hat and bedraggled coat took on a demoniacal appearance.

Asa Heshel closed his eyes, but he could not fall asleep. A
Russian soldier grumbled something or other about all Jews
being spies. He told a long story about a rabbi who concealed
Russian plans in his phylacteries and took them to the Germans. The Russians had caught him and hanged him. A Pole
recounted a tale about a murder committed in his village by
recruits. The Jews in the car talked to one another in subdued
voices. At Ivangorod the train halted for several hours. The
soldiers went out to drink tea. A young Jew with a light
beard, in a ragged and patched coat, loaded sacks onto the
train. The candle in the car had burned itself out and the conductor had not come to renew it. A soldier started to paw a
Polish girl. The girl shrieked: "Keep your hands off me!"

It was well into the dawn when the train approached Lublin. In peasant huts on the outskirts of the city, smoke already
rose from chimneys. The sky lightened and the earth grew
gray. The puddles of water along the edges of the fields took
on a bluish color. Steam rose from piles of refuse, as though
the very soil were aflame somewhere in its inner depths. On a
ragged piece of pasture land a lone cow stood, its face turned
upward in an attitude of pre-dawn sadness.

At Lublin all the Jewish passengers except Asa Heshel got
off. The car filled with soldiers carrying guns, cartridges, mess
kits. The train halted for a long time. On a parallel track a
long train rumbled slowly along. The cattle cars were filled
with soldiers. A tall soldier in a coat reaching to his ankles,
and with spurred boots, engaged Asa Heshel in conversation.
"Where are you traveling to?"

"To the conscription offices."

The soldier laughed. "You don't look like material for a
fighter."

"If they take me, then I'll be one."

"Nonsense! You'll never find a Jew in uniform. They hide
themselves under their grandmothers' skirts." He let out a
roar.

"Hey, brother, give him a piece of pork," a small soldier
suggested.

"A good idea." The soldier took a sausage out of his pocket, cut off a slice, and handed it to Asa Heshel.

"Here, eat this."

"Thank you, I'm not hungry."

"You see, you're afraid." He guffawed.

"They don't eat pig, because it squeals," the other soldier announced.

"Even when it's dead?"

"Yes, in a Jew's belly."

"Ah, a comic rascal!"

Asa Heshel got up and went over to another seat, in a corner. He put up his collar and pulled his hat low over his forehead. He sat half dozing, half brooding. "They'll kill me here, before we get to Reivitz," he thought. "Maybe the best thing to do would be to jump off while there's time." At that moment the train jerked forward. The farther it went from Lublin, the noisier it became. The soldiers were quarreling, shrieking at one another, and making gestures with their bayonets. One tried to throw another's baggage through the window, the owner holding on to it for dear life. Then a group began to play games. One was chosen to bend over a bench while the others swatted his posterior. The small soldier pointed toward Asa Heshel.

"Turn him over."

"Hey, you, Jew, do you want to play?"

"No."

"Why not? Are your pants full?"

"Boy, leave him alone," the tall soldier called out.

He whispered something to the others and they burst into laughter. Asa Heshel looked toward them and saw they were eating the cakes Hadassah had given him. He sank deeper into his seat and pulled his hat farther down over his face. The chill seemed to penetrate to his bones. The hair prickled on his scalp. Everything was senseless: his journey to present himself for service; the shrieking of these oafs. Who was it he was going to fight for? What did he have to do with the nations and their quarrels? What did he care about the human race in general?

It was nine o'clock in the morning when the train pulled to a halt at Reivitz, but it seemed to Asa Heshel that it was already late in the day. The station was full of soldiers. Behind the food counter two fat girls fussed around. Arms, swords, and guns were stacked everywhere. Out in the street Ukranian peasants—they had Jewish beards, Asa Heshel noticed—loaded sacks of wheat on a freight train on a siding. They were dressed in sheepskin coats, with fur caps on their heads and rags wound around their feet. A tall Cossack in a high fur hat relieved himself openly along the rails. Some peasant women laughed. A small sun, white as tin, shone down from behind the clouds. Asa Heshel remembered that once carts had waited at this station to carry passengers to Izhbitza, Krasnostav, Yanov. Now there was not a single vehicle to be seen. From somewhere a tall Jew appeared with a sack over his shoulder. He had a pockmarked face, a pointed beard, and large melancholy eyes. He walked up to Asa Heshel. "Are you going on from here?"

"I'm bound for Yanov, but I don't see a passenger cart."

"You'd better come with me into town. They'll, God forbid, do you an injury."

Asa Heshel picked up his valise and followed the stranger into the city.

2

The general practice was that after a recruit had taken his preliminary oath he was permitted to go home until the time for the final induction. During that period recruits would say their good-bys to their relatives, gather together the clothing they would need, and put their affairs in order. But this year the military head of the Yanov district gave orders that the Jewish recruits were to be kept in the town jail in the interim, making the excuse that too many of them deserted. The cell Asa Heshel found himself in was on the second floor of the building. There were a couple of benches in the cell. There were lumps of clayey bread on the sill of the barred window. Asa Heshel looked out. The window gave onto a large courtyard, in which some Austrian prisoners of war, bearded, filthy, in heavy shoes and ragged uniforms, were working. The talk Asa Heshel heard was a mixture of German, Hungarian, and Bosnian. The prisoners were digging pits, breaking stones, drawing handcarts full of sand and gravel. Russian soldiers with bayoneted guns kept guard over them.

Asa Heshel wanted to stretch out, but all the benches were occupied. Two youngsters, one fair, the other dark, were playing cards. A recruit was distributing tobacco, which he took out of the uppers of his boots. Between the recruits and the civil prisoners a dispute at once arose. One of them, in a patched jacket, an open shirt, and paste-covered pants, prodded Asa Heshel's shoulder. "Hey, you, clumsy! Got any tin?"

"I don't know what you mean."

"Money! Money!" the other explained, rubbing the tips of his fingers against his thumb.

"They took away everything I had when they examined me."

"Hand over the trotters." He pointed to Asa Heshel's boots.

The pale youth came to his defense. "Hey, you, tough guy! Lay off him."

"And what if I don't?"

"If you don't, brother, I'll tap your bung!" He got up from the bench, crouched, and posed his fist against the other's nose.

The other put up his hands. "A brave guy, eh?"

"Hey, boys! What's the argument about?" This was from one of the prisoners who had been sitting and paring his toenails with a penknife. He was tall and broad-shouldered, with the build of a giant. His checked shirt was fastened with a mother-of-pearl collar button. A small mustache sprouted on his lip.

"This specimen here wants to take the young fellow's boots," another answered him.

The giant shook his head deprecatingly and turned to Asa Heshel. "Where are you from, youngster?"

"I come from Warsaw."

"From Warsaw, eh? Where did you live?"

"On Shviento-Yerska Street."

"Come over here. Nobody's going to do anything to anyone from Warsaw while I'm around."

It developed that several of the jail intimates were from Warsaw, brought to the prison from Lublin. They crowded around Asa Heshel, asking for news of their familiar haunts: the City Market, Yanash's Court, the city hall, the Old Town. The prisoner who had tried to get Asa Heshel to give up his boots suddenly remembered that he had a mother in Warsaw, somewhere on St. Boniface Street. One of the others asked Asa Heshel if he wanted a cigarette. He declined.

"So they can hear the firing there already, eh?"

"Yes. At night."

"The Russians stink, eh?"

Asa Heshel moved away to a corner of the cell and sat down on the floor. He had not slept a wink the previous night, and he had waited around at the conscription headquarters from early in the morning. He leaned wearily against the wall and sank into an apathetic dullness. He had hoped that some miracle might save him. In his anxiety he had vowed to give eighteen rubles to charity. He had had all sorts of dreams and premonitions. But the higher powers, apparently, were not interested in sparing him.

The cell door opened and a guard ordered the inmates to form in groups of six to go for their meal. Someone pushed Asa Heshel and he got to his feet. With the others he passed through a long corridor and reached a large room with tin-covered tables. He picked up a tin bowl and a blackened spoon and waited while one of the attendants filled the bowl with some sort of brownish stew and handed him a lump of hard bread. The group was marched back to the cell. The prisoners wolfed the food, cursing and joking. The cell grew dark. From the corridor came the sound of cell doors banging. The men huddled closer together, talking and gesticulating. In the semidarkness the faces were vague and weird-looking. One of the men started to recount some story about a wedding match that never came off, and about a wedding ring he never got back.

"Hey, comrades, who wants to play cards?"

A guard brought in a lantern and hung it from a hook on the ceiling. There was an immediate scurrying around, some of the men moving the benches to the sides of the cell, others spreading coats on the floor. Two youths started a game of checkers on a board drawn with chalk on the floor, using lumps of bread as pieces. One of the men started to tell about the prison in Shedletz and about the political prisoners there. They formed their own governing body. On the first of May they stained a white shirt red with blood and used it as a flag. There was a girl, a consumptive, who was locked up alone in a cell. She had poured kerosene over her clothes and set herself on fire.

"And was she burned?"

"To a cinder."

"Well, anyway, that was better than spending the rest of her life spitting blood."

The lantern was left in the cell for only one hour. After that it was taken away. Again the room was in darkness. Some went to sleep at once, snoring heavily. Others talked, joked, and wrestled. One of the men threw a rag across the room; it caught Asa Heshel in the face. There were apparently women in the adjoining cell; through the walls could be heard female chattering and giggling.

One of the men shouted: "Hey, let's bore a hole through the wall."

"What'll you drill it with?" someone asked.

Another gave an obscene answer, and there was a burst of raucous laughter.

One of the men produced a knife and started to poke at the wall with it. Fragments of plaster began to crumble to the floor. To make sure that the noise would not be heard, some of the men started to sing in loud voices. Asa Heshel stretched out on the floor. He was bitten instantly. He picked a bedbug off his forehead.

Gradually the noises subsided. The prisoners yawned, stretched out, fell asleep. The air became even fouler.

When Asa Heshel opened his eyes, the sky outside the window was scarlet. Flaming clouds floated in the east. He sat up. A bloody braid of smoke ascended from the barracks chimney. A light wind blew in through the broken panes. It seemed to him that God Himself was sighing in the dawn.

CHAPTER TWO

In the middle of the night Adele started up with the frightened feeling that someone had shrieked something into her ear. Dr. Leon Hendlers, her stepbrother, had told her that she would not be delivered until the end of the month, and she hesitated to wake her mother, even though she was in pain. She began to walk back and forth. The night lamp threw a dim light. To guard Adele against evil spirits her mother had hung chapters from the Psalms on the walls of the room. Underneath the pillow she had placed the Book of the Angel Raziel. When Adele approached the mirror, she halted, looking at her own reflection. Her belly was round and high. Her breasts were swollen. Her face was full of pale spots. "I'll soon die," Adele thought. For the third time she had dreamed that she was dead, stretched out on the floor with her toes turned toward the door.

"Dear God in heaven," she murmured, "have mercy on me. For the sake of my dear father."

Suddenly she laughed. "How pious one becomes in trouble!"

The pain had lightened somewhat. She lay down again and dozed off. It seemed to her that she was alone with a creature, half dog, half turtle, with a knotted tail, many-footed like a centipede. Where would such a freak have come from? It was a bad sign. She made a convulsive movement with her hand and started up again. The child heaved inside her womb. A searing pain cut her back. She managed to get to the door. Her mother was there. Rosa Frumetl had heard her daughter's groans. She was barefooted, in a nightgown too big for her, her bed cap pushed back on her gray, badly cut hair. Her face was strained and creased. "My dear child! Woe is me! What's the matter?"

"I think it's started."

"I'll call the midwife right away!"

"No, wait, Mother. Maybe it's too soon."

Mother and daughter began to walk back and forth in the room, their shadows gigantic in the light of the night lamp.

"Mamma, you look sick. Does something hurt you?"

"Only my cares and troubles, daughter. May He whose name I am not worthy to mention help you come through your ordeal. I am already an old woman."

"Shall I get your valerian drops?"

"Ah, my dear daughter! You, with all your sufferings, and you think of me. My pure child."

The door opened and Reb Wolf Hendlers came in. His face was red, his beard round and white. His belly was large and pointed as if he, too, were pregnant. "You're having the pains, eh? Everything is attended by suffering . . . birth . . . Messiah . . ."

Early in the morning, on his way to the hospital, Reb Wolf's son, Leon, dropped into the flat. Reb Wolf opened the door for him. Leon was a giant of a man. His face was ruddy, flushed with blood, like a slaughterer's. Over his high forehead a derby was perched. "Well, Father," he boomed in his coarse Yiddish, "how's she doing?"

"How should I know? Go and take a look for yourself."

"I tell you, she'll have triplets yet."

He laughed noisily and went into Adele's room. Without ceremony he threw back the bedcovers and palpated her abdomen.

"Well, how are you feeling?" he boomed. "The curse of Eve is upon you."

"Have you had your breakfast yet?" Rosa Frumetl asked her stepson.

"Six o'clock in the morning! That's when I eat my breakfast. Black bread and bouillon."

He left abruptly. At the gate he encountered Asa Heshel's mother. Since Asa Heshel had gone off, she had become emaciated as though from consumption. Beneath the shawl that covered her bewigged head her beaked nose protruded. She was bent over, like an ancient woman.

"Well, auntie, you'll soon be a grandmother," Leon boomed.

"God willing."

"Come on, auntie, straighten your shoulders. You're not a hundred years old yet."

He raced away with long steps. At the door Rosa Frumetl greeted Asa Heshel's mother. The two women embraced, kissing each other's wrinkled cheeks.

"How is Adele?"

"May God's angels intervene for her."

Finkel stood in front of the wall mirror to straighten her wig. Rosa Frumetl blew her nose.

"And from Asa Heshel not a word?"

"Disappeared. Like a stone in the water," Finkel answered. Her voice was dry and unmoved; she had no more tears.

She went into her daughter-in-law's room. Adele took both her hands.

"Mother-in-law! You must be frozen!"

She looked at the older woman, and, as always, she felt a sense of astonishment. Mother and son were alike as two peas. The same eyes, nose, mouth, chin, the identical cut of the features. Finkel even had a tic like her son. Like Asa Heshel she was continually biting her lip. A sort of pious melancholy flowed from her, the generations-old dolor of the Jewish mother, the mothers who bled and suffered so that murderers should have victims for their knives. And was she any different? What would happen to her child? Who could say that in another twenty years there wouldn't be another war?

A sudden shriek was torn from Adele's lips. It was not her own voice. Her loins were ripped, as though with a knife. Finkel started up from her chair and began to wring her hands. Rosa Frumetl, the maid, and the nurse rushed into the room together. Reb Wolf, hearing the scream, hurried to the telephone to call the midwife. Finkel stayed with her daughter-in-law until she was delivered. Adele shrieked all through the day and half the night. At three in the morning a boy child issued from her. Finkel looked at her new grandson through tear-filled eyes. The image of his father! Both grandmothers swayed back and forth, their arms about each other. Adele fell asleep the moment the child was delivered. There was a strange smile on her bloodless lips.

Someone awakened Finkel at nine in the morning. After the long watch she had fallen asleep on the sofa in her clothes. There was a telephone call. Finkel did not know how to handle the apparatus. Reb Wolf had to help her out. Her daughter, Dinah, was at the other end of the phone. She had left her six-weeks-old infant with a neighbor and had come down to let her mother know the good news that a letter had come from Asa Heshel. He was well. His regiment was in Galicia.

Finkel raised both arms, her eyes lifted aloft, and she poured out her thanks to the Creator of all things. The All-Merciful had seen her sorrow, He had heard her prayers, and she, the rebellious in spirit, had in her bitterness questioned His wisdom. She immediately decided that this day she would fast and would plead with the Holy One to forgive her her sinful thoughts. It was not until three stars showed in the sky that night that she tasted some food.

CHAPTER THREE

During the evening Dacha suddenly sat up in her sick-bed. Her face was parchment-colored, her eyes preternaturally large and bright. She called for the maid, but there was no answer. Hadassah was out getting a prescription. Dacha picked up a silver spoon that lay on the table beside the bed and banged it against the back of the chair. Finally the maid came in.

"They leave mè alone. I even have to die alone," Dacha groaned.

"But mistress, all I was doing was trying to get a little rest. All last night I didn't close an eye."

"Change my shirt. Bring me a basin to wash my hands."

The girl went to the wardrobe and brought the only shirt that was there; it was elaborately embroidered, but torn—one of the things that had remained from Dacha's trousseau. When Dacha saw it she grimaced. "Is there no other?" she said. "Nice way to run a house!"

The maid helped her to change. Dacha had become pain-

fully thin during her illness. Her ribs stood out; her breasts
had become flabby. A sweetish sickish odor arose from her
body. The fresh nightgown was too big for her and dropped
over her shoulders; the embroidery about the sleeves and over
the front was frayed. Dacha's face grew sterner. "Bring me
the mirror," she commanded.

The servant hesitated for a moment and then brought the
looking-glass. Dacha looked at her reflection for a long time.
"A corpse."

"Maybe you'd like something to eat, mistress?"

"For what? For the worms?"

The maid brought a pitcher of water and a dipper to the
bedside table and helped her mistress wash her bony fingers.
Dacha's lips tried to mumble a prayer, but she could not remember the words. Suddenly her strength left her. Her eyes
rolled upward. The servant put some pillows behind her head
and leaned her back. The sick woman's lips kept on mumbling. All at once there came to her mind the words of an old
song she had sung as a child: "Your lovely cheeks so rosy
red. . . ."

She made a vague effort to hum the melody. She remembered the tune, but the rest of the words had gone from her
mind. After a little while she dozed off. She dreamed that it
was Friday, the day she was to be married. The winter day
was short. Soon it would be time to light the Sabbath candles.
Her bridegroom was waiting in front of the synagogue. The
musicians were playing. But she, the bride, had only one shoe
on; the other foot was bare. She lifted the cover of the oaken
chest, but it was bottomless. The door opened and a crowd of
women poured into the room. Their faces were yellow and
half rotted away. Their eyes were sightless. In their wrinkled
hands they carried double-braided Sabbath loaves. They
danced around her. Her dead mother was among them, in
tattered shoes, and with a handful of straw. She seized Dacha
by the hand and dragged her with her.

"Mother, where are you taking me?"

"To the black canopy . . . in the dark grave. . . ."

Dacha opened her eyes, to see Hadassah standing at the
side of the bed. "Is it you, Hadassah?"

"Yes, Mamma."

"Where have you been?"

"At the druggist's."

"Call people in. I want to make the confession."

Hadassah turned white. "What people?"

"Don't ask me any questions. There's little time."

When Hadassah was at the door Dacha called her back. "Where is your father? Where is he wandering around, the heartless fool?"

"I don't know."

"What will be your end? I know all your wicked deeds."

"Mamma!"

"Be silent! You're unclean. Your lips are unclean."

"Mamusha!"

"Whore! Get out of my sight!"

Hadassah broke into tears and swayed, as though about to fall. Fishel appeared at the half-open door. Seeing the stern face of Dacha and the weeping girl, he took a step back.

"What are you afraid of?" Dacha said harshly. "I'm not dead yet."

Fishel came forward.

"How are you?" he asked.

"May my enemies—" Dacha started. She was quiet for a moment. "There are lucky people in the world. Live easy and die easy. My life is cursed. My mother was a pious woman, but a bitter one. All she did was punish me and drive me to work. Ah, God, never a minute's peace. I was the oldest. All the burdens were on my shoulders. Ever since I was five years old. My father was a holy man, but not of this world. What could he understand? 'Dacha, tea! Dacha, bring me my pipe! Dacha, go and borrow some money; not a copper in the house for the Sabbath!' I had to go and borrow from strangers; I stood at the door like a beggar. They sucked my blood. Woe to me, I was not yet eight years old."

"Mother-in-law, they didn't mean any harm. One has to forgive."

"I forgive them. But what did they want of me? The other children played, danced, sang, while I was sunk in grief. My mother, blessed be her memory, spent her time enjoying herself with her cronies."

"Mother-in-law, don't think of it any more. This is no time to—"

"I know. I'm sinning in my last breath. Both worlds lost."

Dacha closed her eyes and dozed off again. One side of her face was contorted in what looked like a smile, the other was serious and stiff. Hadassah went into the living-room. After a moment of hesitation Fishel followed her.

"What does the doctor say?" he asked her.

"I don't know. Leave me alone."

"Hadassah, I want you to listen to me. There's something I've got to tell you."

"Not now."

"Hadassah, I know everything. It is forbidden for us to live together."

Hadassah looked at him in astonishment. The tears rolled down her cheeks. "What do you want to do?"

"We'll have to get divorced. I'll raise no objections."

"All right."

"You know how I loved you. With all my heart and soul. But if things have gone this far, then we've got to put an end to it. According to the sacred law."

"I understand."

"It's forbidden that we be under the same roof."

His glasses misted over. Red spots appeared on his cheeks. He smiled with embarrassment and waited for a final word of kindness from her. Hadassah started to say something, but the doorbell rang and she went to answer it. Three men came in: Dr. Mintz, her father, and Abram. Dr. Mintz, the stub of a fat cigar in his mouth, the lapel of his coat flecked with ashes, was puffing and panting. He pinched Hadassah's cheek as he passed her. Abram came in soberly and quietly, discarding his cigar at the threshold. Nyunie was wearing his coat with the fox collar and lapels and the fur-edged hat. Since Dacha had become ill, he had taken to trimming his beard. From day to day it became shorter.

"Come into the kitchen and light the stove for me," Dr. Mintz ordered. Hadassah followed him and lit the gas stove. Dr. Mintz took a shallow pan and sterilized a hypodermic needle and some other paraphernalia in it. The gas flame threw a pale light. Dr. Mintz walked over to the sink, washed his hands, and spat out the remains of the cigar.

"You look bad, Hadassah," he said. "I don't want you to let yourself go. You'll need your health."

"What for? I'm ready to die."

"It's too early for that, my girl. You'll not be doing anybody any favors."

He turned toward the sickroom. Abram came into the kitchen and put his hands on Hadassah's shoulders.

"Have you heard anything from Asa Heshel?" he whispered.

Hadassah trembled. "No," she said. "Nothing."

"Then in that case he's managed to get away."

Nyunie went into his own room. Only a little while before,

he had eaten a heavy meal of chopped liver, noodle soup, goose, and apple sauce, but he was hungry again. The war and the scarcity of food seemed only to sharpen his appetite. In the drawer of a table in his room there was a piece of honey cake and a pear. He felt ashamed of this constant hunger, especially at a time when his wife was at the point of death. He closed the door and chained it. He chewed energetically, his beard catching the stray crumbs. "Ah, bitter as gall!" he thought. "It's close. Any minute. Too bad for Hadassah. . . ." He swallowed the last mouthful and went over to the bookcase. On the lower shelf was a book on ethnology. Nyunie took it out and opened it somewhere in the middle. He began to read. The section described the customs of a mid-African tribe; circumcision was practiced, not only on the young males, but on the girls as well. The ceremony was conducted with pagan ritual and wild dancing. Instead of a knife, a polished stone was used for the operation. Nyunie tugged at his beard. The description aroused a sensuous longing in him. He had lived out his years with a sick woman, a pious woman, a harsh woman, the daughter of a rabbinical house. Either she had had no desire herself, or she had been sick, or she had been disturbed by some ritual difficulty. The thought came to Nyunie's mind that as soon as the prescribed thirty-day period of mourning was over he would go to see the widow Gritzhendler and have a direct talk with her. The idea terrified him. He took out his handkerchief and spat into it.

"Faugh! What's happening to me?" he thought. "God forbid! She'll recover! Everything will be all right."

CHAPTER FOUR

At the beginning of January there was a double funeral in the Moskat family: Dacha and Joel died on the same day. The funeral processions joined at Gzhybov Place and proceeded together. The day was wet, with rain, hail, and snow in the air. The cortege was a small one—small for the Moskat clan. There were several droshkies following the hearses. Hadassah, dressed entirely in black, was supported by her two cousins, Stepha and Masha. At the cemetery Hadassah could see through her veil two newly dug graves, one close to the other. Joel had been a big man. The attendants who lowered the body into the grave strained under the burden. Wrapped in her shrouds, Dacha's form seemed strangely tiny. Her body was quickly lowered into the wet ground, and immediately the clods of earth were strewn over it. Fishel, true to the dead woman's request, recited the Kaddish over his mother-in-law's grave. He swayed back and forth, his thin voice broken with tears.

"*Yisgadal v'yiskadash* . . . magnified and sanctified be His great name in the world which He hath created according to His will. May He establish His kingdom during our life and during our days, and during the life of all the house of Israel. . . ."

The women sobbed. The men sighed. Abram kept a firm hand under Hama's elbow; she was noticeably faint. Nyunie was wearing his heavy coat with the fox-fur collar and lapels and his fur-edged hat. His kid boots were encased in a pair of shiny galoshes. Among those who had followed Dacha's body to the cemetery was the widow Bronya Gritzhendler, the owner of an antique shop. She dried her eyes with a silk kerchief, and Nyunie darted glances at her.

On the way back Hadassah, Nyunie, and Fishel shared a carriage. When they arrived home the neighbors brought a loaf of bread, a hard-boiled egg, and a pinch of ashes for the mourners according to the custom, but Hadassah was unable to eat even a mouthful. The wall mirror in the living-room was covered with a sheet. In the bedroom a mourning candle burned and there was a piece of linen soaking in a glass of water. Hadassah went into the room she had occupied before she was married and locked the door behind her. She lowered the window blinds and lay down on the bed fully clothed. She remained there all day and through the night. The maid knocked at the door a few times, but Hadassah refused to answer. For the first half hour or so Nyunie sat on a low stool, wearing a pair of cloth slippers and reading from the Book of Job. But the complaints of Job and the words of comfort of his friends soon became tedious, and Nyunie went into his study. There he lit a cigar and lay down on the sofa. The telephone rang. It was Bronya Gritzhendler.

"Nyunie," came her voice, "I want to know if there's anything I can do for you. And may you be spared from any more sorrow."

"It's you. A thousand thanks. Why don't you come over? It will cheer me immensely."

He took out the volume on folk customs, turned the pages,

and glanced at the woodcuts. He had no patience either to sit on a stool in his stockinged feet or to listen to the pious Jews who would come to the house to hold prayer services during the period of mourning. Now that Dacha was dead, he no longer needed this mask of piety. There was nothing to stop him from shedding these ancient Eastern garments and putting on European clothing. His only worry was Hadassah. During the night her coughing waked him several times. Her mother's death and Asa Heshel's induction into the military service had left her crushed, he reflected. But what could he do? She wouldn't even let him talk to her.

During the third night of the period of mourning Nyunie woke up frightened. From Hadassah's room came gasping and groaning. Nyunie pushed his feet into slippers, put on a robe, and went into her room. The electric lamp was lit. Hadassah was half sitting up in the bed. Her face was white, her lips bloodless.

"What is it, Hadassah?" Nyunie called to her anxiously. "I'll call Dr. Mintz."

"No, no, Papa."

"What'll I do, then?"

"Just let me die."

Nyunie shuddered. "Are you crazy? You're still a child! I'll call the doctor right away."

"No, Papa. Not in the middle of the night."

Nyunie woke the maid. They made Hadassah tea with raspberry juice and a coddled egg. They gave her rock candy. But Hadassah's cough persisted through the night. Dr. Mintz came early. He put his hairy ear against Hadassah's naked back. Nyunie and Fishel waited in the outer room. The doctor came out to them, his forehead creased.

"I'm not pleased with the way she is."

"What should be done?" Fishel asked, his face pale.

"She'll have to go to Otwotsk. To Barabander's sanatorium."

Nyunie scratched at the tuft of his beard. Unbidden ideas came to his mind. Good that Fishel was a rich man; he'd be able to take care of the expenses. And Hadassah's absence from Warsaw at the sanatorium would be propitious to his own plans in relation to Bronya Gritzhendler. To banish these selfish thoughts he hastened to a show of concern. "Tell me, dear doctor, it isn't dangerous, is it?"

"It must be stopped in time," Dr. Mintz answered shortly.

He put on his heavy overcoat and plush hat, lit a cigar, and went out, without waiting for his fee. He knew everything about Hadassah. All rumors sooner or later reached him. Fishel followed him into the stairs and thrust a banknote into his hand. "How long will she have to be there, doctor?"

"Maybe a year—and maybe three," Dr. Mintz answered gravely. "You made a bad bargain, eh?"

"God forbid!"

Fishel followed Dr. Mintz to the street. "A bad bargain," he thought. "What made him think of that? These assimilated Jews think they're the only ones with hearts in their breasts." He gazed after the carriage as it rounded the corner. He plucked at his sidelocks and bit his lips. Hadassah had cheated him, had heaped shame and disgrace on him. But his love for her could not so easily be rooted out. "The poor creature, lost to this world, lost to the next. Yet it might be that she is more precious in the eyes of God than all the pious pretenders. In her own way she is a pure soul. Who knows whose sins she is called on to atone for? Maybe she is the vessel for the spirit of some holy man whose purification it is her lot to accomplish."

As he climbed up the stairs he decided that under no circumstances would he now divorce her. He would support her in honor. He would make it his task to see that she was healed. With God's help she would get well, and she would get over her foolish notions. He went into the flat and toward Hadassah's room. "How are you feeling?"

"Thank you—"

"Dr. Mintz says you'll have to go to Otwotsk. You need fresh air."

"I need nothing now."

"Don't say that. With God's help you'll be well. I'll watch over you. Thank God, you're not among strangers."

"Why? What good have I done you?" Hadassah regarded him with a puzzled look on her face. Fishel's eyes, behind the shining lenses of his glasses, smiled. His cheeks flushed. "Why should he still care for me?" she wondered. "Who is he, this man I married? Is this what his study of the Talmud teaches him? But the Talmudists say that a woman is one of the meaner of God's creatures."

Directly after the mourning period Hadassah was taken by train to Otwotsk. Fishel sat in the second-class car with her. Hadassah held a book bound in black velvet, Novalis's *Hymns to the Night*. Dr. Barabander, the owner of the sanatorium in Otwotsk, had already received a report from Dr. Mintz and had prepared a room for the patient. Hadassah was put to bed immediately on her arrival. The room had a door that led out to a veranda. Clumps of snow rested on the pine trees. Icicles hung from the eaves. Birds twittered as though it were summer. The winter sun was setting, and threw purple shadows on the wallpaper. Fishel left. A nurse hung a temperature chart at the head of the bed and put a thermometer in Hadassah's mouth. It was good to be here, away from Warsaw, from the family, from the Gensha cemetery, from Fishel's shop, from Papa. What would Asa Heshel be doing now? Was he thinking of her? Where was he? In what barracks, what trenches, amidst what dangers?

She fell asleep. Toward the middle of the night she started up. Frost flowers were engraved on the edges of the window panes. The moon cleft its way through the clouds. The stars twinkled. The heavens remained eternally the same. What did they care about the petty sufferings on the tiny planet called Earth? Yet Hadassah voiced a prayer, in Polish. "Dear God! Take the soul of my mother under Your merciful wings. Guard my beloved from hunger and danger, from sickness and death. For it is You who have put this love into my heart."

She waited tensely for a moment, all her senses on edge.

"Mamma! Do you hear me? Answer me!"

Instead of an answer from her dead mother, she heard the thud and rumble of a freight train. The headlights threw a bold shaft of illumination on the pines, which seemed to flee into the distance.

CHAPTER FIVE

One afternoon when Koppel sat smoking a cigarette at his desk in the Moskat office, the door opened and Fishel entered. He greeted Koppel, wiped his misted eyeglasses with a piece of chamois, and said: "Are you busy now?"

Koppel returned the greeting and asked his visitor to sit down. Fishel lowered himself to the edge of a chair. "How are affairs going?" he asked.

Koppel puffed a cloud of smoke directly into Fishel's face. "Which affairs? Mine or yours?"

"The family affairs."

Koppel felt like saying: "What business is it of yours?" Instead he said: "Everything's dead."

"The trouble is that the family has to have food to eat, and clothes to wear. I'm not talking only about my father-in-law. The others, too. Queen Esther is a widow, unfortunately, and she's got to take care of a houseful of children. They're really going hungry."

"That you don't have to tell me."

"Uncle Nathan is a poor man, practically a beggar. Pinnie hasn't got a grosz to his name. Abram doesn't know where his next meal is coming from."

"Tell me something I don't know."

"Something's got to be done."

"Go and do it."

"The whole thing's got to be figured out. My grandfather-in-law—God rest his soul—left a sizable fortune."

Koppel overcame his impulse to grab Fishel by the coat collar and heave him down the stairs. "What is it you want? Make it short."

"The thing's got to be examined. Why, for example, hasn't the estate been divided?"

"Do you expect me to give you a report?"

"God forbid! But why should they suffer from want when something might be done? I hear that part of the estate is a piece of property in Vola and that the city wants to construct a garage for tramcars there. If that's the case why should it be postponed? It would be better than nothing."

"I have nothing against it."

"My father-in-law's no businessman. Pinnie is impractical. Nathan is sick. So far as Pearl is concerned, she has her own means and doesn't care. In fact, there's no one to keep an eye on things."

"Then keep an eye on them yourself."

"How about the books? There's not even any accounting."

"The bookkeeper's blind."

"What kind of excuse is that?"

Koppel lost his temper. "You're not my boss yet. I don't have to give any reports to you."

"I have a document here that says you do."

Fishel carefully took out of his pocket a folded sheet of paper. Written in a flowery script, in a mixture of Hebrew and Yiddish, it read:

We, the undersigned, give authority to our relative, the scholarly and wealthy Fishel Kutner, to administer our houses, forests, yards, lots, granaries, stables, warehouses, and

*other properties that we have inherited from our father, the
pious Reb Meshulam Moskat, may his memory be blessed, in
Warsaw and in other localities wherever situated, until the entire estate is divided among the heirs in accordance with the
law. The above-named Fishel Kutner is to have the right to
receive reports from the overseer, Koppel, and to divide the
rents and all other income arising from the said estate. He
shall also have the authority to negotiate with prospective
buyers of the property of the said estate, both real and personal as though he were himself the owner. The overseer
Koppel is hereby directed to give a complete accounting to
Fishel Kutner. The said Fishel Kutner is hereby empowered
to hire and discharge employees at his discretion. We have
agreed to all of this of our own free will on the night after the
Sabbath, on the 27th day of the month of Kislav in the year
5676 in the City of Warsaw."*

The document was signed by six of the Moskat heirs; only
Leah's name was missing.

Koppel peered at the paper for a long time. Many of the
words he could not make out, because of the ornate handwriting; others, in Hebrew, he did not understand. But the main
idea was clear: Fishel was now the boss; Koppel would have
to make an accounting to him; if Fishel pleased he could
throw him out. And all of this had been done without Leah's
knowledge and without her consent. They had got together in
a secret conspiracy and pulled the supports away from under
him. Koppel's face turned as gray as the paper he clutched
between his fingers. "I see," he murmured. "Yes, I understand."

"What I want to know is exactly how matters stand," Fishel
said, this time in a firmer tone.

Koppel stood up abruptly, almost overturning the half-
filled glass of tea near the edge of the desk. "You can take the
whole thing over," he said. "I'm going home. Thirty years is
enough."

Fishel shook his head. "God forbid you should think we're
driving you out."

"Here are the keys." Koppel opened a drawer of the desk,
took out a bunch of keys, and threw them down. He reached
for his hat, coat, and umbrella.

Fishel shook his head again. "You're an impulsive man,"
he said. "You jump at conclusions too suddenly."

"I don't like underhanded tricks."

"Nobody's doing anything to hurt you. It was my idea you should stay here, in your post. I even suggested a raise in your wages."

"I don't need your raise. When the old man died I shouldn't have stayed on one day."

"Just a moment, Reb Koppel. Don't run away. I'm no more than a messenger here."

Koppel did not answer. He hesitated for a moment, deciding whether or not to say good-by. Finally he went out without a word, closing the door after him more loudly than usual. How strange! For years they had eyed him with suspicion, maneuvered against him, complained about him and slandered him. But never had they been able to budge him from his post. And now this Fishel appears, with a piece of paper, and he's through. Everything, seemingly, comes to an end. He went down the steps slowly. In the courtyard the janitor took off his hat and Koppel acknowledged the gesture with a wry smile. He threw a last glance around the courtyard. He suddenly felt an astonishing sense of lightness, as though his job had always oppressed him. He walked along the Gzhybovska, taking deep breaths of the cold air. "So it seems I'm destined to go to America," he thought. "It's already been decreed in heaven."

He went over to Leah's house, but she was not in the flat. Since it was too early for him to go home, he went over to the Oxenburgs'. Mrs. Oxenburg was seated on a stool, plucking a chicken. Two provincial servant girls were seated on a bench, shawls over their heads. Mrs. Oxenburg was talking to them about jobs. In the corridor Koppel ran into the older of the Oxenburg daughters, Zilka. She was carrying a large bag of flour. Koppel asked her jestingly where she had stolen the stuff and the girl answered in the same vein. He pinched her breast. In the dining-room Isador Oxenburg was seated at the table laying out a deck of cards. He was mumbling: "Spades. Always spades."

"What's the matter, Isador?" Koppel called. "Don't you greet anybody any more?"

"Oh, it's you, Koppel. Come in, sit down. And I congratulate you."

"What for?"

"Your friend Mrs. Goldsober is getting married to Krupnick."

"Impossible! When? Where?"

"Right here. You'll get an invitation."

Koppel smiled. but somewhere inside him there was a knot of anger. Everything was swinish. If a man could turn his back on all this bitchery and run away to some island . . . He left without saying good-by and went home. Bashele was in the kitchen trying to sharpen a knife on the iron edge of the stove. She examined the blade.

"Koppel! So early?"

Koppel sat down on the cot where Yppe slept. "Bashele, I've got to talk something over with you."

"Well?"

"Bashele, our life together is no life."

Bashele dropped the knife. "As long as I'm satisfied, what else do you want?"

"I want a divorce."

"Go away. You're joking."

"No, Bashele, I'm serious."

"Why? I'm a faithful wife to you."

"I want to marry Leah."

Bashele's face paled. but her lips still smiled. "Are you playing some trick? Or what?"

"No, Bashele. It's the truth."

"And what about the children?"

"They'll be taken care of."

Bashele did not stop smiling. "It's just too bad," she said.

"And then you can get married to the coal dealer across the street."

The instant these words were uttered, Bashele broke into a fit of wailing. The tears gushed from her eyes. She clutched her hand to her breast and ran into the other room.

Koppel stretched himself out on the cot: putting his boots on the freshly arranged coverlet. He lay watching the winter dusk descend. His glance fell on the knife. "Maybe cut my throat," he thought. "It wouldn't matter any more." He closed his eyes. There was an unfamiliar silence that seemed to carry in from the street. A hidden force was driving him away from here, liquidating all his affairs, tearing him away from family, from friends. How could it all have happened? Mrs. Goldsober hadn't even mentioned it to him. He turned toward the wall. He heard Bashele come in, move about, light the lamp, fuss with the pots. He could hear the fire in the oven crackling, the water in the kettle seething. It boiled over and sputtered on the iron top of the stove. Yppe came in, the brace on her lame leg knocking on the floor, and whispered something to her mother. "This is the way it must be with a dead man," Koppel thought, "the corpse lying in the house until the funeral."

CHAPTER SIX

1

The house of prayer in Bialodrevna was empty. Because of the war the worshippers did not assemble this year, not even on the Channukah Sabbath. On weekdays not even ten men— the minimum for a quorum—gathered for prayers. Israel Eli, the beadle, who was also the rabbi's treasurer, was without funds. Everyone demanded payment—the grocer, the butcher, the fish dealer, the baker, the serving woman. Israel Eli came to the rabbi with his tale of woe. The rabbi led him into the rooms of his dead wife, which had been closed up for years. The furniture had become warped from the sun; the wallpaper was peeling. There were spiderwebs in the corners. White worms crawled from the cracks in the floor. The rabbi opened a dresser drawer. In it were rings, gold hairpins, a bent brooch, an ivory figurine, an assortment of other objects. The rabbi lifted up a string of pearls. "Take these and sell them," he said.

"Her jewels? God forbid!"

"What do I need them for? I'll not marry again."

"Maybe Gina Genendel will repent and—"

"Those who fall into the pit return no more."

Israel Eli took the string of pearls to Warsaw, where he pawned it for two hundred rubles. While he was in the city he paid a call on a couple of wealthy Bialodrevna Chassidim. They all asked the same question: why does the rabbi continue to stay in that dangerous region? All the other Chassidic rabbis, from the courts of Amshinov, Radzimin, Pulav, Strikov, Novo Minsk, had long since settled in Warsaw. Israel Eli returned to Bialodrevna and paid off the creditors. The rabbi apparently had dismissed the entire matter. He did not ask Israel Eli where he had been or for an accounting.

He paced back and forth in his room. His scant beard was turning gray. but his eyes were still as bright as those of a young man. He stood against the window and looked out over the court yard. "Israel Eli," he said, "be good enough to ask Reb Moshe Gabriel to come to see me."

Israel Eli went out. The rabbi continued gazing out of the windows. The fruit trees in the garden stood bare, their branches covered with snow. The footprints of birds were visible, as though they were the footprints of the shades who, according to the Gemara, had the feet of fowl. Above it all heaved a sky of torn clouds, with pillars of stark light cutting through them.

"You sent for me, rabbi?"

"Moshe Gabriel, yes. I should like to know where we're headed for."

Moshe Gabriel touched his wide sash, his skullcap, his curly sidelocks. "If I only knew."

"What is one to do? Reb Moshe Gabriel, teach me how to be a Jew."

"I should teach the rabbi?"

"Don't be so modest. Where shall I find faith?"

Moshe Gabriel paled. "It's not faith that is needed."

"What then?"

"It's sufficient to say over one of the Psalms."

"Say it, then. I'm listening."

"Ashrei ha' ish asher lo halach . . ."

"Translate it, Reb Moshe Gabriel. I'm a plain man."

Moshe Gabriel read on, sentence by sentence, translating into the Yiddish:

"Blessed is the man that walketh not in the counsel of the ungodly, nor standeth in the way of sinners, nor sitteth in the seat of the scornful.

"But his delight is in the law of the Lord; and in His law doth he meditate day and night.

"And he shall be like a tree planted by the rivers of water, that bringeth forth his fruit in his season; his leaf also shall not wither; and whatsoever he doeth shall prosper."

The rabbi listened to each word, his brows drawn together.

"And what did he mean, the psalm-singer?"

"Exactly what it says."

"You have a good and simple faith, Reb Moshe Gabriel. I envy you."

For a long time the rabbi was silent. He lowered his lids and passed his hand over his lofty brow. The veins in his temples throbbed. He began to pace back and forth, his eyes still closed. "What should one do after reading the Psalms?"

"Study a chapter of the Mishnah."

"And what does one do at night?"

"Sleep."

"And what is the use of sleep?"

"It is necessary."

"You've become a literalist, Reb Moshe Gabriel."

"There is no other way."

"You are right, Reb Moshe Gabriel. The Lord does not demand much. A verse of a psalm and a chapter of the Mishnah. He doesn't expect us to tell Him how to run the world. That he knows Himself."

After a while Moshe Gabriel went out. In deference to the rabbi he took a few steps backward. On the far side of the threshold he stood quietly for a moment, running his finger through his beard. "The strength of a saint," he reflected.

A young boy in a wrinkled coat and with disheveled sidelocks ran up to him in excitement. "Reb Moshe Gabriel, your wife is waiting for you!"

"My wife?"

"Yes. At Naftali's inn."

Reb Moshe Gabriel stared at him in disbelief. After a while he started toward the inn. He passed the well, a row of stores, the tavern. Although liquor was not to be had, owing to the war, a harmonica was playing and the peasants inside were singing in drunken voices. In the inn kitchen an enormous boiler of laundry steamed on the stove. In a room off the kitchen straw sacks were heaped on the floor, a reminder of the days when such hordes of the faithful made the pilgrimage to Bialodrevna that many slept on the floor. In the main room Reb Moshe Gabriel saw Leah. She was wearing a fur coat and hat, in the city style.

"Good afternoon," Reb Moshe Gabriel greeted her formally.

"A good year. Where is Aaron?"

"Aaron? In the study house."

"Close the door. Sit down. I have to talk to you."

Moshe Gabriel closed the door and sat down on a chair, taking such a position that he would not be looking directly at her. He sniffed the worldly odor of perfumed soap. He put his handkerchief to his nose.

Leah coughed. "I'll talk plainly," she said. "I want a divorce."

Moshe Gabriel bent his head. "If you wish it."

"When?"

"On condition that you give me Meyerl."

"Meyerl is going to America with me." The words came out involuntarily.

"To America? To become a goy?"

"There are good Jews in America, too."

"No. Meyerl stays with me. So far as Masha is concerned, she's no better than a gentile already. And as for Zlatele, I leave her to God's mercy. She goes to their schools, and no good will come of it."

"And you think Meyerl will stay with you? Forgive me, Moshe Gabriel, but you're a hanger-on of the rabbi, the same as a beggar."

"Rather a beggar than a heretic."

"No, Moshe Gabriel. I'll not give the child up to you. It's enough what you've done to Aaron. Dear God, what you've made of him! It isn't my fault, Moshe Gabriel. It's been the way you've lived. All these years. And if you don't give me a divorce, then I'll go away without one. And let the sin be on your head."

"You're capable of that, too."

"I'm capable of anything."

"Well, then—" Moshe Gabriel fell silent. The wall clock with its long pendulum and weights creaked and rang twice. Moshe Gabriel got up from the chair. First he glanced toward the mezuzah on the lintel, then he went over to the window and looked out.

Leah took off her fur coat. She was wearing a red dress. "What do you say?" she asked.

"I will give you my answer."

"When? I can't stay here, in this wilderness."

"After evening prayers."

"Is this where you live? Where do you sleep? I mean, where does Aaron sleep?"

"With me."

"I want the divorce papers to be made out here, in Bialodrevna," Leah said harshly.

"It's all one to me."

Leah bit her lips. That was the way he had been all the years of their marriage. Far away, in another world. She felt an urge to engage in a noisy quarrel, to argue about money, to insult him—for the last time. But there was no way to get at him. Although he was away from home, his face had a clear look, his beard was neat, his clothes were spotless. From behind his gold-rimmed glasses his blue eyes looked off into the

distance. Leah remembered what she had once heard of a
saintly rabbi—that the name of God always appeared before
his vision. Him and Koppel; what a comparison, she suddenly
thought. She became angry. "Send Aaron to me."

Moshe Gabriel went out at once. Aaron was standing at a
bench in the study house, pouring hot water from a teakettle
into a cup. His narrow face had a wintry pallor about it; his
sidelocks were awry. From his unbuttoned shirt collar his
pointed Adam's apple showed. A few stray hairs sprouted on
his naked chin. Moshe Gabriel watched him as he put a lump
of sugar into the cup and stirred it with a holy-ark curtain
wire.

"What are you doing, Aaron? That's a holy utensil."

"Everybody uses it."

"Aaron, your mother is here."

The boy's face turned white. "Where?"

"At Naftali's inn. She's come for a divorce. She's going to
America."

Aaron tried to put down the curtain wire, but it fell against
the teacup and the tea spilled over. He left. Moshe Gabriel
stood by the prayer stand and lit a cigarette at the flame of an
anniversary candle. It seemed there were unions, he thought,
that were destined to be broken. He puffed out a ring of
smoke. A special providence. He rubbed his hand over his
forehead to drive away the unwelcome thoughts. Koppel.
Love. Love between two bodies. If—God forbid—Koppel
were to be unsexed, then he would have done with this love.
"And thou shalt love the Lord thy God with all thine heart,
and with all thy soul, and with all thy might. . . ." "Yes,
Moshe Gabriel, love Him whose name is blessed. How long
will you perplex yourself with these trivial thoughts?" He suddenly remembered the answer he had given to the rabbi. He
opened a volume of the Gemara, sat down, and swayed over
it until the night fell.

2

Late one evening Leah sat on the sofa in her living-room,
busy with needle and thread, doing some repairs on a pair of
Meyerl's torn trousers. There was a ring at the outside door.
The house servant was not at home, and Leah went to answer
it. She called out: "Who is there?" but she could not make out

the reply. She opened the door. At the entrance stood Abram, the snow heavy on his coat and hat, his beard snow-whitened, a cigar in his mouth. He was carrying an umbrella held up against his shoulder. Leah stared at him in surprise; never before had he appeared so enormous. He was breathing heavily and puffing out thick clouds of smoke. Leah quickly got a brush and began to brush the snow off his galoshes. "Don't stand there like a *golem*," she said. "Come in."

He followed her inside. The corridor was unlit; only the dim light from the living-room relieved the darkness. Abram began to stamp his feet and cough. Then suddenly he approached Leah and put both his hands on her shoulders.

Leah started in alarm. "What's the matter with you? Are you out of your mind?"

"Leah, is it true?" Abram asked.

Leah knew what he meant. "Yes," she answered. "We've been divorced."

"And is the rest of it true, too?"

"Yes. Take your paws off me."

"It's impossible!" Abram took a few steps backward.

"It's true, Abram. If you don't like it, you can blot my name from the family records. I'm going away just the same."

"And where are you going to go?"

"To America."

"Now? In the middle of a war? How is it possible to travel?"

"If you want to go, there are ways."

"And what about the children?"

"You don't have to worry about them. Meyerl and Zlatele are going with me. Masha wants to stay here. She's old enough to know her own mind. Let her stay. Aaron seems to be ashamed of his mother."

"And Moshe Gabriel will let you take Meyerl?"

"I swore an oath that I'd let him stay here—but I'll break it."

"Leah—Cossack!"

"Look, Abram. If what I'm doing doesn't please you, go back where you came from. I'm sick of all of them, the whole mess."

"What are you shouting for? I won't eat you. I always knew that you were a rebel, but that you'd go as far as this—that never entered my mind."

"Abram, go home."

"Don't throw me out. You're seeing me for the last time. If you've fallen for Koppel, then you're digging your own grave."

"What have you come for? To curse me? Maybe I could expect it from the rest of them, but that you should start to slander—"

"It isn't a question of slander."

"You've made Hama's life miserable; you've broken up the family; you drag around with abandoned women. And you've got the impudence to accuse me. I'll be married honorably, like a decent Jewish daughter."

"Mazeltov! When is the wedding?"

"I'll let you know."

"Then good night."

"Good riddance. None of you are worth Koppel's old shoes. My father—God rest his soul—practically sold me off. My brothers are tearing at each other over the inheritance. I spit on all of you! America is a free country. We'll begin a new life. People aren't ashamed to work for a living there."

"Give my regards to Columbus."

"Get the hell out of here."

Suddenly Abram burst into laughter. "Idiot," he said. "What are you so excited about? If you love Koppel, that's your headache. You'll be the one to live with him, not me."

"I'll be proud of it."

For a while both were silent. In the dimness Leah's eyes shone with a pale green light. Sparks flew from Abram's lighted cigar onto his beard.

"Why have you posted yourself here in the corridor? Unless it's not elegant enough for you, come inside."

"No, Leah. Someone's waiting for me."

"Who? Your actress? You waited longer for her."

"Well, never mind, Leah. Everybody sees the other person's defects. So far as I'm concerned, I've got enough troubles. I'll tell you the honest truth—I envy you. You're acting like a crazy woman, but at least you've got courage. Me? I'm a stinker in everything I do."

Leah shook her head. "As I live, Abram," she said, "I'm beginning to think you don't know what you're saying."

"Well, what of it? The mood I'm in today, don't be surprised at anything I do. What you see before you is a walking corpse."

"What are you? A comedian, or drunk, or something?"

"I'm anything you like. If you have the courage to divorce

Moshe Gabriel and marry Koppel, why didn't a blockhead like me have the courage to divorce Hama and marry Ida? She's a great artist. She loved me and I loved her. I can't live without her. That's the honest truth."

"The old story all over again. So far as I know, Ida's back in Lodz with her husband."

"Yes, Leah. Everything's my fault. I'm a worthless coward. I suffocate without her. I'm so lost I could bang my head against the wall."

"You really deserved everything you got."

"If it weren't for the war I'd know what to do. But we're stuck where we are, she with the Germans and me here. I can hear her calling me—at night. We have a way of knowing—"

"What sort of way? What are you babbling about?"

"Aah, never mind. I don't know what I'm saying. I had a glass of wine too much. Nyunie took me to Fuker's wine cellar. He's a bridegroom all over again. With Bronya Gritzhendler. There's a couple for you. You could fracture your sides laughing. She twists him around her finger." He paused for a moment. "As for this actress of mine, she's driving me insane. Aah, did I get dragged in! Aah, am I a fool! Listen to what I'm telling you, Leah; I'm in a jam. I have to have a hundred rubles. Otherwise I'll have to throw myself off the top floor."

Leah stared at him with wide-open eyes. "So that's why you came to see me?"

"Idiot! Certainly not."

"What do you need the money for? A doctor?"

"Not for a rabbi."

Leah sighed heavily. "A man of your age."

"It's all her fault. First she starts to make speeches that she wants a child. It makes no difference to her what people say. Gets drunk on all those crazy books. Artzybashev. Kollontai. And now she's ready to kill herself ten times a day. It's the fifth month."

"The fifth month? She might die."

"I'll be the one that will die. She'll be the death of me."

"I haven't got a grosz. I thought you were a smart man, but instead you're a fool. A man of your age should know better."

"Yes, Leah. You're right. I'm a beaten dog. Well, good night."

"Wait, you lunatic! Where are you running away to? I can give you a ring. Go and pawn it. But please, no matter what happens, you've got to redeem it before I go away. You'll bring me the ticket from the pawnbroker. It was left to me by my mother, God rest her."

Leah went into the other room, leaving Abram alone. He put his hand to his head and began to sway from side to side. There was a stabbing pain in his heart. He felt a cold wave shoot up his spine. He was hungry, thirsty, tired, ashamed, full of longing for Ida, full of the fear of dying, everything all at the same time. "Maybe this is the last night for me," he thought. "She's right. I'm a fool."

Leah came back with a small red box. Inside, on the cotton padding, lay a ring, its diamond reflecting the colors of the rainbow in the dim light.

"A beautiful stone," Abram said.

"But please don't squander it."

"No, Leah. No. Let me kiss you."

He spat the cigar butt from his lip. He put his arms around her and kissed her fervently on the forehead, cheeks, nose. Leah pushed him away. "Drunk as Lot!"

"No, Leah, no! I love you. You're a noble person. I want to make up with Koppel. I want to be at the wedding."

Leah's eyes filled with tears. "Ah, dear God, that I should live to see this day." Her voice trailed off.

3

Everyone knew the story of Abram's new affair. Since Ida had returned to her husband in Lodz, Abram had been going around with an actress from Odessa, Ninotchka. Ninotchka had been brought to Warsaw by a man who was part owner of a theater. This man boasted that Ninotchka was his mistress and that he had taken her away from a wealthy pawnbroker. Ninotchka behaved like a lady. She made it a point to let it be known that she had graduated from a Gymnasium. She quoted Pushkin and Lermontov by heart. She insinuated that she was mixed up with the revolutionary movement. She had brought with her a suitcase full of play manuscripts—mostly translations of the works of Ibsen, Strindberg, Hauptmann, and Andreyev. The Jewish actresses in Warsaw had immediately taken a dislike to her. They began to spread all kinds of rumors—that she was converted, that she had deserted her two small children, that she had stolen from the theater, and that she sold herself for money. She appeared in a

melodrama in Warsaw, and got good notices, but she was
forced to withdraw from the play because of backstage intrigue. The director of an American Jewish theater was supposed to have offered her a contract to appear in New York
at a salary of two hundred dollars a week, but again her enemies had interfered, and at the last minute the whole thing
had come to nothing. By the time Abram met her, she was no
longer on the stage. She suffered from palpitations of the
heart. She had taken an attic room in the home of a gentile
woman in the summer resort of Mrozy, where Ida had an
apartment. Ida and she became friends. Ida painted her portrait. Ninotchka spent whole evenings talking to Ida and
Abram about her plans for an art theater to be endowed by
Jewish organizations, about her successes in Druskenik, where
her mother had had a first-class hotel, and about her acquaintances among famous Russian producers, actors, writers, and
directors. She went to sleep at two o'clock in the morning; she
opened her shutters at noon. While she was still an intimate of
Ida's, eating frequently at her apartment and scolding Abram
because he did not sufficiently appreciate Ida's talent and ide-
alism, she took him to her attic room, supposedly to read him
a drama she had adapted from a Gorki story, and she stealthily began to carry on an affair with him. It was largely because
of Ninotchka that Ida had packed her bags and left for Lodz.
At the railroad station Ida had said to Abram: "Adieu forever, you dirty beast!"

Abram immediately bombarded her with special-delivery
letters and telegrams, but Ida did not answer them. She had
left Lodz and lived somewhere in a resort town near by.
Meanwhile the war began. The Germans occupied Lodz. Ninotchka had rented a room on Ogrodova Street in Warsaw and
began to take singing lessons from a professor. Whenever
Abram was to visit her, she would phone him in advance to
tell him what to bring—rolls, smoked salmon, cheese, wine,
chocolate, even floor wax. Although she was his mistress, she
would not address him with the familiar second-person singular. She constantly reminded him that he was old enough to
be her father. Abram spoke Russian well, but she continually
criticized his grammar. In the evening she liked to put a candle in the candlestick, sit down on the floor, and recite her
grievances: the wrongs done to her at home, in school, in
the dramatic groups, and in the Odessa theaters. She talked
and wept. She smoked cigarettes and nibbled at raisins, nuts,
and caramels from a paper bag. In bed she sighed, cried,

quoted poems, pointed out to Abram that he was a grandfather and had a weak heart, and spoke about her lovers in Odessa, calling them by pet names.

Abram swore at her in Hebrew, which she did not understand: "Ugly pest! Stinking carcass!"

Now Ninotchka waited for Abram outside Leah's house, under a balcony. She was wearing a fur jacket, a broad-brimmed hat, a green skirt, and high snow boots. Her hands were hidden in a muff. She hopped from one foot to the other to keep warm. She looked at Abram with a large, angry eye. "I thought you were going to be there all night."

"I got the hundred rubles."

The pair walked in silence, at a distance from each other. Abram dragged the point of his umbrella behind him on the pavement and shook his head. Koppel, the overseer, the son-in-law of Reb Meshulam Moskat! His, Abram's, brother-in-law! What an ugly end!

On Ogrodova Street Abram went up to Ninotchka's room, which opened directly from the hall of the building. He stopped frequently to rest as he climbed the steps. His heart was thumping. He recalled Ida's words: "Adieu forever." Ninotchka walked ahead of him. At the threshold she reminded him angrily to wipe his feet. The room was cold and in disorder. Near the cold stove stood a pail containing a few lumps of coal. On the piano there were pots, glasses, cups, and a bowl of rice. An iron stove lid, half wrapped in a towel, lay on the unmade bed. Ninotchka used it at night to keep her stomach warm; she suffered from cramps.

Abram sat down on the edge of the bed. "Ninotchka, make something to eat. I'm dying of hunger."

"Well, go ahead."

Nevertheless, she began to prepare the oil stove. She trimmed the wick, pumped, cursed. Abram closed his eyes. Suddenly he burst out laughing.

"Have you gone crazy, or what?"

"I got myself into the nobility. Koppel the overseer is going to become my brother-in-law. If the old dog had only lived to see it!"

CHAPTER SEVEN

1

During the first few days in the barracks Asa Heshel was sure that he would not be able to stand the sufferings he was going through. Every night when he lay down on his bunk he was terrified that he would never again get up. Because of the urgency of the situation the general staff was trying to drill the new recruits in military techniques in record time. Instead of sending them deep into the Russian interior for the training period, as was the usual procedure, they kept them in barracks not far from the front. Asa Heshel's very bones ached from the constant drilling. His stomach rebelled at the noisome soldier's fare. In the middle of the night the officers would sound an alarm, and Asa Heshel would have to dash out of his quarters half-dressed. In the morning during assembly he shivered with the cold. The other recruits picked on him. He was constantly threatened with court-martial. Of all the raw recruits, Asa Heshel was the rawest. But weeks went by and he survived. In the evening, before taps, after he had cleaned and polished his rifle, he would sit down in the barracks and try to read a few pages of Spinoza's *Ethics*. A harmonica played; a group of peasants danced a *kamarinska*. The kerosene lamp threw a brazen light. Some of the soldiers would be drinking tea, others writing letters. Some would be telling jokes, others sewing buttons on their uniforms. The Christian soldiers would laugh at him. The Jewish recruits would gather about him to ask what he was reading. They could never understand how, at a time like this, a man could devote himself to poring over such small characters.

He sat here in the barracks before taps and carried on a dispute with Spinoza. Well, then, let it be admitted that everything that was happening was necessary. That the entire war was nothing but a play of modes in the infinite ocean of the Substance. But for what reason had the divine nature required all of this? Why should he not put an end to the entire tragicomedy? He read from the Fifth Part of the *Ethics*, where Spinoza discussed the intellectual love of God.

Proposition 35: God loves Himself with infinite intellectual love.

Proposition 37: There is nothing in nature that is contrary to this intellectual love of God or that can remove it.

Asa Heshel raised his eyes from the page. Was it really so? Could one in truth love all these Ivans? Even this one with the pockmarked face and the shifty piggish eyes?

Asa Heshel bent his head. He had come here with the intention of becoming a dutiful soldier. He wanted to demonstrate to himself that he, too, could endure what others endured. He had always looked askance at the youths who maimed themselves to avoid military service, or deserted, or bribed the doctors. It gave the enemies of the Jews the pretext to declare that the Jews always looked for special privileges. But try as he might, he could not live with the others. He had no patience with their talk or their games. The whole business of drilling and learning the military art had no interest for him. He was disgusted with the coarseness of the soldier's vernacular. He avoided all of them, and they avoided him. After all, what was he doing among these people? He was a Jew; most of them were Christians. He was born an intellectual; they were ignoramuses. They had faith in God, in the Czar, in women, children, country, and soil. He had nothing but doubt about everything. Even according to the very Spinoza whom he so much admired, their lives were more virtuous than his, with all his pride, his modesty, his individualism, his intolerable suffering, which were of no use to anybody.

He put back the copy of the *Ethics* in the wooden barracks box that stood under his bunk. He went out for a while into the yard. Soldiers squatted in partitioned, doorless chambers, doing their needs and talking to one another at the same time. In the kitchen the cooks were peeling potatoes and throwing them into huge vats. A Ukranian was singing in a heavy bass, which emerged as though from a grave. Asa Heshel had been here only a month, but it seemed years to him. He stood there haggard, sleepless, unshaven, in boots that were too big for him, with calluses on his hands, with a wide belt around his waist, and he had the feeling that he was a stranger even to himself. He had no fear of death; he felt only that this life was simply beyond his powers to endure. He had one desire, to be sent to the front.

2

Before the Purim season Asa Heshel's regiment was sent to the front. General Selivanov was beleaguering Przemysl. The Austrian garrison was making efforts to break out of the encirclement and it was necessary to bar the escape route. The march to the front followed a familiar path, along the borders of the river San. For three whole days Asa Heshel was even able to stay in the town of his youth, Tereshpol Minor. A gentile swine-slaughterer had moved into his grandfather's house. In the yard stood a wooden tub in which the pig was scalded after it was killed. The study house was being used as a storage place for fodder. On the day Asa Heshel arrived the ovens were being lighted in the ritual bathhouse, and the village gentiles were entering. It was strange to see Tereshpol Minor emptied of Jews.

In Bilgorai, where Asa Heshel spent a day, there was an epidemic. Infants were dying from measles, whooping cough, and scarlet fever. Housewives kept running to the prayerhouse to weep at the holy ark and to light candles for the souls of the sick. The pious women measured graves in the cemetery with candlewicks. Asa Heshel went in to pay a call on the Bilgorai rabbi, who was a distant relative on his grandfather's side. The rabbi's wife received him warmly and spread a meal for him. Although the rabbi had heard that Asa Heshel had departed from the accustomed paths, he nevertheless immediately engaged him in a discussion of Talmudical matters. The women who had come to ask ritual questions gazed in astonishment at the spectacle of their rabbi discussing Talmudic wisdom with a soldier. The rabbi's great-grandchildren came into the room, tried on the military cap, the belt, and the bayonet. To save Asa Heshel from the sin of remaining bareheaded the rabbi gave him one of his own skullcaps to wear. The town was full of soldiers, cartloads of supplies, and troops of cavalry, but the Bilgorai rabbi spent his time musing over a difficult quotation from Maimonides.

When the regiment moved and was somewhere between Bilgorai and Tarnogrod, a violent rain broke out. The wagons stuck fast in the mud. Horses stumbled and fell, breaking their fetlocks, and it was necessary to shoot them. Blood poured from the carcasses, mixing with the rivulets of rainwater. Crows flew about and tried to pick at the eyes of the fallen animals. Somewhere ahead the road was apparently blocked, and it was necessary to wait until the advance columns could move. Soldiers took advantage of the delay to go off into the fields and attend to their needs. The cooks set up their field kitchens. Someone started a bonfire, but the rain quickly quenched it. The soldiers, hungry and tired, grumbled and cursed. The officers shouted, riding from group to group, yelling and waving their crops. Time after time orders were given to advance, but after a few yards it was necessary to come to a halt again. Asa Heshel remained where he was, laden with full equipment, hung with belts of cartridges and with a gun at his shoulder, his mess kit dangling at his waist, staring out into the fog. His shirt was drenched. The soles of his boots were thick, but still the water soaked through them. He was tired and unshaven, and there was a chill darting through his ribs. The man beside him, red-haired, a cobbler from Lublin, kept up a ceaseless cursing. "The God-damn Czar! A plague in his mother's belly! Nothing but a war will please them, the capitalist swine!"

"Hey, you, Jew! What are you growling in that cursed jargon of yours?" a lance corporal shouted. "Are you insulting the government?"

"Don't you worry your head about it."

"Just you wait, you lousy Jews, you'll be court-martialed."

There were no barracks in Tarnogrod and the men were billeted in the Jewish houses. It happened to be a market day. The soldiers broke the clay pots and basins that the booth-keepers had put in front of their stalls, overturned the booths, and even tried to loot the shops. Most of the horses of the neighborhood had already been commandeered; the ones that were permitted to remain had distinguishing stamps on their pelts. But the military needed more horses and they began to confiscate the remaining beasts from the peasants. The owners resisted, trying to hold back the animals by their tails, while the noncommissioned officers lashed at the peasants with the butts of their rifles. They handed pieces of paper, military scrip, to the owners of the animals, but the peasants threw them away contemptuously. "Thieves! Robbers! Murderers! Go and wipe yourselves with 'em!"

The women wept. The men lamented hoarsely. A tall peasant in a sheepskin coat and wooden-soled boots grabbed an ax and made a swing at a sergeant. He was seized, bound with ropes, and led away to the town jail. Behind him ran his wife,

waving her fists and shrieking. The soldier kicked at her with
his boot and she fell in the mud.

It was Thursday. Because of the heavy rainfall the troops
waited in the village over the weekend. The colonel issued an
order to the Jewish bakers to bake a batch of bread on Saturday. The bakers were terrified at the prospect of desecrating
the Sabbath, but the officer threatened to hang every last one
of them if they refused. The rabbi ruled that the emergency
was one that permitted the violation of the Sabbath injunction
against work, and the bakers were constrained to fire up their
ovens on Friday night. Some of the old women complained
about the rabbi's ruling. They uttered baleful warnings of
plagues that would strike the town. On the Sabbath Day Asa
Heshel went into the prayerhouse. A table had been spread
for the Jewish soldiers. The village girls served the Sabbath
stews, the fresh white bread, and the potato pudding. One of
the soldiers, a small man, who in his village had been a choir
singer in a synagogue, began to chant Sabbath songs.

> *How friendly is your rest, Queen Sabbath!*
> *Therefore we will hasten forth to meet you, Anointed*
> *Bride.*
> *All who take joy in you—*
> *Their reward will be great;*
> *From the birth-pangs of Messiah*
> *They will be raised into paradise.*

After the Sabbath they marched toward Galicia. There, on
the enemy's territory, the Russians had indulged in every kind
of cruelty. They seized the most prominent householders and
sent them off as hostages to Siberia. The officers turned a
blind eye to all the looting. The Ruthenian Christian population and their priests came to meet the Russians carrying
bread and water, bearing crucifixes and holy images, and
greeting them as "brothers." The Poles lived mostly outside
the towns. The full rage of the Russian troops was vented on
the Jews. Cossacks donned the looted fur hats of the Chassidim, adorned with the customary thirteen sable points, and
put around their shoulders the cherished silk and satin robes.
The study houses were turned into stables. The holy books
were trampled into the mud of the streets. Jewish boys were
dragooned for forced labor. Many of the rabbis and the
wealthy had already fled to Vienna or to Hungary. The Gali-

cian Jews, who were unaccustomed to persecutions and were staunch patriots of the Emperor Franz Josef, had only one hope to comfort them: that these Muscovites would be quickly driven out and chased back to St. Petersburg. The famous rabbi at Belz had even found an indication in the Zohar that the Russian invader was Gog and Magog.

3

On the 22nd of March the Austrian commander of the fortress of Prezemysl surrendered after a siege of less than four months. Over a hundred thousand prisoners were taken by the Russians. All Russia celebrated the victory. Asa Heshel's regiment was stationed in Prezemysl and charged with guarding the prisoners. They were of all kinds: Magyar hussars in red trousers, Polish uhlans in feathered shakos, Czech dragoons with brass-rimmed helmets, Bosnian Mohammedans in fezzes. Instead of military boots the soldiers wore shoes. They spoke a veritable babel of languages: Polish, Bosnian, Czech, Yiddish. The Russians held their sides with laughter.

"A barefoot army! A bunch of fishwives!"

After the Passover, Asa Heshel's division was moved south, to the Carpathians. The road to Sanok swarmed with soldiers. Wagonloads of wounded streamed back from the front. The fields sown with winter wheat were beginning to turn green. A spring sun shone down from a pre-Pentecost sky. Storks circled overhead, as if in a ceremony, bees hummed, field crickets chirruped. Wherever the eye turned it encountered flowerets—white ones, yellow ones, dotted, lined, adorned with petals and tassels. The thunder of the army could not drown out wholly the croaking of the frogs in the swamps. Peasant women and girls came out of the villages and made eyes at the enemy troops. At one point gallows had been put up, and a peasant, who had been taken for a spy, had been hanged. His bare feet dangled above the ditch. A butterfly danced about the fur shako.

The soldiers marched with a thunderous rhythm of feet. The bayonets glistened in the sunlight like the bristles of a gigantic brush. Trumpeters and drummers led the way, and the peasant infantrymen brayed out a song about girls who had gone into the woods to gather mushrooms.

Asa Heshel marched along, but he never felt like singing. Thank God that the boredom of the barracks was ended; on the march he could think his own thoughts. In the midst of all the tumult he was meditating on Spinoza and Darwin. How could these two philosophies of life be reconciled? How could the pantheistically static be squared with the Heraclitean dynamic?

"Hey, you, Jew! Keep off my heels!"

"I'll bet he's crapped in his pants."

Asa Heshel felt an impulse to reply, but suppressed it. The soldier on his right had huge fists, and he was trying to provoke a quarrel. He was forever correcting Asa Heshel's pronunciation of Russian, his way of marching, his way of carrying his rifle. Every now and then he would stick his hand into Asa Heshel's belt to show that it was loose; or he would joke loudly about the book that Asa Heshel carried in his haversack. For some unknown reason this peasant lad, who came from a village beyond Vladova, had become his enemy. A surly hatred toward Asa Heshel glowered in his little watery eyes, sat on his pug nose with its wide nostrils, and on his long, horselike, protruding teeth. Asa Heshel had not the slightest doubt that if the lad were to find himself alone with him, in some forest, he would commit murder. But why? What harm had he done him? What had the Jews done to him that he should always be cursing them? If hatred could never be good, why had God created it? Oh, what was the sense of all this thinking? God had drawn a veil over His secrets and would let no one pull it aside. The only question was what was to be done. Fight for one's life? Serve the Czar? Desert? Why should he, Asa Heshel, want to conquer Hungary?

The division rested in Sanok. Thence it was to be sent forward to Bialogrod, on the front lines. But a couple of days passed and no orders arrived. The town was in a state of confusion. Half the troops tried to buy out whatever there was in the shops; the other half tried to plunder. Householders put barrels of water outside their doors for the soldiers to drink. Asa Heshel saw a Cossack parading the streets in a rabbinical gaberdine. In the market square a great sale went on of looted merchandise and household goods. And in the midst of all this frenzy the Jews were at one another's throats. The Chassidim of the rabbi of Belz were quarreling furiously with the Chassidim of the rabbi of Bobov. The president of the synagogue was demanding judgment against an orthodox ritual slaughterer. In the study house the daily occupation went on, and youngsters in earlocks and rabbinical garb chanted their lessons. Young men were hiding in attics and cellars for fear of being carried off by the Russians to forced labor. On the outskirts of the city, trenches were being dug, heaps of garbage and skeletons of horses were being cleared away. The seriously wounded were lodged in the city hospital; the lighter cases were shipped in transport ambulances toward Russia. An epidemic of typhus threatened, and even cases of cholera had been reported; the authorities therefore hastily assigned a barrack for disinfection of the civilian population. Orthodox Jews were compelled to shave off their beards and earlocks, and girls had their heads shorn. Immediately there sprang up a group of "fixers," who, for a bribe, obtained forged disinfection certificates for those who would not submit to these indignities.

In the midst of all this chaos Asa Heshel received three letters from Hadassah. The envelopes had been opened, then gummed up again with brown packing paper; here and there lines had been deleted by the censor. Asa Heshel wondered what on earth Hadassah could have written that had any military significance. It was only now, when he held the sheets of paper in his hand, that Asa Heshel realized how frightfully he longed for her. He did not read the letters through, but snatched at sentences here and there. There were notations on the margins, and little additions between the lines.

In the letter that told of her mother's funeral and of her own sickness Hadassah set down expressions of endearment, called him by intimate love-names, referred to matters that only the two could have understood. Asa Heshel read on and felt the blood leaving his face. The words stung him to sharp desire for her. His mind turned, despite himself, to the little houses of prostitution on the Lemberg road, to the peasant girls there, who were to be had for half a loaf of bread, a package of tobacco, a pound of sugar. The young men in his regiment who came from Bilgorai, Zamosc, and Shebreshin were forever talking of the women they were getting, of their adventures in homes, barns, attics, and even the open wheatfields; and not only with peasant women, but with the Jewish girls and Jewish wives whose husbands were away in the army and who were behaving like whores.

The regiment had been assigned to a position near Bialogrod, by the Carpathians, but days passed without the order to proceed being given. The troops scattered into the near-by villages and requisitioned hens, eggs, and even calves. The Jewish soldiers began to do business. In spite of strict orders against the use of alcohol, the officers got drunk regularly in their club. Asa Heshel found himself with a lot of time on his hands. In a deserted Jewish home he found a full bookcase. There were albums such as he had seen at Hadassah's. On the gilt-edged pages verses were written in Polish and German, quotations from Goethe, Schiller, Heine, Hofmannsthal. A diary had been left behind. Among the books there was a complete set of the Talmud, bound in leather.

Asa Heshel lay down on the sofa, which had been ripped up by bayonets, and closed his eyes. (When he closed his eyes he was no longer a soldier.) The sun shone on his face, and a red glimmer broke through his eyelids. A fantastic mixture of sounds, all fused together, came to his ears: the rumbling of wheels, the explosion of guns, the barking of a dog, the laughter of girls. There was a gurgling of gases in his stomach: he had never become used to the Russian diet of cabbage. There had been times when he had suffered from hypochondria. As a youngster he had believed that he would die on the day of his *bar mitzvah*. Later he had convinced himself that his end would come on his wedding day. He had always worried that he had tuberculosis or catarrh of the stomach, or that he would become blind. But now, when he actually expected to proceed to the front, where men fell like flies, his spirit was calm. It had divested itself of the fear of death. His mind was filled with Hadassah and with all kinds of sex fantasies. He saw himself as a maharaja with eighteen wives, lovely women of India, Persia, Arabia, Egypt—and a few particularly beautiful Jewesses. Hadassah was the queen of the harem. Each wife brought him her serving girl, a dark-skinned, black-eyed slave, and he was gracious to her and lay in her lap. Hadassah was jealous, but he assured her again and again that his love was for her alone, and if he was carrying on with the others, it was only because the custom of the kingdom demanded it.

He suddenly felt himself stung, and he opened his eyes. All the efforts of the officers to keep their troops clean were in vain: there were lice everywhere.

4

Marching orders came finally, but for the reverse direction. A gigantic force, composed of German and Austrian troops, under the command of Field Marshal Mackensen, was attacking the Russian center in the vicinity of the Dunayetz and breaking through to the river San. The retreat turned into a rout. Artillery, food stores, piles of ammunition were abandoned. The enemy had outflanked the Russians, and there were rumors that entire army corps had been shattered and that hundreds of thousands of troops had surrendered. Asa Heshel hoped that he would be taken, too, but luck was against him. His division slipped through the pincers. He marched enormous distances: through Prezemysl, Yaroslav, Bilgorai, Zamosc. He passed again through Tereshpol Minor. He ceased to feel the exhaustion in his limbs, the ache in his back, the rumbling in his stomach. Day and night followed each other rapidly in a hot delirium. All fear, all worry for the future, vanished. Lust and mental activity ceased. Torrents of rain fell, winds blew wildly, shells exploded about him, but nothing mattered. Even the longing for rest and sleep became dim. There remained only one thing—a great astonishment: "Is this me? Is this Asa Heshel? Have I really got the strength to go through all this? Is my body really so sturdy? Am I Reb Dan Katzenellenbogen's grandson, my mother's son, Adele's husband, Hadassah's lover?" Somewhere in a field, together with other soldiers, he stacked his rifle and stretched himself out on the ground. He lay amid trampled corn and for a while held his eyes open. A blood-red moon hung in the sky, divided by a wisp of cloud. A column of mist went up from the near-by river. Someone had built a fire, and sparks rose out of the flames. "Who am I? What am I thinking of?" But the more he searched in himself, the less was he able to untangle his thoughts. Everything had rolled up into a tight coil: the heaviness of his body, the dampness of the earth, the groaning of the soldiers. A worm crawled over his forehead. He squashed it. All natural loathing seemed to have left him. What had Adele had there? A boy, or a girl? He was suddenly convinced that it was a girl. But even this thought did not torment him. What, after all, was the difference? And he became dumb and mindless as a stone.

CHAPTER EIGHT

In the middle of the summer the Russians began to evacuate Warsaw. On the Praga bridge—whose supports had been mined—moved long columns of wagons and trucks, motored and horsedrawn. The wives of officers and government officials carried away with them to Russia all the furniture they could—chairs, pianos, sofas, mirrors, and even tubs with palm trees. Orderlies lashed at the dray horses, cursing at the tops of their voices. The bridge was too narrow for the traffic; there was a hopeless jam of tramcars, bicycles, wagons piled with homeless Jews, soldiers in full equipment. In the barracks soldiers were busy selling boots, uniforms, underwear, all kinds of flour, groats, and fats. The buyers dragged away the illegal merchandise without any attempt at concealment. There was panic at police headquarters. The police were inducted into the army. In their place there had been formed a civil militia, citizens wearing brassards on their sleeves, and with rubber truncheons instead of swords. Among this militia were some Yiddish-speaking youths; the Jews of Warsaw took this as a sign that better times were in store for them. On the last day of the evacuation the janitors went about from house to house warning householders to keep their windows closed because the bridges were to be dynamited. The pessimists predicted that at the last moment the Russians would start a pogrom, set fire to the city, and loot the shops. It was whispered that the sewage canals were laden with explosives. But apparently the Russians were not bidding a permanent farewell to the city; the police commissars and the rank and file all voiced the same phrase: *"Nitchevo.* We'll come back."

And for the last time they extended their palms for the usual bribes.

The Moskat family, like many other Warsaw Jewish families, divided into two factions, those who supported the Russians and those who cast a hopeful glance toward the Germans. Pearl, Reb Meshulam's oldest daughter, declared firmly that the Germans would mean nothing but misfortune. It was whispered in the family that she had fifty thousand rubles stowed away in the Imperial Bank of St. Petersburg. Queen Esther warned the others that under the German occupation "there'll be no grub." Fishel began to traffic in enormous quantities of merchandise—oil, soap, blubber, candles, herring, and even sacks of feathers and goose down that he had got cheap on Gensha Street. His yard on the Gnoyna was packed with barrels and cases and crates. He was already making inquiries whether it would be possible to do business with the Germans, whether they were open to bribes, and whether it was true that they understood Yiddish.

"What's the difference to me?" he said with a shrug. "This gentile or that one."

Nathan Moskat was a bit of a German from the old days, when he and Saltsha used to stop off in Berlin on their way to Marienbad. He spoke a smattering of crude German and could even write out an address in the pointed German script. And he had on his bookshelves a copy of the Bible in Mendelssohn's German translation. Now he spent most of the day on his balcony, in a flowered satin dressing-gown and silk skullcap, his feet thrust into a pair of plush slippers, watching with joy the way the Russians were retreating from the city. Pinnie came to visit and discuss politics. He prophesied that when the Germans occupied Moscow the Japanese would turn on Russia, seize Siberia, and tear the bear limb from limb.

"I tell you, Nathan," he beamed, "we can start to say Kaddish for them right now."

Nyunie had just celebrated his marriage to Bronya Gritzhendler. He spent his time with his wife in her antiques and book shop on Holy Cross Street. He could hardly contain his impatience for the Germans to arrive, and for the time when he would be able to don Western clothing. Already he had a proper suit and hat hanging in his clothes closet. Of his full beard only a small chin-tuft was left. Students and teachers were coming into the store to inquire after collections of German works, dictionaries, grammars. It was a pleasure to have a young wife, one who wore her own hair instead of a matron's wig, to spend his time among books, maps, globes, decorative pieces of sculpture, to talk with customers about Klopstock, Goethe, Schiller, and Heine. Ever since the German troops had been advancing on Warsaw there was something of a western European atmosphere about the city.

"Well, Bronya, my love," Nyunie remarked, "we'll soon be abroad without having to cross a border."

Abram grew more optimistic from day to day. True, the tenants weren't paying rent. Hama was busy the whole day peeling potatoes in the kitchen. His daughter Bella now lived with him. His grandchild, the little Meshulam, was in the throes of the measles. Avigdor, his son-in-law, had no job and spent his time rolling cigarettes and reading the Yiddish newspapers. But Abram was seldom at home. Ninotchka had come safely through the abortion, and at her flat on Ogrodova Street there gathered every evening a group of writers, actors, musicians, and others of the intelligentsia. Ninotchka would light two tall candles, seat herself on the carpet, bohemian fashion, declaim poetry, and sing songs.

The evening before the Germans made their entry into the city Abram spent at home with the family. Stepha had brought her fiancé, the medical student. There were other guests besides: Masha, who was an orphan now that Leah had gone to America, and Dosha, Pinnie's youngest daughter. The girls danced about and laughed, whispering secrets to one another. Hama served tea, potato pudding, and vishniak. The baby refused to go to sleep, and Avigdor brought him into the living-room. To amuse the child, Abram got down on his hands and knees, barked like a dog, mewed like a cat, and howled like a wolf. He made such a spectacle of himself that even the melancholy Hama burst out laughing. She shook her bewigged head and put her handkerchief up to blow her reddened nose. "What's there to be so happy about?"

"You dark-minded woman! What are you worrying so much for? We'll die—like the richest millionaires. And we'll rot—like the kings and emperors."

Abram went to bed at two o'clock in the morning but he was awakened before dawn by a loud crash. The sound of two more explosions followed. The Russians had blown up all three bridges across the Vistula. Window panes, torn out of their frames, plunged down into the courtyard. Dogs barked. Children wailed. Abram sat up in bed and thought that soon now it would be possible to travel to Lodz. He'd be able to see Ida. Who knew, maybe she'd completely forgotten about him. Maybe she'd found someone else to take his place. He fell asleep again, but dreams disturbed his rest. For all that his beard was gray, his blood plunged vigorously through his veins. Young and virile desires chased through his brain. In his confused dreams he thought he was kissing Hadassah, and then the image would change and it would be his daughter, Stepha.

The ringing of the telephone awakened him in the morning. It was Nyunie. His voice stammered over the wire. "Abram, *m-m*-mazeltov! The Ger-ger-germans have c-c-come. We-we-we're in P-p-russia now."

"Hurrah! *Viva! Potztausend!*" Abram yelled joyously. "Where are you, my idiot? Let's go to welcome the Huns."

He started to run around the flat in his bare feet. Hama and his daughters awoke; the baby started to squeal. Abram put on a white summer suit, a straw hat, and an open shirt with a sports collar and grabbed his stick with the staghorn handle. He hurried down the steps, singing. Downstairs he hailed a droshky and gave the driver Nyunie's address. From there he,

Nyunie, and Bronya rode on to Senator Street. The sun shone brightly; a soft wind blew from the Vistula. The janitors were dousing the sidewalks and house entrances with rubber hoses. Young women and girls hurried along carrying flowers. The balconies were packed, the streets full of pedestrians. On Senator Street Abram caught sight of the German troops. Officers were sitting stiffly on their horses, with spiked helmets on their heads, swords at their waists, and spurred boots. There was nothing about them to indicate that they had just come from the battlefront. Wide columns of soldiers marched along, most of them middle-aged men, broad-shouldered, round-bellied, and spectacled, with porcelain pipes between their lips. They thumped their boots against the cobblestones, singing in hoarse voices, an absurd bleating, which called forth laughter from the watching crowds. Shouts of greeting came to the conquerors:

"*Gut' Morgen! Gut' Morgen!*"

"*Gut' mo'en! Gut' mo'en!*" the soldiers called back. "Where's the road to St. Petersburg?"

"Have a cigar!" Abram held out his hand to one of the soldiers.

"*Danke schön.* Have a cigarette," and the soldier handed Abram a cigarette, one that had no mouthpiece, but a thin gold edge. The columns of soldiers seemed to stretch endlessly. Flocks of pigeons wheeled over the rooftops, changing from a fiery gold to a leaden black. Window panes reflected the sun's light. The black, white, and red flag already fluttered over the castle. Wagonloads of special police rode on toward the city hall, in blue capes, most of them wearing dark glasses. Shooting was heard from the Praga section; the Russians apparently were not entirely finished. They were still entrenched on the other side of the Vistula. Yellow-faced deserters began to creep out of the Jewish houses, in ragged clothes. Here and there a German patrol seized a Russian soldier and either led him away to imprisonment or shot him on the spot and left him to lie on the ground in a pool of blood. Early in the afternoon posters appeared on walls and fences, in German and Polish. Groups of people gathered to read them. Boldest of all stood out the words: "*Streng verboten*"—"Strictly forbidden. . . ." Toward evening Abram made his way to the Vienna Station to inquire whether trains were running to Lodz. There was excitement on Marshalkovska Street. Troops of cavalry rode by. A band was playing. In the restaurants and bars German soldiers were already drinking and carrying on with women. From Chmielna and Zlota Streets streams of prostitutes poured, faces powdered and rouged, their eyes shaded, and with beauty spots pasted on their cheeks. Drunken shouts and abandoned voices echoed in the air. The Vienna Station was locked and guarded. Abram tried to say something to one of the German guards, but the Swabian, with his horse's face and bulging eyes, pushed him away, almost flinging him into the gutter. "Get the hell out of here, you damn Jew!" The soldier made a threatening gesture with his gun.

PART
SEVEN

CHAPTER ONE

The express train from Bialystok to Warsaw was a few hours late. It was to have arrived at the Vienna Station at four in the afternoon, but at that hour it had only reached a junction point. There it halted for a long time while cars were uncoupled and new cars joined on. The platforms held a crowd that had purchased tickets but could not make its way onto the train. Polish passengers bolted the doors, refusing to allow admittance to the Jews who wove helplessly back and forth, laden with luggage and bundles. A woman carrying a child wept, begging for mercy. She had lost her matron's wig in the shuffle and stood about with her close-cropped head. A soldier picked up the wig on the point of his bayonet.

In one of the second-class cars sat a young man with a high forehead, deep-set eyes, and blond hair, already thin at the top. His gray suit was creased with the journey, his collar turned up at the corners, his tie awry. His pale face was streaked with dust from the train's smoke. He was reading a magazine, from time to time gazing out of the grimy windows. The train had stood at rest for more than an hour. Locomotive and freight cars jammed the wide rails. Conductors ran up and down the platform, swinging the lanterns, which gleamed palely against the daylight. From the window of a first-class compartment a broad-shouldered general, with the square beard of a Great Russian, looked out. His cold eyes gazed stonily with the look of one who was free from all human anxieties. Although Poland had just assumed its statehood, his broad chest was already covered with Polish medals.

In the second-class coach, apart from the young man with the magazine, there were an officer, two women accompanying him, an old woman in black, with a veil on her hat, a landowner with a goat's-beard tuft on his chin, dressed in an old-fashioned Polish caftan, with two rows of buttons and loops. Bags and valises were piled on the rack. The officer, a lieutenant—a short, fair-complexioned specimen, with a red face, watery eyes, and his hair close-cropped—had hung up his jacket, his four-cornered hat, and his sword. He sat with his legs crossed, puffing at a cigarette, gazing down at his reflection in the toe of his polished boot. "What are they waiting so long for—the bastards!" he grumbled.

"Only the devil knows," commented one of the women with him.

"Satan's spawn," the lieutenant complained. "Didn't close my eyes all night. Polish officers have to spend days on these cursed trains, while the place is lousy with Jews. A fine state of affairs."

The landowner sat forward in his seat. "If the lieutenant will forgive me," he said, "where I come from they didn't stand on any ceremony with the Jews. They drove 'em out, and—finished!"

"And where do you come from, sir?"

"Not far from Torun. The Germans call it Thorn." He spoke with a German accent.

"Oh, yes. In Posen and Pomerania it's different. Here the cursed swine are all over."

"They say on the Lithuanian border they side with the Lithuanians, and in eastern Galicia with the Ukranian bandits."

"They got a lesson in Lemberg," the lieutenant said. He turned his head and spat through the open window.

The young man with the magazine huddled a bit deeper into his seat. It was the beginning of May, but the sky above the station was a deep summer blue. Mixed with the smell of coal and oil, the wind bore a faint tang of forest and river. Someone was playing a harmonica or a concertina. From the upper shelf the landowner lifted down an ancient traveling bag. He untied his straps, opened several locks, and fumbled inside, finally bringing out a bag of cookies. "If the lieutenant would deign to—"

"Thank you." The officer lifted a cookie between two fingers.

"And the gracious ladies?"

"Many, many thanks."

The landowner looked toward the blond youth in the corner seat, hesitated, and then said: "Would the gentleman like one?"

The young man sank even further into the seat. "No thanks," he said. "Thank you very much."

All the others turned to look at him at the same time—the officer, his two women companions, even the old woman in black. The landowner withdrew the box of cookies. "Where are you from?" he asked suspiciously.

"I? I'm a Polish citizen. I served in the Czar's army until Kerensky."

"And after that—with the Bolsheviks, hah?"

"With the Bolsheviks, no."

"How can a Polish citizen get out of Russia?"

"I managed."

"You smuggled yourself into Poland?" the landowner persisted.

The young man did not answer. The officer's brows drew together. "Are you a Jew?" the officer asked, using the insulting second-person singular.

"Yes, a Jew."

"Why didn't you say so when you were asked?" the officer yelled at him angrily.

There was a momentary silence. The two women with the officer looked at each other, faint smiles on their faces. The old woman's head shook and the white hairs on her chin quivered. The young man's face turned chalk pale.

"What were you doing in Russia?" the officer asked.

"I worked there."

"Where did you work? In the Cheka? Been a commissar? Robbed churches?"

"I've robbed nobody. I've been a student, a teacher."

"A teacher, hah? What did you teach? Karl Marx, Lenin, Trotsky?"

"I'm not a Marxist. That is why I left. I taught children Hebrew, as long as they allowed it."

"None of your tricks, now! Who sent you here, Comrade Lunacharsky?"

"Nobody sent me. I was born here; my mother lives in Warsaw."

"In what part of Russia were you?" asked the officer.

"In Kiev, Kharkov, Minsk."

"What are you, an agitator or propagandist?"

"Sir, I told you I am not a Marxist."

"You son of a bitch, what you told me isn't worth a pinch of powder. You're all liars, thieves, and traitors. What is your name?"

The young man's face became ashen. "Are you from the police, sir?" he asked, terrified by his own words.

The lieutenant moved as though to rise. "Answer, you cursed Jew! You're speaking to a Polish officer." He glanced at the curved sword hanging from the rack.

The young man closed the magazine. "Asa Heshel Bannet," he said.

"A-sa-he-shel-ban-nett," the lieutenant repeated ironically, dragging out the Jewish-sounding syllables. One of the women broke into a loud titter. She took a lace-edged handkerchief from her pocketbook and held it to her mouth. The other woman made a grimace of disgust.

"Oh, Stashu. Leave him alone."

"Who do they think they are, these Trotskys—riding second-class?" the officer continued, half to her and half to himself. "Decent Polish people have to hang on to the sides and the roofs, while these cursed traitors spread themselves out easy. Where are you going to, eh?"

Asa Heshel got to his feet. "It's none of the lieutenant's business," he said, again surprised at his own courage. The officer started, his thick neck flushed red. The blood rushed to his cheeks, to his low forehead, and to his ears, which lay close to his head.

"What!" he shouted. "We'll soon find out." He thrust his hand to his pants pocket and brought it forward again, holding a revolver, small, toy-sized. The old woman's jaundiced face turned white. The two younger women made an attempt to grab his elbow. He shoved them away with a heave of his shoulders. "Talk up," he roared, "or I'll shoot you like a dog."

"Go on and shoot."

"Conductor! Police!" the lieutenant began to yell. He knew that the revolver wasn't loaded. The landowner shouted with him. Asa Heshel reached up and grabbed his valise, whether to hurry away or to use it as a weapon it was hard to tell. The women began to shout for help. A crowd immediately gathered on the platform outside the car. A helmeted policeman came up, his sword in a black sheath. The lieutenant opened the car door and leaped out.

"This Jew's insulted me. He comes from Russia. A Bolshevik. I've witnesses."

"Come along to the station," the policeman said immediately.

"I've not insulted anybody. I'm on my way to Warsaw to my family."

"We'll see about that."

Asa Heshel took his bag and climbed out of the train. The policeman asked some questions of the officer, making notes in a small notebook. At that moment the station master blew his whistle loudly. The lieutenant darted over to Asa Heshel and, standing behind him, hit him a hard blow with his

clenched fist. Immediately after that he jumped onto the train.
One of the women threw out a crumpled hat at Asa Heshel's
feet. The policeman took Asa Heshel by the wrist.

"What's been happening?" he said. "Don't you know
enough not to start any trouble with officers?"

He moistened his lips with the tip of his tongue, rubbed his
thumb against his first two fingers, and whispered something in
Asa Heshel's ear. Asa Heshel put his hand in his pocket. It all
happened very quickly. The train had already started to
move. Asa Heshel handed the policeman a banknote. The policeman grabbed Asa Heshel's bag, put it on the steps of the
moving car, and Asa Heshel seized the handrails and leaped
up, bruising his knee against the iron stair. He held on to a
side rail while the train gathered speed, puffing and squeaking
along the tracks. There was an alarmed cry from inside and
the car door opened. Asa Heshel pushed himself in. He found
himself in a third-class car. The car was crowded. A tall Jew
picked up his bag and helped him in.

"A narrow escape, eh?" the tall Jew said. "You can thank
God."

CHAPTER TWO

1

From Byalistok Asa Heshel had sent Hadassah a telegram,
but he was not sure that she had received it. He had heard
that in Poland the censorship held up letters and telegrams.
Now he stood in the railroad station and stared about him.
Red-capped porters scurried through the cars, squabbling
over the baggage. There was a dazzle of electric lights, inten-
sifying the darkness. In the main hall of the station long lines
stood before the ticket windows, guarded by Polish police.
Soldiers lay snoring on the floor, the soles of their shoes thickly studded with nails. Others stood at the lunch counter drinking beer out of steins. It took Asa Heshel quite a time to find
the baggage room, to deposit his suitcase. He had intended to
come out on Marshalkovska Street, but found himself, instead, in a square at the rear. Issuing from the square, he ran
into a wild confusion of droshkies, automobiles, and push-
carts. He turned right and almost collided with a horse's head;
there came to him a blast of equine sweat and breath. He

turned left and was dazzled by the headlights of a car, which passed so close that he felt the heat of it and was almost bowled over by the sharp smell of gasoline. When he finally emerged on Marshalkovska Street he found it densely crowded. He stood still for a moment and took a deep breath.

Yes, this was it! Warsaw!

He looked up at the glowing sky. He had come through everything: the barracks, the war, the Revolution, hunger, typhoid, pogroms, arrests. He was back in Warsaw, the city that had woven about him the mysterious nets of love, hope, and happiness and then had flung him forth, as Asmodeus had flung forth King Solomon in the fable. Was it possible that he was not even thirty? Was it conceivable that here, in these streets, there were his mother, Dinah, Abram, Hertz Yanovar, Gina, Hadassah? Was she actually here, in the flesh? Whereabouts was Sienna Street, where Adele lived? His child was there, his, Asa Heshel's son, whom he had never set eyes on. Good God! He had put forth roots in this metropolis: he was someone's father, someone's son, brother, husband, lover, uncle! No ruffianly little army officer could change that fact, which was part of the history of the cosmos.

He hastened on without knowing whether he was making for Krulevska Street or for Mokotov. Perfumed women in bright-colored dresses, with flowered hats, walked with dancing steps. Students of various fraternities, in braid-embroidered caps, marched three and four abreast, taking up the whole sidewalk. Newly created army officers with long swords dangling at the waist saluted one another. Music poured from the cafes. Mannequins stood in the shop windows. Asa Heshel stopped under a lamp, drew out a little notebook, and looked through the faded addresses. His head began to ache. He was filled with impatience.

At the corner of Krulevska Street, not far from the stock exchange, Asa Heshel saw a little café. Excited voices came through the open door. Inside, at marble-topped tables, merchants argued and gesticulated; they were of all kinds: some wore the long Jewish coat, others wore jackets; some wore soft hats, others hard derbies; there were the clean-shaven, the long-bearded, the short-bearded. Many of them were engaged in examining, through a magnifying glass screwed into the eye, diamonds that were passed rapidly from hand to hand; it seemed quite extraordinary that the stones did not get lost. Foreheads perspired, eyes sparkled joyously. There was a glint of gold-filled teeth. A perverse thought came into Asa

Heshel's mind, born of the sheer spirit of confusion: "Here they are, the famous international Jews, the Ahasueruses! How like the caricatures of them drawn by the anti-Semites!" He entered and began to look through the telephone book. There was a clear plan in his mind. He was not going immediately to his mother's; it would not do for Adele to know that he was back. He had to see Hadassah first. He kept turning the pages and could not find Fishel Kutner's name. Was it possible that he had no telephone? Then suddenly he perceived that Fishel Kutner's name occurred not just once, but three times: the home, the store, the office. "How on earth did I miss it?" He took out a pencil and noted the home number. Then he lifted the receiver, but there was no answer from the operator. Somewhere in the distance two stifled female voices were carrying on a conversation. It occurred to him that the talk of ghosts must sound like that. At last the exchange girl answered and he gave her the number. His heart began to thump painfully, and his throat contracted. He heard a high-pitched man's voice. "Hello! Who is that, please?"

"Is this the home of Hadassah Kutner?"

"What do you want?"

"Can she come to the telephone?"

"She's not in town. . . . Who is that?"

"I'm—oh, a friend of hers."

There was a brief silence, and then the high-pitched voice —it was Fishel's—repeated: "She's not in town." The receiver was replaced.

Now, when it was too late, it occurred to Asa Heshel that he ought to have asked where she was. He began to make his way out of the café, stumbling against the tables as he walked. So the road to Hadassah was closed off. She was somewhere in the country, on holiday. The last postcard he had received from her had taken half a year to reach him. At the door of the café a young man with a little yellow beard, and in the clothes of a Chassid, stopped him. "Anything to exchange?"

Asa Heshel heard the words distinctly, but did not grasp their meaning. "What shall I exchange?"

"Dollars, pounds, kroners, marks. You'll get more than at the bank."

"I'm sorry; I've got nothing. I've just come from Russia."

The young man scrutinized him from head to foot. "From Bolshevik-land, eh?"

"Yes, from there."

"Things are bad, aren't they?"

"They're not good."

"They don't let Jews remain Jewish, do they?"

"It's hard."

"It's not good here, either. They've all got one idea—to make life impossible for the Jews."

The young man turned and clumped away in his heavy boots.

2

Abram was not at home. A young woman's voice answered the telephone, speaking Polish.

"May I know who's calling?"

"Oh, I don't think the gracious lady will remember me. I've been away from Warsaw quite a number of years. My name is Asa Heshel Bannet."

"Oh, but I do remember you. I'm Abram's daughter, Stepha."

"Yes, we met once."

"Father isn't home. If you need him urgently I can give you a telephone number where you can reach him. Would you like to write it down? He speaks of you often."

"Thank you. How have things gone with you?"

"Oh, not badly. I'm married, you know. Are you staying in Warsaw?"

"For the time being."

Asa Heshel thanked the young woman, hung up, then made another call. Again a woman's voice answered, but not a young one this time. Asa Heshel waited. There seemed to be some sort of discussion or celebration going on in the room. There were loud voices and laughter. Suddenly Abram's voice thundered into the telephone, so that Asa Heshel had to snatch the receiver away from his ear.

"What? Is that you?" bellowed Abram. "Good God! Am I actually seeing your face—I mean, hearing your voice? Praised be God, who resurrects the dead! I was absolutely certain you weren't above ground any more. A man picks himself up and vanishes, and not a word from him, year after year! Somebody must have rubbed the magician's lamp! Where are you? Where are you talking from? Where the devil have you kept yourself? I thought maybe you'd become a commissar, or a Cheka agent. Well, what are you waiting for? Why don't you come over? And why don't you say something? God, what a sensation you're going to make!"

"I just arrived this evening. I'm in a café on Krulevska Street."

"Oho, on the black market! Where's your baggage?"

"I left my suitcase at the station."

"Well, what are you standing there for, like a graven image? Grab a taxi and come over. I mean, if you have the money for one. Or else take a streetcar. I'm on Holy Cross Street, number seven. Ask for Mrs. Ida Prager in the studio. You don't even have to ask. You'll see it yourself. It's got a skylight. Who gave you my phone number?"

"Your daughter, Stepha."

"No, that's impossible. Anyway, come on over. And how on earth did you find Stepha? I've been looking for her all over. Gets married and forgets she ever had a father. What a rascal you are, not to have written me even once! I mean, before the Revolution."

"The mail wasn't going through."

"Oh, yes it was. You wrote to Hadassah all right, damn your eyes. So what's happened? Have you become a Bolshevik?"

"Not yet."

"Scoot over here at once."

Asa Heshel left the café. His feet were lighter now. He asked a bystander what streetcar to take and then rode slowly down from Krulevska Street. The gate to the courtyard into the house on Holy Cross Street was not closed. Asa Heshel looked up and saw a lighted skylight on the slanted roof. He went up. He did not need to knock; Abram was standing at the door, tall, broad-shouldered, stooping a little, his beard half gray, his face a deep red, as if sunburned. Behind the bushy brows two young black eyes sparkled. "You!"

Abram threw himself at Asa Heshel and embraced him. His breath was heavy with the smell of cigars.

"Look at him! Here he is, right out of hell. What's the matter? Have you grown taller or have I shrunk? Brother, I'm an old man now, that's all there is to it! What are you standing at the door for, like a beggar? Come on in. It's our own crowd. Where the hell have you been? Look at him! He's still wearing a hat and an overcoat! I thought you'd be wearing a cap and blouse. So Czar Nicholas got his! We lived to see the end of him! And the bourgeoisie are street-sweepers now, eh? The

Messiah's come—Judah Leon Trotsky himself. And here in Poland we're getting it in the neck."

"I know."

"Oh, you do? Did you get your share yet? How the devil did you get here? What train did you take? I suppose you don't give a damn for us any more, but we haven't forgotten you. You have a son here, haven't you? Well, let me tell you, he's too damn good for you. I saw him a little while ago, I don't remember where. A big lad. Looks just like his father, two peas in a pod. A clever brat. Tell me, brother," and for a moment Abram lowered his voice, "have you seen Hadassah yet?"

"No."

"Well, you'll be seeing her. She's more beautiful than ever. Become a grand lady. She's been living in Otwotsk for several years. She was sick; the doctors sent her to a sanatorium. Then she stayed on—what's she got in Warsaw, anyhow? In Otwotsk she's got not a house but a palace. Fishel's made a terrific amount of money. He got the Moskats into his hands and gobbled them up. Money just rolls toward him. But what's the good? She hates the sight of him. Where are you living? I mean, are you going to stay with your mother? Let me see now, you have a mother, haven't you?"

"Yes, on Franciskaner Street."

"Have you been there yet?"

"No, not yet."

"Eh? The same old Asa Heshel! What's the sense of it? Don't think I'm going to lecture you. What I say is, to hell with everything, to hell with the whole world! I'm still the same Abram. I've had my ups and downs, too. I nearly became a millionaire, and now I haven't a penny to my name. I'm too trusting, that's what it is. I've had influenza and I've had inflammation of the lungs; the burial society was already licking its chops, but you know how it is when God wants to work a miracle. Seems they've got as much use for me up there as down here. You know what I'd like to do? Pack up and go to Palestine. Not to die, like the old pious Jews, but to take a look at the Jewish country. What d'you think of the Balfour Declaration? They were dancing in the streets here. This studio is Ida Prager's. I think I told you once—a great artist. Well, why don't you come in? They won't eat you up."

"Could you come down with me for a little while?"

"What? Whom are you scared of? Nobody's going to report you."

"My record's all clean. It's something else. You see, I want to be in Warsaw a couple of days before Adele finds out about it."

"Oho, is that the kind of bird you are? I get the idea. Come in—none of the family's here. I'll introduce you to Ida. That's all rubbish about your being found out. Nobody here knows your wife. I tell you there isn't another woman like Ida anywhere in the world. You can laugh, if you like, but it's only now, when I'm getting on in years, that I'm beginning to understand the real meaning of love."

Abram took Asa Heshel by the elbow and led him down a corridor to a large room with a skylight. The walls were covered with canvases stretched on wooden frames. Here and there a piece of sculpture wrapped in burlap stood on a pedestal. There had apparently been an exhibition of some sort. The paintings were in every genre: realist, cubist, futurist. Some figures were standing on their heads and others floated in the air. The studio was filled with young men and women. Couples talked secretively in corners. Two women wrapped in one shawl sat on a chaise-lounge and shared a cigarette.

A little man in a velvet coat, with a huge shock of hair and no neck, was speaking loudly, emphasizing his remarks with a stubby finger. "Forms are like women. They grow old, wrinkled, withered. What meaning has a Matejko for us today? What can we, in our stormy, revolutionary age, get out of a Poussin, a David? The old art is dead!"

"Rappaport, you can say anything you like, but please don't insult old women," called out a woman. "I hope you understand why."

There was laughter and applause. Abram stamped his foot impatiently.

"Hey, loud-mouth, have you still got your trap open? Once upon a time, painters used to paint; now all they can do is gabble. Matejko's no good and you're a first-rater! Why, you idiot, you can't even draw a radish!"

"There he goes! Gets offensive right away."

"Ida, darling, I want to introduce you to a young man. We've often spoken about him—Asa Heshel Bannet, Hadassah's friend."

Ida Prager, a gray-haired woman in a black dress, with a string of pearls on her throat and diamond studs in her ears, lifted a lorgnon which hung on a chain. "So you're Asa Heshel. I know you, of course, I've heard so much about you. When did you get here?"

"Today."

"From Russia?"

"I got here from Bialystok."

"That's really sensational! What's the news over there? You know, one who comes from these parts is like one who has returned from the other world."

"Just what I said!" broke in Abram. "Ida, darling, I want to tell you something," and he took her aside to whisper to her.

"Why, he can sleep here."

"That's not a bad idea. And what about eating? Wouldn't do you any harm to gain ten pounds, Asa Heshel."

"I'm not hungry."

"Where you come from, everyone's hungry. I'll make you something to eat," Ida said.

"Wait, Ida darling. We'll go downstairs. We've got to have a good talk. After all these years. I was the one who introduced him to the family. Who'd have thought it would lead to this mess? Hey, you, Rappaport"—Abram threw his voice across the room—"tear the old masters down, make mincemeat of them. Some day they'll throw the Leonardos, Rubenses, and Titians out of the Louvre and put in your long-nosed caricatures."

Ida made a gesture of indignation. "Abram, shame on you! You can't talk like that. You forget he's my guest. Don't pay any attention to him, Rappaport. He really doesn't mean it."

Rappaport came over. "I've got nothing against him. He represents the viewpoint of his class."

"Come on, Asa Heshel. If I stay a minute longer I'll tear out a handful of his curls. What's *your* class? You're just as much of a bourgeois as I am."

"You've still got their psychology."

"Dauber! D'you think that because they shot Nicholas that makes you a master? David is old and you're new. You ought to wash your mouth before you dare mention his name!"

"Abram, I won't stand for that," cried Ida, angrily.

"All right, all right, we're going. Every tenth-rater jumps on the revolutionary band-wagon and sets himself up as a genius. Bunglers! Fakers! My grandson paints better than you!"

Abram flung out of the room. Asa Heshel turned to say good-by to Ida. She held out a slender hand and smiled at him. The corners of her eyes were filled with wrinkles, and a double chin showed above her throat. Here and there the rouge had cracked, like whitewash on a wall. There was a deep sorrow in her look, the despair of one whose life had become entangled in an error that it was now too late to set right.

"You'll come back, won't you? Don't let him run around. He should be in bed by now."

Ida shook her head, as if intimating that Abram was much sicker than he knew.

3

As they emerged from the courtyard Abram came to a halt and banged on the pavement with his cane. "And now, my lad, let's have the truth. It's five years since you disappeared as if the devil had swallowed you up. And how about eating? Or did you lose the habit? There's a restaurant across the way."

It was a non-Jewish place, a combination of a saloon and food shop, with red hangings on the walls. To the right as they came in was a large poster showing a Bolshevik with a little goatee—half Judas, half Trotsky—thrusting a bayonet into the back of a blonde Polish woman with a snub nose, a cross on her breast, and a child in her arms. Behind the counter, on which were ranged roast ducks and cakes, stood a thickset little man with a shining bald head and upturned, beer-colored mustaches.

"Good evening, Panie Marianie," shouted Abram in Polish. "Where's Joseph? I'm dying of hunger. And this young fellow here also wants to eat."

"Good evening, gentlemen. Please sit down. I'll serve you myself. Today we have sausages and sauerkraut—first class! Or perhaps the gentlemen would prefer soup?"

"I'd like soup, please," said Asa Heshel.

"As for me, Panie Marianie, be good enough to give me a glass of brandy and a sausage."

"Certainly, Panie Abram. A good one. I understand."

"And now talk," said Abram to Asa Heshel. "You can be quite open with me. Hadassah has told me everything—I mean she told me some time ago. Now her father confessor is Hertz Yanovar. He married Gina. I guess you know that. That Kalischer woman is gone, thank God. When you left, Hadassah fell very sick. Her mother died about that time, and her father got married to some poisonous sort of creature. He was always a half-wit; the woman walks all over him. His own daughter avoids him. She never visits him and he never visits her. And as for Fishel, somebody really ought to put him in a book. He's as pious as all hell and makes loads of money. When the Germans came, he made himself useful to them. Now that the Poles have a government of their own, he makes money from them. The moment he buys, the exchange goes up; the moment he sells, it drops. Hausse and Biasse, bulls and bears! We've got a new lingo here. Anyway, that man bought and sold and juggled until he'd stripped everybody. And he's really not a bad kind of fellow. As a matter of fact he's the only support of the Bialodrevna rabbi. Nobody understands why he hangs on to Hadassah—he gets absolutely nothing out of her. There's something crazy between you and Hadassah. If you were so mad about her you shouldn't have let yourself be drafted."

"I'd do it again rather than cut off a finger or take my teeth out."

"You could have gone into hiding. When the Germans arrived, all the deserters came out like rats."

"I didn't want to be a rat."

"All right, you've paid the price for it. When a man's in his early twenties he has time for everything. Now tell me, where the hell did you keep yourself? What happened?"

"I was in the army until a couple of weeks before the Bolshevik Revolution. We retreated all the way from the Carpathians to the Ukraine."

"Quite a trip, if you ask me. Where were you when the Bolsheviks got into the saddle?"

"In a village near Ekaterinoslav."

"What did you do?"

"I was a tutor in a wealthy Jewish family. The man had bought an estate there after the Kerensky Revolution."

"And then?"

"It's all confused. We didn't learn of the Revolution until the middle of November. The Bolsheviks confiscated the estate. The men formed an *ispolkom* and shot a couple of officers. Then came some Drozdov bandits and shot the *ispolkom*. After that, I think the Austrians came. I could have sneaked through to Warsaw, but I fell sick with typhoid fever. That was when Skoropadsky was in power."

"Always in the same village?"

"No, I went over to the city. I was planning to leave, but I had a relapse. Meanwhile Denikin's troops came, and after them Machno's—and then the Bolsheviks broke through again, and after that Denikin came back . . ."

"Is it really as bad as they say with the Bolsheviks?"

"It's everybody against everybody. Hobbe's philosophy in practice."

"Did you see Petlura's pogroms?"

"I saw everything. The entire human tragedy."

"We've seen things here, too. I'm far from being a Bolshevik, but they couldn't let the Czarist bandits take over again."

"The Czarist bandits weren't all they killed."

"I thought you might have become one of them yourself."

"No, Abram, never. How is Hadassah? When did you see her last?"

"I haven't seen her for some time. She's all right. Reading books and doing nothing. Hertz Yanovar has become a real parasite. Founded some kind of society, and all of us are members. He asks everyone about his dreams, writes them down, and sends them to England. There they pickle them, I suppose. Hadassah is his main supporter. She tried to do something for the Zionists, too. She's better now, but she's a sick girl. Tell me, what's your philosophy? What is one supposed to do?"

"I have no philosophy."

"You don't believe in Spinoza any more?"

"Yes. But what's the good of it?"

"I don't want to interfere in your business, but Hadassah wants to get a divorce, marry you, and have a couple of children."

"I refuse to have any children. About that my mind is made up."

"What a mess! You have a nice son. Whenever I see him, I have to laugh. Asa Heshel number two. I can understand everything you've said. It's a mood, and it'll pass. What about Zionism? You used to be a Zionist."

"I don't believe we'll be left in peace unless we're strong."

"We may become strong."

"How? We've been trying for three thousand years."

"So what kind of God is yours? He can't be a fool."

"You can't see His wisdom when you look at a tortured child, all covered with lice, or when you're squeezed into a cattle car and you have to do your needs through a window."

"Suppose some good comes from all this evil?"

"What good?"

"Better conditions."

"I don't care, Abram, and that's the truth. I've made up my mind that the human race is no more important than flies or bedbugs. I couldn't have lived through all these years without that thought."

"Cold comfort! And anyway, even bedbugs would improve their conditions if they could."

"When conditions are better, more brats are born, and the need is just the same."

"What do you advise—birth-control?" asked Abram.

"If it could be applied internationally."

"Nobody could control the Chinese."

"So they will have to stay hungry."

"You certainly know how to twist things. You haven't grown up at all. What did you do there? What are you going to do here for a living?"

"I did many things. I was even a teacher in a People's University in Kiev. They all became professors."

"Do you still remember Polish?"

"The family with whom I lived came from Poland. The girls spoke only Polish."

"If you're serious about Hadassah, you'll sooner or later have to provide for her. You'll have to give something for your son. I guess your mother may need help, too."

"Yes, Abram, I know the situation."

"A bad situation. You don't look well."

"I haven't slept for days. I can't tell you what difficulties I had on this journey."

"I see it. That's the reason I'm not asking too many questions. I hope you didn't leave any bastards there."

"I didn't go that far."

"Well, Hadassah is in Shvider. I think I told you. Her villa is called Rozkosh. It's actually between Otwotsk and Shvider. How are the two of you going to get together?"

"Hasn't she a telephone?"

"No. You'll have to stay with me tonight. Bring your suitcase from the station. You can still get a streetcar. If the courtyard gate is closed, tell the janitor that you're going up to the studio. He's one of our people; we grease his palm every now and then."

Abram rose from his chair. Asa Heshel saw his face become distorted. It took him awhile to straighten out and walk to the door.

4

Asa Heshel stood outside the restaurant and stared into the
night. It was a queer thing, but he had no desire to see his
mother, or his child, or to return to Abram's house. He was
even frightened by the idea of meeting Hadassah. His head
ached, and there was a dryness in his throat and in the back
of his nose. "What's wrong with me," he asked himself. "Am
I going to be sick, or what?" He reflected that it was getting
very late—too late to return to Ida Prager's. But his legs refused to budge. "What did I say to Abram? Am I really as
desperate as that?" A drunk in bedraggled clothes came out of
Yassne Street, stopped at the gutter, and urinated. A policeman with a saber and a black helmet came from Marshalkovska Street. Asa Heshel turned to leave. He did not have a
passport; all he had was his birth certificate, tattered, patched,
and half illegible. He reached the Marshalkovska and saw a
streetcar approaching from Krulevska Street. "It's really very
simple," he thought; "just throw myself on the rails, with my
head under the wheels." No, he might survive, a cripple. The
car dashed by, rocking and roaring, as if it suspected his suici-
dal impulse. Asa Heshel crossed the street. A bevy of streetwalkers appeared from somewhere, rouged, powdered, bedi-
zened, in red stockings, and with cigarettes between their lips.
They were laughing and screeching; evidently there had been
some kind of row, perhaps a police raid. Asa Heshel heard a
police whistle. He stuck his hand into his back pocket. Where
was his baggage check? Lost? Here it was, in his other pocket.
He took out his handkerchief and wiped the perspiration from
his face. "Let me imagine I'm already dead," he thought.
"One of those who wander about in the world of chaos. Nothing more can happen to me, neither good nor evil."

He reached the railroad station. The main room, vast,
brightly lit, was not so crowded now. The light shimmered
from the lamps like golden nets. A sound of snoring came
from the benches. There were lines still in front of the ticket
windows. Policemen walked to and fro, their rifles slung over
their backs. In another hall a detachment of soldiers waited in
full kit, probably ready to be shipped to the front. Asa Heshel
watched one soldier take a cigarette from a comrade's lips,
draw in deeply, and exhale the smoke through his nostrils. A
long, bony soldier, with a freckled face and green, watery lit-

tle eyes, laughed heartily, showing a mouthful of wide-spaced teeth. How could he laugh, Asa Heshel wondered, when he was being sent to be slaughtered, like an animal? What sort of faith did *he* have? Was it the faith of Polish patriotism? No, just healthy nerves. His father and grandfather had not spent their days sitting in the study house, bent over the Talmud.

5

He stood before the zinc-covered counter in the baggage room, holding the check in his hands. But no one was about. All kinds of valises lay on the shelves—large ones, small ones, leather, wood, with locks, with hasps and staples, with outside pockets. "In the midst of the cosmos," he thought, "this little system exists by itself, a thing apart, with its own laws and values. It turns with the earth's turning on its axis, it circles about the sun, it wanders with the wandering of the galactic system in endless space." Strange, very strange! A young Pole with a long face came in at a side door. Asa Heshel handed him the check, and the other dragged the suitcase down from one of the shelves. Asa Heshel lifted it. Why was it suddenly so heavy? Just as if someone had put stones in it. Where was he to get a streetcar? Perhaps he would have to take a drosh-ky. The big clock showed five minutes to midnight. Now he regretted the time he had lost. He felt deeply ashamed to go with the suitcase to Ida Prager's house. Might it not be better to go home, to his mother's? Yes, that was what he would do. At that instant he heard a woman ask: "When does the express leave for Otwotsk?"

"Twelve fifteen."

The instant he heard these words Asa Heshel decided to go to Otwotsk, exactly as he was. Fishel was in Warsaw. Hadassah was alone there with the maid. What was the name of the villa? Rozkosh. The idea seemed to him to be so clever that he was astonished he had not thought of it before. Why should he beg shelter from Ida Prager? He had a sweetheart, had he not? He saw the woman who had asked about the train to Ot-wotsk taking her place in the line of ticket-buyers. He put down the valise (now no longer under the protection of the baggage man) and stood behind the woman. Could he manage it in seventeen minutes? Would he be able to find Hadassah's villa? What would the maid say? The whole thing was crazy. He kept one eye on his suitcase, the other on the ticket window. The ticket-seller seemed to be taking his time. A broad-shouldered man stood at the window, bending over, apparently getting information. The big hand on the station clock stood paralyzed for a little while, then moved forward. The men and women in the line began to mutter. What was happening? "Is the man asleep?" asked a little Pole with long mustaches. "Our Polish officials!" growled a thickset man whose nose looked as if it had been split in the middle. "Hey, panie, faster!" shouted someone. "I hope he isn't a Jew!" flashed through Asa Heshel's mind. The man in front, as if feeling that everyone was against him, bent over deeper. Asa Heshel, too, felt enmity toward that broad-backed person who blocked everyone's path and was bringing his plan to naught. Such persons should be killed! At that instant the man straightened out. He was lame and had to use a crutch. The feelings of anger were touched with something akin to shame. Now the line began to move rapidly. Asa Heshel got out the money for his ticket. But what was he to do with his suitcase? Take it along? No, that was senseless. He'd have to check it again. The lad in the baggage room would definitely think him out of his mind. If only he could take out a shirt and a toothbrush. His face was covered with a thick stubble.

He got his ticket and hurried to the baggage room. Again the lad was absent. Now everything was lost. There were only five minutes left. Where in God's name did that wretched idiot keep disappearing to? Why didn't he stay on the job? That's how the world was—full of dawdlers. He might very well be gone for a full half hour, the swine. But there he was, suddenly. Asa Heshel handed him the suitcase, and the other turned a pair of astonished eyes on him, then asked for ten pfennigs. He fiddled around with the string that fastened the ticket to the bag. Less than three minutes now. Asa Heshel snatched the check and ran wildly to the door. The conductor, with his spectacles pushed down to the tip of his nose, seemed to be ready to close the gate and pulled a face as he punched two holes in the ticket. The train was still standing at the platform. A young man ran in front of Asa Heshel. A woman laden with packages also tried to run, her hips and buttocks swinging. She reminded Asa Heshel of a cow. He overtook her and jumped aboard. He held the door open for her. There was a mixture of goodwill and malice in him: he wanted the woman to get aboard the train, but he was also aware of a childish desire to see her left behind.

The train remained standing for almost another two min-

utes. It was apparently setting out on a long trip. The racks
were filled with valises, baskets, sacks. Most of the passengers
were leaning back against the headrests of the seats, trying to
doze. The benches were crowded. In the air there was already
the sweet-sour odor of mid-journey and sleeplessness. Asa Heshel stationed himself at a window. How queer, he thought,
were the twists in the chain of causality. He had only just
come to Warsaw, and here he was, leaving it. Who knew but
what he would again be away for five years. Everything was
possible. Suppose he were suddenly to get a hemorrhage in
Otwotsk, and were to be taken to a sanatorium? What insane
thoughts! What would happen if he were going through the
forest and were to come across the miserable little officer who
had beaten him up? Suppose that the officer was unarmed and
he himself had a revolver? Would he shoot him down? Was it
proper to invoke the law "Thou shalt not kill" in such a case?
The Ten Commandments lacked all preciseness. He who had
said "Thou shalt not kill" should also have said "Thou shalt
not beget."

The train began to move. Asa Heshel looked out: a midnight city, with somnolent factories, houses, squares. What
would Abram say when he discovered that he had not returned? There was the Vistula! How oddly the lights were reflected in the water, like memorial candles. The river carried
on at its appointed task; it flowed from Kracow to the sea.
Nothing mattered to it—capitalism, Bolshevism, Russians,
Germans, Paderewski, Pilsudski, Christians, Jews. . . . What
was Hadassah doing now? Did she have a premonition that he
was coming to her? Perhaps this very day, she had resolved to
put him forever out of her mind. Perhaps she had guests. Perhaps she had a lover. Everything was possible. If time was
nothing more than a mode of perception, then history consisted merely in turning the pages of a book that had long ago
been completed. "If I at least had a clean handkerchief! If I
had at least shaved! They hate kissing a bristly jaw."

The engine bellowed like an ox and spat out rolls of smoke.
Clouds of steam dashed by. Sparks flew through the air like
shooting stars. Somewhere in the car a Pole was complaining
angrily and cursing the Jews. *"Zhydy! Zhydy!"* The word was
taken up by the others. What were they so infuriated about?
What had the Jews done to them? They blamed them for
everything. If the baggage swayed, if the lamp flickered, if
the water-closet was occupied. A woman holding an infant on
a cushion cried: "Here, you little bastard, take my breast!"

"Madame excuse me," said someone, "maybe he has stomach-ache, or he's raw between the legs and has to be powdered." The mother took out her swollen breast and offered it to the infant. "He's biting my nipple, the little beast."

The train fled rapidly, without a stop, through Miedzeshin, Falenitz, Michalin, Usefov, Shvider. Here was Otwotsk. Asa Heshel tried to get off, but the door would not open. "Hey, pull harder! Those feeble Jewish hands!" The door gave, and he got off. Scattered lamps glimmered in the surrounding darkness, throwing yellow nets on the sand. The air was laden with pine, wood-fires, tuberculosis. How many people died here every day? Every sanatorium had its little morgue. Asa Heshel asked a passer-by for the road to Shvider. Down the Warsaw road, he was told, and then to the left. What on earth had made Fishel name his villa Rozkosh—pleasure? Did Fishel, too, believe in the pleasure principle? Asa Heshel stopped another passer-by. "Where is the villa Rozkosh?" No answer. Deaf! Or perhaps dumb. Hadassah was surely asleep by now. What a crazy adventure! "If only I don't go impotent! That would be a real tragicomedy. The impotent lover! I mustn't think about it. The very thought is dangerous. There's a devil inside me. Why isn't the moon shining? It's mid-month, I'm pretty certain."

Was he still in Otwotsk or had he reached Shvider? Where was the boundary? There was a house! There was no lamp at the entrance.

He stood before the door, which had a sign over it. Was it Rozkosh? The first letter was definitely an *R*. Or was it a *K*? If he only had matches. There was a light upstairs. That might be Hadassah's bedroom. Was the outer door open? Yes, it was open. "I'll be taken for a thief. That would really be funny, if I got arrested for trying to rob Fishel's villa." He suddenly remembered the night when he had sneaked across the Austrian frontier.

He half opened the door and called out: "Hadassah!"

It seemed to him that the light in the upper room had moved. She was there! It was she! "We'll see in a moment if I have intuition!" He waited awhile and then called again: "Hadassah!"

A roaring and thundering gradually filled the air; a train was rounding the rails toward the house. The headlights threw two pillars of light on it. He saw everything as if it had been suddenly projected on a screen; the house, the veranda, the paths between the flowerbeds, the stunted pine trees marked with white numbers. He looked up at the sign; yes, it was Rozkosh! The train passed and darkness returned. From afar came a distant screech, as of a demon who had played someone a low trick and then vanished into the night.

CHAPTER THREE

1

Preparations for the Sabbath were under way at Finkel's flat on Franciskaner Street. Dinah had already carried the Sabbath stew to the baker's and had washed and combed the children, Tamar and Jerachmiel. In the middle room Finkel was setting the table, fixing the candles in the seven candlesticks, silver and brass. She performed the ritual blessing over two candles, for herself and Asa Heshel. Dinah blessed the other five, for herself, Menassah David, Tamar, Jerachmiel, and the newborn child, named after his departed great-grandfather, Dan. The food was already prepared in the kitchen, the soup with rice and beans, the stewed meat in its savory gravy, the carrots. The gefuelte fish was cooling on a large platter, garnished with onions and parsley. In front of the candles Finkel placed two freshly baked loaves, covered with an embroidered cloth. Near them lay a pearl-handled knife. On the blade the words "Holy Sabbath" were engraved. In the middle of the table stood a carafe of currant wine and the special beaker for the ritual blessing. On the beaker was engraved a likeness of the Wailing Wall in Jerusalem. Finkel and Dinah lived a thrifty life. The family income was earned from the sewing Dinah did and the lessons her husband, Menassah David, gave. But poverty never shamed the Sabbath. Finkel put on her silk headkerchief, her wide-sleeved blouse, and the flowered dress that she still had from her trousseau. Dinah tied a velvet ribbon around her matron's wig. After both women had lighted the candles, they covered their eyes with their hands and recited the prayer that had been handed down in the family from mother to daughter for generations. "Exalted God, let the glow of Thy countenance shine upon Thy handmaid, my husband, my children, and protect them from all evil. In the merit of the Sabbath candles which I here do light in Thine honor, illuminate us with Thy holy light, pour Thy grace on our Sabbaths and our weekdays, bestow upon us the strength to abide by Thy commandments. And quickly, oh quickly, speed Messiah, the son of the house of David, so that he may redeem us, speedily and in our days, amen, selah. . . ."

While the women were performing their rituals Menassah David dressed himself in his Sabbath clothes. His coarse boots were polished in honor of the holy day. He donned his threadbare satin gaberdine and mangy fur hat. He was a short, broad-boned man with a reddish beard and pale-yellow sidelocks. His hands and feet were too large for his undersized body. In his early youth he had studied religious law, hoping to become a rabbi. Because of the war he had not received his diploma. Further, he had become a follower of the highly mystic and controversial Rabbi Nachman Bratslaver, whose disciples were known as "Dead Chassidim." A "Dead Chassid" could not easily obtain employment as a rabbi. As he dressed, he smiled and murmured to himself, finally calling out aloud: "Man must not resign himself. Resignation exists not."

"What is it you're shouting, Papa?" little Jerachmiel asked. The boy was three years old. He wore a yellow skullcap, and his curled sidelocks dangled beside his tiny features.

"I say that man must rejoice. Dance, my son! Clap your hands! Joy will triumph over all evil."

"What sort of nonsense is he talking to the child?" Dinah complained from the bedroom. "Are you trying to make him one of your Dead Chassidim?"

"And what about it? The souls of all God's children were assembled at the Sinai mount. Come here, my son. Let me hear you sing the rabbi's melody.

> *Listen not to Satan's voice,*
> *Dance, my little one—rejoice."*

Finkel came into the kitchen. "As true as I live, Menassah David," she said, "you're making yourself foolish. An innocent dove! He's got plenty of time to learn such things."

"Mother-in-law, I tell you there's no time. The Messiah is at our heels. Come, my son, sing with me:

> *If you have sinned, do not be sad.*
> *Repent, and live again, my lad. . . ."*

Finkel looked at her son-in-law with an expression compounded of amusement and dismay and laughed, showing her toothless gums. Dinah came in from the bedroom with the infant in her arms, carrying a black ribbon to tie in little Tamar's braids.

Tamar, the five-year old, had brown hair, a wide little nose, and a face full of freckles. She was clutching a piece of egg cake in her fist. "I don't want the black ribbon," she shrieked. "I want the red one."

The door from the outside corridor opened and a hand set a valise on the floor. Dinah turned pale. "Mamma!" she cried in a startled voice. "Look!"

Finkel turned, confused. Asa Heshel stood inside the doorway.

"My son!"

"Mamma! Dinah!"

"Asa Heshel!"

"Blessed is he who comes! I'm Menassah David. My! To come in right on the eve of the Sabbath!"

"Tamar, this is your Uncle Asa Heshel. This is Jerachmiel —named after the Yanov grandfather. This is little Dan—"

Asa Heshel kissed his mother, his sister, and the children, including the infant in Dinah's arms. Dinah bent down to pick up the valise, but Finkel shouted: "What are you doing? It's the Sabbath!"

"I'm so confused," Dinah said, blushing. "I don't know what I'm doing! So unexpected!"

"Do you know what?" Menassah David interrupted. "Come pray with me. The prayerhouse is right here in the courtyard. Your grandfather—of blessed memory—prayed there."

Menassah David smiled, revealing a mouthful of widely spaced and uneven teeth. An unworldliness that Asa Heshel had long ago forgotten seemed to radiate from his fleshy face.

Dinah showed her impatience. "You're starting that already? He'll say his prayers here at home," she said.

"What harm am I doing him? All I want is to take him to God's holy place. It's never too late to come to God. One good deed outweighs a multitude of sins."

"He's one of these Dead Chassidim," Dinah said apologetically. "You've probably heard of them."

"Yes. The Bratslaver."

"Well, you see," Menassah David remarked, "my rabbi is renowned over the whole wide world. Take my advice and come pray with me. Or, you know what, let's dance."

"Have you gone crazy?" Dinah shrieked. "He'll think you're a lunatic."

"Who knows what is madness and what isn't? A man mustn't be sad. To be melancholy is to be an idolater."

Menassah David raised his thumb and index finger and snapped them. He lifted his foot and began to sway from side to side. It was all Dinah could do to make him leave for his prayers.

Finkel's expression was a mixture of tears and laughter. "That I have lived to see this day!" she murmured. "Praise to the Blessed One."

"Don't cry, Mamma," Dinah pleaded. "It's the Sabbath."

"Yes, I know. I'm weeping for you."

"Look, children, I've brought presents for you," Asa Heshel said. "And for you, Dinah. And, Mamma, for you."

"No. Not now. After the Sabbath."

Little Tamar put a finger in her mouth in embarrassment and held on to a fold of her mother's skirt. Jerachmiel ran to the kitchen-table drawer and took out a spoon. The infant, who had been staring with his wide-open baby gaze, shook his too large head and began to cry. Dinah soothed him.

"Sh—sh. Your uncle has brought you a cookie. Nice, nice cookie."

"The child is hungry. Give it the breast," said Finkel.

Dinah sat down on the edge of the metal bed, near the covered sewing-machine, and fumbled with the buttons of her blouse. Finkel took hold of Asa Heshel's wrist. "Come into the other room. Let me look at you."

She led him into the living-room and closed the door after them. Standing near him, tiny and shrunken, she was like a dwarf alongside a giant. She wanted to spit out as a charm against the evil eye, but she restrained herself. The tears ran down her wrinkled cheeks. "Why did you come so late? It's a shame before the neighbors."

"The train just came in," he lied.

"Well, sit down, my child. Here, on the sofa. Your mother has become an old woman."

"In my eyes you're still young."

"Cares and worries have aged me. How can you know the things that have gone on here? It's a miracle that we're alive. But all that is past and now you are here. Blessed be the Name I am not fit to mention."

She took a handkerchief from the folds of her dress and blew her nose. Asa Heshel looked around the room. The walls were ragged and peeling. Although it was summer, the double windows were closely drawn. There was a sour smell of soap, soda, and diapers.

Finkel opened the old prayerbook and then closed it. "My son, my son! Now it's the Sabbath and you've just arrived. My joy is boundless. God forbid that I should cause you pain now, but still I can't keep quiet."

"What have I done?"

"What you are doing is wrong. You have a wife and a child. It is to them you should have gone first. Woe is me, you don't yet know your own son. A treasure, a sage, may no evil eye—"

"Mother, you know that everything is over between us."

"She's still your wife." Finkel fell into a silence. She folded her hands in front of her and shook her head disapprovingly from side to side. "What have you got against her? She's a dear, devoted woman. And, God help me, she's suffered so much on your account. If you only knew what she has done for us in these hard years, you would realize how you wrong her."

"Mother, I don't love her."

"And the child— Is it the child's fault?"

Finkel opened the prayerbook again and her lips began to move silently. She went over to the eastern wall, where she swayed and bowed. The flames of the lighted candles sputtered and cracked, petals of tallow dripping down their sides.

After the silent prayer Finkel took three steps back from the wall. "Asa Heshel," she said, "since you are here, I wish you too would read the Welcome of the Sabbath. It will certainly do you no harm."

She brought him the prayerbook, the one she had received from her mother-in-law, Asa Heshel's grandmother, the pious Tamar.

2

It was Fishel's long-established custom to close his shop at noon on Friday. He went to the ritual bath and then repaired to the Bialodrevna prayerhouse, where he remained until the Sabbath had set in. Because of the unsettled times and the constant fluctuations of money exchange, Anshel, Fishel's assistant, often came to him in the prayerhouse to ask whether to buy or sell. Fishel would grunt, make vague gestures, and turn away. Nevertheless, Anshel understood what was the proper thing to do. After the evening prayers Fishel would go home, and Anshel would as a rule accompany him. The elderly serving woman, a distant relative of Fishel's, would have prepared the Sabbath meal for both men. Anshel, short and dark, with nearsighted eyes and a beard that almost covered his entire face, had been a widower for years. Fishel's status was like that of a divorced man, for his wife was rarely in Warsaw. Both men would recite the blessings and eat the Sabbath feast, discussing Chassidic matters. In the Bialodrevna prayerhouse the unmarried men would exchange jokes about Fishel, and the women could not seem to understand why he did not put an end to the situation. Surely he could make a brilliant match if he wanted to. Even the Bialodrevna rabbi had more than once let it be known that in his opinion what was happening was not proper.

On this Friday, when Fishel and Anshel reached home after the prayers, the serving woman met them in the corridor and announced that Hadassah had come to Warsaw. Anshel hesitated on the threshold. Fishel showed some confusion, but he quickly recovered his poise. He held fast to Anshel's sleeve, refusing to let him retreat. "Idiot, where are you running to? There'll be enough food for you too."

In the dining-room Fishel and Anshel murmured: "Good Sabbath" to Hadassah. Then they began to pace back and forth over the room, crossing each other's paths. In the traditional fashion they welcomed the good angels who accompany every Jew to his home on the Sabbath. They chanted the verses in praise of the Virtuous Woman from the Proverbs. Fishel sat down at the head of the table, Anshel to his right and Hadassah a little distance away from him at his left. Fishel made the benediction over the wine and handed the beaker to Hadassah so that she might sip of it. He cut the Sabbath loaf and gave a slice to his wife. After the fish both men began to sing Sabbath songs. Fishel poured some brandy for Anshel and took some for himself. "Health!"

"Health, prosperity, and peace!"

"How about you?" Fishel asked, looking toward Hadassah. These were the first words he had spoken directly to her. Hadassah shook her head.

When the meal and the ritual blessing were over, Anshel left. Hadassah went at once to her own room. Fishel paced back and forth, biting his lips. For a while he stood at the window, looking out into the street below. Stars glimmered in the sky. The dark courtyard was crowded with barrels and cases—all his merchandise. Then he opened the bookcase and took out a volume of the Zohar. He turned the pages and read. There were four kinds of souls, the book said, corresponding to the four worlds that God has radiated out of Himself. Usually Fishel and Anshel stayed up late on Friday nights, quoting the rabbi's sage sayings, discussing rabbinical politics, throwing in a remark now and then of more prosaic business matters. But tonight Fishel did not know what to do. Why had she come home? he asked himself. It was not her custom. Maybe she had seen that she was treading a false path. He would forgive her anything, he decided. "I remember thee the kindness of thy youth," he quoted. A man could not always live his life according to strict law.

He opened a volume of the Midrash and sat down at the table. The gas lamp was never lighted on the Sabbath; instead, two candles flickered and an oil lamp. The pages were yellowed and creased, spotted with blobs of tallow. Here and there Fishel noticed a hair lying on the page, plucked from his grandfather's beard. He shuddered. "Surely he has long been in the higher sphere," he thought. "Who knows to what height he has attained?"

As Fishel murmured over the volume, the door opened and Hadassah came in. Before, when she had sat at the table, she had worn a kerchief. Now her head was uncovered, showing her hair combed back over her forehead. It seemed to Fishel that she had become strangely youthful.

"I have to talk to you," Hadassah said.

"What? Sit down."

"I want to tell you that—that we can't go on this way." She seemed to be confused by her own words.

Fishel closed the volume. "What is it you want? The way things are now, you're doing whatever you please."

"I—I—this is no life," Hadassah went on, her voice trembling.

"I won't discuss it now. It's the Sabbath. Can't it wait until tomorrow evening?"

"What difference does it make? I want a divorce. It will be better for you, too."

Fishel's throat went dry. "Why? Has anything new happened?"

"He is here," Hadassah broke out, as though to have it over once for all.

Fishel's face matched the tablecloth in whiteness. "When did he come?"

"A few days ago."

"What of it?" asked Fishel.

"You once promised that if he came back, you would give me a divorce. Now he's here."

Fishel looked at Hadassah's face. The softness that had formerly dwelt in her eyes was no longer there. A gentile toughness emanated from her. "Well, is he willing to have you?" As he spoke, he was aware of a hollowness below his chest.

"We are already man and wife."

"What? He has a wife and child."

"I know all that. We are already living together, at Klonya's mother-in-law's."

"Well, this is different, this is different," Fishel murmured. His cheeks turned red and then white. He had a desire to scream: "Whore! Unclean woman! Leave this house! A thousand curses upon you!" But he restrained himself. First, because it was the Sabbath; then, what good would screaming do? She was already completely depraved, worse than converted. "Why did you have to come today?" he asked. "Did you want to desecrate my Sabbath?"

"He's in Warsaw, too. He came to his mother," Hadassah said, hardly knowing why she told him this.

Fishel pondered and rubbed his forehead. Her words made him think of the confessions of sinful women quoted in the Jewish law books. "I see. I'll give you an answer tomorrow evening."

"Thank you. I'll stay here," said Hadassah. She stood still for a few moments. Then she turned sharply. Fishel looked after her. She took her first steps quickly, as though preparing to run, then she slowed her gait and walked uncertainly toward the door. She held the knob with her left hand, blocking her own exit. Fishel lifted himself as though to call her back. Then he sank back into his chair. "Let it be as it is," he thought. "Who falls into the pit never emerges."

He went into his bedroom. The two beds, one placed at right angles to the other, were made up. There was a fresh smell of lavender from the sheets and coverings. Fishel was not yet tired. Nevertheless he applied himself to the recitation of the nighttime prayers. He undressed and stretched his body out on the cool linen.

He had thought that he would not be able to sleep, but the

moment his head lay against the pillow he fell into a doze. At
first he dreamed he was studying a Talmudic tract in the Bialodrevna prayerhouse; then that dream faded away and he
dreamed instead that the dollar had fallen and that there was
a panic on the Bourse. They were paying ten dollars for a single Polish mark! "What's the sense of it?" he was asking Anshel. "But America's a rich country. It's all speculation." Then
he noticed that Anshel, under his long capote, was wearing a
pair of women's drawers, lace-embroidered at the edges.
"What has happened?" he wondered. "Can it be that Anshel
is a woman after all?"

Suddenly he woke up. It seemed to him that a breeze was
blowing across his face. He opened his eyes. He did not remember what had happened, but he awoke with a feeling of
heaviness in his heart. Or was it his stomach, he wondered.
Then he remembered. Strange, but although Hadassah had
not lived with him as his wife for years, he had always found
comfort in the thought that she was legally bound to him. She
lived in his house, he provided for her needs. He had been
sure that sooner or later she would repent and return to him.
Now everything was different. "We are already man and
wife," the words repeated themselves. He sat up and looked
into the darkness. He knew that according to God's law he
should hate her, but it was not in his nature to hate. It occurred to him that his feeling must be what worldly books call
love. He had a desire to get up, go to her room, plead with
her to have mercy on him and not bring shame on her saintly
mother in paradise. He went so far as to get out of bed and
walk to the door, but there he stopped.

"No, it's no use," he murmured to himself. "Suppose she
were dead," and he heard his voice whispering the prayer for
the dead: "Blessed be the true judges. . . ."

3

Saturday evening Asa Heshel set out for Adele's. He had already spoken with her by telephone. He had also provided
himself with a few things for little David: a tin whistle, a
wooden sword, a few toy soldiers, a bar of chocolate, a bag of
candy. When he left, Dinah was in the kitchen preparing the
Sabbath valedictory meal. The air was filled with the odor of
beets, garlic, and citric salt. His mother had undressed her

grandchildren and was putting them to bed. In the middle of
the room Menassah David stood in his satin gaberdine, a velvet hat covering his skullcap, and he half recited, half sang:

> "The Lord said unto Jacob,
> Fear not, My servant, Jacob,
> The Lord hath chosen Jacob,
> Fear not, My servant Jacob,
> The Lord hath redeemed Jacob,
> Fear not, My servant, Jacob."

His mother asked Asa Heshel whether she should prepare
his bed, but he was not certain that he would return that
night. He had made a midnight appointment with Hadassah.
They might perhaps go by train to Klonya's, in Miedzeshin.
Everything depended on Fishel's answer. Asa Heshel promised his mother that if he did not return that evening he would
send a postcard. He was on the other side of the door before
he had finished talking.

On Nalevki Street he boarded a streetcar. Here in Warsaw
one could still feel in the air the ending of the Sabbath. Chassidim walked in the street wearing their velvet hats. Here and
there one could glimpse through windows the light of candles.
Sienna Street was bleakly illumined by a few gas jets. In the
distance a high factory chimney pierced the heavens. A feeble
old woman was doddering along the sidewalk, carrying a pair
of men's boots in a basket. From an upper floor came the
sound of someone strumming a piano. Asa Heshel stopped for
a moment in his walk. What an immense world! What a variety of destinies! Here he was, going to meet a wife whom he
had never loved, and a child of his on whom he had never set
eyes.

He entered the gate of the courtyard. He remembered the
house in which Adele lived as handsome, but the plaster was
peeling from the walls. In the middle of the yard there was a
glistening garbage box, newly smeared with tar. The windows
were reflected in the asphalt as in a dark pool. He rang the
bell, and heard footsteps. There Adele was, standing at the
door. He scarcely recognized her. She had bobbed her hair
and was wearing a short dress. Her face was white with
powder, her eyebrows were plucked. A distinctive sharpness,
which he had long forgotten, lay on her arched forehead, her

bony nose, her pointed chin. She made a quick gesture as if to embrace him, but stepped back suddenly. "Yes, it's you!"

She led him into the room that he had known years before, when his mother had come to Warsaw. He recognized the carpet, the writing-table, the sofa, even the pictures on the walls.

"Sit down. I've just put David to bed. I want him to fall asleep."

"Yes, I understand."

"You don't look well. I've become stout from the potatoes we ate three times a day. We got swelled up from the water."

"We didn't have any potatoes over there."

"When did you get here? In the middle of the Sabbath?"

"I got here Friday evening."

"Why didn't you telephone?"

"Dinah told me they don't answer the telephone here on the Sabbath."

"What a lie! She knows perfectly well that my mother is in Shvider. Well, I suppose it would have been doing me too much honor. Who am I, after all? Only the mother of your son."

"Could I see him?"

"Not now. He's lying there talking to himself. And is he clever! He asks questions that only a philosopher can answer. Well, tell me about yourself. You don't seem to get any older. I'm all gray. Frankly, I didn't believe you'd ever come back."

"It might very well have happened."

"My stepfather wanted to have me declared a deserted wife. He wanted me to go to the rabbis. As if that was my biggest worry. . . . His son is a doctor, and he thought of marrying us to each other. I'm going to speak openly to you. Why did you come back? To whom? I should think five years was time enough for a man to make up his mind."

"Nothing has changed."

Adele turned a pair of yellow eyes on him. "I understand. You don't have to draw a map for me. I only want you to know one thing: he's your son and you have certain obligations toward him."

"I'll do what I can."

"I'm not asking you for any favors. He's your child legally. I could demand his support for all these years, but what's past is past. He costs me at least thirty marks a week. Everything is terribly scarce. I'd look for work, but he needs me. He goes to school, but I have to take him there and fetch him. Children get run over. My mother is getting very old. Well, what about you? What's become of you?"

"I'm the same rubbish."

She looked at him askance, as if measuring him. Yes, he was still the same Asa Heshel. When he had come in, he had seemed for a second older, but this new expression had immediately disappeared. He still had in his face that mixture of youth and age which she had noticed the first time she met him. God, how David resembled him!—even to the movements of his face. She had a strong desire to bring the boy in to him, but she decided to wait.

"I suppose you had women enough over there," she said, amazed by her own words.

"Sometimes."

"So you weren't faithful even to your beloved Hadassah."

"That has nothing to do with faithfulness."

"No? That's something new to me. Not that I worry about her. What are you going to do now, if I may ask? Are you going to settle down? Fishel will probably divorce her. He can't bear the sight of her any more."

"What about us? Will you let me get a divorce?"

"Why not? But you'd have to pay me."

"You know I have nothing."

"She has. He's given her all sorts of money, the idiot! He's taken away the entire Moskat fortune. You'll be kind enough to get me ten thousand American dollars and sign an agreement to give me fifty marks a week for the child. I mean at the present exchange rate."

"Is that all?"

"Yes, my dear, I loved you once—even more than you know. But everything is dead. Why did you run away into the army? To show Hadassah you're a hero?"

"It's too late to begin it all over again."

"Well, what have you found? What have you reached? What do you expect to do in Warsaw? Become a shoemaker?"

"Excuse me, Adele, but I came to see the child."

"Tell me, when did you actually come? You must have been here the whole week."

"Why do you say that?"

"I know your dodges. The first thing you did was to run off to her, even before you went to your mother."

"It's true."

"What have you got there on your left side? A heart or a stone?"

"A stone."

"Yes, that's it. But why are you like that? Are you really so madly in love with her? Or do you hate everybody else?"

"What difference does it make to you?"

"No difference. But I'm still entitled to know something about you, after five years of absence. My God, it seems to me an eternity!"

"I have nothing to tell."

Nevertheless, after some hesitation he began to speak. She asked and he answered. He told her about his months in the barracks, the almost three years on the battlefront. He was far from being a hero, but he had been in danger many times. He had squatted in trenches. He had had typhoid fever and dysentery. He confessed everything to her: he had gone to prostitutes; he had made love to the daughter of the owner of a sawmill near Ekaterinoslav; he had had an affair with a kindergarten teacher in Kiev. His talk seemed to Adele to be a jumble of unrelated things: Petlura's pogroms and a People's University where he had taught; Denikin's bands and some Hebrew library where he had worked on a catalogue; the Bolshevik Revolution and a book of Hegel's that he was supposed to translate. Adele listened and bit her lip. It was the same old story all over again: starvation, dingy rooms, idle dreams, useless books. He still had neither profession, nor plans; neither real love for anybody, nor responsibility. He looked tired and sad. His eyes were red, as if he had spent sleepless nights. He admitted that he had spent the night of his arrival with Hadassah in Otwotsk. They had later gone to Miedzeshin. They had taken a room there at Klonya's mother-in-law's. Tonight they were supposed to sleep at Hertz Yanovar's. Adele's face turned pale. "You shouldn't have come back. You'll make her unhappy, too."

"I'm afraid so."

"You're crazy, Asa Heshel, crazy to death. You don't run wild in the streets, but you're insane just the same. I have only one hope left—that your son won't take after you."

"Don't worry, he won't. You'll see to it."

"God knows I try. He's already asking the same questions that were an obsession with you. If you have a spark of decency left, see to it that he doesn't have to suffer want in addition."

"Yes, Adele. I'll try. Good night."

"Lunatic! Why are you running away? You came to see the child, didn't you?"

Adele went out. Asa Heshel stood at the window and looked into the courtyard. How dark it was, how gloomy the walls looked against the reddish, starless sky, how empty everything was in him! He was not even eager to see his child. Adele was right, he was insane. He suddenly put out the tip of his tongue and touched the window pane, as if to convince himself that he was really there. Perhaps he should not go to this rendezvous with Hadassah. Maybe she could still return to her husband. What a mad thing to have come back—without a God, without a goal, without a skill! What a frightful responsibility he was taking on himself! Disgraceful as it was, he had already become impatient, even in these few days. "It's all the same thing under different names: impatience, boredom, cruelty, bashfulness, laziness. They are all burdened by the same passion for death; the Reds, the Whites, that Polish officer in the train, Abram, Hadassah. . . ." He heard something behind him. Adele had come in, carrying little David. The child was barefooted and wearing pajamas. He was rubbing his eyes with his fist and staring at his father, pale, astonished.

"That's your *tatush*," Adele said to him in Polish. "And this is your son."

Asa Heshel looked at the boy. In that one instant he saw more than had been revealed in all the photographs Dinah had shown him. The boy resembled him; resembled his grandmother and his great-grandmother. The child scratched his nose hastily. His lips began to quiver, like an infant's, as if he were about to start crying.

"Give Daddy your hand."

"Mamma, I'm sleepy." And little David burst into tears. Asa Heshel unpacked the toys.

"Here. This is a whistle. This is a sword. This is a soldier."

"For real?"

"No, only to play with."

"Mamma, I want to sleep."

"What's the matter with you? Get down. I haven't the strength to carry you."

She put the child down on the carpet. He stood there with his pajama trousers hanging loosely on him, his jacket too big. His head was close-cropped except at the top, where a few blond curls remained. He yawned, stretched himself, and blinked. Asa Heshel watched him, astounded. There was a freshness about the child mingled with a strange maturity. Asa Heshel recognized the cut of his head, the ears, the temples, the premature look of world-weariness in the eyes. A sudden love welled up in him for this cross youngster. In that instant he realized for the first time the meaning of the words "to be a father." "I mustn't," he thought. "I daren't bind myself to him. She'll never stop blackmailing me." He bent down and kissed little David on the forehead.

"David, darling, I'm your daddy. I love you. . . ."

The youngster looked at him slyly, with a touch of the grownup. A smile awoke in his tear-dimmed eyes. "Stay here. . . ."

PART
EIGHT

CHAPTER ONE

During the years that Asa Heshel had spent in the army and later in Russia. Hadassah kept away from the family. Her father had married again. Her aunts Saltsha and Queen Esther sided with Fishel. Of the whole family there were only three cousins who visited her in Otwotsk and whom she occasionally saw in Warsaw: Masha, Stepha, and Pinnie's youngest daughter, Dosha.

Masha had converted to Christianity. Her baptismal father was her father-in-law, Pan Zazhitsky. She went to church daily. Reb Moshe Gabriel observed the week of ritual mourning for his daughter as if she had died. Leah wrote from America that she disowned her. The uncles and aunts spat at the mention of her name. But Hadassah could not hate a woman who had made such a sacrifice for love. For that matter, was she herself any better? Had she not dishonored her marriage vows? Let those who were without sin cast the first stone. Besides, what difference was there between one religion and another? Did not Jews and Christians pray to the same God? When Asa Heshel was in Switzerland, Hadassah had often thought of entering a nunnery and of spending the rest of her life in consecrated solitude, as was done by Christian girls disappointed in worldly things. If she was opposed to apostasy, it was for one reason only: it was the Jews who were the persecuted, not the Christians. If what the Evangelist said was true, that the meek would inherit the earth, then the Jews were the real Christians.

When Masha apostatized, Hadassah broke off with her, but not for long. Masha began writing to Hadassah in Otwotsk. She suffered and was lonely. Hadassah came to meet her in Warsaw and learned that Yanek's family had never forgiven her her Jewish origin. Her father-in-law would mutter, cough, and curse through the nights, blaming his son for his sickness. Her mother-in-law showed her hatred from the very first day. Her sister-in-law avoided her. After a time Yanek and Masha moved out of the house and took a room somewhere in Mokotov, but the situation remained an unhappy one. No one wanted the pictures Yanek painted. Who had time for art during a war? Yanek sent his paintings to the exhibitions, but

they were returned. He would stay in his room for days at a
stretch, read the newspapers, and repeat that he was good for
nothing, that he had not had the right to take a wife. Masha
got a job in a flower shop, but the place depressed her and
threatened to reduce her to a state of melancholia. Most of
the customers bought wreaths for funerals. Masha began to
suffer from cramps and nightmares. Man and wife started to
quarrel; and when Yanek was in a rage he would call her a
"filthy Jew-girl!"

Hadassah and Masha met regularly once a week. The cousins would go to a gentile restaurant, far from the Jewish
quarter, and have dinner there. Hadassah always paid. Once
Masha came out to Otwotsk in the middle of the night. There
had been a violent quarrel, and Yanek had seized her by the
throat and reached for a knife. The two young women stayed
awake until dawn, and Masha poured out all her troubled
soul. Yanek did not want to work. He had no strength. He
had heart trouble, and often spoke of committing suicide. He
was a poor drinker, but he could not keep away from the bottle. He became disgusted with painting and burned his canvases. He was convinced his fellow artists, Mlotek and Ru-
benlicht, were plotting against him, in revenge for his having
married a Jewish girl. Masha suggested that he consult a
nerve specialist, and he accused her of wanting to have him
consigned to an asylum.

When the Germans promised Poland independence and re-
cruited men for the Polish-German army, Yanek volunteered.
His father had died shortly before. Yanek was sent by the
commission to a hospital, but was released from service for
reasons of health. He at once turned against the Germans and
applied to Pilsudski's Polish military organization. Here he
met with luck for the first time. He was commissioned in the
secret service. He painted portraits of Pilsudski's aides, some
of whom headed the Pilsudski Brigade in Hungary. He began
to earn money and to bring home guests who, although they
were in mufti, like Yanek himself, addressed each other as
"captain," "major," and "colonel." They drank, sang patriotic
songs, curled their mustaches, kissed Masha's hand, and wept
drunkenly over the fate of the Polish fatherland, which for a
whole century had been divided up between the swinish Russians, Prussians, and Austrians. They knew that Masha was
Jewish, so they always spoke of the famous Jewish patriots of
Poland, Samuel Zbitkover and Colonel Berek Yosselevich,

and swore that Poland would be a paradise for the tormented Jewish people, even as the poets Mickiewicz, Norvid, and Wyspianski had foretold.

When the Germans arrested Pilsudski, Yanek, who had never written poetry before, was moved to indite a song, which was printed in the illegal newspaper of the military organization. He also painted a heroic picture of Pilsudski at the head of his brigade. Masha did not consider herself an art critic, but even she realized that the picture was a cheap imitation of Mateiko. Yanek's Jewish friends called him a dauber. Yanek raged at them, at Masha, and at the Jewish people who, he said, consisted of nothing but anarchists and degenerates. He rented a studio and stayed away from home for days and nights at a time. He wrote Masha long letters about his love for her, which could never die, and his disillusionment with women, with the Jews, with the hope for true justice. He quoted the anti-Semitic works of Lutoslawski, Nowaczynski, and Niemojewski. He sang the praises of Pilsudski, whom he called the Messiah. He would turn up at home in the middle of the night, dead drunk, kneel beside Masha's bed, and weep. "My angel! I'm a sinner! Don't thrust me away from you! Pure and holy soul!"

Then, when Pilsudski was liberated from the Magdeburg fortress, and Polish independence was declared, Yanek became a major in the Polish army and a frequent visitor at the Belvedere Palace. His portrait of Pilsudski hung among the works of the old Polish masters; his song became a popular marching tune for the army. He obtained an apartment on fashionable Uyazdov Alley. He had made up with Masha. He had an orderly and there were two maids. Colonels, generals, and diplomatic personages were frequent visitors. Masha went out horseback riding in Lazhenki Park. She stopped writing to Hadassah and no longer came to Otwotsk. Hadassah had never seen her new apartment. Madame Masha Zazhitska became a prominent personality in the new Poland. Her photograph appeared in the illustrated magazines. She was invited to serve on women's committees. She was given an honorary title in the Red Cross. Hadassah remained Fishel Kutner's wife and waited for the return of the obscure yeshivah student who had become lost somewhere among the Bolsheviks. Masha often reproached herself for having cut herself off from Hadassah. She would start up in the night, awakened by pangs of conscience, and vow to herself that she would seek out Hadassah the next day, pay her the few marks she owed her, buy her a present, and invited her to the house. But when the day came it was so crammed with commitments that she forgot Hadassah. Weeks would pass during which it never occurred to her that she was a granddaughter of Reb Meshulam Moskat and the daughter of Reb Moshe Gabriel, and that her brother Aaron, newly married in Warsaw, was the son-in-law of Kalman Chelmer. Masha felt sorry for the Jews, but it seemed to her that there was no sense in getting mixed up with this peculiar tribe, with its sickness, its corruption, its complications. Everything seemed to be there in one tremendous mix-up: Communism, the black market, atheism, religious fanaticism. Her family had become poor; her mother was wandering around somewhere in America with her servant lover. No, there was nothing to regret. Now that Yanek had achieved a career, her parents-in-law were dead, and Poland had become an independent state, Masha had one desire: to burn all her bridges behind her.

CHAPTER TWO

1

From Hadassah's Diary

June 26.—Today was a sad day in my life. I can compare it only to the day I got married. Fishel divorced me. I spent the whole day at the rabbi's, sitting on a bench. The scribe wrote on parchment with a quill. The two witnesses had to be taught how to sign their names in the traditional manner. The rabbi used the official "thou" when he spoke to me. He used such queer words—half Hebrew, half Yiddish. He looked into thick volumes, and gave me his kerchief as a token. I certainly wasn't sorry that it was all over, but I cried anyway. F. sat with his back to me all the time, and he swayed as if he were praying. I kept on thinking of death and of mother. I had to stand up and cup my hands, and when F. laid the divorce paper in them, he gave me a strange look. Then the edges of the divorce paper were cut with a penknife, and the rabbi told me: "If thou desirest to get married, thou shalt wait three months and one day."

I'm afraid I'll wait more than three years. Adele will never give him a divorce.

July 3.—Today an old dream of ours came true. We are in
Zakopane. He has seen higher mountains; he knows the Alps,
but I am seeing the mountains for the first time. They're even
more beautiful that I imagined. Suddenly a mountain grows
out, and then it disappears as if the earth had swallowed it.
The woods on the backs of the mountains look to me like
green beards. The hotel is so noisy. They all slam doors. They
give you so much to eat that it's terrible, and the women still
complain that it's not enough. The girls laugh so loudly that
you can't sleep at night. Asa Heshel is very restless. He said
that the modern Jew is not a human being. He's so full of
contradictions. He seems to be satisfied that I'm his mistress
and not his wife. If he knew how much I suffer because of
that! The clerk asked for our papers, and saw immediately
that we weren't married. There are many people from Warsaw here. As soon as we enter the dining-room it becomes
quiet.

In the evening.—He went for a walk alone. We had another argument. Dear God, why do we quarrel so much! Instead
of resting. he's always angry and tense. He doesn't say a word
to the people at our table. He had to borrow money for the
trip, since he refuses to take any of the money I got from F.
Gina lent it to him.

July 8.—Yesterday there was a lot of excitement in the
hotel. A soldier from Haller's army attacked the owner and
cut off his beard. The poor man is going around with a bandaged cheek. I didn't sleep all night. Asa Heshel groaned and
tossed about until dawn.

July 9.—The women here go around half-naked. It's
strange that the Jewish women should be so much more "liberated" than the Polish ones. They're already asking me why I
don't wear shorts. All the gentiles wear dresses. A. H. and I
are so shy. I'm even ashamed to go swimming when there are
men there. Asa Heshel goes around all day in his suit and tie.

July 13.—Thank God, we left the hotel. Now we're living
in the village of Zavoya, near Babia Gora. It's such a huge
mountain. and it stands there all by itself. At sunset it smokes
like a volcano. They say that one can see eagles here. One
thing is bad: there are fleas in the bed. The peasants are so
dirty. A kettle is built into the oven, and they cook in it three
times a day—either barley or potatoes. Our room is full of
holy pictures. The peasant has three cows and a few sheep.
but he keeps them up in the mountain. There isn't enough
fodder down here. Before the war the peasants used to go to

Hungary every summer to work in the fields. Now the frontier is closed. Three of the owner's daughters are servants in Krakow, in Jewish homes.

July 14.—Every time I say anything about having a baby, he becomes furious. He doesn't want to father new generations. Humanity could perish, for all he cares. I cannot understand why he is so pessimistic. He's especially afraid of having a girl. It must be a hangover from his Talmudic studies, although Grandfather also knew the Talmud, and he loved his grandchildren. How can he love me, if that's what he thinks of women? When he talks like that, I have to cry. He seems to be disappointed in everything. Still, sometimes he can be so gay, and play like a child.

July 15.—I didn't sleep all night. The fleas bit murderously. He woke up in the middle of the night to examine the straw mattress with a candle. He cursed everything and everybody, and was resentful that he had come back from Russia. He said that I would have been much happier if I had stayed with F. I cried. He kissed me for a long time and swore that he loved me more than anything. He's sincere, but his love is so uncertain. Every minute he has another plan. First he wants to go to Palestine, and then back to Switzerland. Sometimes he wants us to stay in Otwotsk, then he wants an apartment in Warsaw. Now he's decided not to go into military service if he's called up this year. I can understand how he feels, but it's beneath our dignity to be deserters. After all, we Jews have lived in Poland for many hundreds of years already.

July 16.—He's got the job in the theological seminary, Tachkemoni. We got a letter from Hertz Yanovar. Thank God, now we'll have something to live on, although we don't know yet what they'll pay. Here it's cheap. You get strawberries for almost nothing, and they're very sweet. Butter, too. The girls bring great piles of wood from the forest. Before, Asa Heshel didn't want this job—he considered it hypocritical to teach in a religious school—but now he seems glad. It could help him stay out of military service, since seminary students are exempt, and the teachers may be, too. Today he promised me that he would do everything possible to divorce Adele. He even said he'd let me have a baby if I could guarantee it would be a boy. As if that depended on me!

July 17.—I got a letter from Masha. She suddenly reminded herself that I'm her cousin. It's like the proverb: "When there's trouble, one comes to the Jew." Yanek makes her miserable. Now he's a colonel and has to go to the front. She never writes openly; everything is always wrapped in phrases. She wants me to come to her place in Villanov. She's surrounded by so many generals and their wives. I certainly won't go, although Yanek could help Asa Heshel.

August 6.—Today is my birthday. Twenty-seven years. In three years I'll be thirty. This is fantastic. Where did my years go? Everything passed like a dream. I used to think that at this age one was very clever. But I'm so green in every respect. Sometimes it seems to me that all I can do is love and suffer.

I reminded him about my birthday several times, but I knew he would forget, and he did. When I got up, I didn't say a word. He didn't mention it either, and I made up my mind to keep quiet. But I have such a weak character. At lunch I told him and he gave me a kiss. I had hoped he would give me something this afternoon—a flower or a bar of chocolate— but he's forgotten it again.

August 7.—The peasant got a Krakow newspaper. Great battles are taking place. The Polish army is suffering heavy losses. Strange birds have invaded the village. They eat the grain in the fields, and the peasants say that they speak with a human tongue. They're always screeching *"Day yeshch, day yeshch"* ("Give food, give food"). After the harvest they disappear. Our peasant is so old and good-natured. He's small, and carries such long trees that he chops down in the woods. He's almost in love with me, the poor man! Whenever he sees me he takes off his funny little hat. He tells me Hungarian stories, and about a ghost that emerges from the river on summer nights, disguised as a calf, and chants songs until he lures someone into the river.

Three quarters of the peasants, he says, starve before the harvest, and they have to buy their bread at the baker's. They consider that a disgrace. It seems that there are Communists here. The old man sides with them. He says that in Russia the peasants don't have to pay taxes. If a Jew spoke that way, it would be dreadful, but the peasants are not afraid of anything. His wife is a nasty woman. She complains that not enough people in the village die, and that's why the need is so great.

August 9.—Today we were on the mountain where the peasant keeps his cows. His daughter actually lives with the animals. In the middle of the stable there are a few stones she uses for an oven. Everything looks like thousands of years ago. She sleeps on hay. Earthen pots with sour milk stand on the shelves. She gets up at four o'clock to gather grass. There isn't enough flat pasture land. Asa Heshel was delighted with the whole thing. He said that he would like to stay here with me. The girl wears such a shabby dress. She fell in love with him, and she showed it openly as if she were a cow herself. . . . I had to laugh. She gave him a cup of warm milk, fresh from the udder, and she wouldn't take any money.

August 10.—We didn't sleep until dawn. He doesn't believe in anything—not God, or humanity. Everything is so black. The weather had been nice up to now, but today the sky is overcast, and the Babia Gora is all lost in the clouds. He went to the post office. I feel so depressed and I don't know why. I have to control myself, to stop myself from crying. I'm afraid that he doesn't know what love is. He recognizes only physical passion.

2

A day in August.—We're in Otwotsk again. The trip was terrible. The train was full of soldiers. The Bolsheviks are attacking on all sides. Asa Heshel has to report to the military office the day after tomorrow. He got his job at the seminary, and also one at a girls' Gymnasium, Chavatseleth. But now he has to drop everything. Dear God, ever since I've known him he's been constantly reporting for service. Klonya had a miscarriage. Yanek was wounded at the front. I have only one desire—to fall asleep and never wake up.

Tuesday.—We got up at dawn today and went to Warsaw. The military office is on Zlota Street. There was a long line of recruits waiting outside. I was the only woman. The gentiles made fun of the Jewish boys. I stood next to him, and I felt very sad. How different he was from all the others! The boys got acquainted with each other, talked, laughed, treated one another to cigarettes, but he didn't say a word to anybody. He spent the whole time looking into a book. He was hostile to me, as if the whole thing were my fault. I was sure that they would reject him, but he was accepted. Next week he has to report to the induction center.

Thursday.—He came to Otwotsk last night, and left for Warsaw this morning. He had slept at his mother's, not at Gina's. I can't even reach him by telephone. Why does he make a secret of everything? They all side with Adele. They all belong to one clique, and I'm an outsider. I won't stay in Otwotsk when he leaves for the army. I'll become a nurse.

Friday.—He was supposed to come today, but it's one in the morning and he's not here yet. He hasn't even written a card. I knew we would have all sorts of trouble, but I never thought we would quarrel so much. He gets locked up inside himself and it's impossible to talk to him. He's in a bad situation, but am I any better off?

Saturday night.—This morning I went to Klonya's in Miedzeshin. How different things are there! Vladek is at the front, but nobody makes a tragedy of it. Her mother was there, and her father. I had dinner with them. It was her mother-in-law's birthday. I have never seen such a huge cake, as large as a kneading-trough. After dinner they played a game. They all formed a circle, like children. Whoever was "out" had to pay a forfeit. Klonya's father had to forfeit his watch, and the "judge" told him to kiss me. The old man blushed like a child, and I couldn't help laughing. How I envy these simple people!

Sunday night.—Yesterday, late at night, he came. I don't know what happened to him, but he was cheerful and talkative, and he even brought me a gift—the poems of Leopold Staff. Today Uncle Abram and Hertz Yanovar visited us. All say that the war will be over soon, even before he finishes his training. Uncle Abram, Hertz, and he took sticks and brooms and marched like soldiers. I wrote a letter to Masha.

Wednesday.—He's at the induction center, somewhere in Shiletz. They won't allow any visitors. Last night I slept at Ida's, in the studio. Uncle Abram sleeps with her in the bedroom. I lay on my cot and couldn't fall asleep. Over my head, through the skylight, I saw the stars, and I felt as though I were in heaven. Ida's all gray. The moon was shining, and the pictures on the walls seemed to come alive.

Thursday.—Today I was at the induction center and I spoke to him. Masha called up a colonel and got permission for me. He was overjoyed to see me. It's a large house with a fence around it. The recruits walk around the courtyard like prisoners. They all looked at me. I was one woman among hundreds of men. If it weren't for the soldier who accompanied me, they would have torn me to pieces. The soldier opened the door and I saw Asa Heshel. There are no beds there, only bunks along the walls, one above another. He was sitting on a little box, reading his beloved book, Spinoza's *Ethics*. He was terribly surprised to see me. I wanted to kiss him, but they were all looking. We left for the courtyard and they all whistled after us.

Rosh Hashonah.—Asa Heshel is in Zhichlin. I've never been so lonesome on a holiday. Shifra went to hear them blow the ram's horn, but what right have I to go to a synagogue—I, a woman who leads a sinful life? I was afraid they would drive me out. I sent Papa a New Year's card, but up to now he hasn't answered. Klonya invited me to Miedzeshin, but I would be ashamed to be there on our holidays. I've lost everything—my parents, religion, all support. The leaves of the cherry trees in the courtyard are beginning to fade.

The night after Yom Kippur. Masha was here all day. Her life isn't much better than mine. Yanek is in the hospital; he got a light wound in the thigh. She told me terrible things about him. He's become a real anti-Semite. She plans to go to America, to her mother. We walked as far as Shrudborov. I fasted, and Masha wouldn't eat either. I prayed from mother's prayerbook, and Masha prayed with me. Strange, she still remembers how to read Hebrew, even better than I do. I dream about Mamma every night. She's dead and alive at the same time, and she cries. Is it possible that she knows my situation? I think about her very seldom during the day. I sent my nurse's application off, but there hasn't been any answer. I hear that they don't accept Jews.

Wednesday. Pilsudski is really saving Poland. It's almost sure that Asa Heshel won't have to be in the war. I'm glad about it, but somewhere I had a desire for him to be one of the liberators of Poland. We women always want our men to be heroes. That is silly. I got a postcard from Zhichlin. He writes so briefly.

November 12.—Today I returned from Zhichlin. I was there four days. How funny he looks in his uniform! They gave him clothes that are too big. The soldiers don't actually do anything. They know that they'll be discharged soon. He got a furlough and we slept in a hotel. He introduced me as his wife, and they all called me "Mrs. Bannet."

November 16.—I received a letter from Adele. Her mother must have dictated it to her. It's full of curses and threats. Dear diary, I'm placing the letter between your leaves; let it be a witness of all my sufferings.

At night.—One thought plagues me—have I acted properly? Did I have the right to take him from his child? They all think that I've committed a crime. Even those who consider themselves progressive. They talk and read so much about love, but when it comes down to it they're a bunch of fanatics. Rosa Frumetl goes around maligning me. She's doing it systematically. She goes from house to house. I get all the reports. I've always asked God to guard me from hatred, but it's more and more difficult to keep from hating. Dear God, I forgive everybody. Sometimes I feel as though my neck were in a noose. If I tell him anything, he becomes irritated.

I thought that where there was love, everything was shared, but he's different in this respect too. He's always busy with his own thoughts and he doesn't say anything. It's as though he were always waiting for something and had no patience. Even his letters are hurried.

Monday.—Shifra told me today that she's leaving me. She's going to get married. To Itchele. He came back to her after all. I couldn't afford to keep her, anyway. But it will be so difficult without her. She almost brought me up, although she's only five years older than I. As long as she was around, I felt that Mother was still with me. When she called me "mistress," I always imagined that she was speaking to Mother. I'm going to give her my smaller brooch.

Tuesday.—Today it's been raining all day. He's supposed to come this week, but everything is so indefinite. I can't stand Otwotsk any more, but all doors are closed to me in Warsaw. In her letter Adele calls me "harlot." Probably I am, in everybody's eyes.

He could help me a lot. His love could make up for everything. Other women are so sure of themselves and of their husbands. But I, who have sacrificed so much, am always in doubt.

CHAPTER THREE

1

On the third evening of Channukah, Bashele fried some pancakes. Chaim Leib, the coal dealer, whom she married after Koppel divorced her, went off to play cards with a neighbor after supper. Bashele had put too much oil in the Channukah lamp, and a single wick still spluttered. She grated the raw potatoes and put fat in the frying-pan. The kitchen soon became heavy with the sizzling and the smell of burning fat. No matter how earnestly Bashele begged the children to stay in the living-room they preferred the coziness of the kitchen. Manyek, her married son, who worked as bookkeeper in a vinegar factory, sat on the edge of the cot where Yppe and Tiebele slept. Next to him sat Rita, his wife. Manyek was a dandy. His hair was parted and smeared with pomade. In his stiff collar he wore a tie with a diminutive knot. When he sat down, he carefully pulled his trousers up above his ankles, so that the crease might not be disturbed. He had something of a reputation for his elegant manners. The women of Praga adored having him as a partner for a tango, a shimmy, or a fox trot. It was precisely for these reasons that Rita kept a watchful eye on him. She herself was tiny and dark, a little on the plump side, with fleshy lips and small flashing eyes. Up to this very day the other Praga girls could not understand what Manyek had seen in her.

"What's she got?" the girls used to wonder. "No features and no figure. A stuffed doll."

Shosha, Bashele's oldest daughter, was now twenty-four. She was going with a chalutz, who was preparing to emigrate to Palestine. That was Shosha's lot; the youths who were attracted to her were always idealists. She herself was a domestic girl. She read no newspapers and hardly knew the difference between a Socialist and a Zionist. She had left school when the war started and had stayed at home, helping her mother with the affairs of the household. Now she had taken a job in a chocolate shop on Senator Street. It had looked as though Shosha would grow up to be quite a beauty, but there was something missing. Her features were too childish and her bosom was too big. When she had nothing else to do, she would read aloud from her school books—stories about kings, forest spirits, and hunters. Bashele would complain: "Just look at her! Like a seven-year-old!"

It was nothing short of a miracle that a young man had happened to come along. His name was Simon Bendel, from Dinev, in Galicia. He was a giant of a youth, with thick, curly black hair, a narrow face, pointed chin, and lean long throat. His customary attire was a blouse, a military belt and breeches, puttees wrapped around his legs above the heavy shoes. His father owned some land. Simon knew how to plow, sow, milk cows, and ride horseback. On the chalutzim farm in Grochov they had told him that there was nothing more they could teach him, that he was ready without any further instruction to go to work on a settlement in Palestine. All he needed now was his certificate. Whenever he came from the

Grochov farm to Warsaw. he spent all his time with Shosha. He taught her to speak Hebrew with the Sephardic accent, and took her with him to the young pioneer gatherings. Shosha would come home late at night and Bashele would ask her: "Did you have a good time?"

"So-so."

"What did they talk about?"

"All sorts of things."

"And you really want to go to Palestine?"

"Why not? It's our own country."

For the Channukah holiday Simon had brought Shosha a gift. It was a silver Star of David on a chain to be worn around the throat. Now he was sitting on the edge of a chair in the kitchen, never taking his big dark eyes off Shosha. Manyek looked at him curiously, wondering what on earth he could see in Shosha. To him it was a constant source of surprise that his sister had sense enough even to sell chocolates.

Rita kept glancing at Simon, asking him questions like: "Is it true that the sand in Palestine is very hot?" "Is it true that the Arab men are very handsome?" "Is it true that you have to buy water there by the quart?"

Simon answered all questions like an authority. He took a map out of his pocket, spread it out, and, pointing with his fingers, showed how the earth could be irrigated artificially and how desert land could be transformed into fertile soil. He reeled off a lot of Hebrew names of colonies and settlements, talking like one who was a native Palestinian.

Shosha kept on smiling all the time. "Simon," she said, "tell them about the Arab with six wives."

"Why? I told that already."

"Tell it again. Oh, Mamma, it's so terribly funny."

Yppe, who was younger than Shosha, was crippled. She had had one leg. thin as a stalk, in a brace since childhood. She was small. dark, ugly, and bad-tempered. She worked in a bead factory. Now she was seated on a low stool, pawing through a pile of corals she had brought home to work on. The beauty of the family was Teibele, the fourteen-year-old. She was in the fourth class. She was seated at the table in the living-room, working from a mathematics textbook. She had a talent for the subject; she took after her father in that respect. Whenever her mother was angry with her she would complain: "The spit of her father!"

As Bashele stood at the stove. turning the pancakes, she heard familiar steps outside the door. She pricked up her ears.

It wasn't Chaim Leib; his steps were heavy. There was a knock at the door. *"Kto tam? Who is there?"*

There was no answer. She unlatched the door and turned white as chalk. Koppel stood at the threshold. Over the years he had got somehow both younger and older. He was wearing a light-colored coat, a cream-colored hat, and tan shoes with wide heels and pointed toes. A cigarette dangled from his lips. He looked around, half curious, half frightened. Bashele brought her hands together.

"Don't faint. I'm not dead." Koppel said in his impudent manner. "Good evening, children."

The smile disappeared from Shosha's lips; her face lengthened. Yppe opened her mouth wide. Manyek stood up. "Good evening, Papa," he said.

"Let me see—that's Shosha. That's Yppe. Where is Teibele?"

Teibele came in from the other room, a pencil in one hand and an eraser in the other.

"Teibele, it's father," Manyek said.

"I know. I remember," she said in Polish.

Bashele at last found her tongue. "To come in without warning. You never let us know—"

"I didn't know myself that I was coming. I managed to get on a boat at the last moment. Where is Chaim Leib?"

Bashele stared. In her confusion she forgot for the moment who Chaim Leib was.

Manyek answered: "Uncle is out."

"Oh. Well, I didn't come to cause any trouble. I wanted to see the children."

"Papa, this is my wife."

Rita blushed. *"Bardzo mi przyjemnie,"* she murmured in Polish. "Honored to meet you."

"So you're my daughter-in-law. Yes. You look just like the photograph."

"And this is a friend of Shosha's."

Koppel measured the stranger with his searching eyes. "A soldier, eh?"

"I'm not a soldier. I'm a chalutz."

"A Zionist, eh? You want to send us all to Palestine."

"Not all."

Bashele took the frying-pan off the stove. She had just remembered the law that a divorced woman was not permitted to remain under the same roof with her former husband. Red flecks showed in her cheeks. "So sudden—"

"Don't be so terrified, Bashele. I'm not spending the night here. I'm staying at the Hotel Bristol."

"Take your overcoat off. You'll catch a cold."

He unbuttoned his coat, revealing a checked jacket, the kind one saw only in the movies. The collar of his shirt had long points, and his tie was a blinding mixture of red, yellow, and gold.

"Go ahead. Eat your supper. I won't disturb you."

"Mamma was making pancakes. For Channukah," Shosha said.

"Ah, pancakes. I thought they made them only in America. Well, my children, here I am. A divorced father is still a father. You, Teibele, you've probably forgotten me altogether."

"No, I remember. You used to wear such long boots."

"What boots? Everything looks the same. Tell me, what are you doing? Do you go to high school?"

"She goes to the Gymnasium," Manyek answered.

"Gymnasium, high school, the same thing," Koppel said. "Yes, nothing's changed. The same courtyard, the same janitor. He recognized me. Panie Koppel, he said. He's become a real old tramp. I gave him half a dollar. He wanted to kiss my hand."

"He's nothing but a drunkard," Shosha remarked.

"What? Well, what else has he got to do? Over there they've got prohibition now. But people find ways. New York is full of drunks."

Koppel stopped short. He was surprised himself at the things he was saying. "What am I babbling about?" he wondered. What would they know about all that? "That Yppe—she looks terrible. Shosha hasn't grown up. Bashele is an old woman. Hard to believe that she's six years younger than me." He felt a lump in his throat. He took a lighter from his pocket and lit his cigarette, which had gone out, lowering his face as he did so.

2

Koppel stayed only an hour. Before he left he handed Manyek thirty American dollars—Bashele refused to take the money—and announced that he would be back again the following day. He went downstairs and walked along Mala Street. He turned up his coat collar and pulled his hat over his forehead. Was Isador Oxenburg still alive, he wondered. And Reitze? Were they still living in the same flat? And what about that peppy little woman, Mrs. Goldsober? Koppel walked along, stopping every once in a while to peer around. After New York, Paris, and Berlin, Praga looked like some small town. It was only ten o'clock, but a midnight quiet seemed to hover over the streets. Strange, he had forgotten a good many things in the six years he had been away—the rows of gas lamps, the gutters, the scattered telephone booths, on whose walls theater and opera notices were posted. He passed by a half-fallen house, the red brick walls supported by planks. Through the lighted windows he could see lines of wash hanging on ropes. In New York a building like that would have been condemned.

As Koppel approached, the janitor was about to close the gates of the court in front of the house where the Oxenburgs had lived. He handed the janitor a silver coin. "Do the Oxenburgs still live here?"

"Yes, panie."

"Are they both alive?"

"Where does the gentleman come from?"

"From America."

The janitor took off his cap, scratched his head, and put the cap on again. "Yes, they're both alive. The Pan Isador is sick."

The janitor was holding a box of smoky naphtha lamps. Behind the gate was a bunk covered with a sheepskin. Koppel now remembered that this was where some Warsaw janitors slept at night, so that they would be on hand to admit latecomers. "How are things here? Bad?"

"Bad? Couldn't be worse. When the tenants haven't got a grosz, what can the janitor expect?"

Koppel handed him another coin; then he made his way into the courtyard. He walked by a pile of refuse, an unharnessed wagon with its shafts sticking up in the air, and a toilet, the door smeared with tar. The stench made Koppel screw up his nose. They wouldn't believe a thing like this in America, he thought. He climbed the dark stairs, knocked at the familiar door, waited. In a moment he heard footsteps and the door opened. He saw a huge mass of flesh. It was Reitze. Over the years she had grown twice as vast. Her shapeless body blocked the doorway.

"Reitze!"

"I can't believe it! Koppel!"

She stretched out her enormous arms and drew him within their clasp, kissing and cooing. Then she half dragged him through the long corridor to the living-room. He saw a familiar sight. A table, chairs, playing-cards. They were all here: David Krupnick, Leon the Peddler, Itchele Peltsevisner, Motie the Red. At the head of the table sat Mrs. Goldsober. Then Koppel saw Zilka, the Oxenburgs' older daughter.

Reitze made a flourish with her hand. "Everybody! Everybody! Look who's here! It's Koppel."

"As true as I'm alive. Koppel!" Motie the Red shouted.

David Krupnick stared at him in astonishment. "Did you fall out of the sky?"

"A real American," Itchele Peltsevisner exclaimed.

"What are you standing at the door for?" Leon the Peddler inquired. "Are you too swell to talk with us?"

He came up to Koppel and kissed him. Itchele Peltsevisner also wanted to kiss him, but he had forgotten that he still had his cigarette in his mouth, and he almost burned Koppel's nose. Zilka embraced Koppel without saying a word. Koppel noticed that she was wearing black.

"Where is your husband?" he asked.

Zilka broke into tears. "In the cemetery."

"When? How did it happen?"

"Three months ago. From typhus."

"Yes, God poured out His wrath on us for good," Reitze rasped. "He died like a saint. I pleaded with them: 'Don't drag him to the hospital. They only poison people there.' Half of Warsaw came to his funeral."

"Mamma, Mamma, please stop."

"What have I said?" She turned to Koppel. "You didn't even write us a letter. A man goes off to America and disappears."

"Where's Isador?"

"Bedridden—may you be spared. You won't recognize him. Well, what are you standing for? Here, sit down. Zilka, bring him something to eat."

"I'm not hungry."

"In this house you've got to be hungry. It's my living now. I've begun to serve meals. Don't you even ask about Regina?"

"How is she? What's she doing?"

"What does any girl do? She gets married and becomes a woman. Ah, Koppel, Koppel. Tell me, what kind of place is this America? To go off and forget everybody! They must lose their memories there."

"Never mind, never mind," Mrs. Krupnick, the former Mrs. Goldsober, interrupted. "Tell us, how's your wife?"

Koppel threw a side glance at her. "Leah's still in Paris," he answered.

"In Paris! Dear God in heaven! Where people find themselves!"

"Where is Isador?" Koppel asked again, turning to Reitze.

"My God, look at the way he misses him all of a sudden. In there. Go on in. He'll tell you a million things—but they're all lies. All he does is lie there and figure out all sorts of fantasies. Is it my fault that he's paralyzed? All these years I warned him. 'Isador,' I said, 'a man isn't made of iron.' Three o'clock in the morning he'd get up and start with the bottle. I was scared he'd scald his guts. But it went to his legs."

"Mamma, please stop it," Zilka said sternly.

"See the way she teaches me manners. What are you so worried about? Koppel's known me for years. Even though he lives in New York. Is it true that the money rolls in the streets there?"

"Sure. They sweep it up with shovels."

"Ah, the way we were jealous of you. And the trouble we had. People dying like flies. The Germans—God's curse on them—played the gentlemen. *Bitte,* put the noose around your neck. *Bitte,* drop dead. And everything was ration cards, coupons. And the bread. Baked with chestnuts. Heavy as rock. A whole winter we ate nothing but frozen potatoes. I lost thirty pounds in a few weeks. My petticoats fell off me. Zilka became a smuggler."

"Mamma!"

"All right, all right! I can't say a word any more. The eggs have got smarter than the hens. Well, go in to Isador. But don't stay in there, Koppel, darling."

Koppel went into the bedroom. There was a small lamp burning. Isador was lying flat on the bed, his face yellow as wax. His mustache, which Koppel remembered as always neatly curled, was now ragged. One eye was half closed, the other stared straight ahead. On a night table lay a deck of cards and a sputum cup.

Koppel hesitated at the door. "Good evening, Isador."

Isador returned the greeting in a strong, healthy voice.

"You do recognize me?" Koppel asked.

"Like a bad penny."

Koppel laughed. "Well, thank God you still recognize a person," he said.

"Do you think I'm out of my mind? When did you come?"

"Today."

"Straight from America?"

"I stopped off in Paris."

"Have you been to see your family?"

"Yes."

"You're no fool. As for me, they've got me wrapped up and ready for the ash heap. They don't even give me anything to eat."

"That's impossible."

"Shut up. Give me a couple of dollars. I tell you, I'm a stranger here. They're just waiting for me to kick the bucket."

"You imagine things."

"I'm a healthy man, Koppel. The only thing is I've got no legs. If I had the money I'd get them cut off and buy myself a pair of crutches. If it wasn't for the society I'd be rotting underground. They keep on coming over every Saturday. It's in the bylaws. Not long ago they brought me a cut of meat, but Reitze swiped it. They don't let me have any brandy. Here I stick all day and stare at the ceiling. And all sorts of ideas go through my mind. Well, tell me, are you at least satisfied now?"

"No."

"What's the matter? She's a fancy lady?"

"It's everything together."

"Have you got dollars?"

"Like straw."

"Then it isn't so bad. Go and get me a bottle of schnapps."

"Right away."

"Go now. They'll be closing the saloon. Half of the society is dead. There's a lot of new members now. Isador here, Isador there. but I don't know a single one of them. Tell me, do you still chase around with women?"

"There are plenty of them in America."

"So you're a lucky man. Grab it all while you can, brother. When you're in my condition you can't do a thing."

3

When Koppel returned to the living-room, the card game had stopped. The deck lay on the plate in the middle of the table with the kitty in it. They were apparently talking about him; as he entered, a sudden silence fell. It was only now that Koppel got a real look at the group. David Krupnick had become coarse and clumsy, somehow smaller, as though he had grown in reverse. Itchele Peltsevisner's hair was thinning and his scalp looked scabby. There was a mole on his left cheek. Motie the Red had a mouth full of gold teeth. Leon the Peddler looked worn and sick. Even the house seemed to Koppel to have changed. The curtains on the windows were ragged and torn. The walls were peeling. The ceiling was patchy.

Mrs. Krupnick removed her asthma cigarette from her lips. "Are you going already, Koppel?" she said. "Where are you running to?"

"I'm going to buy a bottle of something for Isador."

Reitze half rose from her chair. "I knew it right away," she said. "The drunk. The moment somebody comes in he begins to take advantage of him. Koppel, as true as that we both should live, I tell you it's a sin. The whole misfortune comes from it."

"It won't make him any sicker."

"Wait. Don't run away. I've got some brandy here in the house. He's really a disgrace."

"I'm afraid that Koppel is ashamed of us paupers," Mrs. Krupnick remarked.

"I came here to see you, didn't I?"

"To see me?"

"To see all of you."

"Tell us about America. Is it true they walk upside down there?"

"You can if you want to. It's a free country." Koppel turned toward Leon the Peddler. "How are things with you?"

Leon slapped his forehead with his hand. "I was sure you'd forgotten my name already," he said. "How should I be? If Poland is a country, then I'm a king. I try to sell jewelry, and what people want is bread. There's only one kind of merchandise to deal in these days—dollars. For dollars you can buy the blue dome of heaven. How is everything with you, Kop-

pel? As true as I'm alive, we talked about you every evening.
And not a word from you. They were all angry. But I told
them: 'Listen to me.' I said, 'a man like Koppel doesn't forget.
The only thing is that in Columbus's country a man has no
time to write.' "

"It's true," Koppel said. "When you get to America, you
don't want to write. Everything seems so distant. As if you
were in a different world."

"You know what. Koppel? You're really an entirely different person," Reitze remarked after some hesitation.

Koppel bristled. "What's different about me?"

"I don't know. You're so serious. You used to be such a
joker. And you've got kind of older. What is it? Working too
hard?"

"Everything's in a hurry there. What you do here in an
hour we do in a minute."

"What's the hurry? They die there too, don't they? Well,
anyway, I suppose we'll get used to you. Where are you staying?"

"At the Hotel Bristol."

"My God! You must have made a fortune."

Koppel said nothing.

"Even in America you don't get rich from honest work," Itchele Peltsevisner remarked.

Koppel threw him an angry glance. "Is your work honest?"

"Who can I steal from? Except maybe from my horses."

"Hey, men! Never mind the fighting." Reitze interrupted.
"Zilka, go into the kitchen with Koppel and pick out a good
bottle of brandy. If your father is such a fool, let him have
it."

Koppel left the room with Zilka. It was dark in the corridor, and it smelled of gas and dirty linen. Zilka took his arm.

"Careful." she said. "Don't fall. Such a bunch of rough-
necks. It sticks in their throats that you live at the Hotel Bristol. Are you going to be in Warsaw long?"

"A month."

"I'd like to talk to you about something. But not here. Everybody's got long ears here."

"Come and see me at the hotel."

"When?"

"Tonight if you want." Koppel felt a sudden alarm at his
own words. What was he saying? She might slap his face.

After a moment's silence Zilka let go of his arm. "I could come tomorrow," she said. "Whenever you like—afternoon or night."

"At night would be better."

"What time?"

"Around ten."

"I'll be there. If I'm a little late, wait for me. Here's the brandy. See that Papa doesn't drink too much."

"It'll be all right."

Koppel took the bottle of brandy with one hand. The other arm he placed around Zilka's shoulders. He drew her toward him and kissed her full on the lips. She kissed him back. Their knees met. "Yes," he thought, "a man must have initiative. Let Leah stay there in Paris as long as she likes."

They went back to the living-room. Mrs. Krupnick looked curiously at them, a strange smile on her lips, as though she had divined what had gone on.

In the bedroom Isador raised his head on the pillow and looked at Koppel sharply. "So you're here at last. Sit down. I was just thinking they'd talked you out of it. Enemies, that's what they are. Pour it, brother. So-o-o. Take a drink for yourself. I don't like drinking alone. *L'chaim!*"

Isador took up the glass with trembling fingers. His mouth opened, revealing his long, blackened teeth. With his weakened hands he could not toss off the liquor quickly, in his old expert way. He sipped it slowly, handling the glass clumsily and spilling the liquid on the bedcover.

"Another?"

"Pour it."

After the fifth glassful Isador's face began to flush. "To-day's liquor—" he growled. "Water. In the old days you could really taste it. How is it in America? What do they drink there?"

"Whisky."

"Ah! Go ahead. Pour it. So-o-o. Yes, brother, I'm finished, I tell you. Here I am, in prison. The old Isador Oxenburg is gone. A restaurant—that's what my home's become. Reitze is just like a cook. About my daughters I'd rather not talk. One decent son-in-law I had, a fine man. They finished him off."

"He died of typhus, didn't he?"

"Well—Regina married a tough guy, a friend of my son. They didn't even take me to the wedding. Here I was, suffering like a dog, and they carried on till daylight. Yes. There's only one wish I have—to be buried in Warsaw. I don't want to be buried here with the Praga fakers."

"What's the difference?"

"Never mind. Tell me, how is it with your wife? Are you still her servant?"

"What are you babbling about?"

"Well, never mind. Once there was a man called Isador Oxenburg; now there's nothing but a heap of useless bones. Me, who could pick up a barrel of ten *pud*. Police Inspector Woikoff himself used to salute me. I had only to look at a woman and—"

"You still remember, eh?"

Isador thumped his chest with his fist. "How long ago was it, twenty years, when Blond Feivel died? Half of Praga went to the cemetery. I was riding in the first carriage with Shmuel Smetana. He bet me that he'd put away a small barrel of beer. At the twenty-third mug he passed out. His guts were splitting. Ah-h-h. What was I talking about? I don't want to be buried in Praga. And I want to hire a pious Jew to say Kaddish after me."

"I'll take care of it."

"What? Stay here, Koppel. Stay here for my funeral."

He closed his eyes, and his hands fell to his sides. His face turned bluish and stiff. Only his mustache moved, rising and falling. His pale lips wore the smile that sometimes appears on the face of a corpse.

CHAPTER FOUR

A week after Channukah, Leah and her son and daughter arrived in Warsaw. Zlatele was now nineteen and a student at college. She was known as Lottie. She was engaged to be married to a boy in New York. Meyerl's fellow students at high school called him Mendy. The trip to Europe in the middle of the winter had interrupted the school terms of the two children. Leah had wanted to wait for the summer vacation before making the trip, but Koppel was too impatient. Leah herself could hardly wait to see Warsaw again. Deep inside her was the hope that she would be able to talk Masha into leaving her gentile husband and coming to America.

The journey was a far from peaceful one. Man and wife

quarreled constantly. Koppel as usual, complained that Leah was playing the high and mighty lady, treating him as though he were still the overseer of her father's affairs. Leah threatened that if he didn't stop his eternal nagging she'd throw herself overboard. For a couple of days she refused to leave her cabin. Koppel spent his time in the bar or playing cards. Koppel did not want to stay in Paris more than three days, but Lottie and Mendy were in no hurry to go to Poland, so Koppel had gone to Warsaw himself. Now they were all in Warsaw, stopping at the Hotel Bristol. Leah had brought with her an enormous trunk, with numerous locks, its sides pasted with customs, hotel, and steamer labels. The porters struggled with twelve pieces of luggage. Passers-by stopped to gape at the American tourists. Leah had grown fat over the years. The blond hair under her hat showed signs of gray. She talked to the children in a strident voice, in a mixture of Yiddish and English. The children could not stand her English-Yiddish jargon and her funny accent.

"What do you have to yell for, Ma?" Lottie asked her. "They'll think we're crazy."

"Who'll think? Who's crazy?" Leah shouted. "Shut up. Get hold of that satchel with shoes. And you, Mendy, what are you standing like a *golem* for?"

"What do you want me to do, Ma?"

"Keep an eye on the *goyim*. Don't be a dummy."

"It's starting again. The same nonsense," Koppel murmured. "Nobody wants your rags."

"Is that so? That's all you know. In Paris they stole a cape from me."

"Well, Lottie, what do you think of Warsaw?" Koppel asked the girl.

Lottie took after her father, Reb Moshe Gabriel. She had small features, dark hair, blue eyes. In New York she was thought to be good-looking, but Leah never understood what others saw in her. The girl ate like a sparrow. She had no bust. She read too much, and her eyes had become myopic. She dressed simply—too simply, Leah thought. Now she was wearing an old green jacket, a dark dress, and an unadorned hat. In one hand she was carrying a French book and in the other an English magazine. She turned to answer Koppel's question.

"So-so," she shrugged. "Kind of drab."

Mendy was already tall, and stout like his mother. He was wearing a green hat with a feather, which he had acquired in

Paris, a jacket with a fur collar, and gray woolen socks. He clutched a bag of peanuts, chewing at them and dropping the shells on the sidewalk.

"Do you like it here, Mendy?" Koppel asked.

"I'm hungry."

"Wait, glutton. We'll soon eat lunch."

The news of Leah's arrival soon spread over Gzhybov Place, Panska Street, Gnoyna Street, Tvarda Street, wherever the Moskat tribe was to be found. Saltsha and Queen Esther kept the telephone busy. It was no small matter for the Moskat clan to address Koppel as brother-in-law. Nathan took a firm oath that he would not permit the upstart into his house. Hama, Abram's wife, wept bitterly when she heard the news. All of them had the same questions: Would Leah see Masha? Would she meet her gentile son-in-law? What would Moshe Gabriel say and do when he saw his Americanized children? How would Aaron speak to his mother? Pinnie ran to get advice from Nyunie in the book and antique shop on Holy Cross Street. Students were fingering the volumes on the shelves. Bronya stood at a table, polishing the belly of a naked Buddha and looking around at the customers with her sharp eyes. Pinnie greeted her, but Bronya pretended that she did not see him. She did not like the Moskats. The two men retired to a rear room.

"Well, what do you think?" Pinnie asked. "My God, it'll be a madhouse. All Warsaw will laugh at us."

"And if they do laugh?" Nyunie answered. "He's still her husband. Am I right or not?"

Pinnie grasped his brother by the lapel. "Is it our fault? We didn't marry him. She did."

"What are you whispering about there? What's going on?" Bronya called through the open door.

Nyunie trembled. "It's nothing, nothing."

"Where's the new catalogue?" Bronya continued in a harsh voice.

Nyunie began to scratch his beard. "How should I know?"

"Who should know, then? Count Pototski?"

"Bronya, darling, Leah has come from Am-m-m-erica," Nyunie stammered.

"That puts no money in my pocket."

She slammed the door, stirring up a cloud of acrid dust. Pinnie started to sneeze.

"What's she so angry about?"

"Ask me something easier."

Both brothers decided to ask Leah and Koppel to their homes and not to add to any scandal. Apart from the fact that brothers should not humiliate a sister, Leah was filthy rich and might be in a position to do them favors. In the evening the two went to the hotel, Pinnie in a too long overcoat, a silk hat, and muddied boots, Nyunie in a fur coat that had grown too tight with the years, a fur hat with ear muffs, kid shoes, and galoshes. The hotel employees looked at them suspiciously. The elevator operator told them to use the stairs. They started to climb, gesturing with their hands, stumbling into one another.

Pinnie bent down and touched the carpet. "How soft! A pleasure to walk on."

"In paradise you'll walk on butter," Nyunie answered.

When they reached their sister's room, Pinnie blew his nose and knocked at the door. Leah opened it, squealed, and threw herself at them. "Pinnie! Nyunie!"

She broke into laughter and tears. Lottie and Mendy, standing behind her, gaped at the two small queer-looking men who were their uncles. Koppel turned pale and spat out the cigarette butt that dangled between his lips. "Children! Your uncles!" Leah cried.

"How do you do?" Mendy said in English, after some hesitation.

"Lottie, what are you staring for? Koppel, why are you hiding there? Ah, dear God, that I've lived to see this day!"

Koppel came toward them with his familiar light step. Nyunie flushed.

Pinnie took off his misted spectacles. "The same Koppel!"

"What did you think? That he'd grow horns on his head?" Leah said. "Take off your coats. Nyunie, you look like a lord. Pinnie, you're all gray."

"I'm not a youngster any more. I'm a man of sixty."

Leah wrung her hands.

"Mamma, Mamma! It's like yesterday when you were married. How the years fly by! Well, sit down. Why are you standing? How are you? How's everybody? How's Hanna?"

"How should she be? She complains, as usual," Pinnie answered.

"Why shouldn't she complain? She probably can't stand your nonsense any more. How's Nathan? And Abram? I telephoned to everybody, but they were never home. Or maybe they're hiding from me. Koppel and me—we could quarrel from morning to night, but so far as you're concerned he's my husband."

"Maybe you'd like a drink?" Koppel interrupted.

No one answered. Koppel went over to the commode, filled some glasses with a reddish-looking liquor from a round bottle, and put them on a tray. He carried the cognac over to the group silently, with the expertness of a waiter.

Leah darted a sharp glance at him. "What's the hurry? Put it down."

"Koppel, you're still a young man," Pinnie remarked.

"In America no one gets old," Koppel answered.

"Really?

"In America you can see men of eighty playing golf."

"So. And what is this—this 'golf'? Maybe you've got an American cigarette?"

Koppel took out a silver cigarette case and struck a match on the sole of his shoe. Pinnie looked on in surprise. "American tricks," he remarked.

"In America matches are free," Koppel said. "You go in to buy cigarettes and you get the matches for nothing. Am I right, Mendy?"

Pinnie clutched at his beard. "This is Meyerl?" he exclaimed. "Do you still remember how I taught you the Gemara Baba Kama?"

"Yes, I do."

"What do you remember?"

"The first Mishnah. 'The ox, the ditch, the tooth, and the fire.'"

"What a memory! And you," Pinnie turned to Lottie, "I hear you've got a young man already."

Lottie turned red. "I'm not sure yet," she murmured.

"Then who should know? From what I hear, in America it's all love, love."

"Today it's love and tomorrow it's good-by," Lottie answered.

Pinnie put his glasses back on his nose. He furrowed his brow, squinted, and bit his lips. He could not make up his mind what to think about these Americans. There was something about them—something was missing, but he could not seem to grasp what it was. Was it the changed accent, the clothing, the gestures? They looked somehow familiar and yet alien, they looked Jewish and gentile at the same time. The words they spoke, the phrases they used, were as though taken from a book. There was a simplicity, a seriousness, a self-assurance on their faces that one saw only in foreign countries. What was lacking was the homeliness, the manner, the expression. Ah, the difference a few years make, Pinnie thought. He looked at Nyunie, baffled. "A world, eh? Ah, dear God in heaven."

CHAPTER FIVE

1

During the years they had been in America Zlatele and Meyerl had written many letters to their father. But Moshe Gabriel had answered them only infrequently. He could see little difference between his apostate daughter Masha and these "American" children of his; as long as they attended worldly schools, profaned the Sabbath, ate unkosher food, they were cut off from the community of Israel. Several times he had received money from Leah, but invariably he had refused to use it, turning it over instead to Aaron.

"What happened to Jacob happened to Joseph." What happened to Moshe Gabriel happened to Aaron. Aaron had married, but did not live with his wife. His father-in-law, Kalman Chelmer, had died of typhus. Aaron's wife had opened a store, but Aaron was not a good businessman. They quarreled constantly, and finally she drove him out of the house. Aaron left Warsaw and went to Bialodrevna to join his father. He plunged deep into the lore of Chassidism. It was understood among the Chassidim that when the rabbi died, Moshe Gabriel would become the Bialodrevna rabbi, and Aaron would be his heir. Once a month the youth wrote a card to his mother in America and from time to time received from her a draft for twenty-five dollars. It was partly because of these remittances that his wife was not too insistent about a divorce.

It was in the Bialodrevna study house that Leah and her children met Aaron. Leah could not understand how she recognized him. She remembered him as a youth with a few hairs sprouting from his chin. But this man had a disheveled beard, an unbuttoned collar, a gaberdine down to his ankles, and sidelocks dangling to his shoulders.

Leah took a step back. "Aaron, it's you!"

Aaron's pale face became as white as chalk. He made a

move as if to run away. Lottie began to murmur something in English. It was all Mendy could do to stop from breaking out into laughter.

"Aaron, don't you recognize me? I'm your mother."

Aaron hastily began to button his gaberdine. "Yes, Mother, I recognize you."

"My child—come here. Me you may kiss," Leah said, frightened by her own words. "This is your sister Zlatele. This is Meyerl."

Aaron took courage. "It's you, Meyerl. You've become a big boy."

"You look like a Jew," Mendy stammered.

"How should I look, like a gentile?"

"He means a Chassid," Leah hastened to explain. "My God, the way you've let yourself go! If you'd at least comb your hair once in a while. Where's your father?" She gazed at Aaron with wide-open melancholy eyes.

"Is this Zlatele?" Aaron half stated, half asked. "Like a real lady."

"I recognized you immediately," Lottie answered, and took a step toward him.

Aaron said nothing but went off to announce the visitors' arrival to his father. He was gone quite a long time. Moshe Gabriel came in with reluctant steps. He had been in the middle of his daily hour of study of the Zohar. He was anxious to see his son and daughter, but why did Leah have to come with them? True, according to law he might talk with her in the presence of the children, but just the same the matter was awkward. He smoothed his beard and curled his sidelocks. The way he saw it, it was all a cunning design of the Evil One. As he reached the door of the study house his glasses misted and he saw everything as through a fog. "Good morning."

"Papa!"

Lottie ran to him, threw her arms around him, and covered his face with kisses. Leah felt a lump rise in her throat. In direct contrast to Aaron's neglected appearance, Moshe Gabriel looked, as of old, neat and cared for. His beard, now graying, was combed. No, he had not changed. He half pushed Lottie aside. His daughter, yes; but a female just the same. Mendy held out his large warm hand.

"Hello, Pop," he said.

"Meyerl, is this you?" Moshe Gabriel took off his glasses and wiped them with his handkerchief. He looked at the boy and shrank back. He remembered him as a soft and delicate child, and here before him stood the strange apparition of a tall, stout, big-boned youth. "Big. He's grown to be big, may the evil eye not harm him."

"*Bar mitzvah* two years ago," Leah said. "He made a speech."

"Do you put on your phylacteries?"

Mendy flushed.

"It's hard to follow all the pious ways in America," Leah explained.

"It's hard anywhere. If it were easy, there would be no temptation."

"Mendy, tell your father what you've studied."

"The Torah—the Law."

"The Law. A Jew must live by it, not only read it," Moshe Gabriel announced gravely.

"I haven't got the time."

"What do you do?"

"I go to high school."

"This is what the prophet meant when he said: 'They have forsaken me, the fountain of living waters, and hewed them out cisterns, broken cisterns.' Without the Torah there can be no lasting existence."

Leah interrupted in the boy's defense. "He can't make a living from the Torah," she said firmly.

"The Torah is the source of life."

"Papa, do you think I've changed so much?" Lottie asked.

Moshe Gabriel did not at first grasp what she meant. Now he looked at her appraisingly. She pleased him. Her face was delicate; it had not yet lost the image of God, he thought. Aloud he said: "You're a grown-up girl."

"Papa, I'd like to talk to you alone."

"What about?"

"Oh, many things."

"Well—you're not going yet."

"Forgive me, Moshe Gabriel, but what's the point of sitting here in the study house?" Leah said. "I can understand that you don't want to see me. But the children would like to take some joy in their father. Why don't you go with them to Warsaw?"

"What business have I in Warsaw?"

"They'll take a room for you in a hotel."

"Out of the question."

"Then at least take them to your room."

"I live here in the rabbi's house. It isn't tidy there."

"Oh, I'll straighten it up," Lottie proposed.

"God forbid. You're a guest."

"I'll tell you what," Leah said. "Mendy, you come with me to the lodging-house; we'll get something to eat. Lottie can stay here with her father. Later we'll come back for her."

Moshe Gabriel was silent.

"Is that satisfactory to you?"

"Let it be so."

"And you, Aaron, come with us," Leah commanded.

Aaron looked questioningly at his father; Moshe Gabriel nodded his head. He could tell that Aaron was eager to be with his mother. A mother is a mother, Reb Moshe Gabriel reflected. That is the way of the world. Leah called Lottie over and whispered something to her. Aaron looked uncomfortable, smiling shyly. Strange that this was his mother, a lady in a hat—and that her husband was Koppel the overseer. "It's like something they describe in the newspapers," Aaron mused. He was afraid that he wouldn't know what to say to her; afraid that she might make fun of him, or want to take him with her to America. He threw a glance toward Lottie. She met his eyes, put two fingers to her lips and threw him a kiss. He felt his ears burning. He turned to his father.

"Good day."

"Where are you running?" Leah shouted. "We'll go together. You'll come with us. I'm your mother—not a strange woman."

Nevertheless Aaron left before the others. He hurried through the doorway, catching a fold of his capote on a nail and tearing it violently. It was growing very cold outside, yet his forehead was covered with perspiration. Unbalanced, Leah decided. Worse than his father. She felt the tears start to her eyes. "It's all his fault," she brooded, not sure herself whom it was she meant, Moshe Gabriel or Koppel. She hurried along to catch up with Aaron. When she reached him she took his arm, but he tried to free himself. She held on tighter. Yes, she had lost her youth. Now she was an old woman, the mother of a bearded Jew. But here, in Bialodrevna, there was no reason to be ashamed of it. Leah and Aaron walked on, Mendy stepping along in advance. He had been eager for this trip to Europe, but now he was fed up. He was tired of everything—the family, the hotels, the filth, the monotonous food, this constant talking and listening to Yiddish. He longed to be back in New York or in Saratoga Springs, where his mother took him during the summers. Mendy's mind was full of thoughts of baseball, football, horse races. He had been in the middle of a serial about Buffalo Bill. He and a friend of his, Jack, would sneak into a burlesque show once in a while. It was fun to sit in the balcony, a cigarette between your lips, chewing gum, and watch the strip-teasers take off one piece of clothing after another and finally stand there naked. He was bored by all of them—those queer uncles and aunts, who, even though he stood a head taller than any of them, kept on pinching his cheeks as though he were a baby. He made up his mind that when he got back to New York he'd never look at those greenhorns again. He'd never come to Europe again, except maybe to England.

2

When the others had left, Lottie turned to Moshe Gabriel.

"Can we go, Papa?" she said.

"Let it be so."

Moshe Gabriel went out into the courtyard, Lottie following him. She was his daughter, true, but just the same Moshe Gabriel tried to keep at a distance from her. Somebody might think that he was transgressing the law by walking with a strange female.

Lottie had almost to run to keep up with him. She reached him and put her hand on his arm. "Papa," she said, "are you in a hurry?"

The courtyard was unpaved. The snow was unswept. She had left her galoshes in Warsaw. Soon her stockings were wet. Moshe Gabriel glanced about him on all sides. A little distance off, there was a tree, but to his misted vision it suddenly seemed to be a man. He said, low but audibly: "It's my daughter."

"Papa, who are you talking to?"

"Never mind. I imagined for a minute—"

The flight of stairs that led to Moshe Gabriel's room was thick with mud. It had been months since the servant girl had bothered to sweep here. The room was cold; only seldom was the stove lighted. A pile of manuscripts lay on a table, with bricks placed on them to keep the pages from turning in the breeze. On a reading-stand a pile of open books was heaped, the uppermost one covered with a kerchief, for it is not proper to leave a holy volume exposed. On a small coffer lay a long pipe. Against the wall stood an iron cot, covered with a blanket, an uncovered pillow lying on it. Moshe Gabriel made a gesture with his hands. "A mess."

"It's not so bad," Lottie said.

"I'm used to it by now. Most of the day I spend in the study house. Well, how are you, my daughter? In America you speak, I suppose, what do you call it—English?"

"Oh, I speak Yiddish, too."

"I hear that you are quite a scholar in their things. Do you go to the university?"

"Yes, Papa, in my second year."

"And what do you study there? To be a doctor?"

"No, Papa. Science."

"What's that, electricity?"

"Some of everything."

"Do you at least remember that you're the daughter of a Jewish house?"

"Don't worry, Papa. The anti-Semites don't let you forget it."

"True, true. Even if a Jew is a sinner, he's still a Jew. He is still of Jacob's seed."

"They say that there are too many of us in the colleges."

"About that they're right. 'What has a priest to do in a cemetery?' What has a Jew to do with their schools?"

"But I can't study in a synagogue."

"A Jewish daughter's duty is to marry, not to run around in the Gymnasia."

"What is there in marrying? I want to learn, to get knowledge."

"To what end?"

"I want to be able to earn my living."

"The right way is for the husband to provide the livelihood and for the wife to attend to her wifely duties. 'The king's daughter is all glorious within.' The Jews are called children of kings."

"The men in America nowadays want women to have jobs."

"So that they may philander?"

Lottie's face turned red. "Yes, Papa," she said. "That's what it is."

"And I hear, too, that you're betrothed."

Lottie nodded, then bowed her head. "That's what I want to talk to you about," she said.

"Then speak."

"Ah, Papa, I just don't know how to begin. We're two different kinds of people. I'm like you. I like to read. I want to have a quiet life. He isn't that way; all he wants is to run around."

"Who is he? Where does he come from?"

"His father is a doctor. A rich man."

"And the boy? What is he? A charlatan?"

"No. But—but he likes to enjoy himself, to go to cabarets. He says he loves me, but just the same he goes around with other girls."

Moshe Gabriel sighed. "Run away from him as you would from a fire."

"Oh, Papa, if you'd only come to America!"

"What would I do in America? Still, who knows? What was it the rabbi of Kotsk said—'The Torah wanders.' One day it may even come there."

"Oh, yes, Papa. There are plenty of synagogues in America, too. And I miss you so, Papa. Oh, Papa, let me kiss you."

Moshe Gabriel felt his face flush. "Why? It's not necessary."

"Just because I love you, Papa."

"If you love me, my daughter, then follow in my path. If you yourself have become so estranged, think of how your children will be."

"No, Papa. I'll not have children."

Moshe Gabriel looked at her, baffled. "Why not? The prophet said: 'He created it not in vain, he formed it to be inhabited.' It is God's will that man should exist."

"But mankind suffers so much."

"All good comes only through suffering."

"Jews have special problems. They call us names. They don't let us into hotels. We can't belong to their clubs. So many are Zionists."

"It's an old story. 'It is known that Esau hates Jacob.' The more the Jew follows in the footsteps of the gentile, the more he is despised."

"Then what is there to do?"

"Penance! 'And repent and be healed.' God gave us a law, a way of life. If not for the Torah, then the nations—God forbid—would long ago have swallowed us up."

"Ah." Lottie was silent for a while. "Papa, there's something else I want to ask you. But don't be angry. Do you—do you ever see Masha?"

Moshe Gabriel felt the blood rush away from his face. "That apostate! May her name be blotted out!"

"Papa!"

"Don't utter her unclean name. Faugh!" Moshe Gabriel stopped his ears with his fingers and spat. He got up from his chair and began to pace back and forth. He shook his head from side to side. "I am no longer her father and she is no longer my daughter. Rather she die than that she bring forth new enemies for Israel."

Lottie bent her head. The tears streamed from Moshe Gabriel's eyes and remained trembling on his beard.

"Mine is the fault," he suddenly groaned, and thumped his fist over his heart. "I should not have been silent. The moment your mother began to send you to the schools of the gentiles, I should have taken you and the others and fled. Fled far away. Saved you while there was yet time."

He covered his eyes and remained standing in silence for a long time. When he dropped his hands, his face showed naked grief. The sacs under his eyes seemed to have grown larger. To Lottie it seemed that old age had suddenly descended upon him.

CHAPTER SIX

1

Simon Bendel, Shosha's boy friend, received a notice from the chalutzim organization that a certificate had been issued in his name for emigration to Palestine. Nine other young men and two girls had also received certificates. There was much excitement at the training farm at Grochov. Since the Palestine certificate was good for an entire family and it would be a shame to waste it on a single individual, the young men had to get married right away.

Simon Bendel put on his jacket and took the country line to visit Shosha in Praga. He came to tell her the news that he was preparing for the trip to Palestine. He spoke to Bashele plainly and to the point.

Although Shosha had told her mother several times that she

was ready to go to Palestine with Simon, Bashele had taken it
for little more than idle talk. For surely it was absurd to think
that Shosha would actually go off, travel away more than a
thousand miles, over seas and mountains; it was more than
Bashele could imagine. But now here was the young man in
person, sitting in front of her, showing her a piece of paper, a
certificate, black on white. From his heavy boots rivulets of
water dripped onto the kitchen floor. His face was red with
cold. A cloud of vapor steamed from his bushy hair. He
looked like a soldier to Bashele, in his tight breeches and the
puttees wrapped around his calves and the heavy leather belt
around his waist. He appeared like an ogre who had suddenly
come to carry off her daughter to the very ends of the earth.
His remarks were studded with the names of strange places
and cities—Lemberg, Vienna, Constanta, Tel Aviv, Haifa. He
was talking about the sea, ships, barracks. He was asking
them to procure a copy of Shosha's birth certificate and a
copy of the registration books so that her passport could be
prepared in time. Every word he uttered dropped like a stone
into Bashele's heart. As for Shosha, she smiled and brought
tea and bread and butter to Simon. She telephoned to Manyek
in the vinegar factory where he was employed as bookkeeper,
and Manyek called his father. It certainly would have been
wrong to marry off Shosha without her father's knowledge.
Koppel was not at the hotel, and it was Leah who came to the
telephone.

"Who's there?" she asked. "Koppel isn't home."

"Do you happen to know when he's coming back?" Manyek asked.

"That's something nobody knows," Leah shouted.

And it was true. Koppel would disappear to be gone all
day, and sometimes not come home at night. There was much
confusion among the visitors from America. Lottie had received a letter from her fiancé informing her that he was
breaking their engagement. When she read the news, she had
pulled off her diamond engagement ring and had thrown it
out of the window. Mendy had chased outside to try to recover it, but he came back to report that he had been unable to
find it. Leah suspected that the boy had actually found the
ring and was hiding it somewhere or had sold it. Mendy had
been quick to make acquaintances in Warsaw among a crowd
of boys and girls whom he took to the movies. In order to
conceal her miserable lot from her family, Leah kept away
from all of them. Queen Esther and Saltsha had finally made

overtures and invited her to their homes, but Leah had managed to avoid the visits. She ate alone in restaurants, and went out on long walks, from the hotel to the bridge and from there back to Three Crosses Place. She was as lonely in Warsaw as in New York. She would stop in front of a shop window, gaze vacantly at the things on display, and murmur to herself: "Koppel, the thief. Yes, I got what was coming to me."

Koppel spent most of his time at the Oxenburgs'. Reitze prepared a room for him and fed him all the dishes he fancied: tripe, marinated fish in sweet and sour sauce. The Polish mark was dropping in value daily and the American dollar was climbing. No matter how extravagantly Koppel scattered his money, living still was dirt cheap. He bought for Zilka, the widow, a fur coat and a gold watch. He saw to it that a doctor visited Isador Oxenburg, and paid a masseur to massage his ailing legs. He helped the younger daughter, Regina, to get a flat, paying key money to the vacating tenant. He was even lavish in his favors to his old cronies, Itchele Peltsevisner, Motie the Red, and Leon the Peddler. David Krupnick had stopped visting the Oxenburg apartment ever since Koppel had installed himself there. His wife, however, the former Mrs. Goldsober, was there frequently and stayed late. She smoked her asthma cigarettes and played poker with Koppel. He must have forgotten all he knew about the game while he was in America, the others decided, because hardly an evening went by when he did not manage to lose at least a few marks. Mrs. Krupnick would always make the same comment: "You certainly must have a lot of luck in love."

Koppel made a regular business of searching out all his old friends and acquaintances. He learned that Naomi, Reb Meshulam's housekeeper, now ran a bakery on Nizka Street. One evening he went there to look for her. Koppel learned from Naomi what had happened to Manya. She had married, but was not living with her husband. She was working in a crockery store on Mirovska Street. She lived at the home of her employer somewhere on Ptasha Street. There was no telephone in the house, and Koppel took a droshky. It was already late and he had some hesitation whether or not he should call on her at such an hour. He passed a dim court that gave off odors of garlic and rotten apples. In a small Chassidic prayerhouse a group of the devout was dancing. Koppel stood watching the ecstatic Chassidim forming in a circle, separating, stamping with their heavy boots, shaking their bearded faces. He felt an urge to go inside and make some sort of contribution, but he overcame the impulse. He climbed a few flights of dark stairs and knocked at a door on the third floor. He heard footsteps at once, and then Manya's voice asking: *"Kto tam?* Who's there?"

"It's me. Koppel."

"Who? The old man's not here.'

"Open the door, Manya. It's me. Koppel the overseer."

There was silence, then the sound of the chain being unhooked, and the door opened. In the dim light of the corridor Koppel saw her, older but still with a girlishness about her, in a fashionable dress, wearing earrings and a necklace of imitation coral. Her flat features were powdered, her Kalmuk eyes penciled. "Koppel! It's really you!" she shouted.

"Yes, it's me."

"Mother mine, if a thing like this can happen, then I don't know what—" She clapped her hands and broke into a peal of laughter. "I knew. I always knew that you'd show up again."

"What made you so sure?"

"Oh, I knew all right. I know everything."

She led him into the kitchen. The householders were not at home. The room was spacious, with a tiled floor and copperware basins on the walls. A deck of playing-cards lay on a stool. The cot against the wall bore an indentation where Manya had been sitting on it. She began to fuss about Koppel, sniffing with her wide nostrils. "The same Koppel. No change."

"And you, too, Manya," Koppel had reverted to the familiar second-person singular. "You're the same."

She looked at him suspiciously and again broke out laughing. "I'm a nobody," she said. "You're the one that got to be Reb Meshulam's son-in-law. That's something."

"It's not worth a grosz."

"Just listen to him. How did you find out where I was?"

"From Naomi."

"How did she know?"

"That you'll have to ask her."

"Koppel to the bone. Not changed a hair. When did you come? Is Leah in Warsaw too?"

"Yes, that bargain is here."

Manya made a grimace. "So that's the way it is, eh?" She was silent for a moment. "Here. Don't stand at the door, you're not a beggar. Sit down on the bed."

"I hear that you got married."

"My God, the man knows everything. Yes, I got married. I fell in like a blind horse in a ditch."

"So. No good, eh?" Koppel lit a cigarette.

"Look at the man. He's here less than five minutes after God knows how many years and he expects a complete report. Here, I'll give you a glass of tea. The night is still young."

Manya flitted over to the stove and put on a kettle of water.

2

At about half past eleven there was a ring at the door. Manya's mistress and master were returning. Manya quickly turned off the gaslight in the kitchen and ran to open the door. Koppel stayed alone in the dark room. As he sat there in this strange room, on the edge of Manya's cot, he suddenly had the feeling of being a youngster again, a little clerk on Bagno Street, chasing after servant girls. Smells he had long ago forgotten came to him from an open pantry door: chicory, green soap, citric acid, washing soda. He had to use all his self control to avoid sneezing. In the corridor he could hear the master of the house muttering something or other and shuffling his feet on the mat. The mistress was laughing. He took a cigarette out of his pocket and put it between his lips, in readiness to light it as soon as it was safe. That idiot, that Manya, he reflected. Why had he bothered to get mixed up with such an ignoramus, with her belief in dreams and her constant fortune-telling with playing cards? Valuable time wasted. He could have spent the evening with Zilka. He bit his lower lip. Go and figure out that a lump like that would take it into her head to play the lady. Marriage, children, respectability—she had the gall to talk about things like that! To divorce Leah and marry her!

He stretched and put a hand up to his mouth to stifle a yawn. "Why the devil did I have to plead with her?" he reflected. "She'll get a swelled head." There was only one thing he wanted now—to go home and sleep.

Manya opened the door and came in. "Koppel, you're still here?"

"What did you think? That I'd get out through the window?"

"They've gone to sleep. The old lady almost walked in here." Manya started to giggle.

Koppel took a deep breath. "Well, never mind. I'm going now."

"You don't have to rush if you don't want to. I'll walk down with you."

"Don't do me any favors. I'm asking you for the last time. Yes or no?"

"No."

"A hundred dollars."

"Not even a thousand," Manya murmured.

He put on his coat and hat and stuck his feet into his overshoes, which stood near the kitchen door. He could see Manya's glowing Kalmuk eyes. He took her by the shoulders. "Well, let me at least give you a kiss," he said.

"Sure. No charge for kissing."

He pressed his lips against hers and she kissed him back ardently, even pinching his lips with her teeth. He had a strange feeling. He wanted neither to stay there with her nor to go away. There was an obstinacy in him, as in a man in the middle of a card game stubbornly trying to win back his losses. "All right," he said. "What is it you want? What exactly do you want?"

"I told you already. I want to live a respectable life."

"What's to stop you from getting married any time you like? I'll give you a dowry."

"I've got a dowry of my own."

"Then good-by, my high-toned friend."

"Good-by. And don't be angry with me."

She opened the outer door and he went down the steps. He walked slowly and wearily. In his pocket he had steamer passage back to America. First-class cabins for himself, Leah, and the two children. But as he felt now, he was far from sure that he would not postpone the journey back. Leah was getting worse from day to day. She cursed him, shrieked, created all sorts of scandals. Ever since she had had her change of life she was half crazy. How could he go on living with a woman like that? What good was the Riverside Drive apartment in New York to him? Suppose he brought the whole thing to an end, once and for all? He started to do some quick figuring. Even if he gave her twenty-five thousand dollars he'd still have plenty left. He'd marry Zilka. Maybe they'd even have a child. No, he wouldn't marry her. He wouldn't marry a woman who was willing to go to bed with another man, and her husband not three months dead. Bashele, on the other hand, had married a coal dealer. My God, how could a woman spread clean sheets for such a dirty creature?

Koppel wanted to take a droshky, but he waited for fifteen minutes without seeing one. Nor did he see a taxi. A streetcar went by, but he could not tell what its route was. He started to walk toward the hotel, tapping at his back pocket where he carried his traveler's checks. But what good was money? Even Manya, the servant, threw it back at him.

Not far from the hotel entrance he saw a girl, hatless and with a creased jacket much too big for her, in a too long, old-fashioned skirt. He stood and looked at her. One of those streetwalkers? No, they did not dress like that. Maybe she was a beginner out for the first time. He crossed the street toward her, strange thoughts blundering through his mind. Suppose he should go over to her and help her. She looked like a gentle child. And why was she staring at him so curiously? Suddenly he froze in his tracks. There was something familiar about her, though he could not say exactly what. She was waving to him and running toward him. It was Shosha. Koppel felt a sudden dryness in his throat. "What are you doing here?" he stammered.

"Oh, Papa, I've been waiting for you—"

"Why? Why didn't you go upstairs?"

"I didn't want to. Your wife—" she stopped abruptly.

"What's happened? Speak clearly."

"Papa, he got a certificate to go to Palestine. He wants to get married right away."

Koppel rubbed his hand against his forehead. "Well—well —what's that got to do with your hanging out here in the street?"

"I've been looking for you for the last three days and—"

"Well, why didn't you write me a letter?"

Shosha shrugged her shoulders. The tears came into Koppel's eyes. He took his daughter by the arm and then glanced up along the front of the hotel building. There wasn't even a place he could take his own flesh and blood to. And, God almighty, the way she was dressed. He remembered with shame that he had not given them more than fifty dollars since he had come to Warsaw. "What was the sense of staying out here in the street?" he muttered. "Where's that boy of yours, that what's-his-name?"

"He lives with the chalutzim."

"Where? He's probably sleeping already."

"Oh no. He's waiting for me. We have to fill out papers."

"Just a minute. I'm tired. Hey, driver!" A droshky was passing and Koppel hailed it The two climbed in. Koppel leaned back against the seat. He asked Shosha to tell the driver where to go. Then he turned to his daughter. "What's the hurry about getting married? Do you at least love him?"

"The certificate will soon expire—"

"And what'll you do there in Palestine?"

"We'll work."

"You can work here too."

"But Palestine is our own country."

"Well, anyway, that's your affair. Only he looks to me like a kind of wild man."

"That's only his way."

Koppel put up his coat collar and lapsed into silence. Anything was possible, he thought, but that he would be traveling in a droshky with his daughter to some chalutzim somewhere, that very night, he had not imagined. He was only half awake.

The droshky came to a halt. The two climbed out and Koppel paid the driver. Shosha pulled the bell at the gate. The rooms of the chalutzim were on the street floor. They were brightly lighted, as though it were still early in the evening. Boys were packing bundles, driving nails into crates. A girl was sewing up a canvas duffel bag with a heavy needle and a length of rope. On the walls there were a map of Palestine and a portrait of Theodor Herzl. An uncovered table at the side of the room was strewn with Hebrew books and newspapers. Koppel stared around him in astonishment. He had read vaguely here and there about Zionism, the Balfour Declaration, chalutzim, but he had never given any special thought to these things. And now Shosha was one of them.

A short girl with heavy legs came over and whispered something to her. Shosha knocked at a side door. Simon Bendel came out, in a shirt open at the collar and showing his wide, hairy chest.

"What's going on here?" Koppel asked. "What's all the rushing around?"

"We're leaving in two weeks."

"For Palestine, eh?"

"Where else?"

Koppel scratched his head. "Well," he said, "I'll give her a dowry. It will be all right."

"We don't need a dowry," Simon said after some hesitation.

"Why not? Money comes in handy anywhere."

The youth dropped his head and did not answer; after a while he left the room. Koppel looked at Shosha. "It's late," he said. "Aren't you going to sleep tonight?"

"I'm going home right away. In just a minute."

She disappeared also. Koppel sat down on a bench near the table and picked up a book that lay there. It was in Hebrew. He turned the pages. There were pictures of agricultural colonies, girls milking cows, chalutzim guiding plows. Things were going on, he reflected. Things were going on with the Jews that he knew nothing about. He had no control even over his own children. What would happen to Teibele and Yppe? What would become of them with that coal dealer for a father? He had lost everything—his wife, his children, the world to come. A strange notion possessed him. Suppose he should go along with these youngsters. Suppose he should go to Palestine. After all, what they were building there was a Jewish home.

CHAPTER SEVEN

Shosha received from her father a dowry of five hundred dollars, a diamond ring, and a gold chain. The wedding was held at the home of an official Warsaw rabbi. Koppel provided money for new clothes for Bashele and the girls and gave presents to his son and daughter-in-law. At first Bashele's husband declared that he would not go to the wedding; why was it necessary for a stepfather to be there, when the girl had her own father and mother present, thank God? But Koppel insisted that he come. He visited Chaim Leib in the coal store, extended his hand, and said: "You belong there more than me, Chaim Leib."

And the two talked so long and warmly together that finally they went over to the near-by inn for a drink.

The wedding canopy was not to be set up until nine in the evening, but by eight o'clock the guests had already begun to gather. On the groom's side there assembled a group of chalutzim in sheepskin jackets, broad-peaked caps, and heavy boots. They dragged mud onto the rabbi's polished floors, dropped cigarette stubs and ashes. They spoke in a mixture of Yiddish and Hebrew. The beadle scolded them and told them to observe a little decorum. The rabbi's wife, an elegant lady with a matron's dyed wig, opened a door to glare at them. It was difficult to believe that such a nondescript group could talk so easily in the holy tongue. Bashele's sister, from the Old City, brought her wedding gift with her wrapped in a kerchief. Shosha's cousins and the girls she had gone to school with whispered to one another in Polish, throwing curious glances at the chalutzim. The beadle complained that there was too much of a crowd. "What do they think this is?" he asked. "A wedding hall?"

Simon Bendel wanted to go through the ceremony in his military breeches and puttees, in the chalutz manner, but Koppel insisted that he wear a suit, a hat, and a tie. The chalutzim constantly kept up a play of pulling him by his necktie. Shosha was wearing a black silk dress and patent-leather shoes, a tulle scarf over her hair. Her mother flanked her on one side; her sister-in-law, Manyek's wife, on the other. Koppel arrived late. He had had himself carefully barbered for the occasion and had put on a dinner jacket, patent-leather shoes, and a starched shirt with gold cuff-links. In one hand he carried an enormous bottle of champagne and in the other a box of honey cakes and cookies. He shook everybody by the hand, his remarks peppered with English words. When Bashele saw him she began to cry; her sister had to take her into another room until she could compose herself. Now that Koppel had made up for all the offenses he had committed against her, her anger was gone. Chaim Leib had washed and soaped himself over and over again, but the grime of the coalyard still lay deeply encrusted on his face and his thick neck. His fingernails were framed in black. His gaberdine was too short. His boots, freshly polished, had muddy uppers. He stood apart from the others, watching reverently as the white-bearded rabbi wrote out the marriage certificate. "Is the bride a virgin?" the rabbi asked.

"Yes, a virgin," Koppel answered after a slight hesitation.

"It says here in this marriage contract that the husband takes upon himself the obligation of supporting his wife, providing her with food and clothing, and living with her as a husband. If he divorces her, then he is obligated to pay her two hundred gulden, and if, may God forbid, he dies, then the debt rests upon his heirs."

Bashele burst into a sob. Shosha put her handkerchief to her eyes.

The ceremony proceeded as custom and law dictated. The

beadle brought out of a closet a canopy supported on four poles. Candles were lit. A beaker was filled with wine. The groom put on a white robe to remind him of death. Two women escorted the bride as she circled the groom seven times. The rabbi intoned the benediction. Simon took a wedding ring from his pocket and placed it on the index finger of the bride's right hand, saying: "Behold, thou art sanctified to me with this ring according to the law of Moses and Israel." The couple sipped from the beaker of wine. Chaim Leib was holding a braided candle. The flame spluttered and flickered, throwing grotesque shadows on the walls and ceiling. After the ceremony there was a fervid exchange of greetings and good wishes. The chalutzim became gay. They formed a circle, hands on shoulders, and began singing in Hebrew:

> *"Work is our life,*
> *It will save us from all ills."*

"Quiet, quiet," the rabbi scolded them. He had no time to waste on the celebrations and carryings-on of this throng, nor was he in any mood to listen to these modern songs, which smacked of heresy.

A tall, lean youth with a pointed Adam's apple took umbrage. "What's bothering you, rabbi? We are building a Jewish home."

" 'Except the Lord build the house, they labor in vain that build it.' "

"Come on, Benjamin. It's a waste of time to argue."

The chalutzim put on their sheepskin jackets and left together. Everyone was against them—the orthodox Jews, the Socialist Bundists, the Communists. But they were not the kind to be frightened off. If the Messiah had not come riding on his ass by now, then it was time to take one's destiny into one's own hands. They tramped out, thumping the floor with their heavy-soled boots, and singing:

> *"In the land of the fathers*
> *All hopes will come true."*

The others left shortly after. Shosha's aunt and the cousins took a streetcar. The young couple climbed into a droshky with Bashele and Chaim Leib. They had been given the room where previously Koppel had been accustomed to retire to weave his plans.

Koppel asked his daughter: "Well, how does it feel to be a newlywed?"

"Like a human being, Papa. No different," she answered.

"Koppel, thank you for everything you've done," Bashele stammered.

"What's there to thank me for? My own daughter!"

The droshky rolled away. Koppel put up his coat collar and gazed after the vehicle until it turned a corner. That he should have married off his daughter, here in Warsaw! It was something that he had not imagined. How long ago was it that Shosha was born? How the time flew by! Soon he would probably be a grandfather. You can rely on a guy like that. Koppel bit his lips. He lit a cigarette, breathing the smoke in deeply. Strange how things were! For years and years he had loved Leah; he had almost expired with longing at the sight of her. And now that she was his wife, he was ready to thank God when he could be away from her. He wanted to go to bed, but he knew that Leah would not let him rest. Now she was probably angry that she had not been invited to his daughter's wedding. Koppel went into a delicatessen store to telephone. He called the Oxenburgs'.

Zilka answered the phone, talking to him in Polish. "Oh, Koppel darling," she said. "It's you. Is the wedding over?"

"Yes, the mischief's done."

"Congratulations. What are you doing tonight? There was some woman here looking for you."

"Who? Who was it?"

"I don't know. A dark woman, with kind of slanting eyes. She said you should call her."

Manya, damn her guts, Koppel thought with a feeling of triumph. "Well, it doesn't matter," he said.

He took a taxi over to the Oxenburgs'. Zilka was waiting for him at the entrance to the courtyard. She was wearing the caracul jacket that Koppel had given her. She was hatless. From her white powdered face a pair of greedy eyes looked out at him. Koppel was eager for love, but this female had only one thing on her mind, to get as much money as she could from him. In the midst of his most ardent caresses she would whisper: "Koppel, give me a dollar."

Koppel was not hungry now, but Zilka wanted him to take her to a restaurant. That small mouth of hers, powdered at the edges to make it appear even smaller, was like a yawning pit. She ate everything and anything: goose, stuffed derma, calf's foot with garlic, tripe. And she could pour all sorts of liquor into herself—vodka, cognac, beer—as long as Koppel had to pay the bill. The only indulgence she could not stand was the real thing. At that game she would turn cold as a fish. She had no patience for his demanding amorousness. She worried all the time lest he might tear or spoil her embroidered underwear. Besides, she kept on sighing over her dead husband. When he left her, Koppel was never satisfied. Now that Manya had come to look him up, it was on Koppel's mind to teach Zilka a lesson. He neither greeted her nor kissed her hand, as had lately become his custom. He did not even take the cigarette from his lips.

He did not go home to sleep that night. It was late in the morning when he returned to the hotel. He was prepared for Leah's shrieks and curses. He had his answer ready for her. If she did not like it, he would give her a divorce and pay her alimony. As he walked into the lobby someone came toward him, someone profoundly familiar and yet equally strange. It was himself, Koppel, his own image reflected in a mirror. The face was yellow, the hair at the temples almost gray.

PART
NINE

CHAPTER ONE

The idea that happiness and morality are identical was not only a postulate of Spinoza's *Ethics*—which Asa Heshel still pored over in his free hours—it was also the outgrowth of his own views. All his reflections led him to the conclusion that the only goal of humanity was enjoyment. Had not the Torah itself promised rain in time as a reward for obeying God's commands? Were not the world to come and the coming of the Messiah in reality no more than the promise of joy? Had Marxism any other goal than the achievement of happiness? Yes, that is what he, Asa Heshel, had himself yearned for morning and night. But many forces had operated to block his aims.

His own nature remained a riddle to him. According to Spinoza, joy could be achieved only in community with others, yet he, Asa Heshel, avoided mankind. He did not drink, did not dance, did not belong to any group or organization in which he might make friends. He sat by himself in his study and brooded over emotions and passions that could only lead to unrest of the mind. He had long ago given up any hope of finding answers to the eternal questions. Nevertheless they gave him no surcease. He agreed with the philosopher of Amsterdam that the sage meditates least on death and the ideas that minimize joy. But he could not free himself from his emotions. He paced back and forth between his bookshelves, knit his brows, bit his lips, murmuring a Chassidic melody that had stayed with him from Tereshpol Minor. He voiced in his mind complaints to the God whose eternal watchfulness he doubted.

There was a knock at the door. Hadassah looked in. "Asa Heshel," she said, "Dacha is sick."

"What's the matter now?"

"Her throat. Please telephone to Dr. Mintz."

For a moment the two looked at each other. With the passing of the years Asa Heshel's hair had thinned. His back was stooped, though Hadassah had cautioned him many times to stand erect. Mintz, the son of old Dr. Mintz, had assured her that Asa Heshel was perfectly sound, but she still worried about his constant pallor. Why did he eat so little? Why did he wake in the middle of the night and find it impossible to get back to sleep? Hadassah was worried that some sort of concealed illness lurked in his system.

Hadassah was still beautiful, although the events of the passing years had left their mark on her. At first Adele had refused to give Asa Heshel a divorce. They had lived together without benefit of clergy. It was as though she lived a life of excommunication. And when at last Adele, after much bargaining, had consented to a divorce, and Hadassah and Asa Heshel had married, there were fresh troubles to plague her. She had gone through a difficult pregnancy and an even more difficult labor. Dacha—the child had been named after Hadassah's mother—was delicate. Asa Heshel had wanted a boy and could make no peace with the thought that he had a daughter. Besides, there was always a lack of money. From his earnings as a teacher he had to contribute to the support of his son, of his mother, of his sister and her children, for Dinah's husband earned only a pittance from the Talmud lessons he gave. And there were other things, too, to make Hadassah regretful. Her gold-blond hair showed signs of fading; the first fine creases were beginning to appear at the corners of her eyes. Her figure, however, still remained girlish.

Asa Heshel approached her. "Did you look into her throat?" he asked.

"She won't let me."

"Well, don't worry. She'll be all right, you little idiot." He embraced and kissed her. Hadassah closed her eyes. As always when he was tender to her, she felt lighter at once. For all she had been his wife for years, she was never satiated with him. In the daytime he was seldom at home. In the evening he was usually occupied with preparing his lessons for the next day, correcting papers, or reading. Frequently he would go out to visit Hertz Yanovar, or elsewhere, Hadassah had no idea where. Sometimes, over the merest trifle, he would go off into a silence for days. His good moments could almost be counted. Now that the child was not well, Hadassah was in mortal terror lest he fall again into one of his sullen rages, especially because the constant visits of Dr. Mintz ate up half his income. But one never knew how he would react. Now he stood with his arms about her at the threshold, kissing her eyes, her nose, her throat, taking the lobe of her ear between his lips. He led her to the sofa and took her on his lap. He began to rock and soothe her as though she was a child. "Sh-sh, sh-sh, Hadassah'la," he murmured to her. "I love you."

The tears came into her eyes. "Ah, Asa," she murmured.

The door opened. It was Yadwiga, the maid. She could not be taught not to enter a room without knocking. Seeing the mistresss sitting on the master's lap, the girl stood gaping. Her broad face, with the high Slavic cheekbones, flushed, making her eyes glow an even lighter blue.

"Ach, *przepraszam,* excuse me," she said, and started to retreat.

Asa Heshel called her back. "What is it you want, Yadwiga?"

"I put on the water to heat for the child's throat," she said.

Hadassah looked at her with a shining glance. "Put some in a glass with salt and let it cool."

"The boy from the coal dealer was here."

Hadassah's face turned serious. "I'll be over there later."

Yadwiga still hesitated at the door. It was time to prepare a meal, but the larder was empty. No meat had been bought and there was only a little milk left. She wanted to ask her mistress what to prepare for supper, but somehow the sight of Hadassah on Asa Heshel's lap, the appealing way in which her slipper dangled from the tip of her foot, gave the girl a warm feeling in her breast. Her feet were glued to the floor. "Don't worry, mistress," she said. "I'll take care of everything."

She went away. Hadassah felt some embarrassment, but at the same time she enjoyed having the maid witness her triumph. Asa Heshel looked toward the double window. As he sat thus, how difficult it was to believe that he had known her now for fifteen years! If anyone had told him when he first met her on Panska Street that she would be his wife one day, the mother of his child! How strange time is!

Aloud he said: "So you haven't paid the coal dealer yet?"

Hadassah tensed. "No."

"But you took ten zlotys from me to pay."

Hadassah thought for a moment. "I must have spent it on something else."

"On what?"

"On a present for you. I wanted it to be a surprise."

"Those surprises of yours will drive me to bankruptcy."

Asa Heshel knit his brows. It was foolish of her to waste money on all sorts of nonsense when there was hardly enough to pay for the basic necessities. But what could he do? He had talked to her about it a thousand times. She had given him her sacred oath that she would be less extravagant. There was no doubt that the woman had a positive mania for wandering about the shops and acquiring bargains.

Hadassah went to the child. Asa Heshel telephoned to the doctor. The winter night began to fall. Outside the daylight turned into a bluish glow. This was a day when Asa Heshel had no classes. He had started to look over his old manuscript, but now the day was gone. In the lingering dusk he brooded over himself, his life. What had he accomplished during his years? What had become of him? He had remained trapped in Poland, laden down with work, deep in debt, weighted down by family burdens. How long could he carry the yoke?

He lay down on the couch and started to doze. Here he was in his thirties, but the unrest in him had not yet been quenched. He still ached with the ancient youthful doubts, dreams, and desires.

CHAPTER TWO

1

In the evening, after dinner, there was a sharp ring at the door. Hadassah was attending to the child in the bedroom and the maid was out. Asa Heshel went to open. Abram stood there, his huge fur hat, long fur coat, and high galoshes white with snow. A cigar was between his lips. Asa Heshel had not seen him for a long time and hardly recognized him now. The broad figure was bent, the beard white, the deep sacs under the eyes covered with a mossy growth. He came in coughing and panting, stamping his feet to rid them of the snow, thumping his stick, whose silver-plated staghorn handle was half broken.

"What are you standing there staring at me for?" he shouted. "Don't you recognize me any more?"

"You look tired. Did you walk up?"

"The janitor wouldn't give me the key to the elevator."

Asa Heshel paled. "Why?"

"An anti-Semitic dog!"

Abram took off his coat, his scarf, and his galoshes. Underneath he was wearing a black jacket and striped trousers. He wore an artist's flowing tie. His belly had grown enormous;

his coat could not button over it. A silver watch chain dangled at his vest. He took out a handkerchief and wiped the perspiration from the bald patch on his head and the stray locks of hair that grew around it, and from his red forehead, sighing as he did so. "Well, you see what's become of me," he said. "All I'm good for is to render into fat."

Hadassah came out of the child's room and flung herself into Abram's arms. She covered him with kisses. The three went into the living-room, where Abram threw himself down on a couch, the springs groaning and sagging under his weight. For a long time he sat there breathing deeply. Gradually he regained his composure. "Well, what are you standing over me that way for? I'm not dead yet. Hadassah, guess what I brought for you. Here. Close your eyes and open your mouth."

Abram lifted his shaking hand to his inner breast pocket, rummaging around. He brought out a packet of protested notes, a foreign passport that had long ago expired, some lottery tickets, letters—a whole miscellany of papers. His pocket must have had a hole, for some of the contents had fallen into the lining. Digging his hand deep down, he brought up a pair of sun glasses; he had lost them months before.

"I must be in my dotage already," he muttered.

Just then his fingers clutched what he was looking for. It was a folded clipping from a Yiddish newspaper. He shook it and two tickets fell out. He settled his eyeglasses on his nose and began to read aloud in a strong voice: "A Ball of all Balls! A thousand attractions. A hundred prizes. Voting for a beauty queen and seven princesses. Jazz band. Buffet of the finest foods. Oriental dances. Salon decorated by the greatest painters. Special revue by distinguished stars. Recitations of modern and classical poets. A Jewish magician, Mr. Trick of America, in a performance which has baffled the greatest scientists. A Jewish strong man, whose name must be kept secret for the present, rending chains and breaking iron, as well as female hearts. Each guest will automatically participate in a lottery and may win such gifts as a Channukah lamp, an alarm clock, a lorgnette, a Japanese fan, a *bonbonnière,* and the finest gift that any Jew might wish—a set of the works of Mendele Mocher Sforim, in a de luxe binding. And in case you're wondering what this event is, it is the masquerade ball of the Jewish press, to be held on the third night of Channukah, at the . . ."

Abram interrupted his reading, then began again, first

blowing his nose. He thumped his fist on the table as he read, swallowing some of the words in his haste. The rest he declaimed in an exaggerated manner with all the vocal nuances of the Polish-Yiddish dialect. From time to time his voice broke into a loud asthmatic wheeze. At the end of the announcement was a list of the judges who were to choose the beauty queen. Among the painters, writers and actors whose names were printed in fat type was: "The well-known community figure and Mæcenas of the arts, Abram Shapiro." Abram's face flushed to an apoplectic red. "And you'll be the one to win," he boomed, "whether they like it or not."

"I really don't know what you mean, Uncle," Hadassah said.

"Don't be so naïve," Abram growled. "I've seen the other candidates. Apes, every last one of them."

Abram subsided into silence. Only the day before, he had promised Dr. Mintz that he'd watch his diet, stop smoking his heavy cigars, keep away from liquor, avoid getting excited over every trifle. Dr. Mintz had warned him that another attack might spell his finish. But what could he do about the ridiculous character he had? The smallest thing would set him off in wild excitement. Hadassah kept turning her gaze from Abram to Asa Heshel.

"Oh, Uncle," she said, "I can't think about balls now. My little Dacha's sick."

Abram's big black eyes immediately grew moist. "What is it?" he asked.

"I don't know. It's something different every day. It's getting to be impossible."

Abram got up from the couch. "Crying already, eh? And I, idiot that I am, want to make her a beauty queen when she's nothing but a mournful Jewess. Well, children get sick. My Bella's house is a regular hospital. One of the brats gets out of the bed and the other gets into it. The place is a mess. The doctors take away every last penny. Well, after we've kicked the bucket they'll overturn the world. Tell me, Asa Heshel, how about you? You don't seem to be bursting with happiness."

"It's a wonder I stay alive."

Abram shook his head dolefully. "What's the matter with you? These things happen in the best of families."

"I'm sick of all this family stuff." He was sorry the moment he spoke.

Hadassah looked at him in astonishment. "It isn't my fault that the baby's sick."

"That's only one of the things that's wrong with us."

Hadassah's cheeks flushed. She made a convulsive movement of her throat, as though she was swallowing something. "Any time you want to go, you're free."

Abram looked at the two, puzzled, and tried to pass it off as a joke. "People in love always pick at each other."

"Oh, no, Uncle. It's no use. He's serious about it."

Hadassah began to make small futile movements at the table, picking up a glass, putting it down again, turning to the right and to the left, fidgeting with her hands. Abruptly she went out of the room.

Abram shrugged his shoulders. "What do you torture her for?" he asked. "You love her, don't you? Ah, you young people—"

Asa Heshel went out too, leaving Abram alone. Abram picked up the newspaper clipping, which he had put on the table, and restored it to his pocket. He carefully placed a salt-shaker on the two tickets to prevent them from blowing away. He had recently seen much. He had witnessed hatred and bitterness everywhere. He found it impossible now to stay at home. Since Hama had died, the flat had been unlivable. Even the mice had fled. His daughter Stepha had quarreled with her husband and was now on the brink of a divorce. Bella bore on her shoulders the whole burden of making a livelihood. Avigdor, the fool, had become a petty trader on the Ghzybov, earning barely enough to buy the water for the barley. And now it seemed that Hadassah, too, was part of an unhappy household. What did they want, these people? Why were they all eager to tear one another to pieces?

Abram got up and went into the bedroom. Hadassah was not there. A dim lamp was burning, and the child lay sleeping in her crib. Abram looked at her for a long time. The long features were pale, with a porcelain-like pallor. The brown hair, the round brow, the too red lips, the closed eyes, the little white nose, all these reminded him of a doll. He remembered what Dr. Mintz had told him some time before, that the child might not live long.

Abram sat down on a chair and picked up one of the child's playthings. His thoughts reverted to the press ball. He needed a tuxedo, a new shirt, a pair of patent-leather shoes. He knew that Ida would not go to the ball unless she had a new dress.

He had promised Bella a hundred zlotys. Where was he to get the money? The house in which he had inherited a half interest was in almost complete ruins. Any time in the next few days a municipal squad was to come to evict the tenants. A man would have to have the heart of a scoundrel to collect rent from such paupers.

No, it was not the same Warsaw. And he was not the same Abram. But just the same a man went on living. And he'd have to find, somewhere or other, a couple of hundred zlotys. And he'd have to have the money at the latest by the coming week. If not, he was done for.

He put his hand to his beard and began plucking at the hairs. He knew that Hadassah still had a pearl necklace, left to her by her mother. He could pawn it for at least five hundred gulden and then pay three months' interest in advance. Before the period was up he would surely, somehow or other, be able to redeem it. After all, wasn't he at the very threshold of carrying off a real stroke of business? The important thing was to keep up appearances.

2

From Asa Heshel's house Abram went to see Ida, on Holy Cross Street. The times when Abram had traveled around the town in droshkies were past. He climbed into a streetcar. Ida's studio and her flat next door were on the fifth floor of the building. The elevator was not working, and Abram climbed up slowly, stopping every once in a while to rest and catch his breath. He smoked his cigar and cocked his ears. He knew everyone in the building, every child, every man, every *shikse*. On the first floor lived a government censor of Hebrew books. Abram would stop for a chat with him from time to time. On the second floor lived an aged Polish Countess, who went about on crutches with plush pads on the arm supports. Abram often greeted her or opened the door for her. The Countess's servant girl had once confided to Abram that she was pregnant. Abram had written a letter to a doctor he knew, and the girl had been able to get an abortion for thirty zlotys.

Abram listened. His heart was bad, but his hearing was sharp. He could catch every sound. From the attic room came the sound of a piano. It was the hunchback, who always had a

procession of girls coming to him. A man with asthma
coughed, spat, and wheezed. That was Pan Vladislav Halpern,
the administrator. A phonograph blurted out a popular song.

Abram closed his eyes. He loved good music. Often he
went to hear the Philharmonic concerts. But the simple songs
that housemaids and courtyard singers sang went straight to
his heart. How beautiful the world was! How lovely girls were!
—And how cleverly the year was divided into its seasons—
summer, autumn, winter, spring! How wonderful that there
was day, and night, and men, and women, and birds and cattle! There was only one thing that wasn't worth a plague:
death. Why should he, Abram, have angina pectoris? What
would he be doing through the long winter nights over there
in the Gensha cemetery? And even admitting that there was
such a thing as paradise, what good would it be to him? He'd
rather have the Warsaw streets than all the wisdom of a Jewish paradise.

He climbed the last flight of stairs and opened Ida's door
with his key. Ida was apparently asleep. He turned on a light.
The skylight was covered with snow. On the floor were scattered canvases, brushes, paper, paints. On the iron stove stood
a pot of unpeeled potatoes. A pair of stockings was drying on
the oven pipe. There was an old portrait of Abram on the
wall, an Abram with a black beard and glistening eyes. In recent times Abram had had scant pleasure out of Ida. She was
always ailing, always quarreling over the merest trifle. She
had stopped sending pictures for exhibition to the Jewish art
societies. She wasn't young any more. She was a woman along
in the fifties, if not even older than that. Her daughter in Berlin was already a mother. But there was still fire in Ida. She
still staged jealous scenes. She could never forget his betrayal
of her with Ninotchka. Abram sat down on a chair, puffing at
his cigar. He took out the string of pearls that he had got at
Hadassah's. He looked carefully at each pearl. How old, he
wondered, were they? Dacha had got them from her mother,
and her mother had got them from her mother when she was
married. Yes, people died, but things lived on. The least cob-
blestone in the street was millions of years old.

As he sat there blowing smoke rings, Ida came in from the
bedroom. Over her nightgown she wore a wine-colored robe.
There were slippers on her feet. Her graying hair was bound
in a scarf. Her face was smeared with cold cream.

Abram burst into loud laughter. "You're still crawling
around."

Ida immediately flared up. "What do you want me to be, paralyzed?"

"Ida, darling, I've got money. You'll have a new dress for the ball."

"Where did you get the money from? I don't need a new dress."

Abram looked at her with a mixture of joy and astonishment.

"What's the matter? Has the Messiah come?"

"Abram, I must have an operation."

Abram's expression changed. "What's happened?"

"I have a growth on the spleen. I didn't want to tell you. I had an X-ray examination. I have to go to the hospital next Monday."

"What's been going on? Why didn't you tell me before?"

"What's the difference? There was a consultation today. For two hours."

Abram lowered his head. He had not expected this. He had noticed that Ida's face had become yellowish. He suspected gall bladder. It was never possible to get any information from her. She had a habit of keeping secrets from him. But now the blow was on him. The cigar smoke against his palate lost its aroma. "I hope it isn't dangerous."

"What's the good of hopes? What I'm afraid of is that it's a cancer."

The cigar fell from Abram's lips. "Are you out of your mind, or what?"

"Don't shout. It isn't my fault."

"Not every tumor is a cancer."

"No." Ida smiled. In a moment her face seemed to become young and girlish, full of the charm that had kept him bound to her these twenty-five years. From behind the fine creases at their corners her eyes shone with a feminine joy in life, that Polish-Jewish look of hopefulness that no misfortune could efface. This was the Ida who had left a husband and child in Lodz, with servants and wealth, and had come here to him, Abram, a rake, and a married man into the bargain. It was the Ida who had year in and year out quarreled with him and made up with him, who had torn up her canvasses in a rage every few months and then started painting again with renewed faith in the importance of art. Now she stood looking at him, half sadly and half scornfully. "Don't take it so to heart, Abram. I'm an old woman."

Abram blushed. "Not to me," he muttered. "Not to me."

"Come. Let's go to bed."

Abram followed her silently. A red-shaded lamp was lighted in the bedroom. On a table by the bed stood a phial of medicine and a Polish book. Ida took off her robe and got into bed. Abram started to get undressed. Everything was clear to him now, her recent nervousness, her touchiness, her veiled remarks about death. He unlaced his shoes, sighing. He took off his trousers and stood in his long underwear. Above the waist band his belly protruded. He put out the lamp. For a while he sat on the edge of the cot on which he usually slept. Then he went over to Ida's bed and lay down beside her, his arms around her. They were both silent. He put his thumb and forefinger around her wrist and counted her pulse. A fragrant warmth came to him from her body. He could see her shining eyes in the darkness. He knew her too well to make a mistake. He sensed a mysterious joy in her. Suddenly she murmured something strange: *"Mazeltov."*

He wanted to ask her what she meant by wishing him good luck now, but he did not venture it. Ida lifted his hand and kissed the tips of his fingers. She caressed his cheeks and beard. "Abram, there's something I want to ask you," she said after a while.

"Yes. What is it, dearest?"

"First, swear to me that you'll do what I ask."

"Yes, anything."

"Abram, I want to be buried beside you."

He shuddered. "No. You'll live, you'll be all right."

"No, Abram dearest. This is the end."

He had to promise her that he would buy two adjoining graves.

"Ida, do you believe in the life hereafter?"

"Do you?"

"I believe."

"You're lucky. To me, man is no more than a leaf of a tree."

She put her head on his breast and dozed off. Abram stayed awake. He stared out into the darkness. Everything within him seemed to become hollow and hopeless. He longed to pray to God, but he did not know what to say. He remembered that almost the selfsame words had been spoken to him by Hama. She too had made him promise that they would be buried side by side, in the Moskat family plot. Ah, even the dead . . . he had to swear falsely to them too. . . . He suddenly saw Hama's face on the bier, white as cheese, the mouth open, the hint of a smile on her bluish lips. It was as though they were saying to him: "You can do no more to me, neither good nor evil." He tried to drive away the vision, but it emerged again and again, full of dreamlike verisimilitude. A terror took possession of him. "Pure soul," he half whispered, "back, back to your rest."

Ida awakened. "What is it? Why aren't you sleeping?" she asked suspiciously.

Abram tried to answer, but his tongue was paralyzed. He put his face on her hair, and his tears fell on it.

CHAPTER THREE

The few hundred zlotys that Abram got from the pawnbroker on Hadassah's pearl necklace he used for Ida's expenses. There were doctor's fees. There was the rent for her studio and flat. On Monday Abram got into a droshky with her to take her to the hospital. The operation was to be performed in three days. Abram insisted that Ida have a private room, so that he could visit her every day. He put a five-zloty note in the nurse's hand and asked her to take particular care of the patient. At five o'clock Abram was asked to leave.

Ida put both her arms around his neck. "If this is the last time, then God bless you."

Abram's eyes filled with tears. "Little idiot, you're talking nonsense."

He left the hospital and got into a number-sixteen streetcar. There was only a single passenger besides himself. He looked through the car window at the streets in the Vola section, half empty, dimly lighted, with red brick buildings, closed factories. The stores were deserted. Streetwalkers loitered in doorways. Abram wiped the misted window. As a rule he refused to permit himself to drift into a melancholy, but Ida's illness had banished all his equanimity. At Marshalkovska Street, near Zlota, he got off the car. There was a Greek bakery near the Vienna Station. He went in and bought a loaf of raisin bread that could be eaten without butter. Then he went home. At the door he paused. Opposite, on the first floor, a Channukah lamp was burning. Two oil wicks were lighted. Abram stared in astonishment. So it was Channukah already! He had momentarily forgotten.

The flat was freezing cold. This year double windows had

not been installed. The gas and electric light had been turned off. Abram lighted a candle that stood in a brass holder in the bedroom. He sat at the edge of the bed and nibbled at the raisin loaf. One of his back teeth was loose, and every time he chewed he felt the sharp ache. He undressed, got into bed, and fell asleep. He dreamed that he was carrying a heavy load, clattering with it up a spiral staircase. His knees were buckling under him, but he had to go on and on. He glanced over his shoulder. It was a millstone. Did he need to grind flour, or was he already in Gehenna? Had his soul transmigrated into a miller's?

He broke into laughter and woke up. He suddenly recalled that the ball was to be held the next day and that he was one of the beauty-contest judges. What difference did it make? He would not be there. With Ida as sick as she was, he was not going to run off to any ball. Besides, he did not have the proper clothing. By the way, where could he have put the tickets?

He got out of bed and hunted through his pockets until he found them. Without any particular plan he went over to the clothes closet. Once upon a time he had had a tuxedo, hadn't he? Maybe it was still wearable. Yes, there it was. He felt the silk lapels and the braid on the side of the trousers. In the darkness he put the coat on. Yes, it still fitted. And didn't he have patent-leather shoes somewhere? They were probably cracked, but he could soften them up with polish. And he had a pair of shoe-trees somebody had once brought him from Germany. Where could they be? Probably in that locked wardrobe. Where were the keys? Yes, they were in the writing-desk.

He moved about the room. In the darkness he took out shirts, ties, collars, starched cuffs that Hama had put away in the old days. He wondered now how it had ever been possible to lay aside as worn-out such fine things. Poor Hama, she had been right; he had just thrown away money. What he was doing now was contemptible, but, after all, who was there to see him? He slapped his body and sides to keep himself warm. "Dear God, what a pouch I have!" he murmured to himself. And a pair of breasts like a woman's. His hand touched his groin. He was overtaken with desire. "To have an affair with another woman," he thought. "Once more before I die." He got back into bed and covered himself with the blanket. He chewed on another piece of the raisin bread. In his years of woman-chasing Abram had learned that a man's will always prevails. If a man makes up his mind, a woman will happen along. It was a kind of magnetism.

Soon he fell asleep. In the morning he awoke refreshed. He washed with cold water at the kitchen sink, singing in a hoarse voice. He picked up the pile of clothing he had put aside in the middle of the night, packed it in a valise, and went off to a tailor he knew. The snow lay dirty and wet. Street-cleaners were clearing it away with picks and shovels. Birds hopped about, poking after stray morsels of food. Abram suddenly recalled the phrase in the prayerbook: "God feeds all things, from the giant elephant to the eggs of a louse."

The tailor was ailing. In the couple of years since Abram had seen him last the man had become as bent as an ancient. His mouth was toothless. A tape measure hung about his thin neck. There was a thimble on his crooked middle finger. He was cutting a piece of canvas with an enormous pair of shears. His yellow eyes looked at Abram doubtfully. "Not today," he muttered when Abram told him what he wanted.

"Murderer! You're killing me! I've got to go to a ball tonight."

From the tailor Abram went in search of a shoemaker. The patent-leather shoes would need to be half-soled. At the entrance Abram saw a sign with a boot on it. The cobbler's shop was in the court, in the cellar. Abram started to climb down the muddy steps. The corridor was pitch-black. He bumped into boxes and crates. He pushed open the door to a small room with an uneven ceiling and a grimy, dust-laden window. On a cot, half hidden by piles of stuff, lay a child in a diaper soiled with excrement. At the rusty stove a bedraggled woman knelt, tending the fire. A small man with a parchment-colored face sat at the table, pale watery eyes looking out of his fallen cheeks. He was pulling the sole from a shoe with a pair of pliers, the exposed leather spiked with nails, like a mouthful of jagged teeth.

Abram sat down on a chair. The air was full of mustiness. Acrid smoke steamed out of the oven. Th child wailed. The mother picked herself up from the floor, went to the bed, and offered a flaccid pendulous breast. In a corner of the room, among spiderwebs and a pile of refuse, there was a bookcase full of pious books. Abram took down a Pentateuch, the binding split, the pages mottled and wormeaten. He opened it at random and began to read:

"And the Lord hath avouched thee this day to be His peculiar people, as He hath promised thee, and that thou shouldest keep all His commandments; and to make thee high above all nations which He hath made, in praise, and in name, and in honor; and that thou mayest be an holy people unto the Lord thy God, as He hath spoken."

CHAPTER FOUR

1

The two tickets that Abram had brought to Asa Heshel and Hadassah were the cause of a good deal of excitement in the household. Hadassah was eager to go to the ball. It had been years since she had been to any sort of function. As long as she had lived with Asa Heshel without benefit of clergy, the pair had been invited nowhere. Then came the long period of her pregnancy, the bearing of the child, the illnesses of infancy. Besides, Asa Heshel invited few to his home and had accepted almost no invitations. But how long could a person isolate herself? She was still good-looking; it was criminal to sit like an old crone warming herself at the oven. Asa Heshel admitted that she was right, but still he had an aversion to balls, parties, celebrations.

Nevertheless, he decided to let Hadassah have her way. He hired a tuxedo, bought a pair of patent-leather shoes, a starched shirt, and a bow tie. Hadassah bought an evening dress. The preparations precipitated another quarrel between the two. It all cost so much money. There was the hairdresser, the manicurist. Masha also had a ticket for the affair, and the cousins made their preparations together. They were busy laundering, pressing, and mending. The telephone rang constantly. Masha kept on bringing over dozens of odds and ends, coral, bracelets, earrings, strings of imitation pearls. Asa Heshel watched with embarrassment how the vanity that slumbers in every woman had overpowered Hadassah. And all the excitement was having a bad effect on her health. Things she picked up would fall from her hands. She scolded the baby, sometimes even cursing. When Asa Heshel reprimanded her she would break into tears.

"What do you want of me?" she complained. "I'm unhappy enough as it is."

The tension had its effect on Asa Heshel too. He neglected

preparing his lectures. He could hardly get any sleep at night. On the day of the ball Hadassah awoke with a temperature. Asa Heshel insisted that it would be dangerous for her to go out, but Hadassah swore she would not stay at home even if it meant her death. She dosed herself with aspirin, and her fever subsided. At nine o'clock, when Hadassah and Masha came out of the bedroom where they had been dressing, Asa Heshel gazed at them in astonishment. Two beauties stood before him, one blonde, the other dark, of the kind whose photographs one sometimes saw in a magazine. He hardly recognized his own image in the mirror. His hair was freshly cut and he was shaved. The evening clothes fitted him well. Some of the gentile tenants of the building, riding down with them in the elevator, gaped at these elegant Jews who, for all their eternal complaining that the last bite of bread was being taxed out of their mouths, could still manage to go to balls.

The three had to wait downstairs for some time before they could get a droshky. Hadassah was wearing only a light coat; Asa Heshel chased about for a full quarter of an hour before he could find a droshky. In the meanwhile Hadassah was chilled through and beginning to cough. Her eagerness to go to the ball and show her good looks subsided. She felt weak and listless and was aware of only one desire: to get through the ordeal as quickly as possible and take to her bed. They sat in the droshky silently.

Masha, who had taken a glass of liqueur before they left the house, became impatient. "What are you so quiet about? It isn't a funeral we're going to."

The droshky came to a halt. Outside, in front of the building where the ball was being held, the sidewalk was packed. Asa Heshel had never seen such a crush before. More tickets had been sold than the hall could accommodate. Women shrieked, men quarreled. Someone tried to force open the doors. A troop of police arrived. A girl called out: "Jewish arrangements!"

The crowd gave a sudden push forward. Hadassah was carried with it. She felt her dress rip. Terror seized her that it would be torn off, leaving her naked. The girls behind the checking tables could not manage to dispose of the heap of coats, hats, parasols, boots, galoshes, and wraps flung at them. They ran out of checking tickets and hangers. Hadassah wanted to hold on to Asa Heshel's arm, but a shift of the crowd separated her from both him and Masha. The mob swept her forward into the ballroom. A band was playing and the dance floor was so crowded that the couples just stood shaking on one spot. Trumpets pealed out, drums throbbed. The over-heated atmosphere was full of shrieks, giggling, and laughter, a confusion of odors and colors. A man in a rabbinical fur hat swayed with a woman whose mask had slipped down to her nose. On the stage, in front of the musicians, towered an enormous figure with a helmet on his head and a breastplate of mail. It was the strong man who had been mentioned in the advertisements. Hadassah wanted to get out of the place; she was hemmed in on all sides. Someone put his arms about her. It was a lean youth, with sharp features and a crooked nose.

"Give me a kiss, beautiful."

She tried to tear herself away, but the youth held on to her tightly. There was a smell of pomade and sweat about him. At that moment Abram emerged from the crowd. "Hadassah, darling."

The stranger disappeared at once. Abram seized her by the shoulders. "What's the matter? Where's Asa Heshel? My God, you're as beautiful as the seven suns."

Hadassah broke into tears. "Oh, Uncle, get me out of this!"

"Idiot, what are you crying for? My God, what a mad-house!"

Abram started to push his way through the throng, holding on to Hadassah, his enormous belly forcing a passage. In all this turmoil he stopped to greet people, to kiss the hands of some ladies, and to wave at others, calling out compliments in a wild mixture of Yiddish, Polish, and Russian. He clutched a stout man who wore an official band on his sleeve. "Ashamed of yourself, that's what you ought to be," he scolded him. "Worse than in Berdichev."

Abram managed to push his way into the adjoining salon. Here people were crowded around buffets, eating butter buns and drinking beer and lemonade. A woman was kneeling, re-pairing an enormous tear in another woman's dress. A girl hopped on one foot, holding a shoe with the heel dangling. A bewildering variety of masked figures went by: Russian gener-als with epaulets, Polish grandees in elegant caftans, Germans in spiked helmets, rabbis in fur hats, yeshivah students in vel-vet skullcaps, sidelocks dangling below their ears. It was some time before Hadassah realized that these were merely mas-querade costumes. Abram himself seemed entirely changed. Strips of paper and bits of confetti were strewn on his coat and in his beard. A balloon had come to rest for an instant on top of his bald spot.

"You got out of it all right," he shouted to Hadassah. "One woman—she was left in her drawers." He broke into a peal of laughter and kissed Hadassah warmly.

She caught a whiff of the liquor he had been drinking. "Uncle, I want to go home."

"Here, you just sit down. I'll go find your cavalier."

He led her to an unoccupied chair against a wall and went off to look for Asa Heshel. From the left Masha came along, holding on to the arm of a red-cheeked, wavy-haired man, with a round belly. One of his eyes smiled, the other seemed to wander about with a dead serious expression. "If only she doesn't notice me," Hadassah thought.

At that very moment Masha came up to her. "Little mother!" she said. "Look at this."

She dragged her companion forward to introduce him to Hadassah. A doctor something-or-other, Hadassah could not catch the name. Masha rattled on vivaciously, while the doctor bent ceremoniously and kissed Hadassah's hand above her glove, then turned and walked away.

"Don't forget the bonbons," Masha called after him, and to Hadassah she said: "A very sympathetic type. A captain in the reserve. And a Jew. But I think converted. What are you sitting here for? My God, what a mob! Phooey! What's the matter with you? You've been crying. Don't take it so seriously. Spit at it. Where's Asa Heshel? I've been searching all over for you."

"Uncle Abram is here."

"Really. Where is he? His sweetheart is in the hospital, and he goes around having a good time. Just take a look at my dress. The place is a madhouse, as I love my grandmother! Phooey, what a scabby crew!" Masha was quiet for a moment. Then she said: "Yes, we're getting old. Have you got a pin?"

2

Abram started on his errand of finding Asa Heshel, but it was only a moment before he had forgotten not only what he had set out to do, but also that Hadassah was waiting for him. Only a little while earlier, to give himself additional spirit, he had swallowed a tumbler of cognac. He knew that he had been chosen as one of the judges of the beauty contest, but he could not figure out where he was to meet his colleagues or where the candidates were to be brought for inspection. He recognized one familiar face after another: Women who, according to Abram's befuddled thinking, should now have been doddering ancients, instead swam before his vision young, hair becomingly coiffured, slim as brides. Men he had imagined as dead of the typhus epidemic or lost somewhere in Russia called him by name and shouted greetings. A woman in a red mask clutched at his lapel. "Abram, dear! How old you've grown! A grandpa!"

"Who are you? Give me a kiss."

Abram tried to hold her, but she nimbly escaped his clutch and darted away. He started after, his knees strangely unsteady. He was not sure whether he was stumbling forward or being pushed backward. Where was she, this summer bird, where had she flown? Abram tried tentatively to stop some of the masked figures that flitted by him, but they brushed past. One of the girls stuck out her tongue at him; another thumbed her nose; a third shouted "Freemason!" after him.

Abram halted in astonishment. It was years since he had heard that underworld epithet. The music stopped, then started again, a cacophony of horns, drums, sounds like the wailing of a thousand cats. The couples swayed, jiggled, swung right, left, heaved back and forth. Abram became more and more confused. What was this? A shimmy, a Charleston, a rumba? Pigs! Made you want to vomit. An ocean of abandoned female flesh. He fumbled for a handkerchief and wiped his perspiring face. His shirt and underwear felt wet and clammy against his skin. His shoes burned his soles. A girl bumped into him and then shouted in his ear, as though he were deaf: "Hey, old man! Why don't you go home to sleep?"

He stumbled on a few steps more. Now he heard a thin voice in his ear: "Herr Abram, how are you?" He turned around. It was Finlender, the hunchback, whom he used to meet at Hertz Yanovar's. Yes, he remembered. Those were the days when he was full of ideas about issuing a journal; Finlender was to be one of the editors. The whole idea had disappeared into thin air, and Finlender had drifted away from the group. But now here he was in the flesh. His hair was a mixture of gold and silver. Abram swayed toward him as though to embrace him. "What do my eyes see!"

"And I thought for a minute you'd not recognize me."

"What are you talking about? Finlender! You're the same. How are you? What are you doing? Are you married yet?"

"What? No."

"Where are you living? Do you ever run into Dembitzer?"

"Dembitzer's dead."

Abram started. "When? How?"

"A heart attack. It was in the newspapers."

"So. And what about the other one—what's his name—the one with the hocus-pocus—the telepath?"

"Messinger. He's here. He's at the ball."

"Here? And the other one? That woman. The one who used to raise up the spirits."

"Kalischer. She married some manufacturer in Lodz."

"No more spirits?"

"No more."

"And Hertz Yanovar? Is he here too?"

"He's here. With Gina."

"Where are they? I've lost sight of everybody."

Abram fumbled in his breast pocket. He wanted to give Finlender a visiting-card, but he could not find one. He shuffled off. What was the difference? All words, words. At that moment he heard someone calling him. "Panie Abram! Panie Abram!" He looked around and saw a woman in a black domino, with a fur jacket over her ball dress. She was of medium height; her hair was braided and parted at either side and studded with combs and pins and flowers. Old-fashioned gold earrings dangled from her ears. Her gloves reached to the elbows.

Abram measured her with his eyes. "Come on, little mask, let's dance."

"The night's still young," the other answered, in Yiddish. "You've aged. You're gray as a dove."

"A man can't get younger, only older," Abram answered. "Who are you, little one?"

"That's a secret."

"You look familiar. Tell me, have you known me for long?"

"Oh, threescore years."

"You couldn't be Reb Berish Kameika's daughter-in-law?"

"Hardly."

"One of the Przepiorko clan?"

"Wrong again."

"Then who *are* you?"

"Just a Jewish girl."

"Of course, what else?"

"I hear that Nathan's sick."

Abram felt a rush of elation. "So you know Nathan too? So you're one of our crowd! Don't play any tricks on me. Take off your mask. Show me your gorgeous face."

"I thought you'd guess."

"Ah, my beautiful little mask! You really intrigue me."

Abram put his hand on her waist and pushed his way with her through the crowded dance floor. He wanted to get to the buffet room, to buy her a drink. It was getting more difficult for him to breathe. Thank God, he wasn't alone and lonely here at the ball. He could still find a woman to be interested in him. She went with him willingly. He inhaled her perfumed odor. He saw other faces he knew. Broide, the Bolshevik, moved about with the lame seamstress, Lila. He saw Gina with a short girl, someone who used to lodge there, Abram remembered. Abram saluted them proudly, bowed and waved his hand. The women looked after him, half curiously, half scornfully. Abram knit his brows. Try as he might, he could not figure out who the woman with him was.

"Who else do you know of the family?"

"Who don't I know? Pinnie, Nyunie, Koppel."

"Koppel? Then in that case you're a prewar piece of stuff."

"I wasn't hatched yesterday."

"Koppel's in America. I hear he's been in trouble there."

"Yes. For bootlegging."

Abram stopped. "As I live, you know everything. Can you read the future, too?"

A pair of brilliant black eyes looked at him through the narrow slits of the mask. Abram had an uncanny feeling: perhaps this was the Angel of Death. By now he was sober. He remembered his bad heart, Ida's operation, Hadassah waiting for him while he went off in search of Asa Heshel. "My God, what's happened to me? I've sunk low." He had an urge to abandon this stranger, to flee home and take to his bed. Instead he clutched her with renewed firmness. "Happen what may, one way or another I'll die." He realized in a flash who the woman was. It was Manya, Reb Meshulam's servant, Naomi's helper. The Black Manya, as they used to call her.

3

For all his searching, Asa Heshel was unable to catch sight of Hadassah. Besides, he had no particular desire to find her. What would be the point of dragging around with his own wife? The jazz music deafened his ears. The stark lights blinded his eyes. He wandered into the buffet room and took a glass of beer. He sat down at a table. What the devil were they carrying on for, these exiled vagabonds? They had lost God and had not won the world. "I can't go on like this," he murmured. "I'll be suffocated." Suddenly he heard a familiar voice.

"Nun, gezweifelt ist genug. . . ."

He opened his eyes and saw Hertz Yanovar, in a wrinkled tuxedo and an artist's flowing tie. Since Asa Heshel had last seen him his side whiskers had grown entirely gray. Near him stood a tall girl, dark and slender, with long, even features and big black eyes. Asa Heshel noticed that her hair was not cut stylishly short. The silk dress she wore was unadorned. Although she was brunette, her skin olive, there was an indefinable non-Jewish quality about her, as among the women of France or Italy whom Asa Heshel had often met in Switzerland. He did not know why, but somehow the girl reminded him of a nun.

Hertz Yanovar was talking to him. "I want to introduce you to a beautiful lady," he was saying, in Polish and in an excited voice. "Panna Barbara Fishelsohn—Asa Heshel Bannet."

Asa Heshel stood up and murmured acknowledgment. "Please sit down."

"My honored friend here is a philosopher," Hertz Yanovar said in his flowery Polish, half ironically. "And this beautiful lady is also a thinker. Just returned from France. And studied under the renowned Bergson."

"Some more of Mr. Yanovar's exaggerations," the lady interrupted. "I'm a simple student."

"Modesty is the crown of all the virtues," Hertz Yanovar declaimed. "I had the honor of knowing Panna Barbara when she was only a little child. Now she's grown a head taller than me—mentally as well as physically."

"Please don't take him seriously. He's had a glass too much."

"Wouldn't you like to sit down for a while?" Asa Heshel asked. "You too, Hertz."

"I must go back to my better half. Where is your lady?"

"Hadassah? We became separated."

"Separated, eh? It's Freudian. The subconscious wish to stay a cavalier. If I were in your place I wouldn't be sitting so peacefully. Hadassah is still a lovely woman."

Asa Heshel blushed. "You talk nonsense, Hertz," he said.

"Maybe yes, maybe no. Just let's hope she won't get bored in all this bacchanalia." He waved his hand in a gesture. "Well, au revoir. I leave you in charming company."

Yanovar bowed, clicked his heels, and threw the lady a kiss. He spun around on his short legs and hurried off. Panna Barbara looked after him. "The poor man. He can't drink."

"Maybe you'd like something?"

"No, thank you. Nothing."

"You really attended Bergson's lectures?"

"Oh, just a few."

"And how long were you in France?"

"Five years."

"Studying philosophy?"

"I specialized in French literature. I understand that you're a professor in a theological seminary."

"Just an instructor."

"I've never met any Jewish seminarists. Tell me, do they dress like rabbis, with sidelocks?"

"No. They wear European clothing. Just like anybody else."

"But why? Aren't they orthodox?"

"The really orthodox ones study in a synagogue."

"Oh, yes. I remember. My own papa went to a yeshivah."

"Your father is a rabbi?"

The girl smiled. Her mouth opened slightly, revealing longish teeth. "A pastor."

Asa Heshel could hardly believe his ears. "Really?" he said. "Where?"

"Here in Warsaw."

"What church?"

"A mission of the Evangelical church. They have a chapel on Krulevska Street."

"You were probably born in the Christian faith," Asa Heshel suggested.

"No. I was converted when I was four."

For a long time there was silence. Asa Heshel now remembered that Hertz Yanovar had once told him about some convert, Fishelsohn, who had been a rabbi in a Talmudic brotherhood and who had written some book or other. The girl beside him had lowered her head and was glancing at her well-manicured hands. "Mr. Yanovar used to visit our home. At one time my papa wanted me to know Hebrew. He used to give me lessons."

"I hope that you managed to learn something."

"Only a little, I'm afraid. Instead of studying, we used to chatter all the time. I've heard about you ever since I was a little girl. How you ran away from the provinces, how you came to Warsaw, the whole story."

"Oh!"

"He even told me that you were writing a book."

Asa Heshel bit his lip. "It wasn't a book," he said. "It was to have been my dissertation. I never finished it."

"As I recall it, what you proposed was the establishment of a research laboratory for experimentation in pure happiness. I remember how the theme interested me at the time."

"I've almost entirely forgotten it myself."

"The only problem is where such a laboratory should be erected. Unless in a vacuum."

"Why in a vacuum?"

"Because any concrete place is tightly bound up in the surrounding social standards, and of course in the ideological superstructures that—"

"A Marxist, eh? I never really talked about pure happiness."

"Philosophers always seem to be in love with purity—with pure reason, pure morals, pure happiness. By the way, do you dance?"

"Unfortunately, no."

"Have you a cigarette?"

"Sorry, I don't smoke."

"So. Tell me, what do you do?"

"I worry."

"Well, that's a fine occupation. While you're worrying, the world is being captured by the Mussolinis, the Pilsudskis, the MacDonalds—"

"Let the world go to the devil."

Panna Barbara emitted a short laugh. "A decadent, eh? You have all the symptoms. Would you come with me? I'd like to watch the dancing."

The two got up. The waitress behind the buffet table ran after them. Asa Heshel had forgotten to pay for his beer.

4

The music had stopped when Asa Heshel and Barbara reached the ballroom. The center of the floor was still crowded. The dancers were standing in pairs, all eyes fixed on the stage. The entertainment was going on. The strong man was performing feats of strength, breaking chains, bending iron staves, allowing his naked chest to be thumped with a hammer in the hands of a youth. After he had left the stage, a magician made his appearance. He was a smallish man in a frock coat and white cravat. He made some flourishes with a handkerchief over a glass, a candle, and some coins, talking in a high thin voice. From the back of the room it was difficult to make out what he was saying. When he left, rows of chairs were placed on the stage, and the men who were to choose the beauty queen took their seats. Asa Heshel tried to pick out Abram among the judges, but he was not there. He looked about him in the crowd for Hadassah or Masha or Gina, but he could not make out a single familiar face.

Panna Barbara made a grimace. "All of Nalevki Street is here," she said.

"Nalevki Street also has the right to live."

"I didn't say no." She opened her pocketbook and took out a little mirror and a powder puff. "You seem to be in a bad mood," she said. "It's peculiar, but I also get into a bad mood whenever I go to balls, especially Jewish balls."

"Why don't you go to Polish balls, then?"

A shadow passed over her face. "I'm in the position of being suspended between the two peoples—Poles and Jews. Because of his missionary work, Daddy was always involved with young Jewish men. I once studied in an Evangelical institute, but I lost all contact when I left for France. You, too, seem to be something of an outsider."

"I have been an outsider all my life."

"Why?"

"I don't know. I've always lacked the kind of faith that holds people together."

"When did you come back from Russia?"

"In 1919."

"Well, didn't the Revolution have any influence on you?"

"I never was a Marxist."

"What, then? An anarchist?"

"Don't laugh at me, but I still believe that the capitalist system is the best. I don't mean that it's good; it's very cruel, but it's human nature and the economic law."

"What nonsense! At least you're sincere. The others hide behind false theories. What about Zionism? Aren't you a Zionist?"

"It's hard for me to believe that they'll ever give the Jews a country. They never give anything to anybody."

"That's true. That's why one has to fight."

"Fight for what? What has been the result of all the wars? What have we got from revolutions? Hunger and a flood of silly speeches."

"If that is all you saw in Soviet Russia you're really to be pitied. If I had such a viewpoint I would have hanged myself long ago."

"Skeptics want to live, maybe even more than believers."

"For what? I heard you have a child. How can anyone with such an attitude bring up children?"

"I never wanted them."

"So you were raped! You should be ashamed of yourself. You hide behind a screen of cowardice. May I ask you a personal question?"

"Ask anything you want."

"I have heard so much about you that I feel as if we were old friends. Is your wife also like you—I mean antisocial?"

"Yes, but in a different direction. She is by nature a believer. One of those for whom love is God."

"Well, so she has achieved her god."

"A bad god. A god who keeps on deserting."

"Poor woman! I should like to know her. Hertz Yanovar speaks of her in superlatives. Didn't you say she's here tonight?"

"Yes. We lost each other."

"Oh! Maybe I'm inquisitive, but that's my nature. If you don't want to answer, just tell me."

"Please, ask me. I'm glad to have someone talk to me."

"When did you interrupt your studies? Why didn't you finish your book? Have you lost ambition?"

"Oh, it's a long story. I came back from Russia, and I had to assume responsibilities. I have to provide for my mother. My sister is very poor. I have a son by my first wife. I have a little daughter by my present wife. You cannot imagine how I have to struggle just for the barest essentials."

"I can imagine it very easily. I myself had quite a struggle in France. What about your book? Have you given it up completely?"

"First, it's written in German. Second, it's a bad German. And third, it's not finished."

"I'd like to read it."

"Why bother? It's just a waste of time."

"I'll decide that."

"It's full of mistakes and erasures. My handwriting is bad."

"I have a typewriter home. I could type it for you."

"But why should you?"

"Ah—just because. The revolution won't suffer. When are you free?"

"Evenings."

"Come and visit me. Give me a ring. We're in the telephone book. Pastor Fishelsohn. Don't worry about Papa. He's a very tolerant man. Besides, lately he's been quite sick. On what is your system built?"

"On Spinoza and Malthus."

"A peculiar combination. What do you preach?"

"Sex-control, in the broadest sense of the word."

"What's that supposed to be?"

"More sex and fewer children. The bedroom is the key to all social and individual problems."

"You seem to laugh at your own theory. My father is like that, too. He speaks seriously, he even screams, but to me it seems that he's fooling. Why don't you try to find your wife?"

"How could I find her? A needle in a haystack."

"You have an answer for everything. Hertz Yanovar also had a philosophy once. The darkness, or something. It made quite an impression on me. When are you going to call me?"

"Very soon."

"I'm going now. I just came out of curiosity. I have a headache. Will you take me to the cloakroom?"

At the cloakroom Barbara collected a caracul coat, a pair of fur-lined boots, an amber-handled umbrella with a silk tassel. At a counter near by she stopped to buy a pack of gold-tipped Egyptian cigarettes. She lighted one, letting the smoke drift out of her nostrils. She looked at herself in the wall mirror and handed the girl twenty groszy.

"Maybe you will help me get a droshky."

"Of course."

A light snow was falling, swirling and drifting in the wind. At the corner of the building stood a droshky, with a convertible top. The horse was shaking its wet head, arching its ears. The driver was seated on his perch, his shoulders hunched in, a hood over his hat. The candle in the droshky's glass-enclosed lamp flickered and spluttered. In its light the walls of the building shook, like decorations in a theater.

"A nasty night," Barbara said. "When shall I hear from you?"

"Very soon."

"Don't make it too long," she called from within the coach. "Good night."

The driver pulled at the reins, and the droshky rolled off. Asa Heshel stood looking after the carriage. Flakes of snow melted on his hair, hung on his eyebrows. The wind whipped at his jacket. Far away in the purple sky chimneys and church steeples cut against the heavens. Asa Heshel followed the coach with his eyes until it rounded a corner.

He went back into the ballroom. The crowd was applauding something. Someone was shouting hoarsely. A broad-shouldered man, swarthy as a Turk, with a shock of black hair, was talking in a throaty voice. "Everything is politics with that bunch. Truth and justice—that they spit on."

"What happened?"

"They chose a beauty queen, and they picked an ugly ape. Someone with influence, I suppose."

"What do you care?"

"The law is the same for a penny as for a hundred gulden, as the Talmud says."

At that moment Asa Heshel saw Hadassah. She was standing looking at the stage. He had never seen her so beautiful. He suddenly remembered Abram's promise that she should be queen of the ball. A wave of pity rushed over him. Here she stood, his beloved wife, the mother of his child, a woman who had thrown away a fortune to be with him. What a disappointment he must be for her! How many angry words had he spoken to her! How bankrupt was his life, his career, his love! He approached her and put a hand on her shoulder. Hadassah trembled. She looked at him, frightened, and then her face lit up. "It's you. Where were you? I've been looking for you all evening. I thought that—" and her eyes became moist.

"What did you think?"

"Nothing. Such noise! What cheap people! We shouldn't have come. You were right. Have you seen Masha?"

"No, my dear. Come, let's sit down somewhere. You look beautiful."

Hadassah became serious. She could not understand his sudden warmth. She had expected a rebuff. She took his arm. "Come, let's leave. Let's go home."

CHAPTER FIVE

1

Abram started up from sleep in the middle of the night with a sharp pain in his left arm and a pressure around his heart. It was dark. Beside him in the bed a woman lay asleep. Who was she, he wondered. Could it be Ida? No, Ida was in the hospital. Hama was dead. He tried to remember what had happened during the evening, but could recall nothing. His head felt heavy on the pillow. His brains were like sand. He remembered his digitalis pills and tried to get up, but he could not seem to raise his back. He could not see a door in the darkness, nor a window. "Dear God in heaven, I'm finished," he thought. He wanted to nudge the woman to wake her up, but he could not seem to raise his arm. For a while he dozed off again. He dreamed he was in a slaughterhouse. A butcher was binding an ox, preparing its throat for the knife. How strange! He, Abram, was the ox! He tried to shriek, but someone held his jaws firmly together. The flayers came toward him, with their bloodied boots. "Murderers! Villains! I'm a man, a human being!" Abram shuddered violently and started awake, drenched in a cold sweat. The bed was trembling beneath him. There was a taste of blood in his mouth. He lay silent and tense. Dear God, this was the end.

The woman beside him woke up. "Abram! What's the matter?"

"Who are you?" Abram managed to grunt.

"It's me. Manya."

"Where am I?"

"What's the matter? Are you sick or something? We came here from the ball."

"Ah."

"Does something hurt you?"

He hardly knew what to answer her. Suddenly the electric light was turned on. Manya was standing beside the bed, barefoot, in a long nightgown. Her face had become faded, flaccid, and wrinkled. Under her chin another chin wobbled. The narrow Kalmuk eyes stared at him in a kind of dull terror. "What is it? Is it your heart?"

"A little—pressure—"

"What shall I do? The master and mistress will be here soon."

Abram looked around him and saw that he was in a kitchen. The floor was tiled. Pots and pans hung from hooks on the walls. On the stove stood a teakettle. A strand of withered flypaper hung from the overhead lamp. Abram had an urge to laugh. Of all places he had to pick out this place to die in. "Pills—I have pills—in my trousers pocket—" he managed to get out.

Manya turned quickly to the trousers, which lay on a chair. The pills were not there. She became entangled in the suspenders. From the vest pocket an enormous watch fell to the floor. Manya picked it up and held it to her ear.

"Did it stop?"

"Yes."

"Ah." Yes, it was an omen. He was dying. In five-and-thirty years the watch had never stopped. He closed his eyes. Warsaw would have plenty to talk about. Manya walked aimlessly back and forth, wringing her hands. "Abram!" she whispered frantically. "You'll have to go home."

"Yes, yes. I'll get dressed."

She hurried to the bed and pulled the covers back. Abram lay in his undershirt. He shivered, trying to huddle his legs up. She helped him to dress, putting on his trousers, socks, and shoes. She made him get up and put on his vest, coat, overcoat, fur hat. Now she found his underwear and put it in the coal box. Abram had only one thought: "I've had it coming to me . . . I've had it coming to me. . ." Manya hurried to dress, too. She drew off her nightgown, standing there naked, with her pendulous breasts, broad hips, flat belly, hairy legs. One of Abram's eyes was closed; through the other he looked curiously at her feet, the crooked toes overlapping. So this was the bargain he had given up his life to possess! It occurred to him that he ought to pronounce the prayer for forgiveness, but he could not capture the words. As he sat on the edge of the bed he must have fallen into a doze, for when he started up, Manya was completely clothed. The stabbing in his chest had stopped. Manya helped him to his feet, and with trembling steps he walked with her out of the room into the corridor. There his strength left him, and he fell to the floor. Manya pawed over him, pulling and tugging, but he made no movement. "Ah, my God! Mamma, for God's sake have

mercy on me," she muttered. In the dimness his face was like
the face of a corpse. She ran out of the house, the snap lock
slipping into place as she banged the door behind her. She had
forgotten her key! She started back, but it was too late; the
door was locked. She stumbled down the dark stairs. "God in
heaven, God in heaven, Mamma, Mamma," she kept moaning, over and over again. She had an urge to knock at a
neighbor's door for help. Why was the night so long? In the
courtyard she glimpsed a white shadowy form. "Dear God,
it's he! He's coming after me!" She stopped stock-still, frozen
with terror. She heard a man's voice.

"Who's there? Who is it?"

"It's me. Manya."

"Manya? From the crockery shop? What are you doing
here?"

Manya realized that it was one of the workmen in the bakery on the courtyard. "Someone got sick upstairs. Fainted.
An uncle. From the provinces."

"Where are the others?"

"Out of the city. Away. Not coming back until morning."

"You better call for the ambulance."

"Help me! Help me! As you've got God in your heart, help
me!"

"I've got the loaves in the oven. Better call a policeman."

She stumbled on, the baker after her. He caught her by the
shoulder.

"You're lying," he said. "It isn't your uncle."

"What do you want? Leave me alone."

"A whore. That's what you are, curse your mother's
womb."

He clutched at her breast and rubbed his face against hers.
She struggled silently. "I'll shout for help."

"Whore! Your father's father! Beat it!" He spat and threw
her off. She almost fell. She was about to faint. In the darkness she heard the baker urinating. Disgust rose in her. She
rushed to lean against a wall, doubling over and vomiting.
"Ah, God! Ah, God!" she kept on moaning.

When she raised her head she saw that patches of gray light
were beginning to show in the sky. The stars were fading. She
wiped her face and went to the courtyard gate. It was already
open. She hurried through the empty street, her knees quak-
ing. The night of terror was gone. She moved in purity and
piousness. She raised her eyes to the glowing hems of the
clouds. She murmured a promise to the Unseen that if He re-

leased her from the trap she would become a decent daughter of Israel.

Abram was not dead. After a while he rose from his coma. He sat up and listened. There was a ringing in his ears. The blood foamed through his veins. He now remembered everything. Where was she? Had she run off and left him? There was only one thing he wanted now: not to die here, in this strange place. He summoned all his strength and struggled to his feet. He opened the door, slowly felt his way down the stairs, holding on to the stair rails, resting and panting after every step. (Never had he imagined that it would be such a formidable task to put one foot ahead of the other.) His teeth chattered. In the courtyard he moved along the wall. He opened one eye and saw a red sky. A word, a phrase, hung on the tip of his lips, but he could not recall it. A white apparition loomed in front of him. It was the baker. "Here, panie, I'll help you. I'll get a droshky."

He lowered himself to the ground. Wisps of smoke rose from chimneys. Windows opened. He heard the shrill voices of women. Someone was holding a drink of water to his lips. "Is this the end?" he thought. "Not so terrible." He smiled into his beard. Up above, beyond the rooftops, the newly risen sun flamed out.

2

It was some time before the baker's apprentice managed to find a droshky. The driver refused to take the sick man unless there was someone to accompany him. The baker climbed up to the flat of Manya's employers to see if the girl was there. The door was open. He spent a few minutes in the flat, then came down. With the driver's help he put Abram into the carriage and climbed in after him. Abram was able to give Ida's address to the driver. The droshky rolled off, the passers-by gaping in surprise at the two strange passengers. Abram's head leaned back against the side of the carriage. His fellow passenger held him by the sleeve. For all his exhaustion, Abram was aware of everything: the smoke, the smell of freshly baked bread, the newly swept gutter. A newsboy was hawking the morning papers. The droshky came to a stop at the building that housed Ida's studio. The janitor came out. He and his wife helped Abram up the five flights of stairs. He must be drunk, they decided. They laid him down on Ida's bed and went out, not thinking to call a doctor. The janitor shook his head. "Fine times, these," he murmured. "Even Jews are becoming sots."

Manya wandered through the streets for a long time. Most of the stores were still shuttered and locked. Here and there a milk store or grocery stall was open. A delivery man carried some loaves of bread artfully suspended on his flour-covered coat. Trucks unloaded cans of milk and forequarters of beef. A wagon loaded with refuse came out of a courtyard. Manya looked about her. She was on Nizka Street, where Naomi and her husband had their bakery. She hurried to the place. Naomi, formerly Reb Meshulam Moskat's servant, was already seated near the gate, guarding a basket of freshly baked loaves and rolls. She was wearing a heavy gray coat. A large pocketbook hung from her waist. She looked up at Manya and wrung her hands. "My goodness, what are you doing here?"

Manya started to stammer and swallow convulsively, the tears streaming from her eyes. Naomi stared at her. At first she could not understand what the girl was saying. When she finally understood, her hand itched to strike the wanton. She called for her stepdaughter to come and take over the business. Then she stopped a droshky and ordered the driver to take them to Ptasha Street, where Manya lived. Naomi swayed from side to side, blowing her nose in a fold of her apron, as though she were riding in a funeral coach.

"My God! My God! To do a thing like that. And your father was a decent Jew."

"I should be cut to pieces," Manya moaned.

"All right, all right. Stop your wailing. God knows I don't envy you."

Naomi became exhilarated. She liked the excitement of complicated situations, liked to have to do with the police, to fuss around with corpses and funerals. Ah, Manya, that common strumpet! And the Moskats, too, had a good scandal in store for them. Let them know that she, Naomi, was an honorable woman. She could hardly wait for the droshky to get to its destination. She lifted herself in her seat, clutching Manya by the arm, as though afraid she would jump out of the carriage. She wiped her forehead with her sleeve. "What a way to die! Woe to his years! And you—may a flame consume your guts!"

"If only I'd died in my sleep!"

"It would have been better for you."

Naomi did not lose her head. She went into the janitor's quarters and told him everything she had learned. She talked loudly in her ragged Polish. The janitor listened, peering at her with his small, half-closed eyes. Naomi told him to get a master key. They walked out and across the large courtyard, Naomi in the lead, the janitor following, and Manya after them. They climbed the stairs. The janitor pushed against the door and it opened. There was no corpse. The flat was empty. They looked through all the rooms. Naomi broke out into raucous laughter. "A devil!"

She rummaged in her pocketbook and brought out a five-zloty note, which she handed to the janitor, putting her finger to her lips in a meaningful gesture. The janitor took the money, scratched the nape of his neck, muttered something, and shuffled out. Naomi's glance fell on the coal box; there was some white cloth there—Abram's underpants. She whispered quickly to Manya: "Hide these."

Manya went out of the kitchen to put the clothing into the basket of soiled laundry. She passed the owner's room. The drawers of the writing-desk were open. The floor was strewn with papers. A chamois purse lay open and empty. Manya began to shriek. "Help! Thieves!"

Naomi was quick to respond. She threw open the door and started to shout at the top of her voice. Now she was beginning to be afraid for her own skin. Suppose they thought that she and Manya had done the thing together? And who knew —maybe the filthy whore had brought her here deliberately to cover up her own theft. She rushed up to Manya and flung her fist at her. Manya stumbled back against the wall, letting the underpants fall to the floor. Neighbors appeared in the doorway, half-clothed. The janitor, who was already on his way downstairs, turned back at the sounds of the commotion.

"Call the police," Naomi yelled. "Right away." She pointed an accusing finger at Manya.

The janitor took off his cap, took out from it the banknote Naomi had given him, and flung it back at her. One of the neighbors, who had a telephone, rushed to call the commissariat. Manya remained where she was, terror in her small, hunted eyes. Out of all the excitement there was one thing clear to her: the whole book of judgments and recriminations was being thrown at her head. Now she was being paid back for all her sins.

Naomi clutched her by the shoulders, shook her back and forth. "What have you done here? Talk! Talk plainly, or I'll lay you out cold."

"Go on. Go on and kill me."

"Whore! Thief! Why did you drag me over here?"

Naomi seemed to be suddenly seized by a new thought. She took a step toward the door. "What's this mob doing here? Let me out."

The group of people gazing curiously at the two made way for her. She pushed past them, steering her way with her belly. She had her stepdaughter as a witness that this thief had come to call her. She hurried down the stairs, her face set, her eyes angry. Downstairs, near the gate, a dog came barking at her. She kicked at him, catching him on the leg. The animal went limping away. "What a dirty mess," she thought with scorn. "Tries to get me in a trap, curse her guts." The droshky that had brought them was still standing outside. The horse was munching oats from the nose bag. Apart from the fact that Naomi did not want to walk the long distance back, it would be good to have the driver, too, as a witness.

3

At three in the morning Masha left the ball. She took with her a torn dress, trampled shoes, a *bonbonnière*, and a headache. It was too late to find a droshky; she took one of the late streetcars. Marianna, the servant, opened the door for her and Masha proceeded at once into her boudoir. It was some time since she and Yanek had shared a bed; Masha slept on a made-up sofa. Now she threw herself down and put out the lamp. She was too tired to undress. She pulled the coverlet over her and fell asleep.

Early in the morning the ringing of the telephone woke her. The instrument was on the toilet table near her sofa. Half asleep, she picked up the receiver and put it to her ear. She heard a woman's voice, harsh and hoarse.

"Mrs. Zazhitska? You'll please excuse me. This is Gina Yanovar. Maybe you'll remember me."

"Yes, I remember you."

"Dear lady, forgive me. I've just had a terrible misfortune. We were at the ball last night. I noticed you there. You looked wonderful. We got home to find the house full of policemen and detectives. You see, I'm forced to keep lodgers.

My husband, unfortunately, is unable to find any employment. And we have a lodger, Broide is his name, with his wife, Lila—"

"This Broide is a Communist, isn't he?"

"That's just the tragedy. He promised me he'd keep his politics out of my place, but you can't trust those people. They found whole bundles of propaganda in his room. And they've arrested my husband. God knows he's innocent, he's got nothing to do with it." Gina began to sob.

Masha closed her eyes in weariness. "What is it you want from me?" she said. "How can I help?"

Gina gasped. "Dear lady, he'll never survive it. It'll be too much for his strength. I beg you—I plead with you by all that you hold dearest, to talk to your husband, the colonel. Please, please, whatever your scruples are. A single word from the colonel can save him." Gina's voice again broke into tears. In her desperation she spoke a mixture of Polish and Yiddish. She said something about her husband's papers—his reports on psychical research—which the police had taken together with Broide's Communist pamphlets.

Masha stopped the flow of words. "My husband's sleeping now," she said. "I'll talk to him later."

"Oh, oh, I'll never stop thanking you. God bless you, you still have a Jewish heart."

Masha hung up the receiver and tried to fall asleep, but again the telephone shrilled. This time it was Hadassah. She talked in so low a tone that Masha had to strain to make out what she was saying. Hadassah told her that her Uncle Abram had had a heart attack, that he had been picked up somewhere in a courtyard on Ptasha Street; a baker's apprentice had brought him in a droshky to Ida Prager's studio. And there was some confused business about a robbery; a girl called Manya, who was once a servant at Grandfather's, had been arrested. Masha listened, one hand to her temple, as though the fierce throbbing might split her skull.

"But, darling," she managed to interrupt, "I really don't understand a word you're saying. I'm more dead than alive."

"I haven't closed an eye all night," Hadassah said.

Masha promised to call her later and sank back on the couch. How on earth did Uncle Abram get to Ptasha Street. What did it have to do with this Manya woman? And what were they holding her for? The whole thing was crazy. She opened a bureau drawer and took out a bottle of valerian drops. She glanced at her reflection in the mirror. Her face was deathly pale. Her hair, which she had had so carefully dressed the day before, was now disheveled. There were dark rings under her eyes. "My God, they bury better-looking carcasses than me," Masha thought, remembering a favorite phrase of her mother's. She heard someone sighing and coughing. Yanek came in barefooted, wearing only his short drawers. His ribs stood out like barrel hoops. A thin chain with a scapular on it hung around his neck. His lean legs were hairy. There was anger in his dark eyes.

"What the devil is all this bedlam so early in the morning?" he growled. "Can't your lovers wait till a decent hour?"

"For God's sake, Yanek, stop torturing me. I have no lovers."

"What time did you get home? And who the hell dares to disturb my rest? I'm a Polish colonel!"

"But, darling, it was Hadassah. My Uncle Abram had a heart attack."

"The damned parasite should have croaked long ago."

"How can you talk that way? Dear God, it's my uncle. And they arrested Hertz Yanovar. His wife is hysterical."

"For Communism, eh?"

"You know very well that Hertz Yanovar's no Communist. It's somebody who lives in the house. Broide and his wife."

"Well, what the devil has it got to do with you? What do they expect? That I'll stick my nose out for these Jewish Bolsheviks? If it was up to me I'd see every one of them hanged."

"What are you getting so excited about? Hertz Yanovar's innocent."

"They're all the same gang. Those damn Jews of yours are eating up the country like a bunch of termites. And they'll never rest, the bastards, until the red flag flies over the Belvedere."

"You're crazy."

"You're one of them yourself. You go to their filthy balls. You're a plague in my house!"

"Then I'll go. I'll go today."

"Who gives a damn? March!"

"Boor!"

He went out of the room, slamming the door behind him. Masha sat brooding in silence. She knew that Yanek would come back to apologize to her. He would call her tender names: "Little soul—little heart—little pigeon—little mother —" Then he would go away and come back late at night, drunk, boasting of the way the officers' wives were throwing themselves at him. She covered her face with her hands. "God in heaven, I'm so tired. If they'd only let me sleep!" She fell back on the couch and buried her face in the pillow. "I've no more strength. Let things happen. I can't help it." She tried to fall asleep, but thoughts buzzed through her brain. She yawned, stretched, wiped the tears from the corners of her eyes. "I'll go to a convent, that's what I'll do. At least I'll get some rest that way." She fell asleep. When she woke again, the room was flooded with sunlight; a fresh snow had fallen. From the kitchen came the smell of soup greens and frying. Marianna was already preparing dinner. Masha went into the bathroom and lighted the gas stove. She sat down on a stool. The maid came to the door, knocked, and opened it.

"There's mail," she said.

She held out three envelopes. One was from America—from her sister Lottie. Her stepfather, Koppel, was in trouble with the law for selling liquor. But the family was provided for. Mendy was a lawyer, married and the father of twins. Lottie was not married. She was an instructor at a college. Lottie complained that she kept on sending money to Bialodrevna, but never got a reply. How was her father? How was Aaron? Why didn't someone write?

The second letter was from a Catholic society to aid war orphans. Masha was asked to come to an entertainment at the orphanage.

The third letter was long. It bore the signature Edek Halpern; he was a young man she had been friendly with before she had married Yanek. He had left her and had married a girl from Vlotslavek. Now he was asking Masha to intervene with the officials about a sawmill he owned, which the government had confiscated without indemnity. Masha sighed. Ah, what a bunch! A dirty lot. Everything with them was money, favors, protection. She tore the letter in four. The water for the bath was ready. She undressed and looked at herself in the mirror. How small she looked without her high-heeled shoes on! How thin her body was! Skin and bones. She had practically no breasts. And she could have no children; she was too small, the doctors had told her. No one loved her, that was the truth. Neither her father nor her mother. Nor her husband.

She looked away from her reflection. Above the washstand stood a bottle of iodine. She drew out the cork and sniffed the vial. Suddenly she lifted the bottle to her mouth, threw back her head, and swallowed a mouthful. It was as though her hand had done it on its own account. She regretted it at once. There was a burning sensation on her tongue, her palate, in her throat. She tried to shout, but no sound came from her sealed lips. She turned and rushed naked into the kitchen. "Help, help! " she gasped.

The maid stared at her and started to howl. "Jesus! Mary!"

Neighbors poured into the apartment. Someone called for an ambulance. One woman snatched up a pan with milk and poured it down Masha's throat. Masha was more surprised than terrified. She had not meant it. Why should she have done it now? She closed her eyes, resigned to never opening them again. They carried her out of the room, pressed her stomach, urged her to vomit. After a while she was aware that a tube was being forced down her throat.

Yanek came rushing in and knelt down by the bed. "What have you done? Why? Why?"

She did not want to open her eyes. Whatever was going to happen, let it happen in the darkness.

The news traveled like wildfire through the Moskat family. They did not know what to talk about first, Abram Shapiro's heart attack or Masha's attempted suicide. Hadassah was struck dumb. Only Gina had heard nothing. She telephoned, to urge Masha again to intercede for Hertz Yanovar. Yanek answered the telephone. He heard the Jewish accent and he shouted at the top of his voice: "Go to the devil! Beasts! Bastards! Dogs! Traitors!"

CHAPTER SIX

The officials of the political police on Danilovichevska Street apparently considered Hertz Yanovar a real haul. They took away his suspenders, removed the laces from his shoes, and put him in a fifth-floor cell by himself. All this happened not much after dawn. Hertz sat down on the edge of the broad bunk that stood in the middle of the room. He looked about him. The walls of the cell were scrawled with a miscellany of names, dates, Communist slogans. He tried to look out of the window, but it was too high. He put his head between his hands. Time after time he had warned Gina that her Communist lodgers would ruin him. But who ever listened to him?

He lay down on the bunk, closed his eyes, and tried to

sleep, but his bones ached and his body itched. What was it? Bugs, maybe, or nerves? He wriggled about and scratched. According to the philosophy he held, he should be ready for anything—sickness, loneliness, squalor, even death. If there was any meaning at all in existence, it would be comprehended beyond the bourne, in the darkness that knows without knowledge, creates without a plan, and is divine without a god.

But now that the catastrophe had come, he could not accept it with any stoicism. To fall into God's hands was one thing, but to fall into the hands of man was fearful. Ever since his childhood he had been afraid of police and officialdom. He had no pass, no birth certificate, no military papers. He hardly knew whether he was properly registered in the records. He knew in advance that he would stammer and blunder at the examination, contradict himself, make his situation even more difficult. He was even nervous lest, out of fear, he might denounce others. He remembered that Broide had served three years in the Pawiak Prison. He knew revolutionists who had been sent to penal servitude and hard labor. How could they have survived it? He himself felt already broken.

He raised the collar of his coat and put a handkerchief under his head. He could hear noises, shufflings, shouts at the other side of the door. The key turned in the lock. A guard thrust in a blind eye.

"Time for the toilet!"

He got up and went out into the corridor. The hall was crowded with prisoners, whispering and gesturing to one another. The guards herded them into a large room, the walls covered with tiles. Along one side was a line of water taps. Men were washing, gargling, combing their hair with their fingers, drying themselves with pieces of paper. Across the room was a row of open toilets where men were relieving themselves. Hertz stood against the urinal, but out of anxiety he could not function. A youngster tapped him on the shoulder.

"Hey, professor. Yes or no. Make up your mind."

They were led out into a kitchen. Each man took a tin tray and spoon. They filed past a table where they were handed bowls of some kind of brown grits and a slice of bread. The blood rushed to Yanovar's face. "This is man, the crown of creation," he thought.

The prisoners were brought back to their cells. Hertz

sniffed at the bowl and put it down on the floor. He began to pace back and forth, his hands folded behind him, in the position he had used to assume in the Bialodrevna study house. He knit his brows as though he were wrestling with a Talmudic interpretation. "If I were guilty," he thought, "all right, let them do what they want with me. But as long as I've not been convicted of anything yet, why humiliate me? Is this justice? Ecclesiastes was right: 'In the place of judgment is wickedness.' "

The door opened and a tall uniformed officer entered, with a pockmarked face, long neck, and angry eyes, gray as tallow. "Come with me."

Hertz followed him. They went down a flight of stairs, the steps edged with iron. Black doors lined the walls. They went through a long court. In the middle was a patrol wagon, with barred windows. They entered an office. The floor was strewn with sawdust. On the wall hung a portrait of Pilsudski. At a desk sat a flaxen-haired woman, working on her fingernails with a file. A stout man with wine-colored spots on his bloated face, his fleshy nose peppered with pimples, leaned against a chair. His stubby fingers were pawing through a sheaf of papers.

"Your name?"

"Hertz Yanovar."

"Chertz Yanovar," the officer mimicked. "What are you? A technician? A secretary? A functionary? A delegate from the Comintern?"

"I'm not a Communist," Hertz began in a trembling voice.

"That's what they all say, the sons of bitches."

"Gracious pan, I'm innocent. I'm not even a Marxist. My wife keeps roomers. We couldn't pay the rent unless—"

The officer raised his eyes from the papers. "What's your profession?"

Hertz did not know what to answer. "Nothing special. I do research for a book I'm writing."

"A writer, eh? What do you write? Proclamations?"

"God forbid. I'm the founder of a society to investigate psychical phenomena."

"Where is the society's headquarters?"

"At my flat."

"Have you got a permit?"

"I didn't know one was needed."

"Illegal, eh?"

"Just a few of us get together and—"

"Who are the members? Their names and addresses."

Hertz recited the names of half a dozen of his friends. The officer wrote them down with a red pencil. "How long have you known Broide?"

"Oh, a long time. From long before the war."

"And did you know that he was a member of the central committee of the Communist Party of Poland?"

"I only knew that he was a Leftist—"

"A Bolshevik?"

Hertz was silent.

"Answer when you're asked something!" The officer thumped his fist on the table.

"That's what they say."

"And how does it happen that you rent rooms to people like that?"

"I don't rent the rooms. My wife does. I don't mix in that."

"Your wife's name?"

"Gina Genendel Yanovar."

"How long has she been a member of the Communist Party?"

"Who? My wife? God forbid. She doesn't belong to any party."

"Do you know that your house is a nest of Bolshevist canaille? Are you aware that your house is a meeting-place for agitators from Moscow?"

"I swear by everything I hold holy that I know nothing about it."

"Where do you live? On the moon? Do you know a woman by the name of Barbara Fishelsohn?"

"Oh, yes, since she was a little child."

"When did you see her last?"

"Last night. At a ball."

"Aha! Who was she with?"

"She came alone, I think. I introduced her to a friend of mine."

"His name and address?"

"He's someone who's far away from all these things."

"We'll decide that. His name and address."

"Asa Heshel Bannet. He's a teacher in a theological seminary. He lives on Bagatella Street, number—"

"Was he at the ball alone?"

"No. With his wife."

"What's her name?"

"Hadassah Bannet."

"Hadassah Bannet, eh? Who else was with him?"

"A cousin of his wife's. Masha Zazhitska, the wife of Colonel Jan Zazhitski."

"Where does the colonel live?"

"In Uyazdover Alley. I don't know the number."

"What's the colonel got to do with this group?"

"What group? My God, the colonel is miles away from such ideas."

"Do you know the colonel personally?"

"I was introduced to him long ago. When he was an unknown painter."

The officer threw a side glance at the woman sitting at the desk. "You hear that?" he said. "The business starts in one of those nests on the Shviento-Yerska and reaches as far as the house of a Polish colonel. His wife is Jewish, isn't she?" He turned his glance back to Hertz Yanovar. "What was her name before?"

"Masha Margolis."

"Masha Margolis. Hadassah Bannet. Asa Heshel. Gina Genendel. There's only one thing to do. Get rid of all of them. Like rats. Into the Vistula with the whole lot of 'em!"

CHAPTER SEVEN

Day after long day passed, and still Hertz Yanovar was kept in the prison cell. From moistened crumbs of bread he had fashioned a set of chessmen and with the end of a spoon had scratched out a chessboard on the surface of the bench. He had smeared the pieces that were supposed to be black with dirt and dust. He sat for hours moving the figures around the board. He bit his lips and tugged at the beard that had sprouted during his imprisonment, muttering to himself in a singsong: "If the king moves here, then I give it the finishing blow. And if, on the other hand, the queen butts in, then I threaten them both with the knight. . . ."

When he got tired of this game, Hertz applied himself to mathematics. He scrawled all sorts of algebraic symbols on the wall and made an attempt to solve Fermat's last theorem. He knew that his efforts were useless, especially as the best mathematical minds had been unable to find a solution, but anything was better than burying himself in the darkness of his own thoughts.

Hertz clambered up on the bench and looked through the barred window. There was no view of the street to be had. From the city there came a muffled roar. Roofs, chimneys, and columns of smoke heaved up under the winter sky. Weathervanes turned in the wind. A cat crawled along a roof gutter. It snowed for a while, and then a wintry sun shimmered down. Yes, Hertz Yanovar thought, they had him cooped up here like an animal in a cage, while the outside world went about its business. Who could know? Maybe Gina, too, had already made her peace with the situation, just as if she had become a widow.

As he stood so, there was the sound of a key in the cell lock. He got down from the bench and sat on it. The pock-marked police officer came in. "Yanovar? Come with me. Bring your things with you."

"Where are you taking me?"

"To be hanged."

Yanovar had nothing to take with him. He followed the officer down the stairways and across the long courtyard. This time there was no sign of the patrol wagon. It was probably out rounding up suspects. It was refreshing to catch a few breaths of the sharp frosty air, to tread on flagstones and soft snow. His footsteps felt youthfully light. It seemed to him that he could smell the fragrance of forests, fields, and the coming spring. There was a single tree in the courtyard, surrounded by an iron paling. The tiny snowflakes on its branches reminded him of blossoms. He was again led into the office, where he saw the same heavy-set officer with the wine-colored blotches on his face. The woman assistant was fussing about with an extinguished candle in a glass holder.

The officer threw an angry glance at Hertz Yanovar. "What's he doing here?"

"For Pan Katchinski."

The policeman carefully took Hertz Yanovar by the elbow and led him into a newly decorated room, where there was a bookcase, a sofa, woven cane chairs, and a writing-desk covered with a green cloth, on which lay a single sheet of paper. At the desk sat a young man of about thirty, slender and clean-shaven, with a head of blond hair combed straight back, and with the high forehead of an intellectual. He wore a green blouse, unadorned by any decoration, the collar tightly buttoned around the throat. It was difficult to be sure whether this was military attire or civilian. There was an air of seriousness and relaxation about him, the aura of one who has divested himself of all ordinary cares. "Pan Yanovar? Please sit down."

"Many thanks."

"Will you smoke?"

"Thank you."

"Please. Maybe you'd like a glass of tea?"

Tears started from Hertz Yanovar's eyes. "No, yes, thank you. Thank you with all my heart."

"Stach, have some tea brought in."

The policeman clicked his heels, turned, and went out. Katchinski lit a match and held it to the tip of Yanovar's cigarette, but no matter how fervently Hertz drew at the mouthpiece, the tobacco would not ignite. The match burned down almost to Katchinski's fingertips. Beads of perspiration stood out on Yanovar's forehead. He took another furious puff and drew in a mouthful of smoke. "Excuse me, I'm a bit nervous."

"It doesn't matter at all."

Katchinski's pale eyes looked now mildly, now searchingly, at Yanovar. It seemed that he was weighing carefully every word he spoke.

"Mr. Yanovar, we are sorry about this whole incident. You are the victim of a misunderstanding."

It was all Hertz could do to restrain his tears.

"I am happy that the truth has come out at last. I was afraid that—" He could not finish the sentence.

"Someone has interceded on your behalf," Katchinski continued. "One of the most splendid personalities in the new Poland—Colonel Jan Zazhitski."

"Really. That is very noble of him. I met the colonel when he was still a beginner—in a studio on Holy Cross Street."

"Yes, I know. It is to be regretted that you have to keep such lodgers as Broide and the others."

"I warned my wife many times. It's all a result of the bad conditions."

"Naturally. But just the same it's better to be careful. The usual detective does not go very deeply into things. If he happens to find subversive literature in a home, then everybody suffers."

"Yes, I can understand that. I'll see to it that no more of that sort is taken in."

"Quite right. The colonel spent an hour here with me last night. All on your behalf. He told me many noteworthy facts. He knows Jewish life thoroughly."

The door slowly opened. The girl who had been fussing with the candle came in, carrying a glass of tea with a tin spoon. On the saucer lay a single piece of sugar. Katchinski smiled.

"Panna Yadzha, it seems to be impossible for you ever to bring in a full glass."

The woman threw a sullen glance at Yanovar. "It spilled."

"It's an old woman's weakness, never to fill the glass."

The girl went out, her heavy feet clattering over the doorsill. Katchinski's face resumed its former seriousness.

"Please drink your tea, Mr. Yanovar. Tell me, what sort of person is Asa Heshel Bannet? You know him, don't you?"

"Very well. He's a close friend of mine. He teaches in a girls' school, Chavazeleth. He also was connected with a theological seminary."

"He's not a red?"

"By no means. He has a philosophy all his own. He argues that all social problems can be solved by means of birth control. My own belief is that he puts entirely too much emphasis on these matters."

"How so? That is very interesting. It has been reported to me that he has something to do with a woman Communist, a certain Barbara Fishelsohn, a converted Jew."

"I know her, too. I would hardly call her a Communist."

"What would you call her, then?"

"A parlor radical. A fellow traveler. What she needs, if you'll pardon me, is a man."

"Quite possible. Mr. Yanovar, I should like to talk to you privately, man to man, with no relation to my official duties."

"Of course."

"Mr. Yanovar, the percentage of Jewish Communists is astonishingly large. The proportion is simply fantastic. Do the Jewish intellectuals know this? What do they think of it?"

"That, sir, is the unfortunate situation the Jew finds himself in. We are not permitted in the civil service, nor are we permitted to take posts in factories. Anti-Semitism creates Communism."

"Well, assuming that it is so, do the Jewish leaders realize that Communism among the Jewish masses evokes an anti-Semitism tenfold, a hundredfold, more intense?"

"We know that, too. It's a vicious circle."

"Mr. Yanovar, I do not want to frighten you, but the situation is unbearable. Today the Jews are the spreaders of Bolshevism throughout the face of the earth. I'm not exaggerating. This puts the very existence of the Jewish race in danger."

"But what can we do about it? Here in Poland we are absolutely without power. The Jewish community has no influence over the younger generation. The only salvation is for the powers to give us Palestine. In a country of our own we will be able to supply the necessary measures."

"You are a Zionist, I see."

"I see no other way out."

"I don't want to hurt you, but Zionism is a failure. Palestine cannot absorb the Jewish overpopulation in Poland. And I won't even mention the Jews of other countries."

"Nevertheless, without a home of our own we are a lost people."

"But just figure it out for yourself, my dear Mr. Yanovar. It is quite impossible to be a Polish citizen and at the same time make every effort to discard that citizenship and assume another one. Does that not, in the best case, put you in the position of temporary citizens?"

"The position we Jews are in is such that we have lost the initiative. We are powerless not only in relation to the Christians, but to our own brethren as well. If the peoples of the world want us to live, then they have to discover the way."

"What sort of way? From the purely democratic standpoint it is out of the question to take a country away from the Arabs and to establish a Jewish state."

"And what would be your advice?"

"I don't know, my dear Yanovar. Have you read the book *The Twilight of Israel?*"

"No. I saw it in a bookshop window."

"A highly learned work—but pessimistic throughout. I was discussing it with the colonel. Well, good-by, Mr. Yanovar. I hope you will forgive us for the discomfort you have suffered. You are free now, you may go."

"I am very grateful to you. Yes, the situation is extremely sad."

"Time solves all problems. One way or another. Adieu."

Hertz Yanovar went out. At the other side of the door the policeman was waiting; Yanovar would still have to go through a few formalities. There was a paper he had to sign; then he had to receive back the money that had been taken from him, as well as his suspenders and shoelaces.

CHAPTER EIGHT

1

During the winter vacation it was again possible for Asa Heshel to stay up late at night and to sleep through the morning. For a while he returned to the habits of his bachelor days. Hadassah would go to sleep, but he would sit in his study, leafing his manuscript. The pages were like his thoughts—a mixture of fantasy and metaphysical concepts. His notebooks were full of systems of conduct. (From his earliest youth he had waged a losing war against laziness and diffusion of thought.) He could never learn to stifle the emotions of pride, shame, regret. His arguments with Hadassah had turned into a kind of madness; they screamed, cursed, even struck each other. Yadwiga, the servant, would cook their meals, but the food would become stale while they quarreled. The little girl would cry, but her mother would pay no heed. Hadassah took sedatives; she still could not sleep. Time after time Asa Heshel resolved to make an end of the constant disputes, but he found it impossible. She never stopped complaining; she accused him of visiting his son too often and spending too much time with Adele. She talked about his love affairs in Russia. She suspected that he was carrying on with the girls of the Chavazeleth, and was even jealous of Masha, Stepha, and Klonya. She began to dislike Hertz Yanovar and maintained that it was he who kept Asa Heshel from his home. She said cruel things about Asa Heshel's mother and sister. She was always taking Dacha to doctors, and spent their last pennies on all kinds of bargains. Every day brought new troubles. Asa Heshel began to fear that Hadassah was losing her mind.

Now Hadassah was asleep. Asa Heshel paced up and down in his study. He went to the window and looked out over the fields and lots of Mokotov, which lay covered with snow, glimmering in the lights of the scattered street lamps. He returned to his desk. He had expected to do some work during his vacation, but the time was nearly all gone and he had accomplished nothing.

He was overcome with drowsiness and began to undress. He began to think about the women he had had. If time is an illusion, as Kant believed, he still had them. Somewhere, in a different sphere, he was living with Adele, with the daughter of the ritual slaughterer in Berne, the kindergarten teacher in Kiev, with Sonia on the estate near Ekaterinoslav. What nonsense! He thought about Barbara. Wasn't it strange? He hadn't wanted to go to that ball; Hadassah had forced him. She had actually led him to her rival. Another example of how casuality and teleology can go hand in hand. Hadassah herself had become frigid; a trick of the subconscious—punishing oneself and others for dreams that had not come true.

He went into the bedroom and lay down on his bed. He pricked up his ears. Was Hadassah sleeping? He covered himself and straightened his pillow. Thank God, he had a place to rest his head. He remembered a night he had spent on the roof of a train. In order to prevent himself from falling, he had tied himself with his belt to a crossbar. A spark from the locomotive had fallen into his eyes. He had been verminous and hungry. If somebody had told him then that he would have an apartment on Bagatella Street with Hadassah. . . . He curled up and tried autosuggestion, according to Coué's formula—"I will fall asleep, I will stop worrying; from day to day I will become more courageous, healthy, tranquil." Strange, but although he had been a teacher for years, he could never enter the classroom without fear. He still blushed, sweated, trembled. Daydreams still consumed most of his free time.

He began to doze. He was both in Russia and in Warsaw. He was having an affair with one of his students. The police were after him. All this was somehow connected with algebra and a funeral. "What's the matter with me?" he said to himself in his sleep. "Why have I become entangled in this net?"

Suddenly the telephone rang.

Asa Heshel thought it was the alarm clock. He heard Hadassah get out of bed and open the bedroom door.

Hadassah came back into the room. "It's for you."

"Who is it?"

"Some woman."

"Who is she?"

"The devil knows."

Asa Heshel got out of bed with a sigh. Could Adele have the impudence to call him at this hour of the night? Maybe something had happened to David. On the way out of the room he stumbled against the edge of little Dacha's bed. The light was turned on in the corridor. In the wall mirror Asa

Heshel caught sight of his reflection, a disheveled image, with sunken chest, a pale face, and sleepless eyes. He picked up the receiver. "Who is this?"

"Did I wake you? Forgive me. It's an emergency. This is Barbara."

"Yes, Barbara?"

"The police have searched my house," Barbara said in a muffled voice. "They wanted to arrest me. I managed to get away. They were asking questions about you."

"About me? Where are you now?"

"At the Central Station. I don't know what to do. I haven't got my pass with me, or any money."

Asa Heshel was silent. He could hear his breath through his nostrils. "What do you want me to do?" he asked.

"Maybe you can come over to meet me. Then I'll be able to tell you everything. You'd better bring a valise with you."

"A valise? Why?"

"So that you'll look like a traveler. Good-by."

Asa Heshel heard the click of the receiver. He stood without moving for a moment. The lamp on the writing-desk threw an uneven glow. Hadassah came into the room in her nightgown. Her face was bloodless. "What's happening? You don't even let me get a night's sleep."

"Hadassah, they're looking for me. To arrest me."

"Arrest you? What for?"

"I don't know. I'll have to leave the house right away. I think it has some connection with Hertz Yanovar. He gave the officials everybody's name and address."

Hadassah was silent. Ever since Masha had made a suicide attempt and her Uncle Abram had had a heart attack in the room of a servant who was a thief, she was ready to believe anything. She shook her head. "Who was that woman? You're lying to me."

"I'm telling you the truth. I swear to you by everything that's holy."

"I don't believe your oaths any more. You're a liar and a traitor. Go on, go to your worthless women! And don't ever come back. Never! Never!"

She wrung her hands. The tears rolled down her cheeks. Asa Heshel went into the bedroom and dressed hurriedly. In the darkness he fussed about with his collar, collar buttons, tie, and shoelaces. His fatigue had left him. In him there arose a new energy that had been hidden somewhere in the deeps of his nervous system.

Dacha awoke. "Papa, what are you doing?"

"Go to sleep. I'm just getting dressed."

"Where are you going?"

"I'll be back soon."

"Did you hit Mamma?"

"God forbid. Where do you get such notions?"

"Because she's crying."

Hadassah's sobs could be heard from the other room. Asa Heshel wanted to explain the situation to her, to assure her again that he was going only because he was compelled to. But he knew that it would be a long-drawn-out affair, using up urgent time. It would be better now not to try to patch up the quarrel. He opened a clothes closet and rummaged about till he found a valise. Without putting on the light he emptied some shirts, socks, and handkerchiefs into it from the dresser drawers. Hadassah entered the room. He stood there in his hat and overcoat. He could see her white nightgown as a pale patch.

She turned toward him. "I'll not let you go."

"You're not the boss here yet."

"Asa Heshel, I beg you! Listen to me. Don't go!" She started to plead with him. "Asa Heshel! For God's sake, don't leave me alone! Have you no more love for me?"

Something tore at his heart. He wanted to reassure her, but there was no time now. Instead he turned harshly on her. "What are you standing there like an idiot for? I'm not going away to have a good time. She called me up because it was necessary to warn me. These Polish officials are madmen."

"Where are you going? It's the middle of the night. I tell you, that woman wants to destroy you."

She clutched at his coat lapel and thrust herself in his way. He tore himself out of her grasp and pushed her aside. The child began to wail. "Tatush, you're hitting her!"

Asa Heshel hurried out and ran quickly down the steps. In the outside courtyard he came to a stop. All the house windows were dark. The janitor, apparently, was already asleep; the window off the entrance was covered with a blanket. But just then there was a ring of the outside gate bell, and the janitor came out in his undershirt, holding his pants. He glanced at Asa Heshel and the valise he was carrying. "You're going away?" he asked.

"Yes. To Lodz."

"Is there a train so late?"

"The last one."

Asa Heshel immediately regretted the remark. In the event of an investigation the lie might have serious consequences. Outside, over the opposite rooftops, hung a pearly dimmed midnight moon. A late streetcar rumbled by. Asa Heshel ran toward it and leaped aboard. He knew that he was letting himself in for trouble; nevertheless, he had an urgent desire to get to the railroad station quickly. He was breathless, and astonished at his own hurry. "What's happening to me now?" he thought. "Am I in love with her?" He paid the conductor and sat down, wiped the mist off the window and looked out. The storekeepers had gone in for a new fashion, he noticed; they were keeping their windows lighted although the shops were closed, in the foreign manner. Along Marshalkovska Street women loitered. Their shadowed eyes shone with the gloomy lust of those who have lost all fear of peering into the abyss. Asa Heshel got off the car a little distance before the station. The waiting-room was half empty, garishly lit. The windows at the ticket-sellers' booths were all down. The hands of the large wall clock showed half past two. He glanced toward the benches. Barbara was sitting there, wearing a caracul jacket, hatless, and carrying a blue valise. She was talking to a woman who held a small dog on her lap. She saw him, got up, and came over to him. She held out her gloved hand, looking at him with an expression that was half worried and half gay. "I knew that you'd come."

"We can't stay here," Asa Heshel said. "We'll have to go somewhere else."

"Where else can we go? It's bitter cold outside."

He took the valise from her and started to walk ahead. A policeman looked curiously at them. He made a motion as though to stop them, but then continued his stroll. A fence separated the train tracks from the street. A solitary locomotive puffed out clouds of steam. There was the clang of milk cans and the shouts of porters. Barbara put on the beret she was carrying in her hand with her pocketbook. "Where are you taking me?"

"I have an idea. A wild one, but this whole thing is wild."

"Give me your arm. You poor boy, I pulled you out of a nice warm bed."

"What happened?"

"Ah, it's all so mixed up. You see, I have a friend—we went to the Evangelical school together. Well, I went to visit her; they live on Napoleon Place. All of a sudden I was called to the telephone. You probably noticed when you visited me the name of one of our neighbors—Pastor Gurney. He has a seventeen-year-old son—the boy's been in love with me ever since he was a child. I asked: 'Who is this?' and he said: 'Peter.' 'How did you know I was here?' I said. I was really frightened. I thought that maybe Father had fallen sick. 'Don't say anything; just listen to me,' Peter said. 'The police have been at your apartment. They were there for about two hours, going through all the books. I listened. They wanted to arrest you. One of them is still waiting outside. They also asked who visited you. Your father gave them a name—Bannet.' . . . Can you imagine? If it wasn't for Peter I'd be in prison now."

"Where did you manage to get the valise?"

"At my friend's. I could have stayed the night, but I figured that the cops might find me. Her parents are such conservative people. And I wanted to warn you."

"Have they anything on you?"

"I haven't done anything. They have absolutely no evidence against me. But you know how it is—in the meanwhile they can hold you in jail. Maybe they found a few pamphlets. So many provocateurs have found their way into our ranks. The Trotskyists are the worst informers. Now I'm sorry that I ever came back from abroad. You can hardly imagine how free everything is in France. Here it's awful. I'm not worrying about myself, but my father must be terribly upset. He's got a bad heart. And I haven't got any money. What's to be done? You know Warsaw, don't you?"

"A hotel would be too dangerous."

"Of course. But there must be some places where one can stay a night without a passport. Tomorrow I'll go to a lawyer and straighten everything out. I'm sure you're perfectly all right. A hundred-per-cent reactionary like you."

"But I'll have to prove it to them."

"Well, if you're frightened you can go back home."

"I'm not frightened."

"Really? I thought you'd answer the telephone, but it was your wife. When I said I wanted to talk to you, she didn't make a sound. I thought she had hung up on me. She must be very jealous."

"Who wouldn't be?"

"Poor thing, I'm so sorry. Although one person has no right to be jealous of another. Your body is your own, as Madame Kollantai said. Where are we going?"

"Have you heard of Abram Shapiro?"

"I think Hertz Yanovar once mentioned him to me. Who is he?"

"That's a long story. He's my wife's uncle. He's sick now; he had a heart attack. And he's living in the house of a woman friend of his—his mistress, really. Ida Prager, a painter. She's in the hospital; she's sick herself. The flat is a kind of studio. Maybe we'll be able to spend a few hours there."

"Where is it?"

"Not far. Holy Cross Street."

"The question is whether the janitor will let us in. Each house here is a prison in itself."

"I think he will. A lot of people come to the studio. I'll give him a zloty."

"Well, you see how smart I was? My heart told me that you'd be the only one to help me. Ah, everything is so mixed up. Tell me, is Mr. Shapiro married?"

"He's a widower."

"Who takes care of him? Anyway, there's nothing else for us to do. I insulted you last time. I regretted it immediately afterwards. There's really something very nice about you. I'm not saying this to flatter you. You're an *enfant terrible*. Your wife, too, sounds like a child."

"How can you know what my wife is like?"

"Oh, I could tell it by her voice. Why aren't you happy with her?"

"I doubt whether I could be happy with anyone."

"Why not?"

"This whole marriage business is not for me."

"It's good that you know it. It's true—you could never love anyone. You're a victim of your own philosophy. If pleasure is all that counts, there is no reason for ever giving. Only for taking."

"That's the quintessence of all civilization."

"We Communists don't believe that. We wish to give as well as to take."

"I've only seen them take."

"You're just a naughty boy and I ought to twist your ear. Someone must have abused you when you were a child and you simply can't forget it. What are people to do? They have to eat."

"There are too many mouths to feed. Every janitor has a dozen kids."

"What have you got against janitors? I guess it's the time of night. At a late hour like this everything is upside down."

"As far as I'm concerned, it has always been upside down."

"Yes, you toss back and forth in the world like a sleepless person on his bed. Papa is right. A Jew of your kind must have a god. Papa is clever and irrational. I, personally, have given up everything. When I was a child I was terribly pious. I would get out of bed during the night to kneel before the picture of Jesus. I had one desire—to become a nun. I wasn't satisfied with the Evangelical church. I envied the Catholics. I had a purity complex. Later I fell in love with a boy, a Christian—but he was smart enough to get married to someone else. That was a blow to me, I can tell you. I became ambitious and wanted to be independent. In France I lived as though I was in a dream. I thought I knew French, but when I got there, no one understood a word I said. I went to live with a family and they treated me like a daughter. Oh, I forgot to tell you—Papa got married here in Warsaw; that was the reason they sent me away. My stepmother is an English-woman, the widow of a missionary. What a match that was! She was brought up somewhere in India. They lived in different worlds. Thank God, she went back to London. Yes, my friend, and in the meanwhile I discovered that people had to eat and so I joined the Communist Party. Are we there?"

Asa Heshel rang the bell. Barbara fidgeted about, tapping her soles on the pavement. After a while footsteps could be heard. Asa Heshel took out a silver zloty. The janitor opened the courtyard door a crack.

"Who is it you're looking for?"

"Pan Abram Shapiro. In the studio."

"Who are you?"

"We're relatives of his."

"*Nu . . .*"

Asa Heshel motioned to Barbara and she went first. The janitor returned to his quarters.

"You're an experienced liar," Barbara said.

"Crazy, too."

On the fourth floor they halted. Barbara sat down on the sill of the landing window, her feet dangling. Asa Heshel set down the valises.

Barbaras eyes bored at him in the darkness. "What are you thinking of, child?" she whispered.

"I have a feeling that all of humanity is caught in a trap. No going forward and no going backward. We Jews will be the first victims."

"The end of the world, eh? Papa to the bones! What does your Jewishness really consist in? What are the Jews, after all?"

"A people who can't sleep themselves and let nobody else sleep."

"Maybe that comes from a bad conscience."

"The others have no conscience at all."

"I must give you credit for one virtue: you're a consistent reactionary. I guess that's really why I like you. Socialism will wipe it all away—chauvinism, poverty, middle-class philosophy. In a certain sense people like you are useful. You help dig the grave for capitalism."

Barbara got down from the window sill. They began to climb the last flight of stairs.

2

When the two stood before the door of the studio, Asa Heshel suddenly became frightened by his utter stupidity. People did not walk into homes in the middle of the night—not to speak of breaking into the house of a sick person; and with a stranger at that. During all the period Abram had been ill Asa Heshel had not once been to see him. He had postponed visiting him from one day to the next. He had a distaste for seeing the changes that Abram's heart attack had brought on him, or hearing his resigned remarks. He had always had an aversion to doctors, medicines, funerals, all the people one meets in hospitals and at cemeteries, who seem to entertain a hidden glee over the misfortunes of others.

In recent days he had gone about in a sort of fog; he had answered no mail, forgotten to pay bills, walked around with his pockets stuffed with neglected papers. He had borrowed some money from the loan organization of the Teacher's Association, and the time had come to pay the first installment, but he did not have the necessary fifty zlotys. The last days of the winter vacation were already here, and it was high time to start preparing his lessons for the resumption of classes. He was weeks behind with the money for Adele, and he neither called her nor went to see David. He even avoided his mother and Dinah. Now he realized that this business of breaking in on Abram would simply embroil him in a new net of complications. Hadassah would learn whom it was he was going about with. There would be more excited gossip among the family. They would find out about it in the school. For a moment he was ready to tell Barbara that they would have to turn around and leave. But he was too exhausted. What difference did anything make now? Let happen what would. He pressed the doorbell. For what seemed a long time there was no sound from the other side of the door. Then they heard footsteps. The door opened. At the threshold stood Avigdor, Abram's older son-in-law, Bella's husband. Apparently he had not yet gone to sleep. He wore a three-quarter gaberdine and a small skullcap. His wide-boned face was milk-white. His pale eyes peered with short-sighted astonishment from behind the lenses of his glasses.

"Good evening. You probably don't recognize me," Asa Heshel said.

"I recognize you. You're Asa Heshel. Why are you standing at the door? Come in. *Sholem a leichem.*"

"Thank you. A late visit, eh? It's an unusual situation. . . . This lady is Miss Fishelsohn."

"Good evening. My father-in-law has been asking about you all the time, wondering why you haven't been to see him. Your wife is here every day. He refuses to listen to the slightest word against you. When he takes a fancy to anyone, he stays that way to the end."

"How is he?"

"Not too well. But you know him. He doesn't give up so easy. He's sleeping now. He's been a little better, but the danger's not over. Someone's got to be with him all the time. Tonight's my watch. Last night Stepha's husband was here. What's happened? Why are you carrying valises?"

"You probably heard that they arrested Hertz Yanovar."

"They let him go already."

"Yes, but he gave them everybody's names and addresses. I found out that they're after me to arrest me."

"You? What for? What sort of nonsense is that? The trouble is that there's no place to sleep here. My father-in-law is on the big bed, and I manage on the cot near him. To tell you the truth, I can't fall asleep anyway. I keep thinking all kinds of things. Well, we men will make out somehow. The lady will have to try to sleep in a chair."

"Oh, thank you, but I'm not sleepy," Barbara said in Polish. "The whole thing is a misunderstanding. They have absolutely nothing against me."

"Of course, my dear lady, but once they get you into their clutches it's bad. The best thing is to have nothing to do with them. I'll make some tea."

"Oh, please don't bother."

"It's nothing at all. You put on the kettle and the gas stove does the rest. Well, come inside. I'm not afraid. Let them arrest me. Just let them take care of my family and I could stand their jails."

The studio was a scene of confusion. Canvases were strewn about. Books, papers, and magazines lay around. Through the dusty, cracked panes of the skylight could be seen patches of snow and gaps of the night sky. In the middle of the room stood an iron stove with crooked pipes stretching away from it. Towels hung on them, drying. Avigdor went into the kitchen and soon returned.

"I put on the tea," he said. "If you'd like something to eat, there's some bread and butter. Tell me, what's the news? In the world of business things aren't good. I know a Jew over on Nalevki Street, and he says that with us it's like the worshippers at the Eighteen Benedictions; one goes out first, and another gets through later—but all of us have to go out sooner or later."

"You have a store?" Asa Heshel asked.

"What do you mean, store? One lives from hand to mouth. I wanted to go to Palestine, but they wouldn't give me a certificate. You have to belong to a party. If not, you're not a human being. They say that the rabbi of Ger is going to settle in Palestine. The Bialodrevna rabbi is opposed to the whole idea. Not so much the rabbi as Reb Moshe Gabriel. The old generation knows only one thing: Messiah will come. God knows, he's taking his time."

"Do you go to the Bialodrevna prayerhouse?" Asa Heshel asked, just to say something.

"Every day. Sometimes in the morning and sometimes in the afternoon. Wait, the tea must be boiled already." He hurried out of the room.

Barbara smiled at Asa Heshel. "A very curious little man," she said.

"He's not so curious at all," Asa Heshel replied. "People like him are the backbone of the Jews."

"Another one of your exaggerations. What is he? A little storekeeper. Nobody."

"In your eyes, maybe. Not in mine. It's these little nobodies who for two thousand years have carried all of Jewry on their backs—as well as all of Christendom. It is they who have always turned the other cheek."

"For whose sake should one turn the other cheek? Mussolini's?"

"I don't say one should. I'm not a Christian."

"Neither are you a Jew."

At that moment from the other room they heard a wheezing, a snorting, and a heavy footfall. The floor squeaked. Asa Heshel and Barbara raised their eyes. The door to the bedroom was thrown open, and at the threshold stood Abram.

3

Asa Heshel had thought that Abram's illness would leave him emaciated, but he was even heavier than before. His round belly and broad hairy chest were visible under his unbuttoned bathrobe. His face was red. The hair around his bald spot was unkempt. He stood and looked at Asa Heshel and Barbara out of his big black eyes, which had not yet lost their luster. His fleshy forehead, over the bushy brows, had a crooked crease running across it. Barbara looked at him in astonishment. He reminded her of the satyrs in the windows of antique shops.

It was a while before Asa Heshel was able to speak. "You got out of bed?" he asked. "Were you sleeping?"

"Yes, it's me—the dead man," Abram answered in an altered voice. "Make your confession, I have come back to choke you."

Avigdor came in from the kitchen with two glasses of tea. When he saw Abram, he took a step backward. The glasses shook in their saucers. "Father-in-law! What's the matter with you? You aren't allowed to get out of bed."

"I've done many things that aren't allowed," Abram answered harshly. "One more sin . . ."

"Father-in-law, you're killing yourself. If Mintz knew, he'd be furious."

"Let him be. These quacks are no help, anyhow."

Asa Heshel got up and placed a chair for Abram at the table. Abram took a step in his worn-out slippers. He tried to ease himself into the chair slowly, but collapsed into it. He clutched at his breast. "I could manage to stand anything. The

only trouble is my legs don't want to keep carrying me any
more. The load's too heavy."

"I'm sorry we woke you up. Something happened suddenly
and—"

"You didn't wake me. I sleep enough. I hibernate, like a
bear in a cave. I heard your sweet voice, so I came out. So
you came at last, did you? Blessed be the guest."

"This is Pan Abram Shapiro. And this is Panna Barbara Fishelsohn. A peculiar visit, eh?"

"I'm honored to know you. Nothing in the world's peculiar.
What induced you to visit me? You ought to be ashamed of
yourself for having kept away."

"I *am* ashamed. You know the story with Hertz Yanovar.
He gave them everybody's names. The police are looking for
me."

"They're looking for me, too. Just ask my son-in-law. A police investigator was around here. They suspect me of some
robbery or other. I'm lucky that I'm a sick man. Anyway,
what are you afraid of? You're as much a Communist as I am
a thief."

"But they keep you in jail for two weeks just the same."

"If you run away they'll keep you in jail for two years. Go
over to Breitman, the lawyer. He's a pal of mine. So far as I'm
concerned, brother, I've got one foot in the grave already.
Once I had it in mind to leave you a fortune in my will, but
now I'm afraid you'll have to finance the cemetery plot for
me. Well, as long as you're here you're here. Tell me, miss,
are you a Warsovian?" He turned to Barbara and addressed
the question to her in Polish.

"Yes, but I've just come back from abroad."

"There are two Fishelsohn families I know about. One is in
the piece-goods business and the other deals in leather. Which
category do you belong to?"

Barbara bit her lip in embarrassment. "To neither, I'm
afraid."

"Not, God forbid, a Litvak?"

"God forbid!"

"Once I knew the genealogy of all Warsaw. Now I've lost
track. There's a proverb: 'Family prestige is in the cemetery.' "

"Father-in-law, now that you're up, maybe you'll take your
medicine," Avigdor said.

"What difference does it make? It's as much help as cupping a corpse. You must be tired, no?" He turned to Asa Heshel and Barbara. "Where shall I put you up? We don't even have bed linen."

"Thanks a lot," Barbara answered. "If you don't mind, I'll just sit here for the night."

"Why should I mind? Once I was a gallant—I would sleep on the floor and give my bed to a lady, but now it's too late even for that. I haven't got the strength any more. Where did you get such burning eyes? They could shoot out sparks."

"It's possible that I have burning eyes, but I hate such eyes."

"Heh? Why? I try to compliment her, and it turns out it's just the opposite. The eyes are supposed to be the mirror of the soul. Jewish eyes are famous for their fire. The gentiles are afraid that we may burn them. Forgive me, Asa Heshel, but the gentiles' blue eyes are as cool and watery as their heads. Maybe that's the reason you're so heartless."

"Father-in-law, here's your medicine; may it cure you!"

Abram drank from the spoon and grimaced. A few drops fell on his beard. "Phooey! Thank you. Where have you been abroad?"

"In France."

"Paris, eh? I was there once. A long time ago. A gay city, hu-ha! They're not such beauties, but the women have something about 'em. Chic. *Comme ci comme ça, oh la-la.* And the Paris pickpockets know their trade, too. They cut the pockets right out of my coat. I went up to the top of the Eiffel Tower and saw all of Paris as though on the palm of my hand. And the what-do-you-call-it, Notre-Dame, and the Place de la Concorde. You get hot sausages and mustard there. Well, anyway. Tell me, do they let Jews live in peace there?"

"The reactionaries stir up trouble against all the minorities."

"There too? Here in Poland it's bitter as gall. The whole world's got together to suffocate us. These days I've got time to read the newspapers. They all have the same theme—Jews, Jews. Jews are all Bolsheviks, bankers, Masons, Wall Street speculators. All the sins of the world they ascribe to us. The others are all pure white spotless lambs. Trotsky, Rothschild, and the rabbi of Ger all sit down to eat Sabbath pudding together. The Elders of Zion spend all their time in some cave figuring out ways to destroy the world. And that Hitler is a vicious beast. If, God forbid, he gets in power, then it'll really be bad."

"You'll excuse me, but the capitalists are doing all they can to make sure that he gets the power in Germany. The Jewish capitalists included," Barbara said.

"Oh! Just the same as the anti-Semites put the blame for everything on the Jew, that's the way you Leftists put all the blame for everything on the capitalists. There's always got to be a sacrificial goat. I'm far from being a bourgeois; if I stay sick a litle bit longer there won't be enough money left to buy me a shroud. Just the same, I can't abide nonsense. What does the capitalist do that's so bad? He buys and sells."

"Then, according to your opinion, who's to blame for the present crisis?"

"Human nature. You can call a man capitalist, Bolshevik, Jew, *goy*, Tartar, Turk, anything you want, but the real truth is that man is a stinker. If you beat him he yells. And if the other fellow is beaten, then he develops a theory. Maybe it'll be better in the next world. Come into the bedroom with me for a while, Asa Heshel. Miss Barbara will excuse us."

Abram grasped the sides of the chair with both hands and grimaced as though he were suffering an intense pain in his bowels. Asa Heshel helped him up. Abram took a few steps and then halted. He took a handkerchief from the pocket of his robe and wiped the perspiration from his face. In the bedroom vials and bottles and boxes of pills were strewn on a chair, and unwashed plates and glasses stood about. There were books and papers everywhere. Abram carefully deposited his bulk in the bed, leaning back against the three pillows at the head.

"Ah, I tell you, I'm a broken shell," he groaned. "When I lie here, I can manage to suffer it, but when I get up, the whole damn thing isn't worth a pinch of snuff. A man's heart, I tell you, brother, is a worthless vessel. Well, I didn't expect I'd last this long. And, if you want to know the truth, I spit at the whole mess. I've thought of being cremated, but what's the difference! I suppose the worms have to eat too. They've got wives and children also. Let's talk about more pleasant subjects. How are things with you? What kind of adventures are you having? Who's that girl? I don't want to be the one to judge you, but I must say that's no way to carry on."

"I told you, they're out to arrest me."

"Naturally, if you run around with people like that they'll arrest you a dozen times. They'll very politely stow you away in jail. And I'll not bail you out. Hadassah cries her eyes out. She's not one of your wailing women, but I can see that she's getting more than she can take. Have you got a better friend than her? For years and years she waited for you. On account of you she turned her back on everything. And now this is the way you're paying her back. What is it? Don't you love her any more?"

"I do love her."

"Then what are you torturing her for? Come on, speak plainly."

"Abram, I'm not a family man!"

"You just discovered it? You want a divorce, heh?"

"I want to be left in peace. I cannot carry the burden any more."

"What do you want to become, a tramp?"

"I can't stand it any more. I'm mortally tired."

"You really look tired. Maybe you'd like some cognac. The doctor prescribed it for me."

"No, it won't help."

"Sit down. People like you get tired of their own thoughts. Who is that woman?"

"The daughter of a missionary."

"And a Communist into the bargain?"

"So she says."

"Aha! Well, as you sow, so shall you reap. I'm content. Soon I won't be here any more. Bitter times are coming for you youngsters."

"They'll destroy all of us."

Abram lifted one eyebrow. "Who? What are you talking about?"

"We've been driven into a trap—economically, spiritually, in every respect."

"So we should at least stick together."

"Why? We don't love one another that much."

"A fine thing! Here I am on my deathbed, and I have to comfort him. The end of the world hasn't come yet."

"The end of our world *has* come."

"You're a lunatic. You've let yourself fall into a melancholy. What do you want to do? Sit down and weep?"

"Personally, I can't take it any more. Dacha is sick. Hadassah has nothing but doctors on her mind. She kills me with her nagging."

"Shut up! You're not letting me die in peace. Tell me, exactly what is it you want to do? Get converted?"

"I want to leave everything and get away."

"Where to? Ah, brother, I had hopes for you. You've been a bitter disappointment to me."

"Not more than to myself."

"You're a coward, brother. That's the whole thing. You want to run away from everything. You'll hang around with this new discovery of yours and in a little while you'll be high and dry again. Unless you want to commit suicide."

Asa Heshel did not answer. Abram's large, dark eyes gazed steadily at him from behind the heavy brows. The crease in his forehead deepened, like a wound. After a while he dropped his head back on the pillows and closed his lids. He lay motionless. Then he opened one eye. "Come and kiss me."

Asa Heshel bent over the bed and kissed Abram on the brow. Abram raised his arms and put them around Asa Heshel's shoulders. "I believe in God," he murmured. "I die a Jew."

CHAPTER NINE

1

Barbara spent the few hours that remained before dawn in a soft chair. She put her feet on a hassock, covered herself with her caracul coat, and slept. Asa Heshel did not close his eyes. He heard Abram snoring in the bedroom. Every few minutes Abram woke up, sighing. Avigdor got off his cot, shuffled across the floor, returned to sleep. Asa Heshel walked around on tip-toe. A long-forgotten adventurousness seized him. It was good to be in a strange house with a strange woman, without money, in a complicated situation. He stood at the window and looked out. "I'm killing myself," he thought, "there's no doubt about it. But why, why? Because I have no faith. That minimum of faith without which one cannot exist. That humility which is friendship, the desire to bring up children, the readiness to sacrifice oneself for others. One cannot even make a career without it. But how can I rescue myself? In what can I believe? I hate God, I hate Him and His creation. How can one love a dead God, a paper God? I am *kaput, kaput.*"

He sat down on a chair and dozed off. He started up, then fell asleep again. He huddled into his coat and put his hands into his sleeves. "Why does he sigh so much—Abram? What is he thinking of? He's afraid of death, in spite of all his bravado. They're all afraid and they all die. What a cursed order!"

At dawn he fell asleep. When he awoke it was daylight. The rising sun threw a purple sheen on the pictures. Barbara stood in the middle of the room, erect and pale. Her big black eyes, like those of a huge bird, looked nowhere. "You're up at last," she said. "It's bitter cold. Maybe we can go down and have a cup of tea."

The gate was already open. Across the street was a coffee house lighted by a gas lamp. A single guest sat at a table. The waitress had not yet come to work. The owner himself brought them tea and rolls. Barbara did not drink her tea immediately, but cupped the glass in her hands to warm them. "What are you going to do now?" she asked.

"I'm going over to my mother's. Although, if the police search my house, they'll discover her address and come after me there."

"Where does she live? I'll tell the whole story to my lawyer. Where and when can you meet me? Let's say six o'clock at the opera house."

"If I don't come, you'll know I was arrested."

"The same with me."

They ate and were silent. The coffee house filled with people. The street became bright. A newsboy brought papers into the restaurant. Barbara bought the *Morning Courier*. She glanced at the headlines and grimaced. She read the editorial. She looked alternately angry and sad. Asa Heshel watched her. How alike all believers are to one another! How they hate others' beliefs! How sure they are of their own! He closed his eyes for a while. It was warm here, almost hot. There was the smell of coffee, milk, and freshly baked cakes. He took out a pencil and a piece of paper and began to draw lines, circles, letters, numbers. If the police were after him, everything was lost. He would never be allowed to teach again. And even if they didn't arrest him, the situation would still be far from good. He was in debt to everyone. He drew a bird with an exaggeratedly long beak, with a rooster's comb and the tail of a peacock. Inside the outlines he wrote, over and over, the number five hundred. That was the sum he needed.

When Barbara left, Asa Heshel telephoned his house to find out whether the police had been there. But when Hadassah heard his voice she immediately hung up the receiver. Asa

Heshel had not been over to his mother's for a long time. He took a streetcar that went along Franciskaner Street. Neither his mother nor Dinah ever visited him at his flat on Bagatella Street. They still sided with Adele. Every fortnight Adele was in the habit of bringing David to pay a visit to his grandmother for a Sabbath meal. She still addressed the old woman as mother-in-law. And Finkel still referred to Hadassah as "that one." Finkel had seen Dacha, her granddaughter, only twice, once when she was still an infant, and the second time in recent months. David knew some Yiddish; Dacha understood only Polish. It was impossible for the grandmother to have any conversation with the child. She had asked: "Do you love your papa?"—this in Yiddish—and when the child made no answer, had commented: "A little *shikse*."

Everything that had happened seemed unreal to Asa Heshel —spending the night away from home, visiting his mother so early in the morning. It was as though he were a bachelor again. Now, at this hour, the poverty of his mother's surroundings struck him more forcefully than ever before. The stairs that led to the flat were covered with filth. On the steps some children sat, wrapped in nondescript rags. They were playing with pebbles and fragments of shells. One of the little girls had a rash on her forehead. A small boy in a tiny skullcap, with adult-looking disordered sidelocks, ran out of a doorway, a prayerbook clutched in his hand. He called somebody by a nickname and ran back again. Dinah's daughter, Tamar, opened the door. She was small-boned and short of stature and resembled her father, Menassah David. She had a head of brown hair, a high bosom, brown eyes, and broad, freckled features. She had studied in the newly organized Orthodox Beth Jacob school and knew Hebrew as well as Polish. She had done her part in helping in the house since she was ten. In the afternoons she worked as assistant bookkeeper in a piece-goods store on Gensha Street. When Asa Heshel knocked, she had been at the sink, cutting an onion. She wiped her hands on her apron.

"Uncle Asa Heshel," she said, "it's been so long. Grandma will be glad."

"Where is she? And where's your mother?"

"Mamma went to the market. Grandma's praying. Father's at the prayerhouse and Jerachmiel's at the yeshivah. Dan's at cheder."

"What's the news? It seems like years since I've been here."

"You really should be ashamed of yourself. Only the other

day Grandma was saying: 'He comes as seldom as a doctor.'
How's David? And Dacha?"

"David, I think, is going to some conference. Dacha has
trouble with her ear. What are you doing. Tamar?"

The girl smiled. "What should I be doing?" she said. "In the
morning I help in the house and in the afternoon I go to
work, and that's how the day goes. We've started a girl's
group of the Religous Worker. We're trying to get certificates
for Palestine. And they've started a women's division on the
farm near Mlava."

"Do you want to go to Palestine?"

"Why not? What is there to do here? In business things are
terrible. Nobody pays; everybody buys on credit. And then
there are piles of protested notes. The old man is such a joker.
When a dealer comes to pay a note, he says: 'I see you're one
of the old-fashioned kind. Nobody pays any more.' I tell you,
you could die laughing. Anyway, a girl can't go to Palestine
alone. They give certificates only for families."

"Well, then all you have to do is get married. I hear that
they arrange fake marriages."

"*We* don't. What are you standing in your overcoat for?
You'll catch cold."

The door of the adjoining room opened and Asa Heshel's
mother came into the kitchen. Each time he saw her he experienced the same shock. She was growing more and more
aged and shrunken. She was not yet sixty, but she looked
eighty. There was a shawl over her close-cropped hair. A pair
of spectacles rested on her curved nose. She was toothless and
as a result her lower jaw curved upward. In one hand she was
holding a handkerchief and in the other a prayerbook. Asa
Heshel went to her and kissed her. She looked at him smiling-
ly and in surprise. "We never see you any more." she said. "I
even told Dinah to telephone to find out about you. You don't
look too good."

"I didn't sleep well last night."

"Why shouldn't you get a good night's sleep? A man of
your years should sleep soundly. How's your family?"

"They're all right."

"You're getting to be more and more of a stranger. You've
got no time, I suppose. With all the burdens you've got to
carry it's no wonder. Will you drink a glass of tea? There's
some cake left from the Sabbath. Dinah will soon be here.
She's got a lot of complaints against you. Tamar, make your
uncle some tea. What are you staying here in the kitchen for?

Come in the other room, although, to tell the truth, it's warmer here."

"Yes, Mother, I'll stay here."

"Tamar, wipe off that chair. And clean off the table. In the meanwhile I've got to finish my prayers."

She turned and went back into the room from which she had come. Tamar busied herself preparing tea and slicing lemon. She went out of the kitchen and in a moment came back with the Sabbath cake.

"How's your father?" Asa Heshel asked. "Is he managing to earn anything?"

Tamar shrugged her shoulders. "Nothing. He's got two pupils, but they keep on owing the money. Jerachmiel gets his dinner at the yeshivah. They got some funds from America. Dan helps the beadle on Friday. He gets a zloty for it." The girl showed a mouth of wide teeth.

"How about you? Weren't you supposed to get a raise?"

"I'm thankful that they don't cut me."

Asa Heshel drank the tea and took a bite of the dry cake, leaving the rest of it on the plate. The young ones yearned for a treat like this, he knew. He was behind more than a hundred zlotys in the allowance he gave his mother, but all he had to his name now was four zlotys. And it would be almost two weeks before he would get paid by the school. And he had left no money with Hadassah. So far as Adele was concerned, there was no use even thinking about the sum he owed her. If he could not manage to borrow at least a hundred zlotys at once, he'd be practically starving. He took a swallow of tea and shook his head in astonishment at his own situation. "Abram is right," he thought. "What I'm doing is committing suicide." With the tips of his fingers he began to pick up the scattered crumbs of cake and carry them to his lips.

As he sat over the glass of tea he reflected that it was not yet too late to end the adventure he was having with Barbara. But his existence was too gray; he simply had to find something to hang on to. Among the extinguished souls with whom he was surrounded it was impossible to breathe.

After he had exchanged some words with his mother and Dinah, who had returned from her marketing, he went into the bedroom and stretched out on the bed. The wallpaper was shabby and peeling; laundry hung drying on ropes slung from wall to wall. Dinah had told him that it was no longer safe to hang up wash on the roof; thieves stole it.

The door opened. At the threshold stood Menassah David,

in a ragged coat with its padding showing through the rips.
His boots were patched, the heels run down. Over his skullcap
his soiled hat sat askew on his head. His ragged beard covered
almost all of his cheeks below the smiling eyes. Under his arm
he held a prayer shawl.

"You sleep, heh? 'What meanest thou, O sleeper! Arise, call
upon thy God!' There's no despair, do you hear me? All melancholy comes from uncleanliness. From a single spark a
whole flame can come to life."

"Menassah David? It's you? How late is it?"

"It's never too late. All a man has to do is repent. Redemp-
tion will come just the same; why should a man impede it?
One pious thought can turn the scales."

"Menassah David, maybe you'll be good enough to stop
your babbling." Dinah's voice came from behind him. "Dan
hasn't got a pair of shoes to his feet, and he prattles his sermons."

"Everything will be all right. 'He who gives life will give
food.' The only thing is to have faith."

"Lunatic, let him sleep. Don't pester him."

"And what does sleep bring? When a man sleeps he has no
free will. Get up, Asa Heshel, let's dance."

He began to sway back and forth on the threshold where he
stood. He clapped his hands. For what, after all, was the great
trick in showing ecstasy only in time of plenty? The true
greatness was in giving oneself up to joy when the waters were
rising around one.

2

Asa Heshel dozed off. When he awoke, it was close to three
o'clock. His mother and Dinah tried to make him stay at
home, but he insisted that he had to go. He promised he
would come back the following day. He had risen with the
feeling that time was pressing. Where could he get some
money? He left the house. The snow was falling heavily as he
walked along Franciskaner Street. He stopped at a bookstore.
The window was crowded with volumes in Hebrew and Yiddish—novels, poetry, drama, political brochures, a Revisionist
magazine calling for war against the "Maneuverings of the
Zionists and their policy of mildness toward England."

While he was thus peering through the dusty window he realized clearly that there was nowhere he would be able to get

any money. He thought of calling on Hertz Yanovar, but he already owed him twenty zlotys. Besides, every time Asa Heshel saw him, Hertz read him protocols of his metaphysical society, stories of dybbuks, poltergeists, about a fish who called "Hear, O Israel!" or about a baby under whose cradle a fire burned. Anyway, Hertz was probably not at home. In the daytime he was always in the public library on Koshykova Street. He took off his hat and shook the snow off it. He walked toward Adele's apartment. She would upbraid him, but what of it? He had a key to the flat, but instead of using it he rang the bell. Adele opened the door for him. She stood looking at him with a doubtful expression on her face, as though she were deciding whether or not to admit him.

"Don't you recognize me?" Asa Heshel said.

"Oh, I recognize you, all right. Wipe your shoes."

"Is David home?"

"He's at the conference of the Shomrim."

Asa Heshel wiped his shoes on the straw mat. He could smell the odor of cooking meat and potatoes and fried onions. He suddenly realized that he was hungry. He had a flash of remembrance of Switzerland, when he had come to tutor some children and their mother was always busy in the kitchen, cooking and frying. "Ah, how low I have fallen!" he thought. Aloud he said: "What does David write?"

"He's full of enthusiasm. Just imagine! They put him on the committee. One out of hundreds of delegates. He sent a photograph. He has an ideal. Well, take off your coat. Come inside. Maybe you'll have dinner?"

"I just ate."

"Too bad. You never come here without having eaten first. I was beginning to think that you'd forgotten my address."

In the living-room a half-finished plate of soup stood on the table. Adele sat down in front of it. Asa Heshel leaned back on a sofa. Adele hurriedly finished the soup and pushed the plate away from her.

"Well, what brings you here?" she asked. "You probably wanted to find out whether we had starved to death."

"Have it your own way."

"As long as David has a mother, he won't go hungry," Adele said firmly. "I gave him money to travel with, and a few zlotys pocket money. Most of the delegates are boys from well-to-do families, and I don't want my child to feel ashamed. You don't look well. What's the matter with you?"

"I haven't slept the past two nights."

"What happened? Is your wife in labor?"

Asa Heshel told her that they were after him to arrest him. He mentioned Barbara. He admitted that he had stayed overnight with her at Abram's. He did not know himself why he was confiding all this to Adele; was it to bolster his masculine prestige, to make her jealous, or to let her know, once for all, that she could not place any reliance on his support? Adele listened to him in silence, looking at him with an oblique glance, her nostrils dilated. She surmised at once that he was carrying on a love affair with this Barbara. She had some regret that he was letting himself fall into such a morass, but she had lived to have her revenge on Hadassah. Besides, she had always known that things would work out this way. When a man was false to one woman, then he would be false to everyone else. As far as she was concerned, she had long since written him off as lost. There was only one thing that was wrong: she could not hate him as he deserved. Her anger with him was always tempered by pity. She looked at him as he sat there with his face sickly pale. in his wrinkled suit, his tie knotted awkwardly, and she felt an impulse to warn and help him. Why should a person want to bring about his own downfall, she wondered. That was puzzling. She remembered a journey she had taken with him, from Geneva to Lausanne and from there to Brig. They had eaten at the station restaurant and had looked up at the mountains that loomed above the village like walls, their sides covered with grape orchards.

"Why don't you eat something?" she said. "I have plenty of food here."

"No," he answered. "Nothing at all."

"Then at least have a glass of tea." She went out of the room and came back with a plate of meat for herself and a glass of tea for Asa Heshel. As she ate she stared at him in wonder. How could a man of his age carry on like an irresponsible youth? What was it that went on in his mind? How could a father show so little interest in his own son? Strange that his irregular goings on had somehow prevented her from marrying again. It had often occurred to her that as long as this riddle remained unsolved she could not completely free herself from him. She still had the nebulous conviction that he would find nothing but disappointment with everyone else and would come back to her.

"What's your opinion about David?" she asked. "He wants to go to Palestine. What will become of him there? If he were only willing to go on with his studies he would be a genius."

"The world spits at our geniuses."

"He says that he'll send you a certificate. He takes after you, but he hasn't got your faults. How is that possible, I ask you. He knows all of your carryings on, but he defends you. You should see the boys who come to see him. Personalities, I tell you. Devoted to the cause. Ready to sacrifice themselves. I don't understand where they get it. A new generation."

"Well, he couldn't be worse than I, so he has to be better."

"At least it's good that you understand yourself. Nevertheless, there's no reason to be so defeated. You have your own virtues. Ah, why did things happen this way? I was so much in love with you."

Adele was frightened at her own words, but they could not now be recalled.

Asa Heshel bent his head. "Nobody can build anything on me."

"Why? Why?"

"I'm sick. Physically and spiritually."

"It's true. You're sick." Adele clutched at this remark. "That's why I can't be angry with you. If I were in your place I'd go to see a psychiatrist."

"Then every Jew in the world would have to go to one. I mean every modern Jew."

"Maybe you need some money. I can lend you some. How much do you need?"

"No, Adele. I'll never have it to pay back."

"What do you propose to do?"

"I'll still play around a bit."

"With what?" she asked. "With human lives?"

"With what else?"

They both rose.

"You've committed a great evil against me; but don't do the same to Hadassah. I've got strong shoulders; she's sick. She'll never survive it."

As Adele spoke she had a strange feeling that it was someone else speaking through her lips. It was her dead mother saying these words, her voice and her intonation.

3

Asa Heshel spent that night with Barbara at the house of a gentile Communist on Leshno Street. In order to conceal from the janitor that strangers were staying in the flat, the pair made sure to reach the house early, before the gates were locked, and to leave late in the morning. They were given a small, dark room that contained a bed and a lame-legged washstand. At eleven o'clock in the morning the two got into a number-nine streetcar. The lawyer whom Barbara had consulted the day before had advised her to return home as soon as possible, declaring that the longer she hid herself, the worse her situation would be. The same advice applied to Asa Heshel. Barbara expected that the moment she entered her father's house she would be arrested; a detective was surely waiting at the outside door, or near the Saxon Gardens. The lawyer had promised her that if she was arrested he would get her out on bail; but no one could ever be sure what the charge would be or whether the examining judge would permit bail.

Now she sat in silence, hunched up, looking through the misted car window, which she wiped constantly with her glove. What a strange game fate was playing with her! As long as she had been alone no one had bothered her; now that she had found a lover she would have to give herself up into the hands of the police. She tried to justify in her mind the sacrifice she was making for the proletariat, but somehow or other this morning all of her social zeal seemed to have faded away. These workers outside, the draymen, the janitors, the gentile stall-keepers in the market places, did not know that she was suffering for them. And even if they knew, would they care? That fat woman with the red cheeks, for instance, sitting at the ready-made shoe stall and gulping soup from a pot. Her husband was probably a cobbler, but what did she care about the working class? She spent her time running to church, kissing the hand of the priest, and cursing the Jews and the Bolsheviks. After the revolution she'd be of the chosen, while as for Barbara, she would have to face the accusation of being the daughter of a clerical. Why in the devil's name should she be singled out to be the one to sacrifice herself for them? She tried to drive away these bourgeois thoughts. What she needed now was encouragement. But who was there to give it to her? She regretted now that she had come back to Poland, and even that she had begun an affair with that pessimistic man who had a wife and children and who lacked any vestige of faith in humanity. Dear God in heaven, if her father knew how his Barbara was behaving! He was sure that she was still a virgin. She closed her eyes. After the night of abandonment comes the punishment, she thought. Just as it is written in the holy books.

At the corner of Krulevska Street Barbara got out of the streetcar. She made a motion to kiss Asa Heshel, but their hatbrims were in the way. She wanted to say something to him, but there was no time. She pressed his wrist. The streetcar started to move while she was getting off. Asa Heshel pushed his way to the platform. Through the fog he caught sight of her caracul coat and the pale oval of her face. She waved her hand to him and turned as though she would run after the car, as though at the last moment she regretted leaving him. The streetcar rolled on, over New World Boulevard, the Place of the Three Crosses, Uyazdover Alley. Asa Heshel started to recall the ecstasy that the last night had brought to them—the kissing, the embracing, the ardent talk—but with it all there was a bitter aftertaste. He remembered how Barbara had said to him as they left the house: "Well, there you have your laboratory of happiness!"

At Bagatella Street Asa Heshel got off the streetcar, but instead of going directly home, as he had made up his mind to do, he crossed over to the other side of the street to make sure that no one was waiting for him at the gate. There was no one there. He went into a restaurant and telephoned to Barbara. He hoped that she would answer the phone herself, but instead he heard the hoarse voice of her father. He hung up. After a few moments he called up his own home. The servant answered.

"This is me, Yadwiga," he said.

"Oh, the pan! Jesus Mary!"

"Has anyone been there for me?" he asked. "Have the police been there?"

"The police? Why should the police come?"

"Is your mistress there?"

"Yes, I'll call her."

While he waited at the phone he realized that he was doing everything the wrong way. He should not have asked about the police. It was not impossible that the phone was being tapped. Even in these few moments it was possible that they were already surrounding the restaurant he was calling from. But it was too late now.

Yadwiga came back to the telephone. "Your wife doesn't want to talk to you. You'd better come home."

He went outside, but instead of going home he walked along toward Marshalkovska Street. The fact that the police had not been around was no proof that they were not looking for him. A detective was probably hiding somewhere. He walked along, taking long steps, every once in a while looking back over his shoulder to see if he was being followed. The old man's voice had been shrill, he reflected, thinking of Barbara's father. They had probably arrested her. Suddenly he stopped. He turned around and began to retrace his steps. "I'll imagine I'm a French aristocrat and they're leading me to the guillotine," he thought. "I have another fifteen minutes to live. At least I had a good night."

With every few steps he stopped to take a deep breath. He turned his eyes up to the sky. The heavens were clouded, but the sunlight was reflected from the upper windows of the buildings. The air was so fragrant. Birds were twittering. There would probably soon be a storm. Something sparkled in the dirt on the ground at his feet. A diamond? No, it was only a piece of glass.

He reached the house. He had a key to the elevator, but he climbed up the stairs. How brave Abram was! He knew how to live and how to die. He still had in him those juices which nourished the people in all the dark hours they had endured. He was a Jew biologically.

He pressed the bell at the door. Yadwiga answered. Just as Adele had done the previous day, she hesitated a moment before she let him in. He glanced into the living-room; no one was there. He went into his study. The room had been cleaned and tidied, the windows washed, the floor polished. The books and papers had been cleared from his writing-desk, as though he had moved away for good. It occurred to him that this is what happens when a man dies. On the desk was a notice from the tax office. The door opened and Hadassah put her head into the room. She seemed to have become thinner; she was carefully made up. She had apparently begun to use powder. She looked at him in silence.

"Well, come in," he said. "Get a revolver and shoot me."

"All I want to tell you is that I've sold the apartment."

He looked at her in inquiry. "What do you mean?"

"They've offered me fifteen hundred American dollars. I'm going to rent a place in Otwotsk. Dacha can't stand the Warsaw climate. And besides, there's nothing for me to do here either."

"Have you taken her to the doctor again?"

"I had a consultation."

"Who wants to pay you fifteen hundred dollars?"

"Papa and my stepmother. We've discussed the whole thing. I hope you won't stand in the way. I can't stay here in

Warsaw any more. I'll bury myself in Otwotsk and wait for God to take me at last."

"You want us to separate?"

"Why? If you should come to Otwotsk you'll stay with us."

Asa Heshel could not understand how all this had come about. When had Hadassah decided on this plan, and when had she had time to go into the matter with her stepmother? But he could tell that it was the only way out; it was the logic of events, as the philosophers expressed it.

Several things happened that day. Ida died in the Jewish hospital. The Bialodrevna rabbi died at his evening prayers. The Chassidim wanted Reb Moshe Gabriel to become their rabbi, but Reb Moshe Gabriel refused. After much persuasion Aaron consented to take the holy burden on his shoulders. It was not for long. Aaron was planning to go to Palestine with a group of young Chassidim. The Bialodrevna court was as good as finished.

PART
TEN

CHAPTER ONE

Beginning with the two cemetery plots that, years before, Reb Meshulam had bought from the community office, an entire path of graves had developed. They were all there now, lying one next to another: Meshulam Moskat and his second wife, Joel and Queen Esther, Nathan and Saltsha, Abram, Hama, Dacha, Pearl. Among them, too, were the graves of Moshe Gabriel and a couple of the grandchildren. The marble tombstone over Meshulam's grave towered above the others. The inscription on it recited all of his virtues, his knowledge of the Torah, his philanthropies, his honesty in business. On Abram's gravestone Stepha, his youngest daughter, had arranged for the engraving of his name in Latin characters in the modern manner, in addition to the Hebrew. Above the grave of Moshe Gabriel the Bialodrevna Chassidim had planned to erect a structure with a perpetual light, as was appropriate for a saintly man, but since Aaron had gone off to the Holy Land the Bialodrevna Chassidic court had practically fallen apart and there was neither the money for the remembrance nor anyone to devote himself to having it done.

Only three of Meshulam's children were alive now: Pinnie, Nyunie, and Leah, who was in America. Pinnie still owned one of the buildings he had inherited when the old man died, and from this he drew his livelihood. The Bialodrevna prayerhouse on Gzhibovska Street still stood, and Pinnie spent most of his time there, reading the Talmud or discussing politics. Although war between Poland and Germany seemed imminent, Pinnie was optimistic. Fishel, Hadassah's first husband, was a constant reader of the newspapers, too. He warned that unless a miracle took place Hitler might, God forbid, become the ruler of the earth. Fishel had married a second time and was now the father of children. He, Pinnie, and a few others still remained among the loyal Bialodrevna Chassidim. It was true that their rabbi had gone to Palestine and that the New Year pilgrimages had had to be abandoned. But what of it? Did not a saint remain a saint? Letters came to the Bialodrevna prayerhouse relating that in the colony Nachlat Jechiel— named for the former Bialodrevna rabbi—which Aaron had founded together with a score or so of Chassidim, they still devoted themselves to Torah and prayer. Those Chassidim who had scattered and joined the courts of other rabbis were considered to be men of little devotion. On the Sabbath the band of the faithful would gather in the Bialodrevna prayer-house, feast on white bread and herring, and sing the familiar Bialodrevna melodies. Even the high voices of youngsters could be heard. Later the old-timers would repeat some of the Bialodrevna words of wisdom. Of course things in Poland were bitter; the anti-Semites were never idle. And the young generation was weak and helpless. But had not the prophets of old, the sages and learned men, foretold that such days—the birth throes of the Messiah—would come? It was the eternal fight. When the holy powers increase in strength, they are challenged by the unholy ones. The Chassidim sang and sighed until the stars were high in the sky. To lengthen the span of the Sabbath they would delay lighting the candles.

In the winter the Chassidim gathered every Sabbath night at Fishel's house, on Gnoyna Street, and ate of the traditional meal to usher out the Sabbath bride. Fishel's wife, the daughter of a wealthy family, helped serve the food. Even though Pinnie was Hadassah's uncle, he joined in these celebrations. In his declining years Pinnie removed himself from the rest of the Moskat family. He did not even visit his only remaining brother, Nyunie, who had turned his back completely on decent Chassidic ways. But the heresy had not helped. Pinnie had been told that outside of Nyunie's bookstore on Holy Cross Street a picket line of Polish students stood guard every day to warn prospective customers that the owner was a Jew. And Nyunie had even been on the receiving end of a few beatings from the fascist ruffians.

So what was the good of crawling to ape the ways of the gentiles? Had not there been enough evidence that the more Jews weakened in their faith, the worse things were for them?

Old Meshulam Moskat had been a king among Jews; and, with all their faults, his sons had managed to stay Jews. But the grandchildren had completely alienated themselves from the old ways. Joel's sons-in-law were paupers. Their children had become artisans. Abram's younger daughter, Stepha, had become a nurse in the Jewish hospital; she had separated from her husband, the doctor. Two of Leah's children had grown up in America, hardly to be distinguished from the goyim. Even Pinnie had had very little to take joy in; one of his daughters had died in childbirth, another had gone off with her husband to settle in France. Of the two who stayed in Warsaw, one had married a lawyer, and the youngest, Dosha, had taken a job as a bookkeeper in a bank. So far as Masha, the apostate, was concerned, it was rumored that her husband had walked out on her. Hadassah had hidden herself some- where in a suburb of Otwotsk. The only ones of Meshulam Moskat's grandchildren, except Rabbi Aaron, who still fol- lowed the traditional Jewish ways, were Pearl's children, but the others knew little of them, for they lived in the north of Warsaw and went off on pilgrimages to the rabbi of Ger. More than twenty years had gone by since old Moskat had died, and the Jewish kingdom over which he had ruled on Gzhybov Place had long been in ruins.

The Chassidim talked, rolled their cigarettes, drank their brandy. In the midst of the feasting and conversation Fishel and Anshel, his assistant, would retire to another room. The moment the Sabbath was over and the new week began, the telephone would begin ringing. Fishel was carrying on vast business affairs. If his marriage with Hadassah had worked out and he remained a Moskat son-in-law, he would have taken old Meshulam's position in the family. But Hadassah had left him for an unbeliever. Some women said that Hadas- sah had taken an oath never to show her face in Warsaw again. She was not living in Otwotsk proper, but a little dis- tance away, in the village of Shrudborov, in the heart of the forest. Her husband was living with another woman. The women whispered to each other that Fishel had not forgotten her to this very day. But how could one really know about such things?

After the meal Pinnie would go to his home on Shliska Street. Visiting Nyunie was out of the question. Apart from the fact that Pinnie could not abide his brother's worldliness, Nyunie had moved somewhere to the other end of Warsaw, on Bagatella Street. Who could go wandering around in those sections? Who could know whether the janitor would open the gate for a gaberdined Jew? Besides, Bronya, Nyunie's wife, was a vicious shrew. Pinnie was thus left practically alone. He walked along, looking in at every doorway. Strangers lived in the flat Meshulam had once occupied. Over the years the houses had changed owners.

On the way home Pinnie had to walk fast. Near Shliska Street the gentile neighborhood began, and a Jew might find himself in trouble. The Nara men, the Polish Nazis, were in the habit of walking about with rubber truncheons, letting

Jews have it right and left. It was as much as one's life was
worth to cut through the Saxon Gardens. One of his grandsons, the son of his oldest daughter, had to stand at the university through the lectures because the gentile students refused to allow a Jew to be seated, or demanded that the Jews
sit in "ghetto" benches separated from the others. And those
idiots insisted on their right to sit with the enemies of Israel!

Pinnie scratched his gray beard. Ah, what had become of
Poland? What had happened to the whole world? A den of
scoundrels!

Pinnie was relieved when the janitor opened the gate. Here,
in the courtyard, he, Pinnie, was the boss. Here no one would
dare touch him. The few elderly gentiles in the house still
greeted him with a courteous "Good day." Hannah, his wife,
opened the apartment door for him. In the early years of their
marriage they had quarreled without cease, but now, in their
old age, Hannah waited for him in the evenings, not going to
bed until he came home. When he left the house now, she
kept on hoping only that he would not fall into the hands of
hooligans and get a beating. She knew very well that Pinnie
would be done for with one blow. Besides, she had a constant
need to have him around to talk to about their daughters and
grandchildren. Pinnie sat down at the table while Hannah
brewed some tea.

"Well, what's the news at Fishel's?" she asked.

"May all decent Jews have it no worse."

"They're going to close the bank. The government will take
over everything."

"*Mazeltov*. That means Dosha will be left without a job.
Very nice. And an old maid, too. What a shame and what a
disgrace!"

"The whole fault is yours."

Pinnie flared up. "So you're beginning at me now? Listen to
me. I'm an old man. I've got no more strength to chase
around. But if you're going to start wagging your sharp
tongue I tell you I'm going to pick up and leave. I'll sell the
house for anything, for a few coppers. But I'm not going to
stand for your lunacy."

"My, my, the delicate gentleman's offended. What did I
say? Other fathers see to it that a daughter doesn't sit around
till her hair turns gray."

"And a decent mother rears up decent Jewish daughters,
not *shikses*," Pinnie flared back. "You're the one who dragged

her to their modern schools. You, with your own hands. You with your newfangled ideas. Litvak pig!"

Hannah shook her bewigged head. "Go to sleep," she said. "You're out of your mind."

Pinnie occupied himself in reading the prescribed prayer on retiring. He paced back and forth across the room, murmuring the phrases and losing himself in dark thoughts. What did they want, these women? They were the ones who caused all the trouble, and it was the men who got the blame. It was the men who had to chase about and slave, while they sat around in the house like princesses, making all sorts of complaints. And what was the sum of it all? Men died before their time, and *they* lived on to a ripe old age. Warsaw was full of widows. Pinnie plucked at his beard and the remains of his side curls. That wife of his had given him no rest in his young years and she was torturing him in his old age.

If he weren't a man of breeding he'd take a stick and break her skull. But no, that wasn't his nature. He must bear it and be silent. Maybe it was some sort of affliction for the sins he had committed. He began to recite aloud, pronouncing each word separately:

"On my right hand is Michael. On my left hand is Gabriel. In front of me is Uriel. Behind me is Raphael. And over my head is the divine presence of God. Into Thy hand I commend my spirit. Thou hast redeemed me, O Lord God of truth. . . ."

CHAPTER TWO

When Hadassah gave up her Warsaw flat and moved out to Shrudborov, the family's comment was that she had voluntarily exiled herself to Siberia. They prophesied that she would die of loneliness, and Dacha would grow up wild, without any discipline. They told each other that the region was so snowed in during the winter that it was impossible to get to the store to do the shopping. Besides, there was not a single Jew anywhere around. But the years passed by and Hadassah did not die; and Dacha recovered her health completely.

The apartment that Hadassah rented cost very little money. In the summer she and Dacha were able to gather plenty of wood for the stove, as well as mushrooms and berries. The wives of the peasants of the neighboring farms sold milk and eggs for next to nothing. The house had a garden attached to it; Hadassah planted vegetables and raised a few chickens. The school that Dacha attended was over a mile distant, but the child did not have to walk there alone. The owner of the house, a Russian, had three daughters, and all the children went to and from school together. Hadassah had brought all her furniture and books from Warsaw. She had installed a radio and a phonograph. Asa Heshel contributed fifteen zlotys a week to her support, and her father gave her an additional ten. She managed, too, to earn a few extra zlotys out of her knitting.

On sunny days she sat on the veranda, on a folding bed, the kind used in sanatoriums, sun glasses shielding her eyes, either reading or knitting. When the weather was cold she spent all day in bed. Dacha helped with the household chores when she got home from school. The Russian family had taken Hadassah under their wing. The oldest of the girls would bring in water, heat the oven, and scour the floors. In exchange Hadassah would embroider dresses and scarves for her. The landlord's wife would keep coming in and going out all day, looking for a chance to be of some assistance. She was in the same position as Hadassah; Vanya, her husband, went off to Warsaw for weeks at a time, leaving her completely alone. It was rumored that he had a mistress there, the wife of a former Russian major. The villa, which was the remains of a prewar estate, consisted of perhaps eighty acres, but the soil was sandy, the buildings run down, and the well a forbidding distance away. The Russians who came there for the summer months paid only a third of the rates charged in Otwotsk. The woman never ceased talking about her uncle, the tax-collector, who had been shot by the Bolsheviks; of the officers with whom she used to dance when she was a young girl; and of her husband, Vanya, the charlatan, who was good only for eating, drinking, sleeping, and carrying on with females. Whenever he came home he beat her; she would walk about with blackened eyes. He would stretch himself out on his bed and sleep the day away. Or he would take a gun and go off with his dogs for a day's hunting. Once in a while when he came back with a hare, the family would have a chance to eat some meat.

The woman was envious of Hadassah. True, Hadassah's husband was certainly not a devoted mate, but still in comparison with her man he conducted himself like a gentleman. When he came out on a Saturday morning he always had a gift for Dacha. And he didn't beat Hadassah, or curse her, or

disgrace her in front of others. He sat quietly under a tree and
read a book. He played games with the children. His clothes
were clean and neat. His face was always carefully shaved. He
never failed to greet her and exchange a few polite words, or
to bring some magazines from Warsaw to her older daughter.
He would throw himself into the spirit of the children's
games, climbing trees, chasing after the goat, pushing the
swing. He sometimes brought out the ax and, in his clumsy
city manner, chopped cords of wood for the use of both families. Then he would lie down in the hammock that stretched
between two pine trees and read and make notes with a little
pencil.

Sometimes, on Saturdays, other visitors besides Hadassah's
husband came—Hadassah's friends and relatives. Klonya,
Masha, Stepha, Dosha. Then the place was lively. The women
would bring gifts for the children, chocolates, cakes, little hats
and aprons, toys and delicacies, all packed in fancy wrappings
and boxes. Rooms had to be prepared for the guests, and
there was never any argument about price. The women were
all over forty, but they looked young and stylish. Klonya and
Stepha, true, were a bit on the fat side, but Hadassah, Masha,
and Dosha still kept their slender figures. When they played
ball in the garden, one might have thought that a group of
young things was running around. It was only when one
looked at them more closely that the gray strands in their
short-cut hair and the tiny creases at the corners of their eyes
could be noticed. Hadassah's husband had a bald spot at the
top of his pate and his tall form was slightly bent. Still, Hadassah swore that he had the same figure she had known in
the youth of nineteen.

Each of these ladies from Warsaw had her own habits.
Right after eating, Dosha Moskat would put on a pair of
glasses and settle back to read a book or a magazine, turning
the pages rapidly and seeming to swallow the lines. She kept
on reading until it was time to take the train back to Warsaw.
Masha devoted her attention to the children. She told them
stories, asked them riddles, and taught them sewing. Her Polish intonation was strangely clear and distinct, like an actress's. Stepha would eat heartily, and the moment she was
through would stretch out on a couch and fall asleep. Hadassah and Klonya would join hands and go off for long walks.
Vanya's wife knew the history of each one of them. All of
them except Klonya had the same grandfather, a certain Meshulam Moskat, a millionaire. Their stories were quite clear to

her, yet it was difficult to understand these Jewesses and the way they lived. They smoked cigarettes, went in for serious discussions, laughed without any perceptible reason, and quarreled over matters that really should have had no interest at all for women. They talked about the Jewish problem, Palestine, religion; gave their opinions about books they had read, throwing Yiddish words and phrases into their Polish speech. Their dark eyes glowed. They powdered and rouged their cheeks and stained their carefully manicured fingernails. The other people of the neighborhood always felt a sense of discomfort when this Warsaw group descended on the house. It was useless for the gentiles to have moved away from Otwotsk; the Jews had followed them, bringing with them their big-city garrulousness, their luxuries and sophistication, the scents of their cosmetics. After every one of their visits they would leave behind them a generous sum of money; nevertheless, Vanya always muttered and growled when he saw them coming. He would hide and keep away till they had gone. He would stretch out on his bed in his knee-length boots, smoking, yawning, and spitting. "Why doesn't Hitler come?" he would demand of his wife. "He'll smoke 'em out, as true as God loves me."

"What, you lazy glutton?" his wife would answer. "What good'll Hitler be for you? He'll take away the only goat you've got left. The Germans will do what they did the last time—loot everything and everybody."

"So there'll be one goat less. They'll confiscate the Jewish hotels and they'll wind up in Christian hands. Things can't go on like this forever."

"It would be better for you to bestir yourself and see that your family doesn't die of hunger. The Jewish husbands turn over their earnings to their wives, and you spend every grosz on your whores."

"Shut your mouth, or I'll shut it for you," Vanya would answer. "You'll find the same end they'll find."

CHAPTER THREE

Asa Heshel, along with everyone else, feared what would happen: the Hitler war and the Nazi pogroms. It was not necessary to be a strategist to see the way the wind was blowing. The Nazi wolf was howling at Poland's door. The Jews in Poland were abandoned and helpless. Asa Heshel thought every day of getting away from the country. He had had a chance to get to Palestine, and there had been the possibility of fleeing to South America or Australia. But the days had passed by and he had done nothing. In all this confusion his own immediate life took on the pattern he had long wanted. Again, as in his younger years, he lived alone. He was rid of Hadassah's complaining and Dacha's illnesses, rid of servants and visitors, debts and taxes. David had gone off to Palestine and Asa Heshel was no longer called on to provide for him. Asa Heshel's mother was dead and her body lay in the cemetery on the Gensha. (He had even neglected to put up a stone on her grave.) So now he sat back and took some degree of comfort in the calm that was preceding the storm. For the small room he rented from a family on Novolipki Street he paid fifty zlotys a month. He ate in restaurants. His situation at the school had improved somewhat. He was able to spend money on decent clothes and could afford to buy some books. True, he had not become a professor of philosophy. He had not reevaluated old values or created a new system. But the need to ponder on the eternal questions was still with him. He would sit up until two in the morning playing with all sorts of intellectual speculations. If Spinoza was right, that inadequate and confused ideas arise from as real a necessity as adequate and clear ones, and nowhere in the world of ideas is there anything positive that can be called false, then there is value in continuing to ponder. In God every idea is true.

Through his window he could see the sky, the stars, the planets, the Milky Way. That white mistiness that he now gazed at had emanated from those heavenly bodies thousands of years ago, in the time of the patriarch Jacob, or when the Pyramids had been built. How strange it was to be here, in a room on the fifth floor of a building on Novolipki Street, and find oneself in contact with the eternity of the cosmos! How strange to reflect that the same laws which controlled the sun and the moon, the comets and the nebulæ, also governed life and death, Mussolini, Hitler, every Nazi lout who lustily sang the *Horst Wessel* song and howled for Jewish blood to spurt from the knife.

From reflections on the universe Asa Heshel went over to his own affairs. Hadassah had moved herself into a wilderness. Death was all she talked about whenever he went to visit her. Dacha was growing up wild and undisciplined among the gentile girls of the neighborhood. There was probably nothing she did not know now. And she went about with gentile boys. Who could know what a child like that might not do? Asa Heshel had tried to assure himself more than once that it really made no difference at all whether a girl married or lived with a man, whether she had to do with a Jew or a gentile. Nevertheless, he worried. David was in a kibbutz in upper Galilee, surrounded by Arabs. It was impossible to move away from the place without carrying a gun. Adele became sick whenever one of his letters was late. Dinah's husband, Menassah David, had abandoned the last vestige of responsibility. If Asa Heshel didn't give Dinah some money, there was none at all. It was at least something to be thankful for that Barbara didn't need his help.

When, years before, he had spent that night with Barbara at the home of a Polish woman Communist, he was sure that it would be the first and last time. There had been a warrant out for Barbara's arrest. She had talked about going back to France, or maybe getting into Russia. But she had stayed on in Warsaw and he was still her lover. Her father was dead. The Comintern had liquidated the Polish Communist Party. Some of the party members were in prison and some in the concentration camp of Kartuz Berez. Some had gone over to the Right Socialists and some had deserted the movement altogether. But Barbara, apparently, had remained a functionary. She took trips away from Warsaw. She led a conspiratorial life. She was registered as a bookkeeper in a button factory on Orla Street. She dressed elegantly. She avoided all radical meetings and subscribed to the reactionary *Warsaw Courier*. She even attended the Evangelical church every Sunday. In her bookcase at home there was not a single work on politics or sociology. On the small table between the two windows of her room was the Bible that had belonged to her father, with a gold cross stamped on the cover.

She was rigidly methodical. When she was in Warsaw she would phone Asa Heshel in the morning promptly at a quarter past eight, and they would meet at seven o'clock in the evening at a designated restaurant. Each paid his own way; that had been the arrangement between them from the beginning. When they went to a cinema or to the theater Barbara refused to allow Asa Heshel to pay for her ticket. On most of their evenings together they went to her room after eating. The room had a private entrance. Barbara would turn on the radio and puff a cigarette. After a while she would turn the radio off. They would sit opposite each other on soft upholstered chairs that she had inherited from her father and look at each other intimately, yet strangely. Barbara had a habit of beginning their conversations with: "Well, what has the accused to say?" Or she would ask: "Well, what have you accomplished today for the counterrevolution?"

"I've done my honest share," he would answer.

Barbara would smile, showing her elongated teeth. The two of them had agreed many times to avoid any political discussions, but they often found themselves deep in a dispute. Always the argument wound around the same question: did people know enough about human history to be able to predict its course? Asa Heshel maintained that since not all of the factors were known, it was impossible to foretell any outcome. The idea of a kingdom of freedom stood in opposition to the concept of causality. Questions of justice had no place in a system where each body could be moved only by another body. The concept of equality was at variance with all biological factors. Barbara would listen to him, getting up now and then to pump fuel into the Primus stove. His words questioned the foundations of everything she believed. But just the same it was more interesting than the constant debates of the comrades she met at carefully concealed meeting-places. She would say to Asa Heshel: "Then what's left? To lie down and die?"

"Death isn't the worst thing in the world."

"A very positive approach, I must say."

She would begin to pace back and forth, throwing side glances at him as though she could still not believe that an anti-Marxist, a former yeshivah student, was actually her lover. He talked like a fascist, but he sipped at his tea with all the mannerisms of the Chassidic youths. He bent his shoulders, bit his lips, grimaced. Sometimes he would seem to her like an eighteen-year-old, and then he would take on the appearance of an old sick Jew. He did not conceal from Barbara that he went to see Hadassah or that he still saw his first wife, Adele. When she thought of him during her stays away from Warsaw, he seemed to have more substance and actuality than when they were together. When she had yielded to him that night, years before, the whole thing had seemed to her like one of those pieces of thoughtlessness that one might commit in days of indecision, between one love and another. Yet it was partly because of him that she had stayed on in Poland, that she had not married, that she had become a professional party worker, always ready for whatever dangerous task might be demanded of her. And now things had come to a pass where another World War seemed imminent. What would happen to her then?

Late at night Asa Heshel would get dressed and go home. He was afraid to spend the night in Barbara's room; there might be a police search. Nor did Barbara want to have the neighbors see a man leaving her house in the morning. He would dress in the darkness. Barbara would intermittently doze and wake. In a sleep-laden voice she would remind him to close the door after him. He would get one shoe on and then sit for a while, exhausted. It was strange—neither he nor Barbara had any fear of God, but they were still ashamed of people. As he tied his shoelaces with numb fingers, he would evaluate his life. The years had passed, filled with purposeless brooding, fantasies, unquenched passions. His mother had died in dire need. David had grown up estranged from him. He had destroyed Adele's life as well as Hadassah's. Even Barbara complained constantly. In his chase after pleasure he had neglected everything—his health, his relatives, his work, his career.

He said: "Good night," but Barbara did not answer. He walked down the dark steps. A cat mewed. A baby woke up and cried. He always had to wait a long time for the janitor. Iron Street, where Barbara lived, was illuminated only dimly by gas lamps. Here and there a prostitute stood. Asa Heshel walked slowly, his head bent. Start all over again? How, with what? He stopped, leaned against a wall, and rested. He suffered from anemia. His heartbeat was either too quick or too slow. He had a constant nervous itch. He was susceptible to colds. "How long can I go on like this?" he asked himself. At such times he could actually feel his life ebbing away. At the gate of Novolipki Street he again had to ring the bell. Asa Heshel walked up the four flights of stairs and opened the door. His bed was made up. He undressed and fell asleep immediately, but after some time he awoke, frightened by a dream. His sleep had been full of visions—corpses, funerals, reptiles, beasts. There was rape, slaughter, fire, torture. He was lying with his sister, Dinah, and with Dacha, his daughter. He even had unclean relations with his dead mother. He was trembling, covered with sweat. "What's the matter with me—what do they want of me—what kind of filth is there in my subconscious?" He threw the covers off himself and gasped. A long neglected molar ached. His knees twitched. He was afraid, and full of lust. In the hectic dawn he began to think about Vanya's oldest daughter. Every time he came to Shrudborov, the girl ran after him. She would look into his eyes; she contrived to talk to him, to stay alone with him in the woods. True, she was not yet seventeen, but she probably was not a virgin any more. If only he were not so bashful, and such a coward!

CHAPTER FOUR

Asa Heshel tried to convince himself that he was resigned to the impending war and to the assaults on the Jews, and that he had long ago made peace with the idea of death. But in truth he was full of fear. When he happened to be on the streets late at night, he walked in the shadow of the walls. More than once Nara fascists and members of chauvinistic student organizations had attacked Jews in his neighborhood. It was even more dangerous at times when, like tonight, he had to walk from the Otwotsk station to Shrudborov. On these lonely roads it would not be much of a surprise to get a knife stuck in your back.

As usual, when he arrived at Hadassah's villa the kenneled dogs in the yard began to bark. Vanya's wife came running to the veranda holding an oil lamp. Dacha was already asleep, but with the news that her father had come, she got out of bed. She came in from her bedroom in a bathrobe and slippers. Each time Asa Heshel saw her he was surprised. She seemed to grow perceptibly day by day. There she stood before him half a child and half a fully grown woman, resembling neither her mother nor her father, but rather like a mixture of the Katzenellenbogens and the Moskats. Her hair was chestnut-colored and her eyes were green. Both Asa Heshel and Hadassah had thin lips, but the child's mouth was large and full, with a curve that to Asa Heshel seemed to be bold and passionate. She looked at him joyfully, at the same time frowning, as children do when they are abruptly awakened from sleep. His meetings with his daughter were always embarrassing for Asa Heshel. Dacha knew all about his goings on. Because of the fact that he saw her so seldom, he had continually to remind himself that she was his own flesh and blood. After a momentary hesitation Dacha came over to embrace him.

Hadassah said: "All right, now. Go to sleep, Dacha. You'll have all day tomorrow to see your father."

"Oh, Mother, I don't want to sleep now. I'll be awake all night."

Taking advantage of her father's unexpected arrival, Dacha ate a second supper, chewing at some bread and drinking a glass of milk. She kissed now her father, now her mother, and indulged in all the little whimsies of an only child. She chattered away about her school and schoolmates, the teachers, the boys, the pictures she saw at the cinema. She was familiar with all the Hollywood actresses. She burbled along about sports and automobiles and planes. How different she was from the girls he had known in his youth! And how different Hadassah must have been at her age!

It was about an hour after midnight when Dacha went back to her bed. Asa Heshel and Hadassah, too, made ready to retire for the night. Asa Heshel was the first to undress. Hadassah was still fussing about in the other room, combing her hair and cleaning her teeth. She came into the dark bedroom in a long nightgown and lay down at the edge of the double bed. For a long time there was no word spoken by either of them. All the shame of their married life emerged during these moments of silence. This was the wife whom he had deceived. This was the love he had defiled. This was the same Hadassah who had once come running to him in his room on Shviento-Yerska Street in her velvet beret and with a book under her arm, the same one who had given him his first kiss. And now he was coming to her from the arms of another.

Each lay on his own side of the bed, quiet and waiting. They had to become reacquainted with one another each time. In the years she had lived in the woods, Hadassah had herself become as silent as the trees that looked in through her window. She had never studied any philosophy, but she had learned to appraise things in her own way. She had seen how the ones nearest to her had gone; she had lived through the decline of the family. She only rarely read the newspapers, but she was aware that the Jewish community in Poland was on the brink of disaster. In Kartchev, a village near Otwotsk, the Polish Nazis were already beating up Jews. And news had come to her about Przytek, Brisk, Novominsk. In Otwotsk she had met some of the Jewish refugees from Germany who wandered from house to house, peddling hosiery, ties, and handkerchiefs. What value had her jealousy in the face of the tragic plight of people like this? She had long since found a

justification for the things Asa Heshel had done. Was it his
fault that he wasn't a family man? Could she demand of him
that he wander about Warsaw all alone? It was true that he
was nothing but an insignificant teacher, but still Hadassah
felt that he had been from his very birth a person who could
not be measured by ordinary standards. Once when her stepmother had delivered herself of harsh words against him, Hadassah had said angrily: "He's my husband, and I love him."
From that time on, Bronya had never come back to Shrudborov.

Hadassah lay still and listened. The spring had come early
this year. By the middle of February the snow was melting. In
the forests the moisture dripped from the trees and the
ground was soggy, rivulets of water flowing between the tree
trunks to join the Shviderek River and then the Vistula.
Winter birds piped with human voices. Warm vapors rose
from the soaked earth. In the orchards the fruit trees took on
a juicy blackness and nakedness, as always just before their
branches broke out into a rash of buds. The peasants muttered that the early spring was a sign of war and bloodletting.
The farm animals seemed to become restless with the change
of weather. Vanya's goat kept up a ceaseless bleating, the
roosters crowed constantly. Insects began to come back to
life, buzzing against the window panes. Hadassah moved a little nearer to Asa Heshel. It was good to lie in his arms.

Asa Heshel slept late. Dacha did not go to school. She sat
on the edge of her father's bed, chattering away. Hadassah
went into the kitchen to prepare breakfast. There was the
smell of fresh milk and fragrant coffee. Vanya's daughters
kept popping in and out. Even the women and girls from the
more distant houses came to see the visitor. Hadassah had
never understood how it was that Asa Heshel managed to at-
tract so many different people, when as a matter of fact he
seemed to pay scant attention to anybody.

After breakfast they walked along the road that led to Garvolin. Here the railroad was only a single track. At the edge
of the forest a hare emerged. Dacha pranced ahead of her
parents with one of her friends. In the sky the sun moved behind clouds, reddish and hazy in an early spring gold. Beams
of light pierced the fog, sharp as the blade of an ax. It was
difficult to know whether the muffled sounds all came from
the rustling of the pine branches, from the distant railway, or
from a cart on the road. Hadassah's hair blew in the wind. A
flush appeared on her usually pale face. This was what she

had dreamed of all her life: a cottage in the forest, a child, and her husband by her side.

In the evening Asa Heshel took the train back to Warsaw. Whenever Hadassah accompanied him to the Otwotsk station she had the foreboding that she was seeing him for the last time. She gave him a package of cookies she had baked. She walked with him up and down the platform. Men still looked at her, but she resented their glances. Love had been cruel enough to her.

The train was ready to leave. Asa Heshel turned to embrace her. For a moment she hung on to him. He would never know how much she loved him. He would never understand how much she had suffered on his account from the very day her Uncle Abram had brought him to her father's house for dinner. Asa Heshel climbed into the train and then looked at her through the window. She looked back at him, nodding her head. She was suddenly ashamed that she was past forty, a middle-aged woman. Who could know? Maybe it was her destiny to grow old. She shook her head as though she were saying no.

The train moved on. Hadassah turned to go back home. Asa Heshel had promised to come back the following week, but she knew how little one could rely on his promises. She was certain that this very night he would sleep in the arms of that other woman.

CHAPTER FIVE

1

Before Passover, guests from America and from Palestine arrived in Warsaw. Koppel was an old man in his seventies, his wife Leah in her late sixties. Now the aging pair had traveled to Poland to see their children. Koppel had sent money to Shosha, his daughter in Palestine, so that she might come to meet him in Warsaw. Leah was to meet her son Aaron, who was journeying to Warsaw from the Holy Land not only to see his mother but also to collect some money for the orthodox colony he had founded. Leah expected to take her daughter Masha back to America with her. Masha was no longer living with her husband, and Leah hoped that in America Masha would return to the Jewish faith. With Leah came her younger daughter, Lottie, who had become a teacher in an American college. The news of Leah's impending arrival brought new life into the Moskat family. Pinnie and Nyunie at once made up the old quarrel that had kept them away from each other. The sisters-in-law Hannah and Bronya, who were blood enemies, began to talk to each other again. The Moskat grandchildren began to call their uncles and aunts on the telephone. All of them were possessed of the same thought: to be helped to get out of Poland while there was still time.

The day that Leah and Koppel were to arrive on the Paris express the entire family assembled in Pinnie's house. All but Hadassah, Asa Heshel, and Masha. The flat was crowded with the Moskat grandchildren and great-grandchildren. Pinnie gazed at them and shrugged his shoulders. A miracle of God! He had hardly realized that old Meshulam had left behind him such a multitude. But still it was not the same as in the old days. Then, when the family gathered at the old man's for the Channukah holiday or Purim, they were all cut from the same cloth. But now Pinnie compared them in his mind to the animals and fowl of Noah's ark. There was such a bewildering variety of types: with beards and with shaven cheeks; yeshivah students and modern youngsters; women in matrons' wigs and women with naked hair. Most of the girls talked Polish. Joel's daughters Pinnie hardly recognized. Anyway, he had never been able rightly to distinguish one of them from the other. All three of them were fat and blowsy, a perfect combination of Joel and Queen Esther, may both their souls find eternal rest in paradise. As for their children, they were utter strangers to Pinnie. Pearl's son, Simchah, had gray hairs in his beard. Pinnie's son-in-law, the lawyer, was talking Polish with Abram's daughter Stepha. Avigdor, Abram's son-in-law, and his wife, Bella, had brought a houseful of their children with them. The oldest, Meshulam, or Max, as they called him, had completed a course in the Technicum. He was talking to Dosha, Pinnie's unmarried daughter. Pinnie wandered around the rooms with Nyunie, the "modern" of the two brothers. Pinnie was only a couple of years older than Nyunie, but he looked like his father. He was altogether white. His small figure was bent. There was not a single tooth left in his mouth. His speech was halting. Nyunie's chin beard was gray, but his face had stayed full, his neck firm and unwrinkled. He clenched a cigar between his lips, and across his vest a gold chain bounced up and down.

Pinnie kept on nudging Nyunie and pointing with his finger. "Who's that one over there with the glasses?"

"That's Joel's grandson."

"What does he do?"

"Ask me something easier. He just came out of the army."

"So he had to serve. Ah, me. Who's the virgin there?"

"Avigdor's daughter. What makes you think she's a virgin?" Nyunie asked slyly.

"Feh, Nyunie!"

According to the railroad timetable the train was scheduled to arrive at eight thirty. By eight o'clock the entire family was waiting at the station. Nyunie had presented platform tickets to everybody. Bronya watched sourly as he proceeded to squander the few zlotys she allowed him as pocket money. The Paris train was an hour late. The train from Gdynia was to arrive at ten. Aaron had come from Palestine in a Polish ship. Shosha and her husband had traveled in the same boat. It looked very much as though both trains, the one from Paris and the one from Gdynia, would pull in at about the same time. The Bialodrevna Chassidim fluttered about to be ready to give a welcome to their returning rabbi. There would ordinarily have been vast crowds to meet him, for over the years Aaron had acquired something of a reputation among Warsaw Jews. The papers mentioned him frequently, and everyone praised him fulsomely for the sacrifices he was making in helping to rebuild the Holy Land. But Fishel Kutner, Pinnie Moskat, and a few others of the older Chassidim maintained that in bad times like these the Jews should not make themselves too noticeable. The younger Chassidim were persuaded to keep away from the railroad station. Fishel did not put in an appearance, either, for he preferred not to meet the Moskats. Who could know?—maybe Hadassah might be there. Aaron was scheduled to stay at the house of Fishel's assistant, Anshel, who some years before had married a widow and lived on Bagno Street.

And if the Moskat clan and the Bialodrevna Chassidim were not enough, there was another group who had come to greet Koppel and his daughter Shosha. These were Koppel's other children, Manyek and Yppe, with their families. All of them took platform tickets. The Poles in the station looked on with disgust at the motley crowd of Jews. There was Hitler with one foot practically in Poland and here were these Jews carrying on as though it were the old days. Didn't they see what was in store for them? Or had they already secretly prepared the death blow for Hitler?

At ten minutes to ten the Paris train came in. Koppel and Leah descended from a first-class car. Although Koppel was an old man, he was wearing a light-colored coat, a light hat, and reddish-tan shoes. He carried a cane in one hand and in the other he held a handbag. Leah still looked like a sound specimen of womanhood. Her hair was white, but her face was unlined, well powdered and rouged, and half hidden under her veil. They at once heard her strong voice, which reminded them somehow of old Meshulam's tones. Lottie wore a mannish-looking hat and coat. There was a scarf around her throat, and glasses with thick lenses on her nose. They could hear Leah asking: "Where is Aaron?"

"The Gdynia train is coming in any minute."

"Nyunie! Pinnie!"

Leah embraced and kissed Nyunie, but she did not kiss Pinnie. This was not the Pinnie she knew. This was an old doddering Jew, bent and worn, with a comically shrunken mouth. The tears started to Leah's eyes. She began to kiss and embrace the others, not knowing whom she was greeting. People talked to her, but she could not make out who was addressing her. What seemed to her old women were calling her Aunt. Their mouths stank of onions. Younger girls talked Polish to her, but she could not find the phrases to answer. Pinnie asked her about Meyerl, but for the moment Leah could not remember that she had a son by that name. Then she grasped that it was Mendy. "Meyerl?" she answered. "He's all right. He's got two wonderful children."

"Zlatele, what are you standing so quiet for?" Pinnie found the courage to ask.

"Uncle Pinnie!" Lottie fell into his arms and kissed him on both cheeks. Pinnie lost himself altogether.

"Hannah, where are you?" he called to his wife.

Suddenly Masha seemed to materialize. She had not been at Pinnie's house; he would not have given the apostate admission. And it had been rumored that she would not put in an appearance at the railroad station either. But here she was, wearing a jacket with a silver-fox collar, a dress bordered with fur, and a flowered hat. All the others moved away from her. Mother and daughter embraced in silence. On her first visit back to Warsaw Leah had not seen her daughter.

While all this was going on, Koppel turned his attention to his own family. Manyek, his son, had grown into a man in his forties. There was a strong resemblance between the two. Nyunie Moskat looked at them in surprise. It was as though he saw two Koppels, one old, the other young. Manyek's wife had become stout. Yppe, Koppel's younger daughter, leaned on her husband, a small person with a dim mustache on his upper lip. Instead of the brace she had worn on her bad leg when she was a child, she now used crutches. Bashele had died. Her second husband, Chaim Leib, the coal dealer, had also gone to his long rest. Both Manyek and Yppe had brought their children with them. Koppel had all their photographs in his breast pocket, but now he could not recognize any of them. To him Yppe was simply a middle-aged lame woman. She talked with a sort of stutter, and Koppel could hardly understand what she was saying.

Manyek had developed a noticeable potbelly. He turned to his father and said: "Let's wait here. The Gdynia train will be coming any minute."

"Hey, boss, where do you want me to take this baggage?" a porter called out. He had Koppel's, Leah's, and Lottie's baggage piled on a hand truck.

"Maybe he ought to take it into the baggage room," Manyek suggested in Polish.

"Yes. And bring me the receipt," Koppel answered in his Americanized Yiddish.

"Children, this is your grandfather," Manyek's wife kept on saying to her brood as well as to Yppe's, speaking to them in Polish.

"I've forgotten the language already," Koppel remarked. "Yes, I am the *dziadek*, the grandfather. What's your name? Whose are you?"

"I'm Manyek's daughter, Andzha."

"Aha, Andzha! Do you go to school, eh?"

"Yes. I'm in the sixth class."

"In America they call it 'high school.' Tell me, do they beat the Jews here?"

"Nobody beats me."

"It'll come yet. In Paris all you hear is that there's going to be a war. Do you know any English?"

"They teach us French."

"French is something I don't know. Anyway, they don't speak that language, they gargle it. At your age I was already working for a living. I was a clerk on Gensha Street. I swept

out the store. They paid me half a ruble a week. And if I
didn't steal anything, then I didn't have anything."

Leah came over to them. "What's all this babbling about
stealing? Introduce me to your family."

"This is my wife," Koppel said after some hesitation. "Her
father used to be my boss. I stole the money out of his safe
and then I stole his daughter."

Leah took a startled step backward. "Have you gone
crazy?"

"It's the truth. Once your father—may he rest in peace—
said to me: 'Tell me, Koppel, do you believe in the next
world?' And I said to him: 'When I get there I'll let you know
all about it.' He was smart, the old man. He knew I was stealing from him, but who wasn't snatching it from him in those
days?"

"So help me God, Koppel, you ought to be ashamed of
yourself," Leah stormed at him in English. "The moment you
get here, you begin with your monkey business."

"Never mind, never mind," Koppel growled. "It's the God's
truth."

2

The train from Gdynia was late too. The Bialodrevna Chassidim, led by Anshel, hovered among the Moskats and Koppel's
family. Then they all crossed to the track on which the Gdynia train was to arrive. From the station emerged a group of
Polish sailors in their round hats, short jackets, and wide trousers. The Chassidim took a few hesitant steps backward; one
could easily be beaten up by this band. Pinnie and Nyunie
looked helplessly about them. Leah stared at them in open astonishment; she had had no idea that Poland had a navy. The
uniform was something like the American sailors' uniform,
she thought, except that the Americans seemed to be tall, and
here they were almost like dwarfs. Koppel shook his head.
They also call themselves a country, he reflected. One American ship and their whole navy would be at the bottom of the
sea. In spite of all the trouble he had had in America because
of his bootlegging, he thought of himself as an American pa-
triot. In France he had had arguments with Leah. He maintained that one Brooklyn street was worth all the boulevards
of Paris. He insisted that the French did not know the first

thing about cooking a meal, that the hotels were dirty, and
that the women were something awful to look at.

Gazing at the Polish sailors, Koppel remarked: "Look at
them. Purim masqueraders!"

"Koppel, please!" Leah warned. "Hold your tongue."

"To hell with them all!"

Everyone had expected that Aaron would travel second-
class; instead he got out of a third-class car. Leah saw a thin
figure of a man with a disheveled beard, a wrinkled coat, and
a wide velvet hat. Leah had heard that Aaron was doing farm
work, but one would never have guessed it by looking at him.
He was not even tanned like the others who came back from
Palestine. The Chassidim immediately ringed him about.

Leah did not know whether to embrace him or not. She
pushed through the throng. She heard Aaron say: "Mother!
It's you!"

"Yes. It's me!" And she could say no more.

"Aaron, Aaron! This is me, Zlatele!"

"Zlatele! Blessed be God's name."

"He may be your son, but he's our rabbi," Anshel remarked. "The rabbi's staying with me, on Bagno Street. And
it's time to go. It's late."

"So soon? Well, all right. I'll come to see him."

The Chassidim led Aaron out into the street. Leah's eyes
followed the group as they shuffled along, pushing into one
another. She had lived two thirds of her life here in Warsaw;
she had been back once before on a visit; she remembered Poland. Nevertheless, when she gazed at these Chassidim leading her son away, making their uncouth gestures and contort-
ing their faces, she realized that she had forgotten a good
deal. She began to look around for Masha. Ah, what a strange
brood she had given birth to: a rabbi, an apostate, a teacher
in a college, a Wall Street lawyer! She suddenly remembered
that there was still no headstone on the grave of Moshe Gabriel. As she stood there among the confusion of trains, locomotives, rails, in the glare of the electric lamps, and among
the hurrying passengers, what she had felt for a long time became clear to her: she had not long to live. At the most she
had only a few years left. In Brooklyn, in the cemetery, there
already waited the plot that Koppel had acquired from the
Warsaw society. Then why should she take things to heart?
Why should she keep on endlessly quarreling with Koppel?
Why should she torture Lottie? What was the good of all this

traveling around? She became so lost in her thoughts that she did not see Koppel greeting and embracing his daughter Shosha and her husband.

Pinnie came over to her. "What are we waiting here for? It's getting late. We'll not be able to find any droshkies."

"One second. I must go over to them."

Her years in Palestine had turned Shosha into a real beauty. Leah could only stare at her. She had become somewhat fleshier, but she was still slim. She was tanned by the sun. Her eyes looked lighter. She kept on kissing her father, Manyek, Yppe, and her sister-in-law. She took her handkerchief out of her bag and wiped her eyes; and the rest followed suit, shedding a tear at the thought of Teibele, who had died before her time. Shosha's husband, Simon, stood a little distance apart. He was dark as a gypsy, with an enormous shock of jet-black hair. His big body seemed constricted in the clothes he wore. A pair of enormous hands protruded from his coat sleeves. Simon worked his own orange groves in Palestine. Pinnie did not know him; nevertheless he went up and extended a courteous greeting. The giant clutched Pinnie's hand in his enormous paw and bent over him, as over a child.

All started to leave the station. The conductor collected the platform tickets, at the same time favoring each of them with a searching glance, as though trying to fix their features in his memory. Manyek collected the baggage from the baggage room. Koppel had wired ahead a reservation for three rooms at the Hotel Bristol, one for himself and Leah, one for Shosha and Simon, and one for Lottie. Outside, these five climbed into a taxi. Manyek summoned a droshky; so did Yppe. Some of the Moskat family went away on foot, others took streetcars. That's the way it always was with these Americans, they reflected. They were always surrounded by hosts of people, and it was impossible to get in a word. Anyway, it was pointless to pin too much hope on them. Even if Leah had the desire to take all of them off with her to America, that didn't mean she could. Joel's daughters withdrew in irritation. Their American aunt hadn't so much as looked at them. Stepha walked off with Dosha, Pinnie's younger daughter. They spoke of Hadassah.

"She did a smart thing in not coming," Stepha remarked. "It turned out to be a circus."

"What did you expect? It's impossible to get a thousand greetings over with in ten minutes."

"That Koppel looks like a cunning fox."

"They say he's half mad."

"It's a wonder they had the nerve to come to Poland now. With all the war talk."

"American citizens have nothing to be afraid of."

"You'll probably think I'm crazy, but I honestly wish the thing had started already," Stepha remarked after a slight pause. Dosha stopped stock-still.

"Stepha, you must be out of your mind!"

"This waiting is worse than any reality could be. At least, if they kill you you're dead and you can laugh at all of them."

"Ah, Stepha, you're just talking nonsense. I've got nothing to be afraid of. I'm all alone. But you—you have a child."

"He got a beating last week—I thought they'd fractured his skull."

"My God! How did it happen? Why didn't you say something about it?"

"They ganged up on him like a swarm of vultures. Six against one. 'March to Palestine!' they yelled at him. He was going to a meeting, in his uniform. He belongs to the Trumpeldor organization."

"Yes, the scum of the gutters has floated up to power now," Dosha said with a sigh. "God knows what the end will be."

CHAPTER SIX

The Bialodrevna Chassidim had rented a bakery on Krochmalna Street where they would be able to have their Passover matzos prepared in the strict ritual manner. Rabbi Aaron and the others did all the work. They drew water in a brand-new cask and allowed it to stand overnight. The Chassidim themselves scrubbed the tables, scoured the rolling-pins, the baking-shovel, and the boards on which the layers of dough were cut and scored. They did not roll the scorings in the unleavened bread, but stabbed them into the dough with wooden prongs, in the old-fashioned manner. Anshel, at whose house the rabbi was lodging, had the job of sliding the flat cakes into the oven. Fishel cut the dough. Pinnie and the others kneaded it, rolled it, and poured the water. All the while the faithful sang and chanted psalms.

Everything was done according to the very letter of the ritual. The rabbi himself watched as Anshel's wife heated the oven in the kitchen. In order that the gratings might become

red-hot and glowing, they heaped burning coal on them and
then covered them with sand. The men ate only dry matzos.
The women and children were permitted the other Passover
dainties, matzoh meal dumplings, pancakes, matzoh pudding.
Therefore it was necessary to have two complete sets of cooking utensils and dishes. At first Pinnie wanted Aaron to spend
the feast days at his house, but the rabbi showed clearly that it
would not be to his taste. Pinnie's daughters were not obser-
vant about ritual matters, and Aaron did not trust Pinnie's
wife, either, since she came from Kurland, where the customs
were different. It was decided that Aaron would observe the
seder night at Anshel's. For his part Pinnie conducted a seder
on the first night for the entire Moskat clan, including Koppel
and his children. Leah paid all the expenses. She also sent a
long telegram to Hadassah in Shrudborov and got in touch
with Asa Heshel in Warsaw. She wanted them both present.

Preparing the seder feast for a score or so of guests was by
no means an easy task. Hannah and the girls could hardly
manage it by themselves. Leah wound a kerchief around her
head, donned an apron, rolled up her sleeves, and applied herself to the job. The others told her not to bother; after all, she
was a guest, an American. But Leah would not be dissuaded.
In America she had never had the opportunity to indulge in
the arduous holiday preparations. There she bought a few
pounds of machine-made matzos and let it go at that. But
here, in Warsaw, Jewishness still had its old-fashioned charm.
She washed and scrubbed and demonstrated some of her
long-unused housewifely energy.

So now they were busy draining the meat according to the
prescribed technique, scouring the pots and pans, cleaning the
dishes. From a hook in the ceiling hung the specially prepared
"Chassidic" matzos for Pinnie. The ordinary kind lay in a
covered basket. Weeks before, Hannah had put up the borsh
to ferment, and the night before the seder Pinnie had lighted a
candle and made the required inspection for leavened bread.
The crumbs of bread that Hannah had beforehand placed in
little corners and crevices about the room were wrapped up in
a rag of cloth and burned the following day.

Hannah was afraid that she would never be ready on time.
But when Passover eve arrived, nothing needed for comfort
or enjoyment was missing. Three tables had been set up and
covered with tablecloths. Additional chairs and benches had
been borrowed from neighbors. For Pinnie there had been
prepared the traditional chair-bed. On the stove in the kitchen

the meat stewed in enormous pots and fish simmered in wide copper pans, which Hannah had had no occasion to use for many years now. In the silver bowl that Pinnie had received as a gift from his father, old Meshulam, lay the shank bone, the egg, the horseradish, the bitter herbs, the parsley, and radish root. The wine and mead were ready in dust-covered bottles and carafes. Leah had purchased wine cups, napkins, linen covers for the matzos, gold-stamped Hagadas. Hannah covered the tray of matzos with a throw she had made for Pinnie while she was still a young bride. On it were embroidered the figures of the Four Sons: the wise one, the wicked one, the simple one, and the one who has no capacity to inquire. Hannah and Leah recited the prescribed blessings over the candles. The candle flames spread a warmth about the room. Hannah had covered the windows as a precaution against the evil eye. While Pinnie was away at prayers—and this year the Bialodrevna prayerhouse was packed—the family assembled. In recent years it had become the fashion to bring flowers to a seder service. So many bouquets were brought that Hannah became confused. Every moment the door opened. Koppel had brought his family in two taxis; Shosha, Simon Bendel, Manyek and his wife, Yppe and her husband, and all the children. Shosha and Simon spoke to each other in Hebrew.

Koppel puffed up with pride. "What do you think of that daughter of mine?" he beamed. "A real scholar."

Hadassah, bringing Dacha with her, was making her first trip to Warsaw in years. She wore a new dress, and she had had her hair done. She was still a beautiful woman. The younger generation of Moskat kin hardly knew her. Old Meshulam's great-grandchildren called her Aunt and crowded about her, exclaiming at her looks. Stepha's boy told Dacha how he built airplanes from pieces of wood and wire. He was wearing a brown blouse, with a Menorah embroidered on the sleeve. He bragged that he was being taught to shoot a real gun. At first Asa Heshel had absolutely refused to come. He had not seen his father-in-law for years. But Hadassah had warned him that if this time he were to abandon her she would leave him for good. The meeting with the Moskats was so painful a prospect for him that before he went to Pinnie's house he stopped at a bar and swallowed three brandies. Unused to strong liquor as he was, the drinks immediately exhilarated him.

Pinnie came home from the prayerhouse in his fur hat. He greeted everyone with a lively air. Leah wept when she saw him. He was a leftover from the old stock. Such fur hats as his used to be worn by Joel and Nathan and Moshe Gabriel, and even Abram. His tone was their tone when they would voice the holiday greetings. Pinnie immediately busied himself with the silver bowl. The shank bone had to be on the right, the egg on the left, and the bitter herbs in the middle. But no matter how he turned the bowl the arrangement did not seem to come out right. As in every year at the Passover seder, Hannah had to come to his aid. Nyunie put his hand to the adjustment, too. The brothers immediately began to quibble about the proper ritual technique.

Pinnie donned a white robe and recited the grace. Hannah brought in a jug of water and a basin. Pinnie washed his hands and distributed the parsley. The men were all wearing their hats or skullcaps. A huge diamond sparkled on Leah's finger. Hannah put over her neck the gold chain that old Meshulam Moskat had given her as an engagement gift. A silver Star of David made in Palestine was suspended around Shosha's throat. Pinnie began to recite:

"This is the bread of affliction which our forefathers ate in the land of Egypt. . . ."

Because Pinnie had no son, his youngest daughter, Dosha, had asked the traditional Four Questions each year. This year, with so many boys about, it was decided that they would go through the ritual together. Their voices pealed out in unison. Yppe's child recited the Hebrew words with expertness, pausing after each phrase to render the translation into Yiddish. He was attending an orthodox school. Stepha's boy recited the phrases with the Sephardic pronunciation. Pinnie grimaced. He did not fancy the way these "modern" Jews had Christianized the holy tongue. After the questions were asked, Pinnie addressed himself to reading the prescribed answer: "Slaves were we unto Pharaoh in Egypt. . . ."

All recited with him, some in Hebrew and some from the Polish translation. Leah read the words and wept. She had wanted to bring Masha to the seder, but Pinnie had firmly refused to allow the apostate in his home. He had demanded that she first go through the ritual bath and perform all the ceremonies prescribed for a return to the faith. Koppel behaved strangely throughout. He spoke loudly in English, and got the names of his grandchildren mixed up. From time to time he laughed and made faces. In his old age he had become eccentric. As the seder ceremony went on, Pinnie fell more and more into ecstasy. He swayed from side to side,

waved his arms in the air, and shouted aloud. He picked up
the beaker of wine and his voice was broken with weeping:
"And it is this same promise which has been the support of
our ancestors and of us, for in every generation our enemies
have arisen to annihilate us, but the Most Holy, blessed be
He, has delivered us out of their hands. . . ."

Hadassah murmured the verses in Polish, Lottie in English.
Hannah blew her nose furiously. Sighs broke out from all of
them. Yes, every generation had its Pharaohs and Hamans
and Chmielnickis. Now it was Hitler. Would a miracle happen this time too? In a year from now would Jews be able
again to sit down and observe the Passover? Or God forbid,
would the new Haman finish them off?

Asa Heshel sat silent. He was thinking of his own family.
He remembered the seder at his grandfather's house. He remembered his uncles, his mother. In Tereshpol Minor and in
the towns round about, there were still cousins of his. And on
Franciskaner Street, Menassah David was celebrating the Passover in his own particular way: reading the Hagada and
dancing in ecstasy. In Palestine, David, his son, was observing
the holiday with his fellow colonists. Adele was probably all
alone in her flat. Barbara had bought a ticket for the opera.
Asa Heshel looked at the Hagada and shook his head. Dacha
was sitting near him and holding on to his arm. What did they
talk so much about miracles for, Asa Heshel thought. "They
kill them in each generation. If not for the slaughterers and
pogroms, we'd number in the hundred millions by now." He
looked at Yezhek, Stepha's son, and Dacha, and the other
children. They were all doomed. The brandy that he had
taken earlier began to lose its effect.

Pinnie lifted up the tray of matzos and with a triumphant
gesture pointed at them: "These unleavened cakes, why do we
eat them? . . ."

CHAPTER SEVEN

Toward the middle of May, Adele set out on a journey to Palestine. She got rid of her home, sold her furniture and sewing-
machine, and paid six hundred zlotys for passage in a boat
that was smuggling immigrants into Palestine. Everything was
done through a man who was supposed to know the ropes.
The boat was to leave, not from Gdynia, the regular port, but

from a little fishing village. Passengers were permitted to take along only one suitcase. Adele sold for next to nothing the cushions, mattresses, and sheets she had inherited from her mother; she gave away to the poor the clothes, underwear, shoes, and stockings that she could not take along.

The sea journey, in the small steamer, was supposed to take four weeks; the route lay through the Baltic, the North Sea, the Atlantic, and the Mediterranean. Stops were to be made in Morocco, Italy, and Egypt. Adele asked the manager of the enterprise all manner of questions: would they go by way of the Skagerrak and the Kattegat or through the Kiel Canal? Would they pass through the English Channel or would they have to turn north and round Scotland and Ireland? Above all, would they be able to get past Gibraltar? The manager replied soothingly that everything had been taken care of. As regards Palestine, they would come in at night. No papers would be needed. Adele did not like the glib answers; she was troubled and uncertain, but there was nothing to be done about it. Her heart longed for David. And here, in Poland, war was in the air.

Asa Heshel accompanied Adele to the boat. He also gave her a present to give to his son—a camera. The two of them set out in the evening from the Vienna Station and traveled second-class. Adele leaned her forehead against Asa Heshel's shoulder and dozed. She was tired out with worry and anxiety. As she napped, with the night lamp glimmering in her eyes, she imagined that she was still young and still Asa Heshel's wife; they were on their honeymoon, in Switzerland.

Asa Heshel read a newspaper: concentration camps, torture chambers, prisons, executions. Every day there arrived from Germany new transports of expelled Jews. In Spain they were still shooting loyalists. In Ethiopia the Fascists were murdering the natives. In Manchuria Japanese were killing Chinese. In Soviet Russia the purges continued. England was still trying to reach some understanding with Hitler. Meanwhile she also issued a White Paper on Palestine, prohibiting the sale of land to Jews. The Poles were at last getting it into their heads that Hitler was their enemy; the German press was conducting an open campaign of hatred against Poland. But in the Polish Sejm the deputies still had time to discuss at great length the minutiae of the Jewish ritual laws for the slaughtering of cattle. The opposition papers were hinting that the Polish army, which had cost so many millions, was not in a state of preparedness.

The express sped through the night, sending out its warning whistle. Dark woods flashed by, alternating with blind-faced houses, factories, chimneys. God's world, which seemed to be wrapped in sleep, was wide awake: every tree, every flower, every stalk, was sucking nourishment out of the earth.

In the morning the train pulled in at Gdynia. Asa Heshel saw the sea for the first time in his life. It flashed at him from the distance like a mirror. In the port were anchored several Polish gunboats, rocking on the waves like so many ducks. A bus was waiting for the train passengers, who were supposed to be arriving for a summer holiday at a local village. Most of the travelers were young people—boys and girls—but there were no children. It had been forbidden to bring them along. Some of them talked Hebrew. All of them would have liked to dance the Palestinian *hora,* but no demonstrations were permitted. Still, when the bus started off for the village of Putzk a group of them burst into a Palestinian song—"Long Live the Jewish People."

The driver turned round furiously. "What's the matter with you? Can't you wait with your singing till you're on the boat?"

They arrived at the village, which consisted of little more than a few boarding-houses. Here the Jewish Cultural Society and the League for Agricultural Training had, in the last few years, set up a few summer camps. The bus drew up at a wooden barracks with unpainted walls. Inside, the rafters were bare and everything smelled of fresh wood. The travelers were ranged at uncovered tables and served with fried flounder and bread. Something about these flat fish, with their brown backs and white bellies, suggested remote places. Through the windows they could see the beach and the advancing and retreating waves. The murmur of the water mingled with the silence, the sea mingled with the sky. A Sabbath peace was hovering over the open spaces. Seagulls circled over the water, uttering their shrill cries. Far away, on the horizon, a boat lay under a long sail like a corpse under its cerements.

A spirit of hominess came over the young people. They spoke with one another in Yiddish, Polish, Hebrew, and German. One young woman giggled continuously, while a young man, in a sort of bravado, took off his shoes and walked about barefoot. A few lay down on the benches and slept; most of the others began to play games. Still others went out and strolled along the beach, which was planted with pine trees almost to the water's edge. Far off a steamer appeared on the horizon, a coil of smoke issuing from it. One could not tell whether the steamer was approaching or withdrawing. The sea was neither stormy nor calm; it tossed and heaved. Asa Heshel stood and looked at the marvel: divinity itself had taken on the form of the sea. Adele, standing near him, turned white, as if she were already seasick.

They climbed up the tiny wooded hill and sat down in the moss, pine needles, and undergrowth. On the root of a tree, protruding from the ground, toadstools grew. Near by, a nest of ants swarmed thickly. Busily the tiny creatures dragged their burdens of twigs and grass. They crawled in zigzag patterns. The hum of mosquitoes was in the air, and in the distance was heard the sound of a cuckoo. The cold wind coming in from the Baltic mingled with the warm air rising from the soil.

Adele took Asa Heshel's hand. "Asa Heshel, why have you behaved like this?"

"It's too late now."

"Tell me truthfully, were you ever in love with anyone?"

Asa Heshel was silent.

"If I had been you, I would have married Barbara," she said, not knowing why she said it or what purpose she had in mind.

Then suddenly she became sharply aware that she was going away and perhaps she would never see him again. She looked at him furtively and noticed how abnormally white his fingernails were. She looked at his nose, his mouth, his eyes, his ears. Was he good-looking or ugly? She could not make up her mind. There was something elusive in his features, something unfixed; they made her think of the waves she had been watching, with their constant change of form. At this moment, as he sat leaning against a pine tree, it seemed to her that there was a strange delicacy in the outlines of his face. Golden strands of hair trembled on his high forehead; from the clear blue eyes a childish simplicity looked forth. Only on the sharp lips a bitterness lay. It occurred to Adele that she had never been able to understand what it was that tortured him. Was it the failure to have had a career? Did his heart long for someone? She was on the point of asking him, but suddenly she knew: he was not a worldly man by his very essence. He was one of those who must serve God or die. He had forsaken God, and because of this he was dead—a living

body with a dead soul. She was astonished that this simple
truth had eluded her until now.

Toward evening the travelers were herded into a bus. Adele
kissed Asa Heshel farewell, remained hanging on his neck for
a moment, pressed his hand. He felt her salt tears on his face.
Then he watched her and the others getting into the bus. She
could not get a seat next a window, but she leaned over and
waved to him with a newspaper. At the last moment, just as
the bus started, she cried out: "Asa Heshel!" It was as though
she had suddenly remembered something of the utmost urgency. Asa Heshel ran forward, but the bus speeded away, leaving a stench of fumes.

CHAPTER EIGHT

The newspapers were full of war news. The controlled German
press was demanding the Polish Corridor and Upper Silesia.
England and France had guaranteed the Polish borders. But
this year the Moskat family, as in previous years, rode out to
their summer places on the Otwotsk line. Nyunie had a house
of his own in Shvider. Pinnie rented a cottage in Falenitz for
his own family and Aaron. Lottie was there, too. Leah and
Koppel were staying in a pension in Otwotsk. Hadassah and
Dacha remained where they were at Vanya's house in Shrudborov. Masha had already procured a passport and visa for
America; for the present she was staying in a room at Hadassah's. Stepha and Dosha came out to visit every Saturday.
Abram's son-in-law warned them all that it was sheer idiocy
to stay in Poland any longer. The catastrophe might descend
at any moment. He pleaded with Reb Aaron as well as with
Leah to get away while there was still time. He swore that if
he had the proper papers he would not linger another moment. But the visitors from abroad did not seem to be in a
hurry.

In Warsaw Rabbi Aaron was collecting manuscripts that
had been written by his father, Reb Moshe Gabriel, by Reb
Yechiel of Bialodrevna, and even by the earlier Bialodrevna
rabbi. Aaron prepared the manuscripts and sent them off to a
printer. He himself did all the revising and proofreading. Besides that he was gathering a group of Chassidic settlers for
the colony Nachlat Yechiel in the Holy Land, prevailing on

the Palestine Office to issue the necessary visas. There was a continual pleading at government bureaus, asking for favors, sending influential intermediaries. There was every kind of confusing business with money, documents, proof of citizenship, and questions of military service. The rabbi was busy from early morning till late at night. He knew that it was a time of disaster, but what could he accomplish by running away from it? A shepherd does not abandon his sheep. Deep in his heart the rabbi had a premonition that at the last moment a miracle would happen.

Koppel relied on his American passport. He kept on saying that all these countries in Europe—if you could call them countries—shivered in their boots at the very thought of America. As long as there was an American consul in Warsaw, then, so far as he, Koppel was concerned, they could all go to hell. Besides, he was an old man. What could they do to him? Pour salt on his tail? After all, New York would not run away. When you came to that, he was all alone there, without kith or kin. All he could do was sit in his apartment and listen to the radio or go out to the park and sit reading a newspaper. But here in Warsaw he had a son and a son-in-law, a daughter and a daughter-in-law, and grandchildren. He had looked up some of his old friends. Isador Oxenburg and his wife, Reitze, were long dead. But their daughters had greeted Koppel with open arms. Itchele Peltsevisner was gone too; a horse had kicked him and that had finished him off. David Krupnick had died of an inflammation of the lungs. But his wife still crawled about, smoking those asthma cigarettes of hers. Leon the Peddler and Motie the Red still came to her house to play cards. Whenever Koppel went to see them, he took a bottle of brandy, a pound of sausage, or a box of sardines. The oldsters would sit up till late, exchanging stories. In his advanced years Leon the Peddler was hardly more than skin and bone. He would look at Koppel and say: "So, Koppel. How are you? All right in America, eh?"

"Why shouldn't I be all right?" Koppel would answer laughing. "I stole plenty."

The business of bragging about his thefts had become an obsession with Koppel. Then time after time he would tell the story of how he had looted Meshulam Moskat's safe. And each time the haul grew in size. He talked openly of his bootlegging in New York. Leah pleaded with him not to shame her. His daughters flushed. Manyek warned his father that if he did not stop the disgraceful chatter he would break off with him for good. But Koppel laughed at them. "What are you ashamed of?" he would cry. "Once a thief, always a thief." And he would dig a sly finger into his son's ribs.

At Mrs. Krupnick's, Koppel could talk to his heart's content. He pulled out of his pocket a bundle of traveler's checks and showed them off. He let them look at his bankbooks. He let the "greenhorns" in on all sorts of machinations involving real estate and stocks and bonds and told them about the operations of American gangsters and racketeers. He sneered at the Warsaw underworld; all they knew was how to open a lock with a skeleton key, or to jab a knife into somebody. The gangsters in America rode around in automobiles, shooting down people with machine guns. They could open safes five inches thick. Motie the Red, who was now completely white, once mentioned that not long ago the Warsaw gangsters had dug a tunnel into the Bank of Poland, but Koppel waved the episode away. "Do you call that a bank?" he said witheringly.

Leah avoided him. Lottie refused to talk to him. Simon, his Palestinian son-in-law, would not even look at him. Koppel went into the kitchen in the Otwotsk pension and showed the cook how food was prepared in America. There hot water was drawn right from the sink. There was an electric refrigerator in every house. And there was kosher soap to wash dishes. Koppel broke two eggs into a pan and set it on the stove. Instead of turning the eggs over with a spoon he tossed them in the air.

The cook made a contemptuous grimace. "American tricks."

When Leah caught him at these antics she went at once to her room. When Koppel came in she shouted: "Yes, I deserve it! If I could give up a man like Moshe Gabriel and take up with a dog like you, I deserve the stick."

"If you want I'll give you a divorce," Koppel responded. "And I'll pay you alimony."

Leah put a summer scarf around her shoulders, took her bag and cane, and went off to Shrudborov. She walked on the sandy path, stopping every once in a while to take off a shoe and shake out the dust and gravel. Sometimes at night she had a terrifying feeling that war would break out and she would not be able to return to America, but during the day her terror was dissipated. The sky above was clear and blue. A golden sun hovered over the pine forests, the houses, the telegraph poles. Birds twittered. Trains sped back and forth. Boys and girls played. Phonographs ground out cantorial melodies.

Peddlers in long caftans wandered about with baskets of fruit. They reminded Leah of the years of her youth. Here, in these very forests, she had mooned about Koppel. In Shrudborov Leah felt at home. Hadassah drew her a drink of cold water from the well. Dacha kissed her. Leah always brought a gift for the child. Vanya's daughters danced attendance on her, vying with one another to be of service. Masha came out of her room. Leah threw side glances at her daughter. In the years since she had seen her, Masha had changed past recognition. There was a lot of gray in her shortcut hair. She seemed to have taken on gentile features. No matter how many times Leah tried to get closer to her, she could not manage to break through the wall that separated them. The worst was that Masha had forgotten how to speak Yiddish and talked to her mother instead in a bastard mixture of Polish and Yiddish.

Leah shook her head dolefully. "Aren't you happy that you're going to America?"

"I'm happy."

Masha went out on the veranda, sat down, and opened her book. This American woman with the silver-white hair and the coarse red face was strange to her. She did not know what she would do in that distant America. The talk about her being converted back to Judaism seemed meaningless. She had never been a really devoted Christian, and she could not take the Jewish faith seriously either.

Ever since the time she had swallowed some iodine, the thought of suicide had never left her. She would never try poison again, but there were other ways. Somewhere in her valise she had a revolver. Then again it was possible to hang oneself. From the time she had begun to make efforts to get a passport to America she had thought each day about jumping off the ship. She was too old to begin all over again. She had already lost her menstrual periods.

CHAPTER NINE

For some years now Asa Heshel and Barbara had planned to spend a summer vacation together. But there had always been obstacles. Asa Heshel never had enough money, and he was unwilling to take it or borrow from Barbara. Again it would happen that at the last moment Barbara would have to take

one of her party trips. This year, however, Asa Heshel borrowed four hundred zlotys from the loan department of the
teachers' union, and Barbara had no more party duties since
every kind of party activity had come to a halt.

It was not easy for Asa Heshel to go away with her. Any
day the war might break out in earnest. He was afraid to
leave Hadassah and Dacha alone in Shrudborov. He was
afraid that he and Barbara might be arrested. But it was impossible for him to stand the oppressive Warsaw heat any
longer. He made up his mind not to tell Hadassah in advance,
but to write to her when he had gone. Later on he would send
her some money.

Everything went without a hitch. Asa Heshel spent Saturday and Sunday in Shrudborov. He left Hadassah sixty zlotys.
Early Monday morning he packed his valise and met Barbara
at the Vienna Station. He had paid his landlady a month's
rent in advance. The two boarded the express for Krakow.

The express halted at Skierniewice, Piotrkow, and Ra-
domsk. At the stations hawkers called out cookies, lemonade,
chocolate, and magazines. There were crowds of Jews and
groups of soldiers at each station. In the train a woman was
quietly telling one of the passengers that in Great Poland they
were already busy digging trenches. The rich were providing
themselves with private air-raid shelters. An old man, red-
faced and with big white mustaches, interrupted the conversation, declaring that Hitler was simply making idle threats,
so that Poland would hand over the Corridor. Now that England and France had guaranteed Poland's borders, nothing
remained for Hitler but to gnash his teeth and bark.

The train reached Krakow towards evening. A cold wind
came from the near-by mountains. The setting sun's light was
reflected from the golden crucifixes of the church spires, in
the Gothic windows of stained glass, in the gilded faces of the
old-fashioned clocks. Pedestrians did not hurry, as they did in
Warsaw, but walked leisurely. The streetcars rolled along
quietly. The horses drawing the droshkies seemed to trot as
though in the measures of a dance. The bells of the churches
pealed, calling worshippers to take account of their immortal
souls. A nun strolled along, leading a group of children in alpaca smocks. Seminarists in long coats and wide-brimmed
hats were carrying large volumes, like the Jewish Gemaras.
Pigeons hopped about, picking for kernels. A blind man
walked by, led by a dog. A tranquillity seemed to hover about
the castles of the ancient Polish kings, the monuments, the tow-

ers and cathedrals. Stars began to appear in the sky. Near by
was the Jewish quarter, Kasimir, with its ancient synagogues
and the old cemetery, the resting-place of generations of rabbis, holy men, leaders of the Jewish community. Asa Heshel
took a deep breath. He had not realized himself how much he
needed a spell of rest.

The hotel they were to stop at was on a street planted on either side with trees. Their room was large and had two beds.
There were flowerpots at the windows, and tapestries on the
walls. The towels were embroidered with homely Polish proverbs: "He who rises early, God will treat him fairly"; "Where
a guest is, there is God." In a corner there was a washstand
with a copper dipper and an earthenware jug. Here in this
room everything else seemed to Asa Heshel far away and
unreal; Hitler, the war, the school where he taught, the Moskat family. Barbara took off her dress without bothering to
put on the light and washed in the soft twilight glow. Asa Heshel, dressed as he was, lay down on the bed with the high
posts and the carved knobs. He listened to the quiet that came
into the room through the open window ventilators. There
was only one thing he wanted now: rest, to forget for a
while all worries and burdens.

For the evening meal the two went to a coffee house where
the Polish writer and painter Wyspianski had been a steady patron. Even now drawings of his hung on the walls. At first
Asa Heshel had felt a reluctance to go to the places that were
tourist haunts. Barbara had to persuade him to enter. Chinese
lanterns threw a soft glow. There were two other couples
whispering to each other over their food. The waitress in her
white apron walked on tiptoe. After they had eaten, Asa Heshel and Barbara strolled over to the Jewish quarter. Here the
streets were narrow and crooked, cobbled with large stones.
In the dimly illuminated alleyways they saw an old Jew in a
skullcap, with long sidelocks. Behind the counter of a food
store stood an old woman with a matron's wig on her head.
To the right of her were bundles of wood and stacks of coal.
At her left hung strings of dried mushrooms. A small girl with
a shawl around her shoulders was buying something, which
was being weighed on an ancient scale with a long tongue. In
another street the two came across a group of men and young
boys who were intoning a prayer in honor of the new moon.
They were dancing about, calling to one another: *"Sholem
aleichem! Aleichem sholem!"*

The boys had long, dangling earlocks and wide-brimmed hats, like little rabbis.

Barbara stopped to stare at them. The light of the moon fell on the pale faces and black beards and was mirrored in the dark eyes. The boys skipped like goats, sometimes chanting from the prayerbooks they held and sometimes pushing against one another frolicsomely. Through the open window of a prayerhouse could be seen shelves of books, the Ark of the Law, gilded lions, memorial candles. Barbara thought of her father, who on his deathbed had cried out that he wanted to be laid to rest in a Jewish cemetery.

In the hotel room they did not put on the light. Thank God, they were alone at last. Tomorrow they would travel on to the mountains. Let them ruin everything. This night no one could take from them. Barbara stood at the window. She looked out at the clear sky, at the rows of crooked rooftops. Asa Heshel took a drink of cold water from the pitcher. He suddenly re-called his parting from Hadassah the previous evening, when she had walked with him from Shrudborov to the Otwotsk station. She had kissed him three times when they parted and said: "If I die, I want to be buried near my mother."

Asa Heshel now suddenly realized the strangeness of her behavior. What had happened? Had she known that he was going away? A terrifying thought occurred to him: he would never see her alive again.

CHAPTER TEN

In the prayer and study houses, this year as every year in the month of Elul, the Jews sounded the shofar, the ancient ram's horn, as protection against Satan. The Polish government was taking defense measures in its own fashion. In the parks and squares trenches had been dug to serve as shelters against a possible bombardment of the city. Priests and rabbis turned the first spadefuls of earth. Substantial citizens, Chassidim, yeshivah students, voluntarily reported to help with the dig-ging. Because of the fear of a sudden onslaught by German planes, the work went on at night in complete darkness. All windows were hung with black sheets of paper or blankets. The Polish army was partly mobilized. It was an open secret that the generals and colonels who had really ruled the country ever since the Pilsudski uprising were far from being prepared for a modern war. For all Marshal Smigly-Rydz's assurances that every inch of Polish soil would be defended, it was expected that the Polish army would retreat to the river Bug.

Pinnie Moskat kept a map folded in his pocket and took it with him wherever he went. Every day he carefully demonstrated to the others in the Bialodrevna prayerhouse that Hitler was nothing less than insane. Nyunie wrote a postcard to Hadassah in Shrudborov urging her to come back to Warsaw. He would take her and Dacha into his house. But Hadassah did not want to go back to the city. The fighting would start near Danzig, not near Shrudborov. Aaron, the Bialodrevna rabbi, planned to spend the high holy days in Falenitz. Leah was straining at the leash to get back to America, but Koppel would not listen to any suggestions about leaving. He spent all his time at the flat of David Krupnick's widow, the former Mrs. Goldsober. He brought her gifts and sat playing cards with her. She cooked his favorite dishes. Leon the Peddler and Motie the Red also frequented the house. The old cronies would have a drink of brandy, nibble at some jellied calves' feet, and smoke the American cigarettes that Koppel provided. Koppel treated them all to pineapple, sardines, and caviar. They talked about the Anshe Zedek Society, of which the departed Isador Oxenburg had long ago been president; of the gang wars between the lads of Warsaw and Praga; of the Revolution of 1905; and of the fights between the strikers and the underworld. What had happened to those wonderful days? All gone. Gone Itche the Blind, Shmuel Smetana, Chatskele Shpigelglass. Gone the racketeers, the pimps, the drivers of horse trucks. The pickpockets of the Krochmalna and the Smotcha had become party and union men. The urchins of Janash's Court were now busy organizing Communist demonstrations. All of them had become intelligentsia.

Motie the Red shook his head dolefully. "Gone for good, the old Warsaw. Dead and buried. You can say Kaddish after it."

"Do you remember how Baruch Palant made a bet he could gorge three dozen eggs?" Leon the Peddler asked.

"Ah, the old days."

Koppel told the others that the Americans did not know how to eat. All they knew about was a sandwich. They liked to fight, but always according to the rules. If one of them wore glasses, he had to take them off. And there was a rule against punching below the belt. He also told them about the horse races. Why, there was one horse that had brought its owner more than a million dollars.

Leon the Peddler smacked his lips. "That's money."

"You said it," Motie the Red agreed.

"And you think you have to be there?" Koppel went on. "No. You sit down like a king in a Turkish bath, and you know everything that's going on. The numbers come over—by electricity. And in the meanwhile a woman is giving you a massage."

"Ha, ha, Koppel," Mrs. Krupnick laughed. "The same old Koppel."

"Do you think that just because a man's old he stops being a man? The eyes can see and the heart can yearn. But that's all. As for the rest, it's true, you get played out."

"You can say that again."

"I'm telling you, Koppel, you'll hang around and hang around until Hitler marches in, and then you'll never be able to get out."

"What can Hitler do to me? Put salt on my tail?"

"He says that he'll finish off all the Jews."

Leon the Peddler flared up. "So did Haman. When he saw that Mordecai wouldn't bow down to him he wanted to kill all the Jews. So what happened? Esther came and he dangled at the end of a rope."

"Hitler won't need an Esther."

"So he'll drop dead just the same."

"Have you already bought a place in the synagogue for Rosh Hashona and Yom Kippur?" Mrs. Krupnick asked.

"I'll pray in Falenitz, with the rabbi. After all, I'm supposed to be his stepfather."

The day went by and Koppel hardly knew where it had gone. After the evening meal the old cronies sat down to play cards. Then, before they could look around, it was twelve o'clock. It was difficult to get a taxi in the Praga section, and Koppel stayed overnight. Mrs. Krupnick gave him her late husband's bathrobe and slippers to put on. She made the bed soft and comfortable. Koppel lay down in the darkness, all his senses alert. It was hard to believe that he was in Warsaw again. Could he be the same Koppel who had once been Meshulam Moskat's bailiff? Was he the man who had once been Bashele's husband? Everything seemed like a dream. He began to think about death. How long could he keep on going? Two or three years, no more. They'd bury him in

Brooklyn. On the way back from the cemetery the *landsleit* would stop off at Delancey Street or Second Avenue for a drink. Leah would get the insurance money, twenty thousand dollars. What did she need all that money for? She was an old dog herself. No, he'd make a new will and leave everything to his children. As soon as he got back to America. Well, what else? The worms would feast on him. A little time would pass by and there'd be nobody to remember that there ever had been a Koppel. Could it be possible that there was really a soul? What sort of thing could it be? What could it do, wandering around without a body?

He fell asleep. A few hours later he started up. He put out his hand and felt for his traveler's checks in his trousers pocket, and the passport in his coat pocket. Leah was right. The best thing would be to get out of Poland as soon as possible. Wars were too much for him. A welter of thoughts gave him no rest. The gravestone on Bashele's tomb had fallen. He was to have put up another, but he had forgotten to attend to it. Her second husband, Chaim Leib, lay without anything to mark his grave at all. He began to think about Leah. In America, whichever way it was, she was his wife; here in Poland she was practically a stranger to him. Her daughter Lottie never said a word to him. And his own son, Manyek, also had his nose up in the air, just because he had a job as a bookkeeper. In America a bookkeeper was a nobody; here in Poland every little snotnose thought himself the cock of the walk. He began to cough.

Mrs. Krupnick woke up. "What's the matter, Koppel? Can't you sleep?"

"In your bed I could sleep."

There was silence. Mrs. Krupnick sighed and giggled. "You're crazy, I'm an old woman."

"I'm an old man."

"Don't make a fool of yourself."

Koppel lay sleepless until dawn. Then he fell asleep, but he had a bad dream. When he got up he could not remember what it was, but it left a bitter taste in his mouth. He felt an urge to get dressed and get out as quickly as possible. Mrs. Krupnick brought him some tea and milk, but he only took a sip of the brew. He dressed and went outside, saying that he would be back later in the day. Mrs. Krupnick still lived on Mala Street. In the same house, on the floor below, lived Isador Oxenburg's daughter, Zilka. Koppel did not want to be seen leaving. He pushed his hat forward and put on a pair of smoked glasses. He tried to hurry down the stairs, but his legs did not serve him. Finally he got out on Stalova Street and waved with his stick at the passing taxis, but none of them stopped. At last he got into a streetcar. A longing to be with Leah overwhelmed him. He wanted to tell her that they were both old people now and that it was foolish to keep on quarreling. The conductor handed him a ticket. Koppel looked in his pocket for some small change, but all he had was a twenty-zloty note. The conductor grumbled, but after a while thrust his hand into his leather purse and counted out the change into Koppel's palm, fifty-groszy pieces, twenties, tens. Suddenly Koppel's hand fell and the coins scattered on the floor of the car. A fierce pang darted through the left side of his chest and his arm. He fell backward. The passengers started up. The conductor rang for the motorman.

"I'm dying," the thought flashed through Koppel's mind. "It's the end." There was a single fragment of thought still hovering somewhere in his consciousness—that what was happening now had something to do with the dream he had had during the night.

Koppel never woke up again. He was not aware of being carried out and put down on the sidewalk. He did not hear the ambulance drive up. He had no knowledge that they had taken him off to a Catholic hospital and laid him in a ward. He did not see the young doctor who put his stethoscope to Koppel's chest and gave orders for an injection.

Two days passed and no one in the family knew what had happened to him. Leah was in the pension at Otwotsk. It was only on the third day that the police found out that the dead man with the American passport had a son, Manyek Berman. Manyek, Yppe, and Shosha came to the morgue. Simon would not let Shosha go down the steps to the room; she was pregnant. Manyek and Yppe went down. There was an overpowering smell of formaldehyde. On tin-covered tables corpses lay under sackcloth. The watchman, a lame man with a growth on his skull, lifted the covering from one of the bodies. It was Koppel, but at the same time it was not Koppel. The face had become strangely shrunken and had acquired a bony yellowness. The ears were white. The nose was pointed like the beak of a bird. The false teeth had fallen out. The open mouth was like a yawning cavern. A smile hovered in the corners of the eyes. It was as though the corpse were say-

ing dumbly: "Well, now you see. . . . This is what it is. . . "
Yppe began to sob and clutched Manyek's arm. Manyek lifted the dead man's eyelid. The pupil stared blindly at nowhere.

A few hours later Leah came hurrying into Warsaw. Both
families, the Moskats and the Bermans, busied themselves
with funeral arrangements. Pinnie went to the offices of the
community to arrange for the burial. Leah sat motionless in
the kitchen of Pinnie's house. She did not cry, but kept on
wringing her hands. Everything had been a mistake: her divorce from Moshe Gabriel, her marriage to Koppel, the way
she had nagged at him and shamed him instead of trying to
raise him up and be a helpmeet to him. Now it was too late,
too late.

A Jewish funeral procession gathered at the doors of the
Catholic hospital. Gentiles stopped and stared at the strange
sight. A crowd of mourners and friends gathered. Mrs.Krup-
nick was there, sobbing aloud and blowing her nose. Regina
and Zilka, the Oxenburgs' daughters, were there. Nyunie supported Leah by the arm, in the modern manner. Motie the
Red and Leon the Peddler looked on in silence. Lottie kept on
wiping her glasses. Aaron, the rabbi, had not come to Praga;
he was to join them at the cemetery. Among the mourners
there was a gray-haired woman with dark, flat features and
Kalmuk eyes. Leah recognized her. It was Manya, Meshulam Moskat's old servant. How she had learned of Koppel's
death remained a mystery to Leah.

CHAPTER ELEVEN

The news that a treaty had been signed by Hitler and Stalin
was taken by everybody as the signal for war. Nevertheless
Asa Heshel did not believe that the actual convulsion would
begin soon. He was staying with Barbara in a village near
Babia Gora mountain, at a distance both from Zakopane and
from Krakow. Newspapers were not easily obtainable and
there were few radios in the vicinity. Asa Heshel and Barbara
were agreed that the district around Krakow would be the sa-
fest. He had sent Hadassah some money and had received a
letter in return; she wrote that in Warsaw they were digging
trenches and that the city was blacked out at night, but that in
Shrudborov nothing had changed. Koppel, the bailiff, had

died; Aunt Leah and Masha were planning to leave for America after the Jewish New Year; Lottie was going to Palestine with her brother Aaron. They all sent their love.

On Wednesday morning Asa Heshel and Barbara went to Zakopane. Then they took the bus to Morske Oko and thence proceeded on foot to Charnystav. They spent the night at the inn. On the other side of the frontier, in Czechoslovakia, were the Nazi hordes, but there was no danger of the invasion starting through the mountains. The next day they returned to the village near Babia Gora. It was a warm autumn day, and the peasants were threshing the wheat. A bride and two bridesmaids in embroidered dresses went from hut to hut and bowed low at every door, inviting the neighbors to a wedding. Another wedding was just then being celebrated, and before the church stood several wagons decorated with flowers. The yokes of the horses were adorned with branches. Young men in embroidered shirts, with red and green feathers in their hats, played on violins, drums, and tambourines. Others yodeled mountain melodies. In the fields behind the huts old women were digging potatoes. In the clear air one felt one could stretch out a hand and touch the distant mountain; the far-off roads and paths were sharply drawn among the dark rocks.

The peasant woman with whom Barbara and Asa Heshel were staying had made ready for them a supper of red berries with cream. Barbara boiled some water in a caldron and washed her hair. Asa Heshel went into the yard, where a hammock swung between two trees, and lay down. On the other side of the yard there was a steep, fortresslike embankment, and on its summit the pines were ranged like green-clad warriors. The evening sun was hanging low in the sky, gleaming like a red lamp. The mists that rolled about in the mountain clefts took on a fiery color. A falcon was flying over the cliff. In the stillness Asa Heshel could hear the beat of its wings.

During the weeks that he had spent in the country Asa Heshel had gained a few pounds. His appetite was good, and he slept through the nights. The holiday had brought him into a homier relationship with Barbara than he had ever known before. She played with the idea of having a child by him. They no longer kept separate accounts, but had a single fund. He taught her to cook some of his mother's dishes: browned grits, noodles and chick peas, dough patties boiled in milk. In the afternoons they would go out into the orchard, lie in the grass under a heavy-branching apple tree, and talk of whatever came into their minds. They amused themselves by making combinations of Polish and Yiddish words. Sometimes they carried on arguments half asleep. Everything Barbara said added up to the same conclusion: there could be no social well-being without planned economy, and there could be no planned economy without the dictatorship of the proletariat. The first news of the Hitler-Stalin pact threw Barbara into some confusion, but she soon came to terms with it: England and France had by their policies made it inevitable. First they had raised Hitler to power and then they had tried to turn him against Russia. Asa Heshel's arguments, too, had a definite trend: too little was known to make possible historical forevision. As long as people went on breeding without restraint, human beings would fight for land. Besides, who says that there exists a system that can save humanity? And why should human beings be saved?

Thursday night they went to bed early, and Barbara soon fell asleep. Asa Heshel stayed awake for a long time. He did not pull the shutter to, but stared out into the night, which was thickly sewn with stars. Meteors shot across the sky, leaving fiery trails behind them. Silent summer lightning quivered in one corner of the heavens, foretelling a hot day. Fireflies shone and were extinguished; frogs croaked; all kinds of winged insects came fluttering into the room and dashed themselves against the walls, the window, and the bedposts. Asa Heshel thought about Hitler; according to Spinoza, Hitler was a part of the Godhead, a mode of the Eternal Substance. Every act of his had been predetermined by eternal laws. Even if one rejected Spinoza, one still had to admit that Hitler's body was part of the substance of the sun, from which the earth had originally detached itself. Every murderous act of Hitler's was a functional part of the cosmos. If one was logically consistent, then one had to concede that God was evil, or else that suffering and death were good.

Barbara squirmed. For a while she seemed to stop breathing, as if she were listening intently. Then her breath became audible again, and in her sleep she put her arm under Asa Heshel's neck. He turned to her eagerly and passed his hand over her body, over the shoulders, the breasts, the curves of the belly. This was a human being that lay close to him, one like himself, the product of countless pairs of males and females, a link in the chain of endless activity, the heir of apes, fishes, and dim creatures that had disappeared without leaving a trace. She too was only an evanescent thing; soon she would return to the melting-pot in which new forms were being prepared. Dawn had set in by the time Asa Heshel fell asleep.

Someone was waking him; it was Barbara. The peasant hut with its whitewashed walls and heavy rafters was filled with sunlight. The air was fragrant with the odor of fresh milk and newly ground coffee. Asa Heshel spoke angrily: "Why do you wake me? Let me sleep."

"Asa Heshel! The war has started," said Barbara, barely restraining her tears.

Asa Heshel was silent for a while. "When? How do you know?"

"They heard it over the radio. They've begun bombing us."

Asa Heshel sat up. "So! It's here!"

"We must leave at once."

Outside in the village street there was a crowd of peasants. Most of them had their faces turned upward, scanning the skies. Airplanes had passed over the village, but no one knew whether they were Polish or Nazi. Now and again someone would peep through the window into the room where the city folk were staying. Barbara pulled the curtain to. Asa Heshel dressed and went out. No trains stopped at the village. They would have to get a lift in a cart as far as Yordanov; there they could catch the local to Krakow. Asa Heshel asked a farmer whether he would take them to Yordanov, but the man shrugged his shoulders: who would be fool enough to risk horse and cart on the road at a time like this? Asa Heshel walked over to the post office; one could sometimes pick up a lift there. The village was in a tumult. Doors stood ajar. The old people talked earnestly, the young jested. At the post office Asa Heshel ran into a gentile teacher from Zakopane whom he and Barbara had met when they were climbing the Babia Gora. He looked at Asa Heshel astounded. "What? Are you still here, sir? The Nazis may arrive at any moment."

Asa Heshel felt his shirt grow clammy with perspiration. "I can't get a horse and cart."

"If I were you, sir, I would set out on foot."

The teacher drew a map out of his breast pocket and with a pencil pointed out the nearest Czech villages on the other side of the frontier. Gadza, Namestovo, Yablunka. There were passes in the mountains through which Nazi tanks could come at any moment.

"Perhaps, sir, you could get me a horse and cart somewhere. I'll pay whatever I have," Asa Heshel said.

The teacher managed it. He decided to go along with them. The journey to Yordanov would take at least three hours. Peasants watched the city people as they climbed in. Barbara and Asa Heshel sat on bales of straw; the teacher made a place for himself next to the driver. The horse plodded slowly forward, step by step. Asa Heshel turned his face to the Babia Gora and to the clear sky above its slopes. There came to his lips the verse from the Psalms: "I will lift up mine eyes unto the hills, from whence cometh my help."

CHAPTER TWELVE

1

Asa Heshel and Barbara arrived in Warsaw in stained and rumpled clothes, in tattered shoes, and without their suitcases. He had grown a beard, and Barbara's white dress had taken on a nondescript color. In their six days of wandering they had gone through a bombardment, hunger, thirst. They spent nights in railroad stations and in the fields. They went long distances on foot; they took shelter in ditches. Asa Heshel had come to terms with the thought of death from the very beginning. In one of his vest pockets he kept a razor blade with which he intended to open his veins as soon as the Germans came in sight. Even before they left Krakow, Barbara had argued that it was insane to return to Warsaw. It would be much better, she said, to make for Rzeszow and thence for Volhynia or perhaps even the Rumanian frontier. But Asa Heshel would not have it. It puzzled Barbara: he, Asa Heshel, the unfaithful husband, the father who had abandoned his children, suddenly became attached to his family. He had no right, he said, to leave Hadassah and Dacha in the midst of all this. His married sister was in Warsaw. Men were leaving their homes and following the retreating Polish army; but he, Asa Heshel, the eternal deserter, was pushing through to the half-beleaguered city. At one point they had almost agreed to part. In the end, however, they remained together. During the last days of their journey they hardly spoke. Asa Heshel's behavior was odd. In one of his coat pockets he had an algebra book without covers and some paper. Between bombardments he made calculations in pencil. He was not afraid of danger, he said, he was only bored. And where was one to seek refuge

from this chaos if not in the realm of "adequate ideas"? A tri-
angle still contained two right angles. Even Hitler could not
change that. In Piotrkow he went looking for a bookstore in
the midst of a bombardment. Then he sat on the floor of the
station platform, in a crowd waiting for a train, and read. The
people stared at him with envy and derision. The general
panic had made Barbara less reserved. She entered into conversations with old-fashioned bearded Jews and bewigged Jewesses, in a mixture of Polish and Yiddish. She sought advice,
asked favors, and collected all sorts of information. Asa Heshel avoided everyone. His face, which had filled out in the
last few weeks, had become haggard again. His eyes were
constantly fixed above the heads of those around him, and his
newly sprouted beard gave him the appearance of a Chassid.
Once, sitting next to Barbara in a ditch near a bombarded station, he suddenly asked: "What do you think of God now, tell
me."

"What do *I* think of Him? You're the one who's always
making up accounts with Him."

"He creates easily and destroys easily. He has His own laboratory."

The electric train from Grodzhisk to Warsaw no longer
functioned. Asa Heshel and Barbara completed the journey in
a truck and Asa Heshel gave the driver his last ten zlotys.
They came to a darkened city. Here and there they saw
watchmen wearing armbands. In the middle of the street there
was a trench, with earth piled up on either side. The streetcars
were not running, and no droshky came their way. The windows were lightless, and the strip of sky between the houses,
deep as in the open country, was thickset with stars. A deaf silence reigned over Warsaw, a strange, unfamiliar silence. Asa
Heshel and Barbara got off at Jerusalem Alley and walked
down to Marshalkovska Street; then they turned into Iron
Street, to go to Barbara's room.

On Zlota Street they came across a bombed house. From it
issued an odor of whitewash, coal gas, and smoking cinders.
The front of the house had collapsed; a ceiling lay sloping
above a pile of bricks, plaster, and glass. They made out the
interiors of rooms, with their beds, tables, and pictures. Asa
Heshel was reminded of modernist theater settings. The road
was blocked and they had to clamber over heaps of rubble.
On Iron Street a factory was burning; flames danced behind
the barred windows, and acrid smoke belched forth. In the
half-darkness firemen stood about and directed streams of

water into the flames. A little man came up, demanded something, and flew into a rage. Barbara hardly recognized her own house. She pulled the bell several times, but no one answered. They began to hammer on the door with their fists. Finally they heard footsteps; the little peephole was uncovered, and a pair of piercing eyes looked out. It was not the old janitor, who knew Barbara, but a new one. The key turned and the door opened a crack.

"Whom do you want to see?"

"We live here."

"Where?"

Barbara gave the number of her room.

"You're not allowed to go wandering around at night."

"We've just come back from Zakopane."

"What? How? Well—" The janitor scratched his head in bewilderment and admitted them. They went up the stairs to Barbara's room. The door was open. Had there been a robbery? She wanted to put on the light, but remembered that it was forbidden. She felt about in the darkness, opened the clothes closet. Her dresses and her winter coat were still there. She went over to the writing-desk and tried the drawers; they were closed. Was it possible that she herself had forgotten to lock the door in the haste of her departure? She remembered clearly that she had made the bed before leaving, but now the blanket was half on the floor, and the bedclothes were in disorder. Someone had been here; someone had slept here. She went over to the telephone and lifted the receiver; the dial tone sounded; the world still existed. She took her keys out of her bag and opened the linen closet; in the darkness she drew out a sheet, a pillow slip, a towel. The people who had broken in had stolen nothing. Asa Heshel stood at the window. The courtyard was steeped in darkness. Black windows looked down on it, like the windows of ruins. A heavy-laden silence filled the unlighted spaces. The thought came to him: "All civilization has been extinguished. Only the skeletons of the earth's human habitation lie scattered about like gravestones."

"We're going to sleep in a bed tonight," Barbara said.

Accustomed now to the darkness, Asa Heshel walked over to the faucet and turned it on. The pipe gasped and gurgled. Tepid water began running out of it. Asa Heshel put his hands under it first, then his head, and while he was washing himself he drank. He began to undress. Little stones rolled out of his trouser cuffs. His shoes were tattered and filled with sand. His shirt clung to his skin. He laid his clothes on a chair, sat down on the sofa, and rubbed his feet. God, what distances they had covered since last Friday! He had never imagined that he could do so much walking. He felt his ribs, his belly, his chest. He stretched himself out and closed his eyes. Only now did it occur to him that he had eaten nothing since early morning. There was a rumbling in his intestines. His pulse beat was slow and intermittent. "Is there anything to eat?" he asked Barbara.

"Wait a moment."

She found quite a supply of food in her cupboard: a bag of flour, a paper container of rice, a box of sardines, a dried-up roll. Asa Heshel struck a match and she lit the gas stove. She put the rice on to boil, then broke the roll in two halves and gave one to him. He chewed it and took sips of water. He was not altogether awake. It flashed through his mind that Hadassah and Dacha were probably in Warsaw, at Nyunie's. He suddenly remembered that he had a son, David, in Palestine. There were countries where there was still peace. In America people were going to the theatre, eating in restaurants, dancing, listening to music. He heard the wailing of cats outside; the animal world did not know there was a Hitler; in this way human beings, too, fail to perceive other realities.

Asa Heshel fell asleep. Barbara woke him. He opened his eyes, but he could remember nothing. He did not know where he was or what had happened to him. He heard a voice: "Asa Heshel, the rice is ready." Who eats rice in the middle of the night, he asked himself wonderingly. Barbara handed him a spoon. He carried the half-boiled mess to his lips. She sat down next to him and ate from the same pot, her cheek close to his. "Aren't you hungry? Or what is it?"

"I must sleep."

He got up from the sofa, but he could not see the bed. He stumbled against a table, a chair, the edge of the stove. Then he stood still and waited. He fell into a doze, like an animal. He came to with a start.

"What are you doing? Why don't you lie down?"

He wanted to answer, but the words would not form on his lips. A grain of rice was stuck to his tongue. He clung to the wall, like a child learning to walk. Barbara put her arms about him. "What is it? You're frightening me."

She guided him to the bed. The sheets were cool. His head sank into the pillow.

2

In the morning Asa Heshel was awakened by the roaring of planes and the clatter of machine guns. The room was flooded with sunlight. Barbara was already up and about, in slippers and a dressing gown. A childish joy took hold of Asa Heshel. The sun was shining! People were alive! He was home! He sprang out of bed and put his clothes on. The roar of the planes stopped, and with it the clatter of the machine guns. The windows were open again; radios blared, children shouted, the courtyard below was filled with people talking, gesticulating, pointing to the sky. A festive gaiety seemed to animate everyone. Asa Heshel had awakened hungry, thirsty, weak-kneed, but eager to start moving, to see his relatives. The dull awareness of the Nazis that had haunted him the last few days had dissolved. Barbara turned on the radio. The announcer told of nothing but victories: our heroic troops were repulsing the enemy on every front, at Sheradz, at Piotrkow, at Tchechanov, at Modlin. On the Hel peninsula our gallant soldiers were putting up a magnificent resistance. The enemy was being flung back from the island of Westerplatte, near Danzig. French and English planes were bombarding German factories in the Ruhr. Tremendous protest rallies were being held in America. President Roosevelt had called an emergency meeting of his cabinet.

The news bulletins were interspersed with music and instructions to the civilian population: what to do during bombardments, how to take care of the wounded. Then again reports, orders, warnings, promises full of good cheer. Asa Heshel telephoned Nyunie, but there was no answer. He looked up Pinnie's number and called him.

Pinnie answered; his voice was hoarse and quavery. "Who is that?"

"This is Asa Heshel, Hadassah's husband."

Pinnie was silent. Asa Heshel continued: "I telephoned my father-in-law, but no one answered."

At last Pinnie said: "Your father-in-law has moved in with us."

"Can he come to the telephone?"

"He's just gone out."

"Can you perhaps tell me where Hadassah is?"

Pinnie began to stammer something, broke off, coughed,

and then said, reproachfully: "We thought you were going to stay out there."

"I got back last night."

"How did you manage it? But it doesn't matter. Hadassah is dead."

There was a long silence at both ends of the line. Finally Asa Heshel asked: "When did it happen? How?"

"In Otwotsk. The first bomb."

Again a long silence. "Where is Dacha?"

"Here, with us. Do you want to speak to her?"

"No, I'm coming right over."

While Asa Heshel had been talking, Barbara had been looking through the closet. She had lost her best clothes on the road. She took out dresses, shoes, underwear. She had apparently paid no attention to the conversation, for she asked: "Well, how are your people?"

"Barbara! I must go!" he answered in a hollow voice. "Hadassah's dead!"

She looked at him and turned pale.

"I'll come back in the evening," he said.

"If the house is still standing!"

They stared at each other for a while, then Barbara started out of her trance. "Wait a moment. I'm coming with you. We might lose each other."

He sat on the sofa while she dressed, then they went out together. The street was crowded—Asa Heshel could not remember ever having seen such mobs on Iron Street. People jostled each other on the sidewalk and in the middle of the road. They carried valises, packages, bundles, rucksacks. One tall man held a floor lamp in one hand and a basket in the other. In an open place on which timber lay scattered a crowd of Jews and gentiles were digging a wide trench. The Chassidim threw up the earth with quick, eager strokes and wiped the sweat from their brows. Somewhere in the vicinity a bakery was open; Asa Heshel saw women carrying fresh loaves. Many of the passers-by were in semi-military clothes: girls had soldiers' capotes on; men in civilian clothes wore helmets. Nurses, stretcher-bearers, and scouts wove their way through the throng. Here and there civilians carried gas masks slung over their shoulders. In the midst of the confusion two tall nuns stood arguing. Barbara clung to Asa Heshel's arm, afraid of losing him. She had changed her dress, but he still wore the rumpled suit, the filthy shirt, and the tattered shoes of their journey. As they passed a large shop window Asa Heshel caught a glimpse of himself and was staggered. He could not go like this to Pinnie's. He turned off the street in the direction of his room on the Novolipki.

The Jewish section, too, was densely crowded. Long lines stood before the bakeries. Some of the shops were shuttered; others were still open. Shopkeepers stood on guard. Here and there barricades had been thrown up; planks, tables, chairs, and boxes lay about, and in one place a cart had been turned upside down, wheels in the air. Children clambered on the heaps of sand, bricks, and stones. A bomb had exploded in the vicinity—no one yet knew exactly where. Small groups stood reading Yiddish newspapers printed on one side in gigantic letters. In the dusty air there was a wild confusion that reminded Asa Heshel of fires, of an eclipse of the sun, of Messianic expectation. They passed a barber shop. He asked Barbara for some change. She went in with him. The attendant began to soap Asa Heshel the moment he sat down, without bothering to wrap a towel around his neck. Barbara waited, staring meanwhile at the mirrors. She had a few hundred zlotys in the State Savings Bank, but she had heard that the banks were all closed. Her total possessions consisted now of thirty-eight zlotys and a diamond ring.

Asa Heshel's room on Novolipki Street had been taken over by a sister of the landlord, newly arrived from the country. His clothes, however, had not been touched. He changed in the kitchen, throwing his dirty shirt out of the window. In the drawer of his desk lay an old version of "The Laboratory of Happiness," written in Switzerland. Asa Heshel unscrewed the door of the stove and thrust it inside. Then he went downstairs. Barbara was in conversation with a young Jewish soldier. Seeing Asa Heshel, she made as if to introduce him, but changed her mind, said good-by to the soldier, and rushed up to Asa Heshel. "We must run! While the bridge is still standing."

"Run where?"

"Toward Russia."

"My daughter is here."

"Asa Heshel, we haven't a minute to lose."

"I'm staying here."

For a moment she stood undecided. Then she took his arm and accompanied him to Twarda Street, to his Uncle Pinnie's. She waited outside, for a long time. German planes, flying low, passed overhead. She heard the rattling of the anti-

aircraft guns, the crash of bombs. She saw bursts of yellow
smoke rising above the roofs and chimneys. Flocks of birds
circled above, screeching. People ran about in panic. Someone
warned her to take shelter, but she was afraid of losing Asa
Heshel. She looked up at the sky, which was filled with
sulphur-yellow fumes, and yawned. Now she understood what
Asa Heshel had meant when he said that the war bored him.

Asa Heshel came down again. He had seen the whole family: his father-in-law, his father-in-law's wife, Dacha. Reb
Aaron, Leah, Dosha, Lottie. Others had been there too,
strangers to him. The rooms were jammed, everything was in
disorder. The bedding had been tied in bundles; valises,
trunks, and packages lay about. Leah, wearing a crepe-
covered hat, stood apart, examining her American passport.
The rabbi was in conversation with a young man. Pinnie ran
around babbling unintelligibly. It appeared that a bomb had
exploded close by. Patches of plaster had fallen from the ceiling and walls, uncovering the gas pipes. A yellow dust lay
over everything. In the kitchen Asa Heshel found Lottie seated on a footstool, reading an English book. No one paid any
attention to him. Dacha was eating bread and sausage. She
had grown much taller since he had last seen her; her face
had a city pallor. She ate with the slow earnestness of an orphan who had become a charge on her relatives. She told her
father all the details: Mother had gone to Otwotsk to ask
about a train. Vanya's older daughter had gone with her. Suddenly there was an alarm; the two women ran into a school
building. That was where the bomb had struck. Mother had
died the same evening in Dr. Barabander's sanatorium. The
girl had lost an arm. Mother was buried in Kartchev.

Dacha began to choke; she laid her head on her father's
shoulder and wept in the shrill, hoarse voice of a grown-up.

3

From Pinnie's Asa Heshel and Barbara set out for Franciskaner Street, where his sister lived. On the way they were
overtaken by an air raid and took shelter under an arch.
Again the planes roared low overhead, machine guns rattled,
bombs exploded. When the sirens sounded the all-clear, they
continued past burning houses and ruins. The streets rapidly
filled again. An order had been issued over the radio that all
men of military age were to leave the city. Immense crowds

were fleeing through the streets leading to the Praga bridges. Some went on foot, others in every variety of vehicle: platforms on wheels, carts, droshkies, motorcycles, buses, and taxis. A limousine was tangled in the traffic. Passers-by caught a glimpse of well-dressed ladies and lapdogs behind the gleaming windows.

The half-shattered church on Gzhybov Place, opposite Reb Meshulam Moskat's house, had been converted into a hospital, where nuns attended the wounded. The broad flight of steps was sprinkled with blood. There had been so many deaths in the city that the corpses could not all be removed. The bodies were carried away on boards. The Saxon Gardens were gashed by long trenches into which protruded the roots of trees. Asa Heshel and Barbara plodded on. "This is fascism," thought Barbara; "I fought it and did not know what it was. Now I see it. But what am I doing here? Why am I wandering about the city? I must flee—today!" An ugly idea occurred to her. Now that Hadassah was gone, Asa Heshel would marry her.

Asa Heshel walked with bowed head. He was prepared for the worst. Perhaps Dinah, too, was dead. He recalled the verse of the Psalmist: "For I am ready to halt, and my sorrow is continually before me." His heart was contracted as though squeezed in a fist. Fantastic! He had had a foreboding the last time that he would never see Hadassah again. She had looked at him so strangely, so timidly. If she died, she said, she wanted to be buried with her mother. It had never occurred to her that she would be buried in Kartchev.

Again there was an alarm and the roar of airplanes, and again they sought shelter, this time in a doorway. Asa Heshel leaned against the wall and closed his eyes. "Hadassah, where are you now? Do you know? Do you exist?" Was it possible that past time had no being? Was there nothing but the momentary present? If he could at least weep! But not a single tear came to his eyes. Why was he still alive? He had not realized that the death of Hadassah could so shatter him. There was a great emptiness about him; his feet seemed to be giving way; he was filled with the horror of death.

They came to Franciskaner Street. Again Barbara waited downstairs. Asa Heshel knocked at his sister's door. There was no answer. He opened it himself and went in. He saw Dinah. She ran toward him, her wig all awry, her face yellowed as by jaundice. She flung herself on him, like one distracted, half laughing, half weeping. "Is it you? Are you really here? I thought you'd been caught somewhere. God in heaven!"

They were all at home: Menassah David, Tamar, Jerachmiel, Dan. Menassah David came in without his gaberdine, in his fringed shirt, his trousers held up by a piece of string. In one hand he held a book of Chassidic stories, in the other a cigarette butt. The bearded face, with its earlocks and its curious mixture of grossness and nobility, was alight. He made as if to run to his brother-in-law and embrace him; but he stopped short on the threshold, began to sway left and right and to make strange gestures. Tamar came in, pushing her father to one side. She seemed exhausted, as if she had not slept for many nights. She looked at her uncle, as if astonished and ashamed of the condition in which he found the house. The two boys came in after her. The older one had already sprouted a beard; he wore a skullcap. The younger one was dressed in a tattered gaberdine, and his head was covered with a little cap.

Dinah clapped her hands together and broke into a lament. "Do you see our misery?" she wept. "Look at us! As if we haven't enough sorrows without this!"

"Uncle Asa Heshel!" cried Tamar, and threw her arms around him. "When did you get here? And how? I thought God knows what had happened to you. Through all this fire—"

"Quiet! Don't scream!" wailed Dinah, covering her ears. "All day long the bombs fall. They drive me out of my mind. Why do you stand at the door? Menassah David, stop dancing there. I tell you, Asa Heshel, he's taken leave of his senses."

Menassah David rubbed his huge hands and quoted with a smile: " 'It is a man's duty to bless God for the evil that befalls him, as well as for the good.' These are the pangs of the Messiah—the wars of Gog and Magog. . . . It is beginning, just as the Book of Daniel says. Idiots!"

"Oh, please, please, don't make so much noise," exclaimed Dinah. "They're driving me mad. People with sense are running away, but how are we to run? I can barely walk two steps. I say, let the men leave. Tamar and I will manage somehow. What will they do to us, I ask you. What do you think, Asa Heshel? Speak up, I can't hear you, God help me. Do you know Adele is here? They sent her back."

"Adele?"

"Yes, Adele. The ship wandered about on all the seas, and in the end they sent it back. That's what's happening to us

Jews—pushed here and there, and then thrown out like garbage. She comes here every day and weeps her eyes out. She wants to go away too. What is the other one doing, Asa Heshel?"

"Hadassah is dead."

"What? God help us all!"

"She was hit by a bomb."

"When? Oh, God, that beautiful child! So young! So lovely! What a terrible thing!"

"Oh, Uncle Asa Heshel—" Tamar began in a choking voice, and could not go on.

"Don't all talk and shout at once," cried Dinah. "With all these dreadful things happening, my nerves have gone to pieces. There's always a singing in my ears. Not that anybody's singing, it's only inside me, the *Kol Nidre* melody. Like the wicked Titus, curse his memory! Sit down, Asa Heshel, sit down; it won't cost you any more to take a chair. What's to be done, I ask you. Where are we to run from this hell? We haven't a copper coin in the house. We might as well lie down and die. I don't care what happens to me, but what am I to do with the others, with the youngsters? Tell me, Asa Heshel."

Asa Heshel felt in his pockets. All he had was a few coins.

Menassah David came toward him. "May this be the last of your troubles! Such times! You can't even observe the week of mourning. But the resurrection's coming soon. We'll see the lost ones again. With our own eyes. As long as I have my rabbi, I'm afraid of nothing. He'll look after everything." And Menassah David indicated his book with the cigarette butt.

"Menassah David, stop it. Everyone knows you're a fool." Dinah turned to Asa Heshel. "Those others throw bombs and he dances. And he'll keep on dancing until we're all killed, God forbid. I've got a few pounds of grits, and that's what we're eating. As soon as they're finished we might was well go bury ourselves. They came after my boys for the army, but when they took a look at them at the recruiting office they sent them back. They have no clothes for the soldiers. They say that Hitler is in Vola. God help us all, what we Jews have come to." She sobbed.

The two boys returned to the living-room. Tamar dried her eyes and said: "Uncle Asa Heshel, won't you sit down? Would you like a glass of tea?"

"No, I must go. I'll be back soon."

"Where are you going?" Dinah demanded. "Comes for a minute and runs out! You're not sure of your life outside. At a time like this we ought to stay together."

"But I tell you I'll come back. I haven't even got a room any more."

"Stay here! If you go away, others will come and take your place. They keep coming from the bombed-out houses. These days you can't put anyone out. What a terrible time! What shall we do? Where shall we go? God's anger is on the world! It's a curse!"

Tamar was ashamed of her mother's weeping and lamenting. Red spots appeared on her cheeks. Menassah David, after hesitating awhile, left the kitchen. Asa Heshel kissed Tamar and said: "I'll be back soon."

Barbara was standing in the middle of the courtyard, her eyes blazing, her face pale with anger. "I thought you weren't coming out any more."

"It's my sister."

"Listen to me, Asa Heshel. I'm not going to remain here. I'm leaving today. Tell me once for all: are you coming with me or are you staying?"

"I'm staying."

"Is that your last word?"

"Yes."

"Then it's good-by. God help you."

"Good-by, Barbara. Forgive me."

"I don't see the sense of remaining with the Nazis."

"The whole family's remaining. It's all the same to me. I want to die."

She scrutinized him with unfriendly eyes. "Maybe you're right; but I'm going to keep on fighting for a while. Where are you going now?"

"I want to see Hertz Yanovar."

"What for? Well, I'll come along. It's on my way."

Half of Shiviento-Yerska Street lay in ruins. Wherever the eye turned, it encountered open roofs, shattered chimneys, tumbled walls, hanging windows and balconies. By the railing of the Krashinski Gardens Asa Heshel came upon Hertz Yanovar. He stood there white-haired, his side whiskers gray, his shirt open. He was wearing a velvet jacket and sandals. He seemed to be waiting for someone; the dark eyes were staring into space. Asa Heshel called out his name. He turned around with a bewildered look, then came running forward with outstretched arms and embraced Asa Heshel and Barbara. " 'I had not thought to see thy face!' " he quoted from the Bible.

"Why are you standing here in the street? Where's Gina?"

"Gina's down with inflammation of the lungs right in the middle of this whole business. I'm waiting for the doctor. He promised to come over. He should have been here a couple of hours ago. And you—I thought you'd managed to escape somewhere."

Hertz Yanovar burst into tears. He took out a yellow handkerchief and blew his nose. He stood before them confused, ashamed. "I've got no more strength," he said apologetically. He hesitated for a moment and then said, in Polish: "The Messiah will come soon."

Asa Heshel looked at him in astonishment. "What do you mean?"

"Death is the Messiah. That's the real truth."